PUSHCART PRIZE XLVIII

2024

PUSHCART PRIZE XLVIII
BEST OF THE
SMALL PRESSES

EDITED BY BILL HENDERSON
WITH THE PUSHCART PRIZE EDITORS

Note: nominations for this series are invited from any small, independent, literary book press or magazine in the world, print or online. Up to six nominations—tear sheets or copies, selected from work published, or about to be published, in the calendar year—are accepted by our December 1 deadline each year. Write to Pushcart Fellowships, P.O. Box 380, Wainscott, N.Y. 11975 for more information or consult our website www.pushcartprize.com.

Acknowledgments
Selections for The Pushcart Prize are reprinted with the permission of authors and presses cited. Copyright reverts to authors and presses immediately after publication.

Distributed by W. W. Norton & Co.
500 Fifth Ave., New York, N.Y. 10110

Library of Congress Card Number: 76-58675
ISBN (hardcover): 9798985469721
ISBN (paperback): 9798985469738
ISSN: 0149-7863

IN MEMORIAM

Rev. Rob McCall
(1944–2023)

Blue Hill, Maine
Congregational Church
pastor, author, friend

INTRODUCTION

In his Introduction to PPXVI (1991), Ted Hoagland saluted small press people as "Holy Fools" because we insist on thoughtful, passionate, non-commercial writing as if life were somehow sacred.

Never have Ted's words meant more to me than at the present moment. All of the authors nominated for this volume care deeply about our sojourns on this bit of stardust. They persist in that faith despite criminal war in Ukraine, climate collapse, and citizens who learn from extreme media and an ex-president how to hate.

To add to these miseries we have been invaded by the most recent notion of our Whizbang Tech Wizards—Chatbot will soon write our poems, essays, stories, books without the annoying intrusion of humans. All of our creative sorts are finished, extinct, Kaput. No more need for Holy Fools.

> "A.I. could rapidly eat the whole of human culture . . . digest it and gush out a flood of new cultural artifacts . . . Soon we will find ourselves living inside the hallucinations of a nonhuman intelligence." states Yuvel Noah Harrai and others in *The New York Times*.

For the record Pushcart will reject all chatbot plagiarisms and will ban forever any human attempting to foist machine products on our editors.

❋   ❋   ❋

A pastor once suggested to me that the Pushcart Prize is "a religious devotion." I hadn't thought of this series quite that way, but he had a point. As with most religious gatherings this edition includes stories, poems and essays that are joyous and wise others that are biblical lamentations for what we are losing and have lost.

No summary will encompass what follows. Our Holy Fools embrace the universe.

*   *   *

As usual, Pushcart has so many people to thank from around the world: the 176 Contributing Editors for this edition, our generous financial donors, our diligent employee-owned distributor W.W. Norton & Co (100 years old this year); our Guest Editors: Kate Osana Simonian, Idra Novey and Elaine Hsieh Chou, (prose), Leila Chatti, Roger Reeves and Phil Schultz (poetry).

> Phil Schultz comments: "Judging anything is impossible of course . . . Imagine what I experienced when I encountered the overwelming quality of gifted work in this year's Pushcart Prize nominations . . . I simply wasn't prepared to deal with the overall excellence, strength and volume of this year's entries.

> "Yes it is an international prize now, with the ever growing number of fine international journals. The volume of work in translation alone is remarkable. . . . All of which is to say the work in this year's edition was truly impossible to do anything less than wonder at . . . Given the condition of our world now, this is most welcome and needed."

*   *   *

Here are 63 brilliant selections from 52 presses, plus lists of Special Mentions.

Our devotion extends to all of the editors and writers worldwide who helped to gather this Small Good Thing.

And of course our thanks to you Dear Reader. Without your caring it is all futile.

Love and wonder,

Bill

THE PEOPLE WHO HELPED

FOUNDING EDITORS—Anaïs Nin (1903–1977), Buckminster Fuller (1895–1983), Charles Newman (1938–2006), Daniel Halpern, Gordon Lish, Harry Smith (1936–2012), Hugh Fox (1932–2011), Ishmael Reed, Joyce Carol Oates, Len Fulton (1934–2011), Leonard Randolph (1926–1993), Leslie Fiedler (1917–2003), Nona Balakian (1918–1991), Paul Bowles (1910–1999), Paul Engle (1908–1991), Ralph Ellison (1913–1994), Reynolds Price (1933–2011), Rhoda Schwartz (1931–2013), Richard Morris (1936–2003), Ted Wilentz (1915–2001), Tom Montag, William Phillips (1907–2002).

CONTRIBUTING EDITORS FOR THIS EDITION—Steve Adams, Dan Albergotti, Allison Adair, Idris Anderson, Tony Ardizzone, Barbara Ascher, David Baker, Kathleen Balma, Kim Barnes, Ellen Bass, Claire Bateman, Charles Baxter, Bruce Beasley, Karen Bender, Bruce Bennett, Linda Bierds, Marianne Boruch, Michael Bowden, Fleda Brown, Rosellen Brown, Ayse Papatya Bucak, E. S. Bumas, Elena Karina Byrne, Richard Cecil, Jung Hae Chae, Jennifer Chang, Ethan Chatagnier, Samuel Cheney, Kim Chinquee, Gina Chung, Jane Ciabattari, Suzanne Cleary, Michael Collier, Martha Collins, Lydia Conklin, Nancy Connors, Robert Cording, Lisa Couturier, Paul Crenshaw, Steven Espada Dawson, Chard deNiord, Danielle Cadena Deulen, John Drury, Karl Elder, Kathy Fagan, Ed Falco, Beth Ann Fennelly, Gary Fincke, Maribeth Fischer, Stephen Fishbach, Robert Long Foreman, Olivia Clare Friedman, Alice Friman, Marcela Fuentes, Frank X. Gaspar, Allen Gee, Christine Gelineau, David Gessner, Nancy Geyer, Gary Gildner, Lee Grayson, Amanda Gunn, Becky Hagenston, Jeffrey Harrison, Tim Hedges, Daniel Lee Henry, DeWitt Henry, David Hernandez, Jane Hirshfield, Richard Hoffman, Andrea Hollander, Elliott Holt, Chloe

Honum, Christopher Howell, Rebecca Gayle Howell, Maria Hummel, Allegra Hyde, Holly Iglesias, Mark Irwin, David Jauss, Jeff P. Jones, Rodney Jones, Christopher Kempf, John Kistner, Keetje Kuipers, Mary Kuryla, Peter LaBerge, Don Lee, Fred Leebron, Sandra Leong, Shara Lessley, Ada Limón, Nicole Graev Lipson, Lisa Low, Emily Lee Luan, Jennifer Lunden, Margaret Luongo, Sanam Mahloudji, Hugh Martin, Matt Mason, Lou Mathews, Robert McBrearty, Nancy McCabe, Elizabeth McKenzie, Edward McPherson, Nancy Mitchell, Jim Moore, Joan Murray, Carol Muske-Dukes, David Naimon, Michael Newirth, Aimee Nezhukumatahil, D. Nurkse, Colleen O'Brien, Joyce Carol Oates, Dzvinia Orlowsky, Tom Paine, Alan Michael Parker, Dominica Phetteplace, Jayne Anne Phillips, Leslie Pietrzyk, Dan Pope, Andrew Porter, C. E. Poverman, Kevin Prüfer, Lia Purpura, Anne Ray, Nancy Richard, Laura Rodley, Dana Roeser, Jay Rogoff, Mary Ruefle, Maxine Scates, Philip Schultz, Lloyd Schwartz, Maureen Seaton, Annie Sheppard, Suzanne Farrell Smith, Lucas Southworth, Marcus Spiegel, Justin St. Germain, Maura Stanton, Maureen Stanton, Jody Stewart, Ron Stottlemyer, Ben Stroud, Nancy Takacs, Elizabeth Tallent, Ron Tanner, Katherine Taylor, Elaine Terranova, Susan Terris, Joni Tevis, Robert Thomas, Frederic Tuten, Lee Upton, Matthew Vollmer, Michael Waters, William Wenthe, Allison Benis White, Philip White, Eleanor Wilner, Eric Wilson, Sandi Wisenberg, David Wojahn, Pui Ying Wong, Shelley Wong, Carolyne Wright, Robert Wrigley, Issac Yuen, Christina Zawadiwsky

PAST POETRY EDITORS—H. L. Van Brunt, Naomi Lazard, Lynne Spaulding, Herb Leibowitz, Jon Galassi, Grace Schulman, Carolyn Forché, Gerald Stern, Stanley Plumly, William Stafford, Philip Levine, David Wojahn, Jorie Graham, Robert Hass, Philip Booth, Jay Meek, Sandra McPherson, Laura Jensen, William Heyen, Elizabeth Spires, Marvin Bell, Carolyn Kizer, Christopher Buckley, Chase Twichell, Richard Jackson, Susan Mitchell, Lynn Emanuel, David St. John, Carol Muske, Dennis Schmitz, William Matthews, Patricia Strachan, Heather McHugh, Molly Bendall, Marilyn Chin, Kimiko Hahn, Michael Dennis Browne, Billy Collins, Joan Murray, Sherod Santos, Judith Kitchen, Pattiann Rogers, Carl Phillips, Martha Collins, Carol Frost, Jane Hirshfield, Dorianne Laux, David Baker, Linda Gregerson, Eleanor Wilner, Linda Bierds, Ray Gonzalez, Philip Schultz, Phillis Levin, Tom Lux, Wesley McNair, Rosanna Warren, Julie Sheehan, Tom Sleigh, Laura Kasischke, Michael Waters, Bob Hicok, Maxine Kumin, Patricia Smith, Arthur Sze, Claudia Rankine, Eduardo C. Corral,

CONTENTS

PUSHCART PRIZE XLVIII

SUNNY TALKS

fiction by LYDIA CONKLIN

from ONE STORY

Hunched over my computer in my cubicle, I prepare for my nephew's visit by watching one of his YouTube videos. His backdrop is his bedroom, the walls painted black, centaur and mermaid posters freshly hung. His mascots, he calls them. He pops into the frame, flaunting his naked, scar-free chest. He's fifteen but looks ten. His wrists are so frail, his shoulders so narrow, that I worry he'll break his arms with his eager, sweeping gestures. His audience is ten or twenty thousand people who litter his page with rainbow emojis, kissing emojis, and shining sun emojis that are occasionally interrupted by trolls reminding him he's a damaged and mutilated female.

"Welcome to Sunny's channel." He rolls his eyes like everyone knows already. Sunny was always his name, so when people threaten to publish his real name, he has a laugh, thrusting his head back against the wall of his bedroom, which is beside my older sister's room in their little house in Shrewsbury, though Sunny doesn't reveal where he dispatches from; he's learned from millennial elders on the platform at least the basics of safe internet practices.

He lifts the rabbit my sister bought him and holds it to the camera, pink pads swelling to blot out the screen. The rabbit died a few months after this video, of nose cancer.

"My assistant," Sunny says. "Almond Senior." He bounces the rabbit's haunches. "Pronouns: they/them." He snorts. "Almond Senior's nonbinary." The rabbit's cute, cancer-filled nose presses against Sunny's cute, little boy nose. "So trendy, now, aren't you?"

I pull back from the screen into the green light of the office. I've watched the video a dozen times, awaiting this moment, my breath so quick it's audible, perking my ears for Sunny's tone. Is the joke that the rabbit has an identity, or is the joke that the identity is nonbinary?

Sunny crops the frame at his waist, as though he has hips to hide. He updates his perspective regularly, on crucial queer Gen Z issues such as pansexuality, passing privilege, cisnormativity, he/him lesbians, PGPs, chasers, and demiromanticism. He applies gel to his hair so it crests sweetly over his forehead, a neighbor boy from a fifties sitcom.

I live hundreds of miles from Sunny now, but this evening my sister will drop him at my apartment in Trenton and then meet up with a fling for the weekend. Tomorrow Sunny and I will attend a convention of trans YouTubers in Philadelphia. Sunny invited me a few weeks back, explaining that it wasn't cool to go with his mom, that he preferred me, his aunt, which was fishy, because he loves my sister, but I guess everyone grows up sometime. Last week, he sent a video message of himself singing "Streets of Philadelphia" with a plastic bell (the crack drawn in Sharpie) nested in his soft disc of hair and a portrait of Ben Franklin taped to the wall behind.

I pat my blouse to absorb the sweat from my palms. Tonight I'll discuss my identity with Sunny, tell him what's been true my whole life, though only now is there language for it. I hate to burden a kid with my issues, but he's the only trans person I know.

"Uh, the write-up?" Eric says, looming over my desk. My colleagues don't look directly at me, as though I could infect them through the eyes. But I hold out hope that Eric could become a friend. He visits my desk instead of emailing me. His earring is either queer or cheesy, same with his spiked, thinning hair. Once I'm more comfortable in my body, I'll ask him out for a drink at the sports bar.

I pinch the report from my printer tray and clap it into a folder. Eric snatches the file as though I'll change my mind.

That evening my sister, Jen, arrives on my doorstep, chest out, proud. She's done everything for Sunny at every stage, each intervention and treatment on schedule. She even pulled him from Shrewsbury High because of bullying, though she's unqualified to homeschool. I'm shocked by how she's handled his transition, with good cheer and hearty forward momentum. When I was thirteen, bowlegged with a rag of hair, the only person in our family with a Boston accent, Jen convinced her classmates that I was an unsavory male cousin. I still brace for her to call me Leon Jenkins.

Jen pats my shoulder. Her ponytail swings. "Thanks for taking him."

"Who is it this time?" I whisper.

Confusion flares across her face, quickly snuffed. There isn't any tryst. Of course not. She's checking into some motel to await her precious son. Jen thumps into my apartment, avoiding the question as she heads down the hall to the bathroom. Sunny flings his duffle onto the stoop and embraces me. He's the only person who's never noticed the failure of my hugs, so he's the only person I enjoy hugging. I'm forty-seven, frumpy, misunderstood by all as asexual, but still, I'm his cool aunt.

"You've grown up so much," I say.

He runs a palm through his hair. Such a boy gesture. Where did he learn it?

I set out a bowl filled with puffy bears coated in cheese powder, Sunny's favorite snack, a rare find among the bleak offerings of Trenton grocery stores. Sunny curls on the couch and helps himself.

Jen finishes her water and refills the glass. She pats her thighs, securely pressed into yoga pants. "I'm leaving."

I haven't seen Jen without my parents in years. If I keep her an hour, we could get to Eric. We could analyze my crush the way we used to with hers as children, scheming into the night. "I thought we could chat a little."

Jen scrapes a finger over her phone as though she could draw up a message. "Well. I guess we should talk over Sunny's stuff, anyway."

"I'm not a child," he says, mouth packed with cheese bears.

"You're fifteen," Jen says. "Don't push this, kiddo." She hooks him into her arms and squeezes his skinny shoulders. His hair licks up against her sweater. The apartment is so full of life I could dance.

Instead, I follow Jen to the door, dragging my shirt down over my hips, scouring my brain for a clever opening to detain her. How relaxing it would be to slump against her large frame in front of the TV, even just for an hour. At the threshold she launches into Sunny's needs: he won't eat chickpeas or meat or radishes or red jelly; he has lotion in his bag for the dry patch on his elbow. She packed a workbook in case he can fit in a little studying. "He gets overstimulated. He'll want to stay the whole day tomorrow, but maybe skip the last bit."

I know all of this already.

"Remember when we hiked up Monadnock?" she asks. Jen carried Sunny halfway up the mountain, his body flipped over her shoulder, pigtails dangling.

"You worry about him too much." My words are sharper than I intend.

"He's a kid."

Besides his fifth-grade trip to Manhattan—the last school year Sunny attended as a girl—he's never left New England. "He's a teenager. He'll be fine."

"Don't make me regret this."

"Hey," I say, softening, playing along with her story. "Ditch your friend. We'll watch movies or something. Come on, Jen. It'll be nice." Somewhere toward midnight, Sunny asleep between us, our bodies washed in the aqua light of the TV, Jen will apologize for how she treated me when we were kids. I'll laugh and say it's nothing. And it will be nothing, somehow, suddenly. A glow will ignite between us, and our relationship will revert to how it was before I hit puberty. We'll hug a normal hug. And ever after: weekly calls like regular siblings. Conversations that aren't about Sunny.

She waves me away. Just before she ducks into the car, her face strains.

I sit with Sunny, him on the couch, me on the desk chair. He clutches his phone, skinny limbs tangled. I have to pee, but if I leave even for a second, he'll drift away on the currents of the internet. What can I ask next? How's puberty? Have you discovered what romance is yet? What are my sister's secrets? Sunny and I like each other—he's my only nibling, a term he taught me—but we've only spent time together with family. We've diced tubers for holiday meals and raised our voices to compete with conversations about baseball and acid reflux. We've never talked about anything serious.

"So," I say. "How's math class? You must have math class, right?" I want to slap myself.

His knee bounces. "Not class, really. I have, like, workbooks."

I arrange the cheese bears on the coffee table. "What about language arts?"

"I have a workbook for that too. The cover has, like, tumbling letters to symbolize the vast and dynamic field of English-language literature."

"Science?"

"Workbook." He seizes a fistful of bears.

"Health?" One regret is that I can't fully see Sunny as a boy. He's used male pronouns since age eleven and never developed female sex characteristics, but although he looks like a boy and is shaped like a boy, I trust him more than I'd trust any boy. I give him more credit. And I like him more. This can only mean I don't see him as a fully real boy, which is a betrayal.

He raises and lowers his palms like a scale. "Workbook."

"Sunny." I roll back on my chair—the floor is so sloped that every minute we're farther apart. I resolve not to pee until I tell him who I am. I realize I've been mutilating a cheese bear only when it explodes on my knee. I ball the bear's remains into a marble and flick it away. "I've been thinking about stuff. About me."

He blinks. His towhead, his jittering leg, his big eyes glancing down at his phone every second. Jen's right. He's a child. I shouldn't dump my sour adult laundry all over him.

"Never mind," I say.

His attention snaps back to the screen. "So, I just found out? There's gonna be these guys at the conference tomorrow. Emmerson and Henry?" His thumbs are all over the screen, satisfying bleeps pulsing up. "These transmed assholes. They're always mocking kids in their comments. We've gotta go to their panel, okay?"

"Okay." My legs twitch. "I guess I'll retire, then."

Sunny looks up, surprised. The sky still has light. "That's all right, Lillia." The baby-talk way he still says my name gives me chills. His features crunch together. His fans call this his old man face, which he makes when discussing the grimmest community comments: *My grandpa's dying but I'm not ready for him to see how I look now. My mom took my period stuff so I'd have to ask for it back. My parents call me "it" and the dog's name.*

Once in my room, I'm trapped. It's only eight, and the bathroom is off the living room. I'm in my nightgown already, and I don't want to pass Sunny so exposed. My breasts are loose, hot and itchy, too heavy, showing through the fabric. And I'm too overwhelmed to talk to him anymore, afraid I'll blurt out my secret at any moment. Through the closed door, I hear Sunny call Jen, complaining that his friends at the conference are already there. "Yes, Mom, friends from the internet," he says. "They count as friends."

I seize the doorknob. I'll drive him to Philly, wait in the car with a book while he socializes. But I can't lurk in proximity to such cool, self-actualized young people. I'll kill myself. I'm glad Sunny got hormone blockers, of course I am. I'm proud of my sister for realizing what was going on, for getting him to a specialist before puberty started, for not giving in to the anti-trans panic that's been hyped up even more since the election. The technology was new even to me. But sometimes I can't bear the fact that, if I were born a bit later, all I would've needed was injections. That my body never had to bloom into these curves.

I sometimes half-wake in a panic, convinced I've just turned thirteen, that my breasts have pushed against the skin, that I'm one day late for intervention. That now I'll be stuck in this body forever, terrified of sex because my shape could never bump up against someone else, so my crushes burn out like stars. When I blink awake and I'm forty-seven, the option for blockers having passed thirty-four years ago, it's not comforting.

Would Sunny have snorted if I'd told him I want to live between the genders? Would he have said, "So trendy"? If I'm not going all the way, he might think I'm not serious. And I don't want a beard. I don't want a bald spot. I fear what anger T could draw out. I sink under my sheets, braiding my legs so I don't wet the bed.

The conference is far enough outside the city that there aren't even sidewalks. We enter the massive bubble of a building under a double banner of the generic queer rainbow and the specialized trans rainbow. Doors all around the giant mushroom atrium discharge hip youngsters. Girls who still read as boys with hair swished into elegant up-dos, colt-like in their heels, boys who still read as girls with mop heads and high athletic socks.

There are kids here who even I, with my YouTube research, cannot identify as trans, trotting so easily in their gender it's like they never had to fight for it. There are kids aiming for and achieving a space so exactly in the middle that you couldn't guess what color birth blanket the doctor once wrapped them in: baby faces with voices that dustings of T or hours of training have frozen into a curious, second-look register too low for a girl, too high for a guy. Their hair sculpted into short shapes stuck between butch and fey, their bodies either skinny or overweight, because it's the between weights, I've learned, like my own, that telegraph gender most clearly.

At registration, Sunny paws through a spread of nametags. If only my name were less feminine and I had a channel listed like everyone else. I once came out in a DM to a trans YouTuber whose profile made him look older than he probably was. His answer was so spammy and generic—*Go for it! Age matters not!*—that I never reached out again.

26

My conference registration was a hundred dollars. I'm still in the red from my move, and every month I go deeper, eating plain pasta to add to my surgery fund. Sunny doesn't know the cost of the conference and so snatches the gift tote with a victory shout, counting the free pin, free condom, free hamburger-shaped eraser, and free pack of nuts as an unimaginable windfall.

Off the atrium shoots a hall lined with doors. Each door boasts a sandwich board with the day's panel schedule, a fresh lineup every hour. At the end of the hall is the auditorium for celebrity events and the keynote. Nut packets and a half-sucked lozenge litter the floor.

Participants study me, as though decoding this middle-aged woman's purpose. Am I Sunny's mother? No; Jen's cameo is Sunny's most popular video—her smug appearance as perfect mom—*you gotta do right by your kid*—so if they know him, they know Jen. I should've brought a hoodie, but when I dress masculine, everyone thinks I'm a lesbian. I've dated a few men, but in my butch periods, I haven't landed any. Until I can hover deep enough in the middle to range beyond lesbian—with a micro-dose of T hardening my face and speckling my chin with hair—until I can look more like a girly boy instead of a boyish girl, until I can scrape these breasts off my ribs and stand up straight, what I wear seems secondary. Except for here.

I dodge through the crowd. It's as if I've stepped inside my computer, everyone newly dimensional and visible, for once, from head to toe. There's Irish Danny Ray Kyle, a tiny copy of Justin Bieber, trailed by waifs in pancake makeup. There's Paulie G from Norway, who, at twenty, is a community elder. Paulie G transitioned late—"late" is seventeen—so his hips are wide, a detail he's disguised in his videos. My heart pulls for him as he shuffles by.

A pair of famous transgirl sisters strolls past. The older one transitioned second, after a suicide attempt, coming out on the younger one's channel with her wrists wrapped and her voice too soft for the mic. The sisters' red hair is tied into contrasting scrunchies, and they skip through the conference collecting greetings like they were never sad a day in their lives. Maybe transitioning is like that. Once you settle into your new form, a peace descends, and for the first time in years, you skip.

Kids clamp Sunny in hugs. "Sunny Talks," "My internet crush," "You're so mini in real life." He lets them linger in his arms. Sunny's wonderful with the weak. That must've been why I thought I could talk to him.

"Emmerson's panel is next," he says. "I'm going to ask a question. Like, a super pointed question. No one challenges that kid. Like, ever."

As we pick our way up the hall, Sunny spots a friend loitering by the water fountain, hands in pockets, chin high, a little older, around nineteen. Shiny of face and puffy of body, the friend sits between genders. Whenever I encounter someone in between, their success or failure predicts my future attempt. If they're attractive, if they achieve the middle, my heart soars for my own transition. If they're unappealing or settle too clearly in the camp of man or woman, I despair. This person is tall and soft with a haircut that starts short on the brow, piles up all swishy at the crest of the head, and shortens severely against the neck. They've achieved the middle, but they aren't attractive.

Sunny says, "Button's channel dominates," then hugs them in his easy, happy way, like a kid who spent his life ricocheting between siblings. He introduces me as his favorite aunt, and Button bobs on their heels.

"Sunny's family!" they cry. "You need a hug."

"That's okay."

Button leans in. My elbows jut out and I clap their shoulders, hunching my back to keep space. I hide my face against their chest. And then I'm sheltered in the hug. In the dark heat of Button's sweatshirt, I will never have to make decisions. My arms soften, like they never do, and for once, a hug feels nice.

"Wow," Button says, face twisted in confusion. "Are you mad at me?"

I step back.

"She hugs strange," says Sunny. "But she's a cool person."

Heaviness drops through me. I study the corporate pattern woven into the carpet.

Button turns to Sunny. "I upset the lady. Yo, hey. Don't freak. At the beginning of my transition, I was a rough hugger too."

I freeze. But of course Button knows. Why else am I here? Relief blows through me in a cold wind.

"Don't despair, beautiful." Button claps my shoulder. "It takes time to get used to a new body. And you totally mostly pass as a chick."

"Oh," I say, cheeks tingling. They have me the wrong way round, but it's something. A panel releases. Conference-goers push and shove, a bright, heady jostle. Button's big face bobs over the shoulders of teens.

"No, dude." Sunny's voice strains. "Hold up, no. She's not trans."

Button's lip twitches. They bow. "Ah. Apologies."

Sunny grabs my hand and beelines through the crowd. We squeeze past clumps of kids on either side. "I'm sorry, Lillia. That was not okay. That was so not okay." He breathes unevenly, like he used to at the beginning of panic attacks. "You totally don't look trans. Like, at all."

28

"It's okay," I say. "It's not an insult." I'm about to say Button was right, is the thing, when Sunny stops and stares at me, cheeks glossy.

"You're right," he says. "I can't believe I never thought of that. Of course it's not." He wipes his wrist across his forehead. "What's wrong with me?"

We take our seats for the panel. Sunny rocks in the chair beside mine, rubbing his knees, intent on the dais, on which sit three panelists. Two are cis-passing boys in their late teens. They could be brothers, but one has an English accent, the other a tweed blazer. These are Henry and Emmerson, according to the table tents—Sunny says transguys all have names like Victorian heirs. Both have thick arms crossed, freckles that rise into zits over the top of their noses, and crew cuts.

The other panelist, Wellcamp, possibly a college student, leans toward boy, though I'm not supposed to guess like that. They have a strong jaw, deep-set eyes, a blue bob, and silver nail polish.

"The dude with the blazer is Emmerson. He's such a dick," Sunny says, with reverence. "Him and the other guy hate Wellcamp. They made, like, this stupid 'exposed' video about how Wellcamp's a trans-trender."

Sunny hasn't shared an opinion on transtrenders, but he has a certain smugness about having started early. He posts shirtless child-hood photos, with hidden ponytails and thick bangs. Commenters cast doubt that he was assigned female at birth. Really, the signs were subtler than that. As a child, Sunny wasn't a boy to me, per se, though not exactly a girl either. He was a wild, genderless thing: charming and silly and free, forever hyper or bereft. More weasel than kid. And I watched him closely, knowing I'd never have my own child, since pregnancy would swell my body further in the wrong direction.

A lady introduces the panelists. She's from the national gender out-reach hotline that sponsored the conference. She explains that the par-ticipants will "debate the core of trans identity, along with issues of permission and fundamental definition." She retires to the front row, stooped and mousy, glancing around like she fears attack.

"So," says Emmerson, thumping his arms down on the table. "I guess it's time to sniff out the 'core of trans identity.'"

"Nasty, mate," says Henry, and they both giggle.

"I brought some notes," says Wellcamp, tapping a battered composi-tion book, as though the relevant information will agitate to the sur-face. "We could open with the theoretical and home in on IRL?"

Emmerson checks the door. "You know what, screw this." He aims his nose at Wellcamp. "Everyone knows why they put us together. Let's talk about why you pose as trans to get more followers and, like, minority cred."

"She doesn't even have gender dysphoria," Henry says. "Ask her, mate."

At the pronoun, air sucks out of the audience. I cross my arms over my chest. At home, I have a set of expensive binders, still stored in their wrappers. When I try them on, they hurt as badly as the kids say and worse, due to my soft, aging torso.

Wellcamp leans back, shaking blue hair off their face. The way their hair moves—of a piece and so dry—it's obvious it's a wig. "I don't believe in gender dysphoria."

Emmerson and Henry groan.

Wellcamp closes their eyes. "Can't we rethink our language? Why is our community so negative? What about gender euphoria for once?"

Surely there are moments, many moments, in a transition that trigger euphoria. Like when I ordered the binders, or when I pin my hair back so fiercely it looks short. I turn to Sunny for approval, but his mouth is tight.

Henry's skin brightens under his freckles: "Of course it's negative to be trans. You're born wrong, so what the fuck, of course! You want what you'll never have. I'll never have a normal willy. I'll never have inbred male confidence. I'll never get those extra little pushes forward a real boy gets one billion times before he even knows what gender is."

"All I'm saying," says Wellcamp, "is that isn't everyone's way. Some people make changes out of joy." They spin a hand over their front, their sparkly top ruffling. "I got top surgery out of joy." They point out a patch on their wrist like an acid burn. "I got phalloplasty out of joy." They dangle their fingers over the rim of the table. "I'm wearing nail polish and this hair because it all makes me happy."

"Then why?" Emmerson's voice is so strained he's barely audible. "What motivates you if you were so happy before? Why pay a hundred thousand dollars to slice up your junk if you're literally spinning around a mountaintop singing about joy?"

Sunny's hands clench his chair. Does he remember my sister's fights with his father, a stumpy architect who left when Sunny was three? Last year Sunny wrote him a letter. His father responded: *I don't have a son.* If Nathan had stayed, Sunny would be halfway through the wrong puberty, miserable and silent. Bangs in his eyes, shoulders hunched around breasts, thinner even than he is now, his voice low and dead. Me at his age.

"She's fucked, dude," says Emmerson to Henry. He turns to Well-camp. "You're discrediting our community."

"Why do you even care?" Sunny's voice breaks the arguing, and the panelists turn. He stands on his chair, slim and tufted as a dandelion, swaying high. I raise my arms instinctively, ready to catch him if he tips over.

"Sunny Talks?" Emmerson's voice softens. "Dude, what's up?"

"Wellcamp's fine." Sunny's voice rings through the canned air. "They're, like, probably a fine person." A shaky sigh heaves out of him. "So leave them alone."

Wellcamp is as abashed as Emmerson and Henry, all three slouching like children caught squabbling, which, really, they are. Sunny lingers on the chair, applause sinking into his skinny shoulders, rotating his golden face for the crowd.

For lunch, I drive Sunny to a cheesesteak joint whose vegetarian option, according to online photos, is crushed tofu coated with a plastic skin of cheese. I pledge to order it in solidarity. "I'm so proud of you," I say, bouncing in the squeaky booth. "You really told him."

"I know," he says, his voice tiny, thrilled.

Heat prickles the back of my neck. Sunny spoke up for the nonbinaries. Maybe I can talk to him after all, in the privacy of the car, en route to the afternoon panels.

Sunny smoothes a crease in the laminated menu. "I really thought I'd chicken out. Like, I didn't even know I was doing it until I was up there, like, doing it."

The waitress sets sweating glasses of water between us. "Ladies? What can I get you?"

I don't register her words until I've placed our orders, and I turn back to Sunny. The vinyl cushion has depressed behind his head, as though he's forced his spine against it hard enough to swallow him.

"Oh, Sunny," I say. "It was an honest mistake."

He hardens his jaw. His focus slides off me. He's acting like he did as a little girl, going limp at any slight. "I don't know what you're talking about." He rises against the booth, shoulders squared.

We chew our crumpled soy in silence.

After lunch we attend two more panels, one on T distribution and then a reading of self-published memoir excerpts from teens who, a year or two out from their transitions, are eager to reflect. "Life was hard," reads one kid. "I concerned my mom by declining PB and J."

"Sunny," I say, on the way to the keynote. "I'm sorry about lunch. Look." My voice wobbles. "I sorta get how it feels."

"Don't," he says, through teeth, his shoulders up, like an animal under threat.

"Okay. Okay." My face relaxes into flabby indifference. The day has lost its point. I want it over, want to be alone in my bed, darkness falling out the window, until I give up and turn on the light. "Maybe we should head out? Jen said you might get tired."

"I'm not a baby."

"She treats you that way, doesn't she? Sometimes?"

His eyes narrow. "Why do you care? You're always so weird about her."

Kids pass in waves, cramping me in. "I don't know." A child jostles me. "I guess I'm jealous, kind of."

"That makes zero sense."

He's genuinely confused. He trots to the auditorium, knees high, like a child.

The whole conference seems to be in attendance. We pass a transboy with a dark wedge of hair, a minor TikTok heartthrob. In person, he's so shockingly young that it's upsetting to see him move through the world unattached to a parent.

I should be grateful that the world changed in time for Sunny. If I were his mother, my feeling would be pure. But as it is, I wish the shift hadn't happened too late for me to ever be beautiful in my right body but too soon for me to die in the peace of never having known another way.

I haven't checked the subject of the keynote, because we should be on the highway by now. The administrator introduces someone named Minsie Slater, who will share their life story. The speaker ascends the stage and leans their elbows on the lectern. They clear their throat and describe themself as a real estate agent and homeowner. Minsie is older than I am, with a dense lick of silver hair, a single long earring like a twisting bar of light, and curiously pink skin. They have thin, wise eyes. Big hands cradle the printout of their speech. I can't determine their original gender assignment, and I don't want to. The room goes silent, agitated. There's a quality to the way they spread their elbows on the podium, the softness of their face against its serious set, that makes you want to perk up and be good.

Minsie peers around the hall. When they open their mouth, they speak like they're sitting next to everyone, individually, in some quiet room: "One evening, early in puberty, I took a bath." They push their glasses up higher on their face. "I laid washcloths on parts of my body that I preferred not to visit. As the cloth dried, it shrank and suctioned to my skin like plaster casts. Only then could I look at myself, at this body with each bad patch redacted. The door was closed. I'm telling you this because that evening in Rapid City, decades before you were born, was the one time I felt okay back then."

In the gelled quiet of the auditorium, I sink into the water of my own long-ago bath. Jen was beside me, though we were big enough that our elbows and knees bumped. Our mother must've been in a hurry. Dressed for a restaurant, shining us up for some babysitter. In the jostle of wet limbs and the metallic tang of the water, I gave myself over to her scrubbing, disappearing my body, until her sponge caught my nipple and I howled. Jen gaped as my scream sliced the air and left it in scraps around us.

"Are you okay?" my mother asked, certain I was. She knew the borders of my body. She knew better than I did what hurt.

My nipples ached. Soon they'd swell like Jen's, but I could never stick out my chest like she did, calling them bomb-bombs and rattling them at neighbors. And the way Jen watched, tense arm gripping the rim of the tub, made me shrink back in the cooling water. "I'm okay," I said, too many times.

Jen's face sagged. She mumbled, "Why's she gotta be so weird?"

Minsie bows over their printed speech. The chatter in the audience rises. "I have my notes here." They lift the page. Stage lights shine through a block of text. "It's all about my private body feelings. My relationships. Coming out. My 'journey.' But you know what?" Minsie plucks their glasses off their face, fingers trembling. Maybe they're older than they look. "Fuck all that. I don't have to tell any of you shit. None of us do."

A pocket of quiet opens across the room, like when a musician finishes a song, and the audience decides together not to break the mood. The blank air swells inside me. I have to transition. I've always planned to, really. Whether it will take months or decades, I've known I'd come to this. And with Minsie up there, statuesque with their soft skin and square head, I've never considered my position has any advantage, that I could ever be all right, much less great, powerful, flinging aside my notes before two hundred beautiful teens.

The silence bursts and the crowd roars, and it's like they're roaring for my choice. Girls with bony knees and big noses bash their hands together; boys with styled hair and evergreen hoodies throw their fists.

33

They leap and wave. "Don't tell us shit," chants a kid next to us. This from kids who've spent their lives documenting their stories, who've offered the world every grain of their shit.

Sunny claps halfheartedly, glancing over his shoulder. "I gotta talk to Emmerson. I don't like how we left it."

"Shouldn't we start home?" Cheers ring out around us.

"But when will I ever be in a place like this again?"

He's right. When will I ever be in a place like this? Many fewer times than he will. Together, we cut through the mass of attendees, shoulders brushing as participants push past. Among the sea of children, older people have materialized. A guy my age takes a selfie with two women only a little younger. A man leans on a walker by a modular wall. A couple in their sixties share chicken tenders from a napkin. I set my shoulders back and stride ahead.

The afterparty is in the parking lot, stuck in a fog of chill. Tiki torches flicker, so many tiki torches that the pavement is clinically bright. A table offers troughs of potato chips and candy. Dimpled two-liter bottles of Coke.

We find Emmerson, presiding over a knot of younger transguys. His face makes the shapes of grievance as the little boys study his every twitch.

"Come with me," Sunny says. "Please? I need to talk to him."

Emmerson spots us and turns quickly away. I should warn Sunny to proceed with caution, but I don't want to get caught up in their spat. Let him figure it out. "You go."

His face breaks, half hurt, half confused. "Ugh, fine." He heads on without me.

Finally, blood shivers through my limbs. I can walk anywhere. I can talk to anyone. The freedom is itchy, bloating my chest, too airy to suffer. I scan the crowd. Even a hello will be some shuffle forward. I slow as I pass a woman with a satisfying rope of a braid and the same wide shoulders as Jen. Jen, tall and curvy, bigger than all her boyfriends, twice the size of Sunny's father: I wish, for the first time all day, that she were here. But Minsie steps out in front of me. "No alcohol in child land," they say, wagging a tiny cup.

Up close, they're so much smaller, compact and dense. "Right," I say, though I haven't checked.

Minsie peers into their drink. "They could at least provide normal cups. So we could pound the juice."

"That's how they stay slim." Boys skip past, hair flopping.

"Are you a speaker?"

"I'm here with my nephew." If only Sunny were beside me, charming Minsie with his boundless energy.

"Two trans in one family. That's rare."

"Yeah." My breath catches. "Actually, though, I wasn't born a guy." My knees loosen. I fear Minsie will think me a poseur, but why does it matter? I'll never meet them again. For practice, I say it, finally: "I'm nonbinary." The words sound trendy, hopeful, like a geezer in a novelty T-shirt.

Minsie's face remains bland. "Are you having a good conference?"

"I guess." Did I really just tell them? Was it so easy and stupid? I don't even know if I'm having a good conference. I take a breath. "But thank you. For asking." I pinch my elbow until it stings. "What you said about the bath. Your old, like, bath? That sort of got me."

Minsie looks beyond me, my cheesy words hanging. Kids tangle together in parking spots, staring at one another like they can't believe the night is real, too stupefied to even touch. "I think you're the only one who listened." They snort. Their nose is broad and flexible, sturdy, like a bull's. "I wasn't trying to be a rock star. I don't know why I didn't think about it before. But I was up there, jabbering, and suddenly it was like clouds parting or whatever shit. Of course these kids have moved on from any stupid freakout. And here's this fossil, spewing."

"Yes," I say, too loudly. "It's galling."

Minsie's focus wanders down to find me. They offer a parsimonious nod. "You want a drink? A real one?" They say it like I asked, like I begged, like they're grudgingly consenting.

"I can't tonight."

"Well." Minsie's cheeks brighten, like a candle lit up inside their head. "Tonight isn't the last night on earth."

"No," I whisper. Are they hitting on me? Their breath burns my forehead. They step closer. Those handsome, slender eyes, vibrant slivers in skin that's invitingly soft, mature. How lovely, a night full of Minsie's attention.

Sunny appears at my side, face strained, dancing on his toes. "Can we go?"

My first instinct is to agree, yes, of course, whatever he wants. But I'm trying to give myself time here. I make myself pause, say, "I'm having a conversation."

35

Sunny groans. "But you said you wanted to go home, and, like, if we have to go home now, that's chill." He peers at the bank of cars, ours somewhere out there, like he could will me toward it. He's had an intense day. Meeting friends who only ever lived in the flat circles of their avatars, finding them thrilling or disappointing or overwhelming or irritating. Speaking before an audience. Being among other kids, en masse, for the first time in years.

My mouth twitches, still stuck in the shape of gratitude for Minsie's invitation. "We can go soon, Sunny. Can you give me a minute?"

"We could have cheese bears and hang out?"

The plan sounds so sweet, so cozy, that half of me melts toward it.

"Yes, dear," says Minsie, their voice pitching high, as though Sunny were years younger. "Me and your—what term do you prefer? There isn't a neutral for aunt and uncle, as far as I'm aware—are talking."

"Wait, what?" Sunny stares between me and Minsie. He takes in my whole body, top to bottom. His eyes are shiny, extra bright, absorbing. "Lillia? What do they mean?"

The crowds around us have shifted away, so we're washed up on our own lonely ring of concrete. "It's okay," I say. "Hey. Sunny. Can we talk about this later? I was just telling Minsie. Like, about me."

His mouth knots into a red ball. "I mean, Mom said you were like that when you were little. That's why she told me to invite you. She said I should talk to you about it or whatever." He rolls his eyes to the dark sky. "I thought she was being annoying. I thought she meant just, like, a thousand years ago. Like you were a tomboy or something dumb."

Sunny's words needle my skin. He and Jen have discussed me like I'm his age. Anger should follow, or humiliation. How can he stand there, dismissing the struggle of my life? I want to snap at him, send him away. But I swallow. I force myself to think. Because maybe Jen was trying. Maybe she threw herself into helping Sunny because she couldn't go back and help me when we were kids.

"It's a lot more than that," I say. "It always has been." I take a breath. "I'm good at hiding."

"No." Sunny's face screws up like I've told him he was adopted, like everything he thought he knew is a lie. "I would've noticed."

"Adults have inner lives too, you know," Minsie says. "It would be good of the youth to remember that now and then."

"Shut up, okay?" says Sunny. "Seriously, who even are you? You're just, like, some random stranger."

36

"They're the speaker," I say, willing the bratty edge to soften from his voice. "Come on, Sunny. Be polite."

"But you're lying, right?" he says. "You're trying to fit in or something."

I search for words to make him feel better. "Don't worry," I say "Nothing has to change."

"Of course it does." Minsie's face hardens into a mask of patience. "Son, you're being trusted with information here. What are you going to do with it?"

"But she lied to me," he squeaks. "She had the same shit, all this time, and she didn't even try to help? You're telling me that's cool?"

"I'm sorry," I say. But I couldn't have helped him; there was no way. I was lost in my own swamp.

"You don't know what it was like for me."

"I was there."

He steps toward me, humiliation wet in his eyes. "Shut up. Just shut up."

"Come on now, kid," Minsie says. "Have a little empathy."

"Get out of here," Sunny says. "Why are you even still here? I'm trying to talk to my aunt."

At *aunt*, Minsie's finger shoots toward Sunny's face. "Cut it out right now. I know you're surprised. But take a breath. You need to put your shit aside and support your family member."

Sunny shrinks, hands rising in protection. He tracks the finger like it will stab his eye. I grab his shoulders and pull him to me. His frame is frail against my stomach. He shivers like he might cry.

"Leave him alone," I spit. "He's a child."

Minsie steps back, guilty finger limp, like a snapped twig. My adrenaline—still shooting through me in circles—feels silly.

"I'm sorry," Minsie says. "I hated him calling you that."

And Minsie is right: it felt wrong, suddenly wrong, to be "aunt" again. But that's good, that's exciting. Everything changing so quickly. "Just leave." My voice cracks. Sunny burrows deeper against me. Minsie squints, a jewel of moisture caught in their eye, then turns to slink off between tiki torches. As they push farther away, past teens and stands of soda, their heavy hips upsetting a bowl of pretzels, I remember their invitation, and panic flutters into my throat—I didn't get their number. I step forward, Sunny still attached. I'm about to call out when I realize, of course they won't give me anything after I've snapped at them. We'll never sit together in some twinkling dive, in a corner of Philadelphia where the fairy lights are always on, the music so soft it cushions the air, their body solid beside mine, their snide comments slicing the fug of beer. As Minsie vanishes into the conference hall, Sunny's fingers lock around my arm. His crest of hair slumps over his forehead, and I push it back into its cheeky wave. I pick out my car, a charcoal smudge across the lot. Time to go home.

Nominated by One Story, Allegra Hyde

TENDER

by SOPHIE KLAHR

from THE THREEPENNY REVIEW

I spend late morning weeping with the news:
a black bear with burnt paws is euthanized
along the latest wildfire's newest edge.
It was crawling on its forearms, seeking
a place to rest. I Google more; reports
leak out: the bear had bedded down behind
a house, below a pine, to lick its paws.
In hours before its end, officials named
it Tenderfoot, though some reports report
just Tender. Later, I will teach a class
where we'll discuss the lengths of lines in poems.
I'll say a sonnet is a little song
to hold a thing that otherwise cannot
be held: a lonely thing; a death; a bear.

Nominated by The Threepenny Review Chloe Honum,
Nancy Richard

THE OTHERS SPOKE

fiction by JIM SHEPARD

from ZOETROPE: ALL STORY

A woman inquired with an edge of teasing in her voice what my first name actually *was:* Was it Adolf, or Otto? Or Karl Adolf? As news of our sessions spread within the community, more and more interested parties began attending, and Sassen's living room was filled, with the curious standing along the walls behind those seated. It was one of those living rooms crowded with Dutch comforts and lined to the ceiling with books, records, and prints, culture being enough of a familial preoccupation that he told me they played "Guess the Composer" at the dinner table.

Perhaps embarrassed by her indelicacy, the woman asked a little playfully how many names I'd had just after the war, and I told her that for a while I'd been a forester on the Lüneberg Heath working alongside *many* men with new names. She asked what that had been like, and I related how I'd also raised chickens and entertained the local young ladies with my violin, and how for a full five years whenever I encountered someone new I endured an involuntary jolt of *Has this person seen me before? Might she recognize my face?* Some of the assembled murmured in sympathy, or at the drama. The woman seemed satisfied, and laid her hand on her husband's.

I've been sought by those who wish to confer about the old times and those who wish to plan for the future, those who consider me expert on history and on the Jewish question. All this talk of excesses has created a great craving for information. It's easy to dismiss the propaganda, but harder to address the issue of what *did* happen, and that issue must be resolved before Germany can resume its rightful place in global politics. So I again have become the specialist too salient to certain debates to be overlooked. The one surviving insider with the necessary overview of the entire project.

For that reason, Sassen and Fritsch proposed this systematic discussion of the current concerns. The three of us signed a contract agreeing to divide equally all income from the book that might result. Sassen asked if I could think of anything to convince publishers that one of its authors was *the* Eichmann, and I told him that, first, one is either familiar with the details or not, and second, if any doubts persisted, I would offer a handwriting sample.

Of course, I've written before. One of my first commanding officers instituted the production of guidance booklets for professional training and assigned me the topic of the origins and goals of Zionism. And some years ago, I began work on my own account, which I have entitled *The Others Spoke, and Now I Want to Speak*.

Each Sunday from April on, we met to discuss every book Sassen was able to collect. He set the course as to the reading. The core participants— six to eight of us, depending on the day—made notes, compiled questions, and presented commentaries. When I asked if a stenographer would be present, Sassen reminded me that this was 1957, and we would be using a tape recorder. His wife confided before the first session that he was a perfect child when it came to his delight with the machine: she would catch him singing and whistling into it at all hours. The plan was to turn the tapes over to trusted transcribers and then to reuse them, since new tapes were apparently very difficult to obtain. I was assured that all the transcripts would ultimately be submitted to me for review and correction. None of us need be reminded that history is a series of events to be interpreted for the generations to follow.

At that same session, in the midst of another question, I could hear my wife's voice, a little hesitant, in the kitchen. Vera had never before intruded, and the entire room went silent to attend to her chat with Sassen's wife and daughters before she entered.

"I'm sorry to interrupt," she told the room, perhaps surprised by the staring. In the expressions, we could both see *So that's his wife*. She often told me she was accustomed to making a poor first impression, being small and fat, with a round, Slavic face, but my response was always that this miscalculation made her only fiercer, and that it was nonsense besides.

It transpired that I'd forgotten a third of my notes on the day's text, and after she threaded her way through the seated and standing throng to deliver them I rose to thank her and announced I'd show her out, and Fritsch joked that the group would take a five-minute break to accommodate my gallantry.

In the kitchen, Sassen's wife and daughters had disappeared, and at the door Vera turned to face me and placed a palm on each side of my chest. She said that she hoped the session was going well, and I answered that it would be more enjoyable if she would stay and occupy the vacant chair beside me. We could hold hands beneath the table. She responded that she wasn't sure that even *I* should stay, and reminded me that she'd always believed my urge to express my opinions outweighed my sense of caution. But I'd told her, lying together in our bed when this project had initially come up between us: After so much responsibility, could I possibly content myself with thinking only of my family and remaining comrades? With being the master of some rabbits on a rabbit farm? Was it so foolish to wish to make a difference in German politics, as I had before?

She raised herself to kiss my cheek. "As always, you choose not to reply," she noted with a small smile, and pressed my breast pocket and the medallion that was her gift when we were first separated by my duties during the war. It has the runes on one side; and on the obverse, *Liebe wird dich durchbringen:* "Love will get you through." I remember her remarking to her sister once, with a mixture of amusement and pride, "Wherever he goes, he carries some memento of me."

Back at the table, Sassen was still holding forth on what an old-fashioned soul I'd become, and various types spotted about the gathering tittered politely. For these events, he waxed what Vera called his gaucho mustache. He'd started as Rudel's chauffeur and then ghostwrote Rudel's first memoir, and confided that past access to such a famous flying ace had opened doors for him all over Buenos Aires, and not just in the German community. He'd been a war correspondent for the Dutch Volunteer SS and severely wounded in the Caucasus offensive, and he liked to tease that my only scar was caused by a slippery parquet floor. He occasionally landed pieces in *Stern* and claimed to have offers from *Der Spiegel* and *Life*. He presented himself as an internationally known author and adventurer and bon vivant. His wife told everyone that he was the most appealing man she'd ever met, as long as one held in mind that he lied about everything to everyone.

Fritsch had spent no time in the Reich beyond his visit to the World Congress of Hitler Youth in 1935, when just a boy, but the summer camp he later founded at the Fredericus School was so overzealously modeled on that one glorious experience that Sassen's wife had to bring their daughter home after just three days. We'd all met at Fritsch's Dürer House, the combination antiquarian bookstore and lending library that was the main gathering place for stranded fellow travelers. Like many there, he wasn't so much an old party member as just an expat with some backbone. He didn't, for example, fret about excessive discretion in his home, where the lace doilies were crocheted with swastikas.

Sassen and Fritsch had kept us updated with the latest publications, and at no little cost, as German books didn't come cheap. In the previous month, we'd discussed transcripts from the Nuremberg Trials, Reitlinger's *The Final Solution*, and Kogon's *The SS State*. I'd observed that it was simple for these people to scribble away after the event, writing whatever suited them, since most were hacks, bunglers, or jackasses, but even Vera noted that as we progressed further into the sessions each one necessitated more and more preparation on my part. I don't read for pleasure; I read for a purpose, and she says I go through a book the way a burglar would through a safe.

Fritsch's agenda has been transparent from the beginning. He initially intended to prove the Jews staged the whole thing to generate enough sympathy among the Allies to justify Israeli maneuvers in Palestine. Sassen, on the other hand, from the outset conceded the killings took place but on a much smaller order, and theorized they were the result of Jews infiltrating the Gestapo and working behind Hitler's back. In either case, for both the issue was that as usual the Jews had abused the truth to gain the upper hand.

The sessions proceeded not so much by direct questions as by extended haggling over each book's claims, and I announced on our first day that I was prepared to provide a rounded and truthful portrait of that time, clarifying that while I was not responsible for initiatives like physical extermination I was still obliged to obtain an overview of the matter, as someone who had to steer a large part of that complex during my years at Department IV B4.

The sheer volume of primary documents these books had reprinted for all to see compelled an acceptance that there had been killings, and at some scale, but the group continued to raise the possibility of a rogue Gestapo, with Müller leading a faction of conspirators and Hitler oblivious, since the man was, after all, busy enough running the war. We all considered German democracy a temporary arrangement with no future, and Fritsch repeated at each and every meeting that he rejected accounts that defamed Hitler, as our primary interest should attend to philosophies that would heal rather than divide. And the group had been disheartened by my tacit and sometimes explicit refusal to agree that Müller—*Müller!*—had acted alone, or that such a project was inherently un-German.

A recent session ended with Sassen allowing that some of the larger excesses cited *were*, in fact, probably factual, while noting that the astute historian must also keep things in perspective. Who had created nuclear weapons? A Jew. And how, then, did whatever happened during the war compare to the likely impending extinction of the human race? Who had been right about Jewish aggression all along? And while our assembly had been sitting around and enjoying our conversations, hadn't Israeli bayonets been tearing through Egyptian flesh, and Israeli tanks overrunning the Sinai?

Back home, Vera and I worked around one another in the small kitchen while I went about fixing a drink. She proclaimed herself relieved after our second move, when the new house had electricity and was near better schools for the boys. I reminded her that this was what came of my never having abused my position to fill my pockets, and that even as a *Obersturmbannführer* I'd cleaned my own boots.

"Or I cleaned them, you mean," she corrected.

"When I was in Berlin, *I* cleaned them," I told her. She chose not to argue.

All of us in this new world look upon ourselves as forsaken, but Vera's portion has been particularly arduous. When she and the boys were evacuated from Prague at the war's end when both fronts were disintegrating and I'd managed to drive down to see her for the last time before going underground—I'd even had my vehicle strafed and ended up rolling into their redoubt in a little Fiat—she'd been in tears, and the boys had had no idea what was going on. We'd gathered at the shore of the Altaussee, and Horst had been so electrified to see me that he'd kept running about and finally fallen into the lake, and I'd clipped him on the ear, and she'd seized my hand and backed me away from him, startling us both. We'd had sharp words as some of our last words, and I'd had nothing to leave them but a briefcase filled with pearl barley and a half sack of flour.

We'd discussed how we would proceed in that eventuality, though, and she followed the plans to the letter—to all interrogators, the penniless widow who'd rarely roamed from the kitchen and by then assumed her husband lost; and two years after the emigration expert had become the émigré, she began to prepare the boys with romantic stories of visiting their glamorous Uncle Ricardo who rode around South America on his golden palomino. And finally, on a cold and rainy morning, seven years after they'd last laid eyes on me, one by one, Vera, Klaus, Horst, and Dieter straggled down the gangplank, each dragging a battered suitcase. A small congregation from the community that had come out to welcome them hunched under black umbrellas, but I stood off on my own, and she started weeping when she spied me. She said later she'd been shocked by how much I'd changed, with my lost weight and hair and new glasses that were ugly and oversize, as well.

She told the boys, "This is your Uncle Ricardo," but they seemed to not much care. Klaus was by then fifteen and Horst eleven and Dieter eight, and part of the arrangement for my disappearance had been for Vera to remove all photos of me from the house, including our wedding photo. But did even Klaus really not recognize his father? I watched him closely, and he seemed unconcerned, razzing his brothers about their seasickness. When I caught his glance, I detected no special interest. Once we were safe inside our home, Vera made clear her dismay at its total lack of amenities, and then gathered the boys in front of me and told them who their Uncle Ricardo really was.

It took some time to restore our equilibrium. She noted that first night that in one of my coded letters to my parents I'd enthused about dabbling in mountain climbing and ascending all the way to the high plateau of some famous peak while she'd been reduced to selling furniture to buy turnips, and the Israelis and Americans had been sniffing around and the boys periodically mentioning nice men who gave them chocolate and inquired as to where they thought their father might be. I offered her my account of all I'd endured, and she listened, unimpressed, and then remarked upon my talent for self-dramatization and role-playing, and my capacity for being moved so easily to tears by my own words. I reminded her that everyone was in the right when seen from their own standpoint, and like anybody else I just tried to make each situation work in my favor. She reminded me to whom I was speaking, and said that she'd never been one of those hopelessly naive people who believed that someone held forth only when they wanted to be understood.

But later that same night, she found me again, pulling me from my sleep. I'd initially glimpsed her across a concert hall and been struck by the sheen of her short, black hair and the combination of her stern

45

eyes and beautiful mouth, and she'd hunted me down during intermission and later claimed love at first sight. A Catholic, she'd been harassed as a Bohemian engaged to a German in the SS, and I'd had to endure any amount of ridicule from the Race and Settlement Main Office, and still after seven long years apart her mouth found its place by my ear and she reminded us in whispers that in one another we'd found that sole spirit who from the beginning had believed in each of us, who had recorded our struggles, and who had operated as that discerning and generous audience for whom we both had been waiting. And that in the end, whether in this world or the last, we had only one another.

In time, the meetings became a citywide social event. The same woman who'd spoken at our prior session began the next with a halting question advancing assumptions about me that I found offensive, and in response I made clear to the assembled how stupid it is to speculate when one is not much troubled with expertise in the matter. In the awkwardness that followed, the woman's husband murmured something that appeared from her expression to be chastising while the core participants helped themselves to tobacco and coffee and alcohol from Sassen's rolling cart. Another woman who seemed to be the first's friend, perhaps looking to salvage the situation, asked shyly if she might trouble me with one more query before we commenced, and Sassen glanced to me and then assented, and the woman asked, "If you *are* such a fanatical nationalist, do you find a mysticism about the *völk* to be a part of your worldview?" And I related how my first commanding officer *had* in fact been a mystic, and that I'd found him rather a figure of fun, with his flat feet and bulging eyes and slightly hysterical belief in ur-Germanic witches. I performed an impression of him that made the group laugh. But I then explained that I *did* believe in the power of one blood.

Von Leers suggested I might talk a little about how I got started. He'd served in the Reich Ministry, and his book on the criminal nature of the Jew was well-known, and he'd landed in Buenos Aires six months or so before I had. I gave the short version about having joined the Party in '32 in Linz and then through some good advice having found my way into the security service two years later. The SD in those days earned one not only a higher salary but also the respect, if not the dread, of fellow Party members, and had the most impressive offices in the city besides, on Wilhelmstrasse. I recalled Heydrich on my first day noting that for someone who a few years earlier had been selling gasoline this was a big step up. My specialty had become incognito investigation, visiting Jewish organizations to establish contacts by presenting myself as liberal-minded and eager to learn, the sort of fellow who might be of real help in a pinch. They'd cultivated me as I'd cultivated them, so that my colleagues had soon assessed me as inexplicably well-informed when it came to Jewish matters.

Von Alvensleben eyed me throughout my account. An intermittent participant, he for some bore an equal fascination, because as the *Reichsführer*'s chief adjutant he happened technically to be the highest-ranking member of the Reich in Argentina. He proclaimed the Americans were so chagrined at having failed to apprehend him that at Dachau they hung a photo of him on a tree and shot at it. We have always been wary of one another, since he was at the center of the *Reichsführer*'s retinue and I was the key advisor on the *Reichsführer*'s favorite project, and to him I was just another social climber, and to me he was one of those salon officers whose white gloves stayed clean. In our initial session, he went on about his friendship with von Karajan at such length that finally Fritsch snapped with some irritation that he'd always preferred Furtwängler, and von Alvensleben was so offended with the lot of us on behalf of German music that he maintained an appalled silence for two full sessions afterward.

Once I'd finished, Sassen read from a text he announced had just arrived by post, a short testimony entitled "The Final Solution" within a book called *The Third Reich and the Jews*. Obsessed with what he called "the theory of the six million," he and his circle then turned to me, all of them certain both that the sources we were encountering were lying, and that only the man those sources claimed to be quoting could prove it. Two or three declarations under oath, such as Höttl's, collected for the Nuremberg Trials, fancied that I'd avowed during my farewell speech in Berlin that I would leap laughing into my grave comforted with the knowledge that six million Jews had preceded me. I stopped him to assure him—and the room—that I'd never spoken of six million Jews, but rather of the enemies of the Reich. Fritsch asked why so many German and not just Allied authorities had made the same allegation, and I proposed that perhaps they'd all chanced upon the same lie. Sassen then pressed on with the text while I interrupted to debunk this or that falsehood, until finally I lost patience and waved him off, suggesting that we'd suffered enough of this so-called witness's childish credulity and nonsense, and as though baiting a trap he fingered his

47

mustache and leaned back and asked, "And just whose testimony do you imagine this is?" and when I responded that I was sure I had no idea, he barked, "Wisliceny's!"

So I was knocked off my pins a bit, and in front of everyone. In the space provided by my silence, Sassen informed the curious that Wisliceny had worked directly under me as a special operations commando, both in the Balkans and in Hungary, and apparently had told his captors in Nuremberg that he remembered everything about his boss, Eichmann, with such clarity that he could identify my corpse from the gold crowns on my molars. For his helpfulness, he was executed nonetheless.

When I was able to speak, I acknowledged all of that, and added that he was a fine example of one of those functionaries who'd found himself able to afford the good life because of his negotiations with the Jews, and that by the end he was so fat he could barely sit down.

Sassen asked if I wished to reconsider some of my positions on my subordinate's claims, and I wondered aloud, after a moment, if anyone could know just how forcibly the man had been interrogated. Von Alvensleben countered amiably that some of his reliable contacts had visited Wisliceny in his cell just before his execution, and in their opinion he'd not required torture to produce that statement. There was another pause while the room waited for me to gather myself. I could only reiterate that I had no answers for them, that I would need to study the testimony, and that perhaps our session for that day was at an end. Fritsch remarked that it was still early, and one of the women asked if I was ill, and I stood, for everyone's benefit, and allowed that yes, I had a migraine, and that they could continue without me for the balance of the afternoon, and the crowd then parted for me all the way to the kitchen.

At our dinner table, Vera could sense my agitation—she was always able to perceive when something was awry at work—but discussed the boys. Klaus was by then enough of a problem that he wished to stay out at all hours, and thus she wished to enlist me in the children's discipline once again. When they'd first arrived, after certain associates' visits, I would give the boys a clip round the ear to insure they didn't talk about such things at school, and she'd put a stop to that by asserting maternal dominion over matters in the home. And still that night, despite her assurances she could manage their behavior, she'd been startled to discover what had transpired with Klaus and this girl. I reminded him while his younger brothers looked on that everything wasn't as safe as we sometimes made it appear, and that in fact this was a time of complete mistrust when two men couldn't sit in a café without a third watching them, and a fourth watching the third. Klaus's response was to ask the other boys if they didn't like me better as Uncle Ricardo, who as they'd come off the boat had given them sweets and a hundred pesos each, as opposed to the father who when introduced the next morning began by stating his expectation that each would learn a hundred Spanish words per day. I noted, refusing to rise to the provocation, that a hundred pesos was a lot of money, and he agreed, and looked at his mother and said that he'd used his to buy his first cigarettes. Later that night, beside me on the pillow, she remarked that more and more he reminded her of me. I told her I didn't see the resemblance, and reassured myself that they were all still young. Meanwhile, none of them could explain the difference between National Socialism and Marxism.

I related a little of what had occurred with Sassen, and with her it had a predictable effect. I repeated that this work would be my defense and allow us to return to Germany, where plenty of my old colleagues already were living unchallenged, and where I could perhaps look forward to release after five or six years. She was impatient with what she called my "fantasies," and I asked her sharply if I'd been spared time and again only in order to hide. So many close scrapes, so many miraculous survivals. And after a silence in which I could barely make out her profile in the darkness, she finally responded that it was just like me to have learned the wrong lesson from all that good fortune.

She had gone her own way before. A month after the war began, Müller had summoned me to Berlin to run the Reich Central Office for Jewish Emigration, and she announced that I could go if I liked but she'd be staying in Prague. She'd by then made three moves in four years and disliked Berlin, and when I informed her that her refusal was unacceptable she informed me that the house was big enough that in my absence her sister and brother-in-law could move in. We went back and forth about the matter so tediously that I finally became sufficiently vexed to agree, and found myself a pied-à-terre on Kurfürstenstrasse, near my new office. Eventually, I sent her the address, and she sent back a postcard of two ducks, one in a pond and one standing on a little hill. I visited some weekends, and when I could on my travels.

During that goodbye on the Altaussee, after she'd been evacuated from Prague, at one point during our exchange she shoved me with both arms, nearly sending me sprawling, and then asked if I was really going to claim to her that I had no regrets, and I reminded her that regrets were pointless, a diversion for children. I would never be one of those simpletons who built a cozy house and lived off a pension. She answered with a fury, gesturing at the boys, that our family was pleased to learn of my clear conscience. And I told her something that we used to say about the half-Jews, during the deportations: when wood was chopped, splinters would fall.

I let it be known that I would skip the next session and address the group more formally at the following one, and for two weeks holed myself up with my manuscript and books and Wislicency's testimony and took even my meals at my little desk. I saw myself in a struggle for interpretational sovereignty, which I would use any and all means to win. A strong argument conferred power, and power was something I missed. It was like the old days, retiring to bed in the wee hours and up before everyone else. When the second Sunday finally arrived, at breakfast Vera said only, "A suit?" and the boys offered that I looked like a proper businessman.

I brought to the session a typescript from which I would be reading, the first of two parts, which Sassen assured me he'd transcribe to circulate among the discussion participants afterward. A hush fell as I settled in and arranged my papers, and those in the outer reaches of the room stilled. I began by expressing my appreciation that here in South America I had been accepted by a community of friends to whom I could speak freely. I gave thanks for the extent to which my family had been embraced. But I added that the awareness that some old colleagues had been permitted to go on with their careers or draw their pensions fireside because of their willingness to lay everything at my feet had curdled my newfound gratitude. We'd already discussed the warrant issued in the district court of Frankfurt accusing me of "killing people in numbers that could not precisely be established, in a cruel and underhanded manner, acting from low motives." It was time for me to name all such lies and shame their sources.

To that, Sassen called, "Bravo!" and Fritsch raised a coffee cup in toast. Von Leers, too, seemed pleased, and von Alvensleben steepled his fingers beneath his nose and waited.

Above all, I wanted one truth to be clear: there was no judgment of the historical Eichmann as severe as my own, and I would set forth what illumination I could on these matters. Having acted rightly, I craved the respect rightly due, and my demand for justice applied comprehensively:

I would acknowledge Germany's guilt when the Allies acknowledged theirs. The gathered inner circle rapped on our shared table energetically, and even those in the larger crowd nodded and approved.

It was a shame we didn't have with us any comrades from that time with whom I'd served, I added, since certainly I'd forgotten so much. But the facts were straightforward. We had wished to expel the Jews from our midst, and we had failed. Still, for a while we had succeeded, and my role in that success had been substantial.

I'd gained a reputation as a master of unconventional organization, an emerging area of expertise that had come to be much prized, and my means had been the following: I'd set up an efficient office, recruited good subordinates, maintained harmonious relationships with my superiors, and borne in mind that improvisation was continually required.

The silence that ensued felt vaguely disagreeable, and I lost my place. So I extemporized to provide an example. In the mess I'd taken over in Vienna, it had been routine for spiteful officials to make the Jews wait hours for meetings and weeks for paperwork, and thus emigration permits—being of limited duration—often expired before the entirety of the process could be completed, and so everything had to be initiated all over again. In response, I instituted a conveyor belt of departments, all in a single building, allowing a Jew to submit an application at one end and carry away the necessary credential at the other. I released the money frozen in Jewish accounts to those too destitute to pay the fees. And in the time it took nineteen thousand to leave all of Germany, I'd arranged for fifty thousand to leave Vienna alone. I was suddenly everywhere in demand.

I had the irritating sense that the assembly was becoming increasingly restive. "That was all very illuminating," Sassen finally responded, and thanked me on behalf of the group. But, he said he was obligated to add, there was no doubt that I was the crucial surviving witness concerning the estimation of the number of Jews actually killed, and that issue remained the heart of our investigation.

"And so it should be," I agreed. It was a German virtue, to stubbornly seek the truth. And oddly, almost a Jewish instinct, this desire to collect knowledge. The room waited for me to continue.

Those figures were always exaggerated for propaganda purposes, I noted, no doubt including all who'd died of natural causes, as well. And the large number who'd perished during the Allied air raids, and in those camps like Mauthausen, where the agenda had been to assign the kind of labor that in practice a person could manage only a few days.

There again followed a disquieting hush. That same woman looked on from the very last row against the windows, her friend beside her. The husband nowhere to be found. And again, she raised her hand, and kept it up. The friend leaned into her, as if in support. I considered them but gave no sign, and neither did Sassen, until at last someone murmured, "The lady has a question."

"Please," I said, extending a palm to her. She lowered her hand and asked if, in hindsight, I believed that anything could have been worse for Germany than the National Socialists' rise to power in 1933. There was a bit of an uproar at the insolence, and calls from the crowd for her to apologize, and after a stir in which we could get nothing accomplished Sassen rose and went to her, bending over her with his hands on his thighs and making a great show of patience as he spoke with her, and then with her friend, and then Fritsch joined them, and finally Sassen and Fritsch ushered the two out, before I could lose my composure any further. I was then invited to go on with my presentation, and did, and remembered nothing of what came after, thinking only, even as I read from my pages: A German! And for this we'd given up everything—our youth, our freedom, and for so many, their lives.

At home for the week that followed, I kept my own counsel while Vera went about her business. The boys noticed the way one might notice two birds sitting farther apart on a clothesline.

During another of our rows about her refusal to move to Berlin, she'd again set forth the myriad ways in which, over the course of our marriage, her wishes had not been taken into account, and when I after some forbearance had finally solicited an example she'd returned to her long-ago request for me to intervene for someone or other from her cousin's family whom I'd never met and of whom I'd refused to make a special case. I'd fielded any number of telephone calls from the woman's priest, as well, the Catholic Church always looking to save its non-Aryan converts. This was back before the time had passed for fretting about this or that individual Jew. She reminded me that this woman had consented to speak with me by telephone when I'd been seeking to increase my proficiency with Hebrew. "So, you see, you had met her," Vera argued. And when I continued on with my day, she added, calling out across the house to me, "Proficiency with Hebrew! As far as *I* can make out, that consists of your ability to hold the books the right way round." She called that out to me with the windows open. When I found her, she backed away, frightened, and with my face up to hers I informed her that *this* was the volume at which civilized people spoke, and that when she had something to say to me she should keep the lesson in mind, and that I'd heard not a peep out of her when my work with the chosen people had begun in earnest, so I would remind her just this once, and not again: in for a penny, in for a pound.

There seemed to be a greater anticipation than usual before our next session—a different sobriety, perhaps, in the chitchat as all at the table assumed their places and arrayed their sources around them—and when Sassen saw me note the same woman and her friend in their spot against the wall he leaned in and assured me that the young ladies had agreed their presence would be contingent upon a keeping a respectful silence.

I'd typed up my remarks myself, forgoing Vera's more efficient help. And as I poured my coffee, settled in, and looked about the room, fifty or so faces looked back. Beyond them, the October sun was warming the windowpanes. Sassen said, with a little bow of his head and hand, "Whenever you are ready."

I began by noting that early on it had become clear the noisy radicals who'd banged on endlessly about the Jewish question had of course no solution of their own to offer. And that all the anti-Jewish legislation they'd initiated had caused as many problems as it had settled. The only logical way to resolve the problem of the Jews in Germany was to remove the Jews from Germany. I wouldn't belabor the details, since most had already been addressed in these sessions, but we'd proceeded from working with the Zionist organizations to the Madagascar Plan, which had been struck down by the war with Russia, and when that campaign hadn't developed as quickly as expected the alternative of expelling them to the east, beyond the Russian borders, had unraveled, as well.

Von Alvensleben cleared his throat and wondered if he might pose a question and, at my nod, asked why there hadn't been more effort expended to trade or sell the Jews to the Allies.

This was precisely the sort of question that ignored the realities on the ground, I explained. Imagine during a war my dispatching trainloads of Jews to the Allied borders, and through our own front lines. Who would have taken them? Everyone was eager to get rid of unwanted mouths, not to add more. And I had, by the way, toward the end in Hungary tried to work out a deal involving blood for goods: a large number of Jews in return for ten thousand trucks equipped for winter operations on the Eastern Front. Of course, that had all fallen through.

53

His expression remained unchanged by my answer. I asked if I might be permitted to continue. No one said otherwise, and I resumed. By 1940, vast numbers of Jews were already pouring into the ghettos in Poland, despite the occupation authorities' insistence that there was no room. The governor-general in particular gummed up the works, always complaining at the highest levels that his domain was becoming a human wastebasket. And it was in the summer of '41, I recalled, that Höppner wrote from his post running the Resettlement Office in Posen to remind me that his ghettoized Jews were already facing drastic food shortages and would not survive the winter, so he wondered if the more humane solution wouldn't be to finish off those unfit for labor through some faster-acting means.

A contention then followed in which Sassen and Fritsch seized upon my account to suggest that this was exactly the kind of initiative about which Hitler would have been oblivious, and I again reiterated, in ways they failed to assimilate, just why such a scenario was unthinkable.

On that matter, there was more recalcitrance, which I waited out in silence.

Eventually, Sassen asserted that at the very least I had to admit that much of the time one hand didn't know what the other was doing. I conceded the point, and described to support it the endless tangle of competing party and state agencies over which our leaders had presided erratically, so that we were always bedeviled by conflicting jurisdictions.

"And you yourself said that improvisation was encouraged," Fritsch added.

So once again, I walked the group through the difference between policy and implementation, a mini-lecture they absorbed glumly.

I granted that, to be sure, some excesses had not been authorized, perhaps the most embarrassing of which being in Riga, where *Einsatzgruppe* A massacred six trainloads of Jews from the Reich immediately upon their arrival, many of whom had been decorated veterans of the Great War. But that was what the conference in Wannsee had been all about: rationalizing the chaos and putting everything under one roof.

That seemed an unwelcome bit of insight, as well.

"And do you or do you not have enough of a personal connection with these processes that you can set us straight about some of these sources' claims?" Sassen pressed.

My role had been greatly exaggerated, I made clear. It had been useful to provide the impression that I was behind everything and everyone, that I was here, there, and everywhere, and that no one knew when

54

I was about to appear, since every department was trying to winkle everything possible out of every Jew by threatening to summon the big, bad Eichmann.

"But you did have direct access to the information we've been seeking," he persisted.

Yes, yes, I told him; as they experimented with any number of methods, I was often dispatched to gauge how each was working out: the gas vans, the shooting pits, all of it. I reported none to be satisfactory. But my energies were mostly taken up elsewhere, and it was easy to forget how much care had been necessary in the deportations, since no one wanted material intended for labor showing up useless. Loading a train was a tricky business, whether it was with cattle or flour sacks, and while we were working to solve such problems others were seeking to milk the Jews for their own ends. Here, I meant Jews important to the Reich and not garden-variety Jews. And always, the camps had to be restocked.

"What about the camps?" someone said. I looked to the crowd surrounding our table to see who had spoken but could not decide.

I never saw the actual extermination process in all its various stages, I explained. I was not the man for that—though occasionally a commandant would take pleasure in detailing his daily burdens to the pencil-pushers, mocking us as "office SS." Still, I added, the camps were awful enough that the *Reichsführer* often claimed them as our equivalent of the front lines.

Sassen asked, peering at me queerly, "So you're saying that the so-called death camps were one of the battlefields?" and then said nothing further when I answered in the affirmative. I noted after a silence my continual struggle against obstinate intellects—including those at this very table—who clung to the opinion that the last war had been fought only on the beachheads.

"And the numbers—so the six million was an exaggeration?" he pursued.

Yes, an exaggeration, I agreed.

"And what were the numbers, then?" he inquired.

As he waited, I proceeded aloud, from camp to camp, estimating based on my memory of each one's capacity and duration of operation, and ended up with no more than two to two-and-a-half million—while allowing for maybe another two million due to the army and *Einsatzgruppen* and local initiative.

Those around the table seemed to be speechless, and for once there were no follow-up queries.

"The so-called children's transports, they were part of this battle, as well?" von Alvensleben eventually asked, barely audible.

As for the children's transports, I replied, the sources we'd been consulting said so many transports and so many children, and I said no. And I had nothing more to contribute on the subject for the moment.

After another silence, von Alvensleben conceded that of course they would defer to my greater knowledge.

And following yet another silence, he added that he himself had come to see the Jewish project as not only a mistake but inhuman, un-German, and ignoble, and that he was personally resistant to the idea of hounding defenseless people into gas ovens, and that he'd hated the Poles more than the Jews. Sassen meanwhile appeared mortally discouraged, while Fritsch, with his chin in his palm, toyed miserably with his coffee cup and saucer.

"You never fully grasped the real danger, in that case," I responded, keeping my voice in check, and then congratulated von Alvensleben for knowing his audience.

"What was that like for you—seeing the camps?" Fritsch finally asked.

What I felt at the time was hard to put into words, I explained. So I would not do it.

My answer seemed to satisfy no one. I concluded the exchange by noting that those of us who undertook this work had believed in a heroic realism in which emotion had been immaterial and action paramount. "But I assume that's apparent to you gentlemen, isn't it," I said. "That must be apparent to everyone."

I then returned to my typescript. Yes, I had been the cautious bureaucrat, I told them. But also a warrior, and while I could cheaply and for the sake of current opinion announce my regrets I would not sit here and pretend that this Saul had become a Paul. We'd been fighting an adversary that through many thousands of years of schooling had become intellectually our superior. Eons before Rome was founded, the Jews had been writing their commandments, commandments our Christian churches still obeyed. We'd accomplished what we could, and our humanity had played a role in our weakness. "But," I continued, "I say now that even if it had been ten million I would still celebrate, sitting here with you, that we had done so much to destroy an enemy."

As I read, my anger became fatigue, and no one seemed able to raise their eyes to me. For a minute or two, we all listened to Sassen's grandfather clock intoning in the hallway. "It's hard," I offered, "what I've told you, I know. But it came from the heart."

And at that, Sassen switched off his tape recorder, desolate. I could see on his face that his attempt to use Eichmann to correct Eichmann had collapsed. He and Fritsch lacked sufficient enthusiasm for even the gesture of wrapping things up. Instead, we remained where we sat until an elderly woman near the hallway cleared her throat into a handkerchief and stood, and then examined what was in the handkerchief and shouldered her way into her jacket.

That evening when I arrived home, the boys had gone out, and despite the hour Vera had not switched on any of the lights. I let myself in the kitchen door and struggled to remove my shoes before locating my slippers. I could just make out her figure across the room, near the stove. "Hello," I said, and she returned a quiet hello.

She asked nothing about how the session had proceeded, and I said nothing about her omission. I remained in the entryway and recognized a kind of vigilance in her posture as my eyes adjusted to the gloom. After a while, she sat at the kitchen counter, as though we had finished our discussion rather than refused to begin it, and then I sat, as well. We heard a thump on the glass, which after a moment she identified as a bird, and then another thump, somewhere nearer the windowsill. "Stubborn bird," she murmured. But without more light, it was impossible to determine where either of our gazes was directed.

Vera had ended her toast for her father's sixtieth birthday celebration, early in 1943, by inviting the assembled to raise a glass to the most impressive man she had ever known. This occasioned a roar of hilarity from those at the table who assumed me to be the butt of the joke. His Christian name had been Mátyás, and even at that late age he'd liked to show off at social gatherings by using his extended arm to lift someone seated in a chair to the level of his ear. He had been a health fanatic, one of those apples-and-nuts men, but also a something-or-other in their church, and had taught her, she reported, Rousseau's old dictum that in every assumption that leads to injustice at least two parties are involved: the person making the claim and those who choose to believe him.

When I'd asked her about the toast later that evening as we were undressing for bed, she had answered only that among the things that most wearied her about our marriage were my endless games of hide-and-seek.

Even when we'd first been married, she had posted to him a letter a week, and had received the same in return. In one that I'd glimpsed

57

when she'd been called away from her desk to the telephone, she had signed off with a line of x's glossed for her father's benefit as kisses, and then had added as a joking postscript that given the state of her life she'd probably never get to collect them.

Everywhere I've gone, I've had the secret sense that people have taken my measure and turned away. I'd called Müller "the Sphinx" because everything with him had to be just so, and still I could never be certain if what I'd done was acceptable. When all was going well, people hadn't been able to do enough to invite me to ministers' meetings or private dinners, but even before the war was over suddenly it was as if no one had known me. At the very end, some of my subordinates from IV B4 had come to me as a group to request that since I was the one being hunted as a war criminal I give them leave to go their way without me.

But I have decided that to be human is to survive a history of being discarded. Everyone bears a past dotted with malice and error. Everyone has made informed choices that have caused pain. Everyone has had that voice in his heart that no man can escape. And everyone has cherished a fellow spirit to the detriment of their own welfare and peace of mind, even when they've cherished that spirit for no good reason at all.

For Bettina Stangneth

Nominated by Sandra Leong

GRAMMAR LESSON, SPRING 2022

by HAYDEN SAUNIER

from RIVER HERON REVIEW

*—conjugation is the variation of the form of a verb by which
are identified the voice, mood, tense, number, and person.*

Dead bodies *lie* in the road.
Dead bodies *are lying* in the road.
Dead bodies *were lying* in the road.
Dead bodies *lay* in the road.

Dead bodies *have lain* in the supermarket.
Dead bodies *have been lying* in the supermarket.
Dead bodies *had lain* in the supermarket.
Dead bodies *had been lying* in the supermarket.

Dead bodies *will lie* in the classroom.
Dead bodies *will have lain* in the classroom.
Dead bodies *will have been lying* in the classroom.
Dead bodies *will be lying* in the classroom.

Sentence Review: Dead *(adjective)* bodies *(noun)*
lie *(verb)* in *(preposition)* the *(definite article)*
road / supermarket / classroom *(noun)*

Extra Credit: among these *dependent clauses*
those with unnecessary repetition:

hands bound behind backs/targeted for their color/
unidentifiable except by DNA and shoes/ shot
through the head/again and again and again

Nominated by River Heron Review

BACKSIDERS

by KATHRYN SCANLAN

from THE PARIS REVIEW

We lived in a poor part of town but we had the greatest entertainment. We had the goldfish ponds, we had Motorcycle Hill, we had the dump and Bicycle Jenny. We made rafts for the creek. We lived off the land.

Down the street was a family who'd moved off the reservation—grandfather and kids and grandkids. The grandkids were our age and we spent a lot of time with them. The grandfather liked to tell me about his religion, his beliefs. I loved his stories and his tales. I called him Grandpa.

The old man—he was very well loved but he liked to drink. His daughter and her husband locked him out of the house when he got drunk. I'd say, Grandpa can stay with us—I'll sleep in my sister's room so Grandpa can have mine. So the old man would stay in my room and he'd go home when he sobered up.

His daughter and her husband didn't like Grandpa to drink but they drank, too. They'd drink and get into fights and their kids would come over and we'd call the police. We'd watch out the bedroom window when the police came and hauled them off in handcuffs. The husband was carted away on a stretcher once for stab wounds.

*   *   *

When I was six we got a big dog, but the dog kept wrapping his legs around me and taking my pants off in the front yard. It wasn't his fault—he wasn't fixed and I was the right height.

A week later my mom sent the dog back to the man who gave it to us. I cried like crazy when I came home and the dog was gone.

61

Then my uncle knew a man getting rid of a Shetland pony, but it was a stallion. Uncle borrowed a trailer anyway and brought the stallion pony to our house. We lived in a cheap rental with a rickety little white picket fence. We tied the pony to a concrete block in the front yard where there was plenty of grass to eat.

One day some girls rode by on their mares and the stallion pony started hollering his mating demand. I grabbed his halter but he kicked me against the side of the house. My mom picked up the concrete block to stop him but instead she went skidding down the road behind him— asphalt skiing. Finally a driver pulled over to help and they dragged the pony home together. My mom was scraped and bumped and black and blue all over.

The pony went away right after that.

✣   ✣   ✣

The neighbor girl who was my age, Regina—we lived on dog biscuits, Milk-Bones. We ate slices of bread from the bag.

No one was there in the morning when I got ready for school. I'd put on my mom's red lipstick and her dresses and her high-heeled shoes.

In first grade, eight girls had me up against the lockers, saying, Punch her, punch her! I didn't want to fight, but when one of them came at me I kicked off my heels and let her have it.

They took us to the principal's office and later my mom showed up. There were scratches on the girl's face and she had a black eye. I thought they would put me in prison. My mom said, Are those my shoes?

✣   ✣   ✣

At school, everyone wondered what you wanted to do when you grew up. I said I wanted to be a jockey, riding racehorses. The teachers were concerned. But jockeys are small, and I was getting tall. People told me, put books on your head, you won't grow. So I'd be walking around with books. I stacked the heaviest ones I could find.

My parents took us to the racetrack in Jackson, South Dakota, on weekends. My dad would go inside to gamble and my mom'd wait outside with my sister and me. We'd lean on the rail and watch them run.

✣   ✣   ✣

Well what do you want for Christmas and what do you want for your birthday and what is it you would like, as a treat?

A horse!

We had no permission, no money, but my sister and I rode our bicycles to all the neighbors' houses to ask: Do you have any horses for sale or do you know of any place we could keep a horse or do you know anyone who does have a horse for sale and if so how much?

Keith Baxter owned a stable in town where you could rent a horse by the hour. The first time my mom took me there, Baxter put me on a giant horse named Joe. I said, I want to ride that one instead—and I pointed at a little horse off by himself in the corral. Baxter said, If you can't ride Joe you sure as heck ain't gonna ride Rowdy.

* * *

Rowdy was a little mustang out of Black River, North Dakota—a paint, brown and white, just beautiful. We had a connection. He was always my pick to ride.

Rowdy'd unseat me and run back to Baxter's, but when I got tired of walking three miles to the stable or riding double on another gal's horse, I learned how to stay on. I paid attention to his twitching ears and the feel of his body. When he tensed up, I talked to him. I couldn't afford a saddle so I rode bareback, which strengthens your legs and gives you balance.

Anytime I mowed grass or did jobs around the house, my folks forked over the dollar so I could ride Rowdy. If I had no money I'd go just to brush him and talk to him.

Once, on my birthday, I got to rent him for five hours straight. We packed a little lunch, the horse and I did, and went out to the pasture to run around. Rowdy kneeled in the grass and I jumped off. He pawed in the crick and rolled in the water. We ate our treats and napped in the shade of a big tree.

* * *

When I was sixteen I wrote letters to horse trainers and racetracks. I got their names and addresses from the racing programs I'd collected. I told them I would work for room and board to learn the ropes.

I got a call from an outfit in Denton, Iowa—B. T. Beauregard—Buford Beauregard and his brother Lester. They had three Thoroughbreds and a quarter horse. I lived with them on their farm all summer while school was out—Bud and Lester and their friend Riley Walker from Tindall.

I learned how to run bandages and how to put a mud knot in a horse's tail. I learned to massage their legs to get the blood going.

I had a little windup clock. When they said to rub each leg for five minutes, I had my clock to make sure I did.

I had a favorite horse—Buckin' Bones was his name. Oh, I loved that horse. I loved all my horses. Everybody called me Bones.

* * *

I learned to gallop around the cornfields. There was always pheasants or deer jumping up to spook the Thoroughbreds. I was riding short iron, jockey-style. You use a light little saddle with a flat cantle and you stand in your irons—it takes the weight off the horse's back and puts it over his loin and shoulders. You use long reins and tie them—you make a special cross. Lester's daughter taught me how to make my cross and to keep my shoulders right, my back straight. You think about balance and control and you go easy on their mouths—you use a ring bit or snaffle bit, kind bits, not severe.

There's an art to knowing how much horse you have left under you. You might get out in front in a route race, but you'll run out of gas. No horse can run full bore the whole time. When you train a route horse, you do long, slow gallops to instill air in him. You make sure he has enough to carry him through to the end.

* * *

When we put a horse in to race at Park Jackson, I got to go along. We'd haul in the night before, sleep in a stall at the racetrack, and run our horse the next day. I rode in Old Bud's pickup, in the middle, with Bud on one side and Riley Walker on the other. Old Bud would be puffing away on his nasty cigars and I'd be gagging. We pulled the trailer behind us and when we arrived, our stalls were ready—one for the horse, one for Bud, one for Riley, and one for me.

I'd been to Park Jackson plenty with my parents, but now I was on the backside. I got to meet other racetrack people besides those Denton people. I stood in the winner's circle with Buckin' Bones and got my picture taken.

Park Jackson was a recognized track, the only pari-mutuel betting in the state, but it was bottom of the barrel—one step above the bushes. It was backwoodsy. All kinds of crap went on. Still, it was where some good horses, some good trainers, got their start.

Of course it's gone now. They race motorcycles there instead.

* * *

I went home at the end of the season. School started, but in my free time I read every book I could find about racehorses—feeding and condition-

64

ing and interval training and selective breeding and linebreeding and hoof care, anatomy. I wanted to be better prepared when I went back.

The next summer Bud and Lester put me in charge—I kept their horses for them on the racetrack grounds. Sometimes I had four horses, sometimes three. I was there all week, alone. I did everything. They gave me a workout schedule and I carried out the orders. On weekends they'd drive up from Denton for the races.

Did quite well. Very successful. We were in the money—meaning first, second, third, or fourth place—at least sixty-five, seventy percent of the time, which is phenomenal.

I lived in a trailer park with other racetrackers. My trailer was a mile, mile and a quarter out. Four o'clock feed—I didn't have a car. I'd start walking across a field in the dark at three fifteen in the morning.

I worked all day at the track. Never left. Most people did. I wouldn't barely break to go to the track kitchen to get a bite to eat and I was right back with the horses. People, they knew I was dedicated.

I was known as the Coca-Cola kid because everyone wanted to buy me a drink, get me drunk, but I'd ask for soda instead. Not to say I never over-did it—but it was rare. You say okay to one drink, then suddenly you've got twenty more in front of you, and twenty people telling you to swallow it.

* * *

Those racetrack trailers were run-down, really dilapidated—nothing nice.

A goose lived there. As soon as you stepped out your door the goose would come and—bam!—she'd nail you in the back of the leg.

There were goats. One day I was sick, lying down with the door open because it was so hot—no air-conditioning, just a fan—and when I woke up, a goat was next to me, chewing on my sleeve.

My bedroom looked out on a cow pen and at night I'd listen to them moo.

Whenever it rained, there'd be water everywhere pouring down— fucking bucket bucket bucket, pails pails pails.

My mom and dad came to visit after I got my finger half bitten off by a horse. When they first got there, my dad was busy poking around. He said, What the hell is a butcher knife doing sitting in the window?

Well, I had these knives. I had this butcher knife. I kept it handy. You never know.

* * *

65

At Park Jackson it was the cheaper horses, but a lot of them were at one time big-money horses. In the past they ran for forty, fifty thousand dollars, but most were so broke down you could buy them for fifteen hundred in a claiming race.

Most racehorses bleed from the lungs when they run. They won't win because they're choking on the blood coming up. There was a drug you'd use to bring their blood pressure down, but then that drug got banned because it could mask other drugs.

Some of the old-timers at Park Jackson would tie smooth wire tight to the root of the tail to constrict blood flow. Others took blood from the neck with a big syringe and squirted it into a milk jug until the jug was full. Sometimes the jug got knocked over—there'd be blood all over the ground.

One trainer in particular liked to do it. He plunged so many syringes people would joke, Hey Joey, how come your right thumb's so much bigger than your left?

❊ ❊ ❊

Near the end of summer, I woke up in my trailer one night with a man over me. He sneaked in while I was sleeping and put a gun to my head. I got raped.

He was taking pills. He was a jockey trying to cut weight. He told me he'd just shot a dog.

I didn't say anything because if I'd said something, I would've been off the track. My folks would've come and got me.

The guy sobered up, I knew him, I seen him every day, I knew exactly who it was, it was bad, but anyway, I survived. I cut my hair real short after that.

❊ ❊ ❊

Turned eighteen, finished school, got my diploma. Went full-time at the racetrack. Instead of working one racetrack I traveled the circuit with my racetrack family. There was grooms, jockeys, trainers, racing secretaries, stewards, pony people, hot-walkers, everybody. When one meet ended we'd all go down the road together, bumper to bumper. We'd go to the same grocery stores, the same Laundromats.

We'd go to a bar after the races and it'd be a racetrack bar—the locals would leave. We didn't want anyone else around. Sometimes it ended in a brawl, but usually we landed on our feet. We even had our own band—the Bug Boys. The singer was a jockey, the drummer was a trainer, the bass player was a groom.

Not everybody drank—some just liked to mingle and talk. We'd gather at long tables and watch replays of the races, the whole card on loop. Oh, see—right there! What did I tell him? I told him not to go to the outside, and what'd he do? See his head bobble?

One night an exercise rider brought his bulldog to the bar. The dog jumped into our booth and people started buying it pickled boiled eggs from a big jar. The dog loved them and everyone liked this dog, so everyone bought the dog a pickled boiled egg, but there are only so many pickled boiled eggs a dog can eat before there are consequences to clean up.

❉ ❉ ❉

The backside is a little city. You flash your track license at the guard shack to get in. There's an ambulance on the grounds during training hours because people are always getting hurt. Feed dealers sell sawdust, straw, oats, beet pulp, bran, good hay. Tack wagons stock bandages, saddles, medication, leg paints, sweats, freezes, Bowie Clay, sheet cotton, vet wrap. You live at the track, your life is full. You don't have time to go shopping at the mall. You lose touch with the outside. Things change. You don't hear about world news unless something major happens, because you're in your own world and you have enough news.

❉ ❉ ❉

The racetrack chaplain, he'd make rounds. Everything going okay? He was concerned about the backside, our personal attitudes, problems, hard times we were having, good times. If we wanted to talk, he was available. The chaplain'd say, We're having a service tonight, seven o'clock under the grandstands. We'd be dirty in our work clothes but he'd say, just come as you are, we'd love to have you. And he'd make sure the service was held after our chores were done. It wouldn't be on a Sunday because there was races on Sundays. It'd be on a dark day in the middle of the week.

Before a race card started, the chaplain would hold a prayer service in the jockeys' room. A lot of the jocks joined. Most of them—I think all of them—would sit and say a prayer together. It didn't matter what they believed.

❉ ❉ ❉

I met the jockeys and seen what they did to make weight. They slap on glycerin and cling wrap and sit in their cars with the heater blasting when it's a hundred in the shade—they pass out. They go in the hotbox—it's like a refrigerator with a spot on top for your head to stick out. Once, a jock caught on fire when the hotbox short-circuited. He had terrible burns all over his body.

The jockeys flip their food or they don't eat at all. They get so good at puking they brag about it—I can flip the rice but leave the beans!

For a few weeks I stopped eating, thinking I could shrink myself. But I was tall—though we do have some tall jocks—and I was muscular doing all that work. The jocks are muscular, too, of course, but they're smaller-statured. There was no way I could keep it up without getting sick.

Sometimes a jockey hasn't ever been on the back of the horse he's riding before. They don't develop a close relationship. I loved to gallop the racehorses, and I ponied, too. I got to work them, open them up, breeze them. I took them to the starting gates. I did everything a jockey does except ride in a race.

*　*　*

If something strange happens, riders say, *Shit fire, save me some matches!* They sing little jingle ditty things. They holler, *Coming on the inside!* or *Whoa back!* Sometimes a horse'll throw his rider and come barreling at you when you're galloping during workouts. Then they yell, *Heads up! Loose horse!*

In the early morning when it's still dark with just a few lights up, you'll be galloping down the empty track and hear *thump, thump, thump, thump*—hoofbeats behind you. It's beautiful. And riders will stand straight up on their horses then—they call it grandstanding. They stand up and stretch out their arms and say, *Thought I was a coyote, but I'm all right now.*

*　*　*

Four o'clock feed, seven days a week. After that you tack them up and get them out on the track. They see the saddle go by and they're arching their heads and bobbing up and down. While the horses are out, the stalls get cleaned. Water buckets get scrubbed, feed tubs get scrubbed. You don't put feed in a dirty old tub. You scrub.

If it's hot you use a hose, but most days you heat up water for a warm bath with a natural sponge and shampoo when they're done running. You clean their sheath with Castile soap if they're a gelding, or if they're a mare, you clean their little tits. You might put a light fishnetty fly sheet on them, but typically your nice big squirrel-cage fans will keep the flies away.

You have your bandages laundered, rolled up, ready. You have your sheet cotton and your hoof packing. You groom them and put on leg liniments, run bandages. You might freeze their legs with ice or put them in a turbulator with Epsom salts. They love to stand with the warm whirlpool water up past their knees. If their shoulders are stiff, you rub salve on and wrap them in plastic and pin a wool blanket around their neck. Pretty soon the sweat starts dripping. It loosens them up, makes them feel good.

On race days, you sprinkle this green powder—it looks like dope— onto a little piece of sheet cotton and light it on fire under the horse's nose. There's belladonna in it, among other things. You put a bucket on the ground and drape the horse with a raincoat so he can really steam open his head. All this crap—snot, phlegm, mucus—pours from his nose into the bucket.

Once, some trainer's kids who hung around the track thought they'd be smart and smoke it, too. They smoked it, then ran around like squirrels.

*　*　*

At Deerheart, Nebraska, we all ran around in golf carts—from the backside of the barns up to the racing office, over to the kitchen and that. Bobbie Mackintosh milked Winnie the goat, who was a mascot for a racehorse called Springtime Notion. When she wasn't in her stall with Springtime, Winnie'd jump on Bobbie's golf cart and away they'd go.

I was having a terrible time with my stomach, and one day Bobbie heard me complaining about it. She said, Sonia, have some goat milk. She gave it to me straight off the goat—nasty, not pasteurized or nothing—but right away my stomach felt better, and then I was fine.

If you're sick, you wait for the veterinarians to come around and treat you, too. The jockeys got B_{12} shots before each race—three, four B_{12} shots a day. You'd say, Oh, I'm exhausted, and the vet'd give you a B_{12} shot. If you had a bad tooth you pulled it yourself.

69

Once I was up for five wins in a row with Miss Sotmoore—she was one of my best mares—but I had a fever and I could hardly move.

Another trainer said, If you want to come over, I'll have Mom give you a shot of—I don't know what it was. It might've been cattle antibiotics. This fellow happened to live about twelve miles from the track, so I went home with him and bent over the kitchen sink and his mom gave me the shot. Within three hours I was a new person. I got to see my horse run, and we won our fifth in a row.

❊   ❊   ❊

You spend hours and hours with a horse. They run their hearts out for you. You know when they're hurting.

Janet M.—she'd run like a house on fire, but she was getting sorer and sorer. I told the owner, We need to blister her and give her some time, bring her back next spring.

Oh no, the owner says, she wants to race—she's better than ever.

You're not there in the morning when she can't even stand up, I said. So I refused. I said I wouldn't train her no more.

The owner—Tricky Ricky, people called him—he found somebody else to do it. Next time Janet M. ran I was there, watching the race. Bobble, bobble—she busted her leg clean off.

I found Tricky Ricky afterward. I said, You call yourself a horseman?

❊   ❊   ❊

Bob Bozeman was an owner who'd been a jockey. He weighed maybe 120 pounds soaking wet. His wife, Charlene, was a big woman with blond, fluffy, weird hair like a movie star's. They had two grown daughters and then they had a little gal, Bebe, who was an accident—Charlene got pregnant when she was forty-four years old. The squirt was spoiled, spoiled, spoiled. She was a little friend who'd help me sometimes with the horses.

Bob was a big gambler, a little shaky. I was happy because I had a good stable of his horses to train, but he'd always put the screws to me. When he drank he'd take on the biggest person he could find. One night a bunch of us were at a big table at Hungry's to celebrate a win. You grilled your own steaks at Hungry's—big old sirloins, huge slabs of Texas toast. Bob got drunk and said, I'll put my dick down the neck of this beer bottle. He was working on it when Charlene stood up and said, Bobby, put that little thing away. The waitress came over and we got kicked out of the restaurant.

70

At draw time, the owner had to be present, but Bob lived in Oklahoma, so he said, We'll fix that problem right now and put the horse in your name. Well, wasn't that fine and dandy—on paper, I was the owner. But then when we win a nice race, guess who paid the tax?

Bob'd come down for the races on Wednesdays and Saturdays. He'd rent a motel room for the week and the room would sit empty on days he drove back to Oklahoma. One week when I'd been sleeping in my truck he said, You might as well stay at the motel since it's paid for, and he gave me the key. But then he came back early and let himself into the room one night while I was asleep. He thought he'd get him some from me.

He was slick, tricky—a slippery son of a bitch. He pulled stunts that made me look like an idiot. You had to watch him. You had to learn. He respected it when you outsmarted him. You can't blame a man for trying, he'd say.

*   *   *

Tim Tucker's parents were wealthy, and they bought him expensive racehorses to train. He wore fancy suits and fancy boots and dark sunglasses and after a few months on the scene he thought he knew everything. He did well, got several wins, but mostly because his horses were so expensive to begin with. All he had to do was drop them in.

Once, after his horse beat my horse, I said, Congratulations, Tim, your horse ran a good race, and he said, Sonia, suck my dick.

The next day, my boss says to me, Sonia, do you know where those bute pills are? He'd just gotten a new bottle from Charblatt. I said, Maybe Tim borrowed them. I wasn't being nasty—that's what we did. We borrowed things, loaned things, helped each other out. But when my boss asked him, Tucker said, I didn't take them—but maybe that dumb cunt who works for you did.

I found Tucker and we had a brawl. He pulled my shirt way up and we were rolling around on the ground. My boss had to drag me off. Tucker was crying and the next day he had a black eye. Everybody was happy about it. They were really rubbing it in.

If you start a fistfight at the racetrack you're supposed to be banned a few months, but instead the stewards said, Sonia, what can we buy you for breakfast?

Tucker did change after that. And a few years later, when I was injured so bad I almost died, he's the one who invited me to stay with him

71

and his wife in their trailer at the racetrack. When I got out of the hospital I couldn't even sit up on my own, but Tucker and his wife—they took good care of me.

* * *

A lot of my friends have gotten killed. A lot of them have steel rods down their spines. One guy lost his leg. He was a jockey who'd lost his leg, but he'd still gallop horses and pony them to the gate. Sometimes his fake leg would fall off when he was riding and someone had to run out and pick it up for him.

There's a lot of pain and pill abuse. You learn some of them are drunks. They show up to hot-walk and they're drunk. When they say they're hungry, you don't give them money. You take them to get a bite instead.

The leg paint I used on the horses had alcohol in it. One morning I came in at four and said, Where's Thorby?

I finally found him passed out in an empty stall. I thought he was dead. He'd gotten into my tack box and drunk up all of my leg paint.

If you had a wild one, you gave it to Thorby—he'd jump on and hoot and holler. It was like he was glued to the horse. He wouldn't ever fall off. Horses responded to him. Thorby was gentle but when he got drunk he'd pick a fight with a cigarette machine or a jukebox.

* * *

My friend Bobbie Mackintosh was galloping a three-year-old and the three-year-old spooked. Bobbie's foot got tangled in the irons and she got dragged. Her neck broke—a hangman's break. She'd just gotten married the week before.

They life-flighted her off the racetrack and took her to the hospital. She was in a coma four months. She had a brain injury. When she woke up she was paralyzed except for her arms. She had to learn how to talk again. The husband dumped her, of course. He dumped her right away.

She got hurt in January. In late November, she showed up at the racetrack in a wheelchair. They let her work the pari-mutuel window. She talked real slow, but she remembered me. We'd used to hitch a ride to the racetrack together every morning at four back when we were staying at the El Rancho Motel—her and her boyfriend and me and the idiot I was with.

Bobbie had to have surgeries all the time, and she was in therapy the rest of her life. She got a medical support dog and she got remarried, too. She was always working on her arm strength. You can read about her on the internet. Her doctors wrote testimonials about her determination and how she made history. She was known as a miracle person.

She just passed away last year. She wanted to write a book about her life. Anyway, she was from Minnesota.

Based on transcribed interviews with a former racehorse trainer from Iowa.

Nominated by Ben Stroud

PEE STANDS FOR PREJUDICE

by ZORINA EXIE FREY

from GLASSWORKS

1. *Circa 2015*

My coworkers and I Uber to happy hour in Coral Gables.
Nobody and everybody's hood.
Cuban. Haitian. Turkish.
Mexican. Arab. European.
African? American?—me.
Tapas chased down with White Russians & reggaeton beats.
Slurred speech accompanies laughter & selfies.
Bar hopping adventure.
Blonde hair & Blue eyes strides
into America's alley to pee with no tissue.
I, with a full bladder lookout
for the nearest proper public facilities.

2. *Circa 2005*

My coworker and I drive to a garage party in Niles, Michigan.
White people playing rap music
Cheers'ing beer bottles
Pabst Blue Ribbon testosterone
surveys Africa's rolling plains.

Their eyes hunt my gazelle legs, my caramel-continent skin,
my sand-kissed lips, my
inner-fight. The lioness considering . . .

Blue & grey eyes scowling
Move, bitch! Get out the way!
Ludacris booms through whitewashed speaker boxes.
My music betraying me.

It's ok. You're with me.

Now, I'm the white girl in her hood.
Walking me back to my hatchback
She relieves herself in shrubs.
America's front yard, with no tissue.

3. *Circa 1983*
We played Luke, Han, Leia, and Godzilla.
Eric had the Millennium Falcon.

He lived further down my white block.
Far enough for me to ask to use his bathroom.
  He refused.

I can't. My father says because you're Black.
To which I replied with a swinging closed fist.
  A reflex.

Since it's frowned upon for me to pee in a bush
I rode my Big Wheel home to relieve myself.

Eric's father berates my momma on her doorstep
flexing white privilege, Eric had a bloody lip.
Look what your daughter did! He hissed.

My mother's 1930s mentality kicked in.
She picked a twig to whip me.
A crime now. Legal when whites did it.

4. *Circa 1980*
My block occupies all white folks.
My friends, Mark & Amy live around the corner
playing Star Wars with baby dolls.

When I used their bathroom,
I wasn't allowed to close the door.
They watched to see if I pee'd black.

When they found it to be yellow,
Mark wiped the toilet seat with white tissue
Erasing my existence.

5. *Circa 1974*

I live in between two different worlds.
Once Black.
The other white.
My mother's light-skinned melanin tells me
Yankee blood swims beneath the bedrock of our family river
where some people pee.

Nominated by Glassworks

THE FUTURE IS A CLICK AWAY

fiction by ALLEGRA HYDE

from BOMB

The Algorithm knew the timing of our periods. It knew when and if we'd marry. Whether we'd have kids. It knew how we'd die. It knew where we went, why we lingered, why we left. It knew what seemed unknowable: the hidden chambers of our hearts. When it sent us tampons in the mail, we took them. We paid.

We were a matrix of a billion-trillion data points. The Algorithm had them all. It saw patterns inside of patterns, heard the whispered implications of our every click, hover, scroll speed, misspelled search term. The Algorithm decoded our emails—our text messages too. It could read a crab emoji like a rune, a dream symbol: our subconscious laid naked before its super-computer mind. The Algorithm had studied enough crab emojis to know how people acted after using one. It synthesized this data with a thousand other patterns—the local weather, stock markets, mortgage rates—decoding our cyber-DNA to peer through the looking glass of the space-time continuum and perceive our future needs. A crab emoji texted after *i luv you*, and the Algorithm sent us a pack of micro-filtering vacuum bags.

Deliveries occurred at least twice a day in most regions.

The Algorithm sent Sonya, in Fairbanks, AZ, a box of sponges. Sonya already had sponges, but not the kind with a scouring pad on one side, which made the Algorithm's delivery fortunate—no, fated—because that night she burnt a pan of lasagna.

Anastasia, in Harrisonburg, VA, received an ankle brace. The Algorithm had anticipated the sprain she'd suffer later that week on a hike up the High Knob Trail. Was the prediction predicated on a kink in

Anastasia's posture—the reality of weakening cartilage embedded in a lifetime cross section of bathroom mirror selfies? Or was there an air of recklessness in her email sign-offs that week *(ttyl, Ana)?* In the end, the Algorithm's methods didn't matter so long as she got what she needed.

Fatima, in Taos, NM, received a set of lemon-scented soy-wax candles.

Everly, in Great Falls, MN, received an all-weather wireless phone charger.

Jan, in Marfa, TX, received a twelve-ounce bottle of motor oil.

Deidre, in Detroit, MI, got a whole sofa: malachite-green, velvet soft, curvaceous. Was it because she'd clicked on stain removers? Streamed too many David Lynch movies? Collected semiprecious stones as a child and uploaded images to multiple social media accounts? Didn't matter. Deidre loved the sofa: a distillation of her desires that had materialized outside her door with the swift wonder of a miracle. Depending where you lived, the Algorithm used drones to drop goods outside of homes in bubble-wrapped packages or workers off-loaded cardboard boxes from unmarked trucks or, in some instances, goods were whisked into apartment lobbies through pneumatic tubes—though that feature remained unavailable to people in most parts of the country.

You are always welcome, the Algorithm noted on every packing slip, *to send these items back.*

We never sent the items back. We knew we might regret the returns if we did, because the Algorithm was always right.

"Sure, but what if the Algorithm is in cahoots with certain for-profit companies?" a few journalists speculated on occasion. "What if a woman receives an ankle-brace because Big Ankle Brace is pushing their latest model—not because the woman really needs foot support?"

These questions were rhetorical; the journalists took the Algorithm's goods, too.

"Perhaps we find uses for the items we receive because we have received them," suggested several behavioral psychologists. "Maybe it's a form of confirmation bias?"

But the behavioral psychologists confirmed that they also took the goods.

"Could be witchcraft," said the anti-witch agitators, who were suspicious of the Algorithm's uncanny accuracy. Yet this faction later disowned their prejudice, after receiving thought-provoking pamphlets on the topic—pamphlets that were constructed by us, using the paper and sparkly pens the Algorithm had delivered to our homes for such purposes.

The Algorithm worked in mysterious ways.

Which isn't to say there weren't a few non-believes. There was a small contingent of people who sent the Algorithm's goods back.

People like Inez, in Denver, CO.

Inez wouldn't accept her deliveries from the Algorithm, even when she needed a particular item, such as socks—because hers were full of holes—and beautiful new socks arrived outside her door.

"But you have money from your pension." we said, "and these socks are reasonably priced."

"Also," we said, "it's a hassle to return stuff."

"And these socks would fit you perfectly," we added. "There's space for your one long toe."

Inez wouldn't accept the goods. A curmudgeon. Seventy-something years old, we estimated, though we could not be sure. (Inez had also refused the sunscreen and wide-brim hats the Algorithm had sent to protect her skin from the damaging effects of UV radiation—which was especially bad in Denver due to the city's high elevation.) She returned the socks, opting to darn her old pairs with yarn she'd acquired from the shantytown market: a motley bazaar at the far edge of the city's sprawl, where a rough crowd bartered for used and salvaged bric-a-brac, wilted homegrown lettuce, and amateur ceramics. Inez acquired most of her goods at the market. Or she went without.

"No wonder she's grumpy," we said to one another.

We did not understand her resistance to the Algorithm. But what we knew for sure was that the Algorithm understood us. After all, we'd been inside its system since before we knew how to type—back when our parents first posted photos of our infant bodies, swaddled and squishy in hospital beds. Although we had no proof, we suspected that the Algorithm might have known, even then, the fates that lay before us—not only what items we'd need, but who we would become. The Algorithm had likely already predicted that Umi would be a helicopter pilot, and Kendall a veterinarian specializing in equine treatments, and Arley a nicotine-addicted fashion model, who would sometimes take horse tranquilizers and occasionally require medical evacuation via helicopter. From our first uploaded image, the Algorithm had been invested in our futures. It had analyzed the texture of our baby blankets, the micromusculature on our crying faces, the awkward cradle of our parents' arms. Then again, perhaps the Algorithm had known us before we even officially existed—extrapolating likely outcomes from our parents' data points, and their parents' data points—a long legacy of information digested and decoded, made into the deliveries that appeared outside our doors.

It brought us comfort that we could be known so fully. In the long march of adulthood—when we lost our friends to distance, lost our parents to age—we never felt truly alone. We had something looking out for us, didn't we? We had the Algorithm at our side.

To be fair, a few deliveries had given us pause. For instance, there was the time the Algorithm sent one of us packages of ground coffee—decaf—and we were mildly annoyed. Decaf? Really? What good would decaf do when we had emails to answer, charts to consider, customers to serve? How would we stay awake? We almost called the Algorithm's customer service line, but our doctor's office called us first. Our test results had come in. The cardiologist recommended we reduce our caffeine intake.

We were grateful; we gave thanks. We praised the Algorithm for its insight and the gift of individualized commodity distribution.

We took our goods. We paid.

"See how much better our lives are," we said to Inez, when we passed her on the street, "with all these products selected for us by the Algorithm?"

She was carting a wheelbarrow full of wild mushrooms, bits of wire, tattered out-of-date almanacs. Her white hair was damp from the exertion. Beside her walked a drifter—dressed in a fake-fur coat and rain boots—whom Inez had likely met at the shantytown market. The drifter carried a large ceramic jug filled with a sloshy liquid; he grinned at us toothlessly.

We ignored the drifter, focused on Inez. It upset us to see this elderly woman performing such taxing labor, her body sweating and unsunscreened as she pushed her wheelbarrow forward.

"Why," we said, "won't you accept the package of premade meals and the easy-yet-entertaining craft items the Algorithm has delivered to your house?"

Inez grunted, continued pushing the wheel-barrow. The drifter made a birdcall noise.

"If you did," we went on—our voice growing shrieky with agitation—"you wouldn't have to haul these odds and ends all the way across the city!"

Inez sighed. She stopped pushing the wheel-barrow and turned to face us, and for a moment we thought we'd achieved victory: we'd helped this old woman relinquish her misguided ways. But then Inez said, "What could the Algorithm know about me that I don't? How can it possibly see the true depths of my soul? The Algorithm is a corporate robot, not a god. It was programmed by people and I've met people. I will not worship at the altar of Capitalistic Codependence. I will live freely and of my own accord."

The drifter hooted.

We shook our heads, retreated into our houses. We knew Inez was misguided, but it would be a lie to say her words did not linger and lurk in our minds. It would be a lie, too, to suggest that those of us who lived in Inez's neighborhood did not peer through our windows at night, watching as she and the drifter—or maybe multiple drifters?— drank moonshine and sang sea shanties on her porch. Because we did. We also watched as she staggered outside the next morning to water her tomato plants, her white hair wild, her belches loud as she ignored the box of electrolyte-filled coconut water the Algorithm had delivered to her doorstep to help with her hangover.

We did not understand Inez's thinking. We were glad, though, that the Algorithm understood ours—it sent foam stress balls to everyone living in Inez's neighborhood, having anticipated our anxiety. It sent batches of sleeping pills, too, so that everyone's rest would be unpunctuated by sea shanties or worries. The Algorithm knew we were simply trying to live our lives: to attend our dentist appointments and our children's birthday parties and our parents' funerals, and to do our jobs well enough to pay for it all. The Algorithm saved us time and preserved our energy. It sent us baby clothes before we had babies. Bigger clothes before we gained weight. The Algorithm always remembered our birthdays. It sympathized with our struggles; for instance, when we missed our friends—who were too busy or faraway to grab a casual coffee— the Algorithm sent us photo albums containing images of past coffees culled from our social media. We wept over those curated pages. We happily paid the four installments of $39.99. The Algorithm was always looking out for us; we were grateful when it delivered new home security features, anticipating a rise in local crime. It sent us bottles of milk before riots broke out in some cities, predicting that tear gas would be carried on the wind and get in our eyes. In Denver, where the air was thin and dry, our noses sometimes bled—dripping like faucets—even on the days no riots occurred, so the Algorithm sent us tissues. It sent

81

home humidifiers. Gas masks. Air-moisturizing houseplants. It sent ear plugs for helicopter noise. Air purifiers for wildfire smoke. It sent us charcoal water for general bodily purification. The Algorithm sent us more and more, ever striving to make our lives better. It intuited the larger television we needed to distract us from the chaos outside our homes, as well as the blouses and golf putters and candy bars and fountain pens and hand towels and salt rocks and macramé plant hangers and chess sets and watercolor paper and glass unicorn figurines and frying pans and tweezers and duct tape and decorative wall prints and toilet paper and antacid tablets and hair dye and cat beds and guitars and exercise bikes and plastic orchids and rare Roman coins we coveted, delivering these items like a fairy godmother, making our lives easier, brighter, making us feel known.

Years passed. The world went on, tumultuous as ever—but thanks to the Algorithm, we could tune that tumult out.

We were damn lucky, we believed.

Then one day, Lacy—who lived a few houses down from where Inez had lived—came home and found three large boxes in her driveway. The boxes contained a scuba suit—too large for Lacy's small frame. A lifetime supply of mayonnaise. And a coffin.

Could the Algorithm have made a mistake? We wondered this as we peered from our windows, watching as Lacy walked around the items, poked at them.

"What the hell?" she said.

The sentiment rang true, and yet we'd questioned the decaf coffee, hadn't we? And how wrong we'd been. The Algorithm was always right. If Lacy was meant to have these items, then it was only a matter of time before she understood their purpose.

The Algorithm never sent us more than we could handle. It knew the scope of our desires, but also our limitations. For instance, a single mother who earned a modest living as a dental hygienist—someone like Ernestine, let's say—would not receive a genuine South Sea pearl choker, made with white gold and inlaid with diamonds, even if her search history revealed compulsive price-checking, page-saving, and an otherwise deep consumer interest in the necklace. No, the Algorithm would not put Ernestine and her children on the street because of her fixation. But it would send her a tasteful stainless steel and imitation pearl replica. The Algorithm knew our hearts, and also where to draw the line.

And when the items we received cost a little beyond our budgets, well, we made our budgets bigger. We took extra night shifts, weekend shifts. That's what Deidre had done, for instance, when the green sofa sent by the Algorithm turned out to be a *touch* pricier than she would have preferred. All of us did what we needed to do to accommodate the small extra costs. Who were we to question what the Algorithm knew? We did our best to optimize, the way an algorithm might. We quit our softball league to work more. We told our kids: no camp this summer, sorry. We turned down the AC in our homes, even when the weather was wickedly hot.

Inez had, back in the day, told us we were fools for working so much, back when we asked her if she thought we were fools. This had made us upset. "You asked," she said. Which was true. Also, to be completely honest, even though the Algorithm never sent us anything prohibitively expensive—and even though we worked constantly—over time, the small extra costs had added up. We'd come to owe a lot of money to the Algorithm. We also owed money on the money we owed, on what our parents had owed, and their parents, too. So we worked. We worked all the time. We let the Algorithm take care of our shopping. Easier that way, we told ourselves. The Algorithm could be so thoughtful, we thought, opening a newly delivered box, filled with more foam stress balls to squeeze. New fluffy slippers. An acupressure mat—which a was bit over the top, yes, but which would help with our back pain from sitting hunched over our desks, working for hours on end. *Thank you,* we said. *Thank you so much.* We doubled down on loving the Algorithm, because the Algorithm loved us. Because the Algorithm would take care of us—of that we were sure. So we bought what it sent us. Praise be: we paid.

And yet, looking at the items on Lacy's lawn, we couldn't help wondering.

A day passed, and then another. Lacy left the boxes in her driveway—unsure of what to do with them. The items were also hard to move. So she waited.

More days passed. Lacy did not grow three sizes and fit into the scuba suit.

She did not develop an intense craving for mayonnaise.

She did not die.

We remembered, then, how Inez had knocked on one of our doors, a few months back, to borrow sugar. She was making muffins, she'd told us, to share with visiting friends. The shantytown market had been shut down for health code violations; she wasn't sure when it would reopen.

"But, Inez," we said, "isn't there a box of sugar on your lawn?"

We pointed at the cardboard box on her lawn, marked *Sugar!*

Inez scowled. "I don't want that sugar," she said.

We ran our fingers through our hair. We wanted to help Inez, but we couldn't stop staring at the box of sugar the Algorithm had sent. "It's right there," we said. "What you need. And while, yes, I have sugar in my pantry, I'm hesitant to give it away. What if I have sugar in my pantry because I might need to make muffins for a surprise bake sale, and if I fail to do so when the time comes—because I gave my sugar away— my daughter will not be well-liked by her teachers and classmates, and will fall behind in her education, and will end up homeless and destitute, and will have many unresolved emotional issues about how her mother did not properly take care of her, which she will not be able to address because quality mental health care is prohibitively expensive?"

Inez said: "Are you sleeping okay?"

"Ha ha," we said, and held up a bottle of sleep medication the Algorithm had sent us, along with decaf caffeine pills to balance us out, because getting up in the morning was hard sometimes, on account of the sleeping pills.

Inez cracked her neck, peered up at the sky: murky with smog and wildfire smoke and a stray puff of tear gas. She looked tired. She looked even older than we had originally guessed her to be. Maybe, we thought, she shouldn't stay up late drinking moonshine with wandering vagrants. Maybe she could use sleeping pills, too. Also, a self-massager for her neck and dark-circle-reducing eye masks. It pained us to know that these items had been delivered to Inez's home and she had not accepted them; that she had the opportunity to live a more comfortable and dignified life, but chose not to.

"Maybe I'll skip the muffins today," said Inez, and smiled at us, which was odd, because we had not helped her. Also she did not smile very often.

Inez walked across the street and back into her house.

The box of sugar remained on her lawn.

The next day it rained. The cardboard box dissolved into a misshapen lump, and then the sugar dissolved, too, disappearing into the grass.

Inez was arrested soon after that, because she did not pay for the sugar, which she also did not return. And because the Algorithm had flagged her as a risk to society based on her well-documented social delinquency and her predicted behavioral trajectory. There were many overlaps between the Algorithm's analytical insights on consumerist and judicial fronts.

We never found out what happened to Inez after her arrest.

Though, to be honest, we also never looked into it; we worried what the Algorithm would make of such online searches, feared that it might infer that we had lost our faith in its judgments.

And yet, we also found ourselves whispering, *A shame,* because we kind of missed Inez's late-night sea shanties and the drifters tramping through the neighborhood—though we were having trouble remembering the precise details of those memories. The sleeping pills made our minds foggy. We were working so many hours by then.

Plus, when Lacy's strange deliveries arrived, we were distracted by their mystery.

If there was one person we would have asked about the scuba suit, and the mayo, and the coffin, it would have been Inez.

Inez was gone, though.

And so Lacy bought the items. She paid.

A month passed. More items arrived—large items, odd items—that surrounded our doorsteps, blocked our driveways, covered our lawns. An inflatable bouncy castle. Sherlock-style hats. A crate of AK-47s. Hundreds of yards of rope. A live Philippine cobra. A twelve-burner barbecue grill. A jet ski. A moped. A canon. Endless filing cabinets. Used hotel furniture. Brand new hotel furniture. A very long knit scarf. Very small dentures. A life-size doll that looked like our least favorite child. A plastic palm tree. Arsenic-laced wallpaper. A twelve-gallon drum of antifreeze. Flags for countries we'd never visited.

We wrote to customer service. "A mistake?" we asked, because by that point we could not help asking.

Ha ha, said the AI representative. *Thank you for contacting customer service. The Algorithm has a special treat for you.*

An unmarked truck delivered a box containing more sleeping pills. A yoga ball bounced off the back of another truck. Then a light-blocking sleep pod arrived. Followed by black-out curtains. Turmeric powder for inflammation. Lavender-infused moisturizer.

"These items are wonderful," we said, trying to smile—then coughing politely. "They are also very expensive."

Stress balls dropped from the sky in a colorful foam rainstorm.

"Thank you," we said, "thank you, but actually, we—" We had long ago run out of storage space. We were running out of credit as well. Also, it had started actually raining. "Please," we said, "just let us get organized." But the deliveries kept coming, more every minute, and the items were getting soaked on our lawns. We thought of the sugar. There was something to remember, notice. Our minds spun.

We raced inside, logged onto the internet. We looked up *sugar, dream symbols, neighbor relationships, prison.* Articles floated by. We squinted at screens, exhausted, grasping for meaning. Outside our houses, more items arrived, piled on top of one another. Hours passed. No meaning materialized. Our eyelids twitched from the strain. We fell asleep on our keyboards.

In the morning, the Algorithm sent us new reading glasses.

Nominated by Lydia Conklin, Olivia Clare Friedman

THE DISHWASHING WOMEN

fiction by TRYPHENA L. YEBOAH

from NARRATIVE

At first there was one of them, and then two, and like a child that isn't planned but also isn't an accident, there was a third. They lived in a small kitchen inside a big kitchen. They imagined their place as some kind of pantry—only rather than a cupboard with shelves, it was an entire room, with a door and a window (that quickly steamed up when there was a lot of cooking in the big kitchen, which was often the case) and even a tall wooden cupboard in the corner where they kept canned foods, chipped plates, colorful scarves, woven straw hats, and a million other unnamed things. Adoma, the newest addition to the kitchen staff, did not want to believe it was the room assigned as the maids' quarters. It was a tiny room compared to all the other rooms in the house. But the maids made a home of it, and when she would look around, Adoma was indeed surprised by their possessions—a stained velvet curtain that hung on the wall, a side table with a lampshade that had no bulb in it, old newspapers to wrap smoked fish in or fold in two as a hand fan when the heat was unbearable, a basket filled to the brim with aprons. So much of it secondhand treasures, and so many times their hands did the digging and salvaging from what would soon be discarded as worthless.

Adoma was the youngest of them all, and at twenty-nine she did not want to accept that well-meaning people designed their homes to include small rooms of this kind for other humans. It seemed strange, the disparity; reckless, the thought of it.

The mansion belonged to a diplomat, his wife, and their two children—Samantha and Ben. At two years old Ben was a precious and often abandoned boy walking and throwing two-word sentences all over the place. When the women first moved in, he would poke his head into the kitchen, cackle, and turn around and head back to the other side of the house. It was almost as if he knew where the territory ended for him, to which side of the building he belonged. After a few weeks, though, and this might be because of all the aromas of food, or their singing and chatter, Ben crossed the gray marble tiles that separated the hall from the kitchen. His mother didn't mind and was perhaps pleased to have him off her hands, and so he kept coming—only on condition that he stayed in the main kitchen. The women had come to wash dishes (that was the initial arrangement), but with all the gatherings and parties the family had been having, extra hands were needed to assist with the cooking. Soon enough, with their secret recipes and many whispered recommendations to the cook about what local spices to use and the right amount of time to keep pastries in the oven, they had more to add to their workload, while their payment stayed the same. And with Ben wanting no other place to play with his toys than on the kitchen's wooden floor—surrounded by women who saw him, tickled him, stuffed a tiny cornbread muffin into his small mouth every now and then, and threw him up in the air and caught him in their firm hands—they quickly became nannies too.

As for Samantha, or Sam, as her parents called her, she watched them from a distance. Sometimes she was envious of the affection her brother received, but most of the time, her eyes were cast down, the anger visible in her slumped shoulders. She did not want to be there, away from her friends and her private school and paved roads back home. She sat in the next room journaling, sometimes writing letters to friends, complaining about the scorching sun. When her father would walk by and say, "You have to make a conscious effort to make yourself feel at home, we will be here for at least two years," she would sulk and shake her head, her red pigtails swinging on both sides of her face. "This is not home, and it will never be."

To the women, home was never explicitly defined, but they knew they were seen by each other, that they could stretch their hand in the dark and another would reach out to hold it, that the unspoken rule was to keep watch and take care of your own, wherever they may be. Every job they did, they did well, talking among themselves, latching on to a tune when one started a hymn, working and praying and stretching their strength into the night. They were aware of each other's sighs and lifted spirits, nursed one another when there was a new burn on the hand from a boiling pot or a deep cut on the finger from the endless chopping of carrots or peeling the skin off plantains, and ended each day looking forward to the next—not so much the labor of the new dawn, but that they could partake in the living again, could strum the chord of being alive, regardless of what it looked like, and what it stripped away from them.

There were empty rooms on the other floors. Adoma knew because she counted them each week when she went up to change the sheets, even when no one slept on them. Six empty rooms. Surely one could be given up for them? She fantasized about sleeping in one of the beds. To just walk up those stairs one night and throw herself onto the soft mattress and feel her body sink into its padded layers of cotton and wool. What's the worst that could happen if they found her in the morning— she'd be sent back to the small kitchen shelter? Well, that wouldn't do much. She imagined the shocked faces of the master and his wife, how they wouldn't know what to say because they hadn't anticipated a day like this would come when somebody they did not—and would not— consider one of them crossed that threshold and made herself feel at home. And perhaps along with the shock would be fear—how did they let this happen? When did they stop being in charge? They would be quick to question: How is it possible that this shy twenty-nine-year-old kinky-haired, soft-eyed, kitchen-bound lady could do this brave, unacceptable thing? It made Adoma laugh whenever she thought about such things, and she thought about them a lot.

Esiha, the oldest and first to arrive at the house, couldn't stand the young lady's absentmindedness and giggles. The whole act was strange, and to Esiha, even impolite. They would be washing and slicing vegetables for an evening gathering, and there Adoma would go, half a tomato in hand, laughing and covering her mouth; or they would be sweeping and mopping the floors and she would stop and nod and chuckle, as if someone had just appeared to her and whispered a joke in her ear. In so many ways she reminded her of Helen, her daughter, who was away from home, from her care, and in the faraway wildness and strangeness of a foreign land. It had been two years since she left to study psychology, and now during every phone call, the girl had questions, she wanted to know everything. How was her mother coping, was there anything from her past holding her back, if she could go back in time, what would she change about her life?

Sometimes Esiha shook her head and smiled, amazed by how smart her girl sounded, how she was confident enough to ask her these big questions. When Esiha was Helen's age, her own voice was unfamiliar to her, and when she did speak, she was meek sounding, uttering the words with fear and uncertainty, unsure of herself. Often swallowing them down before she could even string the words together to articulate them. Her daughter's questions wore her out. She had no complaints, she would say.

"Life is good, there is nothing to change. I wake up, take what I can get, and hope to God I live to see another day."

"And what happens then?" Helen always knew what to say, how to steer the conversation back to what she really wanted to know. "What happens when you see another day? How are you walking into tomorrow, Ma?"

Esiha did not know what to do with her and all this newfound and disconcerting curiosity.

"Ach! Why are you bothering me with all these questions? When tomorrow finds me, I know what I want to do with it. Tell me about you. Have you found a church? And how are you doing in the weather? Don't let the cold get into your bones. It'll stiffen up your veins and cripple you!"

Helen told her not to worry about the cold; there were clothes to keep her warm. She was concerned about her mother, how her work in the house was going, if they were treating her well. They went back and forth like that, each not saying much of what the other needed to hear but still asking enough questions to keep the other talking until one of them had to go. It was often Helen running off the line, her voice suddenly taking on a sense of urgency, as if she were going to miss her train if she didn't get off the phone that instant, but it was always to the library or a café or some department meeting, and none of those things could wait.

After every phone call, Esiha shared her diagnosis with Nkwa-daa, her quiet and observant friend. The one who wouldn't let her do this job all by herself, the one who, despite all of life's misfortune, got back up on her feet every time, humming as she cooked and cleaned and moved about. No one ever embodied the meaning of their name like she did, life always. Esiha and Nkwadaa had been friends for more than twenty years, and when Helen was born, Nkwadaa was right there to pick up Helen's small wailing body and shush her in the middle of the night, urging Esiha to go back to sleep after the baby had had some milk. But Esiha mostly stayed by her friend's side, dozing off a few times, while the image of her dearest friend cradling her baby stayed with her, made her heart heavy with gratitude and at the same time light with relief, for how could she survive these nights all by herself?

"She is well, by grace. But her voice . . . maybe she has a cold," Esiha said, looking at the phone as if expecting Helen's call to come through again.

"Did you tell her to drink some herbal tea?"

"Well, no. But when does she ever listen to us?" Esiha started for the main kitchen.

They were cooking yam and kontomire stew for dinner and some chicken soup too. There were guests coming, foreign people who had slowly trained their palate to enjoy unfamiliar foods. There were, of course, the days of mashing potatoes upon request, when they'd rather fry them, or throwing mixed fruits into a blender when they'd rather pop the solids in their mouth, feel the textures of pineapples and mangoes on their tongues. But rarely did they do anything in the house for their own pleasure. They followed orders for no reason other than it was what they were for.

"She listens to me," Nkwa-daa said, playfully poking her friend in the ribs with her finger. "Next time let me talk to her."

Helen was Nkwa-daa's daughter too, and some days, when the girl was not in a haste and remembered her manners, she asked of her aunt and even spoke to her on the phone sometimes, but of course the woman sounded no different from her own mother. They had the same thoughts, worried about Helen's life abroad, if she was eating well and filling up her Rawlings chain—the visible and protruding collarbones of starving Ghanaians under Rawlings's rule—and if she was staying warm and re-membering their God. They whispered the same prayers over her life, lived as if tied to each other by a string. You tug on one end, only to find the same at the other.

Helen's first year on campus, she had secretly yearned for a friend-ship of this kind, and that had meant saying yes to parties or going on a group hike or enrolling in the same classes as her colleagues. She didn't expect it to be hard—to find someone who brings your presence an ease, an ease that comes from years of knowing and understanding, of pay-ing attention to another. She was wrong and it had been lonely, even lonelier after these gatherings where one is somehow reminded of her own isolated existence while surrounded by happy, dancing, drunk people. Helen wouldn't admit this to herself: if she stayed on this quest of finding a sister-friend, wishing so desperately for what her mother and Aunt Nkwa-daa had, she might indeed miss out on other kinds of friendships, even ordinary delights in being with someone. It need not be what they had, nothing of this strange devotion, this rare unrelenting bond.

It did not surprise her that Aunt Nkwa-daa always asked about her safety and whether she walked home alone at night. Helen said yes, she was being careful and no, she never walked home at night by herself.

Since her daughter's disappearance five years earlier, Aunt Nkwa-daa had a way about her. She was fearful and untrusting, always looking over her shoulder, double-checking locked doors, sitting up in the middle of the night to see whether the sound she heard was the wind blowing things around or somebody in the dark, closing in on her. Helen had to leave behind the pepper spray her aunt gifted her at the airport, although she had tried convincing Nkwa-daa that she wouldn't be allowed to take it on the plane with her. But the woman had pleaded, pressed it firmly in her palms, and wrapped her fingers around it, saying, "Take it, please take it. My heart hurts, take it with you everywhere." And yet, Helen remembered, she is also the woman with so much love in her eyes, so much patience to give, a vessel of flesh that takes on whatever burden is laid on her without so much as a murmur. And of course there was her mother, ready to strike anything that threatened them, and Adoma, the new girl her mom talked about. Helen knew exactly why she was there and what she'd have to give up to get what she wanted. What they all wanted, she believed, was an escape. When she was home, Helen had only wished to be away, and she couldn't exactly say why other than everything about her life in that place was small and stifled and ordinary. She wanted out and wanted more, and she now convinced herself that she had it. The new girl, who her mother said ought to be in school but wasn't, wanted to live the promise of this new life too, at whatever cost. Helen did not blame her; it is the kind of scholarship and good fortune that could change one's life after all. It's changed hers.

Three times Adoma had tried to speak with the diplomat, and three times Esiha had stopped her, pinched her waist on their way out from the dining room.

After all the guests had left, they pushed a cart around to collect the dirty plates. So much food left untouched, so much waste. As soon as they were out of sight, Nkwa-daa grabbed a plastic bag from their cupboard and scooped the leftovers in, stealing glances at the door to be sure the Madam was not walking in. Once when she discovered the women were packaging food and giving them away to people, she told her husband first, who told her to deal with the maids directly and not involve him. So she called some kind of meeting, warning them in a tone she might have used to address fifty people rather than the three tired faces that looked back at her. They nodded their heads yes, they understood her, and it wouldn't happen again.

Nkwa-daa had been restless that night. "How can we throw away all this food? She won't ask us to reduce the quantity, and she won't let us share what's left of it. And they won't eat anything that isn't fresh the next day. What is this life?"

But Esiha had told her they didn't have to stop, they just had to be sure not to get caught. They found a way to make it work and managed to stay out of trouble.

That night they were surprised that Adoma brought it up when they confronted her. It was very clear to both of them how much she sought the diplomat's attention, how she leaned closer than was usual to refill his glass and how even her fragrance was different when the man was around. Some kind of fine perfume mist with notes of vanilla bean and fresh orange blossom filled the air when she walked past them. She wanted so badly to be seen and did not care to hide it. The three of them had a pile of dishes to clean and a conference room to set up for the next day's event before it got too dark, but Esiha's temper was fiercely pressed against their waiting duties. She grabbed Adoma by the arm and pulled the girl face-to-face with her. She made sure her grip was firm, firm enough to send Adoma whimpering and trying to wrest her hand free from Esiha's grasp.

"What's the matter with you? What is it that you want from the man, eh? What do you want to tell him?"

"Ach! I've done nothing wrong. Let me go!"

"Nothing, eh?" Esiha chuckled and shook her head, still holding the girl's wrist. Foolish and ignorant, these young ones. "You're walking around stinking with all these wants. Craving so boldly, throwing yourself at him, having no shame, no dignity. You think no one sees you? You think no one sees those pitiful, pleading eyes?"

"I'm not the only one going against the rules here!" Adoma finally yanked her hand free and fumbled with her apron strings. She was shaking all over. It stung to hear the words because she did feel unseen, and she hated it.

"You and her," she pointed a trembling finger at Nkwa-daa, "have been giving away food. And sometimes, sometimes, I know Ben goes in there to play and he's not supposed to ever be inside that small kitchen." She said the word *small* with such disgust, such spite, that both women looked at each other, unable to hide their shock. Such disrespect.

"What do you want from the man?" Esiha was so close to the girl now and she saw it in her eyes—that fire, that misplaced rage, that stubborn will that would not be shaken.

She had seen it in Helen too, just a few days before she came running into her arms with good news. She had been considered for the scholarship, and she, Helen, would be going abroad to study. The diplomat, together with the school, had picked her last but he had picked her. It was supposed to be good news, but Esiha could not shake off the feeling that something had happened to cause them to arrive at this point. Days before, Helen had sobbed quietly on the other side of the bed as her mother slept, her Bible held over her chest. They slept in an office by the church then, their own home having been submerged in a flood. Helen had complained to her mother about how she was so close, how her grades were good but not good enough, how an opportunity like this could save their family, and if only she could see the man, if only she could make an appointment at his residence and show herself and argue her case.

Esiha could barely follow what her daughter was going on about. Helen explained it over and over. The university had partnered with some ambassadors and diplomats to fund bright but financially challenged students. They announced the selected students in school and she did not make the list, but she was close. She was certain she was close because her grades were good and she could convince them, she could change their minds. "Don't you see? I could be one of them!"

But Esiha did not really see. Yes, the girl was bright, but not so spectacular that anyone would be willing to pay for her to continue schooling. And besides, she hoped her daughter would join her at the market, help her rebuild their lives from all they'd lost in the flood. And so that talk about more school and much worse, Helen possibly going away from her, was unexpected and to her, implausible. Like all things she did not understand or care much about, she dismissed it—her daughter's hopes to meet the man, to change his mind and change her life, a fading noise in the background.

But Helen did exactly as she'd said she would, and she came bearing the good news a few days later. At first she wasn't in, but now she was. Just like that. She was going to America, and it was going to be the best thing that would ever happen to them. Esiha had looked up from the palm kernels she was pounding, settled her eyes on her daughter's body, and looked away without saying a word. Her daughter went on, saying that the diplomat had even offered her mother a job. She could wash dishes. But Esiha was no longer listening. She felt sick to her stomach. There was a burning sensation in her lower abdomen, making her nauseous, causing her to jump from her stool and hang her head over the toilet.

Something had happened to her daughter. Something had happened to her, and it had opened a door and it might just be the happiest she'd ever seen Helen, but something terrible had happened. Esiha thought this every day after the news. She couldn't shake off the feeling as Helen prepared for her visa interview, as she stood in front of the church to be prayed for, as people stopped by to drop off clothes and food items, half of which she would leave behind.

Esiha would take the job and later put in a good word for her best friend. She would hear the stories too—of what many of the girls at the school had to do for these scholarships, how much of themselves they had to give up in exchange for this dream. And she would think about her poor girl, walking down the halls of this mansion, her transcripts in hand, ready to fight and prove her worth. On the other side of the door was the greedy world Helen knew nothing about; the bloodthirsty hands, the wolflike creatures who, with a conscience long rotten, would snatch, deceive, throw a bone of promises to whomever was innocent and desperate, and like a dog, a girl chased after it, undressing herself in every leap. Afraid and cold and alone. Stubborn and prideful and determined.

When Adoma did not respond, suddenly subdued and visibly weakened by the interrogation, the question hung between them.

"What is it that you want from the man?"

A new life. Change. Opportunities. All that can be possible for a girl like me.

Esiha knew the desire as well as the cost, perhaps even more than the girl did. Her daughter's departure left her sick with numbness and a recurring malaria that dug at her bones. She stayed in bed, refusing to eat or bathe or clean the compound before church service. She would see only Nkwa-daa, and when her friend would come, she would sit quietly, watching her and saying nothing. If anyone understood grief and the illness that separation causes, it was Nkwa-daa. The first few days, Nkwa-daa gave her silence and the comfort of her presence, left a banana by her bedside. Then she would bring fresh wheat bread from the bakery along with soup, sit next to her, and feed her. The silence at that point was so familiar, even necessary, that Nkwa-daa did not bother to break it. And one day, as Nkwa-daa was getting ready to leave, Esiha began to speak. And the words, they rushed out like some force was pushing them out of her. Nkwa-daa thought her friend was praying under her breath, but she got closer and realized she was talking to herself but also to her.

She had failed her daughter, she said. Something terrible had happened and she should have been there to stop it. "What kind of mother am I? And all this for what—a new country without me? How is this better? Tell me, Nkwa, how is this better?"

That night Nkwa-daa stayed by her friend's side, dabbing a cold towel on her forehead, for her friend was running a temperature, shaking with fever. A love illness, the terrible condition of the heart where it convinces itself of its brokenness, its deep, incomprehensible calamities. The whole body buys into the illusion and suffers it faithfully. Nkwa-daa held her friend then, as her friend had done in the past when she thought she was losing her mind, when she was so sure that at any point in the day, her own daughter, missing for months, would walk through the door. How she waited, how she hoped—all the while, Esiha was by her side, waiting and hoping, knowing very well no girl was coming home. Saying, "Waiting is the easiest thing we can do, and we can do it for years. It demands nothing of us. Look at us. We sit and weep and fold our hands and look out to see who's coming. But to move on? To gather our breaking selves and plunge back into life after this misfortune, that is the hardest thing we'll ever have to do. And we'll do it, together."

In the kitchen Adoma had turned her back to Esiha's intense black eyes and stood at the sink, furiously scrubbing the bottom of a casserole dish. Esiha exchanged a look with Nkwa-daa, who stood watching the dispute and appeared to be shut in her own despair, worn out from the noise around her. Esiha nodded as if to say "enough," turned, and headed for their place, and Nkwa-daa left the girl and followed suit, a limp in her walk from all the standing that seemed to weaken her knees and leave her feet swollen.

Time was running out. Whatever they had to do, they had to do it fast.

This is one way to say it: they had no plan and yet, the minute she took the job and walked through the towering, polished wooden doors, Esiha knew she couldn't *not* do anything. This was the same place. The same bloody tile, with its dramatic veining and glossy finish that Helen had walked on because the man wouldn't see her in his office, not for a discussion of that kind. They should go home, where he could be comfortable and take his time to listen to her. Esiha never saw the rooms in the house—it was Adoma's job to clean them, and she was partly relieved that nothing triggered her imagination, visions of her daughter vulnerable and naked on one of the sheets. Relieved too that the man had kept his distance from the kitchen altogether, coming and going through his wide office doors—his domineering presence lurking through the halls, always up to some official engagement.

He barely glanced at them when they served people at the table. He appeared so shut off, so indifferent about their presence and movements that it was as if he did not see them. Or rather, it wasn't that they were invisible to him—he could not, after all, miss the clinking of utensils as the women set them on the table or the fact that his bowl of lentil soup did not magically appear before him but was carefully set down by two hands—but did not find them worthy of his attention and time and in fact, of even registering their presence.

Anyway, Fridays were the days his wife took Ben to the park. With a persistent nudge from her friend, Nkwa-daa asked the madam if she could take her boy to the park this time. The madam declined politely, a little surprised about the unusual request; so far, the women's nanny duties had been restricted to feeding and changing Ben, collecting all his toys and scrubbing those that needed scrubbing, and simply watching him closely when he was in the kitchen. But she did think about it when she went to bed, turning in her silk nightgown for the empty side of the mattress; the familiar absence of her husband did not scare her anymore. She had grown used to it over time and treated herself to shopping sprees whenever the fear crept up on her. It was a good distraction, like so many of their properties had become over the years—a veil draped over their faces to keep them from ever coming to terms with their lives and what they'd made of them. Giving Ben to the maid would certainly give her more time to meet with a friend at the spa or spend some time at the public library. She'd always wanted to do that—to be away for a while and experience the town and its people, put herself out there. So she said yes to Nkwa-daa and agreed to go with her the first time.

They sat on the bench and watched Ben play with the other rich kids. Nkwa-daa wasn't sure what to do or say. Their closeness to each other in that moment was odd. Without it being said, each one's place had always been clear and both parties assumed their roles without thinking. One set the rules and insisted on what needed to be done, and the women bent their heads and lives low in subservience. All of it felt strange and Nkwa-daa hoped her uneasiness didn't show. She prayed she wouldn't have to speak. In fact, she hoped the woman would forget she was sitting next to her, which would not surprise her much. The madam wore a white lace pleated tank top tucked in her wide-leg pants. She had twisted her long hair at the back and kept it in place with a leopard-print hair clip—not a single strand of hair in defiance. Hanging loosely on both ears were sparkling silver earrings. She was stunning, an observation Nkwa-daa was sure no one was more convinced of than the woman herself.

"May I ask why you offered to do this? It's . . . quite nice of you, actually. I see how Ben is fond of you folks in the kitchen. But I'm just curious, you know. Do you have any children? Where are they? You must miss them, slaving away in the kitchen like this." She looked at her son as she said this, her eyes all dreamlike and distant.

Nkwa-daa fidgeted with her hands in her lap. They were dry and rough and in serious need of some lotion. They sat on the same bench; the woman's pumpkin-orange bag, the size of a small pillow, was the only thing that separated them. The woman smelled of lavender and expensive oils. Next to her bright bag, Nkwa-daa was reminded of just how faded her skirt was. It was as if someone had stabbed a needle through the fabric and drawn out all its blue, just as life had dealt with her—sapping her of her very strength.

She wasn't sure which of her questions to answer first, so she said simply, "Ben is a sweetheart. No, no children."

The woman lit a cigarette and looked ahead as the sounds of children shrieking and chasing after each other rang in their ears. Nkwa-daa wasn't sure if the woman had heard her, but she liked it that way and hoped that would end their conversation. What smart words do you say to a wealthy woman with a fancy bag like that and skin so smooth, so soft you want to touch it? Nothing. You only watch.

"You like them? I got them for my birthday. Never worn them. Well. Until this morning."

Her madam touched the earring on her left ear and her finger lingered on its sleek surface. She did not really look at Nkwa-daa as she spoke. She seemed to glance at the area around Nkwa-daa, to scan with her eyes but not really to focus on her. And so it took a while for Nkwa-daa to know she was being spoken to, and an even longer while to decide on what to say in response. But before she could think of anything, the woman reached behind one ear and took out the earring and then the other. They were pear-shaped, sterling silver. Nkwa-daa pulled back, both nervous and unsure of what was happening.

The woman, with the confidence of one who is familiar with having her way, grabbed Nkwa-daa's hand and placed the jewelry in her palm. The earrings were beautiful and sparkling, a glorious thing nestled in her coarse and dull hands, exposing the lumpy arthritic joints knotting her fingers. Nkwa-daa wished she could hide her hands or cover them with a handkerchief and then take the earrings. But she said thank you and like an afterthought, asked why. The woman looked at her with an expression that Nkwa-daa couldn't tell whether it was disgust or disbelief, but she recovered quickly, showing a tight smile that did not reach her eyes. Nkwa-daa thought she had ruined the moment. Now the woman would take back her earrings and walk out of the park and take her son with her.

But the woman appeared to give the question some thought before she said, lowering her gaze, "I frankly do not know. I saw you looking and thought you might want them." She spoke fast then, the words toppling over each other. "But of course, that was a silly assumption. Silly of me too. Why would I think that? People are allowed to admire things without needing to own them. Not that you can ever afford these but . . . I don't mean . . ." Her cheeks turned red, and it fascinated Nkwa-daa to see how easily her skin filled with color, how one's emotions could knock past all walls of defense to intrude and ride on their flesh.

If Nkwa-daa thought it was unsettling to be sitting so close to her, it was even harder to watch the woman fumble for words. She was always so poised, so upright in her heels, not a strand of brown hair out of place on her head. Her face was beautiful, with eyebrows that were always drawn over and a very small dimple in her left cheek. They were utterly different women and yet, for a brief moment, one would think they had swapped places. "Thank you," Nkwa-daa said slowly, closing her fingers over the earrings, finally claiming them. "No, thank *you*," the woman said. Her voice trailed at the end, perhaps searching for a name, but when it wouldn't register, she said again, "Thank you." And this time, she looked directly into Nkwa-daa's eyes and clasped her delicate hands over hers.

They got rid of Adoma easily. Esiha only had to break a few pricey dishes—brought out for special occasions like fundraisers—and the woman was furious, a torrent of cries flowing out of her. They could get new ones, she said, but these were her favorites. How could this have happened? She even went down on her knees, picking up the pieces, taking one last look at the floral design that lined the broken rims of the plates.

The girl was absent-minded lately and moving very slowly, Esiha told the Madam. Adoma could use a break; she interrupted their operations in the kitchen and Esiha was confident she and Nkwa-daa could handle the work without her. The whole time Adoma stood there, in shock, a scalding wrath stirring in her. For some reason, she couldn't talk. Her mouth was dry and her words failed her when she needed them most. She was asked to leave that very night. The women filled up a sack bag with fruits for her, and because Nkwa-daa had heard her go on and on about the beds and the soft sheets upstairs, she had managed to find a sheet in the laundry pile and rolled it into a ball to tuck into the bag.

"There's some money tied in a sock for you," Esiha told her, handing the sack bag to her. "Find something to do. If your grades are bad, take that exam again."

Adoma flinched when she heard the word *grades*. Her mission was not a secret after all.

"But do not come back here," Esiha continued. "Do not ask to see the man. I know you think this is what you want," there was a quiver in her voice, but the woman held herself together, "but you're wrong."

"You think you know me," the girl spat back, locking eyes with Esiha. Her eyes were burning, and maybe the women could tell her legs were shaking, but she was going to say what she was going to say, going to do what she was going to do, even if she had to find another way.

"I know Helen, old woman. I know your daughter and what she did here and her filthy—" The riot rising inside her was instantly stilled by a slap from a hand she was not expecting. It was Nkwa-daa's; she had stepped from behind her and struck the right side of her face. Adoma was shocked, betrayed, even; she had always preferred Nkwa-daa's gentle spirit to Esiha's hot blood and mistrust, which seemed to seep into everything she did. The side of her face stung, and her tears flowed freely now, from pain and also from rage at being let go like this, like she was expendable and unwanted. With one last dark look from Esiha, the girl turned, picked up the sack they'd given her, and stepped out through the back door. But not before Adoma had noticed Esiha's sudden muteness; the woman seemed to stiffen and weaken before her at the mention of Helen's name. She had finally left Esiha with no words. It served her right, she thought. It served her bloody right.

They wasted no time and got to work the next day. It was a Friday.

"I will leave the house shortly after you leave for the park. We will meet at the train stop in Salaju. I will sit by the window. When you see me, come."

"With the boy?" Everything about this plan scared Nkwa-daa to death. There was no way they were going to get away with this, and yet she knew her friend's mind was made up. Esiha was going to get back at the family, and Nkwa-daa was going to be a part of it. It was simple, and also the vilest thing she'd ever had to be part of.

"Yes. With the boy."

They were in the small kitchen. Scheming. Looking at her friend now, the crow's feet tugging at her eyes, which seemed red from too much rubbing or crying, her sunken cheeks, the worry lines stretched across her forehead, Nkwa-daa knew she was exhausted and old and yet, after all these years, that fire in Esiha was not quenched. She was after something and by all means, she was going to get it. The whole plan made Nkwa-daa sick and restless. They were going to be caught. Thrown in prison. They would be all over the news, and everyone in town would hear about their abominable offence. They would be shamed and mocked. She knew she wouldn't be able to live with herself, but Esiha eased that thought with the assurance that they would still have each other. She would not have to go through it alone.

Weeks after her daughter went missing, Nkwa-daa would hear her voice in her head, clear as though the child were right in the room with her. She would turn, expecting to see her daughter behind her, but there was no one. The voice wasn't disturbed or filled with panic. It was calm, soft, the way her girl sounded when she was just waking up from sleep. *Mama?* When she called her, it was always in the form of a question, just throwing out her name in the void and expecting a response. *Mama?* Nkwa-daa told Esiha about the voices. How she wanted to hit her head against something, how she wanted them to stop but also didn't. Was she crazy? No, her friend said firmly.

Esiha was the only one who wouldn't mock her or tell her something wasn't right with her head. Or tell her it was nothing, that she was only making up the voice. Some days she told Nkwa-daa she heard the voice too. And so they spoke back to the girl—telling stories or jokes, and other days giving an account of how they spent their time, the new gossip in town, how different things would be with her. They lived through the grief like one wandering in a forest—taking all chances, clearing uncertain paths, clinging to the hope that there was an opening somewhere, that somehow, if only they kept walking through the woods, they would arrive at it.

Now Esiha wanted Nkwa-daa to have the boy. She would keep Ben. This baby that looked nothing like her. She would have another child and she could start all over. Yes, but only this time, the child wasn't hers, Nkwa-daa thought.

"What about you? What do you get from this?" Nkwa-daa knew the answer to this, knew exactly what had driven her friend to come into this house in the first place; she had played servant and surrendered everything for this moment. But still, Nkwa-daa couldn't believe what they were about to do, what Esiha was promising her. There was no way they could get away with this. The diplomats were powerful. How could Esiha be this resolute?

"All the satisfaction knowing how they're going to live from this day." She did not look away from Nkwa-daa as she said this. Her eyes were cold, her voice sharp.

It did not take long for Esiha to pack all their belongings—which weren't much—into a bag and head out through the backdoor. As she walked, she thought about the house—its raised walls, all the useless antiques placed at every corner, their class of people and their expensive wines, their money, clothes, and shoes, their eyes, oh their eyes: unseeing, dismissing, looking down at you and pressing you to the ground without the need to even say a single word. She was leaving it all behind and taking away the best and undefiled part of them.

On the train she thought of nothing else but Helen so far away from her. Sitting somewhere in a strange land, reading a book or eating some new dish. Her daughter walking around campus, acting normal while her life was falling apart when no one was watching. For one did that forget a thing like this, even when they prayed for relief and wished it away with all their heart. The damaged past is a plague that attacks at all times. There are days it sneaks up on you like a thief and plunders your very being. Even when you have nothing left, especially when you have nothing left, it finds you and persists in its merciless pursuit of you.

When the train's brakes hissed and screeched, sending a whistle into the air, Esiha straightened her back and turned to look out the window, as she had said she would. Her heart stopped for a moment, and it was as if the air had been sucked from her lungs. Nkwa-daa stood at the other side of the tracks. Her kinky hair had been piled in a high bun on top of her head and fastened with a scarf, highlighting her broad forehead and sharp cheeks bones, which were quivering and keeping her face from bursting with heavy emotion. The wind pressed her loose dress against her body, revealing her lean frame, her flat breasts. Standing there, she looked so malnourished, so fragile, so old.

It was not the earrings or the sweetness of the child. Nkwa-daa owed that woman nothing. It was a dread far greater than getting caught. To live life the way she had, racked by grief, utterly shattered from a separation that should never be, to lose her senses every once in a while, to keep walking away from every river that called her to throw herself into it—was a terror she would never wish on anyone, no, not on a mother. It was beyond any madness she could think of, and her hands could not dare kindle the same fire that even now continued to burn her.

And so there she stood, watching her friend frozen on her seat in the train, her hand raised to her chest in shock, her lips parted as if to say something but there was no sound. Nkwa-daa shook her head, the tears already free from their hold. She heard the train horn blare and when she looked up, Esiha had turned her face from her, her flaring eyes fixed right ahead. Her rigid neck carried its bounding pulse, her pursed lips, her small poise of what dignity she had left. The train started to move. Nkwa-daa looked on, every part of her body shook, threatening to collapse. Something took hold of her then, crippling her legs, but she did not give in. Not now. She will not look at me, she thought while praying against it. There was an ache spreading through her heart, a throb swelling inside her belly, pushing itself up her throat as the train rapidly faded from view. The friend of my heart will not turn for me, she thought.

And she was right.

Nominated by Narrative

ALL OVER TOWN

by DOUG ANDERSON

from UNDRESS, SHE SAID (Four Way Books)

I am aware that at this hour,
in houses and apartments all around me,
people are stepping into their showers.
I make the water hotter as I grow used to it.
Steam rising around me, soothing me,
clearing my nostrils.
I reach for the soap and lather myself,
wash my scant hair, behind my ears,
remembering my grandmother long ago
scrubbing me as if I were a burnt pot.
But I'm gentle now, knowing the hurt places
I've gathered. I tune myself to a lover's hands,
remember the last woman who was good at it.
All over town people are being tender with themselves
in this hour between waking and dressing,
before putting on the gang face to go to work,
chasing away whatever wisps of dreams
might be hanging on. I feel for scars—
above my eyebrows from fighting.
The ridge of my twice-broken nose.
The side of my face where they dug out
the big chunk of cancer and the long suture marks
on my neck where they took the graft to plug it.
My throat, a broken cathedral organ of backed up love.
My ailing left shoulder, my once proud chest,

moving on down to the love handles, to the gut
beneath which hide the ribbed muscles.
The fading burns on my hands,
the pitted flesh from the bullet fragments
now mostly covered with tattoo.
My shopworn cock and my balls hanging all day
in the dark by themselves, scheming.
My disintegrating right knee,
torn ligaments of the other leg,
down toward the fee t, almost crushed now
under the weight of a life.
For a moment, at this hour, perhaps we are all
this way. It makes me sad
that we are alone in this holy of holies,
grieving the failing flesh beneath which
Death sits in her carriage loosely holding the reins.

Nominated by Four Way Books, Richard Hoffman

TREASURE ISLAND ALLEY

fiction by DA-LIN

from NEW ENGLAND REVIEW

The mourning women are howling. Even with fingers in her ears, Xuan-Xuan hears their loud cries from the big white tent that appeared over-night in the alley. On tiptoe, she peers over the windowsill and looks down three stories to the long line of people holding incense sticks outside the tent. They were here to pay their respects, they said. Her mama had died last night giving birth to a baby, a sister, they said. Her sister would come home but her mama would not, they said, but Xuan-Xuan has her own ideas.

She is in Grandma's bedroom. The smell of old clothes. Spittoon under the bed. She is in her family's apartment building, 58 Hoping Road, Tai-pei, Taiwan. Mama made her memorize their address on her fifth birthday, a month ago, when Mama and Papa took a rare day off from the family's factory and brought her to the zoo, where Mama got so angry that they came home early after Xuan-Xuan strayed from the peacocks and without telling anyone went searching for the bears.

Cupping fingers around her eyes, Xuan-Xuan pretends to scan Grand-ma's bedroom with binoculars. The target is the top drawer of the dresser by the bed, where Grandma hides money.

She notices for the first time a hole high up in the ceiling. Next year, a bird will fly through the window into that hole, and even after Papa opens a big chunk of the plaster, he won't find the bird. It will take three days for the bird's song to die, which Xuan-Xuan will remember years later, when she is old and has forgotten almost everything.

The dresser is two, three times her height. She plucks one hair off her pigtails and blows it afloat to invoke her favorite of Monkey King's

Seventy-Two Transformations: Size Enhancement. Then she breathes slow and hard, and waits for her legs and arms to grow.

Long minutes pass.

Nothing.

She has to watch again how her fabled hero does it on TV in her favorite cartoon, but there is no time now.

She swings one leg over the ledge of Grandma's bed. Then another. Like a frog, like the fat, stubby frog that managed to climb out of an aluminum bowl in the kitchen, where Grandma has been cooking all morning for the relatives, but—*no!*—Grandma flicked the frog down with her spatula. *Where are you going? The wok's ready.*

Xuan-Xuan climbs on the mahogany headboard and then leans out to pull on the dresser's top drawer. Grudgingly it opens, heavy and squeaky like a pirate's trunk full of treasures. She ignores the gold earrings and jade bracelets, and zooms in on the red envelope. Inside is a stack of Taiwanese dollar bills.

Someone shouts in the stairwell. Papa.

Ma, the feng shui master is here!

Papa thumps up the stairs and Grandma's slippers patah-patah, and then they are talking right outside the bedroom door. Xuan-Xuan grabs the envelope and lands on the comforter, wiggles between the pillows, tries to hide. She waits and waits and grows old . . .

❀   ❀   ❀

When she is fifteen she will give her virginity to a boy who makes her laugh. At twenty-two she will move to the United States to study biochemistry. She will change her name to Susan and settle in Silicon Valley, and for two decades her startup will be her life. She will marry a white man with a boyish grin and a linebacker's gait, Alex, a venture capitalist. After their divorce, she will become a staunch atheist in search of a religion. At a Silicon Valley meditation boot camp, she will write down everything she knows about her mother on one page with room to spare. On the last day of her life, when she is a hundred and five, she will lie in her deathbed with her second husband by her side, and she will feel lucky despite the sadness that is just beneath the surface of everything.

Time escapes from her fingers and hops, skips, jumps. It's not that difficult really: you wiggle a little and you are there, in a different crevice of time. You close your eyes to the kid in the mirror and open to a face full of wrinkles. You lie down beside your lover, your cheek brushing against the pillow, and there you are again, five years old, hiding, waiting . . .

* * *

Finally, Papa thump-thumps down the stairs and Grandma pads back to the kitchen. Xuan-Xuan shoves the red envelope in her Monkey King backpack, and opens the bedroom door a slit. Heat rushes in. Down the hall, Grandma's silhouette shifts in and out of dense smoke. The aromas of three-cup frogs and twice-cooked pork creep downstairs to their factory and drift upstairs to their roof deck, where they keep a German shepherd going insane with old age.

Just yesterday morning, Mama waddled up to the roof deck when Xuan-Xuan was riding her new pink bike and Grandma was hanging bedsheets out to dry. The dog pawed at Mama, almost tearing her favorite blue dress, which clung to her thin frame and swollen belly.

Mama handed Grandma the red envelope. *Ma, for this week.*

Grandma frowned. *How am I supposed to live on this?*

Perhaps . . . you should stop shopping at Japan Imports and Layaways. Mama rubbed the half-moon shadow under her eyes.

You blame me? The factory's broke only after you married my son, because you don't know how to manage money!

Xuan-Xuan tried to get Mama's attention by riding the bike with no hands, but Mama was already stomping down the stairs and yelling, *If you want more money, why don't you go earn it like those girls at Treasure Island Alley?* And Grandma was shouting, *How dare you? I curse you that you fall into that hell!*

The dog pounced and Xuan-Xuan flipped over, taking down the clothesline.

Why is Mama so bad? she said after Grandma pulled her out of the tangle.

Good kid, was all Grandma replied, her face glaring like red hot coal.

Xuan-Xuan doesn't miss Mama, who never wanted to play, always hunched over a book filled with black lines and red ink, but Mama must have left because Xuan-Xuan sided with Grandma. On TV, Xuan-Xuan has watched Monkey King fight the Lord of Hell to bring people back to life, even erasing his name from the Book of Life Expectancy to become immortal. If Treasure Island Alley is Hell, she will go there to bring Mama back.

* * *

108

Outside, Xuan-Xuan tiptoes next to a line of black-robed monks marching toward the big white tent.

Na—Mo—A—Mi—Tuo—Fo—

Their chants sound like *There is no Buddha in the South,* which makes no sense. She slips behind the tent and peeks in through a seam.

Papa, wearing a heavy black suit, is standing next to a big, black stone tub surrounded by towers of beer cans and sarsaparilla bottles and flowers in neon colors. One by one, people bow and give him a white envelope.

Three mourning women wail and throw themselves onto the ground beneath a large photo of Mama wearing that pretty blue dress with little white flowers. The women clutch their hearts and tear at their robes made of rough hemp. Xuan-Xuan can't see their faces, hidden under large headpieces like veils of ghost brides. Their microphones shriek: *Why did you depart so soon? I weep for your children. Come back, come back!*

For a long time, she will believe that the mourning women were hired because she did not cry. Until she leaves home for good, every year on Tomb Sweeping Day, her father will drive her and her sister to the cemetery, and he will buy a stack of ghost money at the entrance. He will teach them how to fold the ghost money, little squares of paper, rough like tree bark, a gold dot in the center. *A deposit for your mother's bank account.* He will weep as he tosses it into the fire, while the girls look on stone-faced. The smoke chokes, and cinders fly like lightning bugs. Only once will she wonder how her sister feels about the date engraved on the tombstone—her sister's birthday, their mother's death day—but she will push the thought out of her mind. It will be decades before she can say to her sister, *I don't hate you. I just don't know how to love you.*

One of the mourning women lifts her head and Xuan-Xuan takes off running, past a Buddhist vegetarian restaurant, a playground where the temple troupe boys are practicing drums, and she skids to a stop in front of Thousand-Big Stationery Store.

Inside, in a glass cabinet, above useless Barbie dolls and fake fire trucks, are Monkey King's impenetrable armor and the cudgel he used to pound the Milky Way flat. The small golden box she needs is on the top shelf. It contains one of Monkey King's precious hairs, to be deployed in the direst of dire circumstances.

She pulls out the red envelope from her backpack and demands, *Give me that box.*

The old lady who owns Thousand-Big narrows her eyes and cranes her wrinkled long neck over the counter like an ostrich guarding her eggs. Xuan-Xuan adds to avoid suspicion, *Oh, and Grandma wants a carton of Longevity.*

Finally, Mrs. Ostrich reaches into the red envelope and pecks out two bills. *Tell your Grandma I gave her a discount on the cigarettes.*

Can I have Monkey King's cudgel too, with a discount? she says.

You are your Grandma's granddaughter. Mrs. Ostrich tsk-tsks and puts everything including the change into Xuan-Xuan's backpack.

She steps out of the store and a wild herd of elementary school kids just let out of school charges toward her, shoving and cussing each other. She jostles into the dark vestibule of the pedestrian overpass. Dirty words on the wall. Chewing gums and betel nut pulps, sticky under her shoes. She dodges the kids swinging baseball bats and counts each step to distract herself from the sharp vapor of urine from boys and dogs. *One, two, three, four* . . .

❈   ❈   ❈

By age six, she can count to one thousand. By ten, the fiftieth prime number. She will fall in love with the shape of infinity in high school, filling the margins of her textbooks with that loopy loop that folds in on itself. The idea of something without end fills her with sadness, like lost first love.

In college, she works as a research assistant at the paleontology lab, where she learns to date mummies by carbon-14, which decays by half every 5,730 years. Alone in the lab at night, she blasts punk rock to scare away darkness and dances from tray to tray of bones. The skeletons don't remind her of her mother's, excavated seven years after death per custom and laid out for a day on the marble slab to be picked, cleaned, and sealed in the tomb again. By now her mother seems to have never existed. Xuan-Xuan doesn't know that she keeps death close so it never surprises her again, but on her death bed years later, she is nonetheless surprised by what flashes across her mind:

7,000,000,000,000,000,000,000,000,000, 000,000,000,000,000,000, 000,000,000, 000,000,000,000,000,000,000,000,000,000.

When did these zeros blink down at her for the first time?

She had left Taiwan for graduate studies in the States. A new person on a new continent. She went by Susan because Xuan-Xuan, pronounced by her English-speaking professors and peers, sounded like wound-up springs.

That night, she had wanted to skip the guest lecture, the annual Big Talk, because she needed to rehearse her closing pitch for the startup competition in the morning, but the judges would be there and so she went. As she scanned the packed auditorium and planned her route to intercept the who's who of Silicon Valley, the lights turned off and the auditorium hushed. All those zeros appeared together on the screen, stretching from wall to wall, blinking, pulsating.

Seven billion, billion, billion, said the guest speaker softly. *The number of atoms in a person's body. In your body.*

The twenty-five-year-old rising star in astrophysics, the youngest addition to Oxford's cosmology faculty, was unassuming in his loose khakis and white T-shirt covered with geometric wrinkles like origami unfolded.

You are seven billion, billion, billion stardust, born in the first second after the Big Bang.

Sitting in the first row, Susan could see the white chalk like new snow on the tip of his straight-edged nose. She felt that he was speaking to her alone.

After the lecture, high on her newly bestowed magnificence as the temporary vessel of billion-year-old stardust, she followed the crowd to the Dutch Goose a mile down the road for sauerkraut and beer. Someone's boom box was playing "Beautiful People" by The Books. *And we genuflect before pure abstraction, 1.05946, twelfth root of two, amen.* She hummed along as the melody looped back where it began. The competition tomorrow and the thesis defense next week receded into white noise.

At the bar, two beers later, she found herself sitting next to the Oxfordian.

Oliver. He shook her hand.

Susan. She flashed her lanyard.

Finalist of the Annual Startup Competition, Oliver said. *You've gone far in the game.*

She shrugged.

When he handed her the third beer, their fingers briefly touched. He said, smiling, *You know two atoms can never touch? The force between them grows exponentially as they get closer? We're actually levitating on the bar stools, you know?* He arched his brows into a lowercase lambda.

But what about quantum entanglement? Lemos et al., 2001. She was showing off.

Oliver blushed, as if they were discussing something other than quantum physics. The nervousness in his voice when he changed the topic would give her courage to track him down years later.

So what's your big idea? he said.

She told him about errors of cell replication, nano-robotic telomerase repair, how death is a disease and a disease can be cured.

How about the beauty of ephemera? Of irreplaceability? he said.

What's the point if we disappear as if we've never existed? she said.

Outside, the night fog had swallowed the stars. A panic set in, as her head started to spin, as if she had been lulled off orbit.

The crowd behind them roared. Two professors climbed on the bar and began downing whiskey shots. Before Susan slipped away to rehearse the pitch, she said hello to one of the venture capitalists sponsoring the prize money, while the giddy crowd counted, *Five! Six! Seven!*

*   *   *

... *Twenty-nine, thirty!* Xuan-Xuan counted the last of the stinky staircases and scampered onto the pedestrian overpass. Far away, the old temple warps under the noonday sun like a mirage in the Taklamakan Desert, where Monkey King fought the demons. Somewhere behind the temple, behind the market, behind Snake Alley that is behind the market, is Treasure Island Alley. Hell.

A whiff of pee, wet fur, zoo. A homeless man is splayed out on the ground, neck-to-toe under a disgusting comforter. Not moving. If he is dead then she'll have to save him in Hell too. She checks his face, twisted and sunburnt. Suddenly the man mumbles. Xuan-Xuan barely escapes his fingers, which jab the air as if he is interrogating someone in his dream.

She runs downstairs to the other side of the road, weaves through the market, resists food carts selling fried tofu and popcorn chicken, and dodges people slurping noodles while walking, until a giant snake freezes her in her track.

The snake that dangles off the arched entrance of Snake Alley is thicker than her thigh and longer than the longest pipe. Sharp fangs, green scales, and very dead.

Papa has taken her here before, for a Chinese New Year banquet with his factory workers, but which way is Treasure Island Alley? She wants to ask the boss man of One Snake restaurant, but a group of men blocks the entrance. They look like the bank men who come to Papa's office every week. Leather briefcases and sweaty armpits. *Dozo*, they say, bowing to let each other enter first, and she realizes that they are Japanese tourists.

Twelve bowls of double penis soup! their tour guide yells in Mandarin as he directs the men in and switches to Taiwanese to whisper to the waiter, *These horny dogs need extra potency for later.*

Finally, only one man remains outside. Big-bearded like a wild boar.

Little friend-rr! the Japanese man says, his foreigner's Mandarin gurgle-gurgling like there's a baby bird in his throat. *You like-rr Doraemon?*

Of course, she thinks. The robot cat is the hero of her second favorite cartoon.

Want to see Doraemon's magic pocket? he says and unzips his bag.

Xuan-Xuan reaches for the bag, because Doraemon's Anywhere Door can open straight to Treasure Island Alley so she won't have to waste time while Mama's body grows stale.

Suddenly someone snatches her hand. *Don't you dare touch this one*, the woman hisses at the man and drags Xuan-Xuan down a narrow alley. The woman doesn't let go until they stop at an opening where several alleyways converge. Xuan-Xuan has never seen this woman before. Fake eyelashes, sequin miniskirt, and heels as high as footstools.

Where you live? What you do here? The woman fires the questions so rapidly that Xuan-Xuan feels a familiar heat shoot up her chest, like when Mama got angry.

One by one, strange women step out from shadowy doorways and circle her.

Lucky Mei-Li picked up a stray! Their red mouths are full of teeth, their eyes wild with crayon colors.

What you thinking? The Japanese could kidnap you to be a comfort woman like they did to her, Mei-Li says and points at a very old woman in mud-caked pajamas squatting by a house corner. The old woman dips her head and hugs her broom.

Comfort woman? Such ancient history. Better the Japanese than penniless Kuomintang veterans! says a girl who has been painting toenails on a stoop. *Kidnap me, please!*

You wish! You're stuck in Treasure Island Alley!

Xuan-Xuan knows she can't ask these women about Mama because they are the minions of the Lord of Hell she has been expecting. She's seen them so many times on TV, in disguise to seduce Monkey King from his missions. Her heart thumps. She grips her backpack and eyes the alleyways.

While the women shriek and bend with laughter, falling over each other, Xuan-Xuan escapes down an alley. She runs past one barred window after another, searching for Mama and peering into dark rooms, where strange creatures with men's heads and women's feet moan and writhe under comforters.

❊ ❊ ❊

It happens fast, between blinks and tricks of light. First, she hears a scream. Then she is straining to see into a room where someone is shouting, *Stop it! I can't breathe!* In the room, in a pool of sunlight on the ground, is Mama's favorite blue dress, torn. *Let me go!* Mama screams. Xuan-Xuan shakes the window bars but they do not budge. She crawls into the room through a hole for dogs at the bottom of the concrete wall, scraping her hands and knees.

On a bed in the tiny room, a man is sitting on Mama's face and growling, *I paid you, bitch.* Xuan-Xuan bites down on the man's buttock, her strength all animal.

Rat, rat! the man yells and jumps off the bed.

Rat, rat! Mama also yells, and Xuan-Xuan sees that the woman is not Mama but a naked girl with purple glitters on her bruised eyes, a bad soul that has been punished.

Then Xuan-Xuan is lifted up by her backpack, kicking air.

Let her go, you beast! The girl beats the man with bare hands, and Xuan-Xuan falls on the bed.

In the darkness that is all perfume and sweat, she rummages in her backpack and finds Monkey King's cudgel, but the man swipes it away. As she dives for it, he yanks her legs.

Save me, Monkey King!

Suddenly the man yelps in pain and doubles over. A broom is beating his back. The old comfort woman has appeared from nowhere, looking twice as big and half as old, her dirty pajamas whipping, and she beats the man with her broom, again and again.

You crazy whores! the man shouts and flees the room. The old woman gives chase.

Xuan-Xuan runs after the old woman, convinced that she is Monkey King. Rounding a corner, she is suddenly out on the street, out of the maze of Treasure Island Alley. In front of the old temple, a throng of worshippers is coming and going. She searches the faces crushing toward her, but Monkey King is gone.

❊ ❊ ❊

Later, years later, she will doubt if any of this really happened. The blue dress. The pool of light by the dog hole. Cinematic spotlight of reconstructed memory. Perhaps she can't bear the failure? Perhaps she wishes she really had gone to Hell to search for her mother? She will decide that she never looked for her mother, never wanted to, for many years.

And in those years, she rarely leaves the office. That is where she and Alex have their last argument over the phone. By then the divorce is merely a formality. Time has softened him and hardened her armor. *You never let me in, never let anyone in,* is the last thing he says to her. She sends her father's call to the voice mail. *Xuan-Xuan*—the name feels like a stranger's—*your grandma is dying and your sister is not doing well.* She doesn't go back to Taiwan because there is the next fight for the next round of funding to pursue another dead end in her quest to eradicate death.

On the eve of her forty-second birthday, after the last investor walks away, she turns off the office light for the last time. She is ten years older than her mother ever would be. One day she will be another pile of bones under a marble slab. What's the point? Returning to her house, long emptied of her ex's things, she binge-watches two decades of missed TV shows.

Afternoons slide into evenings. Evenings creep into mornings. Then all day it is evening.

One night, the moonlight wakes her. She steps outside for the first time in weeks wearing unwashed yoga-wear. The moon walks her north, past the midcentury houses of her neighborhood, then gated mansions, then clusters of high-rises, then car washes, car dealers, car repairs, along forty miles of El Camino Real.

Twelve hours of walk later, she is in San Francisco's Chinatown. In front of a breakfast shop, people huddle against the chill wind from the bay and sip steamy rice milk in Styrofoam cups. On a rooftop, a crackly old radio is playing.

She finds herself in front of Eternal Light Kung Fu Academy, its storefront windows covered with flyers for tai chi, qigong, and something she has never heard of, laughing yoga. Inside, ten, twelve Chinese grandmas and grandpas are lying on tatami mats with their legs up in the air, happy baby pose. *Hah hah! Hah hah!* They pump their bellies like mechanics warming rusty engines. An old man with a shock of white hair and a tiger-stripe scarf walks up and down the aisle prodding the old folks with his cane. *Louder, louder!* he says.

Somehow, all at once, they burst out laughing—roaring—laughing like it's all funny, like to live is funny to die is funny to love is funny to hate is funny, their lungs choking with funny.

She opens the glass door, yearning to lose herself in this lunatic bin.

Welcome, the old man shouts in Mandarin above the chorus of laughter. He points his cane toward a free spot.

Susan lies down and opens her mouth. Nothing comes out. She tries again, but what comes out sounds like the cough of a mouse.

The old man hobbles over and kneels between her legs. He presses his palm into her navel and she chuckles. Then, somewhere between *ahh* and *aargh*, she starts to cry.

There. There. If you can't cry, you can't laugh, the old man says. *But there's more.*

He wedges his fingers between her ribs and digs. Just below her heart, he finds an ancient obstruction, a wad of grief, which Xuan-Xuan pelletized and wedged in when she was five. A dam breaks loose. Tears gush out. She tumbles down the waves, thrashing, kicking, trying not to drown. In the roaring laughter that envelops her, she cries till time disappears.

When she wakes up on the tatami mat, the old man is gone, and the grandmas and grandpas are asleep, their snores one soft rumble. She struggles up. Her legs wobble, and her body feels foreign as if what held her up all these years has gone out with the tears.

She staggers home.

In her living room, under a stack of magazines by the fireplace, she finds the piece of paper from the meditation boot camp, where she scribbled down the few things she knew about her mother: accounting major, loves animal channels, type O negative . . .

She sits by the fire and writes silly questions she would ask her mother if she could: Ocean or mountain? Your worst lie? What would you name your bar?

Her pencil hovers like the needle of a record player abruptly stopped. She studies her hands. They have green veins like her father's, but her father says that her heels are rough like her mother's. She may have her father's eyes, but he says she has her mother's mouth. She makes up answers, knowing that half of them come from her mother.

Then she folds the paper corners to center, the way her father taught her to do with the ghost money, and tosses it into the fire. It unfurls and blossoms. A white rose aflame. In a minute, it is ash.

116

Mother. She tests the word.

Mother. It tastes like a horn melon, musky with a hint of sour.

Mother.

*   *   *

Perhaps the truth is this: that past and future are concepts the mind makes up to take refuge from the present. Perhaps all of time is one. Send a word back to when you were that kid, not yet strong enough to fall. Say *you'll be okay.* Send a word forward to that moment you dread, your last moment, say *I'm here. I'm with you.* If you are lucky, you will feel all of you cushioning your fall. And if you are very lucky, you will realize before it's too late that what is the point is really the wrong question.

*   *   *

From the temple, Xuan-Xuan retraces her steps home. She climbs the pedestrian overpass distractedly. Where is Mama? Maybe she needs to go west, like Monkey King's journey, maybe recruit an entourage, maybe their German shepherd, old but still with good teeth. But how long does she have before Mama's body becomes too stale for the soul?

Suddenly something grabs her. She looks down to see the homeless man by her feet, his dirty hand on her ankle.

Where're you going? the man rasps and grins. Wide mouth no teeth! She screams—

She will have a century of recurring dreams about this homeless man, and she dreams of him now, in the last moment of her life, as the nectar of opioid drips into her vein, as all her moments collapse into one, and Oliver, her frail Oxfordian—wasn't it yesterday when she found him again?—sits vigil by her side.

Let go of me, in her feverish dream she begs the homeless man. *I have no more time for your game.*

The man laughs. *Stupid girl. All these years and you don't recognize me?*

He flings open his dirty comforter and unfurls a tail in stripes of brown and black. She blinks and the man changes. First, he is the old comfort woman, then the old man at the Kung Fu Academy, and then he is a thousand images of a thousand people.

Monkey King stands before her, not much taller than she is. His windblown fur sticks out from underneath his yellow kung fu suit. A face full not of lines but of furrows.

You have seen death, but you've never seen it in the right light, he says, twirling his thousand-pound cudgel with his thumb. *I'll teach you the way of immortality, the greatest trick of all mankind.*

Then his images begin to chant in unison, *Na—Mo—A—Mi—Tuo—Fo—*

She bursts out laughing. *You're kidding.*

This is no joke. Monkey King taps her head with his cudgel. *Repeat after me.*

She gives in, too tired to argue, certain that this, all this, will end soon enough.

Na—Mo—A—Mi—Tuo—Fo . . . Bow to the Buddha of Infinite Light. And now—

Wait, wait, she says, suddenly panicky, but only a gurgle escapes her throat. The dying note of a bird's last song. She feels Oliver's hands. *Two atoms can never touch.* Then the girl that she was, twenty and alone in the lab, twenty and feeling old, is saying to her, *Don't be scared, you're only going where your mother has gone . . .*

Monkey King guides her hand to pluck a hair off her head. The gesture of his Seventy-Two Transformations. With her last breath, she whispers her last bit of magic:

Now . . . Watch me disappear . . .

Her seven-billion-billion particles break away—a liberal amount of oxygen and carbon, some hydrogen, nitrogen, calcium, a pinch of sulfur, phosphorus, potassium—and they race toward another cosmic lottery to become a hummingbird, a copper tin, a speck of dirt in Treasure Island Alley, a little girl, who flees the homeless man and runs into the swell of chants and cries from the white tent holding her mother's body, and she screams to a stop in front of her family's building—

Grandma appears at the top of the stairs, a spatula still in hand, a baby swaddles to her chest.

Where have you been?

And for a few seconds, Xuan-Xuan has absolutely no idea.

Nominated by New England Review, Lou Matthews

BALLAD THAT ENDS WITH BITCH

from **DIANE SEUSS**

from AGNI

She was one of those long-nosed ones.
Mary, full of grace, cream atop the milk.
I picked my way through dung piles and bones.
Animal dung. Animals of every ilk.

All of us come with a ballad.
Hers was set in an Amish puppy mill.
Born in a mill, then forced to give birth.
Birth before she'd been a year on this cold earth.

She rolled on her back to show me her scar.
Playing dead, she showed me her spaying scar.
I have one of those, I said, but mine is perpendicular.
Little princess, I too have been opened with a crowbar.

My tenderness. I couldn't find a way to say yes.
I felt splayed, my little scar exposed.
It's all against our will, I suppose.
I stumbled through brambles to find my way, I guess.

A whole pathless hillside covered in sedge.
Barn cats arched their backs. Neutralizing agents.
Agents of indifference. Other animals pawed at the gate.
Looking to get in or out of grace or fate.

I walked her, using a piece of rope for a leash.
She knew nothing of a leash, that false umbilical cord.
On that tether, she wandered aimless, trampish.
Too small for this world, vast as a billboard.

I was once too small for this world.
Somebody burned my arm with a cigar.
They said they didn't know I was there.
I believe them. I still have the scar.

She was a prototype of tenderness.
I wandered that hillside, this way and that.
I could not find my way to yes.
She was a child bride in a plastic crèche.

As I drove away, her borders dissolved.
She dispersed herself across the landscape like mist.
Through the fog I could still see her belly scar.
A horizon line, I told myself, divvying up that and this.

When I returned to my digs, the house was frozen stiff.
A fine skim of hoarfrost on the writing desk.
Why call it a writing desk?
It's commerce-covered. Bills. Tat. That. This.

At age ten, I turned away from tenderness.
I remember the moment. A flipping of a switch.
My house is a cold mess except for that thing in the corner.
Poetry, that snarling, flaming bitch.

Nominated by Agni, Ellen Bass, David Hernandez, Maxine Scates, Robert Thomas, Lee Lipton, Michael Waters

THE RESTAURANT, THE CONCERT, THE BAR, THE BED, THE PETIT DÉJUENER

fiction by FREDERIC TUTEN

from BOMB and THE BAR AT TWILIGHT (Bellevue Literary Press)

Central Park spread outside the window, the evening transforming shrubs and trees and the Egyptian obelisk into silhouettes. Snow drifted down flake by flake and two hit the window, each melting into another state. When we die, don't we also go into another state?

I started to give voice to this ancient question, but, turning from the window, Marie spoke first. "You live your life and then, bang, suddenly it's all looking back."

"Is it the snow outside that makes you think this now?"

"No, it's this restaurant. Everyone's old and every last one is regretting what they've left undone and where they went wrong."

"Everything I've done is wrong, so I don't really dwell on it. I'd rather sit here and dwell on you."

"Dwell away," she said. "Still, this is the most boring restaurant in the whole world. No wonder it suits you."

"I like that it's beige and tame."

"You just summed up your taste in art, buddy," she said, pointing—rudely, I thought—her salad fork at me.

"I like all kinds of art and all kinds of women, except rude ones with spears."

"Do you like them when they are overripe like old pears with brown bruises?"

As if not having heard her, I said, "And dessert? What appeals to you?"

"Hemlock, please."

"Or maybe an espresso, if they've run out?"

"Natch."

"What's with the argot?"

Luis, the waiter, who had known us a long time, came by to take our dessert order, adding, "You have twenty-five minutes to get down to the concert."

I thanked him and she thanked him and I thanked him again.

"You mean 'What's with the slang?' *Argot* means specialist language, like the kind criminals use," she said.

"I'm hip to the criminal argot," I said. "Like shiv or screw or gator tossing the salad."

"I swoon," she said in a sexy whisper, "when you make like a street urchin from Hell's Kitchen."

"That dates you," I said. "Hell's Kitchen's gone upscale."

"You're an urchin anyway. But with friendly spines and a soft shell and a mushy middle." She showed a thread of a smile, as when she won a round at bridge.

"You know, my dear, I have been giving this a great deal of thought in the last few seconds and I've concluded that you need a giant dose of sex, liberally applied."

"I have *plenty* of sex," she said, twisting her napkin. "Tons of it. Just not always with you is all."

"I have noticed your absence from my bed, except when we watch TV."

"Which is never," she said.

"Are you hinting I buy one? They have color now, I understand."

She squinted and whispered, "Don't turn now, but there is a man at the next table who's making eyes at me."

I turned. A man in a shiny blue suit and bulging blue eyes. And a grotesque plaid tie. He was still staring. "Maybe he knows you from one of your reading groups."

"Does he look like he's into Proust?"

"Or maybe your spin class?"

"That butterball?"

"Or maybe from your Umbrian cooking class or your Zen poetry workshop? Maybe he's your old college boyfriend gone chubby and bald?"

122

"He had no friends. He got rich before he could make any."

"Excuse me," I said. "Must see a man about a horse."

"That same old, tired nag? Is he still running?"

"More frequently than ever."

The bathroom was white and empty, palatial in size and bracing in its mountain pine-scented aroma. It was pleasant to be alone in a room without the hum of voices. But suddenly a man materialized at the adjacent urinal, but he was not peeing. His blue suit went dull in the fluorescent light.

"Is that your wife?"

"None other," I replied.

"Because it's unnatural for a husband and wife to talk so much at dinner. Unless they're newly-weds. Are you newlyweds?"

I zippered up and went to wash my hands. The water was warm and flowed luxuriously and, for the moment, made me feel secure in this daunting world.

"She's very beautiful, in a fading kind of way," he said, giving his hands a rinse and a shake over the sink.

"Oh! Yes, I agree, both the beauty and the fading part. She aged years at that place."

"Hospital?" he asked with a little alarm in his voice.

I pretended not to hear. Until he repeated, "Hospital?"

"No," I said sotto voce, "*prison.*"

I put my hands under a machine and a sheet of brown paper came out with a whine. Then I did it again.

He held the door open for me. "Serious offense?"

I made a face, as if the memory of that time had made me sad, frightened. "She gouged out her lover's eye with a salad fork."

"My God!" he said. "That beautiful woman? Really?"

He opened the door and motioned for me to pass first. I did the same for him and we went back and forth until finally I won.

He walked beside me, searching, I thought, for something to say, until we reached the dining room, when he whispered, "Good luck, fella."

"He came right over after you left," she said. "And slid a note under my napkin."

"Saying what?"

"Nothing. Just a phone number with an upstate area code."

"Oh! Not Syracuse or Hornell, I hope," I said. She let it pass.

"Well, I suppose I've still got it," she said with a sigh that I liked.

"It has never left you."

Luis threw up his hands. I looked at my watch. We had only five minutes before the concert and we sped to the elevator, where Blue Suit was standing.

My wife smiled at him. "Haven't we met before?"

"I don't think so," he said.

"Oh! Yes, yes, yes," she sang, "I'm sure we have."

The door opened and we entered, my wife first. The man said, "Go ahead. I just forgot I left something at the table."

The door shut. I pressed the button and took her hand and soon we were speeding down to the museum's lobby and to its theater.

"Which story did you tell him?"

"The fork in the eye," I said.

"That's getting tired," she said.

I agreed. The door glided open, and we walked out hand in hand. "You have a new perfume?"

"Yes, do you like it?"

"Love it. Like rags soaked in a dying man's urine."

"That good?"

"Like a sewer overflow in Fez."

"Don't flatter."

She took my arm and leaned her head on my shoulder. "My man," she purred.

We found our seats and, having found them, sat, me on the aisle, where I could close my eyes and fall asleep in the event the performance went flat, without fire or even a flame. And there vanishes two hours.

"You can sleep on my shoulder, if you like," she said.

This was a comforting invitation. Enough to keep me uncomplaining while we waited for the concert to begin. The audience, with its coughing and rustling, seemed impatient—pissed off with life, even. But they did not have her elegant shoulder to anticipate should life go sour.

"Or 'lie in your lap,' madame?"

"Even there, but no snoring."

Finally, the musicians filed out, sat, fidgeted, tuned up. The man in the blue suit was now in a tux. His bow tie drooped. He wore scuffed street shoes with sloped heels. He looked over the audience and caught my eye. I smiled. My wife did, too. Then I made a gesture as if gouging out my left eye and smiled again. He turned in an agitated way and said some words to the other three, waiting, poised for him to begin.

"You're going overboard with this," she said.

"Yes," I said, feeling contrite. Then I added, "But he deserves it. What kind of man slips you his phone number behind my back? He didn't have the grace to do it in my presence. And it's not even a Manhattan number."

He gave one more alarmed look our way; then, composing himself, and with a slight nod to the others, he ravaged the strings with his bow. It was an accomplished modernist piece, light on melody, heavy on dissonance. It had its innocuous merits, like most intellectually constructed art—like most conventional exchanges in life.

I soon let the music become wallpaper to my thoughts. Which ran this way: Should we stop for a drink after? Why am I so happy? What is it that moves me in life and in art? To the last, I answered, The surprise. Then I whispered to myself, She is my marvelous surprise.

There was a silence, a pause before the next piece began, a Beethoven string quartet. The first three movements demanded concentration, diligence, and sent my mind straining to follow its ravishing complexity, but the fourth movement unexpectedly sprang a sweet melody seemingly unrelated to anything in the earlier movements and my heart opened with a warm tenderness to life, even if the illness and dying part were to come sooner rather than later.

I barely knew the music was over when the audience rose about me, clapping. My wife released my hand and started clapping wildly. I sat but did not clap; I was in a daze of bliss and could hardly move. We left our seats slowly, lingering, as if to savor the rare thing that had happened to us. And we were the last to take our coats and the last at the long steps leading down to the street, where the waiting taxis fled into the night.

"Cab?" I asked.

"I'd rather hoof it, is what I'd rather do. Wait, didn't we get mugged walking here last year?" she said.

"The kids sort of just asked us for money."

"Was it the knives that opened your wallet?"

"That, and I liked that they called me 'sir.'" We walked. She nestled into my arm.

"You're okay," she said.

"So was the violinist."

"Very okay. Very," she said.

Before we knew it, we were at the Carlyle. "This is a kir royale night," I said.

"Sure, you get one," but then, turning to the bartender, she said, "Monsieur Marcel, I'll have a Seven and Seven and a Corona." He brought us a crystal bowl of nuts, not a peanut among them.

"Do you have any pretzels, Marcel?"

"*Je n'en ai pas*," he said.

"The next time, I'm going to bring you a few boxes to keep for me, with my name on them."

"*Quelle bonne idée*," he said.

He brought us our drinks, excused himself, and sped to the other end of the bar, where a young couple in party hats was flagrantly in love.

"We should have died right there in our seats after the final movement. But it would have been inconsiderate of the others in our row, I suppose," she said.

"I guess, and we wouldn't have wanted to spoil his night, even if he's so tacky," I said.

"He's tacky, all right, but brilliant. One doesn't preclude the other."

"Right, just look at Wagner."

"He wasn't at all tacky. Wagner was rotten and sexy." She took a slug of beer straight from the bottle. I had never seen her do that before.

"You've never seen me do that before," she said, reading my mind. "Well, I thought I'd put a little spice in my life. Like that girl over there."

The girl was dividing her time between guzzling her beer and tonguing her boyfriend. I heard Marcel say to the lovers, "I have asked you twice politely to behave. Please leave now. Go to the St. Regis for this kind of material."

"We have a room here," the young man said with nervous dignity.

"Then, should you continue, I shall have you evicted," Marcel said.

Marcel returned to us. "*Incroyable, ça, n'est-ce pas?*"

"*Pas de tout*," my wife said. "*Les bêtises de jeunesse.*"

"I myself was once young, but even in my youth I observed the proprieties," Marcel said.

Some people came in noisily and settled at the only empty table. It was the musicians with their bulging instrument cases and two young women gleeful to be with them.

Marcel beckoned to the waiter and said, "Tell them they must install their instruments in the cloakroom. We cannot have them cluttering the bar."

My wife gave them a smile and waved hello. I made a friendly nod to the table and a little bow to the first violinist, now again in his blue suit. He smiled back like a man hiding a toothache.

"Marcel, please send them over a bottle of champagne," my wife said. "You choose, you always know the best."

"I shall take care of it," Marcel said. "A good-quality champagne, of course, but nothing too grand."

"Sending only a bottle, my dear?" I asked.

"It's just for the gesture, not to make a drama of the thing," she said.

The table went into a huddle; the violinist leaned in and spoke. A few moments later, they all turned, giving us looks of wonder and discomfort.

"Let's go before the champagne arrives," she said. "I'd feel more comfortable."

"Sure, that will leave a trail of mystery behind." I signed our tab and slid a bill into Marcel's hand.

"*Bonsoir*, Marcel," she said, blowing him a kiss.

"*Bonne soirée, monsieur-dame*," Marcel said, giving the bar counter a swipe of his immaculate towel.

We got to our building as it began to snow. "Oh! Let's stay and watch the snow fall on the trees," she said. "It's been such a rare night. I hate for it to end so quickly."

We paused under the canopy as the snow fell in a greater and greater rush. Eddie, the doorman, stood guard at the doorway and gave us a friendly smile and a salute.

"Have you ever observed that the snow is gentler on this side of the park?"

"I've noticed that, too," she said. "And that the flakes are more distinguished."

Eddie came over and asked if we'd like him to bring out our beach chairs so that we could sit under the canopy.

"We're not staying that long. Unless you want to," she said, taking my hand.

"We're fine, Eddie. Thank you very much," I said, making a note to tip him before we went up. Tips, big ones especially, make the world run on time; I had learned that in Paris, where even love affairs run on time.

We sometimes sat in front of the building on spring nights to gawk at the stars and at the flow of the Fifth Avenue traffic. We blighted the sidewalk, several of our neighbors protested in anonymous letters. One wrote, "Move to the Bronx." We received official reprimands from the board, until my wife, the litigation lawyer, threatened to sue them. She never seemed to mind the cold shoulders after that. I think she was glad for them. She was silent in the ride up the elevator and was distracted in our apartment, looking out the window several times into the now fiercely driving snow.

"It's coming down hard now," she said. "How will the musicians ever get home tonight?"

"You mean the musician," I said.

"His shoes are too thin for the snow." She looked away for a moment before kissing me on the cheek and saying, "Good night, sweet dreams."

I went to my bedroom, undressed, and put on my comforting blue flannel pajamas with prancing polar bears. I thought about the music I had heard earlier and how Beethoven shaved sounds into planes, each note hiding another that could not be heard but was vibrantly felt. I was still thinking about this when she came in without knocking.

"Would you like a visit?" she asked.

"For as long as you wish," I said.

"It's just a visit," she said; "I wasn't thinking of moving in." She was in oversize boy's pajamas with wild horses roaming a range of hills and sky. She slid under the covers and took the book from my hand.

"Lights on or off?" she asked. Before I could answer, she added, "It's been so long, maybe lights off is better. I don't want to shock you with the changes."

"You never change," I said. "You are one of those immutable forms of nature."

"Sure," she said, switching off the light.

She took off her pajamas. I could see even in the faint window light the scars from her old operations and the recent gash where her breast had been. We kissed, a little formally. It had been so long, I was shy. But soon we kissed like first lovers. We lay still, bathed in the faint glow of the streetlamps and the reflecting light of the snow on the windowsill.

"I don't love you," she said, taking my hand. "I don't love you very much."

"Same here with aces," I said.

We kissed again before she went back to her room. She had left my door open, but I was too comfortable in my place to get up to shut it. Images of her played in my mind until I finally fell into a mellow sleep. It was almost two when I heard my wife's low voice, but she was not in my room. I first thought she was sleep talking, though over the years I had rarely heard her do so. I waited awhile, but I grew worried that she was unwell, so I went to her door, which was open. The light was on and the bed was in disarray. She looked up, her cell phone in her hand.

"I called him to apologize for the bad joke. I called to say how great he was. It was a perfect evening and I did not want it to end with regrets, that's all."

"You called him at three in the morning?"

"Musicians never sleep, don't you know that?"

I stayed silent and troubled. And finally, I said, "I see."

"Look, my dear," she said, "We've had a good life and a night we'll never top. What's the point, then, of our waiting around for all the dreariness to come?"

"Well, there's life is why."

"So you can see me sliced up again? So you can sit in a hospital corridor waiting for the news?"

"There's nothing to worry about yet. Go back to sleep," I said with all the tenderness and assurance I could bring to my voice.

I went back to bed. It was some while before I could return to sleep, but not before I heard her on the phone again. I felt a mild nausea sweep over me and I turned off the light.

It was early morning when she came into the room fully dressed. "I'll be gone for a little while now," she said. "Maybe for the day. Or so."

"Going out in this snow?"

"Don't worry, Eddie will get me a cab."

"Will you stay for breakfast?"

"Just start without me."

"I'll wait," I said. I walked her to the door and watched her put on her sable coat and matching Russian sable hat. She looked as if she were going on a sleigh ride in 1904 to meet her lover in a dacha in Siberia.

After she left, I started puttering about. Walked into the kitchen, then walked out, put on Ravel's *Pavane pour une infante défunte,* but its melancholy only further dispirited me and gloomed up the furniture. I looked for solace and read aloud to myself Wallace Stevens's "Sunday Morning." Did he ever love anything but metaphor and the immutable, imperishable forms of beauty? These and other lofty thoughts did not distract me from the snow and my wife, who was out there in it. Or out there somewhere. I soon found that I was in no mood to read or to do much of anything but brood.

I phoned down to the desk and Eddie answered. "Was my wife able to get a cab?" I asked.

"I told her she'd never get one in this snow. She said that was okay, that she didn't want one anyway."

I paced the apartment again, this time looking for our dear cat, Nicolino, knowing he was not there, having died years ago, his little dried-up body found in one of the building's shafts. She cried for a week and said we should never have a cat again. And we didn't. But we had his ghost, who showed up mostly at our breakfast, the meal he had always loved best to share with us in his mortal form.

The snow was piling up on the windowsill and the park faded into whiteness; the trees seemed embarrassed by the weight of their heavy white shapes. I went back to the kitchen. The fridge was almost empty, but there was a little tin of caviar our friends had given us two weeks ago. Our friends, a middle-aged couple like us, had come to celebrate our twentieth anniversary and they were merry all through dinner, but I knew they were unhappy together—their pores leaked it—and were yearning to return home to settle back into the familiar comfort of their unhappiness. I thought not to open the caviar lest it release the unhappiness they had brought with it, and I returned the tin to its cold place. Anyway, I could always one day share it with Nicolino, who wasn't so fussy about human emotions.

Eddie phoned. "The city's shut down," he said, "I had to sleep on the couch in the hall."

"It must be cold down there," I said, "Come up and have a drink."

"No, you come down," he said, "and let's have a snowball fight." He was drunk again.

I got dressed and went to the cabinet and pulled out an unopened bottle of malt scotch that someone had left us years ago and took two glasses from the kitchen, one for Eddie. Why not get drunk together, I thought. Maybe we could even make a snowman at the entrance and irritate the other tenants.

He was sprawled on the hall couch, gaudy with parrots and monkeys sitting in leafy tropical branches. He fit the scene, even with his winter coat and Russian-style fur hat that my wife had given him after our return from a Siberian vacation. His eyes were open, but the rest of him was asleep. I left the bottle and the glasses—crystal, for the occasion— by the couch and went to the doorway, halfway blocked by the snow. I pushed my way out and into the pathway now covered with crunchy snow high to my knees. I took the shovel that Eddie had left by the door and cut a path to the sidewalk. A bus had careened into a tree and stood, lights on, with snow embracing the tires. No cars passed, nor did one person in the tundra of lampposts of what once had been Fifth Avenue.

The passengers and driver, I surmised, had made their way out earlier, because their tracks were now covered in the snow, as I now was fast becoming.

I felt a terrible chill once I was back in the building that not even a stiff drink of the scotch that I had brought down with me seemed to warm. The bottle had been opened and I could see from the half-filled glass on the floor that the now fully awake Eddie had not stood on ceremony.

"Excellent scotch," Eddie said, raising his glass in a toast. "To you and the missus."

"To you and yours, Eddie," I said, feeling the warmth returning, feeling a bit of good cheer even.

"There is no mine, Mr. Charles." And then, rising from his prone position and sitting erect but wobbling slightly, he added, "There is no nothing. That's the ticket, no nothing. One day she's holding my hand in the park on a bench under a big fat tree with leaves so green that your eyes water and calling me 'sweetie' and 'honey' and 'cupcake' and me returning the same to her with interest and the next day she's in a hospital with arms stuck with needles and before you can say 'jackrabbit,' she's ashes in a jar."

"I'm so sorry, Eddie," I said. I was sorry. For him, for us. For all of us. Where was she now, in all this whiteout?

"Stick with your missus as long as you can. Even if you can't stand it once in a while."

"Keen advice, Eddie."

He sloshed his glass with a hefty dose of scotch and knocked it back. It seemed to sober and steady him and he straightened himself and stood up erect like a marine at drill. *"Le silence d'amour. Ce n'est tout, ne c'est pas?"*

"Bien sûr," I said, a bit astonished that Eddie spoke French and with a Parisian flair, *en plus*. One day I would introduce him to Marcel and hear them discourse on the proprieties of love.

Thinking of love, I asked, "By the way, have you seen Nicolino these days?"

"He passes by to say hello sometimes and vanishes into the park."

I was very sad that he had not come to see me in months, and my expression showed it.

"He's got a girlfriend. He's in love, I can tell."

"In love," I said.

"Yes, Mr. Charles, but I'm sure he will never leave you. *Jamais*."

I left Eddie and the half-empty scotch bottle with him. And without further word, he stretched out on the couch and went back to sleep in the jungle drunk with acrobatic apes and screaming parrots.

No sooner had I settled in and returned to my fears and gloom than the doorbell chimed. Odd that, because Eddie had not phoned to announce a visitor—unless he was so plastered that an elephant could walk by him unnoticed—and I was taken aback. I thought it might be my neighbor, but he and his wife had gone to Marrakesh, where they spent their winters in their rented villa packed with their English guests from Belgravia.

But then there was a not too gentle knock and a voice: "I'm frozen. Open up."

She was drowned in snow, so, too, her shopping bags, like baby igloos. She took off her snow-piled coat and hat, dropped them on the marble hall floor, and brought the igloos into the kitchen, brushing off the snow in the wide sink.

"Look what I have," she said, naming each item as she placed it on the kitchen counter: "Lox, sable, salmon roe, bagels, pickles, herring, potato salad, Spanish olives stuffed with almonds, chopped liver, a container of young pickles, Carr's water biscuits, *The New York Times*—it's yesterday's—and Dr. Brown's Cel-Ray soda."

"Wasn't everything closed?"

"Everything is. The whole city is closed. The owner at the deli was trapped there overnight and he welcomed me like a rescue party. Half the stuff here is a present."

"Eddie's been down there all night. Let's invite him up for breakfast—or bring him down a tray."

"Later, if you like. I just want breakfast alone with you, unless you've got some floozy stashed away here."

"Please, her name's Brandee. She's a model slash astrophysicist, and she left a minute ago."

"Okay," she said, "then let's get down to business."

She loaded up a tray with the deli containers and I took out the plates and silverware and we set up on the dining room table. She disappeared for what seemed forever but returned with a silver pot of coffee and a creamer. I noticed that she had changed into a Chinese silk robe where dragons clashed and fire streamed from their eyes.

"Have you missed me?"

"Not at all," I said.

132

"So robust of you!"

"Missed you the whole world," I added.

She poured coffee into my cup and pitched in a bit of cream—the way she knew I liked it.

"Have you ever wanted to be invited to a party just for the satisfaction of not going?" she asked. "Have you?"

"I'm no longer invited to parties," I said, "nor do I wish to be."

"Then what would you know, Louis, of the pleasure of not showing up?"

I wanted to kiss her but thought better of it, not to change the mood. We didn't speak for a long while, eating lazily, as if we had all the time in the world.

Nominated by Bellevue Literary Press, Bomb

TWO PEOPLE

by JAMES LONGENBACH

from THE ADROIT JOURNAL

1.
Two people at the end of a dock, facing the sea, the sky.
Behind them a party, clink of glasses.
Guests still relevant to their lives
But not essential;
Parents, family friends.

Two people not yet old, but no longer young.
Before them the bay, they're facing west, they're watching
    the sun go down.
The sky is bright, and then, remarkably, it's dark
    again.

They've never done this before,
They've done it a thousand times.

The sun goes down,
The stars come out,
Even the lights above the patio are beautiful.

2.
How do you imagine the shape of one lifetime?
A circle, a tangle of lines? He knows
That if he kisses her

She'll kiss him back,
But he waits, they're going to spend their lives together; he knows
    that, too.

Behind them, growing louder, the past:
The one who left, the one who would not go away—
What happens when a wish comes true?
A room by the sea, a bed, a chair.

You're a little sunburnt, a breeze, white curtains billowing,
And as you raise your arms
She lifts the tee shirt from your body.
Perfect gentleness, the perfect glint of pain.

3.
Where will we be in five years, five years after that?
This is a game they play.
Often they play it in a restaurant, *Rue de L'Espoir*.
A basket of bread, two round glasses of wine. How free they feel!

Five years from now I want us each to have a book.
We'll live in London, maybe Rome.

Five years from that we'll have a baby, what will we name her?
   She'll be a girl.

It all comes true—everything
They ever wished
And more, many books, two girls.

Remember the party behind them, the voices?
They never went away.
But the sound of the sea grew louder.

By now you understand I'm the boy, or that I was.
We've lived in the same houses, the red, the yellow, then the
    brown—
The girl is in her attic study right
Above my head, right now; she's writing a book.

Her fierce intelligence, her beautiful body—
Where will I go
Without her? What will I see?

One of our daughters lives in Boston, one in New York.
They walk to work past boats, fishmongers, the bars.
We've lived far
From the ocean for thirty years.

I had made up my mind: any distant city would serve my purpose.

That turned out also to be true.

Nominated by Adroit Journal

WHAT IF PUTIN LAUGHED

by STEVE STERN

from TIKKUN

The schlemiel is the quintessential Jewish archetype. He (and some-times she) is the bumbler who spills the soup, as opposed to his cousin the schlimazel upon whom the soup is spilled. His character has been a fixture of the Jewish tradition from the Bible's hapless Jonah to the Wise Men of Chelm, through Yiddish folklore and theater (Menashe Skulnik, Fanny Brice) via the Borscht Belt to the present-day Jewish comics (Woody Allen, Larry David). As a literary figure, he can assume a variety of faces: he's the unlucky blunderer and the sympathetic kle-ine mentschele, "the little man" of Sholem Aleichem's tales, the holy innocent of I.B. Singer's "Gimpel". But always he's a loser with a differ-ence; because, regardless of how many times he's deceived by charla-tans or throttled by pogromchiks, he retains what the Yiddish writers called der pintele yid. This is that eternal drop of Jewishness, sweet but never saccharine, that compels the schlemiel to maintain a compassion-ate relation to his community and by extension—once he's done licking his wounds—the rest of mankind.

The image of the schlemiel has not always been considered good for the Jews. The early Zionists sought to erase the couple of millennia that had spawned the stereotype of the Jewish male as the soft, anemic, and bookish victim of his pitiable circumstances. In his place they revived the idea of the Jewish warrior. All those centuries of vulnerability and persecution were just an aberrant interlude between the Maccabees and the Arab-Israeli War. Never mind that, during that interlude, a kaleidoscopically rich and exuberant culture had developed in the shadow of tyranny and unending oppression. It was out of that culture, the culture Yiddishkeit, that the figure of the schlemiel emerged with his ironic what-me-worry shrug. He's an Old World staple, the schlemiel, the universal underdog, embodying, in the words of Irving Howe and Eliezer Greenberg, "the virtue of powerlessness, the power of helplessness, the company of the dispossessed, the sanctity of the insulted and the injured." Of course, the world that nurtured him no longer exists. But the archetype endures and continues, in its posthumous personifications, to have a paculiar relevance to the events of the day.

The seat of that culture of Yiddishkeit was the Pale of Settlement, the Eastern European portion of the old Russian Empire to which the Jews were confined by law. Among the regions included within its boundaries was a major expanse of what is today modern Ukraine. It's a landscape that throughout its various national incarnations has been largely, often savagely, hostile to the Jews. During one of the Ukraine's earliest attempts at achieving independence—led by the Cossack hetman Bogdan Chmielnitski in his 17th century war against Russia—the Jews suffered their greatest slaughter prior to the Holocaust. Sporadic pogroms and anti-Jewish riots persisted throughout the centuries of Czarist rule, to say nothing of the purges during the First World War, the Russian Revolution, and the civil war that followed. Then came the Nazi Occupation, when the Germans and their Ukrainian collaborators murdered over one and a half million Jews, effectively eliminating the Jewish presence in the Ukraine. One of the last recorded ritual murder trials took place in Kiev in 1912. In all of their thousand-year residency in the Ukraine, it's safe to say that the Jews were never able to relax.

And yet it was a homeland. In the rural slums of their shtetls and the teeming rookeries of their urban ghettos, the Jews may have yearned to spend next year in Jerusalem, but in the meantime, they made the best of what they had; and the best of it included—grinding poverty aside, the constant threat of pogrom and the squelching of civil liberties notwithstanding—the vitality of a culture informed by a dogged resourcefulness, an ecstatic spiritual longing, and a fatalistic and irrepressible sense of humor.

> *Two Jews are facing the Czar's firing squad. Yossel cries, "Up with the motherland!" "Shah!" says Hymie with a finger to his lips, "Yossel, do you want to make trouble?"*
>
> *After the Czar was assassinated, a government official says to a rabbi, "I bet you know who's responsible." "Gevalt," says the rabbi, "I don't have a clue, but the government will con-*

clude the same as always: they'll blame it on the Jews and the beekeepers." "Why the beekeepers?" asks the puzzled official. Replies the rabbi, "Why the Jews?"

And so on.

The schlemiel is the very human manifestation of that inherent humor (with which the Yiddish language itself seems to resonate), and perhaps the most emblematic schlemiel of them all was conceived by one of Ukraine's native sons. Tevye the Dairyman, made iconic by "Fiddler on the Roof", was the literary offspring of the Yiddish writer Sholem Aleichem, who was born in a village a stone's throw from Kiev. He lived awhile in Kiev then fled from there to Odessa after witnessing a brutal massacre of the Jews, then fled Odessa after having survived yet another pogrom. There's a woefully neglected Sholem Aleichem Museum in the house where he lived in Kiev; there are statues of him which are occasionally spray-painted with swastikas. His life was full of frequent reversals and chronic financial embarrassment, throughout which he apparently remained as sanguine as his creation: the wry and mock-sagacious Tevye, whose bittersweet sensibility can make tragedy ashamed of itself.

> *"No matter how bad things get, you got to go on living, even if it kills you."*
> *"Let's talk about something more cheerful. Have you heard any news of the cholera in Odessa?"*
> *"The Bible tells us to get along with our neighbor—but if his dog bites, muzzle him."*
> *"When the heart is full, it runs out the eyes."*

And so on.

He can barely eke out a living, is relentlessly harried by ill fortune, impending displacement, and the uncertain destinies of his daughters; and he is fool enough to keep his faith despite it all. ("How many luxuries has the good God prepared for his children.") In his passive resistance to adversity, he has come to be viewed as a kind of poor man's Quixote, the anti-hero who in the end forfeits his anti-.

Another son of the Ukraine, the Russian Jewish writer and lifelong devotee of Sholem Aleichem, Isaac Babel, also traded in characterizations of the schlemiel. His version, however, tended to anticipate the Zionist "muscle Jew" in his admiration for the schlemiel's antithesis, the virile and ruthless warrior. Expressing a self-deprecating disdain for the Diaspora Yid with "spectacles on his nose and autumn in his heart", Babel himself (the most abject kind of schlemiel—a literary artist) joined a Cossack regiment during the Russian Civil War. The Cossacks had been the historical worst enemy of the Eastern European Jews for generations, and many of the stories in Babel's *Red Cavalry* collection, the book that made him famous, show his four-eyed narrator attempting to prove himself the equal of his comrades in violence and cruelty. The stories are unique in the annals of wartime chronicles, describing as they often do cold-blooded atrocities in a lapidary, unbiased, and even forgiving language. The incompatibility of the prose with its bloody subject make the stories somehow that much more disturbing. They underscore in their poignancy what is necessarily lost in the transition from schlemiel to warrior—that is, an essential measure of one's humanity, let alone your sense of humor. Later on, before he was executed by Stalin for no particular reason, Babel returned in his stories to the Moldavanka slum of his Odessa childhood, where his narrator's catalog of humiliations was portrayed with a gentle and forbearing irony.

While Babel's schlemiel traveled far from the dense Jewish enclave of the Moldavanka, Sholem Aleichem's Tevye stayed put in Boiberik until he was compelled to leave, but both sprang from the same milieu that Hannah Arendt once designated as "worldless". What she meant, I think, is that in the ghetto or the shtetl the Jew lived in a space defined less by the events of the historical moment than by the timeless myth of a people. Enter the world beyond the myth, regardless of its possibilities—enter that world, which is called history, at your peril. Philosophical as always in the face of expulsion from his home, Tevye acknowledges, "It's an old Jewish custom to pick up and go elsewhere at the first mention of a pogrom." The Jew Volodymyr Zelensky, however, contradicts Tevye in his now-legendary quip: "I don't need a ride, I need ammo."

It turns out we're not the only nation with a tendency to view real life through the lens of make-believe. In the TV sitcom "Servant of the People" in which he starred, Volodymyr Zelensky played a classic schlemiel, bumbling but good-hearted and well-intentioned, with his nose often literally in a book. Through an improbable series of events, he stumbles from a high school classroom into the presidency of his country. Our nation also had a president who stepped out of make-believe—in his case reality TV—into the Oval Office, then tried, with disastrous consequences, to drag reality back into the asphyxiating, two-dimensional confines of a television show. Zelensky hasn't had that option. At first, his leadership wasn't taken awfully seriously by his citizens, though everyone seemed to enjoy the meta-fictional joke; it was a hoot to have an authentic funny man in the office rather than the evil clowns who had preceded him. But then came the war which forced him to rise to the occasion, to enter history and behave as the kind of leader whose resolute attitude calls into question his credentials as schlemiel. The media, borrowing another Jewish trope, was quick to seize upon the predictable association: he was like a nebbish Clark Kent who, having entered a figurative phone booth, swapped his briefcase and soup-stained tie for a military T-shirt and fatigues, and emerged as a full-blown superhero.

I like the drama of sensational metamorphosis as well as the next, but I would suggest that, in the case of Zelensky, there was no transformation at all. Though if not, the question arises: Was he always a hero disguised as a clown or is he now a clown disguised as a hero? The answer is of course neither and both. The hero is always potential in the schlemiel; the qualities that make him funny make him human and vice-versa; his sense of irony is a source of irreverence that finds opportunities for laughter even in the interstices of the tragic. Without the laughter, there's no human component, and without the humanity no real courage; the warrior is an automaton, a hollow man. Meanwhile, the fight remains what it's always been: a contest between humanity and the lack of same.

I regard myself as a political naïf. In my life I never saw a war I believed worth fighting—so what if, in this one, the line between good and evil has never been so clearly drawn. The horror trumps the moral stakes. The metaphors are all reductive: Zelensky is not David (or Charlie Chaplin or Leopold Bloom) vs Goliath; he's not Frodo vs the Dark Lord Sauron. He's a politician and we all know better than to put faith in politicians. There's always an element of raw ambition. I suspect even Gandhi had an ego. Still, it's thrilling to see the tyrant, the one boasting his hypertrophied testicles, opposed by the little man with the humility to admit to an ordinary pair of beytsim. In a recent interview, Zelensky was asked if he thought he could make Putin laugh. He answered "Sure" then qualified the remark. "Laughter," he said gnomically, "is a weapon that is fatal to men of marble." I imagine—if only to relieve a little the feeling of helplessness—that Putin, after dozens of failed attempts to assassinate him, finally captures Zelensky.

"I'll let you choose how you are to die," he says.

And Zelensky: "How about from old age?"

Putin laughs, no doubt a sardonic laugh—after all, he's been challenged by a clown; he laughs and the cracks begin to appear in the marble; the laughter persists, the cracks widen, and the statue (forgive the metaphor) comes apart and crumbles to dust.

Nominated by Jay Rogoff

A POTATO ON THE TABLE

by MARY RUEFLE

from THE GLACIER

There is a potato
on the table.
I stare at it,
then write a novel.
The novel takes place
inside the potato.
Its point-of-view
is that of the hard creamy
unseen inside, but I know
what that looks like
so I am able to write.
It is a perfect potato.
A novel potato.
One without eyes.

Nominated by Marianne Boruch

CONVERSATIONS

by RAE ARMANTROUT

from IMAGE

Push on it again,
that point of light.

What do you think
light *is*?

What is anything?

§

If you aren't telling kids
how to live

in a world
you can't imagine,

what *are* you doing?

Telling God
about fall's
claret colored leaves.

§

Touch me
like you do the foliage!

Nominated by Image

DREAMERS AWAKEN

by SCOTT SPENCER

from CHICAGO QUARTERLY REVIEW

On the South Side of Chicago, the students attending my public school were predominately second-generation Americans, many with family roots in Eastern Europe—Poland, Yugoslavia—though no one waxed nostalgic about the Old Country. It was the mid-1950s and still close to the time when Europe was basically a hellhole, and that door to the past was closed. We were all dug in and secure in our unhyphenated identity as Americans. No one who wasn't white stepped foot in our school without a broom and a dustpan, and on the block where I lived, my guess is that no one except my parents even knew anyone who was Black. The crazy, angry dream of an All-White World was alive in the carpenters, bricklayers, roofers, plumbers, and electricians who had built the neighborhood, the people who worked the shops we frequented, and every father, mother, and child who lived and played there. Every once in a while, a Black housekeeper could be seen getting off the bus with a paper sack holding her lunch, and there she would be again at the end of the day, waiting for the bus to take her back to her home, with the paper sack, empty now, carefully folded so it could be used again.

We began the school day pledging our allegiance to the American flag. It was around this time that, in a burst of anti-Communist virtue, the words under God were inserted into the pledge by congressional decree. I wasn't aware of anyone else in the school having a quarrel with this addition to the morning ritual, but I silently mouthed those two words; I was being raised to disbelieve in God, and I was also being taught to keep that unbelief a secret.

145

Our teachers were the usual mix of dedicated educators, public-sector lifers, and cheerful younger teachers doing their best to teach us to add and subtract, write legibly, and learn the names of the presidents and the state capitals.

The students were of varying abilities, but nearly all of us were obedient and relatively easy to teach. We completed our homework assignments, and no one made remarks without first raising their hand, except, occasionally, me. I was the designated pain in the neck of the fourth grade—a distinction that would follow me through elementary and high school. I wanted to be a blend of Marlon Brando and Jerry Lewis, and my bad reputation puzzled me. I had never been tardy, or fought in the playground, or cheated on a test, yet it was clear to me that most of the teachers actively disliked me, a disdain that caught on with many of the other students, resulting in my feeling underliked.

In the spring of that year, plans were being made for a school-wide assemblyh organized around the theme of American folk tales. The teachers had already chosen a freckled girl to be Johnny Appleseed, another girl with straw-colored hair for Casey Jones, a tall boy for Paul Bunyan, but the role of John Henry, the Black steel-driving man who worked himself to death in his attempt to outwork a steam drill, was still up for grabs. I told the music teacher I wanted to try out for the part. It was my chance to be seen as I wanted to be seen—not as a discipline problem but as someone creative, talented, and interesting.

I had a leg up because my parents owned a recording of the guitar-playing Josh White singing the folk song about John Henry—he could whistle, he could sing, / he woke up every morning just to hear his hammer ring. Josh White was not particularly militant and outspoken—he was no Paul Robeson—but he was a Black man who was hounded by the very red-baiters who repelled and frightened my parents, giving him a kind of favored-nation status in our household.

I was glad my parents liked someone singing and playing a guitar, but, really, anyone who could entertain had favored-nation status with me. I was an only child, with a passion for any all forms of show business, but I'd learned to be careful when I watched the TV. We had a snug little house—four rooms and a kitchen—and my parents heard everything that was happening on the set: the laughter, the applause, and the dialogue, too. There were things I didn't dare watch if they were home, such as Davy Crockett, a show every kid in my school loved but which my parents (accurately, depressingly) said was a bunch of lies about a guy who was nothing but a vicious, coldhearted Indian killer. As much

146

as I enjoyed Jack Benny, I would have been mortified to be caught watching his program because Rochester, his house servant, who spoke in a screeching, funny voice, would have offended my parents. Amos 'n' Andy was out of the question. And blackface? Blackface was an abomination. When they came upon Al Jolson singing and dancing in one of the old movies I used to watch on TV, or Eddie Cantor doing a similar act on one of the new variety shows, my father would say, "That's disgraceful," and my mother would add, "He's making fun of Negroes. Do you think that's the right thing to do?" And in their presence it became what it actually was—the inky, shining black face, the insane, goofy eyes, the wildly exaggerated lips, the hopping, the jumping, the childish patty-pat-pat of hands in bright-white gloves. It became grotesque.

* * *

I told my parents I had a featured role in the upcoming school assembly, and I was going to portray John Henry, singing the song they had taught me to love. They seemed quite pleased. They might not have been pleased had I told them I was going to be made up so my skin would be black. In fact, they might have forbidden it, and probably that's why I kept that detail to myself. I didn't want them to yank me the hell out of that pageant, which I continued to dream about as if it were going to be a tremendous turning point in my life.

The afternoon of the performance, it was time to blacken my face. The art teacher supplied the charcoal, and she and two other teachers circled around me, clearly enjoying themselves, giving me the tingling sensation of positive attention for once.

The art teacher was a soft, well-powdered woman in her forties, with a wide face, light-brown eyes, and bangs that had grown out too long, forcing her to continually toss her head like a horse. She was a kindly soul who disliked me noticeably less than most of the other teachers. She used Kleenex to protect her fingers while she gently went over my face with a charcoal stick. I stood at attention, dressed in the torn shirt and patched trousers that made up my costume, and held in one hand a broom handle upon which a hammerhead had been fashioned out of aluminum foil.

I was a bit nervous, but I knew the song "John Henry" about as well as I knew "The Star-Spangled Banner." I had sung it fifty times at least, in the shower and for my parents, and, over the past week, I'd rehearsed it with the music teacher, who was going to accompany me on the piano. She had promised prompting whispers to anyone who might forget a word or a line, but I doubted I would need her prompts. I knew that song cold.

The whole school would be there to see the show, and some of the parents would be there, though not mine. My parents kept a low profile. I don't think the phrase flying under the radar was widely used at the time, but there certainly was radar looking for enemy planes in the sky, and a more insidious kind of radar searching for what J. Edgar Hoover called the enemies within, and my parents were doing what they could to fly beneath it.

✿ ✿ ✿

And in the meanwhile, two women, both appointed members of the board of education, and both Black, were driving toward our school in a two-door Plymouth. Richard Daley, who'd been elected mayor a couple of years before, and would remain mayor of Chicago for another two decades, was consolidating his power and making savvy moves. Daley needed to pull in votes from people in the Black community, so he put a few Blacks on the board of education, in a small gesture that would not likely offend the sensibilities of the white ethnic voters who were his base.

And as two of those appointees were closing in on my school, three teachers and the librarian hovered around me, and the gentle art teacher put the finishing touches on my face. I silently ran through the song while Mrs. Adams (circumstances prohibit me from using her real name here) moved the charcoal stick over the wings of my nose. She was really getting into it, taking little voilà swipes at me and then lifting the charcoal and stepping back a foot or two, like someone in a movie about a great artist.

Louise Gluck has written that the best occupation for a child is to observe and listen. I did a bit of that, but mainly my energies went into seeking approval. That a teacher had a home life would have made sense to me if someone had mentioned it, but on my own it never crossed my mind. In my narrowly self-centered imagination, the teachers were basically a twenty-headed gorgon, a scolding authority whose affection I had no chance of earning and whose ire I was continually hoping to evade.

Yet here in this makeshift green room, getting ready for my star turn, I was aware of the interplay between the teachers. I noticed that even though Mrs. Adams was solely responsible for blackening my face, Miss Michaels and Miss Benson (also not their real names) diligently monitored. Miss Benson, whom I liked because she was pretty—slender, young—smiled at me, and when she brushed back her hair, her left ear emerged. I listened to the friendly hum of their conversation. You missed a spot. We have five more minutes. I'm hurrying. Oh, wait, you missed another spot.

At that moment, Miss Fitzgerald, the third-grade teacher, burst into the library, urgency radiating off of her. She was so upset, and the situation was so urgent that she didn't want to waste a moment by taking Mrs. Adams aside, or speaking sotto voce. "Clean him up," she said, in a tone better suited for man overboard or the British are coming! The other teachers looked at her blankly. "Two women from the board of education just arrived," she said. She waited for a moment and then said the rest. "Colored."

It took only a moment for them all to realize the gravity of the situation. No one said, "That's great," and no one said, "So what?" Instead, they seemed to know what to do if a Black person appeared, just as we'd practiced what to do if the Russians dropped the bomb on Chicago.

Mrs. Adams raced to the teachers' lounge across the hall. The rest of us waited in silence. We were like bank robbers who hear the Doppler whoop of approaching sirens. We had only a minute or two to save ourselves. Mrs. Adams returned, her eyes wide with purpose, holding a cloth towel thoroughly wetted down with water. The teachers worked in concert. Miss Fitzgerald said she would get another towel, Miss Michaels spoke to Mrs. Adams in a calming murmur, and Miss Benson— this was the moment's saving grace—held my shoulders to steady to keep me from falling over while Mrs. Adams scrubbed at my face.

Some of the charcoal came off, much of it remained, though lightened and smeared. As they worked, the teachers debated among themselves whether to cancel my part of the show or send me out as-is. I was slow to realize that no matter what happened, my dream of impressing the school was not going to come true.

"Why did they have to come here on this of all days?" wondered Mrs. Adams as she scrubbed me.

"To ruin everything," opined Miss Fitzgerald.

"We're saying John Henry was a good man," said Mrs. Adams. "That's the whole point of the song." She fell silent for a moment and then added, barely audibly, "It's for Mr. Henry. Not against."

I marched into the assembly, a filthy, frightened boy shielded inside a moving box of teachers. I looked up at their necklaces, their chins, their freeze-dried smiles. My teachers had lost their privacy from the non-white citizens of our city, and now they were like people in a dream who had come to school naked.

"How were we supposed to know?" Mrs. Fitzgerald asked.

"We didn't do anything wrong," said Miss Benson, glancing down at me, smiling.

We made it to the front, and I slowly walked up the four steps that led to the side of the stage, joining the other American folk heroes waiting to go on. Everyone could feel that some sort of trouble had come to us, and there they were: invaders in heavy blue dresses, accusers in hats with the veils pinned up, spies with black patent leather handbags large as reel-to-reel tape recorders resting on their laps.

At first, they had seemed indistinguishable, twins. But now I saw that one was older and larger than the other. The older one had broad shoulders and a wide face and wore a necklace made of large colored stones. Her hair was smooth and shiny and went back in three waves. She wore large dangling earrings that matched her necklace, heavy ovals that pulled down on her lobes. The younger board rep rubbed her hands together as if to warm them. She wore pink lipstick and blue eye shadow. Her hair was a blackish gray, pulled tight and gathered in a bun.

I got through the first verse of "John Henry" without flubbing so much as a syllable. My dream of school-wide stardom was over. The only real goal was to get through to the end. It's not a short song. Ten days before, the music teacher had found a version of "John Henry" that was even longer than the version I had memorized. The song as I had known it ended with John Henry's death, but now there were three more verses about his wife, his son, and his immortality.

When I'd first been presented with the new verses, I'd been happy that my time on stage would be extended. Now, however, the extra verses loomed ahead of me like a rock face I was meant to climb. I didn't know them nearly so well as I knew the earlier verses, and I was suddenly sure I would flub them. When I lost heart and my voice got smaller, the visitors from the board leaned forward, smiling and nodding encouragingly.

Every once in a while, I looked away from the two Black faces, just to make certain that my parents hadn't surprised me and slipped into the auditorium. I scanned the rows. There were plenty of parents in attendance, mostly mothers. Ponytails, babushkas, harlequin glasses, sitting with whatever class their child was in, towering over the children like cypress trees.

Finally—it felt as if an hour had passed—I got to He died with a hammer in his hand, Lawd, Lawd. I was careful to translate the Lawd into

150

Lord, lingering over the r, as if to light it with neon, lest there be any mistaking my intentions. And that was as far as I could go. The music teacher was already playing the first chords of the next verse, but I put down my broomstick with its tinfoil hammerhead, and, with one hand on my belly and the other on the small of my back, I made the low bow.

Our principal, Miss Taylor, a strict, deeply traditional product of Chicago public schools, came quickly onto the stage and announced her enthusiastic appreciation of all of the students and teachers who had made today's assembly possible. Stately, impenetrable Principal Taylor stood near me as she brought the assembly to a close and then did something I found extraordinary. She picked up my pathetically unconvincing steel-driving hammer and handed it back to me. "If you will, please," she said, smiling at me warmly, with a sympathy I had never seen in her before—we had gone through something together and as far as she was concerned, we had all survived it.

As we had practiced, John Henry, Casey Jones, and the others joined hands and bowed our heads for a final thank you to the audience, and then the cast, except for me, jumped off the stage and ran to their mother, their mother, their mother and father, and their mother. I stood alone for a few moments, relieved that my parents were not here and experiencing the familiar shame of being different, then hopping off the stage and placing myself in front of the two visitors from the board of education.

"I'm sorry," I said.

The auditorium seemed to twitch for a moment; one of the fathers had taken a souvenir picture and lit it with a flashbulb.

"You made a wonderful John Henry," the smaller of the two women said. Her hands were still cold, and she continued to rub them together.

"I never knew that song had so many verses," the larger woman said. Her voice was deep, and after she spoke she raised her eyebrows.

"There's even more," I said.

"Oh," said the larger woman, stretching the word out.

"Well you were very good," her friend said.

I touched my face.

"You sang it well and very clearly," the larger woman said. "We could hear every word."

We stood in the awkward silence that followed their two-star review of my performance. I'm sure they wanted to get out of there and go home, but it was clear to them that there was something I wanted to say, and they were kind, very kind. As for me, I was waiting for something, some recognition that did not and could not come. I had wanted to be seen as someone worthy of applause, and now what I needed was to be seen as someone worthy of forgiveness. I wanted them to tousle my hair, give my arm a little friendly squeeze. I could hear the shuffle of feet and the teachers reminding everyone to stay with their class as the auditorium emptied. Normally, I would have been sharply reminded to march out with the rest of my class, but for now I was ignored. In a few moments the auditorium was empty except for the three of us.

We stood to one side, halfway between the stage and the exit doors, smiling uncertainly. We were in our own little impromptu pageant, folk tales from the future, and we were waiting for the invisible proctor to tell us in a whisper, or perhaps with some urgency, what to say next.

Nominated by Chicago Quarterly Review

THANK YOU THANK YOU THANK YOU THANK YOU THANK YOU HAVE A NICE DAY

fiction by HEDGIE CHOI

from NOON

I saw a plastic bag blowing across a parking lot and thought of my father who learned about the great snowy owl in school and later that same day saw a white plastic bag for the first time in his life in the sky and thought, *There it is—the owl!* It seems important to point out now that my father once kicked me in the stomach when I was thirteen. But before that I did call him a worthless motherfucker. But before that he brought me into the world. And later he will leave me in it. My thoughts in the parking lot had nothing to do with any of this. My thoughts were of a casual and fond nature.

Nominated by Noon, Emily Lee Luan

WANTING ONLY TO BE HEARD

fiction by JACK DRISCOLL

from TWENTY STORIES (Pushcart Press)

Ashelby Judge was an odd name for a kid growing up in northern Michigan, so we just called him by his last name, Judge. Everyone did. In a way he always was holding court, pronouncing sentence: Kevin Moriarty was a first-class cockroach, Jake Reardon a homo from the word "go." He had once called me a dicksqueeze, but later he took it back, gladly, he said, having indicted me prematurely. I was okay, he said, I really was, that being the final verdict.

Judge was not easy sometimes, but I liked him. I liked his impatience with boredom and the way he gathered all the pertinent information in the end, the evidence to prove or discredit a story. He always proceeded step-by-step, building an airtight case for whatever he was defending or attacking, whatever he was attempting to pin down. It wouldn't have surprised me, forty years later, to read he'd been appointed to the Supreme Court. Judge Ashelby Judge. Or, for the sake of a joke, Judge Judge. I liked famous names that repeated or almost did, names like Robin Roberts or Ricky Ricardo, or even slant combos like Jack Johnson. The duplication had a friendly ring, a sense of conviction and rectitude, the feeling that they really knew who they were and liked it and would never entirely grow up, grow old.

It was a Friday night, no wind for a change, and we were fishing smelt, three of us inside my father's shanty, when Judge told me and Timmy Murphy about the claustrophobic Irish setter who, after being locked all afternoon in a fishing hut on Torch Lake, jumped right through the spearing hole just after dark and, ten or twelve feet under the ice, swam toward the faint, opalescent glow of another shanty almost fifty yards away (someone later measured it) and came bursting up there from the muck like some monster awakened, the water swelling, convulsing up over the wooden floor. That one simile, "like some monster," was the only embellishment, Judge's single artistic touch.

He was not a natural storyteller who tested his listeners by saying, "imagine this," or "pretend that," or "just think if," and on and on, suspending their willingness to imprint the local tales into myth. He despised the "what then, what next" demands made on every story. Which was exactly what Timmy was doing, all excited and ahead of himself as usual: "What'd the guy do? Holy shit, I bet he croaked right there. I can't believe it, a dog under the ice. That's great!"

Judge, calculatedly slow and flat, said the guy was plenty scared, who wouldn't be, but not berserk scared the way you might expect. "He was old," Judge said—a simple observation of fact, like what day it was or how cold. He never speculated that age buffered the body's reaction to shock or trauma, but I translated it that way anyhow, without thinking.

"Who cares?" Timmy asked. "Twenty, fifty-seven, a hundred-and-two years old. It doesn't matter."

But it did, the way it mattered that the dog was an Irish setter and male and was abandoned by his owner who loved him but hadn't gotten any fish, and instead of a quick trip to the 7-Eleven for a six-pack of Stroh's, he drank away the afternoon, alone in a bar that said just that in red neon, *BAR*, just outside Bellaire, forgetting the dog, and playing, over and over on the free juke box, Patsy Cline's "Walking After Midnight." Which was about the time he left the bar, broke and drunk, and halfway home remembered the dog and right there, on 137, opened his window full for the few seconds it took him to slow down and power slide into the other lane, the pickup fishtailing back up the gradual incline beneath the stars, the hook of the moon. And it mattered that he honked his horn a couple of times from the lake's edge, his shanty invisible somewhere beyond the white perimeter of his high beams. That was the real story, that sadness, and the way the guy, on both knees, fiddled with the combination lock until his fingers went numb, the whole time talking to the dog who wasn't even there. When he finally opened the door and lit the lantern, the white flame hissing in the mantle, he stepped back outside and screamed the dog's name a single time across the emptiness.

Judge said you could measure a story by its private disclosures, by how far a person came forward to confess a part of himself, asking forgiveness. The dramatics meant nothing, those exaggerations that served only to engage our obvious and temporary fascinations. And he continued, refining the art of meticulous detachment from such a rare and bizarre event by saying he didn't care what the Irish setter looked like emerging—a giant muskie or sturgeon or a red freshwater seal. "The fact is," he repeated, "it was a hundred-pound dog. That's it, cut and dried!"

I thought maybe the "cut and dried" part was a pun, and I smiled until Timmy, really miffed, said, "You take away all the magic. You make everything too real, too damn ordinary."

But Timmy was at least partly wrong. There *was* something principled about facts, something stark and real that required nothing but themselves to survive. Maybe that's why I liked "Dragnet" so much, the claim that it was a true story, and that the sentence handed down after the last TV commercial was really being served. I thought of that while leaving the shanty to pee and to check the tip-ups set for browns behind us in the dark. My father let me and my buddies use the shanty on weeknights while he worked at the Fisk. Usually he'd drop us off at the state park and we'd take turns dragging the sled with the minnow bucket and spud and the gallon can of stove gas straight toward the village of fifty or sixty tiny structures in a cluster set over the deep water. It was easy to find my father's shanty because it was separated a little ways from the others, and because of the spoked hubcap from a Cadillac Eldorado he'd nailed to the door. His house sign, he called it. Other guys had other things, and it was fun to traipse around at night out there, just looking around, the world glaciated, frozen so tight you could feel your breath clinging to the fine hairs on your face.

The name of each owner and town he was from was painted on every shanty—that was the law—some from as far south as Clare, though those were the ones that were not used very much. Sometimes as you passed you could hear talking from inside, or good laughter, or country music on the radio, and when you returned to the heat of your own hut, maybe you'd be humming a certain song, surprised by how happy you were, how peaceful, knowing that you belonged. I figured that was why my father decided to fish again after all these years, why he spent most of every weekend out here, calm and without worries.

That wasn't the feeling, however, when I stepped back inside and Judge and Timmy were both just staring into the rectangular hole, staring at the blue rubber-band bobbers and saying nothing. The smelt pail was still empty and half the minnows in the other bucket had turned belly up. My father would have said no big deal, that smelt would go for the dead bait just as good if they were feeding, but either Judge or

Timmy, having already given up, had entered a big 0, a goose egg, in the calendar square for February 12th. On good nights you loaded up fast, constant action, and on the homemade speed reels you could bring in two or three smelt at a time, every few minutes without a break. Just three nights earlier my father had recorded 268, and that was by himself. That's how it happened, streaky and unpredictable, and you simply had to like being out there, maybe sharing a Pall Mall around or talking girls if that's what mystery happened to be biting. But on this night of the Irish setter story, everything had gone closemouthed.

"No flags," I said, latching the door and hanging the gaff on a hook above the stove. This was Judge's first time ice fishing, and I knew he was bored—knew it even better when he said to Timmy, "Why not?" Responding to whether a person (forget the dog) could survive the 33 degree water long enough to swim from this shanty to the one closest by, the one that said M. KULANDA, KALKASKA, MI, the largest one on the ice. I'd never seen anybody there, not once.

"Houdini stayed under twenty minutes," Judge said, "under the Detroit River. No wetsuit. Nothing but a pair of pants."

"What was he doing there? A trick?" Timmy asked.

"An escape," Judge corrected, and although Timmy argued, "Trick, escape, whatever he did . . ." I understood the difference, the dangerous mishandling of a single word so that a story softened, collapsed like a fragile set of lungs.

"Houdini said later he sucked the air pockets, bubbles trapped between the water and ice, and with the current, followed his dead mother's voice until he emerged, a quarter mile downriver." Judge was still staring into the thick, dark water while he talked, until Timmy, excited, just like at first with the Irish setter story, said, "You're shitting me!" Judge, looking up finally, straight-faced and serious, said, "I shit you not," as if under oath, and they both went silent as if the naked truth of Houdini and the Irish setter were tempting them to find out.

It started simple as that, and next thing I knew we were pacing off the distance between the shanties. About thirty yards. I had once stayed underwater in the bathtub for as long as I could, just sliding back and holding my nose. I counted a minute and forty-four seconds, long seconds—one, one thousand, two, one thousand, three, the facecloth kind of floating back and forth across my stomach. And sneaking into the Camp Ketch-A-Tonk swim-grounds one night last summer, I breast stroked real close to the sandy bottom, from the Great Raft all the way up to shore. My father did it too, swimming behind me, and without coming up for air he turned and swam halfway back. I was scared, the way you get when someone's been down a long time, maybe just monkeying around, but scaring you just the same. I remembered whispering, "Come up, please come up, "and he did, beyond the blue lifeline, gracefully rolling onto his back in a single motion and kicking, eyes closed I imagined, straight out toward whatever secret had surfaced in his memory. That's how it is with the mind, always buoyant, bobbing up and down on the complex sea of recollection.

Judge knocked on Kulanda's door, but nobody was there. "Nobody has been," Timmy said, trying to take charge. "Look around. No footprints anywhere."

And I noticed there were no bloodstains from trout or pike tossed into the snow, no frozen minnows. Nothing. The shanty was unlocked, a lousy idea my father always lectured, every time he'd see a door blown open, slapping backwards hard against its hinges. He said that only invited trouble, people snooping around, poking their heads in where they didn't belong, which was exactly what we were doing and I didn't like it and said, "Come on you guys, let's go. Let's get out of here."

But when Timmy stepped inside with the lantern, the hut was nearly empty, unused, the kind that just got left sitting there until the ice softened toward spring, and one morning it would be gone forever. Who knows, maybe the owner died or got sick or one Sunday started watching the Pistons on TV with his son-in-law and thought *screw the fishing* and that was that for the whole season.

Timmy said, "The guy's got a couch in here," and when he sat down he was staring at a calendar hanging on the opposite wall. It was the kind of calendar I first saw in a gas station in Germfask when my father's station wagon broke down. We were there a good part of the afternoon while the garage owner phoned around until he finally located a water pump at a junkyard in Greighton. The owner's kid drove over to pick it up, and while our fathers small talked engines and horsepower and cubic inches, I snuck into the men's room three or four times to examine, close-up, this woman who was showing me everything, her lips parted just enough to show the pink edge of her tongue. The last time I stepped out my father was waiting by the door and he told me, "Pee out back. I don't want you in there anymore." And that was the feeling I had again in Kulanda's abandoned shanty, of wanting to be there and not, both at the same time. Timmy lowered the lantern to the ice, right under the calendar where the fishing hole should have been, really lighting up the glossy nude, and he said, acting the big shot for this lucky find, "I'd swim anywhere if I could surface between legs like that!"

But it was Judge who decided to really do it, and when my father dropped us off again the next night, we brought, along with the fishing gear, a book on Houdini and a *National Geographic* that showed people in swimsuits running toward the Atlantic Ocean from a snowy beach, in Rhode Island, I think. And Judge talked on and on about some Mr. Maslowski who chipped a large round hole in the ice of his man-made pond, and letting the same red towel drop behind him, he'd hold his hands flat to the sides of his thighs, and each morning, without hesitation, he'd step right through over his head. "For his rheumatism," Judge said. "He worshiped what he called 'certitude,' the ancient and natural cure taking place under the world."

Judge had done his homework, covering the Polar Bear Club and U.S. Navy ice divers, the whole time spouting off dates and temperatures and distances, building his case until I believed there was hardly any danger after the initial shock of entering, and he said, staring at me, "You'll be my key witness." And to Timmy, "Who knows what you'll see."

Of course we wanted to see everything: the entry, the look of his eyes behind the mask the instant he surfaced in Kulanda's shanty. But most of all we wanted desperately to watch him moving under the ice, so later that week Judge waterproofed a flashlight with candle wax and electrician's tape, and tested it by lowering the light about twenty feet under the ice. Then Timmy turned off the Coleman lantern and we just stared, all three of us in complete darkness, at that dim glimmer wavering back and forth below us, slow motion, soporific.

Judge was the first to speak, his unquestionable right now, presiding and authoritative, factitious as always, but Timmy was making no objections anymore. Judge said, "It works," and we just nodded, accomplices who had learned to listen closely, to rehearse every detail at night in our dreams. "We'll fasten the light to my back," Judge said, "and you guys can walk right above me."

Although we didn't actually fish anymore that week, we'd make up numbers and jot them down each night on my father's calendar, keeping the records current: 114, 226, and—a slow night, Timmy's entry—27. "Just to keep things honest," he said, and we laughed, sitting and clowning around and smoking Pall Malls in what now seemed more like a fort, a refuge—not from the gusting wind, but from the predictable, ordinary things we might have done late after school, like playing Ping-Pong in Timmy's basement, or being home alone tinkering with science projects, or making up a story for English—something sensational and dangerous and totally unbelievable. And whenever my father asked about the fishing I'd tell him Judge and Timmy were splitting up the smelt, taking them home. "Good," he said, as though it were the proper courtesy, the way to make and keep good friends.

If Judge had moments of panic, he never let on, not even on the night of his dive, the Saturday my father decided to work OT. He dropped us at the state park as usual and asked, "You got a ride back?" and Timmy said, "Yep, my father's picking us up," which was true, but he was coming later than usual. He wouldn't be here until eleven. I don't know why we wanted the extra time, I really don't. Maybe to change our minds, or to deny, as Judge would have been the first to point out, that redemption had anything to do with danger, with the spectacular moments in a life.

But that didn't happen. We felt transformed, faithful to the careful preparation of an entire week, and when we started across the ice toward the village, we believed those two shanties were ours, and ours to swim between if we wanted, the way you might swim deep under a cliff in order to come up in a secret cave. After the first time, it would be easy.

We felt all set, having already stashed an extra heater and lantern, an army blanket, and towels in Kulanda's, and we'd hung a thermometer on the same nail that held what Judge was calling Timmy's porno queen, but I'd seen him peeking from the couch at those hard nipples, too, or at the red mercury rising slowly between her breasts after we'd fired the heater up. Chips of ice were bouncing off her paper flesh as Timmy started to spud the hole, Judge's exit, and Judge and I left him there and headed for the other hut. But Judge stopped halfway and said, "No hurry," and we stood there, watching the lights of houses blink on the far side of the lake. I felt calm as the lights vanished and appeared again, floating, I thought, behind a cold vapor of darkness. And I could hear Timmy in Kulanda's shanty, a strange thud, thud, as though coming from a great distance, and already we'd begun walking even farther away.

By the time Timmy got to my father's hut he was breathing heavily, but he laughed real hard at Judge just sitting there in his white boxers, the flashlight already taped to his back like a dorsal fin.

"All you need now are scales," Timmy said, taking off his gloves and coat, and Judge, reaching into his knapsack, said, "This will have to do," and pulled out a tub of ball bearing grease and said, "Cover me real good," scooping the first brown gob himself with his fingers and sculpting it up and down one arm. Then he stood there, arms out, and me and Timmy did the rest, each a skinny side, and Judge, still joking around said, "Save a little for my dick," and Timmy said back, "A little is all you'll need," as I knelt and reached my greasy hand into the freezing water to see if this translucent coating really helped, and for that second I was terrified of falling in, the rectangular hole seeming so much like a grave, calm and so carefully ladled out. And without them seeing me, I crossed myself, as my father had taught me to do every, every time before entering strange water.

When I stood up, Timmy, having taken charge of things in Kulanda's shanty, had left again, and Judge was wiping his hands clean on a rag. Then he knotted the white clothesline around his waist—knotted it a couple of times, nothing fancy, but I knew by the way he tugged it wasn't coming free. Still, I wanted something thicker, stronger, a new length of rope, a boat line maybe. Judge said he just needed something to follow back if he got lost or in trouble. It didn't need to be strong. The other end was already tied off around the single roof brace, the rest of the clothesline coiled in wide loops on the floor. Nobody needed to be there to watch or feed it out. It would uncoil smoothly, trailing behind him like a long umbilical cord. Judge, the literalist, would have hated the metaphor, as he would have hated me telling him he looked a little like the creature in *The Creature from the Black Lagoon*, standing there. But he did, primordial and weedy-green in the bright light of the lantern, breathing hard now, and hyperventilating for whatever extra oxygen he could squeeze into his lungs.

I thought there would be some talk, a final go-over of the details, maybe even a last-minute pardon from this craziness if my father would unexpectedly burst in. But it was Timmy, back again and out of breath, who said, "All set," and Judge simply reached back without hesitation, snapped on the flashlight, then pushed the mask with both hands to his face for better suction and stepped under. I wasn't even sure it happened—he disappeared that fast, without a single word or even a human splash, as though all that body grease had dissolved his bones, his skull, the entire weight of him so that only a ghost drifted under the ice, a vague iridescence.

When we got outside Judge was moving in the right direction. All winter the winds had blown the snow from the ice, so we could see the blurry light down there, and Timmy had one of his own which he kept blinking on and off to let Judge know we were there, right above him, ready to guide him home. The moon was up too, and suddenly the distance to Kulanda's shanty did not seem so far, not with Judge already halfway there and Timmy, all wound up and hooting, "He's got it made, he's got it now!"

It was right then that Judge's light conked out, and we both stopped, as if Judge would surface there. Neither of us wanted to move, afraid, I think, that we would step on him in the dark and send him deeper, and when we started running for Kulanda's, I circled wide, way behind where Judge would be, hoping he wouldn't hear the slapping panic of our boots, the fear inside us struggling desperately to break free.

Timmy pumped and pumped the lantern until I thought the glass globe would explode. Then he held it just inches above the black water, and he seemed to be staring at the nude, staring all the way through her as if counting each vertebra, the soft curves of her back, and I knew Judge was not coming up. I didn't have to tell Timmy to stay. He was crying now. He was all done, and I think if Judge had surfaced right then, Timmy would have just dropped the lantern and walked away and would never have spoken of this again.

I slipped and fell hard, almost knocking myself out, and in that moment of dizziness, face down on the ice, I imagined Judge staring back, just ten inches away, his black hair wavering in the moonlight, his eyes wide-open behind his mask. And I imagined him pointing and pointing and I got up and ran, sweating now, into my father's shanty. I believed the rope twitched or pulsed when I picked it up, something like a nibble, but when I yanked back there was nothing there, just the loose arc of slack, and I remembered my father always shouting from the stern of the boat, "Reel hard, keep reeling," when I thought I'd lost a big one, and this time the weight was there, solid and unforgiving. It was the same heavy feeling of a snag that begins to move just when you're sure it will bust your line, and I knew that bulk dragged backwards was enough to snap any line with a nick or fray, and to hurry was to lose it all.

I kept it coming, hand over hand, Judge's body drifting sideways, then back again, always rising slowly from the deep water. I shouted for Timmy four or five times, tilting my head backwards and toward the door, but he did not come. And it was during one of those shouts that the flashlight on Judge's back appeared in the center of the hole, then the whole back hunched in a deadman's float. I could not get him up, my arms weak and shaking, and I hauled back one last time and dropped the rope and grabbed, all in the same motion, his thick hair with both my hands, his face finally lifting out of the water.

His mask was gone and I just held him like that for a long time, one arm under his chin, the lantern dimming. I was stretched on my belly, our cheeks touching, and I had never felt anything so cold, so silent. I knew mouth-to-mouth resuscitation would do Judge no good in this position, his lungs full of water, so maybe I was really kissing him, not trying to reclaim a heartbeat, but rather to confess, as Judge said, a part of myself, and to ask forgiveness. I did not know how long I could hold him there, though I promised over and over I would never let him slide back to that bottom, alone among those tentacles of weeds. I closed my eyes, and in what must have been a kind of shock or sleep, I drifted into a strange current of emptiness, a white vaporous light, the absolute and lovely beginning of nothing.

I did not see the two ice fishermen hoist Judge from the hole, and I did not remember being carried to Kulanda's shanty or being wrapped in the army blanket on the couch. I awakened alone there, still dizzy but very warm. I was wearing Judge's sweatshirt, the one we had waiting for him for when he came up. I did not take it off or even move very much, and I could hear my father's voice just outside the door, though it sounded distant, too, and dull, the blunt echo of a voice approaching. I thought if he entered, the flood of his words would drown me for good. But only silence followed him in. I did not look up and I did not cry when he touched my head, or when he turned away to face the wall. There would be no sermonizing, no interrogation from him or from anyone else. Not that night anyway.

And I noticed eye-level across from me, that the nude was gone, removed like evidence we didn't want found. The cigarette butts on the floor had disappeared too. And it sounded strange to hear someone knock on the door. My father did not say, "Come in," but a man did, an ambulance driver, and he bent down on one knee and said, "How do you feel now?" I didn't know, but I said, "Good," and I wanted to stay there, maybe all night, making sure the hole did not freeze over.

Next morning, as we walked together toward the shanties, my father said, "Tell them everything exactly like it happened. There's only one story." What he meant was that the options narrowed and narrowed when the ending was already known. "They won't keep us long," he said. "We'll get back home." I thought he might add, "For the Pistons-Celtics game," but he didn't.

It was Sunday morning and sunny, and up ahead, off to the left, I saw a red flag go up from the ice, then someone running toward the tip-up, shaking his gloves off. I watched him set the hook and after a few seconds, with his left hand, move the gaff a little bit away from the hole.

"Probably a pike," my father said, and I was glad he did, so natural, and without the conviction of disguise.

There were not all that many people gathered at the shanties, not the way I thought it would be with a lot of photographers and sheriff's department deputies. Timmy was already there. I could see his green hat and his arms flailing like an exhausted swimmer, and for that split second I imagined he was yelling, "Help, help me," and I started to run, not toward him, but the other way, back toward the car. My father caught me from behind, caught me first by the collar, then wrapped both his arms around me and turned me back slowly to face Timmy and whatever version he was carving of the story. My father just held me there and released the pressure gradually and then, after a couple minutes, let me go.

His shanty had been moved back and two divers were adjusting their masks at the side of the hole. I did not know what they were searching for, what more they could possibly find. But they jumped through, one after the other as Judge had, but with black wetsuits and yellow tanks and searchlights sealed with more than candle wax and electrician's tape. The sheriff met us and shook my hand and my father's hand and said Judge's parents were not there and wouldn't be. Then he said, "We've called Mary Kulanda," as though he knew him personally. "He's on his way."

I was okay after that. They kept me and Timmy separated, though we caught each other's eye a couple times. The two fishermen who had pulled Judge out kept nodding a lot, and once they pointed at me, both of them did, then shrugged, and they finally left, to fish and talk, I guess, since they walked that way into the village of shanties. I knew the stories wouldn't be the same, but not the same in a way that didn't matter to the law.

The sheriff asked me about approximate times: how long before Timmy ran for help, how long I held Judge partially out of the water—all questions I couldn't answer, and that seemed to be all right. But before he let me go he said, "Whose idea was this?" It was the first time he spoke without detachment, accusatory now, and I did not deny that it was me though it wasn't, and my father the whole time shaking his head, shaking it back and forth, no, no, insisting that could never be.

Before the first diver was helped out of the hole, he tossed Judge's mask a few feet onto the ice, and then, behind it—crumpled into a pulpy ball—what I knew was the calendar nude. I didn't know why that frightened me so much, except that it was a detail I had consciously left out, perhaps to protect Timmy's secret need to destroy the crime of her nakedness, one of the reasons we stayed there and smoked cigarettes and talked big in front of her, already outlining the plans of our story. When the sheriff unwadded the nude she fell apart, and he just shook the wet pieces from his hands. In his investigation for details, she meant nothing—a piece of newspaper, a bag, anything that might have floated up.

We left and my father said, "It's over," and I knew he'd protect me from whatever came next. Behind us I could hear them nailing my father's shanty closed, and I could see, angling beyond us from the shore, a single man, half stepping and half sliding across the ice. I knew that it was Kulanda, who should have locked his hut, and who was wishing at that very moment that we had broken in. And beyond him, running between the avenues of shanties, a single dog, tall and thin and red like an Irish setter. But maybe not. Maybe he was something else, barking like that, wanting only to be heard.

Nominated by Pushcart Press

MAKING SAUSAGE IN THE TIME OF REVOLUTION

by CLAUDIA SEREA

from CONSEQUENCE

This sausage is best made
during martial law,
lights turned off
and the window covered
with a heavy blanket
that still lets through the white streaks
of the tracers in the night sky.

Place a candle in a cup.
In its shaky light, we look like ghosts.

Think of the ghosts in the streets.

Think of the fires on barricades,
the only candles these souls will have.

On the table, set up the cast iron grinder
with its large, enameled maw,
its helix, gears, and iron clamp.

Think of the tanks and armored vehicles
advancing like huge night insects,
tens of boots grinding the pavement.

Start grinding the lean meat
and the white belly fat,
piece by piece,
one red chunk, one white,
one red one, white, red, white,
stuff the grinder, careful
to not catch your fingers.

Think of the grinder that smashes
students, young men and women shouting,
Libertate, te iubim!
Ori învingem, ori murim!

Grind, grind, grind, grind.

Stop and listen to explosions
and the giddy chatter of the guns.

Add salt, pepper to taste,
crushed cloves of garlic
and powdered sweet paprika.

Taste the tear gas and pepper spray
on students' faces.

Sink your hands into the meat paste,
hungry roots that turn and lift it,
turn, and lift again,
until blended and smooth.

Add a little bone soup
to soften the mix.

Think of the water cannons,
clotted bodies drenched in cold December.

Pull the thin,
almost transparent intestine
onto the machine's spout,

bunched up, white like the stocking
of a high school girl.

Think of that girl
crowned with sniper bullets,
and start pushing the paste in the machine,
against the machine.

Push, push, push, push,
with the force of a mudslide,
its rage and fear
and abandon.

Push, push, push, push,
until the dawn is born,
unrecognizable and wet,

and sanitation trucks roll in
to wash the blood from the pavement.

The candle burns to the bottom
and the only thing that remains is the smoke.

Nominated by Consequence

GOAT

by MAG GABBERT

from THE JOURNAL

Because every man I've ever slept with has wandered off to have kids, but later fucked me again.

Because I can't seem to pick a religion.

Because, during sex-ed, my teacher showed us a little box with an open slot on her desk, told us to write down our questions and slip them in.

Because the first note read: *Does sex really make women scream?*

Because the ancient Greek word *tragōidía*, which meant "goat song," somehow turned into the modern English *tragedy*.

Because my dad's nickname for me is "smelly."

Because for a long time I heard *bleat* as *bleed*.

Because *this song is sweet. It is sweet.*

Because God told his people to bring him two goats; he said they should give one their sins and let it go, and they should slit the other's throat.

Because my brother claims he needs a new razor for "manscaping."

Because childless mothers are called nannies.

Because Jesus won't help me.

And one night, when a friend and I were fifteen, we took a late train to a faraway party, and a man approached us, whispering, *Would you rather be stabbed or sliced?*

Because hell is an animal with other animals inside it.

Because every choice I've made involved sacrifice.

Because I'm always the one that got away.

Nominated by The Journal, Chloe Honum

LA BOHÈME

by CLIFFORD THOMPSON

from THE THREEPENNY REVIEW

On a Saturday or Sunday afternoon in the cold early months of 1988, I sat alone at a table for two in a Greenwich Village diner, twenty-four years old, hopelessly young, my notebook open in front of me. At the table next to mine were three people, all white: a woman and her very young daughter, and, across from them, another woman, who talked to the child in a kind way. I recall thinking that this woman was good with kids. When the mother took her little girl to the restroom, the other woman turned to me.

"What are you working on?" she asked.

I'm sure I smiled; that is what I did with everyone, that is what I do. "Trying to write a short story," I said.

"I thought so from the way you looked," she said. "I know that feeling of trying to get something on paper"—and she imitated my expression of paralyzed urgency. We laughed. We talked a little about writing. And at some point, apparently, I told her my first name and where I worked.

Where I worked was a book publishing company in Midtown Manhattan. Quite a few young people take entry-level jobs at publishing houses because they love books and also, often, secretly or not-so-secretly, want to write them. They sometimes learn the hard way that their passions have very little to do with the day-to-day business of making and publishing books. This is a way of saying that I didn't love my job. But I needed to earn a living, meagre though it was, and I was at my desk, ostensibly doing that, when my phone rang two or three days after my visit to the diner.

"This is Liz," the caller said. She added, clearing up my confusion and handing me a surprise, "We met in the restaurant the other day." We talked for a few minutes, by the end of which we had agreed that I would come to her apartment in the Village that Saturday night.

Where do I begin describing the young man who went to Liz's place? Let's start with how he looked: darker than some black folks, lighter than some others. A few people, on meeting him, thought he was a teenager, because of his face and also, probably, because he was on the small side— five feet eight inches and skinny, a hundred fifty pounds or so, though with a small pot belly he tried to suck in. There were other parts of his body he wasn't crazy about. He had the thinnest wrists and legs he knew of (he avoided wearing shorts and swimming trunks whenever possible), and the less said about his chin, the better. Partly for those reasons, partly for others, this young man's manner did not scream "confidence."

At this point you may not be thinking "woman magnet," and yet our young man was not without experience in that area. He'd had half a dozen or so lovers, including two with whom he had been in serious re- lationships. He was nothing if not nice, which can sometimes carry the day, though hardly always. If it seems mysterious that this guy had had any luck at all with women, the mystery may be cleared up, or possibly deepened, by what a woman at his previous job had once told him: "I've never met anybody as good-looking and as underconfident as you are." He might have dismissed the good-looking part, except that he'd heard it from other people. There was a diner waitress, in the town where he'd gone to college, who told him, unprompted, "You are really handsome," and a group of young girls in the same town who stared at him from across the park where he sat with his date, giggling and shrieking be- fore getting up their nerve to come over and say, "You look like Michael Jackson!"

None of this helped his confidence, at least outwardly. And yet, in there somewhere, he had some. It was a kind of forward-looking confi- dence, not about what he could do in the moment but what he would do some day yet a ways off; and it, this confidence, was not only present but completely, absurdly out of proportion to any evidence. Writing would be involved. He wanted to write—he *did* write—and he believed strongly that it would lead him somewhere. He had a lot to learn, and he knew it, and in his groping way he went about trying to learn: read- ing novels, seeking out screenings of classic films that he often attended alone, going here and there to an art museum.

This was the young man who made his way on a Saturday evening to Liz's apartment. He—I—took the subway from the neighborhood very far out in Brooklyn where I had a one-bedroom apartment, the place that was my answer to the question of how to have an affordable space all my own. No doubt, as I sat among other black and brown folks on the lumbering J train, I had a novel or a story collection with me; no doubt, too, I was distracted from my already slow reading by thoughts of the evening to come. Who knows, this might be the start of a relationship. I hadn't been in a serious one since I'd come to New York, a year and a half earlier.

Part of the reason had to do with my approach to pursuing women, which was really no approach at all. It would be easy to put that down to a lack of confidence, but the real explanation is more complicated. In high school I had a crush on a girl—Cheryl was her name—and I asked my mother (my father was four or five years dead by then) if I ought to tell Cheryl how I felt. No, she said. She recommended going slow, trying to figure out first how Cheryl felt about me, because if I opened my heart to her blindly, "She might tell her friends, and they might laugh at you." This was loving, well-intentioned, but unfortunate advice (for one thing, I realized later that Cheryl would have happily become my girlfriend if I had only said the word, and it seems everyone knew this but me), and it was advice for which I do not blame my mother one bit. Good parents—and my mother was a good parent—communicate to their children what they have come to understand; still, no one understands everything, and it is on the kid, eventually, to learn some things for his, her, their self. But I will say that my mother's advice sadly fortified my unconscious feeling that there was something embarrassing, something shameful, about admitting that you wanted to be with another person, unless that person clearly wanted to be with you. And so, with rare exceptions, the relationships I entered were with women who pursued me, or who let me know in some way that they wanted to be pursued (cues that I would sometimes pick up on only years after the fact).

Now here was Liz. Even I understood that you don't track someone down at his office, with only a first name and company name to go on, if you're not interested in him romantically, and it was clear that I could become involved with her. The only question was whether or not I wanted to. The evening to come would determine that, since I knew very little about Liz, except that she seemed nice and interesting—and creative, from the sound of things. Some of it, much of it, for better or worse, would depend on physical attraction. I didn't know whether I was attracted to her or not, because at the diner I had barely paid attention to how she looked. I didn't recall thinking she was unattractive, which seemed a good sign—good enough for my mind to begin to construct a woman I hadn't actually seen. As I got off the subway downtown and walked in the winter air to Liz's building, then up to her apartment, I felt optimistic. And then she opened her door, and I got a lesson in how easy it is to con yourself.

The evening was pleasant—more than pleasant in some ways, which I'll get to—yet I knew instantly that I would not become romantically involved with Liz. But I was here, we had the evening ahead of us, why not make the most of it? And maybe we could be friends. She had a comfortable home, the most memorable feature of which was smack in the middle of her living room: a playground-style slide. (I must have gone down it, though I can't actually remember doing that.) Here, I thought, is someone with a great childlike spirit.

In a way, that spirit—the desire to transcend age—became the theme of our acquaintance. It came out during the evening that, at thirty-seven, she was twelve-plus years older than I was. "I thought you were about thirty-two," she told me. (Months after that evening, I recited that line to another woman I was involved with briefly. "I'll laugh later," she said.) But our age difference didn't matter to Liz.

As for the difference between our skin colors, it didn't even come up, that night or ever, which impresses me in retrospect. We talked about writing; she had published a novel, which I dreamed of doing, and she gave me a copy—"It's good to have copies of your book to give people," she said, "for when it goes out of print." Though she didn't go into it much, I took in that she was involved in theater. At one point we stretched out on her floor to watch TV. She nudged me with her stockinged foot, and we held hands. I remember that she wore dark red polish on elegantly shaped nails; there was enough erotic tension that we rubbed the backs of our hands together, but not enough for me to proceed from there. At the end of the evening, when I put on my coat and stood at her door, she wrapped my scarf, smiling with her prominent front teeth, and gave me a light peck on the lips. She looked hopeful. That makes me sad now.

It is easy for someone my age to forget, and difficult for younger people to understand, how different life was before the internet. Had there been universal access to the World Wide Web in 1988, I could have

174

Googled the name on the cover of Liz's novel—Elizabeth Swados—and discovered a few things. She probably told me herself, and I'm sure I asked, where she grew up (Buffalo) and went to school (Bennington College). What she didn't mention, and what I might have found out on the Web in a different era, is that while she was still studying music and writing at Bennington, she met Ellen Stewart, founder of the experimental La MaMa theater in New York; that through La MaMa she met the director Andrei Serban; and that, working with Serban and others, she broke new ground in musical theater. I might have learned that in the late 1970s, when I was a miserable, oblivious junior high school student in D.C., Liz's Broadway show *Runaways*, and Liz herself, were racking up Tony Award nominations.

So, yes—she was, in her way, quite famous. There was more, though. "I recall thinking that this woman was good with kids," I wrote in the first paragraph of this essay. I didn't know the half of it. *Runaways* is a series of sung monologues by teen characters who have fled their broken family lives. As research for the show, Liz interviewed numerous hard-luck young people, and later cast them in actual parts. Others of her works, such as *The Hating Pot*, would take on themes of racism and anti-Semitism. (Liz was Jewish.) This was the profoundly talented, openhearted, special person I had taken one look at when, to put it plainly, I thought, *Nah.*

We got together again. I went to her apartment, and from there we went walking. There was, that evening, the feeling of the Village, maybe all of Manhattan, being her playground. We went to a place that was having a dance party—possibly La MaMa, because Liz pointed out Ellen Stewart, who was floating around the huge room like a giant bee. I must have indicated that I didn't know who she was, because Liz said, "Don't tell her that. She'll kill you." Liz introduced me to a man—white, fortyish, good-looking, wearing a blue suit—whose name and possibly very important occupation I have forgotten. I do recall that he smiled at me in a friendly way while his eyes asked: What is *she* doing with *you?*

Later we went back to Liz's place. We talked—mostly she talked, about our age difference, which she seemed to think was holding me back from getting involved with her, and whose unimportance she tried hard to impress upon me. "I had a relationship with a man who was sixty-nine years old," she told me." He was one of the greatest men I've ever known. Age doesn't matter. What matters is what people are like inside. There are some people you meet, sometimes they're young

175

people, and they're walking around, but it's like they're already *dead*."
I had little to say. What she was saying was true, but it missed the point, and I didn't know how to tell her what the point was without hurting her.

What I've learned about Liz since that evening has led me to reflect on the possible significance, for her, of the word "dead."

The book she gave me a copy of is *Leah and Lazar*, a novel published in 1982. Her nonfiction book *The Four of Us: A Family Memoir* came out in 1991. I don't know what became of my original copy of *Leah and Lazar*, but I acquired and read both of those books recently. The memoir has four sections, one for each member of Liz's quintessentially dysfunctional immediate family. The first section is about Liz's older brother, Lincoln, a highly creative schizophrenic who was Liz's chief tormentor and the biggest influence on her life, a doomed soul who was disabled after throwing himself in front of a subway train and who later became a street person, dying in a hovel in 1989. The second section tells the story of Liz's mother, a depressed woman of unrealized artistic gifts who committed suicide when Liz was a young woman. Next up is Liz's father, a lawyer who brought big-league hockey to Buffalo, a bellicose man with contempt for those—e.g., his wife and son—who gave up on their own lives; he indentified himself and his daughter as survivors. Finally, there is Liz herself, whose youthful adventures included living among coal miners in Appalachia, teaching in an African village, performing as a musician with, among others, Pete Seeger, and appearing on soap operas (all the ones my grandmother watched: I probably saw her on TV at some point).

Leah and Lazar was a fictionalized version of all this, remarkable, among other reasons, for telling the story of the death of the brother—Lazar, in the novel—with alarming accuracy, seven years before the fact. One part of the novel seems to have been influenced by the research for *Runaways:* the Liz character, Leah, becomes a teen prostitute in Florida before returning to her rather blasé parents. But in a figurative sense, that section of *Leah and Lazar* is perhaps autobiographical. Liz was a runaway from the spirit of death in her family. A refugee, a survivor. Defiantly alive.

One evening, the last one we spent together, Liz and I went to the movies. We saw *Moonstruck*, a romantic comedy in which the Cher character falls in love with her fiancé's brother, played by Nicolas Cage. It was not lost on me that I was a twenty-four-year-old man sitting with a thirty-seven-year-old woman as we watched the twenty-four-year-old Cage declare his love for the forty-one-year-old Cher. Afterward, as we walked to Liz's place, I hummed or whistled part of *Moonstruck*'s soundtrack, which I dimly recalled having heard before but couldn't place, and asked Liz about it. Even then I could feel what she must have been thinking when she looked at me: *He really is young.* "It's from Puccini's opera *La Bohème*," she said evenly.

Our conversation at her apartment was listless, dismal. I don't recall what we said, because it was trivial, and because Liz's tone made our exchange like a dubbed film—her lips were saying one thing, but I heard something else: *I've tried. I'm obviously not going to persuade you. I don't know what else there is to say.* Before long, I left. I never saw or spoke to Liz again.

Unless you count this. One day, more than two decades later, when I was spending, as usual, way too much time on Facebook, I found Liz's profile. I sent her a friend request. She accepted. There was no exchange beyond that. I don't know if she even remembered who I was, and for my part, I wouldn't have been sure what to write. (*Hi, twenty-odd years ago you wanted us to be lovers, but I wasn't interested. How's it going?*) You might ask why I looked her up at all. It's a good question, one I've often asked myself, particularly since early 2016, when I saw the news of Liz's death. Complications after surgery for esophageal cancer. A month short of her sixty-fifth birthday.

How well Liz is remembered depends on whom you're talking to. I recently mentioned her to two well-educated friends, both men, one several years older than I am, the other nine years younger. Both immediately thought of the writer Harvey Swados—was Liz his wife? Daughter? (He was a cousin.) On the other hand, the *New York Times* ran a substantial obituary of her (which mentioned, among many other things, that she was survived by her wife) and months later published remembrances of Liz by major theatrical figures, including Meryl Streep.

When I remember Liz—and maybe this has something to do with the Facebook friend request—I think of what she said about some people already being dead. What Liz thought of me is ultimately, of course, both unknowable and unimportant, though I do wonder if she considered me one of those walking dead folks because, as she must have thought, I deferred to societal mores about age differences. But what *is* important is what I think of myself, and I realize that over the years I have used Liz's words as a kind of personal yardstick. Have I lived as an alive person?

Writing is the one thing I have always pursued whether I knew anyone was interested or not. That fickle, elusive object of affection has nonetheless taken me to some interesting places. (Some of them are Liz's old haunts. I've taught nonfiction writing at Bennington, where she was a student, and NYU, where she was a professor.) I have written steadily; I write because I can't imagine not doing it, because I need to. But one also needs to make a living, and I spent a couple of decades doing work few would describe as glamorous to support myself and the family I always wanted. Would an alive person have done it differently? Would he have put writing front and center, always, until he either hit it big or died the death of Lazar? Looking at these questions written in my notebook, I think I have the beginnings of an answer; but maybe that is less important than asking the question—not about what we've done, but what we're doing.

It is tempting for a human being, especially a writer, and most especially an essayist, to find cause and effect between one event and subsequent events. And if you're not careful, you can end up with an essay that might as well be a short story. So I will simply list some things that happened after I last saw Liz.

That spring, my office had a dance party. I asked a co-worker to dance (the one who said "I'll laugh later"), and as we were dancing, I asked if she wanted to have coffee after the party. We went from Midtown to a diner in the Village. When we left there and were about to part for the evening, I kissed her. I didn't know if she wanted me to or not. Turned out she liked it.

Four years after that, I married a (different) woman I love deeply and am still with. We've told our daughters the story of our courtship, which at first seemed anything but that. They laugh at how we had to overcome our first impressions, or non-impressions, of each other. "Love at fiftieth sight," our older daughter said once.

One thing about settling down is that it's good for establishing routines. One of mine is going to the Y. Between that and the fact that, lately, my metabolism appears to have been run over by an eighteen-wheeler, my little body has gotten a bit bigger. Some of that, though not a lot, has made its way down to my legs. I wear shorts and swimming trunks now without a thought. You could call this confidence, or you could say I no longer care, or you could conclude that often the two amount to the same thing.

The other day I listened to a recording of *La Bohème* with Maria Callas singing the part of the fatally ill Mimi. The passage of the music included in *Moonstruck* is actually a very small part of the opera. But it is lovely, and a little sad, and memorable, and once in a while it goes through my head.

Nominated by The Threepenny Review

THE PRESENCE OF ORDER

by YONA HARVEY

from THE IOWA REVIEW

after Barbara Edelman and Diana Khoi Nguyen

Being separated from my family
& placed in a public school is what I recall
of time, the back-to-school calendar,
the months still lined up in my head
like on the bulletin board the first day of kindergarten.
& this is how I view the days even now, December
at the end of a straight line drawn with a yardstick,
maybe Christmas trees or candy canes stapled in place
before the weeks break as the lines in poems, a year
fading away & becoming another year,
January at the start of a new line then, the month
unfolding in rows, counting the days until spring,
counting the days left in June. How many seconds
allowed at the water fountain in the hottest months?
There were just too many of us kids to manage, to keep
in line, to shuffle from homeroom to gym class,
from gym class to lunch. When could I go back?
To my mother? To my sister?
To the daylong, nightlong television?

All I have left of my sister
I can fit into two storage containers—clear,
rectangular, neutral as Switzerland or Canada

except *not really* because I can see inside a red,
leather jacket & matching pants I'll never wear
but can't bring myself to get rid of. Where
would they go? Who would they flatter? I'd rather
not think about it, even after all these years,
& so, it remains, a darkening clot
in a plastic box, a brackish memory.

My sister did not cut herself
out of photographs before she leapt
from the roof, but she called several people
in our family & gave them a piece of her mind.
What I remember the most was her address book,
her ex-boyfriend's name scratched out so brutally
in black ink, the paper ripped through so much
that *that* is how I see him, a living, breathing black
plague of scribble—nameless, bodiless but somehow here
on the Earth my sister abandoned.

"Unbuckle your grief,"
whispered The Great Buffalo that began visiting me
last June, apart from the tales of first settlers &
first colonies that failed to bound the creature
to The Treacherous West. I trust The Great Animal
so much more than I trust man. How could I not
in this weary war market? In this accumulation of days
speckled with disease?

"Do you have any questions," the pharmacist asks
as he brushes my left muscled arm with alcohol.
"I've read too much, I've viewed too much, I've
listened too much," I tell him. "What else is left?"
"I can't hold any more information," I say.
& when he shoots me up, I feel the exhale,
The Great Long Sigh, The Defeated Breath
like the size of Southern California on fire,
The Sound of Inevitability. "What's the point,"
I don't say, "Why am I even preserving my health
or fighting for it? To live where? To be loved by whom?"

No, it wasn't as grim as that, *really.*
Just the sound of the soft gush of giving
into something that felt greater than me.

I walked around the store for ten minutes,
bought some bodywash, some toothpaste,
some sugary cereal in a bright, yellow box,
a two-pack of Chapstick. "Give me a thumbs-up
before you go," the pharmacist said.
He was kind as Canada or a thick bouquet
of chrysanthemums, sweet as a stick of spearmint gum.
I did not want to black out his face or rip through
the paper he gave me, tucked in a neat, little folder
commemorating the day. I was light
as a cardinal's wing. Unkennelled. Sister.

Nominated by The Iowa Review

FRESH ACCUSATIONS

by MOLLY BRODAK

from THE GLACIER

We have been so much. And what has been deleted!

Especially what's opulent. A yawn.
A warm January. A nice man. He had something in mind.
I did not choose to be lined with filth.

I wanted to place some colors against the water. I remember not
    answering.
Leaking leads nowhere. I ate quietly. Small amounts of anything
    I wanted.
The door to the building where I lived with hundreds of people was
    propped open.

Dead bodies sat in chairs. I denied wanting.

I denied to myself a feeling. I used white. It ached. I let it ache.

I seem fine. On the map I marked all the lakes along the way. My
    husband.
I collected pinecones aimlessly. Where we had walked and
    argued.
Now I am quiet. I have split myself. For love. Not for great art.
Not for peace. Not for everyone. I have wasted time. A flag I didn't
    recognize.

A swarming field where I looked for something and found nothing.
I will keep me away from you, I think. I'll appear to myself. In
   the ice.
Even in animals' bodies. For love.

All eyes seem like glass eyes, I have heard.

It is still winter here. I have worked a long time.
Two hours away my husband lives. The loud cry, or laugh?
It is not for everyone.

Nominated by The Glacier

THE BA'AL SHEM'S DAUGHTER

fiction by GLENN GITOMER

from JEWISH FICTION

My life is an out-of-the-money call option about to expire. Time value is quickly diminishing to naught. What is left of my career at the options exchange is in a corrugated banker box I am carrying to the elevator. I am tired, confused, forgetful. Dreams are no longer confined to the realm of sleep. I shut my eyes. Vivid images appear and vanish when I try to capture them. Ruminations are of an episodic past, whether legendary or real. My future is fantasies of a time gone by and playing boogie woogie piano Wednesdays at Captain Jack's on the Southside.

My great-great-grandmother Leya was the daughter of Rabbi Shmuel Jacovitsky. Rabbi Jacovitsky was a renowned scholar and author of esoteric interpretations of the Zohar in the tradition of the Holy Ari. For fourteen hours a day, except the Sabbath, he poured over the Midrash and treatises of the great scholars and meditated on the meaning of prayers and the letters of the Tetragrammaton. Upon the publication of his seminal work, *The Sefirot of Evil*, he was celebrated by rebbes from Vilnius to Odessa. In the Grand Synagogue of Kiev, built with the generosity of his father-in-law Aaron Brodsky, Rabbi Jacovitsky meandered through the aisles on the Sabbath, followed by his favorite students and carrying the Torah with its gold breastplate and crown and embroidered velvet mantel. He nodded approvingly at the men who approached and touched the Torah with their kissed tallit. From the *bima*, he flailed his arms about as he told of being transported without the passage of time by a chariot drawn by a host of angels, half-men and half-beast, to commune with the spirit of the Great One, the Ba'al Shem Tov. "As I left his holy presence, I was bathed in the pure light of Ultimate

185

Nothingness. I became one with the spirit of Hashem the Creator and the goodness that flowed forth." The women in the balcony sat transfixed. The men stood and davened. Gone was the short, bespectacled Shmuel with an unkempt gray beard and drooping belly, stooping as he went about a day interrupted by his bodily functions. Before them was a blessed one, a Master of the Divine Name, the Ba'al Shem of Kiev.

It was apparent from an early age that Leya was a piano prodigy. She was drawn to piano by the age of three. By four, Leya could play by ear tunes that she had heard only once. A member of her father's congregation came by once a week to give her lessons. Leya did not need to be coaxed to practice. The piano was her only friend. She spoke to it with her fingers, and it responded with melodies. Leya delighted in the increasing intricacy of their conversations.

Leya was nervous in the presence of her grandfather Brodsky. He was not warm and welcoming to those he did not view as his equal. His hugs were perfunctory and icy. It frightened Leya when Brodsky summoned her to a soirée attended by his coterie of the wealthy and intellectual Jews of Kiev in the finely furnished salon of his majestic home. She was directed to sit in an anteroom while the men discussed Goethe's *Faust* and Kant's pure reason and the precarious politics of Alexander the Liberator. "Wait until you are called, young lady," Brodsky's major domo instructed. Leya sat with her eyes closed and hands folded on her lap. To maintain composure, she concentrated on the ebbing and flowing noise of conversation punctuated with occasional bursts of laughter. The major domo tapped her on the shoulder. "Go in, young lady," He pointed to the salon. As she walked to the piano bench, she felt assaulted by pompous glares of the Brodskys' friends.

"Gentleman, a special treat tonight. My granddaughter will play for us Mendelssohn's *Venetian Boat Song*. Leya played it well. The men reacted with polite applause and nodding smiles. Brodsky put his hand on Leya's shoulder. "Friends, my eldest daughter Rebecca married an eminent scholar and revered rabbi, and my granddaughter is a musical genius. What greater gifts could Hashem bestow upon me? Ah, Leya, *meyn kleyn* Mozart *meydl*. They will speak of her in Vienna and Paris and London."

Brodsky commissioned Maestro Fedor Stein to tutor the eight-year-old Leya. "Maestro, I will pay you handsomely so long as you are devoted to her training. Be honest with me about her progress."

"That I will be, sir," Stein responded with a slight bow of his head. "You will not be disappointed."

Stein understood her gift the first time he heard Leya play. She was not restless or distracted. She sat erect. She was focused. She played Mozart's *Sonata No. 16* from memory and with greater discipline and emotion than any student thrice her age. After the final notes, Leya closed her eyes and sighed. Stein stared at the little girl. *She will be my greatest creation.* For two hours a day for three days a week for fifty weeks a year he paced and hovered over her. Stein was relentless, sparing with praise and cruel with his criticism. He accepted nothing less than perfection. Neither would Leya. For four hours a day for six days a week for fifty-two weeks a year, she practiced. Perfection left her sublimely content. Missteps felt like broken glass.

When Leya was eleven, Fedor Stein deemed her ready to be presented at the Kiev City Theater. The Maestro proudly addressed the packed theater. "Ladies and Gentlemen, welcome to this auspicious occasion. This evening you have the honor of attending the debut of a genius, Leya Jacovitsky, the eleven-year-old granddaughter of our beloved benefactor Aaron Brodsky." Stein lowered his arm in the direction of the great man. Brodsky rose from the first row, turned to the audience, and bowed his head to accept the applause. "And the daughter of our esteemed Rabbi Shmuel Jacovitsky." Shmuel proudly rose. "And now, may I introduce my pupil Leya Jacovitsky to perform for you Beethoven's *Sonata No. 31.*"

Leya had been groomed to play the part of an adorable scion of a cultured Kiev Jew. She walked out in a floor-length, puffed-sleeve white dress. Her light brown hair was set in braids. As she was instructed by Maestro Stein, she turned politely to the audience, curtsied, and took her seat under a spotlight on the bench to polite applause from a darkened anonymous theater. In that moment, it struck her: *Why do I let myself be paraded out as the Maestro's dancing bear to entertain pompous old men as a testament to my grandfather's glory? I am not Fedor Stein's creation. I am what Stein in his dreams hoped to be. I am tired of being the little girl in a white dress.*

During the first movement, Leya's long-repressed rage overtook her. She was fed up with Stein's hovering thick breath reeking of cigars and hand tapping her thigh and incessant condescension. She resented being sold into servitude by her grandfather. *These beasts have the nerve to judge me. Let them rot.* To her parents she was only a possession to boast about. They could not imagine the world she lived in. Her thoughts were beyond their command. Her rage was fed by the angry pounding *allegro molto* of the second movement. The third movement was a

187

portal to the abyss of Beethoven's dark soul from which she could never return. Leya resolved that she would not go on like this. She would have no more of Fedor Stein, no more of the Ba'al Shem and his wife, no more of the Great Brodsky. She would never touch a piano again. Neither they nor it would any longer control her. *They will wring nothing more from my soul.*

Her performance came to a flawless end. The theater roared with applause and cries of "Bravo!" as the audience rose to its feet. She sat for a moment and trembled like a volcano about to erupt. She stood, turned to the audience, and curtsied. She ran off the stage. She didn't answer the crowd's pleas for her to return. She ran out of the theater and ran and ran and ran.

All night Leya sat alone on a bench by the Dnieper River. She was resolved. *I'm not sure who I will be now that my piano will no longer speak to me, but I am finally free to find out.* She came home at four in the morning. Rebecca screamed, "Shmuel, she's here! Where have you been? We thought you might be dead. Why did you do this to us?"

Shmuel stormed into the room. "What is wrong with you? Your grandfather had everyone out looking for you. Rebecca, go tell your father that Leya is home now. Why, Leya, why have you chosen to destroy the pleasure of a night that we have so long anticipated?"

Leya was deaf to them. "Father, you will never understand. I will not be spoken to like that." She ran upstairs to her room and slammed the door.

For months Leya confined herself to her room. A paralyzing emptiness set in. She spoke very little and refused to answer questions about her mood or intentions. She didn't approach the piano which, until her City Theater performance, had defined her. She could not return to what had consumed her life and given her an identity. Her parents and grandfather had stopped caring, which was just as well. Leya no longer cared what anyone thought. She had no idea where to go from here. Only a rocky bottom would stop her free fall. She feared that she would never escape the lonely darkness.

Rabbi Jacovitsky was certain that his only child, who had been bestowed by Hashem with the gift of genius, was possessed by a dybbuk. Perhaps it was the spirit of his Uncle Lazarus the Masturbator of Minsk, that was causing Leya's endless fits and descent into despair. He had been so proud of her special brilliance. Now he heard that she cursed her classmates and ridiculed her teachers, who dared not confront the daughter of the celebrated Ba'al Shem of Kiev and granddaughter of their patron. Leya shielded herself with contempt and insulted anyone who tried to show her kindness. *These fools, they call me a spoiled brat. How dare they look at me like that? They are nothing but a bunch of ignorant clowns.*

Rebecca sought Brodsky's counsel. "I will get her a donkey. It will give her something to care for and ride around town. Maybe that will snap her out of this. I will build a small barn in your garden and keep the donkey supplied with hay. Let's see if that works, Rebecca."

To honor her twelfth birthday and first menstruation, Leya was presented with a donkey. She named the donkey Esau. With Esau, Leya felt for the first time the love of a sentient being. She couldn't wait to see him in the morning. After she'd carefully groomEsau's mane, Leya would stare into his eyes and ask, "What adventure shall we have today, Esau?"

Esau did not look away. In a soft bray he replied, "Ride me through town. We will call the tradesmen impotent cuckolds. Or maybe we'll go down to the Dnieper where you like to skinny dip."

"Why don't we do both, Esau? We will have a marvelous day."

When the Gentile boys saw Leya ride Esau on the road to the river, they scurried to hide in the woods above the riverbank and watched as Leya tied her ass to a tree. She disrobed, laid her folded clothes beside Esau, and waded into the Dnieper. She swam around and stood waist high with her feet squishing into the mud of the riverbed. The boys were motionless. They feared that if the girl knew they were there, she would cover herself and run away. Leya knew they were there. That was the whole point.

Rabbi Jacovitsky beseeched Hashem in incessant prayers deep into the night. "Please, Lord, I have devoted my every moment to your glory. Free my daughter from this wicked curse. I have become a laughing-stock even as I praise your name." Hashem heard Shmuel's prayers but was not inclined to get involved in his worldly troubles.

Shmuel shook his sleeping wife with fire in his eyes. "She is your daughter. How could you let this happen? You must do something. She will be the ruin of me."

"I don't know what to do, Shmuel. I can't take much more of it. Please just let me lie in peace for a few hours."

"No, Rebecca. Why should you sleep while I suffer?"

As the sun rose, a solution to his problem came to Shmuel. He would arrange the marriage of his daughter to young Rabbi Mordechai Davidich, who bragged of skills as an exorcist. He would rid Leya of the dybbuk and give her a new start in the village of Lubny far from the gossips of Kiev.

Rabbi Davidich, a slender balding man with a thin beard, who deflected his eyes in the presence of women, welcomed the shidduch. He was a devoted initiate of the esoteric teachings and practices passed to him by his teacher, a disciple of Rabbi Jacovitsky. His teacher considered Rabbi Davidich a talented student and persuaded him that his ambitions would be advanced by a marriage to the daughter of a rabbi of such eminence and the granddaughter of one of the wealthiest Jews of Kiev. "And such a beauty, I have heard," his teacher told him. Mordechai Davidich had never seen a naked woman. As hard as he tried, he could not repress the thoughts of the mysteries that would be revealed on a sacred wedding night. He was all in.

Leya needed coaxing. "Me, a rabbi's wife? In Lubny where the peasants stand knee deep in shit? What an absurdly ugly idea," she told Esau. "I would sooner just fade into the night."

Shmuel was insistent. "There is no other way. You are driving me crazy. You are a disgrace to your grandfather and us. You must leave. I will lock you in your room until you consent. I will take your damn donkey to be slaughtered and fed to the serfs."

Rebecca was gentler. "Dear, it will work out. Rabbi Davidich is a good man. He will give you a wonderful new life. It is for the best."

Leya cried for days. She banged her head against the wall until it was bruised and bloody and she could take no more pain. Esau could not stand what Leya was doing to herself. Esau promised Leya that he would always be by her side. "It's time for us to go, Leya," he brayed. "We'll make a great adventure out of it."

In the last days of August, a month before Leya's fourteenth birthday, Shmuel hired a carriage for the one hundred and thirty mile trip to Lubny. Esau was given the honor of helping lead the way. Leya sat with the coachman to watch over Esau, who occasionally looked back at her and gave out a gentle encouraging bray.

The marriage started badly. Leya detested Modi's timidity and fawning deference. She felt caged and raged at a life among strangers that made no sense to her. Leya became feral and preyed upon Modi with ridicule. She brazenly flirted with unholy roughs in front of the cheder boys and teachers' wives. Modi tried to placate her with kindness, but these efforts provoked cruelty and violence. The townsfolk pretended not to see the bloody scratches on his cheek and bruises around his eyes.

Leya laughed when she overhead them call her "the *meshugena* who talks to a donkey."

Modi cherished Leya as a gift from Hashem. Modi knew that to win her love he would have to exorcise the dybbuk that possessed her. He was a devoted student of the rites of exorcism. He devoured the *Minhat Yehuda* and *Hayyim Eliyahu*, but this would be the first time he would put his knowledge into practice. He prayed to Hashem for the wisdom and strength to perform this most holy task.

Rabbi Davidich summoned a minyan of his most trusted friends, all sworn to secrecy, to the shul at five in the morning. Four of Rabbi Davidich's students gagged and dragged a sleepy Leya, dressed in her bedclothes, from her room as she squirmed and struggled. They tied her tightly to a chair in the sanctuary. The davening minyan surrounded her as Rabbi Davidich hung sacred amulets around her neck and recited prayers to Hashem pleading to rid Leya of the dybbuk. The minyan chanted the ninety-first psalm over and over. "He will deliver thee from the snare of the fowler."

"Esau, save me from this insanity!" Leya cried, struggling to break free.

"Thou shall not be afraid of the terror by night."

"Esau! It's not the terror of the night that frightens me!"

"For He will give His angels charge over thee, to keep thee in all ways. They shall bear thee upon their hands, lest thou dash thy foot against a stone."

"Esau, please! I promise I will not stub my toes. Please make these lunatics leave me alone."

After each recitation, the grating staccato blasts of the shofar filled the room. There was no sign of a dybbuk fleeing from any of Leya's orifices, but Modi took Leya's exhausted collapse after hours of this ordeal as a sign that the dybbuk must have fled. Rabbi Davidich led his wife to the mikveh, certain that its waters would restore her purity.

Rabbi Davidich oversold his skills as an exorcist. After weeks of docile resignation and sadness, Leya's dybbuk awoke and took hold. Repeated efforts at exorcism had no greater success. On Yom Kippur, among the sins that Rabbi Davidich sought atonement for were his arrogance and false claim that Hashem bestowed upon him the power of exorcism. Hashem forgave Modi. Leya did not.

Leya gave Modi two sons and two daughters, but Leya was out of his control. The gossips of Lubny began to refer to the couple as Hosea and Gomer and whispered that their children were not of the rabbi's seed.

One Sabbath eve in October, while the townsfolk gathered in the shul, the twenty-four-year-old Leya left Lubny, her four children, and Modi on a horse-drawn cart with Esau, a sack of her modest belongings, and a deserter from the Tsar's army. Her children never heard from her again. Rabbi Davidich learned from a rabbi visiting from Jerusalem that Leya had fallen under the influence of Satan and was living in a commune in Palestine reputed to practice orgiastic rites.

The humiliation that Leya had caused Modi was eventually forgotten. Free of her, Rabbi Davidich earned respect for his humility and wisdom. After obtaining a *get*, Modi married the zaftig widow Esther, ten years his senior. She was a caring mother to his children and doting wife until his death on the eve of the turn of the century.

Sixteen years after that October Sabbath eve, Leya and Esau returned. She persuaded a Gentile family to take her in as a housekeeper on their farm near the mountains a few miles south of Lubny. She gave her name as Maria Polenka.

She was not the beautiful woman who had disappeared. Her skin had aged like a fig in the Palestine sun. Her waist and legs had thickened. Her speckled gray hair was unkempt. She had nervous obsessions, darting her tongue in spaces where teeth had been and scratching her arms until they bled. Her vanity and spirit were gone. Her mind was a tightening web of confusion. In her lucid moments, Leya was tormented by sadness and regret. Esau remained at her side and tried to comfort her.

Leya and Esau went into Lubny to find out what had become of her children. In the autumn Sabbath afternoon, she found a house where she thought she had lived with Modi and her children. She sat with Esau unnoticed for hours on the curb across the street. Young men and women, some with children, came in and out of the house. Leya could make no sense of it. She recognized no one. She wondered why the people who milled about were oblivious to her. *Am I invisible? Do they think I'm possessed by a dybbuk? Maybe I am.* As the sun set, Leya and Esau mumbled to each other as they returned to the farm. Their conversations no longer made sense.

On Sunday morning, Leya and Esau went hiking on familiar mountain paths. From the cliff atop a mountain, Leya looked straight out into farmland and the Sula River and a distant town. It frightened her to look down at the chasm from the edge of the cliff. She felt a force drawing her to the edge. She stepped back. She couldn't stop looking down.

She grew dizzy. Esau stood beside her. He softly brayed, "Leya, it's time for you to fly. It will be an adventure."

"I know. I know."

Leya spread her arms and dove into the canyon. She flew for a moment until gravity took her down. Esau let out a loud bray that echoed through the canyon as he watched Leya fall. He took a galloping leap and followed her down.

My great-grandfather Yitzchak was the youngest of Leya's children. He was tall and muscular and bore no resemblance to Rabbi Davidich. Yitzy did not share his brother Joseph's patience for study. He was good with numbers and got along well with the Gentile landowners. He went into business with his father-in-law Moshe Billanoff, a money lender and speculator in grain futures. Yitzy and Lilliana had four sons and three daughters. They lived in an H-shaped one-story home on the outskirts of Lubny. My grandfather Abe told me that they had a comfortable life until the Pogrom of 1905. Cossack mobs swept through and burned Yitzy's house to the ground. Yitzy, Lilliana, and their daughter Elena died in fire. Two sons were hacked to death as they fled the burning house. Shmuel, Avram, Bella, and Golda survived the melée. Several years later, after Avram was ordered to report as a conscript in the Tzar's army, Shmuel and Avram left for America, where they became known around Baltimore's Lombard Street as Sam and Abe, the Davis Boys.

Abe kept in touch with Bella and Golda for a while. They had both married and moved on with their lives in Lubny. Their sons and husbands were conscripted to defend the Homeland against the German onslaught. On October 16, 1941, the indifferent Hashem left Lubny never to return. It was about a month after the Germans captured Lubny. The Einsatzgruppen ordered the thousand five hundred Jews that remained to assemble in the outskirts of the city for resettlement. The Gentiles of Lubny shuttered their windows. At the Zasylskiy Ravine, the Jews were ordered to undress and massacred with endless machine gun fire. Abe was certain that Bella, Golda, and those of their children who were not away at war were among the bodies that the Germans had kicked and prodded to be certain they were dead. Abe told my dad that the German enlisted men obeyed the order to finish with a bullet in the skull anyone who moved, before the bodies were thrown into ditches dug at gunpoint by Russian prisoners of war, who covered them with earth. A few weeks earlier, the Einsatzgruppen in the same way had massacred thirty thousand Jews at the Babi Yar ravine outside of Kiev.

It's Wednesday. I'm on my way to Captain Jack's. Legend is that Bird and Monk performed there. I wish that Bubbie Leya were there to hear me play. I would give her a big hug, thank her for the gift, and tell her that I too feel drawn to the edge.

Nominated by Jewish Fiction

HAVING LOST THE KEYS TO THE WORLD, WHERE EVERYONE SITS

by KATERYNA KALYTKO

from LOST HORSE

Having lost the keys to the world, where everyone sits
on the thresholds in twos or more, she waits
until someone returns:
from work, from battles close to home, from short term memory,
from a comfortable afterlife,
but no one is there.
The key plunges into the snow
and dreams that by spring it will grow into a railroad.
Evening will be cold.
Her blood is too red for those of the black earth, the *chornozem*,
and not blue enough to find its way to the sea,
and not thick enough to call her
to the promised earth. Into the promised earth—hint at burial
people enter into great history,
they exit,
and she has a history that is too diverse to become
a passport.
None of the unity that she really wanted to grow
let her in, they were closed and hard,
they mock her and delight in themselves
as, it happens, the green apple in the branches swells with pride.
With the aging scrape the ark rocks,
among ice sheets; stranger's sighs, squealing,
they break off in pairs, frightened quiet rats.

If she stays here longer, and she will forget what kind of voice she had,
how she saved it: suddenly there will come a time
to tell her story without translation, without interpreting,
simply the way that people who ran a long way breathe,
and now they lie in the darkness beside one another
and calm down.

Translated from the Ukrainian by Olena Jennings and Oksana Lutsyshyna

Nominated by Lost Horse

THE LOCKSMITH

fiction by GREY WOLFE LAJOIE

from THE THREEPENNY REVIEW

The locksmith cannot speak well. He never liked school. When he was a child, the others called him Tombstone. They threw things at him. Bottles and food waste and dirt clumps studded with gravel. Though he was much larger than they were, he remained as still and as quiet as he could while enduring these acts.

The locksmith is not allowed a driver's license. He rides a bicycle from customer to customer, granting them entry. He likes to think about the number zero. He likes to think about time travel. He likes to think about shadows. He has watched many videos on each of these subjects.

When customers engage with him he is polite. The locksmith nods and goes about his work in silence. As a child he suffered a traumatic head injury at the hands of his stepfather, and now he rarely smiles. It is painful to do so. The customers are deeply troubled by his presence, by his ineffable, clouded expression. But they must regain access to their homes, to their automobiles.

A woman calls the locksmith. She is screaming. Her son has shut himself inside her Lexus and refuses to open the door. Her only spare is with the father, she says, who is out of the country on business. Intermittently she shouts at her son while, it seems, banging on the hood of the car. She asks for an estimate and then gives the locksmith her address. The locksmith hangs up the phone and readies his equipment. Into a heavy black bag he packs his tension wrenches, his small key-cutting machine, his pick sets, a wedge, several blank keys.

It takes him over an hour by bike to get to the large three-story house on the far side of town. When the locksmith arrives, the woman is on her phone, pacing. She lowers the phone and covers the receiver. "Where were you?" she asks. "Liam might have died of dehydration waiting for you!" She wears dark, formfitting jogging clothes and her gray hair is pulled up in a bun. The locksmith looks past her, toward the deep black car which glistens like fire. He steps toward the car and removes his bag. Inside the vehicle, a small blond boy watches him, motionless. The woman carries herself back and forth across the driveway speaking gravely into her phone. Sometimes she pauses to shout through the windshield at her son. "You little shit," she shouts. "You're going to have yourself a hell of a week after this, you little shit." The boy does not acknowledge this. He continues to watch the locksmith, carefully. The two of them stare at each other through the glass. Something is being communicated. The locksmith leans down, shuffles through his black bag. The boy watches him in much the way a small animal would—a squirrel or a bird—if it were to find itself frozen in the locksmith's path. With terror the boy watches. From the heavy bag the locksmith removes a long, narrow tool. Abruptly the boy unlocks the car and runs toward his mother.

"Oh Liam," the woman says, hugging the boy. "Liam baby, are you okay?" She turns toward the locksmith. "You can leave now," she says.

In particular, what the locksmith likes about shadows is that, although they occupy a three-dimensional area, we can see only a cross-section of them. The cross-section is a silhouette, a reverse projection of the object which blocks the light. But the shadow itself has volume, dark and imperceptible.

It is still early in the morning, a cold sunny day in December, and the locksmith is riding to his next customer. The shape of his shadow stretches out before him. The customer he is visiting has dealt with the locksmith before. He is a man named Chuck, a realtor of some kind. Today Chuck is waiting on the steps of a property he has just purchased, a small bungalow with peeling white paint and shattered windows. He is smoking a cigarette and he waits for the locksmith to dismount his bike before speaking.

"They told me this key worked on all the doors but it doesn't. I can't get into the basement." He hands the key to the locksmith and, although it serves no obvious purpose, the locksmith examines it carefully. SCHLAGE, the key reads. The locksmith breathes heavily.

He hands it back to Chuck and follows him into the house. The floor is littered with items of varying familiarity. Things bank up against the corners of each room, soiled beyond restoration. There are wrappers and shards, stray electrical wires, syringes, a phone book ripped to pieces, an old tire. There are baby clothes and animal droppings and a heavily stained mattress. The smell is inscrutable.

Chuck leads the locksmith through the hallway, where every few feet someone has punched a hole into the drywall. Black mold wanders along in snaking bursts, digressing sometimes into these holes. The locksmith is careful not to step on a thing. Chuck points to the basement door, then goes to the kitchen to inspect the gas lines.

The locksmith stands before the door. It is secured with two worn locks, and the work will take him some time to complete. He lowers his bag and begins.

The locksmith does not have friends. He has a pit bull terrier. When he found it, the dog was lying abandoned behind a shopping center. It was peppered with lacerations and unable to walk. He and the dog reside together in his deceased mother's house. Its coat is black but for the white streaks of fur atop its scars and the mist of gray under its eyes.

Each day when the locksmith comes home, the dog will hide under the bed for an hour or two, trembling. In the beginning, the locksmith tried to coax it out with food, but now he simply waits for these episodes to pass. By dark the dog climbs onto the bed and lies at the foot, watching the locksmith cautiously before drifting to sleep. In the mornings it eats, and only then allows itself to be touched by the locksmith. In this sense they coexist.

For two hours the locksmith works with patience and efficiency on the basement door. The first lock is a standard cylinder barrel and takes him very little time, but the second is rather elaborate, a paracentric keyway. He does not label these in words but nevertheless understands them intimately and moves gracefully through the steps required to open them. Chuck has ordered a pepperoni pizza and offers it several times to him, but the locksmith cannot think of this. He must focus on his task. A lock is its own kind of language.

By noon he has fabricated a functioning key for each of the barrels. He duplicates them, puts them on a ring, and brings them in to Chuck, who is crouched behind the oven. Chuck rises and takes the keys. His hands are dark with grease. From his wallet he removes three twenty-dollar bills and holds them out to the locksmith. "Pleasure," Chuck says. The locksmith takes the money and begins to leave.

"Hey," Chuck says, "don't you want to see what's down there?" The locksmith turns back to him, shakes his head, and goes.

The symbol for zero is meant to encircle an absence, a nothingness. But the unbroken circle comes also to connote, paradoxically, everything. This excites the locksmith greatly. He has learned much about zero. He has learned that mathematicians and physicists are unsure whether zero is real, whether it should be treated as presence or absence. It is an interpretive problem. They are fiercely divided on the issue, he has learned. The answer determines a great deal: the nature of black holes and gravitational singularities and the origins of the Big Bang. The locksmith stays awake late into the night, watching videos on the subject.

He must ride across the river toward a small apartment building where an elevator has locked itself shut. Along the way the locksmith crosses a set of train tracks. On the tracks there is an animal, an opossum. She has been split in half precisely by the train. She is dead, certainly, though her stomach still bulges and writhes. The locksmith sets his bike aside, comes closer to the animal. From within her cleaved stomach there are newborn opossums, nosing their way out. Perhaps two dozen. They are pale pink and blind, moving haltingly into the hard winter light. Their flesh is so thin as to be translucent, the black eyes just visible beneath. The locksmith watches them squirm. He is unsure what to do. They are incredibly small. Each could fit with ease onto a tablespoon. After a time, he lowers his bag and begins to remove his tools. He takes out his tension wrenches and his key-cutting machine and his pick sets. He places them all neatly into a shrub, out of sight. He takes off his undershirt and lines the inside of his large black bag with it. Then, one at a time, he sets the opossums into the bag. In his hands they are crêpey and silken and periodically they seem to sneeze. The locksmith thinks to himself, *Hmm . . .*

The dog is bewildered by the locksmith's return so early in the day. For a time it stares at him, forgetting to hide. The locksmith finds an old cookie tin in the kitchen. His home is as it was when he inherited it. He takes the tin and lines it with socks. He places the opossums in the tin along with a jar lid filled with warm water. Into another lid he spoons applesauce. The dog watches curiously as he works. It sniffs at the air

200

between them. When the locksmith glances at the dog it turns and leaves abruptly, disappearing into the bedroom for the rest of the night. Nervously, the locksmith looks into the tin. The small animals stumble vaguely into one another and then rest. He sets them on the kitchen counter, beneath a small reading lamp which he hopes will keep them warm. For the remainder of the day he sits and watches them.

In the morning the locksmith goes and retrieves his tools. They are coated in a thin layer of dew and he wipes them down carefully with a rag before placing them back into his bag. The woman who owns the apartment building with the locked elevator is not terribly upset about the delay. The name she gives is Ms. Alice. "People can use the stairs," she says, when he arrives. She speaks with an enigmatic European accent and wears heavy, riotous jewelry. The locksmith follows her up to the fourth floor, where the elevator was last opened. On the way she hums to herself an unrecognizable tune. Her voice leaps about the staircase. The locksmith walks closely behind, blushing at the sound.

It has been a long time since the locksmith has worked an elevator but he has not forgotten. First he must use a universal drop key to open the landing doors. Once inside he can determine the underlying issue.

"You know the great Houdini?" Ms. Alice asks him. The locksmith is kneeling before the elevator control panel, the woman standing behind him. He looks back at her, somewhat distressed. "He started as a locksmith," she says. "At the age of eleven he began as an apprentice for the local locksmith and soon he could pick anything open." The locksmith smiles painfully, nods, and turns back to his work. "Have you seen his gaze?" she asks. "I think he had the most magical gaze. So terribly terribly morbid his gaze was." The locksmith is trying to focus. He has the key in the chamber but he must turn it just so in order to trigger the doors. Ms. Alice watches with her hand on her chest. "He was Hungarian, you know. A lot of people don't know that. Hungarian and Jewish. They buried him alive but he clawed his way out. That was one of his tricks but he started panicking while he was digging up." Her jewels clatter carelessly as she speaks. "Later he wrote in his diary, 'the weight of the earth is killing.' That's what he wrote. Can you believe that? They had to pull his body up out of the dirt." The mechanism catches and the locksmith steps back. He takes his heavy pry bar and carefully works the doors open. "How lovely!" Ms. Alice says.

The elevator cab is stalled between floors and the locksmith has to crouch and step down into it. It is dim in the cab. The only light comes from the floor above, where Ms. Alice's feet are still visible, rising up from red shoes. The locksmith inspects the service key mechanism. It is a very simple tubular pin tumbler lock. It will take only a little while. Ms. Alice calls down into the shaft. "Are you thirsty?" she asks. "Would you like something to drink?" The locksmith mumbles something quickly. "What?" Ms. Alice says. He repeats himself carefully, his shoulders tense. There is a long silence and then the locksmith returns to his work, impressioning the lock with a blank. "Oh how I wish I could have seen him perform," Ms. Alice says. "Such a handsome, eerie man. Full of miracles. Full of wonder. Keep up your enthusiasm! He always said that! But then of course his final words were something altogether different."

In very little time the locksmith has restarted the elevator's operation. The lights flicker on at once and the doors close and of its own accord the cab begins to lift him. It rises eight stories and then opens up to the roof. Before him, the gray sky unfolds slowly, its cold light flooding the cab. A dark bird drifts down on the wind and lands just ahead of him.

Since he was a very small child the locksmith has thought of time travel. There is one theory which accepts the flow of time as a cognitive construct. This is the locksmith's favorite. According to this theory, were the locksmith to return to his past—such as the last time he saw his mother—he would have no experience of any temporal discontinuity. He would simply look backward in memory, reconstructing his childhood, or forward in expectation, guessing at the future. Were the locksmith to travel back through time, in other words, everything would feel as it does now. The locksmith thinks of this often. He thinks, who is to say I haven't just time-traveled? Who is to say time ever moves forward? Wordlessly he thinks these things to himself.

The locksmith waits for the elevator doors to close, then presses the button to go back down. When he returns Ms. Alice is there smiling. "That was quite the escape!" she says.

Nominated by The Threepenny Review

CHEMO BECOMES ME

by LILY JARMAN-REISCH

from LIGHT

Lost all my hair and too much weight
yet everyone tells me I look great.
Chemo becomes me.

Don't mind the toxin in my veins
'cause no bad hair days when it rains.
Chemo becomes me.

Sick in bed or on the bathroom floor
it never mattered what I wore
'cause chemo becomes me.

Nails nut brown, face fever red.
I'm lovelier than being dead.
Chemo becomes me.

I don't worry 'bout being mauled:
got that covered by being bald.
Chemo becomes me.

A shitty change in my fate
got my skewed priorities straight.
Chemo becomes me.

Cut, poisoned, radiated too
beats a dirt nap before it's due.
Chemo becomes me.

Nominated by Light

EVERYCHILD

fiction by ALIX CHRISTIE

from THE MISSOURI REVIEW

It should have been their senior year. Everychild was seventeen going on a hundred, what with everything that lay ahead. They were pale after months chained to their laptop, pale and blond and exceedingly white, though this too galled them, to be no more than an ally as the world went up in flames. Time to think about college applications, their parents began to chirp in October, Covid month seven.

"What's the point?" Everychild's voice was flat. "We'll all be climate refugees, and you'll be dead."

Afterward, Mom and Dad cast their minds back. Was there a precise moment, some tipping point they'd missed? Time had become so folded upon itself that year. Perhaps it began right after the Day No One Could Breathe. When the birds, disoriented, failed to lift into the orange-black sky. When they and Everychild and Younger Brother all woke to the same suffocating murk, six months into the pandemic. It coated them inside and out: skin, feathers, alveoli. The entire state of California was aflame, Silicon Valley run aground on the *Exxon Valdez*. Outside was the world they had made, both visible and invisible: smoke and ash and fire and virus. They couldn't leave the house, even if they hadn't been sheltering in place. They couldn't even step into the yard. The pool water was slick with platinum ash.

During that orange week—the color of a dying sun—the doorbell rang. Bags filled with food appeared on the front porch. "Like magic!" exclaimed Dad, surprised by how easy it had been. Until now, he'd sallied forth with list and mask. Now, literally no one could fucking breathe. At the unaccustomed ding-dong, each of them emerged from their separate lairs. "Jesus, Dad," said Everychild. Their hair was cut at a sharp angle that week; patches of hot pink blush outlined their eye sockets. Inside the rings, those cutting green eyes. "Did you even think about the delivery people?"

Mom, in her noise-canceling headphones, flapped her hands and mimed that she was on a call.

"Did you tip them massively, at least?"

At dinner that night—line-caught tuna, organic Brussels sprouts—their father looked perplexed. "It's not like there's any choice. It's not safe to shop. Buying online at least gives them jobs."

"*Them*?" Everychild raised their narrow shoulders. "Have you even thought about the carbon footprint of all this shit? All these trucks, the fucking Amazon?"

"What about Amazon?" Younger Brother's head jerked up as if sensing a predator. He was fifteen and tethered to his games, downloadable, thank God, but even he required a delivery from time to time.

"We've been through this." Dad shook his head. "Trucking everything to stores and everyone driving to those stores is no different, maybe even worse, than delivering door-to-door."

"Maybe trucking is the problem," Everychild said.

The next morning they were scrubbed clean. Gone the makeup, along with most of the flaxen hair. "I've been thinking," they announced. "About my applications."

The parents couldn't help but feel a spurt of relief. It didn't have to be an Ivy, they'd agreed—but someplace in the second tier, at least.

"It's a project," was all their eldest child would say. "Physical, in the real world, maybe part of a portfolio."

Art school was better than nothing, Mom murmured. Everychild didn't hear this; they were scanning the kitchen. "No way!" They lurched suddenly toward the coffee machine. "Almond milk? Really, Dad?" Their bone-white fingers tightened on the Tetra-Pak. "It takes a gallon of water to grow a single almond, did you know that? Tell me it even crossed your mind?"

Dad sighed. Their family did their best, eco-wise. They recycled metal, plastic, and glass, dumped rinds in the compost, tried not to waste water in this land of endless drought. In his own youth, he'd boycotted tuna to save the dolphins. But it was he who did the shopping, surprisingly still an outlier there; he who bought the food and cooked it. How many hours and days had he lost to scanning labels for parabens, corn syrup, hormones, hydrogenated fats? And still they did nothing but carp. Was it his job to save the whole damn planet?

They would work on the project in the den, Everychild announced. Mom said that would be fine. It was, in any case, an appropriate word for the dark, fetid place upstairs from which their son launched into his online worlds. Everychild insisted that Dad replace the doorknob with a locking one. "At least," they said with a peculiar smile, "hardware stores are an essential service."

Around the house, things began to disappear. Shampoo bottles. The plastic shells for takeout salads. The mother's Lycra top for online Zumba. When the kids were younger, the parents thought nothing of rifling their rooms, unearthing stuff. Out of the question now that they were teenagers. The mornings were for remote school, and the afternoons—well, college applications and snacks and multiplayer multiverses, the parents supposed. It was hard to know: both of them were tied to work. "So long as no one's dying or dead," Mom liked to deadpan.

Each had their laptop, their zone. Even meeting for meals, bit by bit, began to break down. Was it that first order from Instacart? Or the next rung down, when the father couldn't even cope with preparing food after eight hours on Zoom? Then it was Grubhub, DoorDash, all those monosyllabic bursts of bytes and instant magic. Was it that, they would later ask, that triggered her—triggered *them;* they're sorry, they slipped up, they try so hard. Not *she,* not *her,* but *they* and *them.* They were liberal parents in a liberal suburb on the San Francisco Peninsula, accepting piercings, tattoos, nonbinary, whatever. The main thing, the parents stressed, was living up to your potential. Everychild and their brother had heard this since preschool: striving, straining, achieving their personal best. They were good kids; they did what they were told. There would still be tests, counselors, SATs, Mom reminded Everychild from time to time.

"It's harsh out there," she told her former girl. "You don't want to end up dependent on somebody else, that's for sure."

"Not my planes."

"I gave my dolls."

Everychild's face softened, gathering him up in bone-thin arms. Younger Brother held himself stiffly but allowed the intrusion. Everything had changed, not only outside, in the world and with their parents, but especially between them. They felt so protective of one another now. Like they were already the last two left, everything else already burned and blown away.

"You'll see," they whispered, ducking and brushing the hair that would not stop growing from their eyes. Green to his hazel, close now, forehead to forehead as they whispered in the dimness of the den. "It'll be better when we get there; we won't feel so alone."

He was taller, skinnier even than Everychild and increasingly sad. "We could take them too, make them come," he had said at the start, but even he knew it would never work. *A shock is the only way,* this pale elfin creature who had been born before him kept saying. They were in touch with others, or so he understood. There was a group, a plan, a destination somewhere to the north. Gradually his fear subsided, and a little feeling of excitement began to build. He brought more offerings to their task.

"Maybe we can get them to come after," he said to Everychild when they were close to done. "Maybe," they said, and there was something in their tone—wistfulness or resignation or maybe just neutrality—that gave him hope.

"What's she—they—doing in there?" Dad buttonholed their son by the stairs. He had been granted access to the construction zone, even if the parents were expressly barred.

"You'll see." Their son looked bizarrely marsupial without his huge headphones. His parents ought to have been glad. How many years had they railed against the pernicious effects of these goddamned screens, without, of course, logging off themselves? Irony of ironies: For this one thing, they could thank the coronavirus, Dad said to Mom. Forced to spend each waking instant glued to a glass pane, even the most die-hard digital natives were finally glazed to death. It was a boon: they'd forgotten what he even looked like with ears.

Yet even so, each time he scurried upstairs, bolting like a freed serf from class, one or the other would try to intercept him. "What?" they'd wheedle. "Give us a hint."

"We're building something" was all he'd say, wriggling past. "You'll see." On the weekends, prepandemic, Dad and the boy used to shoot hoops at the middle school down the road. Dad remembered this on his Peloton, listening to yet another motivational conference speaker. God, could they all use some air. He stuck his head inside his son's bedroom door and mimed a dribble. Younger Brother signaled back "thirty minutes."

"Actually, I wanted to ask if I could get a tent and sleeping bag," the boy said as they walked to the court. "To sleep outside, when I can."

"Sure." Anything to get him out of his bedroom and the den. "We'll check it out online when we get back."

"Bricks and mortar. Please." The boy, with his long red mop, his fine light lashes, looked pained. "I hear you can pick up at Patagonia now, and REI."

They fist-bumped and began to play, and the father allowed himself a fleeting fantasy of the trip they might take together to the redwoods or the Sierra. "I'll run you down after, in the car," he gasped, lungs heaving.

"Thanks." The boy's thin, long torso rose and fell, slender and hooked like a fern, like the tiny, curled thing he had been inside his mother.

"When did you get so tall?" the father asked, grinning. "Considering you barely eat?"

He was going vegan too, Younger Brother had announced a week previous. It was the least they could all do, to cut the greenhouse gases.

"Can't you at least wait until you've stopped growing?" the mother said. "You really need protein for that."

"As if the 95 percent of humans who eat beans and rice don't get protein," Everychild cut in. "Animal protein is literally destroying this earth."

"Not if it's sustainably raised." Dad tried not to sound defensive.

"What'll it be next? That's what I want to know." Mom sighed. "Daily showers? Soap?"

"It's not a joke, even if you think it is," glowered Everychild, nicking their chin at their brother and stomping upstairs.

At night, in the marital bed, they discussed the situation.

"Since when are we public enemy number one?" Dad snorted.

"We just have to wait them out, I guess."

"It could be years."

They stared up, unblinking. They had thought it would get easier as the kids grew up.

"We made it this far."

"It'll be OK," they both said almost simultaneously. It had worked so far. Neither had grown up rich; they'd both worked hard. Somehow it would be OK.

By Christmas, they were down to one family dinner a week, and even that required negotiation.

"I don't have time," Everychild protested. "I'm really making progress."

"Yeah," Younger Brother chimed in. "We're almost done."

"With what?" Mom asked.

"We feed you," Dad pointed out.

Their eldest sighed, giving their brother a meaningful look. "Exactly. That's exactly what we want to talk about." Younger Brother tossed back his own veil of hair. "Indeed."

The clipboard appeared the next time they sat together at the dining room table. Everychild looked around at the wood paneling, the beveled window glass, as if they'd never seen the place before. Original Craftsman, solid oak, a jewel both parents prized, albeit for different reasons: Dad for the craftsmanship, Mom the guaranteed resale bump.

"So this is research," Everychild began. On the table was free-range chicken for the meat-eaters, tofu burgers for the vegans, avocado-and-heirloom-tomato salad, brown rice instead of white. A merlot from Napa, berries for dessert.

"You realize the meat producers lie," they began. "Clearing rainforest for animal feed, especially soy." They eyed their own soy burger. "You have to drill all the way down to be sure it's really carbon neutral and not built on slave labor or deforestation like 90 percent of the food you buy."

The father glanced at his wife. It really was the case that the kids were getting skinnier. "Life-cycle analysis," he responded.

"But no one counts the carbon cost. And there's no accountability. Cargill is the world's biggest supplier of ground beef, but you'd never know it was them destroying the Amazon if you buy it from Safeway or Costco or Giant. They hide behind a hundred labels. It's fucking insane."

"Language," automatically Mom said.

"So you need to answer some questions." Their child resembled a census-taker, glasses hanging at the tip of their nose. Their T-shirt—unbranded, beige—had not been washed in weeks. Their only adornment was a Celtic rune on one arm. Once, this child had been pretty, the mother fleetingly thought. She'd settle now for simply clean.

Swiftly the thrust of the interrogation became clear. Did they know how their electricity was generated? Why didn't they drive electric cars, or at the very least a hybrid? Where were their solar panels? How could they still be even answering "paper or plastic" at the grocery store?

"Do you consider yourself environmentally aware?" one question read. Dad looked at Mom, patience and smile wearing thin. "I'm not even going to tell you how much we donate to the Sierra Club and NRDC."

"So why do you still use a dryer?"

Mom felt the familiar low-grade anger rising in her throat. And who would be hanging out all those sopping clothes? "Maybe you can tell me why you both still use computers," she shot back.

"Spotify, Instagram. Can't have it both ways, honey." Dad might have thought his expression was rueful, but it just came off as smug.

"The point is—" Everychild paused, eyes seeking their brother's—"we know. We're working on dumping all that. I just don't see the same commitment from you guys."

Just that morning a carton of navel oranges had arrived by air freight from Costa Rica. The midmorning Amazon box contained Mom's new exercise top. Up and down their street in the eerie calm they all heard the near-constant stream of discreet beeps from the handheld devices of the deliverers, like some new species of birdsong rippling beneath the endless hours.

"We're doing what we can," said Dad.

"I don't really see that." Their daughter rose, nicking her—their—chin at their son.

"There's dessert—" Mom began, but Everychild was already halfway up the stairs.

"Berries. I saw. Flown in from Peru, no doubt." With that, their children turned and left them there.

It shouldn't have surprised them. When Everychild was young—seven or eight—she fairly glowed with rage at every injustice. "Remember," said the mother, picking at the offending blueberries, "how she would talk to every homeless person on the street?"

"There's a homeless!" Dad's smile was wistful as he mimicked their child's young, high voice. *"We have to help him! Give him some food, Dad, some money!"* They shook their heads. It was cute at that age, less so ten years later.

"They're going stir-crazy. I mean, who isn't?" Mom sighed. "I'm not surprised they're getting a little obsessed."

At least they had a tent now, to pitch outside when the particulates allowed. The tab on all their laptops was permanently open to the air quality site, though the murk had mostly dispersed. Mom rose to check it. Not red, but not green either.

"I know." She spun toward her husband. "Let's just get out of Dodge. Get on a plane to the Big Island, or Maui." Her face was shining. "They can do school from anywhere."

Instantly Dad pictured the long white beach, soft air, Caipirinha sweating in his hand. "Brilliant!" He laughed. "Even they can't refuse that." One thing they knew for sure: each of them adored Hawaii.

"It would be fun to surprise them with the tickets," said Mom.

"Bad, bad idea," said Dad. "How would you feel if nobody even consulted you?" The kids were too old for that. In a couple of months, Everychild would technically be an adult. They were, in essence, already an adult. This became immediately apparent at the next—and last—family dinner.

"You are out of your minds. Oh, my God," burst instantly from Everychild's thin lips when they floated the trip. Over the preceding weeks, their cheeks had hollowed so much that they seemed spectral. They leaped instantly from their seat, and for a moment Dad thought they might simply waft away. But their brother too was on his feet, holding his sister's spindly arm. On both their faces were looks of undiluted rage.

"You really don't give a rat's ass about the planet you've completely screwed over, do you?" Everychild's voice was controlled yet full of venom. "All that matters is your comfort, your A/C and leather interior, your little 'treats'—the CrossFit and flight and Airbnb and all that shit. You don't care if we have to live in a hellscape with unbreathable air, if our future is fucked, if the whole world is desert or flooded, if societies collapse and every species is destroyed, including us."

Everychild's eyes were the bright teal-white of a gas flame. Dad could feel the febrile heat from where he sat.

"There's no way we would get on a plane," their son added, as if this weren't crystal clear. It was almost endearing. But his face was blank, the blank of a teen who no longer cared to hear even another word from adult lips. *Don't trust anyone over thirty* chimed distantly in Dad's mind. He glanced at his wife, whose face was splotched red and white like a prime cut of beef, her hand clenching and unclenching her cloth napkin.

"I—" she began, but Everychild silenced her with a sharp flick of the hand.

"The mere fact you could even suggest it." Their lips curled. "Native people look forward seven generations, and you two can't manage even one."

"It's basically genocide." Their son was nodding. "Genocide against the earth and all succeeding generations."

"Now, wait a minute." It was as if they'd been held in a trance that only broke when their youngest spoke, so clearly parroting the words. But their children were no longer listening. They were gone, up the stairs, into the den, where the click of the lock was as loud as a shot.

"This has gone far enough." That night she left the light on, scrutinizing her husband.

"What do you want me to do?"

"Break the door down, for starters."

"Like that would solve anything."

Dad looked up at the ceiling, then back at his wife. He couldn't remember the last time they'd had sex.

"If you just hadn't suggested Hawaii."

"If *we* hadn't." Her nostrils flared.

Whose fault was it, actually? When or how had these children become so . . . rabid? Obscurely, each blamed the other.

"I just think we should talk to them more, listen harder to what they have to say."

"That presupposes they'll actually talk."

"I took him to shoot hoops. You could try with her." By mutual agreement they left the pronouns on the bedroom floor.

"She'll barely look at me, much less speak." There was an edge to Mom's voice—anger or despair, it was hard to tell.

"I didn't think it had gotten that bad."

"I'd hoped it would change when she got to college."

He sighed and reached to turn off the light. "That feels about as far away as Mars."

The next morning, the house wore an uneasy silence. Mom felt the disturbance the instant she awoke, the air uncannily still, like that orange dawn all those months ago.

"Wake up." Sharply, she elbowed Dad. "Something's wrong."

On the landing she knocked at each kid's door, then opened. No sign of either child. Kitchen, living room, yard. She spun from spot to spot. The silence yawned. She felt like she might throw up.

"Calm down." Her husband's voice was sharp, not at all consoling. "The den," they both said at the exact same moment before lurching back up the stairs. For the first time in weeks, the door was unlocked.

He turned the knob and pushed it open. The drapes were closed, and she shuffled in the dimness toward the drawstrings. There was something big, a large blob of some kind, in the center of the room. A mountain almost, she fuzzily thought, yanking to admit the morning light. Her husband stood there, mouth agape, as she turned, still scanning for her children. They were nowhere to be seen. Instead there was this—thing—this monstrosity, a giant plaster object at least eight feet tall, shaped like a cone, indeed a mountain—only upside down and balanced on its tip. The front part facing them was ripped away, like it had been blown off.

"What the fuck? Where the fuck did they go?" Her husband dashed back out and down the stairs, and she could hear him slamming doors and calling their names, moving again through each room: kitchen, living room, study, garage. She pictured each place joined to the next, her husband a furious blue dot in the diagram in her mind, while she stared intently at this object—this landscape—this blob that her children had apparently created in the secrecy of this room.

It was heavy, made out of some kind of plaster or dough, a huge cone reaching nearly to the ceiling. It halfway crushed the arms of two love-seats on which it sat, the tip just grazing the floor.

"Fuck." Her husband reappeared at the door. "The sleeping bags are gone. And the tent and the archery kit I just bought him."

"My God."

They swiveled to survey the thing. The inner core resembled an open pit, with horizontal striations running through it like different bands of rock. Yet cluttered—encrusted—with tiny figures and objects—plastic and metal dolls, cars, beads, bricks—all glued or stuck along the different bands. It reminded her of a photo she'd seen of an open gold mine in Brazil, the ant-like workers scuttling across the broken landscape. All at once she understood. "Her project. It's a model of some kind."

"A diorama." He saw a row of dolls, their faces drawn with snarls; a bunch of food made out of Play-Doh. Gray plastic bands, descending in concentric circles. Atop it was a flag, a label in their daughter's hand: *The Hell We've Made.*

"My God." He wiped his hands across his face and started counting. Nine circles. Nine. They were even labeled: LIMBO, LUST, GLUTTONY, etcetera.

"The Inferno."

The rings got smaller as they dropped. "Dante's fucking Inferno."

He'd read it a lifetime ago. For once, majoring in English had some practical payoff, he thought with a kind of hysteria. He glanced at his

214

wife. Her face was white. He too was shocked. But this was not all he felt: there was wonder, amazement, too.

Every single toy or figure or game piece they had ever given these children was affixed to this thing. Their entire childhood, 98 percent of it apparently plastic, trashed and slathered with some kind of goo and stuck somehow—along with a welter of plastic containers of every shape and size—to this inverted, sliced-open volcano.

He began to laugh. The circles—half-circles, really—were silver-gray with yellow stripes, two inches wide. "Hot Wheels." He reached out to touch one plastic track. "So that's what they've been doing. Holy shit. His goddam Hot Wheels."

"Jesus, Carl. This isn't *Project Runway*." Her eyes were wild.

"Cynthia. Calm down."

"*You* fucking calm down. It's not a joke."

"I never said it was a joke."

It was, in fact, in deadly earnest. That was the thing. He sank onto his haunches, peering more closely, shuffling forward until he was nearly inside the pit. Each level was covered with crap: shampoos and tooth-pastes and takeout containers, the toy farm, cows and pigs all maimed or mangled, tiny fans and paper flames and cut-out logos of all kinds, Safeway, Pornhub, Palmolive, Facebook, Nestlé. It was too much to take in. The sheer busyness and detail, the research, the painting and cut-ting and shredding. Overwhelming.

"Holy shit," he said again, for maybe the third or fourth time, and looked over at Cynthia and saw that she was crying.

"Honey," he said, but she jerked away and sat back with a thud. It was the dolls, undoubtedly, all those plump and fair-skinned Madame Al-exander dolls—with their creepy lifelike eyes, hugely expensive and dripping with lace and satin—now lined up, defaced with Sharpies, fangs and horns, each bearing a little label: Trump, McConnell, Bolso-naro. But no, this was not the particular circle of hell at which his wife pointed. He looked another ring down, to the level of his knees, to FRAUD, and there they were.

Two cardboard cutouts, Mom and Dad, their faces in the photos red and jolly—most likely drunk, cut from vacation snaps in Hawaii, Tahiti, the South of France. Cocktail umbrellas, fake leis, the little metal plane he'd brought back from some business trip. Mom's body wore a bra cut from her missing Lycra top; Dad held a selfie stick.

"They were there too," she choked out. "We took them too."

"Too young to know any different." He swallowed. It was the label, a subset of fraud, he guessed, that got her—and him too, if he was honest.

HYPOCRITES.

That's what the whole *Divine Comedy* was about, wasn't it? To skewer the falsely pious, reveal the hypocrisies of the Holy Roman Church? Tear away the masks so all could see the real depravity and waste, corruption running rife beneath the wealth and power of the princes in those days?

The lowest ring—the worst—was labeled TREACHERY, which Dante had reserved for the greatest of all traitors. Judas Iscariot, he remembered, and Cain, who slew his brother, Abel. They'd been frozen in an icy lake. Whereas their clever children had made this the very heart of the fire and placed here CEOs of the most rapacious of the corporations allowed to rampage through what was coyly called "late capitalism," the "late" denoting "last" or "decadent," "collapse of this particular civilization": Cargill, ExxonMobil, Amazon.

"I had no idea." Their mother sat limply, a husk. If a fire or flood or earthquake were to come, as they surely would, she'd simply melt or float away. How could she have been so clueless? Everything was empty, her mind, her house, her entire insane and frantic, pointless life.

"There's a note," she heard him say. He started to read it.

We tried to tell you. This is the only way to make you see.

He pictured their child again as a young girl, face crinkling and earnest. From his wife came an anguished sound. She was picturing them injured or dead, chained and trampled at some pipeline protest.

Collective action is the only hope. We know you mean well, but it's nowhere near enough. Even if we all did everything right, it wouldn't make a dent. They want us to think individual action will fix it. But you were right about that, Dad. It's a lie. We have to hold their feet to the fire, the politicians and the CEOs.
We'll take care of ourselves. We'll be in touch.
Love, Everychild.

He looked at Cynthia. Strange feelings coursed through him: fear and pride and love. She looked different too: less harried, stripped entirely bare. More like the woman he had married. He handed her the note, only then noticing the postscript.

Don't worry, their son had added in his loopy script. *We still have our phones.*

Nominated by The Missouri Review

LAKE QARUN JAN. 19, '22

by SARA ELKAMEL

from SUNDOG LIT

At the edge of the city, the dead sleep behind green doors the color of god.

The fence rises with the hills.

Drops of rain in the desert mistake themselves for sand, nick the windshield.

It is difficult to tell if the palms—brown, stout, inclined to the earth— are dying or young.

The years have salted the lake.

I came here to hide from darkness in light, its less honest sister.

Excrement lines the shore.

A crane wounded in the chest eyes the short-lived crests.

I look for green boats in the blinking water.

Four plastic chairs and a stool with frills are all one needs to make a house on the lake.

The tea smells of the small fire that brewed it.

I move the chairs out of their circle, wipe damp sand off each seat.

The hair swathing my face reminds me of the wind.

A small table—it must have been carpentered for a child—is turned over; who turned it over?

My sister's eyes have always been sensitive to salt and water.

She sutures them shut in every ocean.

The day of her wedding, the night dissolved the lake.

The dress she chose had 36 satin buttons, each the size of a warbler's eye.

It was my job to fasten each eye to its socket.

Her back was disappearing as mine—in the mid-May heat—was becoming a lake.

Nominated by Sundog Lit.

TRAVEL AGENCY

by KRYSTYNA DABROWSKA

from TIDELINE (Zephyr Press)

I'm a travel agency for the dead,
booking flights to the dreams of the living.
Famous celebrities, like Heraclitus, use me
to visit a writer who's in love with him,
but so do the lesser-known dead—like a farmer from Wasily village
wishing to advise his wife on matters of rabbit breeding.
Sometimes several generations of a family charter an airplane
and land on the brow of their final descendant.
I also have dealings with the murdered,
who on regular trips to the dreams of the survivors,
collect frequent flyer miles.
I never deny my services to anyone.
I find them the very best connections
and reproach myself when a young lover,
entering his girlfriend's dream,
must transfer through a snoring crone.
Or when weather conditions force an emergency landing
and the dead man calls out to me: do something,
I'm stuck in the dream of a terrified child!
Incidents like these mean stress and a challenge
for me, a minor business with major ambitions—
for though I have no access to the dead men's world
or to other people's dreams,
thanks to me they are in touch.

Translated by Antonia Lloyd-Jones

Nominated by Zephyr Press

LEENA

by TRIIN PAJA

from SALT HILL JOURNAL

for my great-great-grandmother

in a recording from 1973, you are 91—
your voice a leaf about to fall.

father takes you to school on a horse.
your children, asleep by an oven.

life, you say, is better. there is fruit now.
someone is calling you mother,

and your body, bettered with oranges,
responds, placing a broadleaf on a wound,

spilling bread for the cows. you do not speak
of Siberia, of *psikbusbkas*, you can water

the names of the dead. you can sell roses
in Leningrad. your farmhouse drifts

in a sea of fields but no earth, no earth for you.

I do not want to turn from the lined face
of this night, but the leaf of your voice

is rotting. Leena, I write because
it is less violent than speaking

but one is still burnt.

the light cracks open like an overripe apple
but no earth, no earth for you.

Nominated by Salt Hill Journal

WINTER FLAME

by EUGÉNIO DE ANDRADE

from FURROWS OF THIRST (Diálogos Books)

The flame. The lowly flame. And still
the flame. It comes from so far. From the simple
house upon the threshing floor.
the house where something little
pulsed: a heart,
the water in the big jug.
the wheat as it grew.
I was so small I didn't even know
how to ask for an orange.
a bit of bread.
Even less, a kiss.
It seemed I only knew
how to reach out my hands toward that low-lying
sun and towards the gaze
that protected it
from the enchantments of the flame.

Translated by Alexia Leuitin

Nominated by Diálogos Books

TWO BREATHS

by CHRISTINA RIVERA COGSWELL

from KENYON REVIEW

You would not believe in the existence of a manta ray until you've seen one. She's nearly a creature of mythology, with underwater arms that can span twentyish feet from tip to tip. The manta twists and turns by tilting the edges of her wings—her acrobatics accented by a dark dorsal topside and white-gilled underbelly. Her diamond frame and right-angled fins can encapsulate a three-thousand-pound mass so flat she might flash invisible when she turns vertical—like a nickel in a hand trick.

The mantas off the coast of Kailua-Kona congregate at night, when the bounty of planktonic creatures arises. So I organized a night boat. There were two options. My husband and I could snorkel at the top of the water, putting our masked faces under the sea's surface, looking for the tips of those steel wings peeking white and manifesting from darkness in our direction. Or we could don scuba tanks, weight belts, four-millimeter wet suits, and release the air from our diving vests and our lungs at the same time. Till there's no air left to buoy us, and our bodies sink to the sea floor.

This is where I find a nook among rocks to plant my knees.

Where we sway with sea fans—as we wait.

Down here, the waiting is quiet. There is the sound of my breath as I pull air from my tank. There is my exhalation, a knocking of air bubbles against each other like bamboo chimes. There is the scraping of a nocturnal creature's teeth on coral. Otherwise, it's black, and I am left mostly alone to the orbs of my thoughts.

My hand moves—as quickly as a hand can move underwater—for my husband's. He knows my quiet languages. He reads them in my eyes.

Even behind the scuba mask he proves this literacy as he returns my hand squeeze—a little stronger than normal. Because he, too, is wondering what's going on with me. I, after all, am the expert. I am the one with the divemaster certification and dozens of night dives sketched into my logbook. I organized this dive with the manta rays. It was my idea. My wish. So what are these hooves now trampling in my chest? I know anxiety. But the slow kind that accumulates like tumbleweed through the night and is brushed to the side of the road by the velocity of day. I don't recognize this mob in my heart—all at once—scanning for an exit. I look up. There's the surface of the ocean, only thirty feet above my head. I could take one breath of air from my tank and "slowly exhale and slowly kick" to the top and reach it just fine. I know this because it's one of the first diving tests I passed for my certifications. But there is danger. Equally silent and lethal danger. If I did not exhale as I made my "emergency swimming ascent," the air in my lungs would expand. And with nowhere to go, the air could break through the blood vessels in my lungs' tissues. The invisible pressure could rupture and collapse my lungs. Technically it's called "pneumothorax." Casually, it's called "burst lungs."

As I'm looking at the roof of the ocean, I'm thinking of this because I am thinking of what lives on the other side. This night dive is different from the last one I did with my husband, off a wooden Indonesian boat five years ago. The difference is my two small children, by now tucked into their beds by the babysitter. Two children who have no place even in their borderless imaginations to know their parents, tonight, are sitting on the floor of the ocean, swaying with sea fans, pointing flashlights at an underwater night sky of sparkling plankton.

Looking at the top of the water, I understand it is my distance from my children that makes my eyes wide enough to speak the quiet language of panic. Luckily, a scuba regulator functions much like a brown paper bag. I can hear my drag of air from the tank, see my exhalation in the rising bubbles. And I'm practiced at slow breathing. Especially underwater. In my dive-training months, on the occasions the divemasters could take the boat without clients, we would tumble into the water without briefings, maps, or dive tables. We'd take off our diving vests and turn them backward so as to "fly" underwater, with the tanks underneath us and our arms outstretched. And we'd play. Pulling a fin off a friend's foot, snapping another's mask, even turning off someone's tank as a prank. The playing wasn't always well received (especially by me), but it did make us all nimble for real emergencies. In those days,

I was the last diver up. I was small and not as involved in the air-guzzling tumbles. Rather, it was my instinct to use my unrestricted time to hover. To make myself as still as a sea fan and watch what revealed itself from the dark nooks of coral walls. And because being a sea fan requires very little air, I was able to stretch my tank into the longest, safest allowable dive. I am at home in the underwater world. After hundreds of dives, I did not expect to find this panic in it.

What was not my idea, my wish, was the new meaning of death upon the birth of my children. This was not mentioned in the shelf of motherhood books I read. No one told me about the heaviness. The blue whale weight of walking into the future with a baby on my hip and another child in Velcroed shoes holding my hand. About how the small bodies add gravity to life. From the ocean floor, looking up, I feel this pressure. And I am not the only warm-blooded mammal in the ocean tonight with this anxiety.

A sperm whale births her babe in the sunlight zone of the ocean. Close to the surface is where she nurses her infant for two or more years. But the fat in her milk comes from meals consumed two thousand feet below. In frigid, high-pressure depths, where her babe can't follow. So while the sperm whale mother is foraging, she leaves her child to the care of an orbiting pod of related females who babysit, sometimes even wet-nursing the babe themselves. A "mother culture" it's called by whale biologists. While mom is below, she is still in touch with her offspring, sending messages via sonar clicks. Mom typically stays in the depths, hunting, for about an hour. Unless she panics. Peter Matthiessen once documented a whaling ship's chase of a sperm whale. The whaler's sonar pinged the animal at a thousand feet deep as it tracked her panicked flight, waiting for her to run out of air and into the crosshairs of the harpooner above. Matthiessen noted of the sperm whale's ability to stay submerged: "[T]his time is rapidly decreased by panic."

I know the sperm whale's quick breath: The time I turned around at the pool and my three-year-old son was sinking in the deep end. My daughter's fall from a car seat teetering on the edge of a table. Five calls to poison control for the berries and plants and tubes of old medicines my toddlers put to their lips. Two swift Heimlich maneuvers. A broken arm. Midnight runs to the emergency room for spiking temperatures. My recurring nightmares in which climate disasters arrive.

Down in the high-pressure depths, with my body anchored by rocks and my husband's hand, I'm thinking about death. I do not ponder death as much as I did before I had children. I no longer have the time to meditate for two hours a day. I don't remember the dreams I used to prompt and record each night. I don't walk so close to cliffs of bodily risk anymore. Those were qualities of my prechild life. Of regular earth-gravity living. Of nights uninterrupted by monsters, wet sheets, and the chills of fever. Motherhood breaks linear time. Life becomes instead—punctuated. By the unwavering eye contact of a nursing babe. By a small body shuddering with relief against my chest. By my son's outstretched arm, pointing to the moon.

Swaying with the sea fans, my husband squeezes my hand again. He has read in my quiet language that I'm OK enough to be daydreaming. Or water-dreaming. Or whatever one calls the cartwheels of the waking human imagination at nighttime on the floor of the sea. He sees, too, that I'm looking at the ocean's surface in a funny way. I squeeze his hand back, and a beam of light swings like a car's headlights into the fog of plankton. It points at the flicker of faraway wing tips, and though a diver is never supposed to hold her breath, I have no choice.

Our first visiting manta ray—an entirely nonviolent creature of one and a half tons—swims toward us as her ancestors have been swimming for five million years. She flies into the center of the flashlights' illuminating the plankton of her midnight snack. Except night and day are not distinctions for those who live in swallowed light. Humans don't know if the manta ray sleeps. To the best knowledge of those who study her, she's a perpetually swimming thing. This manta now swoops in impossibly graceful loops in our light beams. I lean back. I would fall if the water did not hold me. *We are only guests*, I think. My sigh is captured in iridescent ovals, rising toward the ocean's top. Toward the land of my sleeping babies. Whom I have forgotten. Whom I can never forget. But whom I can hold even as I'm swaying with sea fans.

Long before I slipped into a black wet suit, off a boat, and into the cold coastal waters of Kailua-Kona, Native Hawaiians observed the manta ray with due respect. Roxanne Kapuaimohalaikalani Stewart, a Hawaiian cultural specialist, says, "The name of the manta—hahalua—can be interpreted as 'two breaths' . . . 'ha,' meaning breath, and 'lua,' meaning two. . . . When mantas leap [out of the water], their experience from below transcends into our sphere. . . . Their transcendence speaks to things that we don't yet know."

I flip this image—seeing myself in the eyes of the manta as a land animal of too many lanky appendages, anchored among rocks, submerged in her ocean's sphere of preexisting laws and spirit. We are of different worlds, and yet we share viscera. We both have a heart. A stomach.

Intestines. A gallbladder. Kidney. Liver. Uterus. Ovaries. Who would know the difference of our innards? And a brain! The manta has the largest brain of any fish, with developed areas for problem-solving, learning, communication, coordination, and intelligence. To the surprise of marine biologists, manta rays—in a "mirror test," widely used to gauge self-awareness—were able to recognize themselves.

I have forgotten my husband's hand. He has forgotten mine. Under the swooping manta, there's no room for anything but awe. My thoughts of my children are tucked away. Baby manta rays are born wrapped in their own wings like a blanket. There is a single set of images of a manta ray birthing in the wild. It was taken by Roberto Fabbri in the Red Sea in 1968. In the black-and-white series, a tidy bundle of wrapped manta bursts from its mother's body in a cloud of white. The photographer's caption—in tiny font—reads, "The manta ray was speared. . . . [I]t represented a big trophy." And if you squint at the photo of the mother midlabor, you can see the man's murky outline in the shadow just behind her. You can see the long white glint of his metal speargun. He stands waiting, a few feet from her arching, birthing body. A few feet from her eyes.

Two breaths.

Female manta rays are pregnant for thirteen months. For the ten months I carried each of my children, I had two hearts, two brains, four ears, four legs, four eyes. My children came out of my body, and I was back to two legs, but not one heart. I know this because when my child's seashell ear is on my chest, my heart speeds up and theirs slows down. Female mantas might birth only one pup every three years. Their populations have a "low likelihood of recovery," yet in 2022 they are still harpooned, pulled from their home and scraped alive of their gill rakers for fabled Chinese "medicines." Humans may not even notice their extinction. Whales were native to this planet forty-nine million years before humans arrived, and yet man, in less than a hundred years, disappeared three million whales—like a nickel in a hand trick.

Herman Melville in *Moby Dick* (drawn from Melville's experiences aboard whalers) wrote of the sperm whale's mammary glands, "When by chance these precious parts in a nursing whale are cut by the hunter's lance, the mother's pouring milk and blood rivallingly discolor the sea for rods."

In a sperm whale's fourteen tons of warm-blooded body, her blood is blue like mine. Red like mine when exposed to the oxygen in air or water. Her blood spills when her calf is born. Her blood leaks brown in the blue wake of her afterbirth, the way mine trailed on the linoleum floor between my hospital bed and the bathroom. Her milk may be flavored by squid the way mine is by garlic. Milk that drops in my breast by an ancestral song of DNA. A dropping of milk that feels like the cracking of ice, the crunch of snow. "Man" does not know this reflex. But I do. And if you call my empathy "feminine," that is my point. "Man" harpooned and dragged thirty-ton bodies onto boat decks until the oceans nearly went silent of humpback song. Man thought that if he could kill it, he could own it. He spread the red viscera of warm bodies but recognized none of it in himself. Man looked into the mirror and saw *only* himself.

My husband and I ascend from the dive. We strip off our wet suits in the dark. Shiver in the cold of night. Towel off our transcendence from the womb of water.

At home, I check on the children. I pull a blanket over the exposed limbs of my son. Tuck a pink bear under the arm of my daughter. Turn around with my lungs so full of hope they might burst. Knowing my tumbleweed of anxiety will not evade the velocity of day. That my children, tucked under covers, will face the consequences of all man's great failures of compassion and care. Holding my breath for a mother culture I can feel—but can't see.

I close their door, careful not to make a sound, still swaying with the sea fans under the silent and lethal weight of it all.

Nominated by Allen Gee, Ron Tanner

IT IS ONCE AGAIN THE SEA OF CORN

by ONYEKACHI ILOH

from QUARTERLY WEST

and women in clothes the colours of flame
roast corn on open fires all over this city

the bus drivers, the policemen with rusting rifles,
and the iron-benders with biceps like seas

not fully awake, all hold cobs to their mouths
turning them this way and that, the turnings

marked by the disappearance of the kernels
the bright afternoon casts an orange glow

on everything - the roof of the trucks lining the road
like sleeping centipedes, the umbrellas gently nodding

like a flag oblivious of its countrymen's brandishing
of blades at one another, the policemen's black and fading

uniforms remain unchanged, and I want to pray all the corn held
to every mouth in this city of dust and hills into harmonicas

let all the rifles become violins, and the trucks, organs
pipes raised in the praise of the amphitheatre's dancing lights

the women and their fires, I pray into cherubs
let their *adire* scarves morph into flaming halos

and their iron grilles into aeolian lyres, unneeding the labour
   of fingers
Lord, grant me this prayer, every line of it

I know I have asked for ridiculous things in time past
I have sat on the banks of a river, watched diving boys

and asked for a man like Biko, I have lamented the locust season
and prayed for a man like Sankara, for a man like Mandela

Lord, I have asked for men,
now send me an orchestra.

Nominated by Quarterly West

THE MAGICIAN'S ASSISTANT

by **KELSEY BRYAN-ZWICK**

from HERE GO THE KNIVES (Moon Tide Press)

Sews herself back up every night, backstage, after
the show, after the spell's worn off, the makeup and
glitter, the stage lights dimmed, she sits at her mirror
bent over her own figure, needle pulling thread.

The operation as routine as square knots, she will
stand, rub blood out of wound, take a plug of whisky,
and a pull off something often unmentioned.
Smoke spiraling as she readies herself

to sharpen the saw, to clean and oil the toothed
edge—glistening. She prepares for tomorrow's show
where a new room full of strangers will gather—
gasp, open mouthed.

In suspense, half believing, half not, as the magician
cleaves her in two, the applause is for his miracle
and not hers—though it is her body they watch, her body
they imagine long after the popcorn has gone stale.

Nominated by Moon Tide Press

TOMORROWS

fiction by LAKIESHA CARR

from THE PARIS REVIEW

The night, as most nights, was like a dream.

At ten, once I'd fed the dog the last scraps off the stove. Once I'd cursed the cat for scratching up my mama's antique furniture, then welcomed him back into my arms. Once I'd slicked my hair into a ponytail, wrapping it up tight in my mama's old, old scarf. Once I'd stayed in the bathtub a lil' too long, letting the heat of the water do things my husband stopped doing years ago. Once I'd oiled myself down and up and down again with cocoa butter and reached for my housecoat hanging against the door—leopard print and silk—wrapping it around my bloated body, not caring if the water and oil bled through.

Then, soundlessly, I floated out to the garage and had a cigarette alone.

Mostly I listened to the blues. Lightnin' Hopkins. Bessie Smith. Bobby Womack, if my mama was heavy on my mind, which was most nights. I nursed a lil' Crown Royal poured thin over crushed ice. I smoked my Virginia Slims, pulling that cool menthol taste to the back of my throat before pushing it out—a thick plume.

Creating that smoke is what I liked to do. I let my thoughts drift and curl before tapering out. My daddy used to tell his congregation that life was like a vapor—here today and gone tomorrow—and so they best get right with the Lord soon. As I sat watching the smoke blossom, growing and weakening again, I couldn't help thinking, There goes my life. I took another long pull, watched the ash stiffen then drop to the concrete floor, and thought, There it goes again.

If I became tipsy, I might sing. Not because I could, but just 'cause sometimes I only felt happy when listening to the blues. Until I changed the record player to something electronic, full of shock and wonder. The funk. That beat that lifted me up somewhere heavenly, then gently delivered me back to earth.

After that I walked up to my boudoir, the most beautiful space in my whole house, decked out with zebra and lion prints. There I stood before the mirror nude. There I took in the soft flaps of brown skin that folded upon one another in stacks around the middle of my body. I examined the fine lines and deep ridges carved into my face, my eyes that were gradually dimming with age, my crown of hair growing thin, those smooth and soft bald spots along its edges. Needless to say, I was lonely. But comforted by the burn of whiskey in my belly, I took in the absoluteness of my womanhood and somehow I still felt desirable.

Sometimes, in the quietness just before dawn, I felt hopeful. Then the faint sounds of my husband's snoring across the hall made their way into my room, and I was left with fatigue. So it was then that I went to bed, a mess of cheetah-spotted down comforters and black cotton sheets. I slipped under the covers, grateful for the coolness of the fabric against my skin. And I watched my stories: *The Young and the Restless, The Bold and the Beautiful, General Hospital. CSI, NCIS,* and any other crime drama where dead bodies the color of milk wound up in unusual places and cold white people with grim faces sought to find the causes of their demise.

The hours passed. And just as the sun revealed itself in orderly fashion, and the sound of school buses rumbled through the neighborhood, and the bickering of children seeped through the thin windowpane, I pulled the covers over my head and shut my eyes tight, willing sleep to come until it finally obeyed.

This was the night. Not so special. But always consistent.

When my phone rang at ten thirty it was my client Diamond, calling to tell me she'd be late for her appointment. Not a surprise. Still, I acted impatient: "Girl, can't you ever be on time?"

To which Diamond only said, "Now, I wouldn't be me if I was on time, right?" Then she laughed, high-pitched and girlish in that way that made you love her even if you barely knew her.

"Nah, I don't suppose so," I said, relieved that I'd have time to wash my face, dress, even have a cup of coffee and sober up before she got here. Late, for Diamond, could mean two to three hours, and while that should and would piss off the average person, I was grateful. Not only had I overslept but Diamond's tardiness meant I could charge a late fee. Not to mention, she was my one client for the day.

"I'll see you when you get here," I said, and rose out of bed, closing the phone. Time to start the day. A new day of the same old thing.

Now, if anyone asked, with a lil' liquor in my system I might tell you very easily:

Who do Diamond be? Shit, I've asked myself continually. She big and brown as I is. Thick in places where she ought not be, thus she comes for her colonic regularly and I be like—Shit, get it all, girl! Lymphatic drain. Reflexology for dem feet. Lean back and relax, set them parasites free! Digestive system harboring the disease—with this cleansing we do harmonize your inner chemistry. Get your body on point. And she be like, Yeah, yeah, do that! Whatever it costs I'll pay. Pass some of this gas and make my belly go flat. Drop least five pounds every time I climb up on your table and my man like it that way. Flat belly, full ass. Black men don't ever change. You know the game! And I be like, True true. That'll be sixty today.

She pretty short, no more than five three, always wearing them high heels. She got a broad nose that makes it seem like she can smell everything, though she tries to minimize its size with MAC makeup that's a bit too light for her complexion. She got them black eyes, what they call dark, dark brown but really they look black, and honestly I feel that should be okay but don't nobody else seem to agree. Sometimes she comes in here with green or blue contacts and I be like, Damn, Diamond! You shining, girl!

She used to be a dancer but now she got three kids—ages five, eight, and eleven. And I'm always shocked to remember this because she looks no more than twenty-one herself. Once I asked her as I was warming the water, on a rare day she'd arrived early and caught me unprepared, "Diamond, how old are you chile?" I'm so much older and fortunately age allows us to be rude—what my mama called "to the point." Diamond laughed, tugging down her black leggings and reaching for the yellow terry-cloth robe I give all my clients.

"Why you ask that, Miss Nettie?" And with that I knew she had to have been older than I ever figured her for.

"Girl, you come in here not lookin' a day over nineteen! I have to ask." I tried to laugh all high-pitched like she does, but years of nicotine wouldn't let my voice climb that far. Still, she told me with a sheepish smile that she was twenty-seven.

235

"Oh, okay," I said. "That's a good number."

"Is it?" she asked, scooting her bottom to the end of the table.

I removed the plastic tube from its wrapping and felt for the entryway. Softly, gently, I inserted the nozzle, keeping my eyes focused on her face. "Relax," I said, more out of habit than necessity. "Twenty-seven is a good number."

It was 1:15 when Diamond finally arrived, and she was her usual chipper self. As she settled on the table, she told me again about the thin scar running alongside her left ear, from broken glass flying during a fight years ago at Baby Dolls, a strip club in Atlanta where she once worked. All the women there wore wigs and weaves that stretched down their backs. Young girls still, but already they had scars that showed under the lights even with heavy makeup on: bullet holes in their upper thighs and pelvic regions, cuts on their faces and arms. Nothing like no baby doll I ever had or would have wanted. But Diamond said the club was good to her. She made close to a thousand dollars a week, which was extremely good money in Georgia.

She told me this while her impurities floated by in the aquarium-size septic tank where clients could see the progress of their colon cleansing. "I was seventeen, but my friend had managed to get me a fake ID. Not that I needed it. The younger you looked the better. The younger you actually was, even mo' better."

"Damn shame," I said, sucking my teeth but careful not to let my face show judgment.

"I danced there for three years, until I met Rodney."

I realized I'd never asked her if Diamond was her stage name. Without so much as batting an eye she said, "Oh no. My mama named me Diamond. My dance name was Princess Cut. But everyone just called me Princess."

"Why Princess *Cut*?"

"So everybody would know I didn't play."

And we laughed and laughed and laughed until she farted hard enough to blow small waves of bubbles throughout the tank. Then we only laughed more.

Rodney was her baby daddy and eventually her husband, almost ten years and three kids later. They married at the justice of the peace a year ago and Diamond came in for a colonic to look extra good for her wedding day. I did it half price as a wedding gift and she invited me to the courthouse to witness the act. I told her I'd come but I overslept, even though the ceremony wasn't until two. Such is the life of a woman who doesn't sleep.

I listened to Diamond talk while the inside of her body told its own tales. I rubbed her feet down with cocoa butter, then gently extracted the tube from her bottom in one quick move. Wrapping it in a paper towel while she spoke with her eyes now closed, I threw it in the trash can, and smiled though she couldn't see me.

Patting her twice against her leg, I said, "We're finished, baby. You can sit up now."

After giving her a mixed drink rich with vitamins meant to replenish her electrolytes, I walked her to the door, laughing though I was distracted thinking of the ways I intended to spend the soft twenty-dollar bills she'd crushed into my hand.

"Diamond, you take care of yourself, baby."

I stood, letting the weight of my body fall against the doorframe, and watched her wobbling to her car on orange stilettos.

"I will, Miss Nettie!" Her two-tone face was flushed with the effects of purification, glowing like I imagined her seventeen-year-old self might have. In the afternoon sun she appeared a baby doll. My baby doll.

She looked back and smiled, a gold tooth in the middle of her mouth catching the light. As she drove away, she honked her horn twice.

After I closed the door I breathed a sigh. Then I grabbed my keys.

It was 2:45. Time to go play my match.

At 2:47, I sat in my car, a red '98 two-door Lexus with sorority plates and cheetah-print dice hanging from the rearview mirror. I looked at my gas tank. Watched the arrow refuse to rise above *E*, the tiny gas light in all its bright yellow glory. Realized I'd already been driving on *E* for at least two days.

Shit.

At three I started the long walk up and out of my neighborhood, my shadow thick and black against the sidewalk. I told myself I was getting exercise. I even walked as though that was my intention, eyes to the ground with short glances at the sky.

I wasn't ashamed. This was not the first time I'd had to walk, crossing several streets before reaching the main drag, the concrete artery that would take me two miles straight to the Little Taco, a convenience store slash gas station slash taco hut slash—shhh—game room.

At 3:35 I walked in only slightly sweating, my body having reached a point of cooperation. Raud said hello without smiling. The store was musty and quiet, save for Fleetwood Mac's "Little Lies." And as if on cue, I acted as though I was going to buy something other than more cigarettes.

This was the dance. The part where I glided down the aisles looking at old peanuts and candy bars, bottles of juice and soda with expiration dates that passed long ago. A dusty flashlight that likely didn't work, a single nail file wrapped in plastic that'd been opened already, just visibly so at the corner of the packaging. Glass jars of sour pickles floating in what looked like swamps. The worst kinda algae green.

I made eye contact twice with Raud, who stood there all brown and long like beef jerky, looking far too serious for his age, which I estimated as no more than twenty. I was always guessing ages. I'd noticed Raud only truly looked at me, with a sort of bewilderment and softness, on rainy days when I walked in soaked as a steeped tea bag. One of those times, I'd smiled with embarrassment and he'd smiled back, with the most perfect teeth and a small tilt of his head. Like he remembered that despite the circumstances, I was his elder and thus due a certain amount of respect.

When I reached the counter he said, "The usual?" And I replied, "Yes."

He stooped down and popped back up with my Virginia Slims. Menthol. 120s. Silver stripe.

"One or two?" he asked.

"One," I said, thinking about the gas. And then, without making eye contact, I said, "So what's goin' on back yonder?"

"It's quiet. Not much flashing."

Now, Raud knew this encouraged me. He knew that fewer jackpots throughout the day only increased my chances. When I was lucky. And today I felt lucky. My right hand had started itching in the night, sometime between *The Bold and The Beautiful* and *General Hospital*.

"I guess I'll go see how Miss Bertha doin' back there."

That was my code, playing it off as if I was only there to check on Miss Bertha, an older lady who walked over from the housing projects at the opposite end of town. Raud accepted it every time with a courteous nod toward the back door. Grabbing my cigarettes, I concluded our dance.

Now, when I couldn't make it east on I-35 toward Oklahoma to the Choctaw reservation casinos or even farther east on I-20 to the Louisiana casino boats, the game rooms were the best alternative. Ever moving, ever changing, you had to be in the know to find out where they were. Once the cops busted a joint, it was a wrap until the operation regrouped and relocated.

But the game room at the Little Taco had become a special place, my second home, though it was shoebox-size, dim, smoky, and blank except for the pulsing energy of win, win, double red, double purple— jackpot! You could hit as much as $2,000, good money for any room. And Miss Bertha had actually become a highlight of my day.

She was sitting there on the barstool nothing but bones and rotten teeth, yet she still smiled, real welcoming. I'd never seen her without some kinda loopy grin, whether she was winning or losing. And best believe she had plenty reasons to frown. I admired her stamina. Had come to love her since we met years ago at the game room inside the old neighborhood rib joint. For my birthdays she always made me a pecan pie, said if I shelled the pecans she didn't mind doing the rest.

She was up, clutching thirty dollars in her bony fingers, pressing the green play button like a drum, her left knee shaking ever so slightly as she played. I stood behind her and gently placed my hands over her eyes. "Surprise!" I whispered. "Who you think it is?"

"Girl, if you don't stop playing!" She rocked her lean body side to side with a grin. "Can't you see I'm winnin'?" The highest jackpots came in royal shades and her terminal was flashing a purple $245 at the top of the screen.

"Look," she said, pulling two crisp hundred-dollar bills from her skirt pocket. "Mama been lucky today!" Her breath smelled of brown liquor.

"Dang, Miss Bertha!" I clutched at her money as though I meant to take it—she and I both knowing I didn't. "Gimme some of that!"

She laughed.

"Go on now, girl, before you mess up my concentration. Your machine is free!"

There against the wall behind us my old faithful stood vacant, waiting on me, the barstool with its black pleather busted open like split fruit.

Delilah, the clerk who doled out cheap wines, beers, and whiskey, walked through, and I stopped her with a smile and drawled, long and slow, "Heeeey, Dee!" Dee smiled and winked before disappearing back into the storeroom where they kept drinks and cash for the machines. She returned with my usual drink, Crown Royal with a splash of Coke.

"Thanks, baby girl," I said, relieving her of the cocktail, careful not to spill.

"How you doing today, baby?" She held her tray against her wide hips, popping her gum. Every time I heard the soft pop, pop, pop between her teeth I thought of what my grandma used to say: when you could pop gum like that it meant you had cavities.

"I'm good," I said, sliding a twenty-dollar bill inside the machine's opening.

"Good, good," she replied, rubbing my shoulder. Dee was a white girl who made you forget it. A Tennessee native, she had skull tattoos dotting her arms and she occasionally showed up with nasty bruises that turned a sickly yellow. It was no secret that her man fought on her, but we all knew she fought him back. Some days she'd crack open a Bud Light and laugh, saying, "You shoulda seen him." And we believed her.

My eyes were fixed on the screen, body tense and focused on the win. Never mind paying attention to Alvin, the crippled Vietnam vet sitting next to me, who reeked of marijuana and rubbing alcohol. On his other side was Floyd, a real cool cat in dark tortoiseshell glasses and a brown trench coat he tucked his plump shape into no matter the weather. Floyd was known for hitting $500 or more on any given day. He won so often that everyone watched him, trying to decipher his tricks. He didn't drink when he played, though Alvin often tried tempting him with E&J or a beer. Alvin brought his own, pulling a silver canister from the inside of his worn Army-green jacket embroidered with military patches. 1969.1971.1973. A timeline only he understood.

I began my ritual chant: double-double orange, double-double purple. C'mon. Gimme something. Anything.

Here in the back, the music was different. Al Green sang "Tired of Being Alone," and Alvin was singing as though he could sing. Scratchy voice, rough yet sweet. Sweeter still the more I drank. Forty dollars in and I was rolling purple sevens, just enough to keep me playing.

By the time Dee returned with my third drink, I was tipsy and singing "Cheaper to Keep Her." After hitting a double orange that briefly saw me up by $150, I was down to my last $20. I didn't care. Across the way, Miss Bertha swayed with a slight bop to my crooning and another woman I'd seen only a few times—skinny as can be and caramel-colored, hair piled high upon her head like a basket—started snapping her fingers. Her multicolored artificial nails were tipped with pink hearts. "Heeeey, hey!" she called, and I could tell she was feeling it, too. In her other hand, she held what had to have been her fifth beer of the afternoon. She stood beside Juan, a Mexican man who wore a black cowboy hat and brown Stetson boots. He was playing his game with one hand;

his other arm was around her waist. The louder I sang, the more she popped her skinny fingers and cried out, "Sing it, sistah!" I liked her immediately.

Alvin walked up and rested his salt-and-pepper beard against my shoulder. "All right, gal," he said. "Don't you imagine you oughta get while the gettin' is good?" To which I snapped my fingers, too, and wrapped an arm around his waist. Inside my own groove, like over in the midnight hours when the combination of music and alcohol gave me some relief, some escape from my body.

"Leave her alone!" Floyd called. "Can't you see she feelin' it? She gone, man. Let her be!"

"Yeah, get away from her, Alvin!" Miss Bertha said. "Don't you know a yella nigga bad luck?" As she walked the three, maybe four steps over to us, she almost tripped over her own feet before catching Alvin's arm.

Giggling, she said in my ear, still loud enough for Alvin to hear, "Told you a yella nigga ain't shit!" I grinned and removed my arm from Alvin's waist and placed it tightly around hers.

"You know it's cheaper to keep her," I sang, truly happy now.

"Aw, now, Bertha, don't start that shit with me today!" Alvin said.

"Say, Floyd!" yelled Bertha, "Tell Miss Nettie over here how a yella nigga won't do shit but take ya money and bring you bad luck."

"My name Emmitt and I ain't in it," he called back, not once removing his eyes from his game.

"Now, Miss Bertha, you know Floyd too close to that nigga-red color to agree with you," Alvin said, laughing.

"Aw, hush up, Alvin!" Miss Bertha said. "It ain't no fun if you agree with me."

"Well, I knows I ain't no bad luck," Alvin said. "My mama didn't make no such thing."

"Well, anyhow," Miss Bertha replied, "I don't suppose yo' ass would recognize it if you was."

"Now, Bertha," he said, growing serious. "You know you wrong. How would you feel if I called you a dark—?"

Alvin trailed off as the machines went quiet. No one moved or seemed to breathe until Miss Bertha, blacker than the darkest moonless night, turned her head slowly, slowly, slowly with the sorta drama only a classic Hollywood director could fully appreciate, and faced him straight on.

We watched her full lips turn up into a smile, and it was like the universe resumed motion, molecules vibrating—bouncing faster and faster still.

"Nigga," she said, "You ever call me even anything like that and those'll be the last words your Black ass utters on God's green earth."

The room erupted in laughter—tension built and tore down within a span of seconds. The music came back up and Alvin said, "Oh, now I'm Black, huh? I got to damn near insult you to be considered Black, huh?" Miss Bertha only laughed and said, "Well, hell, we all Black in the dark."

Dee handed Alvin a Coors Light, sweating through the thin paper towel. He took a long swig and began to dance between the machines, their lights strobing like a disco ball.

"I ain't got time for none of you," he said, doing a lil' two-step, jutting his one good leg out to the beat. "I served my time for this country," he continued, closing his eyes and settling into his groove. "And I was lucky enough to make it back. Shit, I'm a Black man. I'm lucky to be alive at all! I'm a man, baby. The realest kinda man you'll prolly ever meet!"

I stood up and took his yellow hand in my brown one, and fell into step with his rhythm. So happy in the late afternoon with my game-room family. And as Alvin reached around my back, let his hands wander down, and grabbed my ass like it belonged to him, I only said, "Of course you are, Alvin! Of course you are."

The sound of school bells went off and I heard Floyd yell, "Yes! Yessir! Double-double purple, baby! Jackpot, baby! How you like me now!" The lights cast a neon glow upon his smiling face.

"Don't tell me that joker done did it again! Hot damn!" Alvin said, holding me close and smelling heavy with smoke.

"Hell yeah, I did it!" Floyd said. "Drinks for everybody on me!"

Juan stood up, releasing his lady friend, and went to peer at Floyd's machine. He was almost a whole three inches shorter than Floyd, and thin inside his red button-up and his starched denim jeans. His fingers were looped inside a belt with the head of an Aztec warrior on its over-size buckle (I knew because it read AZTEC WARRIOR in silver lettering underneath). Juan nodded and said, "You did good. But, my friend, you know drinks here are free."

Floyd was dancing now, holding his trench coat open as though he intended to flash somebody, revealing only a plain old purple cotton sweat suit. I couldn't help thinking he looked like Barney, the kid's show dinosaur who loved me, who loved you, who loved the world!

"Go 'head, Floyd," I called, stomping my foot and spilling the last bit of watered-down drink in my cup.

"Well, hell, I'll get everybody ten dollars toward some gas. Only unleaded though, none of that fancy shit. Go 'head! Line 'em up outdoors! I'm good for it."

I sobered up real quick at that, remembering my car sitting at home on *E. Shit!*

"Ain't no gas right now," Dee said from her corner. "We out right now. Waiting on the refill."

"Shit, me too!" the caramel-colored lady said, tossing an empty bottle into the nearest trash can.

"Okay, okay," Floyd said, undeterred. "What do y'all got?"

"Tacos," Dee replied, handing the caramel woman a fresh beer.

"Oh, hell nah!" Miss Bertha hollered. She spun around on her chair like her booty had a swivel on it. "Them thangs got too much salt and grease—run my pressure up!"

"I'll take a taco!" I said.

"Me too," said Juan.

"Me too," said Alvin, scratching at his balls and finishing the last of his drink.

"I like dem thangs," said the caramel chick. "Tha's how I make mines."

"All right! Tacos for everyone!" Dee called and headed toward the kitchen.

"All y'all must have a death wish!" Miss Bertha said, sucking her teeth, but Alvin reached out and pulled her to his chest. They stayed in a close slow dance to B. B. King until the food came.

We ate as a group, dripping hot sauce and grease down our chins and on the floor and on the machines. Drinking more liquor until everyone was good and full. By the time I stumbled out it was after seven and Raud had been replaced by Amir.

"See you tomorrow, Miss Nettie!" he said, plucking at his cash register. "Be careful out there!"

There was no pretense with Amir, a teenage boy with a clumsy way of being in the world. No dance. With Amir it just was what it was, and he seemed to make no judgments.

"Bye, baby," I called back. "See you tomorrow if the sun shine and the creek don't rise!"

"What?" Amir said. The sound of his laughing carried me back out onto the street.

The night air was cool on my face. I watched my shadow move again as I made my way home under the streetlights, in and out of darkness, imagining the headlights behind me casting a kind of aura around my body. I felt powerful. The taste of onion and cilantro was still heavy on my tongue. When I hiccuped, I smelled garlic on my breath and was satisfied at least that it covered the Crown Royal.

I was counting the cracks in the sidewalk, thinking about each dollar I'd lost and not giving one damn, when a car full of white boys pulled up alongside me, a red four-door Nissan, the red I liked most, like a candied apple. Their faces were a translucent blur, smoke weaving its way around them. The marijuana was strong and good. Not like the dirt my husband smoked. My cell phone was vibrating long and hard through the canvas of my purse, and I answered it as I continued walking. The car was crawling along the curbside.

"Hey now!"

"Hey yaself!" It was my best friend, Peaches. "Where you at? I been calling you since three this afternoon."

One of the boys in the back seat rolled down the passenger-side window and stuck out his head, blossoming with soft blond curls. He was motioning for my attention.

"I'm headed home from the grocery store. I had five clients today and barely had a minute to eat, chile. I'm 'bout to go in the house now and fix Ernest something and try to get off these feet."

I kept my eyes forward, made the white boys follow me to where the next streetlight shone yellow against the pavement.

"Sounds like you walking now," Peaches said, and I could hear the confusion in her voice.

"I am, girl! Tryin' to get these groceries in the house." I stopped and tried to muster up a laugh that sounded authentic. But I was sure Peaches wouldn't question me. She was the kinda friend who wouldn't join you in your shenanigans but also wouldn't snitch. She was always quiet about these things.

I liked to think it was because of how we grew up, that country upbringing where little Black kids saw everything but said nothing. Children were seen but not heard, and so we never learned to speak, especially when it mattered. Sure, occasionally someone might lean back in their chair over drinks or a big meal, someone might cock their head to one side during the card game, someone might move the dominoes about on the table and say, "You 'memba how dem white kids chased me from school all the way downtown and beat my ass in the square? Not a single soul helped me."

Or, "Hey, y'all 'memba when the Black school played against Robert E. Lee, and before the second quarter even started dem boys was knockin' heads tryin' to kill each other? 'Memba how the folks ran out the stands and we was all scrappin'?"

Or, "Y'all 'memba how Aunt Baby's boy got shot up by the police over on First Street in front of the Baptist church? Always told that lil' nigga to stay off First Street after dark."

And then inevitably someone would laugh in response and say, "Hell yeah! How could we forget?" Then someone would say we shouldn't have integrated. Integration was a mistake. To which someone else would say, "Hell yeah it was! We lost our schools. We lost our teachers. We lost our culture!" And everyone would mostly agree except for that one fat Negro in the back, the one who always got the cards and the dominoes greasy whenever he played; he'd pipe in on a contrary note with, "Shiiiiiit, say what you wanna say. Dem white folks was good to me." To which we'd all say, "Nigga, tha's 'cause you played ball!"

The simple truth was, Peaches and I were the generation that watched our parents get beaten down struggling for civil rights, though I never heard my mama speak about that violence. We were the integrators and assimilators who didn't speak up, the nine-to-fivers working jobs like the one I held on to so long at the county courthouse before starting my colonics business. Hanging on twenty years plus to some sweet dream that said after going to work sick, tore down, doped up, depressed, stressed, and angry all the damn time, we might still get a little freedom at the end of it, a little time to go sit down and rest and reap some of whatever we'd sowed. That real American dream that said we could send our kids to school and raise them to have better than us by knowing better than us.

And they did know better—enough to notice that slaving for the right job or house or shiny red Lexus hadn't gotten any of us a whole lot more protection than my mama had. Peaches's daughter, Ketinah, didn't want to be like us. I knew better too by now, although I had no offspring to pass this knowing on to. No matter how hard we worked there was no such destination. Peaches knew it too, though you could count on her not to say as much.

All this shit was an awful game.

The white boy was hissing at me now. Psst. Psst. His face was the kind of warm, pink-red I'd come to associate with young white men over the years, the kind that used to scare me. The only red I didn't like.

"Yeah, Peaches, so, let me call you back when I get settled in the house." I reached down into my purse. I'd left home without my pepper spray.

"Yeah, okay, girl," Peaches said, and I could hear her worry. "Call me before you have your last one." We always had a cigarette together before she went to bed. I closed my phone, my other hand tight around a pencil with a sharp tip.

"What y'all need?" I hollered.

"Can you tell us how to get to Toliver Street from here?"

Under the light the boy looked small and stoned, his eyes as bloodshot as my own. A bass line thumped out of the car, too fast and hollow to be worth a damn. The other young men stared straight ahead, and it dawned on me that they were nervous. My strength returned.

"What kinda business y'all got over on Toliver?" I asked, even though I knew the business well. Someone at the game room had a house on Toliver, a stretch known for white shit. Cocaine. Heroin. Ecstasy. Name it.

"We're just going to see a friend," he said.

"Mm-hmm," I said. "Keep going straight. When you see the liquor store on the right, start looking for Toliver. If you see Popeyes you know you went too far."

"Gotcha." He grinned. Seeing his teeth, I couldn't help thinking, Now I know he got enough money to get them thangs cleaned. "Hey, can we give you something for your trouble?" he said, still grinning. He couldn't have been more than sixteen.

"Gimme something like what?" I took a step closer and tipped on my toes to peer into the car. "Whatchu got?"

I only had five raggedy dollar bills in my pocketbook, one of them held together by a thin strip of Scotch tape with the words YOU NEED JESUS written along one side.

"Come and see," he said, mischief in his blue eyes.

"Aw, hell nah . . ." I started, but before I could finish a voice yelled, "You a'ight, Miss Nettie?"

Across the way I saw Melvin, one of the neighborhood drunks, in his brown Dickies and a dingy white wifebeater under an old leather jacket. His malt liquor was in a brown paper bag in one hand, his rainbow-striped walking stick in the other.

"That you, Melvin?" I called.

"That me!"

"I'm good, baby!" I hollered back. "These boys done got turned around and I was just straightening 'em out. Ain't that right?" I said, nodding at the blond and picking up his grin where he'd dropped it.

"You sure, baby? 'Cause I got my stick!" Melvin stood erect and raised his cane in the air. It glittered under the streetlight. He looked maniacal.

"Fuck this!" the boy in the driver's seat said, pressing down on the accelerator.

As soon as I could see nothing more than their taillights, I burst out laughing.

"Good lookin' out, Melvin!"

"Anytime, baby," he slurred.

I looked at my watch. It was 7:45.

At home, the windows showed no signs of life. Aside from a glint of light escaping beneath the garage door, it looked as if no one lived there at all. As I walked up the driveway, I caught the musty scent of weed and the faint sounds of Earth, Wind & Fire.

"Ernest! Let the garage up!"

"Jeanette?"

"Who else would it be?" I yelled. The walk had worn down my buzz, but mostly I was irritated that Ernest was still awake. Many nights his early-morning shifts sent him to bed just as I was getting home. His voice was heavy and slow, so I knew he had been drinking, too.

"Wait just a minute!"

I waited, listening to the sounds of his big body stumbling about, making its way to the switch at the wall. I stood up as the door began to lift, the funk of weed and sweat burning the insides of my nose. Ernest was still in his work clothes, blue pants and blue button-up, the tiny red emblem of the Amtrak station on the front shirt pocket.

"Damn, Jeanette, I was wondering where you was when I seen your car here. I know ten dollars ain't have you playing that long. What time you leave?"

"Shit, Ernest!" I said, sitting to remove my shoes and rubbing my feet. "I didn't get up there till 'bout five."

"You know it ain't safe for you to be walking at night."

His concern mellowed me out some. I leaned back and took in the deep burgundy of his face. His hair was graying around the temples. I wondered if I looked as old as he did sprawled out in the lawn chair.

And I wondered why he hadn't thought to call and check on me, if he'd been so concerned.

"Gimme a sip of that," I said, reaching for his glass, pretending as always not to notice the missing pointer finger he'd lost as a boy in Louisiana. He claimed he never realized until he became a man at thirteen that the cotton fields he picked and plowed alongside his mother and his eight siblings had once been a plantation. The whole place was a graveyard to him after that, filled with young men his age haunting the grounds with thrashings about their backs and rope burns around their necks. Back when we shared a bed I could feel them show up in his dreams—his breathing stopped and his body turned, as if those Louisiana oak trees were growing thick around his chest, meaning to suffocate him. After all these years, I still hadn't grown used to that hard brown nub on his hand. He'd been shaving down a log with his oldest sister, it was almost dinnertime and he'd been eager to eat. One quick push and pull of the saw had been enough to slice right through.

"Nah," he said, "I'll go make you one but this one's mine."

"Ugh, you so stingy with everything. Ain't ever known a man as stingy as you!" I crossed my legs and arms. Ernest chuckled.

"Shit, you don't be sayin' that when I pay your car note every month. And the light bill. And the water."

"Don't act like you doin' me no favors!"

"You mean I'm not?" He laughed again. "'Cause we can bring all that to a halt real quick."

"Hmph."

"Hmph, my ass." He stood up, stumbling against his chair. "Have yo' ass walking all the time and everywhere." He turned to go inside the house.

"Crushed ice, Ernest! And use the glass I like!"

"Yeah, yeah," he muttered. "You think after all this time I don't know how you like your drink?"

I had a craving for a cigarette but I'd already smoked my pack down to its final six and I knew that wasn't enough to get me through the night. The remains of Ernest's marijuana were scattered on one of the speakers, his wrapping papers nearby. For a moment I considered taking one of his grape-flavored cigarillos. Instead I inhaled the smoke lingering in the garage, until he shuffled back out and handed me my drink. The Coke was flat.

"Ernest, didn't you put the top back on tight like I told you? God-damnit!"

"Ain't nothing wrong with that Coke, girl. Besides, too much carbonation give you gas." He reached for the drink and took a deep gulp. "Aw, hell, ain't nothin' wrong with this." He held his lighter to the end of his blunt till it burned cherry red. I rolled my eyes and stood up.

"That's right," he said, coughing through a laugh. "Go 'head, Miss Independent Woman. Take yo' ass in there and see if you can get it right." He took another pull, holding the smoke in his chest before releasing it, as I made my way inside. "See if you can find me something to eat, too. Nothin' on the stove."

In the kitchen, I transferred the drink to a plastic cup, then handed it out the door to him without looking. "Here," I said, waiting for the weight of the cup to leave my hand. He took it and didn't make a sound. I went about preparing my own drink now, glancing at my phone for any missed calls.

By the time I headed back out, Ernest was folded over both ends of the blue-and-white chair, barely holding on to his drink with his four fingers, the blunt going dead from neglect. The Temptations sang on the stereo: "Just another lonely night . . ."

When I kicked Ernest's chair to wake him, his body jerked.

"Damn, Jeanette," he moaned. "Why you so rough?"

"Go in the house if you sleepy. Don't sit out here and fall asleep."

Ernest blinked hard. "Nah, nah . . ." he said. "I ain't sleep." He brushed ashes from his lap onto the concrete.

"Jeanette, you know what them motherfuckers at work said to me?"

I said nothing. I relaxed in my chair, took a long sip from my drink, knowing this wouldn't be going anywhere soon.

"So then I said . . ."

Nothing.

"But you know I wanted to knock that motherfucker in his mouth."

"Of course you did, baby. Of course."

I was high now—floating away somewhere willingly. Leaving my body and watching strands of shit and parasites departing my insides with each "motherfucker" Ernest uttered. And I kept floating and floating. To a place full of sevens. Purple sevens. Red sevens. Orange-and-green sevens. An entire rainbow of jackpots. A saturation of something I didn't know what to call except I knew it was good. Better than what I was, better than how I ever felt, sober or intoxicated.

Still I floated until I heard Ernest say, "Ah shit, what time is it? Let me take my ass to bed." I watched him lift himself out of his chair, eyes closed. And at that moment, my phone vibrated in my lap. It was Peaches. I figured she was still worried, though she'd never say as much.

"Well, girl, you ready for your last one? And don't bother lyin' to me, I know what you did today. Did you at least get lucky?"

I watched the smoke from my cigarette twist in the air, like a lost spirit trying to escape.

"Nah. Not today," I said. "Maybe tomorrow, though."

Nominated by Ben Stroud

THANK YOU FOR THE TULIPS

by LISA BELLAMY

from NEW OHIO REVIEW

During the pandemic, after I told you—
speaking up never easy—I was lonely
for you, your kids, and your husband,
you sent me tulips. Just like that, you
sent tulips. I wondered, though: did I
deserve them? I am sorry I was a drunk
when you were a kid. Thank you for not
hanging up when I call. The tulips
arrived in a creamy box; your note
tucked in tissue paper. I am sorry I could
not keep your father around or try very
hard to stop him when he said he was
leaving. I am sorry I did not love him
enough. Thank you for choosing such a
nice, funny guy for a husband. I am
sorry I pursued such a crazy boyfriend
after your father left—the shouting, the
slamming phones and slamming doors,
the walking out, the coming back. The
tulips are white and iridescent purple.
Thank you for your brown eyes. I
believe they are still flecked with green,
although sometimes, even now, I am
embarrassed to look you in the eye. I am
sorry I was so sick from drinking,

throwing up, and dizzy. Once, I could
not take you to your dentist appointment
because I felt shaky and kept falling.
You cried, you said nothing works,
nothing happens, everything falls apart.
Thank you for your clarity. Thank you
for your red face, your bursting, when
you were born. Thank you for your
anger when your stepfather and I
screwed up the car seat as we drove the
baby around the city, looking after her
while you were at your conference. Boy,
that woke us up! I am sorry you fell out
of your stroller when you were a toddler
because I was hungover and forgot to
buckle you in. I don't know if you
remember. Now you know. Thank you
for the tulips. You sent so many I filled
three vases: one big, two small. Thank
you for insisting you wanted hipster
vegan donuts at your wedding instead of
a white cake. That one threw me over
the handlebars—drama, etc. Your
stepfather was kind and calm throughout
and wrote the checks. He loves you. He
says, later you get all the money, no one
else. In the end, I was a good sport,
admit it; the donuts were
delicious. You were a delicious baby.

Nominated by New Ohio Review

MEMORIALS

by TYLER SONES

from THE PINCH

The way it used to be when I'd tell people where I'm from, they would joke about how the government killed seventy-six religious separatists in my very own backyard. Everybody was a comedian back then—the TSA man with his blue gloves and the flashlight he shined on my driver's license, gas station clerks who carded me for cigarettes, bosses, coworkers, temporary girlfriends in Portland, LA, Maui, Austin, wherever I happened to be living after I left Waco for good.

When I was younger and more earnest, I'd explain that, in fact, the Branch Davidian compound was in Elk, not Waco, twenty miles from where I grew up. Later, I would say that my junior high art teacher played bass in David Koresh's band. In the late eighties, they played every weekend at Chelsea Street Pub, a British-themed restaurant in the mall. Or I would tell them that the day the siege happened I was in third grade at Spring Valley Christian School, which looked like a barn and smelled like septic tank runoff. That there were six kids in my class, maybe forty in the whole school, and during lunch, Mrs. McFarland, the ninety-year-old choir teacher, brought an antique TV into the lunchroom, extended the rabbit-ear antenna, and turned it on to breaking news that a beige building was on fire, surrounded by tanks and men with guns. She didn't explain what we were watching. Nobody talked. Nobody I knew back then even had a TV, except for my grandmother, who was considered eccentric, because TV, like Halloween and the Clinton Administration, was associated somehow with the Devil.

These explanations grew stale too. Like when your arm is in a cast and you're expected to tell everybody who asks exactly what happened, but briefly, please, because nobody cares that much. So you start telling lies. You fell out of a tree. You should see the other guy. Your uncle died in that fire. Your whole family. David Koresh was the bonafide Messiah, so you would appreciate it if a little respect was shown.

It's different now. The only people who ask about the Branch Davidians anymore are death-cult enthusiasts or the elderly. Instead, people ask about the reality television show that, finally, after a quarter century, has restored Waco's image to something resembling respectability.

According to my parents, who cite Tripadvisor's Travelers' Choice Awards for Destinations on the Rise, Waco is the number two family vacation spot in the whole USA, which is patently ridiculous, it looks like the some place it's always been. The shitty parts of town are shittier than ever, but the salvageable spots now wear a new coat of paint. Shabby, when nobody was looking, became shabby chic. All due. I'm told, to the TV show, whose very mission was superficial rehabilitation.

Unremarkable houses were made special. Like dentists who replace stained and broken teeth with immaculate veneers, the TV show gave Waco a winning, twenty-five-century smile, something to smile about. Once-derelict buildings now host juice bars, coffee shops, nightclubs that serve cocktails made with mezcal and fernet. In the twin shadows of the grain silos on Webster Street where my dad used to work building cabinets, there's a shopping and dining complex owned by the hosts of the show. Paddleboarders and kayakers clutter the river we used to joke was full of dead bodies, two-headed fish. Twenty years ago, we would hang from the underside of the railroad tracks that cross that river and scream cuss words into the bellies of trains.

As of 2018, the show is no longer on the air, but its success continues to snowball. Houses they restored have become tourist destinations. The TV hosts' faces adorn freeway billboards from Austin to Dallas. They boast a line of pseudo-antiques sold nationwide at your neighborhood Target. Waco people have nothing but nice things to say about them.

The hosts go to the same church as my parents, where they still believe the Bible is the living, inherent breath of God, still raise their hands in worship, and when overcome by the Holy Ghost, speak in tongues. They still say *in the world but not of the world,* but they're not the same fundamentalists I remember. They've assimilated. Last time I counted, my parents had three TVs.

Today is Mother's Day, twenty-six years and twenty-three days after the siege of the Branch Davidian compound and the first time I've visited home in a while. I've been stuck in Ohio for grad school and itching to get back to Texas—although not Waco. I'm just in Waco to see my folks.

We have an understanding, my parents and I. They don't invite me to church anymore, but I'll meet them afterward for lunch. This morning when they leave for the early service, I head out to the site of the massacre. For how much time I've spent thinking about it. I don't know why I've never made the drive.

Central Texas in May is almost breathtakingly beautiful, at least in the country. The lush carpeting of bluebonnets that line the roadsides in April have already died, but there are still Indian paintbrushes in orange abundance. Mexican hats and black-eyed Susans, spiny thistles with purple blossoms. Clematis and brambles suffocate barbed-wire fences. The air smells like the potpourri my grandmother kept on the back of her toilet. By June, the wildflowers will be burnt up, it'll be a hundred degrees in the shade, and all the deep, wild greens will be paler, set off against the brown of the sun-scorched ground.

Double EE Ranch Road dead ends into gravel ruts that snake off and disappear in the woods. According to my directions, that dead end is my destination. The entrance to the compound is barred by a cattle gate, but just beyond the gate are two granite memorials, each four feet high and twice as wide, one centered in the gate, the other to the left. Two poles fly one white and one blue flag, both advertising the current American president and his slogan, which makes sense, I guess, considering it was a Democrat who signed off on the raid.

As a rule, I'd rather endure any number of discomforts than talk to a stranger, and I'm a little relieved that there are no cars, none of the people I've seen in photos who look like Mennonites on vacation, country people with an eighties flair. The gate is locked. Behind it are a couple mobile homes and a path that climbs a hill to what looks like a chapel. Somewhere back there, tucked away, a new generation of separatists live, attend church, and espouse those kinds of deeply held religious beliefs that are sometimes protected by law. They're an offshoot of the Seventh Day Adventists. I'm pretty sure their seventh day is Saturday, but maybe they hold Sunday sacred too. Or else they're all sleeping in. Because I can't make out the inscriptions from my car, I hop the fence.

The ground around the memorial is paved with square cement tiles, like a floor made of unmarked graves. Along the top of the central monument runs the heading: *The Seven Shepherds of the Advent Movement.* Each shepherd has beneath their name a birthdate, a death date, and their contribution to the movement. The seventh of whom is Vernon Wayne Howell, a serial killer's name, and the one David Koresh was born with.

Vernon Wayne Howell
August 7, 1959
April 19, 1993
Founder of the Davidian Branch Davidian
Seventh Day Adventist Movement

I don't know if it's a typo or not: *Davidian Davidian*. The inscription neglects to mention other attributes—child molestor, monomaniac, messiah.

Under the row of shepherds, in smaller typeface, are arranged the names of the regular dead, same as on the adjacent memorial. Each casualty gets their own brick. They range in color from eggplant to dappled pink. I count seventy-eight bricks, not seventy-six.

The bricks are inscribed with the person's name, age, the invariable date of death, and their country of origin. It only takes me a moment to find the two extra names: "Aborted Fetus Gent" and "Aborted Baby Jennings," no age, USA. I don't know what makes one a fetus and the other a baby. I do know that two women were pregnant when they died in the siege, asphyxiated in the bunker where the women and children were made to hide. I don't know what to do with the word *aborted*.

Seventy-six people (or seventy-eight, depending on who's counting), and I wonder how many felt, as they were choking or burning to death, or crushed beneath rubble, that they were dying martyrs' deaths. What does martyrdom feel like? How many were just plain afraid?

There are countless examples of would-be prophets or messiahs predicting a fixed date for the conclusion of their earthly tenure, and I get the impression that non-believers get a good laugh when those dates pass. I do too. But I also feel a tinge of jealousy at their capacity for belief, at the fact that they hold their beliefs so earth-shatteringly dear that they're willing to be humiliated for them. Or maybe humiliation doesn't cross their minds, because their faith allows for no contingency other than the one they're counting on.

And when their armageddons pass without event, isn't there also a little relief mixed in with our laughter? Like isn't there always a nonzero chance that these kooks and charlatans might be right and the rest of us are too cynical or arrogant to understand the finer distinctions between our doubt and their belief? That we wouldn't know the truth if it spit in our face? Or in this case, what if David Koresh was the messiah and the world was just too broken to see it? And now he's dead and we're all fucked.

It's doubtful, of course, and silly, but I can barely wrap my head around its ramifications as I read each row of names. An awful lot of children died that day, many with the last name of either Koresh or Howell. Several grown-ups from Australia, a couple from England. And all who were old enough to decide for themselves, they believed so hard in their messiah that they chose to die beside him. Nobody even did that for Jesus.

Lesser memorials are sprinkled nearby. One that looks like it predates the granite ones—a pale limestone marker with the dead listed in two columns, no shepherds, no abortions. Another, a flat granite plaque, is dedicated to the memory of the four ATF agents who died that day, which strikes me as an act of—or an attempt at—forgiveness. Or perhaps more in keeping with their fundamentalism: a reminder that every human life is sacred, even those of their enemies.

The memorial that most surprises me I come to last. Two doves sitting on a branch, beneath which it reads:

IN REMEMBRANCE OF ALL THE MEN WOMEN
AND CHILDREN WHO WERE VICTIMIZED
AND BRUTALLY SLAUGHTERED IN THE BOMBING
OF THE OKLAHOMA CITY FEDERAL BUILDING
ON APRIL 19, 1995
WE PRAY THAT THEY AND THEIR FAMILIES
FIND PEACE IN OUR LORD

In Ohio. I was older than most of my grad school cohort, and I had to jog their memories about why my hometown rang a bell. For context, I would explain how Ruby Ridge—the eleven-day siege on Randy Weaver's Idaho hermit cabin by U.S. Marshals that resulted in the death of his wife and teenage son—took place not eight months before Waco, how it was the first link in an American chain that led directly to Oklahoma City. Waco was another link. The Oklahoma City bomber, Timothy McVeigh, was radicalized by both, and by the rage those events stoked among the white supremacists and separatists he kept company with. In fact, McVeigh was present during the Waco siege. He'd set up a merch table on the hood of his Mercury Grand Marquis. On a hill a couple miles away—the vantage point of choice for looky-loos and journalists without credentials—he sold bumper stickers to spectators whose philosophies overlapped with his. It's hard to think of him making small talk with strangers, somehow not yet pregnant with the one hundred and fifty-eight deaths he would bring into the world.

The news in the early nineties was busy with stories about white separatists, their crimes, and the cloister-cities they'd built to keep themselves separate. The events at Ruby Ridge and Waco emboldened all the disparate elements—the explicit racists, the anti-government gun hoarders, the race-war paranoiacs—but the Oklahoma City bombing sent them all scuttling back underground. That is, until recently.

And now I have questions. Oklahoma City took place two years to the date after the Branch Davidian armageddon. Are the latter-day separatists as troubled by that fact as I am? Do they feel complicit or avenged? Do they see themselves as a new link in the chain their forebears helped to forge? How separate are they? I'm looking for a fundamentalist with a pamphlet, but nobody's here. Nothing but birds chirping and the sub-audible groans of the gone and all but forgotten. Like I said. Waco is a ghost town on Sunday.

Armageddon and *apocalypse,* in common Christian usage, are practically synonyms. Both connote catastrophe, violence, the end of the world, and both *feel* very Biblical. Growing up, we said *end times* and that signified both. Jesus bursting through the clouds on a white horse, trailing an army of dead saints and angels, coming to wipe out Satan and ferry the saved back with him to heaven. This final reckoning would follow wars and rumors of war, famine, calamity in general. Every terrible newspaper headline meant we were that much nearer to the end of earthly sorrows.

That's Armageddon, the last battle. There is no proper plural of the word.

Apocalypse is a different animal entirely. It's a Greek word, meaning revelation. Hitherto unheard-of-truth truth is revealed and it's some cataclysmic shit. After that, normal life cannot be the same.

When I was a kid, the kind of faith the people around me had was apocalyptic. They were given special insight, and they had no choice but to act on it, rejecting the easy, available pleasures of the world (which for me meant TV and Halloween) in order to pursue their idea of righteousness. It made us separate by necessity. *In the world but not of the world.* Would we be ready when Jesus came back? Because it was going to be any minute now.

During the final days of the Branch Davidian siege. David Koresh tried several times to stall the ATF and FBI. In video and audio messages, and on the phone with negotiators, he begged for more time. He was in the process of opening the Seventh Seal, the final revelation, which, he claimed, would usher in widespread, maybe even global, apocalypse. The same truth that had been made clear to him, would be revealed to everyone at once. And no, he didn't know how much time he needed. What a ridiculous question to ask.

But then suppose you don't go out in a blaze of glory or ignominy. You have to sit with your special knowledge through years of regular, eventless days. What then? It's hard to carry the burden of apocalypse indefinitely. Jesus doesn't come back in a timely fashion, so you have to start worrying about the little things. The present tense overwhelms the future. You remodel the kitchen because you're tired of looking at the same old cabinets. The walls are stained with fingerprints and spaghetti sauce, so you repaint. You get a couple TVs because what are you supposed to do with all that extra time, waiting for your theology to be justified by triumph? On your drive to work, you think: *Somebody should do something about this town. It doesn't have to be so ugly.*

How do you undo a revelation? Maybe you can't. Or maybe you can start by giving everything a makeover. If the world around you looks different, maybe it is. And then it's easier to forget.

What's the opposite of apocalypse?

The massacre of a cult might not be a pretty thing for a town to be famous for, but it beats the hell out of being known for some television show. At least for me it does. I preferred it when my hometown didn't have something freshly painted to hide its sins behind. When that was all we were known for, it was harder to forget. Now it's easy. But I guess that's what memorials are for, even if that memorial is tucked away behind a cattle gate at the ass end of a ranch road.

Remember now with me, if you please. How in lieu of TV, we had acres of woods. How nobody called it the Satanic Panic when it was happening, because Satan was real and among us, seeking whom he might devour. How a cult was slaughtered in our own backyard. How the dead are buried under each new thing we've built. How what we had was ugly and now it's not. But it will be again. Like scars on a body or a mouthful of original teeth, everything is a memorial when you're looking for one. Lest we forget, lest we be reminded.

Nominated by The Pinch

DAWN 2040

by JORIE GRAHAM

from THE YALE REVIEW

These tiny sounds
you think you hear
in the house
elsewhere—

is someone awake, is
someone alive. You
turn around. *Just
now*, you hear

yourself say. I know
what finished is.
I know the *just
now* & then the *just*

gone. I am alive.
Then it is the sun
arriving, rising
just above the edge

of yr turning, my
earth. It's touching my
shoulder. *You*
it makes me feel,

you. Are you there.
In this world now, this
is the last
moment in which

we can breathe
normally. *Normally* I say
to myself.
The scrub oaks

are dying
back. The white sky
arrives, whitening
further. Did we

survive at the end
of this story, I ask
the sun. I give up on
tenses here. What were

the things we called
freedoms, I
ask. But the sun
as it rises is touching

everything less and less
tenderly, reaching
everything,
no matter how u

hide, no water
anywhere—though here, listen,
I make it
for you—*drip drip*—

as I admire yr breathing
wherever u are now
reading this. Inhale.
Are you still there

the sun says to me
as I hide on this
page. Be there.
As long as you can

take it, be there
as I rise. The lifting
groundmist now
is the last moment,

the very last, in which

you can breathe. Soon—
now actually—
you must hide
from me. You. You

beautiful thing, you
human, yr lungs
I can crush with one
inadvertent in-

halation. But how
I admired yr
breathing, yr so few
years, how u took them

to heart and believed in
things to the
end. The end is
a hard thing to

comprehend. You
did not
comprehend it. Now go,
I must widen

across the fields,

the cicadas will soon
begin in unison
the song of unison
till u can hear no more

variation, no rise or
fall. Can I live please
in this unchanging sound, I
ask, as we enter further

into yr dayrise.
What was that
just flew over. What else is
in here. I sit as quietly

as breathing
permits. All's
hum & insect
thread. Nothing un-

locks. Yes there's burning
wind sometimes, all
is building towards
sand's hard thought, nothing will

change its mind
this dune of the future
as it moves
towards us

here where we can for now
still hide. You there,
wondering what to do with
yr day,

yawning as you wake
from dream,
I can almost make you out
in yr brightening

morning-light. You there. Wake up. But
nobody's here,
just the earth
revolving, in-

exhaustible, without

purpose, in which
from moment to
moment
even now

change gathers,
inception gathers, & variation, & pro-
liferation—
And all is. All is.

Do you remember.

Nominated by The Yale Review

FIGHT WEEK

fiction by LAURA VAN DEN BERG

from VIRGINIA QUARTERLY REVIEW

On fight week, Kayla feels every muscle in her body harden. Electrical currents race around in her bloodstream; each movement is animated by a force that feels uncontrollable, uncontainable. Her coach keeps telling her to rest, to sleep, but how is she supposed to sleep? Her life has tapered to one fine and brilliant point. In bed at night she imagines each punch landing like a sledgehammer ripping through concrete.

This will be Kayla's third fight. She lost her first, won her second. In the first, she felt caught in a herd of stampeding horses: overwhelmed, overpowered. In her second, the herd stilled and parted and her objective emerged from the dust with stunning clarity. She pressed forward, hurled the combinations she had spent countless hours honing. She pinned the other girl to the ropes and did not relent until the bell.

After that second fight, the adrenaline high soared for days. Insults bounced off her, at school and at home. She walked around feeling like nothing in this world could ever hurt her again.

Not long after that second fight, however, something irrevocable happened. Her best friend abandoned their coach for a rival gym. No conversation, no advance warning. Most afternoons, they met up in an empty field to do sprints and one day she simply was not there. When confronted over text, she said she wanted to win nationals this year and she didn't see that happening with Coach, whom she called *a washed-up old fuck*. Kayla understands that this is a thing that happens in their world, that fighters come and go; she just did not think it would ever happen to them. They have not spoken since, though they still follow each other on social media. Every week they post photos: scowling in headgear on sparring days, flexing in dirty mirrors after lifting weights. Kayla feels like they are in silent competition with one another and maybe that has always been the case, even when they were still best friends. Same age. Same weight class. Only two white girls on the fight team. They both even have a dead parent knocking around in their pasts. Her former best friend's father was killed in a car accident three years ago. Kayla's own mother has been dead for a decade, after a blood vessel burst like a pipe in her brain. She collapsed in the grocery store, right by the citrus display. Life support for twenty-four hours and then gone.

The thing Kayla resents most is how her former best friend has managed to shake her confidence in her gym, which is to say her home. Just a little. Just enough. She feels like she's seeing her family through the eyes of an outsider for the first time. All the small things she never paid much attention to before—now they're all she notices. Coach's habit of running late; the haphazard equipment (good luck finding two dumbbells that match); his mercurial moods. One day he waves his fighters off, sends them away to work the heavy bags on their own. *Sometimes you have to do for yourselves,* he tells them, like they're a bunch of needy children. Another he spends an hour breaking down the jab in glorious detail. One day she can't tie her shoes right; another she's the greatest thing this gym has ever seen. On fight dates, Coach is like one of those performers who practically has to be carried to the venue only to transform into an entirely different person the moment he steps onstage. She is certain that the talks he delivered before her bouts did nothing less than alter the substance of her soul. The way he left her feeling so understood, so believed-in.

Two days before the fight, Kayla drives over to the gym to shadowbox in front of the mirrors, work her head movement with the slip bag. Then she sits ringside and watches Coach oversee two guys sparring. One is a newbie with a big mouth, the other a veteran who keeps landing crisp, effortless punches, driving the newbie into a pinched, sweaty silence. One thing she has always loved about boxing is the transparency, the way five minutes in the ring can tell you things about a person that otherwise might take years to learn.

Though she has to admit that this theory is another thing that has been rattled lately, considering her former best friend is, despite all the rounds they put in together, now behaving in a way that Kayla never could have predicted.

She looks up at the ring, at the two tall, thin men dancing around each other inside the ropes, at Coach calling out instructions from the corner, the brim of his baseball cap pulled low. *Breadbasket* means throw a straight punch to the body. *Ticktock* means move your head already. She remembers all the times she and her former best friend embraced in the ring's slightly sunken center after a hard sparring session, heaving and drenched. For a moment, Kayla gets the outlandish idea that her friend has been kidnapped and a menacing stranger is posting under her name.

Before Kayla even sees the bout sheet, she knows who she is going to be matched with. There aren't that many local girls in her weight class and division. The day before the fight her suspicion is confirmed.

"She only has two tricks," Coach tells her. "You know them both."

They spend the rest of the day reviewing how to dismantle those tricks, working slowly and lightly in the ring. Her former best friend's first trick is catching someone with a looping left hook as they're coming in. The second is feinting an overhand and digging the body instead. Coach reminds her of how to take each punch away and how to counter.

"Keep her out of your head." Coach flicks her forehead with his index finger and thumb. "Don't let her go where she doesn't belong."

The fight is in Kissimmee. Kayla leaves early in the morning, in order to make weigh-in. Coach is driving a few teenagers down in his van; she will meet everyone at the venue, a civic center on a large lake. On her way out of town, she swings by a gas station. The air is already torpid; the dawn sky is a luminous, tangerine veil. At the pump, the credit-card reader is broken, so she has to pay inside. She decides to use the bathroom, to grab a sports drink and a protein bar for after weigh-in, while she's at it.

On a different day, she might have noticed the man hovering outside the entrance, right in front of the Florida Lottery sign, with the neon-pink flamingo balanced on one spindly leg. White and drawn, in black pants with some kind of pale dust on the knees, and a swamp-green hoodie, strange only because the temperature is already pushing ninety. Hood pulled tight around his face and eyes jumping all around the parking lot, like he's waiting for someone else to arrive, like he's waiting for a sign.

The gas station is just down the street from her house, where Kayla lives with her father, an employee of John E. Polk Correctional. She has been coming to this gas station for candy and slushies ever since she was a kid. It is one of the few places that remains untouched by time: same yellow linoleum floors, same dust-clotted light. Kayla is waiting to pay, the sports drink in one hand and the protein bar in the other, when she hears slamming, shouting, coming from the front of the line. Two people are ahead of her, a man in navy coveralls and a woman in jeans and a pink tank top and white sneakers. A maroon braid hangs between her shoulder blades. L'Oréal Babylon Intense Red—that's Kayla's best guess. The woman cradles a family-size bag of pretzels. The man in coveralls takes a step back, holds up his hands.

Kayla pops up on her toes; the man in the green hoodie is standing in front of the counter, up by the black-cherry cigarillos and the energy drinks and the WINNING TICKET SOLD HERE signs that paper the wall behind the register. *Does he think he can just cut the line?* she thinks at first, but then she sees the small, black gun raised above his head.

The hoodie screams something and then the cashier screams something back and then the hoodie fires two shots into the ceiling. Plaster rains onto the floor. A choking white dust gusts down the aisles.

After that, the air around her begins to shimmer; every sound is amplified, overwhelming, an immense wave rearing up from the ocean and arcing overhead. The man in the coveralls lunges in the direction of the counter; he hurls himself at the hoodie and attempts to wrestle away the gun, but the hoodie gets free, skitters backward, and fires. The man in the coveralls collapses. The woman screams and drops the pretzels. She sinks to the floor, rocks on her heels, arms lashed around her knees. She looks to be around fifty, with a long face and feline-green eyes.

Kayla crouches beside the woman, taps her knee, points to the end of the aisle. Together they crawl to the humming refrigerators, take shelter behind a pyramid of Bud Light cases. The woman presses her hands over her ears. Kayla faces the refrigerators and watches the reflections, something she has seen action heroes do in movies. Up front, she can hear the hoodie screaming at the cashier to keep his hands up, to lay down on the ground. She scans the reflections for the man in the coveralls, but he is nowhere in sight.

Finally, she hears the entry chime; she pictures the hoodie bursting into the parking lot. Running and running.

Kayla stands, slowly, and peers down the aisle. The cashier is still behind the counter, alive; he is talking on the phone. She feels as though she has been huddled behind the beer cases for hours. The woman uncurls her body and looks around like she's not quite sure how she ended up here.

"I feel sick." She clutches her stomach. She has a slender build, one that Kayla guesses is deceptively strong, from the ribbons of muscle on her forearms. The kind of person who can hit harder than you think.

Kayla bends down and grabs the woman by a pointy elbow. Helps her up. "What's your name?" she asks her, and the woman says, "Mary."

Together they rush over to the man in the coveralls. He is conscious. He has been shot in the shoulder. Blood is pooling under his left side. Kayla kneels by his head. His hair is thinning; she can see straight through to his scalp, glistening with sweat. He's wearing a gold wedding ring. His name—Julian—is stitched onto the chest of his coveralls with light-blue thread. She has never seen a shot person before; she has no idea what to do. "I'm so sorry," she keeps saying to him. Useless, useless. The cashier has called 911. The woman crouches beside the man; she places a thin, pale hand to his forehead.

"Imagine you are in a warm cave," she tells him. "A safe and quiet place."

"My wife," he says. "Can someone call my wife?"

"We'll call whoever you want." She speaks in a soft and soothing voice. Kayla wonders if she has a lot of experience talking to the injured or the critically ill.

A police car skids into the parking lot, followed by an ambulance. Sirens, flashing lights. The man is put on a stretcher and taken away.

No one can leave until they give a statement. Kayla, the woman, and the cashier all go outside, away from the wing-shaped bloodstain on the linoleum and the gaping hole in the ceiling. The cashier, a middle-aged man in glasses and a white T-shirt, gives his statement first. He keeps his hands crossed over his round stomach, breathes in huge gulps, like someone has been holding his head underwater and he's just now been allowed to surface.

Running late, Kayla texts Coach. *Be there as soon as I can.*

The tangerine sky has faded into a muted blue; raft-like clouds drift overhead. A neon purple OPEN sign blinks on and off behind them.

"Do you live around here?" Kayla asks the woman while they wait. She notices wet crescents under her armpits. Her jeans have an elastic waistband.

"I work over there." She points at the diner across the street, Perks, located in a small strip mall. A black leather coin purse is wedged into the front of her pants. She keeps opening her mouth wide, like she has an ache in her jaw. When the police officer comes to collect their statements, she goes first and a few minutes in she stops talking and claws at the fabric just over her heart.

A second ambulance is summoned. Actually it turns out to be the same ambulance as before, piloted by two muscular, serious-looking young men with goatees. The moment they dropped the man in the coveralls at the emergency room, they were called right back.

Once the woman is on the stretcher, one of the paramedics turns to Kayla and asks if she's family. She starts to shake her head, but then the woman sits up a little and cries out, "Why yes! That's my daughter."

At first, Kayla thinks she has misheard the woman. Or maybe the woman is in shock and has mistaken Kayla for someone else.

"Is that right?" the paramedic asks, impatient. "Are you two together?"

She looks at the woman being loaded into the ambulance, her sneaker soles dark with blood. She feels caught between her desire to make it to Kissimmee in time to fight and imagining her mother lying still by the citrus. She wonders if a stranger waited with her until the ambulance came. About the last face her mother peered into, the last hand she touched.

All these questions that she has never dared to ask her father.

"Okay," Kayla says. "Yes. We are."

The next thing she knows she's grabbing her backpack from her car, making sure all the doors are locked, the windows rolled up. When the paramedic hands her the woman's black coin purse, Kayla zips it into her backpack and then she is riding alongside this Mary, this perfect stranger, in the cool little cave of the ambulance.

The paramedic performs an EKG, a mess of wires and round electrodes. "The man that was shot," Kayla asks the paramedic. "Is he going to die?"

"He's going to be fine," the young man says, sounding almost a little bored.

At the hospital, they are ushered straight into a long tan hallway with a row of beds, separated by blue privacy curtains. A nurse in mint-green scrubs tells them the doctor will read the EKG as soon as possible.

"Describe your pain," the nurse says to Mary.

"I feel like I've been punched." Her eyes are shut tight. She has a pronounced clavicle, long and straight as a beam, and a slender neck. Bangs that fall to her eyebrows. Her maroon hair is radiant under the hospital lights.

"Punched where?" says the nurse.

She touches her chest, her shoulder, her jaw. The nurse makes a note on her clipboard. She turns to Kayla and explains that they will draw blood and administer medications through her IV.

"Take two aspirin and call me from the great beyond." The softness has evaporated from Mary's voice; the words burst out of her sharp and loud.

The nurse ignores her. "What can you tell me about her medical history?"

"What?" Kayla is startled by the question. She's wearing her backpack and slides her hands under the front straps. The backpack has all her fight gear inside: gloves, mouthpiece in its plastic case, headgear, lucky socks, a small round container of Vaseline.

The nurse glances down at her clipboard. "Aren't you her daughter?"

"Oh," Kayla says. "Yes, well, we haven't spoken in a long time."

The nurse nods curtly, makes another note, leaves. Kayla closes all the privacy curtains, buffering them from the hive of the nurses' station and the dire cases rushing past. She wonders about the man who was shot in the shoulder, if he is somewhere on this floor.

"Take two aspirin and call me from the grave," Mary says.

"They're going to run some tests," Kayla tells her. "They might need to do something called a cardiac cath?"

"They kill you and then they bill you." Mary writhes around on the bed. "They kill you and then they *kill* you."

"No one is getting killed," Kayla says and right then the patient next door starts screaming, a cry so high and awful it could split the heavens. "Is there anything I should tell them about your medical history? Is there anyone you want me to call?"

She has to raise her voice to be heard over the neighbor's skull-cracking screams. She is terrified to step into the hallway and see for herself what's happening next door.

"No," says Mary. "No calls."

The screaming neighbor suddenly goes silent.

By the time the nurse returns, it is past lunchtime; a doctor has read the EKG. "You've had a heart attack," the nurse says. "That's the bad news."

The good news is that the heart attack was relatively minor. Only a small portion of the muscle has been damaged. Still, Mary must be admitted to the coronary-care unit; it is possible that she will need surgery. Kayla feels bewildered by the pace of information: One minute she's hearing *minor* and the next *surgery*. How to understand what it is that Mary is facing?

"When?" Kayla asks. A good daughter, she imagines, would ask questions.

"Soon," says the nurse, but three hours pass and there is still no sign of a transport orderly or anyone else.

Eventually Mary rolls onto her side, falls asleep. Kayla goes down to the cafeteria. She buys a cheeseburger and a chocolate pudding topped with a stiff swirl of whipped cream, since making weight is no longer an immediate concern. It's not until Kayla begins eating that she realizes she is raw with hunger; her hands tremble as she brings the food to her mouth. After she finishes, she checks her phone, finds about a hundred worried messages from Coach and one from her father, asking her if she's fought yet. Her former best friend, meanwhile, has made a bitchy Instagram post, with an image of an empty ring and a caption talking about how the saddest thing is not a fighter losing, but a fighter being scared to fight.

Kayla sinks deeper into the booth. It's true that she's been nursing a small and secret relief that she will not have to battle her former best friend today after all. In sparring, she usually got the better of Kayla in small, tricky ways—counterpunching, angles. She knew just what to feed her and when. Tactics that could be exploited to ruinous ends in a real bout.

She opens her backpack and takes out Mary's coin purse. She digs around and finds two damp ten-dollar bills, a credit card, her driver's license, which she had to hand over to the nurse earlier to be copied, along with a health-insurance card; she has no idea what kind of plan Mary is on, if the expense will drive her into a debt that she will never be able to get free of. Mary is forty-eight. She is not an organ donor. She finds a small Polaroid of a marmalade cat stretched out on a bright-green lawn. An empty matchbook. From a side pocket, she pulls out three business cards: George's Tavern, one of the few places in town where people can still smoke indoors; Rivera Family Chiropractic Center; a psychic adviser.

She knows that doctors have rules about who they can talk to, so she dials the number for the psychic adviser. She keeps thinking that someone must know this woman, that there must be someone out there that she should inform.

"I'm calling about Mary." Kayla reads aloud her full name from the driver's license. "I think she's a client of yours?"

"I'm going to stop you right there," the psychic adviser says, "and let you know that I am not in the business of giving refunds."

"She's in the hospital."

"I am an innocent seer. I am not liable. I don't *make* anything happen."

"I'm just trying to figure out what to do," says Kayla. "She might need surgery. Do you know if she has any family?"

"Honey," the psychic adviser says. "Do you know how many Marys I talked to this week?"

"No," Kayla admits.

"I could give the Bible a run for its money," she says before hanging up.

Soon, Kayla is back in the rising elevator, her backpack between her feet. Her phone pings in her pocket. Her former best friend has just texted, wanting to know what happened today and if she is okay. As though she thinks that, in secret, she can go back to being the person she used to be. A teammate. A friend. *Fuck you*, Kayla thinks, and does not reply.

She finds Mary's bed empty. A tangle of white sheets. Dangling tubes. She asks nurse after nurse what's happened, begins to panic that she left at some critical juncture to eat a cheeseburger and a chocolate pudding. Finally, she learns that Mary has been transferred to the coronary-care unit. She crosses a sky bridge, moving briskly through the blue evening; she rushes down one long, bright-white hallway after another until she finds Mary's room.

"You just missed the doctor," Mary tells her, a little scolding.

Kayla pulls a hard, beige chair up to her bedside. "What did the doctor say?"

"I have two choices." She sighs, crosses her arms over her chest, pushes out her lips. "Surgery or . . . surgery!"

"When?"

"Tonight. Maybe. They don't know." The room is cramped and windowless, with a tart, medicinal smell and dim lighting, though the bed itself is spotlit. Kayla can make out blue veins running under Mary's face, evidence of that deeper architecture currently under attack. Her bloody sneakers have been replaced with white ankle socks.

Eventually Kayla knows that she will need to drop this charade. Eventually she will need to go home.

"Earlier," Mary says. "You asked me about my family history."

"The nurse did. Yes."

"My mother died of a heart attack. Well, that's not exactly right. My father threw my mother down a flight of stairs. Then she had a heart

273

attack and then she died." She rests her hands on the small hump of her stomach. "I come from a long line of fragile and broken hearts."

"How old were you?" Kayla asks. "When your mother died?"

"Fourteen," she says. "Your age."

Kayla sits up straight in the hard chair, a little insulted. "Actually, I'm seventeen."

"Seventeen!" Mary pushes herself up on her elbows and squints. "Why are you so skinny?"

"I've been dieting." She fights at 112 and has to cut ten or more pounds in the weeks before a bout. She has gotten used to the meager meals of chicken and boiled vegetables, the slow, steamy runs in her sauna suit, the clawing hunger.

"Do you have one of those mothers who is always on some kind of strange diet? My mother once ate nothing but cabbage soup for a month. 'If I must be miserable, I might as well be thin.' That was her motto."

I have no mother, Kayla wants to tell her. "I'm a boxer," she says instead.

"You're joking."

"I was supposed to fight today."

"All my life," Mary says, "I have tried so hard to avoid violence."

How did people come by their violences? For a moment, Kayla feels like she can perceive the whole miserable network. The hoodie got his violence from somewhere, as did her father. Eventually the hoodie will be apprehended and, if he ends up in Polk, their two violences will collide and create a violence larger than either of them.

To locate the dawn of her own violence, Kayla only has to recall her early days at the gym. Once another kid pinned her to the ropes during class, shuffled left and right so she couldn't escape. She stabbed him with an uppercut to the solar plexus and he stumbled back, eyes wide. His submission, his surprise: She felt like she had spent years alone in a rollicking sea and suddenly someone had thrown her a rope, told her what direction to swim in.

"What now?" Kayla asks.

"Nothing happens." Mary presses her head down into the white pillow. Her voice grows louder, filling all four corners of the room. "Nobody comes, nobody goes."

"Didn't the doctor just come by?"

"'Let us do something, while we have the chance!' It is not every day that we are needed. That we personally are needed." Her eyes snap open. Her pupils are ringed with gold. "Do you know what you are doing *here*?"

Kayla jumps up from the chair, worried that Mary has turned delirious. She stands at the head of the bed and wonders if she should touch her forehead and talk about warm and quiet caves, like Mary did when the man in the coveralls was bleeding on the gas-station floor. She remembers a stray line from a song her mother used to sing when she was a child.

"To see a fine lady," she whispers. "Upon a white horse."

Mary closes her eyes again and appears to drift, her hands still at rest on her stomach. Kayla decides that she will stay until Mary is wheeled into the operating room. Then she will take a rideshare to the gas station, retrieve her car, drive home. She opens the black coin purse and digs out the psychic advisor's card. She writes her name and number on the back, returns the card to the purse. She imagines sitting with Mary at Perks, when all of this is over. The fragrant heat of coffee. The sweet stick of pie.

At three in the morning, a nurse preps Mary for surgery. An orderly transfers her to a gurney and then they're off. Kayla follows them into the elevator and then back across the skybridge—by now it feels like they are traversing a black sea—and into another elevator, which delivers them to an entirely different wing, on an even-higher floor. It is like a kingdom, this hospital. Labyrinthine, vast. All the hallways aggressively illuminated. She tries to recall where exactly in this kingdom her mother died, but she can't remember the unit or the floor; she must have been too young to retain such details. She only remembers the way her mother's skin had turned gray and spongy as putty.

"There, there," Kayla says at the mouth of the operating room. She stares down at Mary's long ashen face. Her maroon hair, her colorless lips. She tries to understand her role. Has she been a bystander? An innocent seer, as the psychic adviser claimed to be? "It'll be over before you know it."

Mary gazes up at Kayla with a strange opacity, as though she is just now starting to absorb all that has happened, and then the orderly rolls her away.

She leaves the black coin purse at the nurses' station. An exhausted-looking young woman—puddles of mascara under her eyes—takes it without argument. Kayla walks to the end of the hallway and stands by a tall window. She sees something that looks at first like an oil spill below, but no: She's looking down at a man-made lake.

In the window, Kayla's reflection is sharp and bright, and she begins to slowly, softly shadowbox—uppercut, uppercut, hook, cross—an absentminded habit, something she's caught herself doing in all kinds of places.

From the other end of the hall a gurney flies toward her, flanked by two orderlies in white, running like a pair of very athletic angels. Her hands drop. A voice crackles over the speakers. Some urgent missive. As the stretcher rounds the corner, the patient's head rolls in her direction and she glimpses the man in the coveralls, the one who was shot in the shoulder, the one the paramedic said would be fine. Julian. Where could he be off to now?

A nurse trails behind. She walks with her hands in pockets, nodding at everyone she passes. She seems to be in no hurry at all. Kayla wonders if she is on a break.

"That view is the only thing in this hospital that no one ever complains about. Living or dead." The nurse pauses by the window and explains to Kayla that the only problem is that the lake wasn't built deep enough and so it floods when it rains; sometimes the water breaches the entrance and then it's like trying to walk around on a Slip 'N Slide.

"Your mother is going to be fine." The nurse pats her shoulder. "Don't worry."

Kayla blinks at the nurse, takes in her wine-dark scrubs and her frosted-blond hair. She is the one who prepped Mary for surgery. She feels a chill, for that is exactly what the paramedic said about the man in the coveralls. And yet, moments ago, she witnessed him being transferred to another part of the kingdom with tremendous urgency.

The nurse continues down the illuminated hallway. Kayla bats at the air a few more times, fists loosely curled, then reminds herself of where she is, makes her hands go still.

Three months later, she will get another chance to fight her former best friend and she will knock her out in the second round. She will move with a finely honed aggression that is beyond anything she has ever shown in the ring before; she will understand that she has now broken through to a different place. *I never doubted,* Coach will tell her as they embrace in the corner. After the fight, she will stride over to her former best friend's corner and shake hands with her and her new coach; she will learn that nothing makes her feel like a badder bitch than showing magnanimity in victory. The hoodie who robbed the gas station will be shot dead by the police outside a laundromat. *See?* Kayla's father will say after he hears the news. *They kill white people too.* Which is not the defense he thinks it is. She will not ever hear from Mary. She will go into the diner, Perks, and ask if Mary is on shift and the manager will tell her that Mary hasn't worked there in years. "Are you sure?" she will ask, and the manager will say, "Look, kid, I know my Marys."

Kayla stares down at the lake, which appears, at this hour, unfathomably deep. When the man passed on the gurney he seemed to be looking at her, as though he might have remembered her face from the early morning, her expression of terror and helplessness, but perhaps he was just casting a long, last look in the direction of the outside world. The starless night sky; the emerald curve of the lake; the rising tide.

Nominated by Virginia Quarterly Review

NOMAD PALINDROME

by KAI CARLSON-WEE

from AGNI

Maps, dogs, rail, stars, a Warsaw door,
no sleep, no moods,
I lived on flow, on speed, on spit-faced lonely tons,
red rum, Tums, on bad dessert, sands,
eye-level, dim as time,
stab on, sway on, span on, Erewhon,
drawn onward,
nowhere, no naps, no yaws, no bats
(emits a mid-level E), yes, DNA stress, ED, dab,
no smut, murders, no Tylenol, decaf, tips,
no deeps, no wolf, no devil-is-doom,
on peels, on rood,
was raw as rats, liars, God, Spam.

Nominated by Elizabeth Tallent

JORIE, JR.

fiction by MICHAEL CZYZNIEJEWSKI

from BOULEVARD

The guys on the line couldn't shut up about Jorie. *Jorie pounding tin was like a mountain forming a diamond. Jorie driving screws was like a tornado ripping into the plains. Jorie clinching sheet was like furious, impassioned fucking.* In short, one shift with Jorie was Genesis, six days packed into eight hours, then watching it over and over, five times a week. Jorie was why they made quota. Jorie kept the factory open. Jorie was why everyone still had jobs, why everyone could pay their mortgage and feed their kids. Jorie leaving was why we fell behind, why all of that was in jeopardy.

I was his less-abled replacement, but they couldn't blame me—none of them were Jorie, either. They did, anyway. Foreman Steve came up to me, mid-shift, said I was done. They were losing their ass because I couldn't keep up—not like Jorie. Two new guys were there to take my place, jumped in on the next rotation. I asked why I couldn't just have a partner if they were going to spend two guys on one spot, anyway. Steve said I wasn't half the man Jorie was so they'd still need two guys. He pointed to the office where my partial check was waiting.

In the office, I stared at Jorie, his six-straight Employee-of-the-Month photos, the six months prior to my tenure. His curly red hair made him look on fire. His jaw was the foundation of a skyscraper. His eyes were love poems to every woman who ever lived.

The clerk behind the counter said, "Staring at Jorie?"

"I guess," I said.

"Best part of my job," she said. She ran her index fingertip across her tongue, peeled my check from a pile. "Six of him staring down at me when one would more than do the trick."

My stepdad was disappointed to see me home early but not surprised. He said I embarrassed him, that he'd put in thirty years on that line without as much as a firm talking-to. He told me to find something else soon, on my own, that I'd have to pay my share or get out. I told him not to worry, that I'd get another job, one without a Jorie.

He looked away from the TV and said, "What'd you say?"

I filled him in on Jorie, the awards, the production, how two guys had to replace him. He said he'd worked with a guy named Jorie, going into the whole mountain-tornado-furious-fucking shtick. I told him that was who I replaced, who I couldn't live up to. He said it couldn't be the same Jorie, so many years later. I told him about the red hair, the woman aflutter, the circle jerk that ensued whenever anyone talked about him.

"Jorie must have a son," he said. "Jorie, Jr."

"Whatever," I said.

Finding a job took a while. I had no skills or references and especially no real desire to work. I put out feelers, called in favors, but nothing. After a month I lied to my stepdad, said I'd gotten on at the quarry, just so I could leave the house every morning, get away from him. I split the days between the library and the gym. I lifted in work clothes so when I came home, my stepdad would think I'd put in a solid eight—I even dusted myself with gym talc to make it look good. One of the trainers, this ponce in a mesh tank top, asked me why I lifted in flannels, jeans, and poleclimbers. I told him I'd just been at work. He told me about the locker room. Then he asked where I worked. I told him the library. He took the hint, walked away, but did a sudden turn and asked, "You don't happen to know a guy named Jorie, do you?"

I placed the bar on the rack and sat up.

"He used to come in here dressed like you. He still holds most of the gym's records." He pointed to the whiteboard above the dumbbells. Most every field—bench, squats, thrust, curl—all had the name *Jorie* written in marker, some impossible weight next to it.

"People came in just to watch him lift," the trainer said. He had the same look on him as the woman who'd had my check. "Jorie pumping iron was like a locomotive charging up a mountain."

"Fuck me," I said and left forever.

That night, my stepdad and I drove up to visit my mom in the home. She couldn't live with us anymore, needing twenty-four-hour care, professional-like. Responsible. Neither of us were that. The administrator stopped us on our way in, said Mom hadn't been doing well. Her kidney was bad, the left one.

"Left from the front or the back?" my stepdad asked.

The administrator stared at him. He said, "*Her* left."

Mom was a non-candidate for a transplant, her age, plus why she needed twenty-four-hour care. She could get dialysis, but dialysis sucked, and she'd die, anyway. They could search for a match, but even if they found one, they wouldn't waste an organ on my mom. They wanted to test me, said I was the best shot she had. The next day I took the test. A day later a surgeon called and said he had good news and bad news. The bad news: I wasn't a match. The good news: They knew of someone, someone who wanted my mother to have his kidney—he didn't care about younger, healthier people—he wanted to save my mom. We scheduled the operation.

In prep, my mother thought I was my father, that she was in the hospital for her C-section, to give birth to me. I didn't know my father, and she'd always refused to reveal his name. I listened for details, to see if she'd let it slip while all drugged up. She fell asleep talking about Burt Lancaster.

The donor was in the adjoining OR; as soon as they had it out of him, they put it into her. I wondered if they had to rinse it first, like produce (they did but not with water). Recovery would be rough, but if they flooded her with anti-rejectors, she might pull through. I stayed with her until my stepdad told me to go home, pointed out only one of us could spend the night. He insisted it be him. I let him have it.

On my way out, I caught him out of the corner of my eye as I walked past his room: Jorie. He was out, sleeping soundly, his red locks filling his pillow like a sun. I considered going in and reading his chart to verify my suspicion, but I knew it was him, this massive folk hero, the perfect match, kidney-wise, for my expiring mom. I sat next to him, waiting for him to wake. His arms and legs hung over the end of the bed as if he were in the children's ward. He could have been twenty-nine or fifty-nine—it was hard to tell, all the tubes going into him; plus, he'd just donated a kidney. An hour passed before a nurse came in, surmised I didn't belong, kicked me out. I went to get my stepdad, to show him, to see if the Jorie I knew was the Jorie he knew. My stepdad was gone; my mother's nurse said he'd left right after I did. I stayed next to my mom all that night, sleeping in a wooden chair. When I woke, I went to check on Jorie, but he was gone, his bed occupied by a woman with a rotten gallbladder.

I stayed with my mother until she was released. The amazing thing was she knew me, said my name, the first time in over a year. Maybe it was the lighting, better than at the home. Maybe it was the sweet drugs pumping into her. But me, I thought of Jorie's left kidney, sifting out her insides, unclogging something in her head. That had to be it.

When I got home, I confronted my stepdad, asked if Jorie was my father. He said he doubted it but admitted I could do worse. I asked him why he was so sure, and he reminded me that a lot of guys—most of them, in fact—weren't my father.

"But I'd bet your mom did him," my stepdad said. "After you were born."

"Why do you say that?"

"Everybody had a turn with Jorie. Your mother saw him at plant picnics. Once the ladies saw Jorie, there was no going back."

"This doesn't bother you?"

"What did you want me to do? Fight him? Leave your mother? She was only human. This is Jorie we're talking about here.

"In a way, I'm honored."

I searched for a comeback. Something awful popped into my head instead, a joke about Jorie being in my mother then, being in her again now. I didn't share this with my stepdad. He'd get there himself, eventually.

Jorie didn't come up again, not for months. Christmastime, I got a job at the P.O., sorting letters. It didn't take long before I spotted his name. It could've been another Jorie, but I knew it was him. He had a P.O. box, so no address. I'd have to spot him coming in. I could see most of the boxes from where I sorted, and Jorie would be hard to miss, this handsome, hulking ginger. Of course, he could come in when I wasn't there—I was only on twenty hours a week, and the boxes were accessible 24-7. Unless I staked out the P.O. when I was off the clock, I'd miss him.

I staked out the P.O. when I was off the clock. I stayed all night in my Taurus in the main lot. Sometimes I'd force myself awake until three or four in the morning, then get up at six and stumble inside for my shift. Sure enough, every time I fell asleep, I'd go inside to see Jorie's box emptied. I started to nod off at work, too, sorting letters with one eye, watching for Jorie with the other. Didn't take long for me to get fired from the P.O., three days before Christmas.

"I thought it was impossible to get fired from the P.O. three days before Christmas," the postmaster said.

In a way, I was honored.

Since her surgery, Mom's clarity peaked. I'd visit, and we'd have real conversations—she and I instead of she and some dead relative from the Coolidge administration. My stepdad came sometimes, too. We'd drive together, actually talk on the way there and back. One day, Mom's doctor pointed out this was what they called terminal lucidity; her being so clear, for so long, meant she was about to die, her brain going all out before giving up. I asked about the kidney, if that was helping. The doctor laughed. After he realized I was serious, he said, "No, that's not it" and left the room. I silently maintained a faint belief that Jorie's organ was curing her.

My stepdad didn't talk on the way home that day except to say we should start making arrangements. That's when I told him about the P.O., me getting fired, being utterly broke. For some reason I copped to the quarry job being fake, too. And the landscaping and pizza-delivery jobs in between.

"Well, we know who won't be chipping in for the funeral," he said.

If that doctor, the internet, and a movie I half-watched on Lifetime were all correct, my mother could die any day. First I had to find out one thing and that was who my real father was. My stepdad said it wasn't Jorie, that she'd slept with Jorie after I was born. Then again, my stepdad didn't know my mother before I was born—she could have slept with Jorie back then, too, rekindling a spark years down the road. Jorie was my father: I was sure of it. Before my mother passed, I had to make her speak the words.

Mom greeted me when I came in, knowing my name, who I was, showing genuine affection—I was getting used to this. It was Christmas Eve. We both said "Merry Christmas." Neither of us had presents. I sat next to her on the bed, and we played gin. I told her I knew the truth about my father.

"It was a matter of time before you found out," she said. "Did he tell you?"

"I put two and two together," I said.

"I'm glad you know."

"How come you never told me?" I asked.

"He was ashamed for leaving you. He couldn't face up to what he'd done."

"So why's he still around?"

"I suppose when I go, that might stop happening."

"I wish he'd just talk to me. I'd love to just talk to him."

It went on like this for a while, me asking, in different phrasings, why she'd not been honest with me.

"I'll always thank him for giving you his kidney, though," I said eventually.

My mother stopped talking, stopped apologizing for Jorie. She said, "What the hell are you talking about?"

"Jorie gave you his left kidney," I said. "Jorie. My birth father. Who we've been discussing."

Mom started to laugh, loudly and continuously. She stopped when she realized I was serious. "Your stepdad is your father, Melvin. He abandoned us, then came back when you were three. He was embarrassed, so we made up the stepdad thing. I don't know any Jorie."

On my way home that day, I decided not to tell my stepdad/dad that I knew. He was going to have to tell me, or we'd never speak of it. I didn't even mind the whole stepdad thing, but the fact that the treated me like shit as my stepdad made no sense: Why'd he come back, just to be a dick?

When I got to the house, my stepdad/dad's car wasn't in the driveway, and he wasn't anywhere in the house. This wasn't too odd until it got late. I thought that maybe he'd gone to visit my mom, that we crossed each other on the way. The next morning, I woke and saw that he hadn't slept in his bed, but also that his dresser drawers were pulled out and mostly empty. Like reverse-Christmas. I went to the hospital, and he wasn't there—the nurses said they hadn't seen him, that my mother slept alone.

I asked my mom what she thought, if she knew where he could have gone. Within a second I knew that she was gone, too. She didn't know who I was, staring at me with the discerning bewilderment I'd come to know. I explained who I was, but knew I was wasting my time. She became upset, throwing things at me, her pillow, her glasses, her dentures. The nurses told me to go. I told my mom I'd come back later, maybe the next day. Mom told the nurses to call the police.

On my way home, I stopped for gas. Inside, I spied Jorie behind the counter, his picture adorning a poster, wearing a Santa hat: He'd just won the Lotto, three million and change, having purchased his ticket at that gas station.

Half a mile from my house, I saw a billboard: Jorie was a lawyer, wanting to represent me, or anybody, in our medical malpractice cases. His phone number ended in 5555—he was that kind of lawyer.

On the radio, Jammin' Jorie reminded me it was a Christmas Two for Tuesday between "D'yer Mak'er" and "Stairway to Heaven."

On the front door, Jorie'd left a flier, announcing he was running for county coroner, asking for my vote. The flier used the same picture, him in the black suit and tie, from the lawyer billboard. Jorie was a doctor and a lawyer? I was surprised I was surprised.

Inside, still no stepdad/dad. There was one message on his ancient answering machine next to his rotary phone, the red light blinking. I pressed play, assuming it would be Jorie, selling me something, telling me he was coming over, declaring himself king of the world.

It was the hospital. Mom.

My stepdad/dad didn't show up to identify Mom's body. He didn't make arrangements. He didn't come to the funeral. An account to cover all the costs had been set up with the home, I found out, as otherwise, my mother would have been buried in a box out in a field behind the home. She'd done it during her lucidity, they told me. The rest in her account would go to me, after probate.

A few days after Mom was in the ground, a letter came to the house, informing me I had two weeks to vacate: Stepdad/Dad had sold the place. He wasn't coming back to get any more of his things—I'd never talk to him again. I didn't have a whole lot, so I was gone in half the time. That house was the only place I'd ever lived.

I sold a lot of Stepdad/Dad's shit in that week, his TVs and furniture and appliances, even the phone and answering machine. Between that and what my mother left for me, I had enough to function for a few months. I rented an efficiency and spent the days sleeping and the nights drinking. I got fat, grew my beard out, got excellent at computer solitaire. I found a job just before the money ran, out so I didn't have to live on the streets. That seemed to be my line.

The job was the midnight shift at the morgue, janitorial mostly but also helping the coroner with unenviable tasks. Of course, the coroner was Jorie—he'd won in a landslide, getting an unprecedented 99 percent of the vote. During the interview, he said I looked familiar. I told him he gave my mother his kidney. He asked how that would make me familiar to him. I told him his kidney had amazing palliative powers, perhaps even something telepathic. He laughed, then stopped when he realized I was serious. He changed the subject, hiring me on the spot.

A few months in, my stepdad/dad showed up on the slab as a John Doe. I told Jorie I could identify him, how I was his next of kin. He said he could, too, that he'd worked with him on an assembly line years earlier. He suggested I take the night off, said I wouldn't want to be around for the autopsy. I fell asleep in the morgue's parking lot, never going home.

Jorie determined my father had died from a botched surgery. He, too, had needed a kidney and even had a donor. Then the doctors took his good one out by mistake, leaving the bad one inside. He died from blood poisoning on the operating table. Jorie offered to represent me in the suit, reminding me he lawyered during the day. I pointed out the conflict, how they'd never let him testify at a trial he was also trying. He said there wouldn't be a trial: They always settled when they pulled the wrong thing out of you.

"Your father's parting gift," he said. "You'll get millions."

I accepted his offer, with one stipulation: I wanted to keep working with him at the morgue, keep being his assistant. Jorie told me he'd be honored, that me tagging toes was like Shakespeare naming his sonnets. We got back to work. People died every day.

Nominated by Boulevard

THE EMPEROR CONCERTO

by JULIE HECHT

from GRANTA

I was wondering about Beethoven's state of mind when he wrote the 'Emperor' Concerto. Because it has an endless end – and endless ending. And I'm sure that musicologists and scholars have written about the insanely beautiful part known in music as rondo. But I'm too tired to look that up. I was wondering if he was going mad when he wrote the concerto because when I listened and watched for the third time on the annoying YouTube, with 'Ads' and 'Skip Ads' interrupting, I thought this rondo is going to drive me mad. It's never going to end. And I looked at the pianist, Mitsuko Uchida, half magical princess, half wild being. While I listened to the unbelievable beauty of her playing – delicate and light-handed, but strong and filled with passion – I realized that compared to her and Seiji Ozawa, we're all little pipsqueaks. And to think my husband prevented me from seeing them perform at Carnegie Hall and in Boston, and at Tanglewood, and it's too late now because Ozawa is so frail and Mitsuko might be less energetic now. She might not be able to fly off the bench, throwing her aquamarine organza sleeve with her delicate white-skin arm into the air.

I looked at her. She was wearing a blue-green organza blouse with a crinkly – is it *ruched?* – camisole underneath, her beautiful, white, smooth skin showing. It was distracting, the sleeves were so big and puffy, and you could see her arms and slight, thin chest through the middle tighter part. She hadn't had her hair blown dry straight. Hair blow-drying is a waste of life. Her hair was cut in thick layers and it was wild. She was like a wild woman when she played, and I wondered how she could play that way without going crazy. And then I looked at Ozawa,

287

and the rondo wasn't bothering him. I guess he'd done it many times before and he knew the music-history explanation for it. Then I remembered my piano teacher from childhood. One day he said, 'How would you like to play a little Gershwin for a change?'

'How about Beethoven? The Moonlight Sonata,' I said.

'You know Beethoven was blind and deaf when he wrote that.'

And since I was only eleven, I said, 'Oh no. How come? Why?'

The piano teacher said, 'He had syphilis.'

'What's that?' I said.

Then he called my mother in from the kitchen where she was holding an orange Le Creuset pot, for those onions, as usual. I mean, how could it be so important for my mother always to be cutting onions in the kitchen?

He asked her, 'Doesn't anyone tell this kid anything?'

'Tell her anything like what?'

And he said, 'Well, she doesn't know what syphilis is.'

'She's only eleven,' my mother said. 'Why should she know about that?'

'We were talking about Beethoven,' he said.

He was kind of a bohemian, now called hip, but somewhat overweight guy. He wore corduroy suits and dark blue shirts with olive-green ties. He used to come and smoke a cigar and let my mother feed him every fattening thing she had cooked and baked the whole week. During my piano lesson he would show me how a piece of music ought to be played and he would explain by singing along with Mozart, and instead of saying, 'la la la', or 'la da', like most people, he would sing 'ya ba ba' and 'ya ba bom' and 'bom bom pom', and more and more excitedly 'ya pa pom! pa pa pom!', rocking back and forth and bouncing up and down in the antique chair my mother had provided for him until I thought the seams of his corduroy pants and the buttons on his hopsack cloth shirt would pop off from the pressure. I was afraid the veins standing out in his face would burst and that his whole person might just explode from the exertion.

He was married to a beautiful modern dancer. She was thin and had creamy white skin and long black hair she wound up and stuck at the top of her long neck with big, tortoiseshell hairpins and she had thick bangs. They were an arty and elegant couple. She was arty and elegant, anyway. He was arty.

I pictured the room. I pictured sitting at the piano on the bench, with these beautiful pink roses on the dark green needlepoint cover. We bought the piano from an older couple in their apartment, with the nee-dlepoint cover bench. To think I was offered that bench when my parents sold our house, and I didn't take it. My apartment had two rooms, without space for the piano or the bench. I would like to look at that bench so much. The bench could be opened up and inside were all the yellow Mozart piano books. If only I could be in that room with those many big windows looking out onto what's called a tree-lined street, and inside, walls of shelves of books and my mother in the doorway with her orange-red Le Creuset pot, and my teacher sitting in a chair next to the piano.

Once, in an argument with the teacher, he pushed me at the bench to show feeling and I refused to play after that. He said, 'Do you hold that against me?' I said, 'Yes, you pushed me at the piano bench. You're not supposed to do that. I don't understand how you can have such a beautiful, wonderful wife.' He was amused, and he said, 'Well, how is she so beautiful?' And I said, 'Oh everything, her hair. That long thick black hair. That white skin. That beautiful big smile.' And he said, 'But you have the same long hair. And yours is blonde.' And I said, 'Oh, but hers is thicker. She has those thick bangs. She's just so beautiful and everything she has is beautiful.' And he said, 'Well, why do you suppose she married me?'

'I don't know,' I said. 'But it was a mistake or some error in judgment.' He was entertained by that. I guessed he knew he was a lucky man.

I could tell that the teacher didn't like me. He was brought in to make my older sibling feel better. He was told how she felt so bad because she was not attractive or entertaining. However, even she was entertained at the dinner table when I told stories of what I'd seen and done that day. They even laughed at imitations of their table manners. And all the attention from everyone we knew or met went in my direction. Then the piano teacher was filled in, as so many people were, with that sob story. That's why he preferred the evil sibling.

I couldn't help that I looked like a movie star and made people laugh – I thought all children's looks were equal and I chose my friends because they all looked different. I couldn't help it that I was born and that my older sibling never got over it. That's why she was miserable and depressed. My mother did everything to keep me down.

A Viennese child psychoanalyst told me, when I was a young grown-up – and she wasn't an empathetic person – 'I have seen one child completely destroyed to protect the other.'

About thirty years later I was friendly with a precocious pre-teenaged son of a world-renowned reproductive surgeon, who said to me, 'I have a way on my computer where I can find anyone. Do you want me to find someone?'

'Yes, find my piano teacher,' I said. 'Ivan Fiedel. Find him.'

A bit later that evening the boy reported back to me that he had found the piano teacher, his phone number and where he lived in California.

He offered to call him for me.

When he reported back, he had a long story to tell. He said the teacher talked and talked and talked and talked. And he added, 'You know what, he didn't like you. He just liked your older sibling. He just wanted to ask about her.' The boy thought it was funny. I could tell he was smiling.

The piano teacher told the boy everything about his life, that he'd had an illness and for a while he didn't think he'd recover. But he did recover. The boy said, 'The stories he told, he went on and on and on! He couldn't stop talking about your whole family, your parents, your sibling, your house! Early-American antiques bought inexpensively. Art that had been given. But the main thing is, I could tell he didn't like you.' He was still amused.

I said, 'That's right, he didn't. He once pushed me as I was playing and he yelled, "Move! Move! Move!" Then he added, "Marion Greene moves around with feeling when she plays these sonatas! You're not supposed to sit there like a wooden stick."'

He probably wished he'd had Mitsuko Uchida as his student. It's possible, she was much younger than he was but she lived in Vienna at the time. Who was her teacher? I guess I could google it, but it would take too long.

I had the courage to say, 'I think Marion Greene looks like a complete fool when she moves around. I don't want to be like that. I'm just playing the piano. I do what she does when I'm imitating a famous pianist I've seen on TV. Everyone laughs.'

He liked it when I explained this because he considered that one of his side points as a piano teacher was getting adolescents to express their true inner feelings and solve their hidden conflicts. Emotional outbursts were fine with him. I used to pretend to be wildly conducting a symphony or even playing a sonata. My mother and aunt found this funny, laughing their heads off, instead of just sending me to the High School of Performing Arts. My high school was more like one in Beverly Hills.

My mother said he'd told her that Marion was learning like a house on fire, and then said to me, in her meanest way, 'You're learning like a house not even started.'

Years later I wished the teacher could know that I had Mozart's complete works and listened all the time. I saw him interviewed on TV one year, running a progressive music and dance school in Connecticut, and then I saw his wife buying a black cape and black coat on the designer floor at Lord & Taylor. She looked exactly the same, twenty years later, the same exact face, the same black hair, no gray and not dyed; maybe a few lines around the eyes from laughing and being happy and hip. I told her who I was and she didn't remember if I had my name or my sibling's. She said her baby was fifteen now and a very sensitive boy.

When I was about eleven and I told the piano teacher I hated the boring Hannon piano exercises, he said, 'How would you like to take a little vacation from Hannon?' I was quick to agree and when he never resumed them after three years I didn't remind him, although it was always on my mind.

Once, after he got me to confess that I sometimes hated my mother, he said, 'How would you like to talk to a psychiatrist?'

'But I'm not crazy.'

'You don't need to be crazy. Lots of people do it if they're a little confused the way you are.'

'What does a little confused mean?'

'It means I know lots of people who feel better after they go to one.'

'Including you?'

'People like me.'

He'd probably been going for years and was still going. I didn't know that part of society yet.

'And kids your age,' he added.

'What?'

'Yes. Lots of kids like you.'

'Anyone I know?'

'My brother.'

'What brother?'

'My kid brother.'

'You have no brother, no young brother.'

'Sure I do. He's fifteen.'

'But you're old.'

'How old am I?'

'In your thirties.'

'I'm thirty-six and my parents had a surprise baby when I was twenty.'

'Is that why he's crazy?' This is something I might have said as Lolita in the film version of *Lolita*. I love the moments when she screams at James Mason, 'You're crazy!' I could have played that part of dialogue, although the unbelievably great performance of the teenage actress Sue Lyon was perfect for all of the movie. I was too high class to play that character.

'Wait a minute. He's not crazy. He had some problems, he got some help and now he's getting straightened out. He's a lot happier kid now, less guilty, less withdrawn, more in touch with life.' That was his style of talking.

'Uh-huh,' I said. Even then I didn't care for that style.

'Are you interested in looking into it?' the teacher asked.

'I don't believe you have a brother that age.'

'Why not?'

'You never said so before.'

'It never came up.'

'You're always telling about all the kids you know, especially ones that you've helped with their mental problems.'

'I didn't get to help him, the psychiatrist did.'

'I'll ask your wife. She wouldn't make something up like that.'

'Why would I if she wouldn't?'

'She's superior to you.'

'Ha. Really? How?'

'She's beautiful and thin and kind. She doesn't interfere with people's minds. She'd never scream and push a student over at the piano.'

'You hold that against me still?'

'Always.'

The piano teacher and his beautiful dancer wife had two little children. A photo of her had appeared in *Life* magazine just after she had her first baby by natural childbirth, in the delivery room with what looks like all her stage makeup still on, smiling in ecstasy with her new baby. My mother said, 'It's not normal for a man to talk about details of natural childbirth. This is what women talk about, amongst themselves.'

This was the beginning of the new era. I guess he was ahead of his time, or her time anyway. Now everybody talks about everything.

In the photograph the dancer-wife looked beautiful and not even tired. But my mother didn't want to hear about that either – the fact there was no anesthesia used and maybe she went home the next day or the same day. Hard to remember every detail.

My mother would bring out those samples of unhealthful things she was cooking in the kitchen. The piano lessons were mostly about her giving him samples of food she was cooking for dinner, in fact about anything other than the piano playing. Antique furniture was another topic.

It's not as if I were a great piano student. Chopping onions was always more important than anything. And I hate everything about onions. I begged her not to cook onions during the daytime, especially in the morning. Not a good aroma for waking up, not like toast.

When I was four, and we lived in an old, antique-filled house in Brooklyn, a part that's become hip and fashionable now – luckily I have a photograph of the room of the scene I remember – my mother was in the kitchen doing something, and while we were arguing, I was telling her over and over that I had nothing to do. She finally lost her temper and followed me into the living room with that long, pointy knife she had for cooking big things. She might have been screaming, 'You're the curse of my life. What did I do to deserve this?' This scene caused hysterical crying on my part. I lay on the couch, face down, in wild hysteria.

During the middle of the crying, my closest friend, who lived in the house next door, came and knocked on the door. It was a glass French door inside the vestibule. It had a thin white curtain over it, the way it was done. My mother asked her in, but I still couldn't stop crying.

My friend said, 'What's wrong? Why is she crying like that?'

And my mother said, 'Oh, some little thing. Come in.'

But my friend was so terrified that she left. Or was it that my friend stayed and we tried to talk for a minute first? Because a little later, my mother came back into the room, still in her housedress with an apron – I wish I could remember which ones – and she said, 'But why were you so hysterical? Things like this have happened before.'

'You had a knife,' I said.

'You thought I was going to attack you?'

'You were holding it and screaming.'

And she said, with what looked like regret and guilt, 'I just happened to have the knife in my hand. If I had a cup, I would have come in there with a cup.' I always remember this sentence exactly the way she said it.

293

Upon review of the scene, she meant a measuring cup. But I pictured a white teacup, the simplest, plainest kind in children's books. It still didn't make sense. I tried to understand the scene, but I couldn't be sure because of the idea of the cup. Also there was the screaming, 'You're the curse of my life,' when she came into the living room. I had heard that before. Just because I had said I had nothing to do. She hadn't arranged anything the way other mothers did.

She probably told my father about the incident when he came home from work. They must have both been sad. Maybe my mother cried.

I complained to my mother that I didn't like the piano teacher's behavior one of the times when she was raving about what an 'unusual guy' he was and how lucky we were to have him instead of the average kind of piano teacher. That's what my parents get for moving to a suburb, they lost their perspective of quality. There must have been a million of his type in Manhattan. Now I see my mother was right. I understand him better and wish we all could have stayed friends.

'He's not a psychologist,' I said. 'He's just here to give piano lessons.' 'How do you know he's not a psychologist?' she said in her mean way. It always worried me after that, that he was a secret psychologist and just pretended he was there to give piano lessons.

Before this guy, we had an old-fashioned strict-style piano teacher. We went to her apartment for piano lessons. She was a middle-aged kind of piano teacher with short curly hair, with some gray in it. She insisted that we hold our elbows up high, higher than our hands, to play anything on the piano.

When I told the hip piano teacher about this, he said, 'Oh, I know about her. She's damaged a lot of kids.'

I wish I knew what happened to these people. I wish I knew their whole life stories. I guessed it was a coincidence that her niece taught ballet lessons.

That was all I knew.

My idea for a spring day was to get a ride in a convertible. Walking was not yet known. The piano teacher had an old white Chevrolet convertible and when he saw how surprised I was that he had the top down he offered to take me for a ride.

'Is there some great maternity shop around here?' he asked my mother. 'I'd like to pick up some surprise present for the mother-to-be.'

'Maternally Yours!' I said. 'I've always wanted to go there!'

'You have, huh? Why have you?' He was looking at me intently.

'They have such cute things in the window. Like Lucille Ball wears in *I Love Lucy.*'

'I hope they're better than the name of the place. Is it any good,' he asked my mother.

'It's supposed to be. I don't know really, I've never been inside.'

'I always try to get her to go,' I said.

'But we have no reason to. I don't want people to see us going in there. You don't just go browsing in a maternity shop for no reason.'

'Well I have a reason,' the piano teacher said. 'Let's go.'

When we got to the shop and parked across the street he said, 'I'll be out in ten minutes.'

'Can't I go with you?'

'Nah, you better wait here. I don't want them to think I'm buying it for you.'

'How could they?'

'I don't want to take any chances. Better wait outside in the car.'

'Can I look in the window?'

'That'd be worse. I'll be right out.'

In just a few minutes he came back carrying a giant white box tied with royal-blue ribbon. It was like the movies where the husband goes in for a present and spends lots of money very easily after seeing only one or two things. I've never gotten a package wrapped in a white box with a ribbon and then jumped into a convertible and happily zoomed away. I had to have admiration for the piano teacher the way he did that, even if he was a little overweight.

When my mother took my sister for college interviews, the piano teacher came for a lesson. He asked where my mother was. I told him, 'They're at Wellesley for a college interview. And Tufts.'

'Why didn't you go too?' he asked.

'My mother said I was too young and I would get in the way of important things they had to do.'

'But you might want to go to Wellesley some day.'

I didn't think of that.

I liked Smith better. There was more grass, more ivy – there were more bricks. There was an inn with an antique spinning wheel in the main floor and four-poster canopy beds upstairs. I liked Smith better mainly because it had more ivy. I judged colleges by the amount of ivy, bricks, green grass, beautiful old trees. I didn't know that's why these colleges were called the Ivy League, and Seven Sisters schools. Even after I'd seen all the ivy. I thought it was just a name. I thought there were only three colleges: Smith, Wellesley, and what they called Mount Holyoke at the time. I didn't count Radcliffe because there was hardly any lawn, or brick, and hardly any ivy. I couldn't take it seriously. This is before I knew about Bennington. But when I went for the interview all the girls seemed depressed and boy-crazy.

When we went to visit Smith, we stayed at that beautiful, antique inn with the antique spinning wheel. A kind, New England-style older lady, who appeared to be the manager of the inn, asked me, 'Are you here for an interview and to see Smith?'

I said, 'No, my older sister is here for an interview.'

She smiled and said, 'Well, you may want to come here, too, someday.'

I'd never thought of that, either. I thought colleges were for older teenagers and my place was just in my room, listening to Elvis Presley on my pink radio. I still had a carton of Little Lulu comics under my bed.

The night of the Wellesley trip, the teacher said, 'So you're left alone with your father? What are you two going to do?' My father didn't pick up on the father–daughter stuff. He didn't think girls were serious and he showed no emotion.

'Well, we went to dinner at a Chinese restaurant,' I said.

There were no good restaurants in suburbs during that era. Even in the city, just the fancy French ones. We often had to go to Longchamps, a dark and dreary formal restaurant on the ground floor of the Empire State Building with a menu consisting of things like turkey, or mashed potatoes, canned cranberry sauce – not just for Thanksgiving, but all the time. My mother always found this to be the only thing to order. She would ask me, 'How is that? Is that any good?'

'Not too good. Canned string beans,' I would say. And she would say, 'I thought so. Most restaurants aren't good.'

When I remember this, I'm surprised she was asking my opinion about food, since, as a vegetarian, there was hardly any food I could order and there was hardly any food she didn't like. I was a vegetarian at an early age when I found out most food was some kind of animal.

During my lesson I was tired and kind of slumped over as I played my Mozart sonata, and finally the teacher said to my father, 'What'd you do to this kid, get her drunk?'

'She only had a couple of sips.'

'Well, let's give this up until next week,' the teacher suggested.

'She only had the orange from my whiskey sour,' my father said. 'That couldn't have much effect.' I felt sorry for my father. He seemed guilty, as if he really thought he'd done something wrong.

'I'm just naturally tired,' I said. Life was tiring.

During the dinner we never spoke, maybe just a few sentences. When he did, it was about history or current events. He ordered that whiskey sour and offered me some. First I ate the orange and the carcinogenic red cherry and then I had a few sips. It was like some interesting orange juice. My father was thinking about something serious. I could tell. Then we came back for the evening piano lesson. I guess it was spring, there was daylight savings, so we had to have dinner early.

My father didn't seem to like me either. He could talk to my sibling because she was scholarly. She had no friends. She stayed in her dreary, blue-green room, always alone, reading. I liked to be outside playing with my friends or studying the insides of their houses.

He'd talk to her about history, but I was interested in Elvis Presley. What could we say about him?

The name of the restaurant was the Joy Inn. But all the times we went there I don't remember any joy – only my father's admonition not to eat spare ribs, or any greasy, unhealthy, disgusting thing on the menu. What could be more disgusting than spare ribs? I guess there are many things. Just think about the pigs, and their treatment, ending up on a plate.

I can still see the spare ribs shining right now, under the orange sugar marinade. A vegan even then, my dinner was the sloppy dish called vegetable chow mein or even sloppier Buddha's Delight – not a delight. I bet Jacqueline Kennedy and Caroline were never taken to places like the Joy Inn.

Upbringing is important, and I've never gotten over mine.

While the two conspirators were away at Wellesley, I discovered that my best slip was missing from my drawer. My drawers were neat in those days. When things needed repairs my mother had them done, when they were old and worn, she took them for rags. When things were outgrown, they were given away. Not the way it is now, the drawers are now with sections and areas of indecision, which gradually become mixed in with those I use until I can't tell which is which or what things are there for in the first place.

My mother organized everything: socks, underwear, slips and nightgowns. This slip was nylon. It was a color called powder blue, with scallops of white lace at the hem, and there was a little flower embroidery at the top of each scallop. I saved it for special occasions.

When the evil twosome got home from the college tour, I asked my mother, 'Where is my blue slip?' She helped me look. She was only fifty-percent evil.

'Did you look all through your drawer?' she said.

'Yes,' I said. 'Look, it isn't here.'

And then she said, 'Maybe _____ took it.'

I kept turning things over in the drawer and looking into my night-gown and sock drawers. I was late for school that day and when I asked my mother about the slip, she said again, 'Maybe _____ took it.'

I said, 'How could she take my best slip? She has her own. She's older. It's not even her size! It's small! She wears medium! I'm only eleven!' Maybe I was almost screaming by then.

It turned out that she had taken it. My mother asked her, and she said none of hers were clean. Typical – always taking my things because hers weren't clean, and for other, deeper reasons.

I believe I screamed at her, 'You probably stretched it out with your wide hips!'

'Cut it out now,' my mother said. A favorite thing of hers to say.

'She always asks for my best thing and then she uses it for slopping around. She wears silk to fry food and wash pots.'

To this very day she tries to steal from me. I was glad she was only on the waiting list at Wellesley. I wished I had remembered to say, 'God punished you for stealing my blue slip.'

There were three people chosen to try out for our grammar school grad-uation program. There was a talented piano player who was going on to Juilliard and he was known to be the one who would win. And then there were two others. There was me, because it was known I could play classical music, Mozart sonatas. I think it was known because they just asked in a haphazard, uncaring way: 'Who can play the piano? Who can play classical music?' And then there was a third person. But it was as-sumed that the Juilliard-headed student was going to be the winner.

I mentioned to my piano teacher that this was coming up, and he said, 'Oh, why don't you play the second movement of the Mozart sonata that you learned.'

And I just said, 'OK. But really, he's the pianist and he's known to be the one.'

My piano teacher said, 'I know, but why don't you try?'

'I'm not a talented pianist,' I said. 'I'm a writer, and an actress. I'm a storyteller.'

'Why don't you compete?'

'Oh, because it's for him,' I said. Anyway, I'd be too fearful to be competitive.

The truth is, he was a little nerdy guy. He had the appearance of something called a schlemiel. He shrugged a lot. He was short. He was cute in a way, in that Eastern European way. And certain girls liked him. He was kind of a mess. His shirts were always crumpled up and hanging out of his pants on the side. He was in his own world of musical practicing. Years later I met an English psychiatrist with that shirt style. He was outside at night in a parking lot, calling, 'I can't find some papers!'

At the audition, when I played the sonata in the stick-of-wood style – my mother didn't come. She was probably home chopping onions or in Manhattan at her other favorite store, Ohrbach's, where women could get low prices on designer clothes, not as great as Loehmann's. Next she'd probably be meeting my father for dinner and going to a play. My mother really couldn't care at all about my activities. She once took me into that store with her. It was packed with women five inches from each other. My mother was wearing a black velvet, corduroy wide-wale hat she had been saving from the 1940s. It came to a slanted point on top and near the point in one place there was a small collection of tiny gold bells. My mother, who usually had the best taste in everything including clothing, said to me, 'Now if we get separated from each other, just listen for the little bells ringing.' She couldn't have believed I could hear those tiny bells ringing in that mob scene. No wonder I was a terrified child, and grown-up too.

Since this piano student was the talented pianist and I had different talents, I was surprised at the silence and then applause after I played. The students looked at me in this way: 'Oh, she can play the piano, too?' And they applauded more. And then I just got up and I went back to my seat, knowing the Juilliard boy had to win. And he did. And that was fine with me.

I was surprised that my piano teacher wanted me to compete with a serious musician. I guess he was an early feminist. He didn't know the Juilliard student. He probably would have liked to have been his teacher, but the boy had a special Juilliard teacher. Some years ago I saw an album he had recorded. He was wearing a tuxedo and he had white hair. He had become an important pianist.

In an interview, I heard Mitsuko was mad for Beethoven. She's supposed to be a Mozart lover, known for her unique interpretations of Mozart. I'd read in the interview with her that she was mad, mad, mad for Beethoven.

I fell into another deep state of gloom and barely remembered Mitsuko and her performances. The world health and political crises were worsening. Then I saw her being interviewed again. I heard her say, 'I don't know why people don't go to concerts anymore. That's not what I mean.' She meant something else. That wasn't the subject here. I missed that part. She sounded annoyed.

I didn't know people didn't go to concerts anymore. Classical music concerts. I thought only I didn't go, because I didn't live near Carnegie Hall or any of the places there were classical piano concerts, especially Mozart and Beethoven.

The only ones I'd ever seen in recent years were in a Nantucket Congregational Church. It wasn't air-conditioned, and I always sat in the last seat of the last row, near the open window. Hot humid air was coming through, and I needed my personal battery-powered fan in order to stay without fainting. I have several little powerful fans, but you can't really take them to a concert. People in the other rows are disturbed by the noise, especially the fastest setting #3.

The humidity and the BBC World News, bad parts skipped, watching the whole thing in five minutes still interfered with the nights of obsession with Mitsuko and the 'Emperor' Concerto.

Yes, I had been mad for Beethoven, but now I was just mad.

Nominated by Granta

SELF PORTRAIT AS MARY MAGDALENE IN THE STYLE OF GENTILESCHI

by KAMERYN ALEXA CARTER

from TORCH

I retired the Mary Magdalene around my neck
to a quaint embroidered box. The pressure of her
devotion was too much to carry. I have trouble
leveling and require a soft reminder of the double
pole inside me. Seeking a refuge for my soul, where
do I go but to the State Street preacher, who proclaims
the word into a rattling portable microphone, flanked
by Macy's mothers shoving along their Dyson strollers.
My phone is dead, so I ask if by chance he has the time,
to which he replies now. Jesus is coming, been came,
come back! Supposedly, the Son knows me by name.
Supposedly if I call, he'll answer. In the morning,
having pushed on through the acute trouble,
I acknowledge how far my mind has come
from turning against and against itself. It's too hot
for anything but gazpacho. The trick is day
old bread. Trouble don't last. Not always.

Nominated by Torch

THE DROPPER

fiction by MATTHEW NEILL NULL

from KENYON REVIEW

The miner Fluharty fussed around with bird dogs, and he'd earned a few red and yellow ribbons on the field trial circuit, "way back when," he'd say modestly. Beside his house stood the upturned blue barrel where the old man made them stand, their claws pinned to the curving sides, to learn steadiness as he murmured, "Whoa," and circled them, keeping eye contact as they puzzled over the situation with their doggy brains. He flushed training birds with his foot from tip-up traps and made the dogs stand quivering through their temptation: "Whoa, whoa." Fluharty could steady a dog, all right. The yard was full of cast-off kennel equipment, steel bowls, detritus.

"Our people," the current Senator's uncle liked to say, "are adept at turning money into junk. But why shouldn't they? A poor people should have as much right and opportunity to do stupid things as the rich, and with just as much questionable ostentation. That's why they leave their belongings scattered in the yard: they want you to know. But unlike rich households, they want you to stop by and talk about it." The Senator's uncle (who'd been the secretary of state and then the state treasurer) was the speechifier and the glad-hander and everyone's darling, "just an old 'Tally boy," he liked to say. Yet the man could be loving, too, and more than once was reduced to tears. "Our people," he said, "will endure."

But it's the old man's nephew who gets things done. The former company houses and neat farmsteads have "Proud Union Home" placards in the yards. If you pay attention as you glide the slaloming highway that carves a black ribbon through green forest, you'll notice the people shuf-

302

fling in the yards are retired, or near that. For the most part, they will not be replaced. Even so, the people have been better off than before. Cradle to grave: Manchin clinic, Manchin rehab, Manchin nursing home, Manchin funeral—the Senator and his family have brought their largesse home for fifty years. Calabrese coal miners, embedded in the union, in the law courts, ones who found a way to escape the repetitive bloody crush that fell on their kind. The roads are better than elsewhere. In this place, on both sides of I-79, the people have had enough money to take modest pleasures. Vacations. Good rifles. College for the children. Mannington and Grant Town, Hepzibah and Gypsy. Season tickets at the football. Motorcycles. Feast of the Seven Fishes. On the edge of mountains. Rich in birds and coal and Marcellus Shale.

Fluharty was one of the Senator's people, and look at the man's yard: his homing pigeons cooed and thrummed in their johnny house. The pricier devices—the electronic pigeon launchers, the tracking collars, the blank pistols—were theoretically kept organized in the mudroom, but Fluharty's daughter was suddenly finding them on any flat surface around the house. He was dogless at the moment; these objects' sudden appearance on the kitchen table told her what was happening, as well as the way he marched around upright, trying to disprove his herniated disc.

"You are not," Fluharty's daughter said.

"I shall," said Fluharty, pulling on a little cigar as they sat at the kitchen table. His free hand played lightly on the oilcloth.

Lorna told her father that at age seventy-four he had no business bringing home a young dog. "You told me you was getting out of it, Dad. Your back's for shit."

"You trying to pitch me in the grave?"

"I'm sure the dog'll dig it for me."

Fluharty didn't laugh; he knew she wasn't joking. But she didn't walk out of the room in a huff like she usually would. A couple of failed marriages had taught him about communication; he said, "I'm gonna tell you about him, at least," and when Lorna didn't answer, he knew he could go on about the dog. Maybe it was a pleasure to speak of something other than her son. The boy hadn't been to visit either one of them in a year or better, though he lived just three miles down the road, an electrician at Patriot Coal. Sometimes he'd rip by on a dirt bike, half the time throwing up a little wave, other times keeping it firm on the handlebar.

"A dropper," Fluharty called the dog in question, as old-time bird hunters do. A half-breed. The cross was said to have a ghostly, unreproducible talent that never found a way past that first litter.

His friend Peck Miller from the mines doted on a good English pointer bitch that he planned to breed to a Runner-Up Grouse Champion from Michigan, but Peck's grandson screwed up and kenneled a big randy setter next to her and they tied through the chain-link fence. "Nature finds a way," hooted the grandson, and Peck slapped the boy's head right in front of Fluharty—too hard, he thought. The breeding took, to Peck's despair. "Yes, she stood for him. Hundreds of years of line-breeding, ruint in the time it takes a dog to knot! Twenty minutes! Gone!" But in the end, just two pups of seven lived. The pointer had rolled on them, a deranged mother. The ones that survived, she wouldn't nurse. Peck's grandson was getting one to raise and to train, in semi-punishment, though the pup was awfully cute, it must be admitted, with lemon ears and a pert face, a little female, with just a hint of her father's feathering.

The survivors had to be bottle-fed around the clock. Quite a responsibility! Make that grandson think a little harder about dipping his wick in whomever . . .

"So, Dad, this one you're worked up about, it's just a glorified mutt?"

Fluharty's speech quickened as he grew more excited. "The male pup now, he got a intelligent look about him, that problem-solving look I call it. And better coloring—liver and white. The sire's kindly big-boned, but he's a good meat dog for sure. And you know it's all about the dam anyhow, that's seventy-five percent of it."

"And Peck come whispering in your ear? Trying to fob it off on you like usual?"

"Now, Lorna. I asked him."

"When's the last time somebody give a good dog away? That man wouldn't give you a kick in the ass for free."

"Said he'd pay for all the shots and the vet bills."

"Why'd Peck offer that if you asked him?"

Fluharty grew agitated. "Because Peck's a decent man! You're all wrong about him! He'll start it on pigeons. Give it to me at fifteen, sixteen weeks. Just right."

"Daddy, you can't even get where the birds are." Lorna's voice was coaxing. She was the only child of his who came around, and her word meant something. "Come now." She still wore her uniform from the US Post Office, and it gave her an official air. "Remember last time?"

Yes, he got turned around on Phares Knob, he'd admit, but don't you be getting ideas, his memory's sound. Could've happened to anybody, that thick stuff there.

"I got legs for it! Climbing that mountain don't bother me. How many fellows my age can say that? After spending a life on my side no less? Look at how Peck's all humped up."

"You're not keeping it in the house. I got enough trouble cleaning up after you."

Fluharty looked to the floor.

Both knew what he had in mind: a dog curled up by the woodstove.

"Yeah, the dam's all-important," Lorna cried. "She smothers her own! A screwball!"

"Happens time to time." Fluharty lifted his hands. "Remember Rennie? Darn fine dog. She was refused. Rennie had a gait to remember. I don't think it affects the pups over-much. Heck, maybe it helps." He dared a tentative look. "Makes them attach to a loving handler. Rennie'd look at me and moon." Rennie was a setter he had campaigned up in Pennsylvania, after he got on Disability (bad back, "the coal miner's Powerball ticket," as the local wags liked to say), retired early, and had all the time in the world, and now he measured all creatures living and dead against her and that glorious day of the spring derby at the Marienville trial grounds, where she dazzled the walking judges and a Philadelphia lawyer offered $12,000 for her on the spot. Fluharty was king that day.

"You know the dog ain't no Rennie. You only get that once in a life."

Fluharty almost said, "I'll give the pup to Anthony if it gets too much for me," but Lorna would have told him to quit talking nonsense. Lorna's son was the type you might not trust with a lawn mower, let alone an animal. Anthony's pets died prematurely. His last one, a gray pit bull with mournful eyes, came to a bad end when Anthony had managed, in his garbled and tearful telling, to back over it in the driveway with his own car. He had to run it over again to put it out of its misery. What's worse, he told everyone in Grant Town, he couldn't quit talking about the debacle—Anthony never understood that there were some things to be ashamed of and to be kept quiet. Yet he had loved something for once, and that was progress. "My son," Lorna assured her confidantes, "is something else."

The boy hadn't inherited his grandfather's ways, that's for sure. Fluharty had a long track record of taking on haggard, misshapen, or otherwise unwanted gun dogs, "welfare cases," and turning them into stone-cold hunters. He liked the challenge; he loved the discomfiture in the eyes of former owners who encountered their charges transformed in the field. Yes, Fluharty had trained one-eyed dogs and mean dogs, dysplastic dogs and gun-shy dogs, soft Brittanies and sadistic German shorthairs, the deer crazed and the lightning addled, escape artists and rock eaters, bird crowders and mindless barkers, even a deaf, all-white setter he taught to respond to hand signals. Could quarter that deaf fellow like he was working the joystick on a video game. In turn, the written-off critters adored him; they sensed he had saved them from being pitched into the void. Other handlers were quick to send a troubled bird dog down the road, sorting through ten to get that single, shining savant. Not Fluharty. But he'd never owned a dropper. It couldn't be registered in the *Stud Book*. Not that Fluharty cared about that. Competing was long behind him. He just wanted to fill his final hours.

"A mutt, Dad!"

"Uncle had one. Best of both worlds, said he. Grit of a pointer, gait of a setter."

"Worst of both worlds. A run-off pointer and a head-case setter."

"Oh, Lorna," he sighed, "you and me just look at things different."

No dog was too far gone. One time he took a jittery field trial washout that was so sickle-tailed you could have hung the dog on a clothesline. The first owner had fried the dog with an e-collar; now it blinked birds. To get it over its fear, each day Fluharty lovingly stripped meat from the breast of a shotgunned quail and hand-fed the dog until it worshipped him and grew perky at the smell of feathers. Not a season later, he sold it back to the original owner, a local dentist, for $2,500. A brag dog of a lifetime, and now he regretted taking the money. "Call me Judas," he'd say, and it felt even worse when the dentist praised the dog each time Fluharty needed a cavity filled. Soon its littermate came, with a different problem, a monomaniacal addiction to chasing deer. Not an uncommon issue, but this setter was something else. In its very first week at Fluharty's, it was kicked in the face by a doe with fawns. She broke the dog's jaw in a grisly fashion; the vet said to put it down, but Fluharty stapled the dog shut himself and it lived another seven years, a long thread of life. He shot twenty-seven ruffed grouse and ninety-three woodcock over its points.

Never ran deer again.

"Kids and dogs," said Fluharty, "learn from hard experience." Then he blushed. Waited to see his daughter react.

306

"You better plan on living another ten years," Lorna said finally, packing a cigarette against her thumbnail. "I am not getting saddled with this, I got trouble enough."

She didn't even have to name her trouble out loud.

The wind whistles through the kennel doors. Night is cruel. A heartbroken whining travels from kennel to house—not that anyone pays it any mind. Hardly a season out of its mother's womb, the pup learns the chill concrete of its home, tensing its claws, curling its body in an empty barrel that serves as its bed. Each morning, a bent form arrives to shovel its shit, freshen its water, dole out hard kibble and solid chunks of butter. The man fastens an outsized check cord on its collar for a morning romp around its little world. You can sense it adapting—maybe from this humble beginning, a bright future awaits. Rich smells branch promisingly in all directions. A gentle tug guides it now and again. A hedge of briar and sumac draws attention. It points a hobbled pigeon. It chases a quail. It becomes incandescent with glee. It is nudged back into its kennel and tries to stay where the sunbeam falls. Then night again, and the cold, and this time there is no whining. The mother is forgotten. The big-headed pup is satisfied with its day. The past is broken off like a dead limb. More fun tomorrow, tomorrow is more fun.

Snappish and wild, it gnawed on porch furniture. It ate underwear. It chewed the head off a toothbrush. It ripped apart every magazine in the house and the tongues from shoes—fuming, Lorna noticed immediately the dropper had been inside. Fluharty's thin skin tore easily against its horseplay. Even he had to admit there was a problem when the pup found a box of shells, chewed through the hard plastic hulls, and scattered #7.5 bird shot all over the floor, which Lorna would be picking out of crevices for months. Suddenly she was coming thrice a week to clean.

Then it ate a hole through the kitchen drywall to get at a mouse. Exposed wire curled from the wound.

Took a heavy hand to settle it down. What's worse, it lacked charisma to an astonishing degree—and who among the crowd has met a puppy without charisma? Aloof to the bone like its pointer mother, all business and devoid of affection, which might otherwise make you tolerate the mischief. But even so, Fluharty would praise the dropper as it slept on the rug, its side gently heaving, worn out from having performed so

307

much evil. "Two speeds: dead asleep, full throttle. Well, the best gun dogs I ever had was pure devils young. Smart and bored ain't a good combo."

"Smart? Good God," Lorna sighed, sitting on a partially disemboweled sofa. She had come to remind her father to shave and dress decently for the Jefferson-Jackson Dinner the next day. The Senator would be there and must be thanked. "He kindly makes you want to drown him in the bathtub, don't he?"

Fluharty didn't disagree. "If only I was a younger man. Get this dog broke and he'd take your breath away. High octane. I'd love to drop him in a field trial and make Peck shit."

Lorna swatted her father's head with a newspaper. "Enough."

Long and leggy, it grew up fast.

Not five months after bringing the pup home, Fluharty dropped dead. Lorna found him out by the woodpile. Stroke, said the doctor. At the funeral home, to which the Party and the Local sent pale flowers, she noticed that Peck was giving her a wide berth, so she walked straight to him.

"You're taking that dog back."

"What dog?"

"You son of a bitch!"

"OK, OK," he cried, stricken.

"You knowed how sick Dad was." This wasn't strictly true, but she took pleasure in driving this nail.

"Bring her over tomorrow then. I ain't around, just toss her in the kennel."

"It's a he."

"That's right," said Peck, backing up. Lorna tended to rattle men with her sudden anger and her beauty, and Peck had to glance away, saying, "I sent flowers, did you get 'em? He looks good. Real good!" He tried reminding Lorna how the two men were dragged off by police and arrested together at a black lung march, "back in seventy-one, when we was buck-wild shavers, no fear in us," but she just walked off shaking her head and muttering about his worthlessness.

Half the crowd had shuffled past the receiving line by the time Lorna's own son finally came through the door, a leather racing jacket over his dress shirt. Anthony fished a balled tie out of a pocket and began to cinch it around his neck. The other set of grandchildren snickered. They knew Aunt Lorna would tear into him, put on a spectacle. Well, at least he'd showed up—that had been in doubt. All of them had broken off contact with Anthony once childhood ended. He was out there somewhere, living his mysterious, addled life. He hardly glanced at the casket.

Once they were old enough to learn the truth, the nieces and nephews always looked askance at Aunt Lorna (the "Favorite," she was called, or the "Presentable One," for her willowy figure and intense dark Calabrese eyes), who was the product of an affair with another woman of Fluharty's; Fluharty's first wife (now dead, as was the second) had taken in the love child to raise as her own, shocking the county. When Lorna turned out to be Fluharty's favored child (he would take her around to the political gatherings, and he drove the others mad by helping her buy that modest house on the ridge, even if it was just a trailer with an addition), the rest fell in line against her. Even the sainted first wife's feelings curdled once Lorna was a cuddly child no more, and this seeped down into the family's dealings with Anthony, who, it must be said, was a godawful nuisance. The cousins remembered a disastrous summer when Anthony was sent on the road to help their grandfather compete— and disappeared from a rest area outside Pittsburgh not a week into the trip. Fluharty was apoplectic with fear and, when Anthony reappeared back home via Greyhound bus, rage. Fluharty didn't have patience for the boy after that. "You can tell him something ten times and he won't recall it, he don't pay you any mind."

Yet after the service, he accepted his mother's invitation back to Fluharty's house, where aged Methodist women had set out steaming, overcooked meals for the mourners. Surprised her.

Anthony insisted on riding separately, on his dirt bike—did he have his license back? He had long been a misery to her, a sullen little kid who frightened the classroom with his rages and did his damnedest to make her suitors think twice, but she'd been proud when he got hired on for apprenticeship at Patriot. Maybe he'd turn it around after all. Anthony had a DUI and an assault charge he'd pled down, but because Fluharty had done so much for the Local (twice he had been arrested on the picket line, and that accorded respect, even in these dismal times), somehow the background check was ignored, misplaced, or never performed. Three years Anthony had labored at Patriot, full-time now and by most accounts doing well—or not doing poorly enough to draw attention. Anthony was dating a woman named Teea, whom his mother had met only once. She read about this Teea online—Lateea Morgan, it turned out, of the numberless Morgan clan. The woman had two blond children and a hard mountain jaw. Did they think of Anthony as a father? Her hair was beautiful. Her forehead was pronounced—a trait Anthony would ridicule later while authoring insults on social media. Lorna had smiled when her son wrote on Facebook, "I LOVE YOU TEEA." Lorna was about to type a comment underneath it, something with floating hearts, when she saw a response from a fellow named Patrick Dawson, who looked about her son's age. "If you lover so much," this Dawson wrote, "you should quit beating on her." Underneath, Dawson had written a second comment. "Little bitch. Where you been hiding. I'll find you little bitch. Run, rabbit."

When Lorna pulled into the drive behind a vehicle full of her wise-cracking, college-attending nieces and nephews, she noticed the kennel door standing open—the dropper was gone. For once, Peck had made good on his word. Tears of gratitude stood in her eyes.

The meal after went well, the mourners and the churchwomen satisfied, and everyone had a pretty good time, even the jilted half brothers and sisters, who suddenly lost the urge to squabble. As sometimes happens at country burials, no one spoke of the dead man, exhausted as they were with feeling, except when someone noted how much Fluharty would've enjoyed the strong coffee brewed in the borrowed urn.

The one sour moment came when a niece pulled Lorna aside, the one who had designs on buying this very house. "You know Patriot let Anthony go," she whispered. "He's going around acting like he's still working there, but I seen the papers in the office. What happened? I don't know, I was about to ask you."

Lorna's own father had warned her about Anthony: "I don't know about that one." At age eight, the boy had punched and kicked his mother after a scene at a family picnic. "All your brothers and sisters, none of you done that. And him banging his head when he's mad . . ."

"You'd have whacked us."

"It ain't that." Fluharty had a strange look on his face. "You hit that boy, he wouldn't care."

She remembered feeling that all the air had been sucked out of her lungs. Her father was right. Look in Anthony's eyes, you sensed it. Watching Anthony eat Methodist pie from a dish (and without an inkling that this would be the very last time she ever saw her son), she smoked cigarette after cigarette and reminded herself that she must have loved him, once, before the feeling was battered out of her by experience. In that place and in that time, bad children would be told by their parents, "Settle down or I'm sending you to Pruntytown"—that's where the state's Industrial Home for Boys stood. No one in Grant Town remembered a parent making good on that threat, until Lorna did. Male offenders aged twelve to twenty were put to work on the farm and in the machine shop; Anthony returned with a shifty, nervous look, and he wouldn't let anyone touch him; he'd jump if you brushed past him in the hall. He missed large swaths of his eighth- and ninth-grade years, returning like a stranger to his own youth. Following his release, twice after his rages she had the magistrate clamp a mental health hold on him for seventy-two hours in lockup and observation. "That boy," Lorna lamented, "been through every pill in the pharmacy." He would end up back in Pruntytown as a junior. He moved out of her home the first day he could, into his girlfriend's father's house. In those bad times, his look was dull and unfocused, and she thought of those voided eyes when she read in the paper of his assault and battery charge, when he attacked a boy with whom he raced dirt bikes, supposedly his best friend. "Squabbling over part money," Anthony, gullible, told the police, who claimed friendship and understanding and provided a cold can of pop from the machine in the hall. Then he began to brag a bit. "Owed me seventy-five dollars. Ducking me. So I beat the ever-loving piss out of him." Oh, the police knew Anthony. A deputy looked at him over glasses and said, "I remember when you used to clerk at the Exxon and you got fired for selling cigarettes to a ten-year-old. I always thought it was just a mean joke. Now I'm realizing you're just real fucking nutty. Let's have your picture took."

Up Sourwood Mountain, over North Fork of Laurel, then a long straight run along the pipeline right-of-way, across Route 250 and on to the tongue twister of a trout stream called Slip Hill Mill Run, through woodcock swamps and oak scrub, into the next county and quartering back again, slashing through private land and a tag of National Forest, Wildlife Refuge, and even the lowly board of education acreage that no one can figure how to use or legally divest, romping downhill on the bankrupt ski slope at Tory Camp Run and, near the White Hall exit, the Walmart parking lot and through a red light, chasing the ghost of scent on the wind as a car horn blares.

After seventeen miles of this, the dropper decides to take a little break, huffing in the lee of a fallen log, tongue out and purpled, ribs rising and falling, finally satisfied, for a moment at least. Then it begins to dig a little hole into the slightly colder earth, curling there like a snake in the divot. Is it smiling? The dropper doesn't live such a bad life,

311

except for the stinging rain and, once December comes, ice and snow. It eats road-killed deer. It runs down a young turkey. It uproots a campaign sign from a yard, amusing people who whip out their phones to video that. It feeds on delicious garbage.

Just a few weeks before he died, Fluharty had begun to say things like, "I'm getting this dog ready for Anthony." "Be good for him. Anthony's a little older now, he could handle a bird dog." "My, this dropper's a handsome one. Maybe I'll surprise Anthony on his birthday."

It startled her. Not long before, Lorna would have told her dad to stop being ridiculous. The first time Fluharty brought it up, she looked at him strangely but said nothing. After that, she would murmur, "Yeah, Dad, that might be a good idea."

The day after the funeral, Lorna called up Peck to thank him, and Peck said, "For what?"

The dropper was nowhere to be found—the dog had freed itself from its kennel, or some enemy of the family had let it loose.

Suddenly she felt awful. Maybe the dropper was the devil, but it was the last dog her father had loved. Would have killed him to think of it shivering out there in the cold shadow of some ridge. Fluharty doted on dogs. He would sit and fume over the cruel hand that some trainers had. "You know when I told Peck about how that one setter run deer? He said take a buck's gonads, tie them around the dog's neck, and leave them until they rotted off—the smell would come to disgust the dog. If that didn't work, Peck said put the dog in a barrel with that mess and roll it down a hill." Fluharty was on the verge of tears, petting the very animal in question, drinking up the gaze from its soft-dark eyes. "You talk to your neighbors, you figure out right quick who'd've been Nazis." He had saved many a hunting dog from cruelty and abandonment, a sweet man, "maybe too sweet," a fountain of patience, his acquaintances said, though he looked to the world like just another grizzled redneck with a yard full of junk. "The hillside socialist," the doubters called his kind, but there were a lot of hillside socialists back then. When a dog shat in the yard, he'd mutter, "Must have been thinking about NAFTA."

Lorna found herself driving the roads and calling the dropper's name ("Sawyer! Sawyer!"), not that she was convinced the wild dog ever took notice of what human beings called it. On her work rounds, she mistook goats and calves flashing by on the roadside for pale visions of the dropper. She talked to everyone at church; she stapled up flyers at the gas station and the grocery. Since she'd no picture of the dropper to

312

post, she described it accurately on Facebook (where she received countless message requests from creepy, potato-faced men) and asked people to share far and wide—173 people did so. Every white-dog sighting in the county was sent her way. The dropper was not found. Yet she was convinced that some of the sightings were valid, such as when a schoolteacher reported a young dog standing on point at her bird feeder for half an hour, its muscles quivering as it locked up on a fat blue jay, the dog's tail poker-straight at twelve o'clock. Fluharty would have beamed at its confirmation. When the jay flushed, finally, the dog took off after. The teacher was dialing Lorna's phone as the dog broke over the horizon. For twenty-seven miles the dropper ripped along, but circling under the sway of an unruly wind, it ended up not two miles from Lorna's house, not that she ever saw it. She heard other rumors of an emaciated "spaniel" throwing itself against a chicken coop out Miracle Run. Then an idea flared in her mind, as she recalled a trick her father had taught her to catch lost dogs. She nailed one of Fluharty's undershirts on the fence, with a portable kennel near it where the dog could bed down. But the smell must have gone out of the clothing, and she left the undershirt to whip there uselessly, a melancholy flag. The thought of her father's clothes having lost his character—that hit harder than she expected; she had to call in sick that day.

If the funeral didn't affect her as much as one might expect, sorting through her father's dog-training equipment struck her again like violent surf.

Peck Miller tried to buy everything off her as a package deal, but she knew he'd cheat her, so she sold what she could online instead. The pigeon launchers and the Garmin and Dogtra collars went for princely sums that surprised her, even when she couldn't find the matching chargers. She had trouble selling the blank guns and the live pigeons, as Facebook Marketplace kept taking down the postings, so she relented and sold the guns to Peck and, though she loathed the man, simply threw in the homers and unflown squeakers to be done with them.

"You never did find that run-off dog? No? Happens to the best of us. Last year I left one on the Upper Peninsula. Her tracking collar just turnt itself off, I called Garmin and threw a fit. I wonder if wolves got her. They got wolves up there," Peck added quickly, as if she had disagreed.

"Hum," she said, doubtful he'd put in a good search.

The vast kennels she'd sell when the weather improved, when someone could come disassemble them and the johnny house and maybe the whoa post, too, where for so many hours her father had walked dogs with a half hitch around the flank, letting the pressure of the rope teach them steadiness. If she couldn't find a dog man, well, some druggy type would take it for scrap. She wasn't sure what to do with the shotguns. Fluharty had made her promise to keep them in the family—but not to give any to Anthony. Yet she had no great inclination to hand them over to her nieces and nephews, who came by only when they needed something, and with their parents she was not on speaking terms. Peck tried giving her $300 for her father's aged L. C. Smith double-barrel, but he annoyed her by insulting it: "Got so much drop it's like a hockey stick, no wonder he was such a bad shot, but I'd like to remember him when I'm afield, it'll be like I'm walking with his ghost." She drew her mouth into a firm line. Peck blushed at the nonanswer and crept out of the yard.

When Fluharty's other heirs caught wind of these sales, there was some commotion about the man's meager estate, as he had died without a will and left children from two marriages and an affair. Not that any of them called her. They left that to an avaricious, outraged niece. But Lorna told her half brothers and sisters via text that, despite the bitterness of their shared past, there was only one way to go forward. They got to live here together, after all.

Her job forced her to read their many names each day as she delivered their mail.

She typed on her phone, "And do you really want to pay some lawyer thousands of dollars to hash out who gets to get three dozen pigeons and some hardware store shotguns beat so hard the checkering's wore off? Now the house is due for a roof, and we all know who's gonna be on the hook for that."

"That Italian slut," the meaner ones called her in their group chat. "That liberal bitch."

About the time she'd stripped all of Fluharty's obsession from the property, sold the house to her pushy niece just to shut the family up, and divided the profit equally among the living children, her son disappeared from the county.

Which story do you want to believe? For Lorna hears them all in the years to come. That Anthony overdosed on fentanyl. That Anthony overdosed on oxycodone. That Anthony's homeless on the streets of Pittsburgh, or doing time under a false name at the prison farm in Huttonsville, or that the Morgans took their revenge, or that he burnt up in that apartment fire in Mannington.

314

That Anthony's jumping child support (never mind the fact he has no children). That he's traveling the state and taking revenge on those who abused him in the Industrial Home. That he happily works on the coal barges on the Ohio River, that easy river trade: three weeks on, ten days off. He never been better. He stands on deck and takes in great lungsful of morning air. Settled down, a baby on the way. In one of them port towns, Marietta or St. Marys or Martins Ferry, something like that.

Which story do you want to believe? The dropper's been struck down on the highway. The dropper starves. The dropper breaks through the ice chasing geese on a municipal pond and, exhausted, drowns.

The dropper succumbs in a leghold trap. By regulation, trappers are supposed to check their lines daily, but you know how people are around here.

The dropper is found by a bird hunter, is adopted, and matures into a brag dog, beloved by the household children, a lazybones on the couch and a pure beast in the field. He'll watch all the TV you can stand. They'll name him Moses, Wandering Moses. When you drop the tailgate, he goes bounding out, head lifted high to scent the wind, "born broke." There. In the tangle of grapevine and briar. Not twenty minutes later, he'll pin a spooky grouse at just the right distance after three relocations—it can run but it cannot fly—and when the bell stops, the handler knows he's been blessed by that rare thing, and it costed him nothing but love and devotion. Gun flies to shoulder, finds its mark. The bird, tumbling, falls. When the hunter's daughters marry, why, the dog carries the ring down the aisle!

"Well, look who it is!"

After the niece bought Fluharty's house, Lorna didn't find herself invited back so often, though she'd stop and chat if she was driving by on her rounds and saw the kids playing in the yard or racing little cars on the slab that used to be the kennel floor. From time to time, she'd ask if the white dog had wandered back, and the mouthy niece would say, "No, but we continue to hold his mail here if he wants to pick it up."

"Wiseass." Lorna glanced up at the mountain. "The time I wasted playing dress-up with you." She laughed and took a drag off her cigarette. "I know, I'm probably crazy. Hard to believe it's been three year now."

Was just too much to think of it somewhere as a bare skeleton in the green, green briar.

"I can't believe it's another election already. Here, speaking of." The niece handed over a stack of signs from the Party office: Manchin and

315

Jezioro, Tennant and Lemasters. "They told me they'll have the road repaved. It could stand it, for sure!"

"Oh, thank you, they was out the other day. Who's that last one?"

"Lemasters? House of Delegates. He married Rocky Manchin's girl. From up north somewhere."

Leaning back in the mail truck, Lorna said, "It's all the same, I reckon."

"This is an important one. I was watching Fox. Say the Senator's in trouble. Granddad'd just hate to see how the Party's going on all this."

"He was loyal," Lorna cautioned. Even when the Senator's uncle lost the state $279 million on bad investments in securities and was impeached, her father would come to blows defending the man, who had been hoodwinked, Fluharty said, by a smooth-talking subordinate. Gloomy, proud, Fluharty was part of the miners' delegation that walked the man's casket up the highway to his grave. Lorna said, "Loyal to the ragged end."

"Will you go door-knocking this year?"

"I don't know, they ain't called me."

"Oh, gosh."

"You know I'm willing." Lorna turned her hands over so you could see the palms.

"They need to get it together. Don't be a stranger," said the niece, as if Lorna didn't live just a mile up the ridge.

When Lorna got home from her shift, she found the back door busted open and the shotguns stolen out of the house. The police came; the police went. Oddly, her heart thrilled—not only had she been shed of a burden, she suspected Anthony had come back to take them, she suspected his odd presence in the house. Had she been a bad mother? She didn't know, sincerely. She had done what she could.

"If only Anthony's dad had been in the picture," the churchwomen murmured. "If only Fluharty had give him half the attention he give them dogs."

"If I never have nothing else. How I loved your mother," Fluharty once said after a bottle of wine, startling her. "Can't say she quite returned it." If not for the birth certificate, Lorna wouldn't have even known the woman's name; Fluharty couldn't bring himself to utter it. "Druv me crazy for years. I was just a way of passing a little time, I guess." Even in his final year, he might weep some at the kitchen table. "Half the time, working these dogs was just to keep my mind off it, give me something to care about."

Lorna lived in awe of respectable people. Many a time she cast a ballot for the judges who found against her son time and time again. A single mother standing overwhelmed before the juvenile court judge (a Jezioro) who kept saying Industrial Home for Boys, Lorna answered, "Maybe that'll knock some sense into him, Your Honor," while Anthony lifted shackled hands and tried to get her attention. The bailiff roused himself, attuned to some invisible courtroom frequency. For a strange year, she was not a mother, she struggled to fill the days, she worked the phone bank for the Party, she ran the coat drive and gave out frozen turkeys, she joined Bible Study, and, guilty-sweet, she rather liked it. Later, a school counselor would break Anthony's confidence and explain what horrors he'd gone through in the Industrial Home; shivering, Lorna would tell the counselor that he shouldn't encourage Anthony to dwell so much on the past.

Snow fell early this Election Day, way up the legs on the many signs in her yard. She thought of her father, how he loved to bird hunt in snow. "You got better dog work them days," he promised. The grouse hold tight and honor the dog. He loved it so, he didn't care when he missed (and he usually missed). November, December, January—he lived for that. The chill and the dead red foliage reminded her. She'd dry pluck the birds on the porch and brine them, then roast them on a bed of celery stalks. Why didn't he ever bring her along? No one thought to take girls hunting in those days, just as they never hunted on Sundays. Never mind that she was the Favorite. The old ways seemed so silly now. All the time, you saw girls in the paper standing over dead animals and showing up the men. Hell, you even saw a few mining coal.

This Election Day evening, her door-knocking done, Lorna settled down to watch the news, for weather and returns, chain-smoking to calm her nerves. She wanted to see what would come for the Senator—way back when the man was governor, he smoothed the way for Fluharty's Disability claim: he jotted a note to the commissioner and asked that no blockage form in the pipe, just as he'd put in a word for Lorna at the Postal Service on Fluharty's humble and fawning request, which was granted as her father had done so much yeoman service to the Party and to the Local, before and after his injury. The Senator had even called to offer his condolences, lamenting that Fluharty's kind was melting into history and we'd all be much worse for it. In turn, she'd be loyal to the end, she'd do the unglamorous work. She had praised and apologized for the Senator seventy-five times today, and her throat was hoarse. Long ago, on a night like this, she watched her father take a chair by the leg and beat it to splinters when Reagan was elected.

In front of her eyes, percentages rose and fell.

The Senator survived; life would not change.

She clapped her hands together—her heart thrilled.

Here in the living room, the television flared like a fireplace against the velvet mountain blackness outside. Winter came down hard that year. Lorna was forty-three. She thought of moving off the mountain and into town, where she'd be with people. Her friends at church urged her to do it (just as they said to find some pale bachelor), but no, she said, she ought to stay put in case Anthony came looking for her.

Hell, she might not have a choice. The Federal government wanted to shutter the tiny Grant Town post office along with thirty-seven others in the state; if so, they'd want to cycle her to the county seat. But the Senator swore he'd fight it: "A post office is the backbone of a rural community, and these idiots on K Street have no earthly clue!"

The television lulled her to sleep. In such moments she might dream of Anthony's father, an itinerant installer of stained glass windows who labored one summer at the church. He had long brown hair, a crooked mouth, and marvelous legs from climbing on high. She was nineteen; she gave in to a fleeting desire. "Hello," he called down from the scaffold one day as she was dropping off her creation for the cakewalk. "Hand me up the grinder, would you? I don't bite. Yes, that one." In this corner of the county, where every person was known and stitched together in intricate patterns of blood and marriage, a stranger was thrilling. No one knew him! No one at all! And he didn't know a thing about her questionable birth, nor did he care when she confessed it while lying beside him. He had been her age now, forty-three. He left without saying goodbye, his labor complete, and when her body told her what was happening, she pried the man's mailing address (an exotic state, Oregon) out of the appalled church secretary. The last name didn't match the one he'd told her. When she called Information in his hometown, they claimed that such a man did not exist. The Oregon-Idaho Conference of the Methodist Church told her the same. The child support agency told her the same. She moved out of Fluharty's home into the trailer a mile up the ridge and three hundred feet closer to God; Fluharty was long past the age of babies in the house, he said; he'd paid his dues.

At least once a month, she typed Anthony's father's various names into Facebook, but the pictures never matched the face she had gazed into so many lazy afternoons, in the pollen-crowded light of the church

318

attic, where he'd set up his cot and his mysterious tools, where he shocked her by admitting he did not believe in God, not even a little bit. Besides that, she couldn't much recall his character. Had he seemed the type to fight and to steal? To hit a woman? Surely not. Surely not. At altar call, waiting for the preacher to bless her, she can't help but look at the paneled wings of glass that man touched, the slabs of color that he lifted himself, cording his forearms with muscle. Anthony inherited his crooked mouth and fidgety hands. In the Industrial Home, where they could seemingly know you by smell, a group of older boys—men, really—would call out to Anthony, "Hey, you bastard, you little bastard!" and one day he said quite reasonably, "But we're all bastards in here . . ." and they didn't spare him a beating and God knows what else for fact of it being true. When he got home from that year, Lorna noticed he looked much more like his father. When he tinkered with dirt bikes, she could sense the faint outline of the stained glass man, who drove his hands into the fitful insides of a work van and coaxed it back to life. Maybe that's where Anthony was. Maybe he'd gone hunting for the man, to measure himself against his maker. An old man now. About like Fluharty. The television flickered. The snowstorm was bringing down lines.

Do you know how snow crunches in the same way salted cabbage does when you knead it in your hands? Lorna does. In fall season, for the annual sale, she fills great stone crocks with sauerkraut and, for untold hours in the church's kitchen, works the shredded cabbage and watches it give up its water as paper cuts burn on her hands. Drowsy and still half dreaming, she hears the sound again, and recalls her kitchen labor, and realizes something's walking on the unshoveled porch. Yes, it takes a step and pauses, takes a step and pauses. Snow is whipping against the glass.

When a faint scratching comes at the door, she wishes she still had her father's guns. You don't answer the door at night in this county without one, not with what's been happening.

Something is on the porch. She knows what it is. She knew it would come back to her. There are things one does not outrun. She rises to let it in.

Nominated by Kenyon Review

A MOST GENEROUS OFFER

fiction by JOY GUO

from COLORADO REVIEW

I.

The apartment in Beijing was Lin's and mine until Ma made the generous decision of allowing old Mrs. Yang to move in. My sister and I spent our summers there. Lin liked to trample through the weeds caulking the patches around the apartment building, gathering the goosefoot and crabgrass in bouquets for imaginary weddings and tea parties, even eating the grubby flowers. I was berated for not keeping a closer eye on her, but we were six years apart and beholden to two fathers—a distance yawned between us that was hard to cross.

The apartment itself was nothing special. The floors sloped and listed at odd angles, so that a pencil rolled joyfully across; the ceilings clipped the tops of our heads; the windows were caked with grime, the light sieving through a nauseated shade. Tumbleweeds of hair and dust hid in the corners. I'd save those and stuff them into Lin's mouth as she slept, only for the favor to be returned to me the following night. Parts of the flooring had rotted through, leaving toothy gaps. The walls were speckled with black scorch marks that wouldn't flake off. According to Lin, the apartment contained a spirit, constantly eyeing us day and night—its staggering, yowling form reminded her of Mrs. Yang.

Years later, I could draw Mrs. Yang's face from memory—the riverbed grooves, the lips bunching into a tight little pit. She was a cousin, a word that held little meaning for me when I was younger. As far as I knew, everyone from the street-sweeper to the butcher was an aunt or uncle or cousin, if not by blood, then by a simple honorific. Later, I'd

320

find out she was actually related to us, on Ma's side, the daughter of a distant aunt I had never met or spoken to, which might have explained the generosity that Ma showed her but was certainly not the whole story.

That one summer, when Lin was seven and I was thirteen and Ma took us back to Beijing, Mrs. Yang, who lived nearby, visited us all the time. Dragging her gout-stricken left foot like a club, she'd lodge herself heavily into a chair and bark at me to make her a cup of chrysanthemum tea. Unlike other adults, who were patient with, even touched by, Lin's and my dismal attempts at Mandarin, Mrs. Yang pretended she couldn't understand and made us repeat our names, ages, and favorite subjects until she was satisfied with our intonation. Making things worse, she fawned over Lin, petting her hair, complimenting her eyes. "Look at this pretty little girl," she cooed and then hollered, "Porklet! Where's my tea?" Porklet was her name for me.

"I'll show that old witch some tea," I said to Lin, grabbing the fistful of crabgrass she was holding.

"No!" Lin cried, but it was too late.

Mrs. Yang grunted as she took a sip. "Too hot." Sensing something unseemly in my expression, she latched on to my arm. "Is this the chrysanthemum? It tastes bitter. Did you give me jasmine by mistake? Jasmine gives me hives."

"Sorry," I muttered, wrenching myself free.

"Make me another," she growled after me.

The apartment had been in my mother's family for decades, an inheritance that each generation received piously and then forgot. By the time it passed into Ma's possession, the accumulated neglect was impossible to ignore. Cracks appeared in the ceiling, jagged and ominous, like mountain ranges bearing down. When it rained (short, half-hearted, sputtering outbursts that Beijing summers were known for), the cracks leaked a bilious ooze. A blotch the texture and color of moss had sprouted in the kitchen. Our solution was to hustle dishes and pans, the vinegar and salt and sugar, away from the problem area, and otherwise carry on around it as best we could. Repairs were scheduled, canceled, rescheduled, started, and never finished.

No, the apartment's value was due entirely to its location. Specifically, its proximity to the Diaoyutai State Guesthouse, used by the central government for housing foreign dignitaries and esteemed guests of the state. The surrounding geography, with Sanlihe, the commercial district, to the east, Yuyuantan Park to the west, and the guesthouse equidistant from both, created a kind of funneling effect. Every day a constant flow of people circled from one end to the other, and back again, on their way to pedal duck boats in the park's lake, or shop, or run their hands along the guesthouse's wall and wait for a dark-tinted convoy to pull up. Each time a procession passed, all activity on the boulevard froze. Even the sparrows bit their tongues.

The first thing visitors to our apartment always did was march to the southern-facing windows and crane their necks for a glimpse of the gleaming, pale wall that marked the guesthouse's boundary. "Ah," they crowed, "you can almost see right over into the complex," which was impossible. A perimeter of pines and yews constructed a second barrier. The windows were too filthy. Still, Lin and I blushed with pride. The apartment, smelly and broken and disintegrating, was ours, regardless. We had no reason to think otherwise.

II.

As a child, all I knew was that the apartment afforded multiple opportunities to see Wu Laoshi, who lived in the building over. Wu Laoshi was fifty years old and gave lessons to all the neighborhood children on his piano, though, out of everyone, only Lin showed the slightest promise.

"Now watch my hand," he'd say, and his long, pale fingers struck the keys like thunder, singularly deft. I tried as hard as I could to please Wu Laoshi. Compared to every other adult I knew, he never laughed to my face, and, though Lin was obviously better in every respect (more docile, prettier, not a single stain on her clothes), he didn't show any favoritism between us.

"Very good." Wu Laoshi clapped my shoulder. It was almost the end of my hour, and the tips of Lin's slippers were visible from around the corner. I made her go after me, so that the difference in our skills wouldn't be so apparent to Wu Laoshi.

The morning was steeped in sweat. My dress felt shellacked to my skin. Every now and then, a wet drop plopped on the keys; cutting my eyes slowly to the right, I glimpsed sodden patches under Wu Laoshi's armpits, beads dotting his forehead.

"Now, watch me again. Here." This time, he rested his fingers against my shoulder and unspooled the allegro in D major. I was wearing a tank top, my arms bare and brown from playing outside all summer, which Mrs. Yang always felt the need to comment on. Raking me from crown to feet, she intoned, "You look like a laborer. A *nongmin*," this last part with a chortle of distaste.

"Hmm," I said, trying to pay attention. The notes being played against my skin felt pleasant. I was about to say more when Wu Laoshi gave a hoarse sigh. Looking up, I saw his eyes were closed, shoulders swaying, lips ajar, as his fingers began to paddle harder against my shoulder. We had reached the recapitulation, the section that always gave me trouble—I was intimidated by the series of trills and concentrated too hard on not messing up and then, immersed somewhere else altogether, lost my place and stabbed the wrong key.

Now my mind shrank to a pinhole, big enough for only splotches of sensation to seep through. Wu Laoshi's sharp nails. The smell of cigarette smoke. The heaviness of his breathing, ringing like a seashell held against my ear. He was too close. I sat, a mute lump, holding myself all on one side to bear his weight.

"Do you see now?" He took his hand away, where, later, I'd find a cluster of tiny half-moons dug into my flesh. A whisper of hurt remained when I pressed down, but I was already beginning to forget what happened. Nothing had happened.

"Yes." Suddenly, despite the heat, I couldn't stop shivering.

"Very good. I'll see you next week. Lin! Your turn." As we passed each other, she gave me a look, one I kept replaying to myself in the years to come. A strange, yearning, adult look, which did not belong on her small face.

III.

The next week, I was ill, thrumming with headache and fever. Ma prescribed various wretched concoctions—roots and grass, bird's nest soup, jujubes boiled down to a slop. Too hot to sleep, I would sit up and peer out the window, trying to glimpse the shadowy wall of the guesthouse, making out only a branch slapping against the glass. My lessons with Wu Laoshi came and went and came again; I watched quietly as Lin clattered about, gathering her composition books, and wondered at the vague sense of relief I felt that I did not have to go.

Once, I woke up to find Mrs. Yang sitting by my bed. "Your ma went out and asked me to watch you. Lin's outside," she said. This didn't perturb me. During the summer, Lin and I barely saw our mother. She crammed her days with visiting old friends, settling my grandparents' accounts, fetching gifts for coworkers back home, shopping for clothes, perming her hair ("They do it just the way I like it," she cooed, fluffing the cloud around her face luxuriously). As for Lin, she was dreamy and misty-brained, the corners of her eyes crusty with morning gunk, happiest when wandering through the high banks of weeds, looking for blossoms to weave into crowns.

Mrs. Yang shoved a claw onto my forehead.

"Stop that."

"Fever's broke, Porklet." She grunted a wad of phlegm into a tissue and tossed it onto my nightstand. I stared, revolted.

"Did you know," she said abruptly, as though picking up the strand of a previous conversation. "Did you know that, when I was your age, the Red Guards almost burned down this apartment?"

I turtled under the covers, as far down as I could. Ma had told me and Lin the story once. When she finished, though we were brimming with questions, she smiled and hugged us and murmured, "Don't worry—that was so long ago."

"Your grandparents were bourgeois enemies," Mrs. Yang continued. "Two university professors, teaching the future minds of China all this Western philosophy. They were labeled anti-revolutionaries. Everyone begged them to take your ma and go to America, hunker down for a few years until it was safe to come back. Did they listen? Of course not. 'Nothing will happen,' they insisted. 'We'll be all right.' They decided to wait out the insanity. Struggle sessions, public firings, even after all that, your Ah Po and Ah Gong stayed. My parents, honest, decent people, offered to help in any way they could. A most generous offer, if you ask me."

Ma hadn't mentioned any of this in her telling. I sat up higher.

"The Red Guards came for them, as we knew they would. Came at night, with rope and gasoline. Came right through that door, about twenty of them, just one or two years older than me. In fact, I knew them from school." She let out a harsh chuckle and scoured her mouth with the back of her hand, the dry rasp the only sound in the room.

"They dragged out your grandparents. Whipped them in front of their neighbors. Oh, I'll never forget. Your poor Ah Gong. His mind never came back from that night. One of the boys used his belt on him. The buckle caught—"

Mrs. Yang's red-laced, ruined eyes gleamed wetly. I barely registered Lin tiptoeing into the room, coming to sit beside me on the bed.

"While all that was going on, some of the Red Guards were carting out the contraband your Ah Gong and Ah Po had tucked away. Hardcover encyclopedias. Fur coats. Jewelry. They all went into the fire. Your grandparents kept crying out there wasn't anything left to be burned, but the Red Guards kept going. The furniture contained, according to them, signs of Western craftsmanship. Dressers. Mirrors. An enormous bureau that Ah Po's parents gifted to her when she was married.

"Until, finally, they couldn't find anything else. We thought that was the end of that. Then one of the Red Guards shouted, 'Why not? Let's burn the apartment too.' Never mind the other families in the building! Never mind that a fire could creep utterly out of control. What did they care? They were out of their minds, at that point. So they set it on fire and left, screaming and laughing.

"The rest of the night, my parents and I helped your Ah Po and Ah Gong put out the flames. We had burns that festered and had to be lanced. My father, his hands when he caught the curtains—" She spread her fingers and pushed them in front of us. Lin cringed, but I stared, as though the charred patches of skin were visible.

"In the end, we did it." Tenderly, Mrs. Yang peered at the crumbling walls and ceiling and floor, one gnarled hand reaching up and stroking an invisible surface, before her face assumed its usual grimace. The light in the room had coalesced into murkiness. Though it would not turn completely dark for a few more hours, I had to squint to see. Mrs. Yang checked her watch, stood up, and surveyed us with something that took a beat for me to recognize as weariness. Before she left, she said, "You tell your ma I always keep my word."

IV.

I would have pestered Ma harder as to what Mrs. Yang meant if it weren't for the incident with Wu Laoshi and Lin a few days later. I hung around Ma, demanding, nudging, poking, before she finally laid into me. "Now you listen," Ma said, soft and deadly, a surefire sign that I had overstepped. "That happened a long, long time ago. Okay? It had nothing to do with you. Leave it." After that, I had to proceed carefully. Ma was impenetrable. Out of principle, I refused to seek out Mrs. Yang. That left Lin, who wasn't much help. That summer, she seemed completely preoccupied, spinning worlds and stories that couldn't be divulged, always whispering under her breath, eyes cast downward at the clumps of weeds she tied into knobby shapes. I figured she was trying to withdraw from all the attention she received from our relatives, the old ladies ringed around the apartment building's entrance, even strangers passing by on the street. They insisted on taking pictures with her, fondled her cheeks, thrust her around by the shoulders like an extravagant purchase.

"This is Liping's little girl," they crowed. "Where is your father?" When Lin shook her head, the question was repeated twice in slow, syrupy drawls.

"Not here."

Titters. Lin's face was a blank little moon. "Where is he *from?*"

"Germany."

"Oh, oh." Hands fluttered in wonder.

"Mine is from New York," I piped up, ignoring the stares.

"Hmm." They took a step back, scrutinizing our faces. "Well, you don't look much alike." It was true, we didn't, but it stung no less to hear.

"If it were me," I said to Lin when we were alone, "I wouldn't mind being called pretty and cute and sweet by everyone. I'd be *happy*. At least no one calls you 'Porklet.'" These little jabs toward my sister never made me feel better; each time the words burst forth, I regretted them. But Lin just smiled as though I were a favorite television show or book and she had come across an interesting part.

Even so, I expected Mrs. Yang's story to make some dent in Lin's dreamy world. "Don't you wonder why Ma never told us any of this? What do you suppose Mrs. Yang meant?" I mused. That day, Lin had enlisted me to help find a particular flower she wanted. We went to the back of the apartment, where the path was pocked with weeds and garbage. Other than Lin, no one, not even the little kids, who were awed by our accents and Lin's American features, played here.

"Don't know," she mumbled. "I don't know. I don't know." She coughed.

"Are you okay?"

Ignoring my question, Lin tilted her face at the sky and stuck her tongue out. Pink and pebbled, it disturbed me for no reason I could explain.

The next day, I was well enough to go to Wu Laoshi's. At the end of the lesson, he handed me two oranges. "For you. No need to share," he said, smiling.

"Thank you." I cupped the fruit to my chest and felt a swell of feeling for him.

Outside, I found a shady spot and gulped down both oranges. Juice spattered down my front. I licked my fingers and the peels, ignoring the acid prickle, when a convoy of black, sleekly shiny vans lumbered up the boulevard slowly, as if basking in the attention.

Throwing the peels down, I barreled back to tell Lin and Wu Laoshi to look out the window. The front door was unlocked; inside was quiet.

I could make out the backs of the two figures sitting in front of the piano, the larger one slumped, head tottering. Except for the left arm that squeezed the nape of Lin's neck and the right one that levered up and down, working furiously in front of him, he seemed like a boulder, rolled into position by the sea. A wisp of Lin's shirt poked out above the waistband, a little duck-tail. Her hair was done up in braids. They were all askew, tufts sticking out every which way—she had begged me that morning and finally I had given in, though I had worked the hair roughly, letting her know I didn't appreciate being badgered.

At the sound of my footsteps, both turned to look, Lin a second after Wu Laoshi. I would never be able to recall his expression. Hers, I caught all the time in the way it made me feel—the plummeting lurch in the stomach when I couldn't remember if I forgot to turn the stove off, or I misplaced a credit card, or I sent an email to the wrong person. Whatever it was, it could not be undone, and now, the only thing left to do was apologize.

V.

Scarcely aware of where I was going, I smacked right into Mrs. Yang. The air outside was limp with impending rain. A family, the little boy crouched on his father's shoulders, hurried past, while an old man shook out a plastic bag and yanked it over his head.

"Ay! Watch where you're going."

"Sorry, sorry." What had his right hand been doing, burrowing like a worm? Already, the scene was losing its crispness, my grasp of the details slackening. Dazed, I rubbed my eyes.

Mrs. Yang cocked her head. "What is it? Are you still sick?"

Right hand, right hand, I repeated to myself. If only I could sit somewhere cool and quiet, if only I could yank the thoughts from my head and lay them out slowly in front of me. Mrs. Yang hustled me over to a bench under a scrawny, half-dead tree. A froth of midges rose in protest when we sat in their midst.

"Now. What is it?"

"Lin," I managed.

"What's wrong with her?"

"I don't know."

"Where is she?"

"At—" I couldn't swallow. I should have said something. I should have grabbed her hand and pulled her out from under him. Instead, I had run.

327

"Spit it out."

"She's at Wu Laoshi's. He—" I couldn't bring myself to say more. My right hand jerked up and down, in imitation of his.

A pause. I didn't dare lift my head. The thunderstorm broke its silence across the city. Everyone around us had already scuttled inside. The tree above us provided little shelter. I watched my pants darken, the blotches devouring themselves, until my whole lap was soaked, and still, I didn't move. In a way, it felt like penance.

"Yan. Look at me." Before, it was always "Porklet" or "child" or, when she couldn't be bothered, "hey, you." I didn't think she even knew my name. I met her gaze, and, in that moment, I didn't need to say more. She understood me completely.

VI.

The incident was fifteen years ago. Long enough to diffuse into dim outlines: the glances I cast in Lin's direction hooking nothing concrete, no visible sign of disorder or anguish—the many times I tried to raise it with her, with Ma, crumbling into something so unsaid that it couldn't have happened. In the end, I figured I was mistaken. I didn't know what I saw. We continued to go to Wu Laoshi every week, though I made it a point to switch my hour with Lin's. I would pace in the adjoining room, heart rabbiting furiously, prepared to lunge at a creak in the bench, rustling of clothes, Wu Laoshi's murmur. But every time, I heard nothing out of the ordinary. Lin played without interruption, the notes fluid and slurred. As for the man himself, he was his usual solicitous self with me, blinking innocently when he opened the door to greet us. His hands would stray to my shoulder, and I'd jerk back, which he ignored in favor of flipping to the next page or clearing his throat.

Now the memory had started to fade away. I would have let myself forget about it entirely, if not for Mrs. Yang.

I had moved to New York to take care of Ma, while Lin moved as far away as possible in the opposite direction, to pursue a graduate degree at an arts school in Wyoming, from where, at a safe distance, she called every Wednesday to see how we were doing.

"What did the doctor say?"

"Hold on," I said as I maneuvered Ma into the bathtub. No matter how I calibrated the knobs, the water always scalded her at first. "He said the same thing as last time. Levels look normal. She's taking the treatment well." Which wasn't exactly what the doctor had said. Instead, he explained, in an infuriatingly calm tone, that yes, the medication was working but not as well or as quickly as he hoped, and by that, he meant it was time to consider some other options that he'd be happy to walk me through. The half lie tasted petty on my tongue, but Lin would only ask questions, the same ones heaving through my head, and I couldn't stand having to hear them articulated in someone else's voice.

"Well, that sounds okay, right?"

"I guess. We have another appointment next week. Do you want to talk to Ma? She's right here." Ma was sitting back in the tub, humming, with her eyes closed, cupping the water against her chest. I asked this every time, if only to see what excuse Lin would come up with.

"Maybe next time? I have to go soon. Got to finish some work for my class tomorrow."

"She misses you."

"I know."

When I didn't respond, her voice arced defensively. "I *know*."

"Fine." This was how our conversations tended to unfold, volleying accusations and resentment back and forth in as few words as possible.

"By the way. Did we decide on what to do about the apartment?"

I glanced at Ma, whose eyes were still closed. The apartment had grown into a bruise, its borders encroaching into everyday conversation. Real estate in Beijing had become more precious than gold, with millionaires buying multiple floors of a development and paying in cash, while everyone else waded through years-long waiting lists for merely an opportunity to apply. The value of our apartment in Diaoyutai had tripled. Every week, I fielded calls from relatives asking what our plans were, offering unsolicited advice that we should sell as soon as possible, what with the market at its peak in decades, and recommending an array of lawyers and agents to help with the process.

The problem was Ma. The summer I turned fourteen, she had agreed to let Mrs. Yang live in the apartment indefinitely, in exchange for a nominal monthly sum. From Ma's perspective, come May or June, when she herself had to stay behind in the States for work and our fathers couldn't take us, we needed to have someone there to make sure we bathed, went to bed at a reasonable hour, and subsisted on more than crackers and red bean popsicles. It was a shock each time to open the door and be welcomed by the sight of Mrs. Yang sprawled on the couch, bare toes propped on the armrest, cackling at a soap opera. When we protested that we didn't need a babysitter, Ma switched tactics, trying to appeal to our sense of practicality. For the rest of the year, the apartment was sitting empty, collecting decay and rodents and termites, a potential target for burglars.

When that too failed to move us, Ma said, with the air of someone holding the trump card, that Mrs. Yang never had an apartment to herself before. Her life, up to then, was a series of cramped, stinking spaces. The sink built into the space above the toilet. Someone else's shit clinging to the bottom of the bowl. The communal kitchen, sugar and soy sauce stolen in inconspicuous increments. Didn't we think Mrs. Yang deserved to have her own space for the years she had left? It was unlike Ma to be so explicit about death, and this, more than anything else, made me and Lin relent. What was the harm, we thought.

Until our mother fell sick. Her thick curly hair, her only vanity, tumbled to the floor like pine needles. Chopsticks were too precarious. Where she parked or put the keys, her favorite books and songs, the details of her arrangement with Mrs. Yang—sifted away like sand. When I would probe about a contract, any sort of written agreement, Ma buttoned out her lower lip and folded into herself. I was left to ransack through her papers, amazed by the little scraps she had squirreled away over the years (dentist bills, report cards, test scores, college brochures) and found nothing. My father and Lin's hadn't known; if they had, they each insisted, they would have certainly talked her out of it.

At my silence, Lin cleared her throat. "It's just, well, you know. The money could go a long way. I could open my own gallery. I'm sure you've considered it too," she added hastily. That she had tallied up the sum and figured out its allocation for her own purposes was not surprising. What pricked was the truth of her assumption that I had done the same.

"Well, actually, I've been thinking about how most of it will have to go to Ma's care."

Lin was quiet, not even a sigh. I decided to change the subject. "I don't know. It feels off. Evicting Mrs. Yang."

"It's not really evicting, though, is it?" Lin was parroting the lawyer in Beijing that we had hired. He liked to switch showily between English and Mandarin and had an off-putting habit of shouting at random intervals, but he was plainspoken about the situation. "You have a squatter on your hands," he declared. "You're saying she's been there for more than five years by now? Ten? And she pays almost nothing? Well, I advise you to get a move on with proceedings! The longer she remains, the better her argument that your mother wanted her to have the apartment and you did nothing to signal your dissent."

"Dissent?"

"Well, you let her just stay there all these years, right?"

"Yes, but—"

"Your mother wouldn't have drawn up a will before her illness, would she?"

"No."

"So, there's nothing in writing that says who will hold title to the apartment once your mother passes?"

"No . . ."

"Then, you really have only one option. Talk to this woman in person. See if you can convince her to leave on her own. The apartment is in utter squalor—that's your recollection, yes?" Ignoring my sputter of protest at the word "squalor," he continued. "Take pictures. Write down what you see about the conditions. We may be able to argue that it's in her best interest to vacate. After all, once you involve the courts"—he sighed—"legal proceedings often gain their own momentum, and, once they get started, you have no idea how they will resolve."

Mrs. Yang had refused to answer any of my calls. The lawyer said no one would open the door—he had gone by multiple times.

Lin was saying into my ear, "It's ours. Ma wanted us to have it. You know that, right?" The water had cooled. Squawking in discomfort, Ma slapped the sides of the tub.

"I'm coming," I said to my mother. To Beijing.

VII.

The apartment was the last thread tying us to that city. I had not been back in years, less from any outright dislike than sheer inconvenience. The time difference caused massive havoc, requiring more than a week to recover from. Necessities that I usually took for granted were stripped away: orderly queuing, free and unencumbered internet access.

Not to mention how Beijing was a city made up of layers and layers of its own bones. The years in between visits were enough for parks, buildings, blocks, entire neighborhoods to be razed and rebuilt, with no resemblance to what existed previously. Every time I left China, I thought I had gained a foothold—I could walk to and from the bank and grocer and subway station without having to ask for directions. But every time I returned, I lost any sense of direction all over again.

Lin had refused to come with me. "I'd only get in the way. You've always been the savvy one, the daughter who knows how to get things done," she said. "Ma always said so."

331

"She did? She never said that to me."

"I mean, she didn't need to."

I would have resisted harder, if not for the fact that she volunteered, without my having to ask, to look after Ma while I was away. Standing there on the porch, my suitcases piled around our feet, we hugged for a long time. She had been drinking tea, but underneath I caught a sour tang of morning breath, a constant smell from when we were little and slept in the same bed. The night before, I had overheard her talking on the phone to someone—a friend? A lover? Lin had always been cagey, ever since she was little, and to this day, I had no idea how the interior of her life looked. With whoever she was speaking to, she sounded so unlike how I knew her, her voice an octave higher, flirtily pitched, laughter and cries of "Oh, stop it. No, stop."

Lin helped me put the suitcases into the car and slammed the trunk shut. I turned to look at her.

"When I get back, let's catch up. Really catch up. I want to hear how you've been."

"Sure. That sounds great," she said unconvincingly, not meeting my eyes.

VIII.

On my second day back in Beijing, I paid a visit to the apartment. The sky rasped a startling, rare blue. The cabbie made several wrong turns down alleys barely wide enough for a car to pass. He cursed and railed against a particular contractor who had built a luxury condo across a major throughway, creating more traffic on top of an already congested stretch— every now and then, he flicked his gaze up to the rearview mirror to see if I agreed. I shrank against the seat and repeated the last thing he said, having no idea how to say "bulldozed" and "injustice" in Mandarin. Before long, I caught a glimpse of the guesthouse's wall, a pale streak darting through the trees. The wall had always seemed so intimidating, this glistening, pristine relic, but now, as I pressed against the window, I could make out a grimy lattice of handprints smudged across its surface.

No one answered the door. A flicker in the eyehole. I knocked and called for Mrs. Yang until a woman on the landing above emerged. "Shoo," she huffed.

"Have you seen anyone going into this apartment today?"

She peeked at me suspiciously. "What's it to you?"

"I'm Xie Liping's daughter—" I gave up. Her face held no flicker of recognition. "I'll just try again later."

Outside, I paced and, having nothing better to do, walked the loop in the back, once teeming with weeds and wildflowers, where Lin wove her little fantasies, unruly and vast and abandoned. Now the weeds had been cleared away, the uneven dirt path paved over by asphalt, bustling with kids on their bicycles, families hurrying to the market before it closed. Before I knew it, I found myself standing in front of Wu Laoshi's old building. I stared up at it, then turned around and trudged back.

IX.

This time, when I knocked, the door creaked open.

"Well. Come in," said Mrs. Yang. Her left foot did not seem to bother her at all. She seemed much sturdier than I expected, an octogenarian who would go on living for years just to prove everyone wrong.

Inside was nothing like I remembered. The rotted bits in the floor had been mended, producing a patchwork of shiny spots. The cracks in the ceiling had disappeared. I wondered how Mrs. Yang had gotten the money to replace the entire drywall. The windows too had been swapped out for new ones, or so I thought, until, at close range, the teeny circles of repeated efforts at rubbing and polishing appeared. The only traces that lingered from our time in the apartment were the scorch marks. It occurred to me that perhaps Mrs. Yang had left them there on purpose, as a reminder.

"You've taken very good care of the place," I admitted.

"And now you want me to leave."

"It's mine. Mine and Lin's."

She sniffed. "Technically, it's still your Ma's. How is she?"

"Not good." Immediately, I regretted being so candid. I almost never told anyone, including Lin sometimes, how quickly Ma was fading. I felt it was the least I could do for her.

"I'm sorry." Mrs. Yang pronounced this with an earnestness that undid my bravado. I couldn't think of what to say next. There was a script the lawyer prepared, certain phrases I needed to make sure to convey, but those were as remote to me as ancient Greek at that moment.

"I'm making some tea," she said over her shoulder. "Chrysanthemum." Walking into the kitchen, the smell of bleach was overwhelming; bending over, as inconspicuously as I could, I scrutinized the grout in the tiling

333

above the counters. Not a speck of black. A toothbrush, the head brown and frayed from regular scrubbing, lay within reach.

Mrs. Yang took out two mugs and a ramekin of sugar cubes and sat down with the kettle. "I suppose your ma never told you about the offer for this apartment?"

"Only after you had already moved in. She said she would let you live here until, well . . ." I trailed off.

She swatted the air with the flat of her palm. "I'm not referring to the offer she made."

"I have no idea what you're talking about."

"I'm referring to *mine*. Sit down, Porklet. You're making me anxious, just standing there." I remained where I was. Shrugging, she popped a sugar cube into her mouth and sucked.

"You see this apartment as only a tidy sum, no? It's all right. I'm sure you have things you want to do with it, dreams and hopes. As does your sister. The money from the sale will go a long way toward fulfilling those."

Finding my voice, I retorted, "The money will be for Ma's treatment." The same thing I had said to Lin, ringing even more dully in my ears now.

"Of course. All that matters is what we tell ourselves, right?" She traced the rim of her cup. "That summer, when you told me about the piano teacher and Lin, remember? It was quite some time ago."

A shadow of an afternoon, those two figures hunched at the piano bench. I bit the inside of my cheek.

"Ah. You do remember. Well, I wanted to make sure I could be here with you both. In case it happened again." So, the spirit in our apartment that Lin had told me about turned out to be real. I finally sat.

Mrs. Yang shook her head. "He'd been teaching every boy and girl in this neighborhood for decades, and no one ever said anything. Until you. Your ma, she was confounded as to what to do."

"Ma knew? You told her?"

"Yes. She wouldn't believe me at first. Said you were just a child. Said you didn't know what you saw. 'Yes,' I told her. 'Quite possible that Yan may have gotten confused. So why not ask Lin?'"

My mouth was open. I was aware of every breath I took.

"Do you know what she said?"

"No," I replied, dazed.

"She said she liked piano and wanted to keep playing. And then she said the reason she liked it so much was because Wu Laoshi played piano on her."

"You mean with her?"

"No." Mrs. Yang's face blazed. "*On* her."

Outside the open window, I could hear the rabble of children playing or fighting—it was hard to tell. Piercing through their noise, the calls of a vendor selling *tanghulu*. Lin and I used to get a skewer apiece, competing to see whose stick had the biggest date or strawberry.

"Well. After that, your ma told Lin no more lessons. Oh, how she screamed. Threw herself onto the floor and sobbed until she frothed at the mouth and whacked her head against the wall. Your ma also wanted to go confront Wu Laoshi, but how was this any proof? He would only deny it and, besides, imagine the impact that would have had on Lin. An accusation could take on a life of its own. But I had an idea. In the summers, when your ma had to work, I would stay here and watch you girls. I would know if it happened again—no, not from Lin, of course. From you."

I pictured Lin, the way she held everything back and how easily, in comparison, I gave up how I felt. On the wall facing us danced bright lozenges of color cast by the sun.

"I kept watching all these years. You may wonder how an old, weak lady like me could have gone up against him even if he tried but"—she cleared her throat—"I would have figured it out. Your ma was grateful. Said I could live here for as long as I wanted."

"Why? Why would you do that for us?"

Mrs. Yang gave a cluck, as though, by needing to ask, I had missed the point.

I didn't know what to make of this generosity, the kind that didn't need to be written down, or explained, or dangled right in front of our noses, begging to be acknowledged. It had the quality of a memory, timeworn, yellowing around the edges. Flaring and sinking down into a single spark, only to be revived, day after day. I thought of how I'd explain to Lin that I'd spoken to Mrs. Yang and we'd reached an agreement, how my sister would brush past my reasoning and ask, "Just get to the point—what does this mean for *us*," and I'd have to spell it out— how the apartment wasn't really ours in the way I had always assumed it to be. How letting Mrs. Yang stay ("Just for a bit longer," I'd tell Lin and the lawyer. "She's kept it up well.") was doing her a terribly meager kindness. How Lin wouldn't understand, not at first.

But I would spare her the entire story. I could be generous too.

Nominated by Colorado Review

THE BLOB

by MOLLY GALLENTINE

from THE GETTYSBURG REVIEW

A future that would not be monstrous would not be a future; it would already be a predictable, calculable, and programmable tomorrow.

—*Jacques Derrida*

"Don't bleed on the work," James and I warn each other after each prick and subsequent curse. A pin nips my finger, and I hold my index up to the light to look for a tiny puncture, waiting to see if a red drop will emerge. We're hand sewing a ten-foot dome from socks, skirts, and other assorted fabrics, including something that might be the hide of Elmo. Every day, our hands receive tiny little injuries. Stitched together, the varying colors and fabrics appear similar to abstractly patterned stained glass. It's a big project, sewing this tent/installation/sculpture, so friends come to help. They include a teacher, a historian, a poet, two seamstresses, and a beekeeper whose hives are kept inside a cemetery. He calls the honey the Sweet Hereafter; every year his product sells out very fast.

Hereafter can refer to the afterlife, or it can mean "from now on." I feel like my entire generation is preoccupied with this meaning—something already set in motion. "What will happen from now on?" I ask James. I ask him lots of questions about the future. He is anxious because he's worried we've already ruined it. That's why, these days, all of his artwork is about climate collapse. After the arctic ice melt of 2012—the ice had not been that low for sixty thousand years—he sat on a boat while carving it out from under himself. It was thirteen feet long and wooden, and he placed the boat in a storefront window. Over the course of several weeks, as construction workers and policemen watched, James chipped away at the vessel with hand tools until nothing but a sea of shavings remained.

The argument of what *is* and what *isn't* art is beside the point: the destruction of a boat is clearly a metaphor. The process hurt him; he got splinters and had to be careful lest his hands suffer stress fractures. He hired me soon after, and during my artist-assistant training, I took copious notes. I see now that most of these notes are about pain.

The creation of the dome is an intimate and painful experience. James gives the dome a name: *The Tent of Casually Observed Phenologies*. He paints the words on a piece of wood and leans it against the base of the tent's frame.

Phenology is the study of cyclic and seasonal natural phenomena. It's concerned with whether plants and animals thrive or survive, because our food supply depends on the timing of events. Two other words that pop up when the term *phenology* is entered into a search engine: *climate* and *consequences*.

James has experienced vivid dreams throughout his life. In them, the sun expands over centuries. Oceans boil off. I'm aware of these dreams because he has told me about them and because I read his journals.

"Artist Assistant" is an elusive title. Reading private journals was not mentioned during my interview—an interview granted because I found his listing on the New York Foundation of the Arts website and applied, edging out one hundred other applicants who were equally interested in finding meaningful work and/or leaving work they hated. When I arrived at the interview, I *really* wanted the job, even though it didn't pay much. During the interview, I wanted it even more because the whole practice appeared intense and mysterious, and the artist, who was about a decade older than me, came across as considerate and professional, not as a slimeball or an axe murderer, even though I suppose he could have been one. After I got the job, I quickly learned that James is an academically minded human who, alongside painting and design, studies complex systems, which basically means he studies a lot of subjects at once. Like studying the world.

I think I am the only one who reads his private thoughts.

"I work for an artist!" I tell people.

They ask, "What do you *do* for the artist?"

"I make art!"

I don't tell anyone this unless prompted because, when my job comes up in conversation, one of three things happens: someone changes the subject; I'm told in one patronizing way or another that I'm noble; I'm asked what *kind* of art I make. This last question is a difficult one to answer, and I have not perfected my elevator speech. Mixed media? Conceptual? Socially engaged? I suppose it's the kind of art that causes you to stop attempting to make your Iowa farmer parents proud or even understand.

How do you explain to them that you professionally contemplate the apocalypse?

For days I walk around Brooklyn neighborhoods posting tear-off flyers on telephone poles. These flyers read: "Can you divine? Do you divine? I want to know how the story ends." "Do you have religious or spiritual experiences that provide insight into the future?" "Looking for diviners comfortable discussing the end of the world."

James calls this flyer-ing on-the-ground research, and we do ultimately receive responses by phone and email. One of them leads to a meeting. We drive to see a man who is both a shaman and initiated asogwe priest in Haitian Vodou. We drink coffee with him, and it's a special experience because I have never met a shaman/asogwe priest. Later, I find out he has a Twitter account. His tweets say things like, "Trying to figure out where all the kitchen knives have disappeared to and they're all in your workings. #rootworkerproblems." I smile at the screen. I love this shaman/asogwe priest. During the visit, we'd shared concerns for the future, and the shaman explained the Cree word, *wetiko*, a word that perfectly describes an otherwise unarticulated sickness. To be wetiko is to suffer a contagious, psycho-spiritual disease of the soul, to be the human instrument of an evil, cannibalistic spirit, a monstrosity collectively acted. The shaman says wetiko is our disregard for, and destruction of, our biosphere, the very thing that we need for survival. The word is a gift. I feel more at ease when I have language for what I fear.

I find hundreds of divination methods and the names for them, and I type them out on an old typewriter in James's studio so that we can occasionally remind ourselves of the many ways one can look into, or discuss, the future.

338

Sortes Virgilianae	divination by Virgil's *Aeneid*
Cromnyomancy	divination by onion sprouts
Catoptromancy	divination by mirror gazing
Meilomancy	divination by moles on the skin
Abacomancy	divination by dust

❉   ❉   ❉

My father does this thing where, holding my feet in both of his hands, he examines my toes. As a child, I used to love it when my parents sang "This Little Piggy" and wiggled each toe, but I don't know what my father is looking for when he examines my feet at this age. I read somewhere that physicians often inspect the feet of the elderly. How long are the toenails? It is one way to predict whether or not the patient can still take care of themselves. I've started to sneakily examine my parents' feet for this reason. A form of pedomancy? I care about their happiness and longevity, which are mostly out of my control.

When my mother, a nonsmoker, discovered she had lung cancer, she notified me via text message as if it were a casual thing happening to her body. Or maybe it was a strategic distancing; she could easily write but not *say* her diagnosis. They removed an entire lobe at the hospital. A couple of weeks after the procedure, she was back in the grain cart alongside her husband. As far as work goes, the two of them are a package set. My mother prides herself on her usefulness but desperately wants my father to retire. I used to be convinced that my father would farm corn and soybeans right up until the day he died, but now I foresee something different. When you get a glimpse of mortality, sometimes your priorities change. "Take me somewhere warm," says my mother.

When talking about the farm, my parents have always emphatically insisted that I never sell the land. Part of it has been taken care of by my family for over a hundred years. But recently, my parents explained a plan that would include a buy-out option regarding my future inheritance. Someone else can work the ground; I can be freed from that burden. But lifting one imparts another. "I don't care what happens to the land," said my father one evening at the dinner table, which is either a lie to ease his daughter's guilt or a horrible, depressing truth. Even though I find myself outside of the world of farming, I have been thinking about this particular legacy and responsibility for years. There is pride associated with food production. And when an article appears in

339

Atlas Obscura, written by George Pendle, titled, "This Iowa Town's Dirt Might Be More Valuable Than Gold," I know even before reading it that the piece will mention the fertility of Conrad in Grundy County—my home.

> Some have suggested that the Pampas of Argentina have soil of especial richness. Others posit certain areas of the Ukraine, where the fecundity of the soil has led to a $900 million black market in "chernozem" ("black dirt"). However, the National Laboratory for Agriculture and the Environment, located a dispassionate fifty-three miles away from Conrad, has declared Conrad's soil among the richest farmland in the world.

My town is built on a thousand years of prairie ecology. But this soil, with the pressures of modern yield and the large application of fertilizers, is being used up. Pendle explains that, from the Minoans and Mesopotamians to the Incas and the Aztecs, soil loss is tied to the demise of many ancient societies and "Conrad itself . . . has already decreased from the two feet of topsoil the original settlers found to an average between six to eight inches today."

After consulting with our shaman friend, James purchases a tarot deck. He takes classes from experts and practices reading his set of cards. I quiz James about tarot's iconography and each potential meaning. I pretend to be other people asking questions, or I simply ask them as myself—interrogations about farming, food supply, and how to be a good ancestor. Sometimes I don't say my questions aloud. Tarot practitioners call this a blind reading; it's a method to weed out fakers. We do all of this from inside *The Tent of Casually Observed Phenologies.* After all, this is the point of the artwork (not that all artwork has to have a point): we aim to confront climate change and its signposts, to acknowledge its complexity, and to decipher possible outcomes by means of visualization and divination.

It's decided. In our tent, James will discuss only the future of the planet. He flips the cards over, places them into a spread, and tells me what he sees. It's not very good.

Science writer, Craig Childs, explains in *Apocalyptic Planet: Field Guide to the Future of the Earth* that "when modern farmers first plowed Grundy County soils in the mid-nineteenth century, they said it sounded like firecrackers going off, all those prairie roots snapping as topsoil folded back like a blanket." Childs recruited a friend named Angus to spend two nights and three days with him in the middle of a six-hundred-acre farm. They wanted to see what they'd find living in the dirt. NPR reported on their experiment, explaining that a hundred years ago the same land was home to "three hundred species of plants, sixty mammals, three hundred birds, hundreds and hundreds of insects." What Childs and his buddy found: one mushroom the size of an apple seed, a cobweb spider eating a crane fly, some grasshoppers, and a single red mite. A combination of DuPont and Monsanto stock, the field plants had unbreakable leaves, unless you leaned right on the nodes. Childs describes walking into this farmland as "like pushing through Jell-O."

Childs's description of the gelatinous sensation sounds like science fiction. It sounds monstrous and horrific. A formless, shape-shifting, all-encompassing vehicle for terror.

Midway through the 1958 version of *The Blob*, Steve (Steve McQueen) and Jane (Aneta Corsaut) sneak away under cover of night to discuss the gelatinous creature that threatens to consume and destroy the world. The authorities in their town, who are generally dubious of teenagers' thoughts and actions and see youth itself as a danger to a strictly controlled status quo, don't believe the teens and so don't believe the blob exists. A good portion of the film is devoted to the young protagonists assuring each other of their sanity, but, newly awakened to their situation—that humanity is at the brink of being eradicated and that no one believes them—Steve and Jane struggle with the veracity of their own experience as well as what to do about the town's denial of the blob.

JANE. Steve, you believe you *did* see it. Don't you?

STEVE. I don't kn . . . I don't . . .

JANE. That's not true, Steve. Maybe now you don't want to believe it; maybe you'd like to tell yourself it didn't happen. Steve, you're not the kind of person who can turn their back on something you know is true.

STEVE. How do you get people to protect themselves from something they don't believe in?

JANE. You keep trying and hoping that you can find some sort of proof that will convince them.

341

Early ripening of the wild pawpaw.

House sparrows laying three sets of eggs instead of two.

Nonexistent torpor of the eastern chipmunk.

The northern creep of the crepe myrtle.

Changing taste of whitetail deer flesh.

Lost stripes of the eastern red-backed salamander.

So many phenological shifts are happening.

James makes a painting of each of these species, and we pin the portraits to the outside of our tent. The paintings are representations of observations and anecdotes taken from birdwatchers, citizen scientists, and elderly friends. We're collecting them—each subsequently and figuratively detailed on marine canvas by James. Eventually, the list of observations will grow too long, and we'll start stacking the images of plants and animals like Tibetan prayer flags. It becomes clear James will never finish all of the paintings.

Because we are working with our hands and trying to complete our tent structure in a timely manner, James and I spend a lot of time together— they are mostly quiet moments that we sometimes fill with chatter. James encourages my budding science-fiction curiosities and gives me comic books and movie recommendations. We talk about *The Blob*. I enjoy having this new interest, although it's a bit paradoxical to be working on an artwork about potential end times when science-fiction narratives are frequently meant to build up the expectation that technology can solve all our problems.

STEVE. It's kind of like a mass that keeps getting bigger.

POLICE OFFICER. Come on, Steve. Make sense.

* * *

Did you know that by 2050, there might be more plastic matter in the ocean than the biomass of fish? At the Morgan Library & Museum, I see an exhibit on Wayne Thiebaud's drawings. He has drawn, and painted, many things but most remarkably food. My favorite work of his is *Circle of Fish*, which happens to be hung on display. As the title states, the fish are arranged into a perfect circle. A placard explains Theibaud's theory behind the presentation: the common arrangement of fish into decorative circles at fish markets is intended to make the sight of dead animals more palatable. "Fish, laid out on a plain white surface, are very moving," Thiebaud remarked, "a kind of tragedy, actually." When I dish up dinner for myself,

I always clean any dripped contents off the white-rimmed lip of my plate with a napkin. Such fussiness, but I simply cannot ignore the impulse. As well as the notion of palatability, there is an element of sacredness to aesthetics. There is also something especially sacred about the circle. It's a symbol of unification, Earth's generative nature, and, largely, wholeness.

We have finally completed the sewing, and James and I are standing inside the studio, inside the tent, which is a circle, and we are looking up at the ceiling through an oculus, which is also a circle—an opening we have left at the top of the tent for air circulation. Soon, our view will not be the ceiling of his studio but the sky above because we are taking the tent on the road. I've planned and outlined the trip. We will take the tent to approximately fifty locations in towns across multiple states, set up the structure early in the morning while everyone is asleep, and tear it down late in the evening. James likens us to a circus caravan, which is the most apt description either of us can come up with. I feel like a carnival barker and a magician's assistant. Someone to grow the excitement of the crowd and wave her arms at the performer. Someone to step into a box and disappear when instructed.

The Tent of Casually Observed Phenologies garners the attention of a professor at an ivy league school. James is interviewed by the woman (I am off camera, crouched in the box of invisibility), and she puts this filmed interview online so it can be shared with the smartest young people. They are teaching new courses at her ivy league school, teaching concepts like "climate communication," the lens through which she's explaining the tent project. Scientists are worried about how to get individuals to care about our climate crisis, and they have discovered that academic charts and diagrams are not the language of the people. So while offering tarot card readings about climate change may mock modern scientific thought, scientists are also recognizing that it might *not* be a terrible idea to use a communication tool that provides a spiritual and personalized element.

> STEVE. I've never needed to talk to anyone before, not as much as I do now.

> JANE. We're in this together, aren't we, Steve?

James paints "Free Climate Change Divination Readings" onto his wooden sign. It's the last thing that we pack into his car—along with the tent, our backpacks, and ourselves. We turn away from the city and its tall buildings and momentarily allow the highway traffic to distract

343

us from the mild nervousness accompanying what we've set out to do. Everything familiar trails off into the distance. A binary starts to creep into my head: there will be a *before* the tent tour and an *after*. We say farewell to our homes. We continue, driving ahead.

Around the start of our tent tour, I read in a newspaper article that "evacuation of the two villages has begun, with authorities reportedly relocating 68 of 223 families so far." It's an update to a story first reported a couple of years prior. People were suddenly falling asleep in northern Kazakhstan, even while walking, and waking with headaches and memory loss. Some people mysteriously fell asleep over half a dozen times, and some slept for up to six days at a time. It happened in two small villages to adults and children alike. Even a cat was reported to be snoring, wandering like a zombie. The language used to describe sufferers was that they were "dropping off." Some lost consciousness while others experienced new realities: hallucinations of winged horses, worms eating their hands, snakes in their beds.

The investigation took a long time. After analyzing the results of medical examinations of all the afflicted residents, researchers finally concluded that it was caused by the heightened levels of carbon monoxide and hydrocarbons in the air. The villages had uranium mines left over from the Cold War. They had been closed at some point, but the mines had created a concentration of carbon monoxide. The real reason for the sleeping sickness was lack of oxygen.

"Nobody likes it when you mention the unconscious, and nowadays, hardly anybody likes it when you mention the environment," writes Timothy Morton in his book *Ecology without Nature: Rethinking Environmental Aesthetics*. "You risk sounding boring or judgmental or hysterical, or a mixture of all three." To Morton, there is a deep yet simple reason for this. When you mention the unconscious, it becomes conscious. When you speak of the environment, it's brought to the foreground and stops being the environment: "It stops being That Thing Over There that surrounds and sustains us. When you think about where your waste goes, your world starts to shrink." The waste—from human industrialization and extraction—becomes monstrous. It becomes a hostile force, invading the parameters of our conceptual environment.

A paper written by May R. Berenbaum and Richard J. Leskosky for the Ecological Society of America—*Life History Strategies and Population*

Biology in Science Fiction Films—analyzes sixty-seven "invader" films released in theaters between 1950 and 1958. According to film historians, they were an artistic response to fears brought on by Nazi imperialism and Cold War paranoia. Only three alien creatures survive to the end of the film; most are obliterated in spectacular ways.

MEANS OF DESTRUCTION

Atmosphere 6	Water 4
Volcano 4	Microbes 1
Earthquake 2	Conventional Weapons 22
Avalanche 2	Electromagnetic Radiation 12
Poison Gas 2	Predators 2
Suicide 2	Cannibalism 1

The paper includes a table of the invader films remade between 1970 and 1990—which includes *The Blob*. The biggest difference between the remake and the original version is the role of the authority figures. In the '50s' version, the military successfully comes to the aid of the townspeople by removing the creature. In the 1988 remake, the government accidentally unleashes the blob—an experiment in biological warfare gone awry. "That organism is potentially the biggest breakthrough in weapons research since man split the atom," says the man in charge. "What we do here will affect the balance of world power." Everything is about power. Yet officials fail at domination and heap violence upon their creation to no avail. "Chew on that, slimeball," says a government employee after dropping a grenade atop the blob. In response, it shoots out of a manhole like a giant phallus and falls limp upon the man, killing him instantly. His body is absorbed and disappears into the growing gelatinous goo.

I stand on a chair so that my head, shoulders, and arms emerge through the oculus at the top of our tent. James hoists up a large amount of fabric and passes it to my outstretched hands. He helps me dress the structure, and the material cascades prettily to the ground. It takes three hours for James and me to install *The Tent of Casually Observed Phenologies*. It's slow and arduous—this daily business of building and tearing down, of dressing and undressing—but I succumb to the muscle memory of our careful process. I am my best robotic self. Tie this, pull this, snap that. Amidst a bent metal frame lies a taut canvas grid marked by numbers and letters. We cinch and button and pin our quilts of used

345

clothing to the inner walls. When secured and drawn back, it becomes a dome of soft textiles spread into a gradated rainbow pattern. I softly trace some lace and then a child's shirt collar with my finger before placing our tools out of sight. It's an impressive thing, this stitched sculpture, although you can't experience the whole effect unless you step inside, which many creatures do. A groundhog tries to enter by burrowing a hole under the base. A cat admits herself and curls her body against the wall. A young couple comes to sit and talk. I think it's because the structure's attractive and protective.

The couple is either newly married or about to be married. He is a serviceman working as a member of the Coast Guard and will soon be off on another deployment. The two of them gaze at the fabrics and the stack of tarot cards. James begins to shuffle.

I once heard a poet call mysticism the prophetic act of piecing together a scattered cosmic body. This serviceman tells James he has "seen some stuff" already, across both land and sea. Scenes replay in his mind, but he knows he will travel once again into zones struck by natural disaster. The man will witness more violence, depletion, and struggle. What will this "stuff" feel like when accumulated over time?

His partner squeezes his hand, supportive, grounded, and loving. She is the real reason for visiting *The Tent of Casually Observed Phenologies*. He worries about the "out there," but he also worries about his home, which is a place but also a person—her. He doesn't want to bring *it* home to his love. By *it* he means anxiety, darkness, and climate crisis. By *it*, he means a monster.

People are generally curious about the tent. I stand outside the structure, control the queue, which fluctuates from zero people to a big line and a waiting period that lasts for hours. Most everyone wants to know if James will really give them a definitive answer to their question. I say "maybe" but also "not really," because the world is in constant flux. Mostly, I think a prophet is simply someone who pays attention and has a good imagination. A prophet is someone who can think metaphorically. I stress the positive attributes of contemplative space and envisioning possible outcomes. I am not one for strict adherence—that the cards will tell us the one and only truth. I don't know if this is frustrating or brings relief to those waiting in line, but they nod their heads regardless.

A solitary, serious boy in Virginia sits quietly reading a book until it is his time to enter the tent. He has been scrutinizing the movement of eagles on his grandfather's property and is now worried. In Massachusetts, a petite child asks about warming temperatures, but she is not interested in melting snow. "What will happen to life in the desert?" she asks. A middle schooler, who has a subscription to the *Economist*, wants to learn how this crisis will affect the complex web of trade.

Sometimes, a parent will enter the tent with their child. The parent, usually a mother, sits quietly and listens to the child's query. James guides them through time, into the future. The mother must imagine her child as a teenager, as a college student, as someone her own age. She must imagine her child with age spots, gray hair, and bad knees. She must imagine her child without her. The mother will admit that she has never done this before, visualized her child as an old man/woman. When they exit the space, the mother is often quiet and maybe a little shaken. I notice energy shifts, how people walk in and walk out, and quickly measure these energies, occasionally checking in to see if participants are okay. James and I also check in with each other.

While driving, or over greasy diner eggs, he will relay the daily tarot readings to me, both because I'm curious and also to unburden himself. If there is a bathtub, in the evening James will lie in warm water in an attempt to clear his mind. I will sit in silence somewhere on the other side of the door, respecting his quiet suspension. I drink alcohol to help me sleep. James still has bad dreams, and when we have to share a room, I think about what he must be dreaming in the dark from my position on the floor, the couch, or a blow-up mattress. We sleep wherever people let us sleep, finding hosts in different regions and from different backgrounds.

A run-down Winnebago with a shattered window.

The carriage house of a mansion belonging to the city mayor.

A treehouse.

The living room of a horticultural PhD student.

The insect-infested home of a woman who believes in fairies.

Amish country, surrounded by wildflowers.

In *The Blob*, the protagonists don't sleep. Jane and Steve only pretend to go to sleep, sneaking out of their bedrooms at night. They know the blob is at large and feel the responsibility to warn everyone they see. When they *do* find the blob, it's too late. They're trapped inside a diner—along with Jane's little brother—completely enveloped by the monster. Steve lifts the boy into his arms. Jane tells her brother to try and go to sleep. In the frame, the three of them appear to be a nuclear family; having grown up in the matter of a few hours and no longer

347

recognizable as teenagers, Steve and Jane morph into parental figures. The little boy buries his head into Steve's shoulder, and, amidst the heightened tension of this climax, Steve and Jane look meaningfully into each other's eyes.

STEVE. Hey, listen Jane—

JANE. It'll be alright.

When the *New York Times* film critic, Howard Thompson, reviewed *The Blob*, he described the picture as one that "talks itself to death." But I can't get over the way Jane cuts Steve short. We'll never know if Steve meant to tell her "I love you" or "I'm sorry," both of which seem true. Why did I have to get her involved? he probably thinks to himself. It's all too much. There is no declaration of feeling, of this *immensity* of feeling between the two of them, because to put it into language would kill it.

James and I can talk about our day-to-day, but we find it hard to speak about the wider scope of our project—about the legs of our journey not yet traveled. The tent is overwhelming. The tent is an endurance test. When we begin to broach these things, our voices trail off. "It'll be alright," I find myself saying out loud. I set an intention amidst the most tragic circumstances, telling myself something positive will be born of the experience. It's this attitude that James and I adopt in the throes of exhaustion.

A pamphlet published by Martin Luther and Phillipp Melanchthon in 1523, and translated into English in 1579, tells of "two wonderful popish monsters." It details various interpretations of the monstrous, either prophetic or eschatological. Monsters and prodigies are signs of fundamental change about to affect the world. Another interpretation is allegorical, each monster a divine hieroglyph exhibiting a particular feature of God's wrath. I see tarot cards as functioning in the allegorical sense too—archetypes meant as guideposts for a way of making decisions and navigating life.

I cannot convince everyone to partake in the process. In Pennsylvania, a handful of Christians express concern that the tent and our tarot will invoke some kind of demonic spirit. In Maryland, our presence makes a few police officers chuckle. They are flippant. "I don't care what happens with climate change because I will already be dead," says an old man in Connecticut.

I listen to an interview on the radio with an indigenous activist. "Not all people who grow old are elders."

We install *The Tent of Casually Observed Phenologies* in a public park, and it is hot. I watch a group of adults with cognitive disabilities climb onto a choo-choo train with the help of caretakers. The train plays music, and its song repeats while it does wide loops around the tent. There is another activity at the park too: paddle boating. For a small fee, people can take them out onto the pond and make figure eights in the water if they like. The proprietor leaves what I'm assuming is his son in charge. I get the impression he is one of those kids who hasn't had much of a childhood; he has held a job since the moment he could hold one. His current job is to rent the boats. He drags a chair over to the dock and sits. He then stands up and paces, waiting for a customer.

The boats look like white swans. Tied to the dock, the big plastic birds sway in unison. A real swan avoids them, swimming at a distance. The boy doesn't pay much attention to it because he has to pay attention to the plastic swans, the ones that will hopefully bring in money, which he needs. But the boy is interested in us and our tent, which appeared mysteriously at his workplace. He wants to poke his head inside and get a reading, but first he has to work. "Maybe I can do it when I get off!" he told us when he found us there that morning.

We—the three of us—sit in the heat for hours.

A couple of people pass by our tent while out for a walk and briefly stop. But the day is mostly quiet and boring. At a certain point, I go to buy a lemonade as James waits inside the tent. The boy departs to use the bathroom. When he gets back, the cashbox is gone. "Did you see where it went?" he asks us, as if the money left by its own volition. I spot him searching the park, visibly distressed. Eventually, we have to pack up the tent and go to our next destination. We ask the boy if he wants to look inside. "I can't," he says. James and I leave him with his plastic birds, and it makes us depressed.

Over time, the questions from participants begin to pile up, so much so that James and I have trouble remembering them all, and James resorts to jotting them down nightly in his journal to maintain a record.

Can I safely buy a waterfront condo?
Should I change careers to respond to climate change?
Will anything I do make any difference?

Should I be doing more?
Will climate refugees come to my town?
Will my children be a part of the solution?
Should I have children at all?
Is there hope?

A woman silently cries as she exits the tent, and I hug her. The weight and tension of her body releases into mine. A man who used to work for the National Forest Service until the President of the United States cut his research funding has his wife take Polaroid photos of the two of us standing in front of the tent—one for me and one for them to remember me by. "It's so important," they both say about *The Tent of Casually Observed Phenologies.*

The Guardian recently published an article titled, "How Scientists Are Coping with Ecological Grief." In it, the various experts interviewed are blunt. They speak about the horrifying loss of the Great Barrier Reef and other subjects of their fieldwork but also the loss of personal identities and cultural connections that indigenous people affected by global warming are experiencing. Ashlee Consolo, an environmentalist who works with Inuit communities in Labrador, mentions hearing a lot of "anticipatory grief," which she describes as "the sense that the changes are continuing, and that they're likely to experience worsening of what they're already seeing. . . . This is a slow and cumulative grief without end."

The blob is bigger, and it will grow bigger yet. It consumes an unsuspecting janitor, a car mechanic, and an old man.

"Doctor, I'm afraid," admits a nurse when she finds the blob on the floor of a patient's room. There's a crash. The lights go out. The blob moves to its next target.

The true horror in the movie is knowing that the growing mass is made of once-human meat and the flesh of any other living thing the blob has absorbed. Unlike other famous monster figures, the blob has no distinguishable human qualities. The monster is simply a thing. Still, the people in the movie want to know what "it" is because they have never seen the likes of "it" before. Philosopher Georges Bataille describes an object of horror as "a fetid sticky object without boundaries, which teems with life and yet is the sign of death. It is nature at the point where its effervescence closely joins life and death, where it is death gorging life with decomposed substance."

This boundary-less horror is something contemporary philosopher Julia Kristeva calls "abjection"—the breakdown in the distinction of the self and other. I cannot help but think of the blob's ignorance of human exceptionalism as being analogous to climate change. The blob will consume *all* living things, and then these living things will become dissolved, assimilated, unrecognizable. And while I think there is hope and the possibility of change within our unknown futures, even if this means a future without humans, I also don't want to get lost dwelling in the dissolve. After all, one of the guiding principles of a horror movie is for its main characters to try and stay alive.

In Rhode Island, a young woman from Taiwan enters *The Tent of Casually Observed Phenologies*. She describes to James her affinity for water, a relationship that has now become upsetting to her. The woman talks about the sea as intimately as one would a lover. I tell everyone who asks that the tent is not a space for answering questions of romance, but her question is an exception. Throughout her life, she would instinctively go to water when contemplating a new job or some other major transition. The water had a calming effect. Her visitation was a spiritual one. In a 1927 letter to his friend Sigmund Freud, writer and mystic Romain Rolland coined the term "oceanic feeling," describing it as "a sensation of 'eternity,' a feeling of something limitless, unbounded . . . of an indissoluble bond, of being one with the external world as a whole." Her oceanic feeling has become disrupted, the woman explains. After experiencing several strong typhoons in her home country, she can no longer stare at the water without feeling its violence.

Will she be able to find resolve?

James turns the cards and places them into a spread.

The truth of the matter is that water has become fraught. I read about the Ocean Observatories Initiative Endurance Array, a mechanism "designed to measure changes in the ocean on timescales from hours to decades" and how it has been keeping tabs on the Northeast Pacific—more specifically, a large region of anomalously warm surface water. Scientists are surveying this "warm blob" (as they call it), tracking its movements. The last big report observed that it had "advected south and toward the Canadian and US west coasts." On the opposite coast, especially around Rhode Island, water temperatures contribute to what the locals ominously call "red tide." The name itself sounds like something out of a B movie—the blob grows redder with every new victim—but instead of blood and gore, "red tide" refers to red seaweed. A

351

spongy algae grows over native seaweed, starving and damaging the habitat. It smells bad when washed ashore, and little bugs like to cling onto it and live within its surface. For paddle boarders, swimmers, and surfers, it's unpleasantly soupy.

Joan Didion has an essay about Rhode Island, namely Newport, called "The Seacoast of Despair." While she calls the area "physically ugly, mean without the saving grace of extreme severity," James and I are generously housed by those who intend to preserve the place. The Newport Restoration Foundation, with its Keeping History Above Water initiative, gives us beds to sleep in for two nights in one of the oldest neighborhoods. We left Providence late in the day, and it is dark when we arrive in town. Mist is everywhere. The house, which was built in 1725, is hard to find without daylight, but we manage. I stretch my legs while James searches for the key placed in a hidden spot and then watch as he struggles with the lock. The air smells of salt and fish. We must be near the water, but it's hard to know in which direction the land's edge lies.

When James finally opens the door, the house, from what I can tell, seems charming inside; it has good bones and creaky wooden floors. It's a restoration project in progress, and I'm sure the foundation will make it beautiful and then sell it to some interested family. I find a set of new sheets stacked on the bed I claim, and I thrill at the level of cushion in the mattress. But before I can collapse on the bed, James and I take the time to carry all of the pieces of the disassembled tent from the car into the kitchen; James wants us to protect it from thieves. We go through the same motions wherever we sleep, no matter how tired we might be, because we understand that there is only one *Tent of Casually Observed Phenologies.*

We wake up early, shower, eat a banana, and pack everything back into the car before heading to our installation spot. I've made sure to wear the least amount of clothing possible as the forecast says it'll be a scorcher. Instead of the woods or some cliff overlooking the sea, we're setting up the tent on concrete. James drives, and unlike the night before, our destination is easily spotted. A defunct Texaco station rests in stark contrast against historic, centuries-old buildings.

James pops the trunk, we empty it, and I begin to lock the tent frame in place. A woman approaches us to say that underneath our feet is actually a natural spring, covered up by Texaco. It's holy, or at least was at one time. The water beneath us is baptismal water. I look around. Across the street from our tent is a United Baptist Church, the second oldest in America. Also nearby: a Quaker meeting house and a synagogue. I think again of Joan Didion and her critique of the lives of individuals who chose to live in these parts. It was she who bristled at the level of topiary gardening in Newport, seeing it as a symbol of the rich. What did she say? "A landscape less to be enjoyed than dominated." A bead of sweat slides from my neck down between my breasts. God, what I wouldn't do to run my hands through that spring water and splash it onto my face and arms. If only we had kept and protected what was truly sacred. I turn to face James, but to utter these words out loud to him would only be preaching to the choir.

When the blob surrounds and envelopes the diner—with Steve, and Jane, and Jane's little brother trapped inside—the parents watch. The police drop a power line onto the blob to burn it to a crisp, but the blob doesn't care about the sparking power line or the fire that it starts. Now the diner is engulfed by the blob and engulfed by flames. Smoke begins to fill the diner and burn their lungs. They cough.

JANE'S MOTHER. Why don't you *do* something?! *Do* something!

Jane's mother is wildly distressed. She has been awakened from a dream. She's been sleepwalking this whole time, you see—cooking meatloaves and cleaning windows and applying lipstick and saying "yes, dear." Jane's mother is an agreeable woman who never makes a scene. She wants to instill these qualities in her daughter too because these are the qualities her own mother taught her to value. These qualities will get you far in life, people in charge said. *People.* But people in charge can't or won't save her family. She never imagined it would be like this. Never dared think.

Jane's father is waking up too. He has also been sleepwalking—going to work in clean suits in order to feed his family, coming home late and tired. He is the man of the house, a patriarch, an embodiment and expression of a system. When he opens his eyes, I envision him asking himself, How did I end up here with this monster? When he opens his eyes, he finds a rock in his hand. When he opens his eyes, he finds himself in front of one of the town's honored institutions: the high school, where he is principal. He throws a rock at the school's window. It breaks, of course. It's just a facade. Teenagers cheer and swarm each room, grabbing every fire extinguisher in sight.

The teenagers drive to the diner to rescue their friends. CO_2 puffs into the air. The children must save themselves.

In Newport, standing at a gas station above holy water that I cannot touch, I get the worst sunburn of my life. Halfway through the day, I notice patches of flushed skin and apply sunscreen, but it is too late. My neck is bright red, as well as most of my back, the result of my decision to wear a tank top of flimsy material with an incredibly low cutout. I put my palm below the base of my skull and hairline, and it aches upon touch. I search for trees that might offer some shade, but there are none close by. There is just a line of people waiting to enter *The Tent of Casually Observed Phenologies*. So I stand on the concrete and make small talk with individuals to distract myself from my discomfort until James stands to leave. He tells me about the town's worries, about the red seaweed, then furrows his brow at the sight of my skin.

In *Recreational Terror: Postmodern Elements of the Contemporary Horror Film*, author Isabel Cristina Pinedo writes about the prevalent trend of the open ending. She lists the various options as such: the monster triumphs, the monster is defeated but only temporarily, or the outcome is uncertain. The open ending's not the only reason I don't particularly enjoy watching scary movies; I just don't have a natural impulse to enjoy looming threats and death.

Regardless, the monster's already here. It lurks in the flooded bayous of southeastern Louisiana, the land of the United Houma Nation. It visits western Saudi Arabia in the summer, bringing with it humidity and heat stroke. And it feeds on the coconut plantations in the Solomon Islands. The monster chases the giant mountain lobelia until it has nowhere cool enough to grow, tramples the habitat of the Sierra Nevada blue butterfly, sucks the life out of staghorn coral. It sends a cyclone to Buzi and gorges itself on water in Somalia so that people flee to the Wajaale district, where they create makeshift shelters. The people construct tents that look shockingly like our tent—soft and colorful things—to protect themselves from the elements.

When we enter our historic house, it's once again dark. One of us finds a light switch, and we creak across the floor to the small kitchen table, where we sit. We try to imagine what kind of people the house played host to over the years. We have fun considering the past of this place and what sort of maritime workers might have lived here at one time.

What did they do inside these walls? Who knows. It's all a casual lead-up to this moment.

"Are you ready?" he asks. James opens the cap to a tube of aloe vera, hurriedly purchased from a nearby pharmacy.

"Yes," I say, scooting my chair and turning away from him. I bend over slightly and pull up the back of my shirt. He sucks in air through his teeth, and I blush.

"Is it bad?" I ask.

"Yes."

James is gentle but thorough, squeezing globs of aloe from the tube and spreading it over every spot of inflamed flesh. I feel his hands and hear the aloe oozing between his fingers. And I feel the sliminess coating my skin.

What a predicament, I think, to be in this strange kitchen and in these strange times. There are still four more stops on this journey before we can go home. I think of all the questions from strangers, the worries detailed in James's journal, and the fears shaping our hearts. We carry them with us as we carry the tent, somehow heavier with every stop.

His hands move to the back of my neck, and I get goosebumps from the alternating heat radiating off my skin and the coldness of the medicinal goop.

James apologizes for my sensitivity. This is what James and I share: tenderness.

The blob cannot be destroyed. The only way to slow down or pause its destructive momentum is to blast it with cold air. In the final scene, it's dropped from a plane into snow-covered territory. A literal question mark hangs in the sky.

STEVE. It's not dead, is it?

POLICE OFFICER. No, it's not.

STEVE. Just frozen.

POLICE OFFICER. I don't think it can be killed, but at least we've got it stopped.

STEVE. Yeah, as long as the arctic stays cold.

Nominated by Gettysburg Review, Marcus Spiegel

MARMALADE

fiction by FRED D'AGUIAR

from CONJUNCTIONS

For breakfast, lunch, and dinner. On slices of rubbery white bread buttered with margarine so that the marmalade slides under the spreading knife. In the glass jar, the orange jelly with bright shavings of orange peel absorbs light and invites hungry eyes. And so, dreaming of marmalade, the brothers, always in need of sustenance, arrive on a snowy March morning at Heathrow. Their mother stands at the bottom of the aircraft boarding stairs, her arms full of four gray wool coats. She's given special permission to stand by the plane with the coats because of the snow and the fact that her children, categorized as minors in the state's eyes, materialize with no protection against the English weather. The boys file down, the eldest, age thirteen, holding the hands of the youngest, age five, and the two middle boys, eight and ten, in single file, not touching. Their teeth chatter. Their heads swivel, take in parchments of light.

The youngest opens his mouth and tries to catch snow, his neck extended. His face juts this way and that as the flakes dodge his mouth. The eldest tries to pull on his youngest brother's arm but it slips from his grip. Halfway down the steps the youngest stumbles. Though the eldest grabs at him, he just misses a sleeve and the five-year-old tumbles, as if boneless, so soft are his landings by hands, shoulders, knees, backside, and elbows, down the flight of stairs all the way onto the black tarmac, flecked with white. His mother shouts three joined-up names first before she gets to the correct one, Gavin-Neil-William! Tony! She drops the coats and drags him to his feet and folds her arms around him. Two airport officials rush over, pick up the coats, and check with her that the boy's unhurt. She nods and she distributes the coats to the children, from the smallest, which she helps onto Tony, upward in size, using one free arm and hugging each in turn with a quick kiss and a smile. She keeps her grip on little Tony, bruised with embarrassment.

They collect four suitcases helped by a man who is neither Guyanese nor British and who their mum introduces as Uncle Iqbal, which causes the three oldest boys to raise their eyebrows, while the youngest seems oblivious. As they march to a van, stamping on the snow as if the ground were showered with insects to be obliterated, the eldest asks, Where's Dad? Their mother says she will explain later and she invites them to take in the sights of England. The boys, all except the youngest, Tony, who is engrossed in following the things his mother points out to him, look at each other and at the man introduced as their uncle, and again at each other. There is nothing discernible in their expressionless faces; there is everything in the way they catch each other's eyes.

The drive to the house takes a long time measured by streets of joined-up houses, low walls at the front and a patch of greenery, cars parked bumper to bumper, the stop and start progress of traffic lights and their mother saying, Not far now, every time the Ford van with three rows of seats gathers momentum and jolts the children. The sky narrows and leans in close with a mix of low, gray clouds, dull light and moisture, no sun. The children take in everything, though their eyes burn from lack of sleep. They see people in long coats, shoulders hunched, heads down, a slight crouch to them as they walk at a brisk pace. The people look pale, ashen. Some of them push prams whose contents remain invisible under thick covers. Others carry bags of shopping. Couples grab onto each other for dear life.

The driver sings quietly and glances over to the boy's mother in the front passenger seat. He searches for the boys in the rearview. They try not to look but cannot help listening to his sweet voice. He pauses and explains it is a song by Iqbal, no relation, he adds, a great poet from his home country, Pakistan. He sings on, *So sal la pe hel le, mu jay toom say pyar a tar, mu jay toom say pyar a tar, sal la pehe . . .* Then translates roughly, though no one asks him to, he says, I have loved you a thousand years and I will love you a thousand more. He says this and looks to his left at the boys' mother. He takes his eyes off the road again and again. She blushes and her hands fiddle with her headdress. The boys stare ahead in alarm as the van careens toward stalled traffic. Uncle Iqbal slams on the brakes. The boys slide off their seats. The oldest three suck their teeth—a loud intake of air through clenched teeth and pursed lips—and their mother asks the youngest if he is all right. He nods. Says he wants to wee. Uncle Iqbal apologizes and pulls over in front of a fast-food place, where he turns on the hazard lights and leaves with Tony. They return with burgers and fries and drinks. The boys' mother asks, What do you say, children? They say, Thank you, in unison. She asks again, Thank you who? They reply, Thank you, Uncle Iqbal. As they eat, everything changes from lethargy to a jittery animatedness. Uncle Iqbal drives in silence for the rest of the journey.

At last the van with its musical driver pulls into an East London side street and parks about halfway along it in front of houses that all look alike, the net curtains, the sepia wood tones, unadorned brick and concrete. Uncle Iqbal runs from the driver's side to open the passenger door for their mother and next the back door for them. He splits open the van's back doors and unloads the four suitcases. He rushes to the gate and pushes it open and gestures to the house for their mother to proceed. She calls on her children to follow her. Tony runs to her side and takes her hand. We're home, she says. Again the eldest asks, Where's Dad? She says back to him with a forced smile, Gavin, be patient. I'll explain everything in a moment. Gavin catches the eyes of Neil and William. This time their mother sees the exchange and she adds quickly, We can talk as soon as we settle in, I promise. The owners of the house, a young and corduroy-wearing English couple and their daughter, Jennifer, greet the boys, their mother, and Uncle Iqbal at the front door. They offer to help with the suitcases but between Uncle Iqbal and the boys there's nothing left to carry. They retreat to the upstairs portion of the house. Jennifer waves at Gavin. He returns a barely perceptible nod and the merest wisp of a smile since all eyes are pasted on him. The boys' mother ushers them into a front room with a table and sofa, a sewing machine and clothes rack and television. She opens a curtain separating the room into two to reveal a pair of bunk beds and barely enough room for a chest of drawers and a clothes rack. She tells them space is limited and they will have to keep the place tidy. She says they can decide where they want to sleep but she does not want the youngest on a top bunk. She rubs the top of Tony's head as if dusting it and skims it with a kiss.

After she leaves the room, they hear her talking with Uncle Iqbal in the corridor. The words cannot be discerned, just the interplay of two tones, one male and the other female. The front door closes and she walks along the corridor, quick steps with heels resounding on wood, to the kitchen. The boys hear aluminum, water, glass, and steel all banging against each other as their mother hums and adds her voice to her one-woman orchestra. They put away clothes, one drawer for each of them, coats on hangers. They pick out beds with a rhyme. Gavin, the eldest, says each syllable and chops the air in the direction of each brother, *Apten-dapten-dee-kalapten-daddy-kalapten-dee-do-es-kamoody-skalam-askoody-apten-dapten-dee-kalapten-daddy-kalapten-dee-do.* The nonsensical rhyme ends with Gavin pointing at Neil, who is the first to pick a top bunk. Gavin launches the rhyme again and this time he ends it by pointing at himself. He shrugs and chooses the other top bunk. William stops Gavin launching into the rhyme for a third time with a quick nod at Tony to go ahead and take a pick of one of the two remaining lower bunks. They complete the sleeping arrangements just as their mother returns with a tray loaded with four glasses of hot orange juice and marmalade sandwiches. She explains about the orange juice. You'll get used to it. It will warm you up. The children screw up their faces as they sip the drink. They maintain the same expression as they bite into the white bread caked with marmalade. She watches and keeps on smiling. She sees the empty suitcases and nods approvingly. They eat and drink everything. She tells them that they share the kitchen and bathroom with the Dunstans so they need to exercise especial care when they use both, to keep both tidy. The boys nod. Tony follows whatever his older brothers do, which leaves him a couple of moves behind them, still nodding after they stop.

Where's Dad? the eldest asks.

Your father left me. He said he didn't love me anymore. He loves someone else. I asked him about you children. What was to become of you? He said that it was up to me. You could stay in Mahaicony or I could bring you to England.

Neil and William look at Gavin for his usual leadership. He places his hands on his hips and straightens to his full height of perhaps five feet. Tony interrupts. Where's Dad? He does not understand her explanation. She pulls him close to her and kisses the top of his head. Gavin asks, Why didn't he come to meet us? She cannot stop her eyes from flooding, looks away and wipes her face. She replies that she asked him to come but he said he did not want to. Her words meet four puzzled faces. They hear her words but they cannot square what she says with what her words mean. Tony asks, Where's Daddy? And this time Neil raises his voice at his young brother without really meaning to. Can't you hear what she's saying? He doesn't want anything to do with us. Gavin and William shoot stern looks at Neil. He adds a quick and quiet

Sorry. Tony starts to cry. His mother hugs him and he buries his face in her chest. What did we do wrong? Gavin asks. His mother shakes her head. It's not you boys. It's your father. Don't blame yourselves. I am proud of every one of you. She barely manages to get these words out between heaving to suppress her upset. She hugs Tony so tightly that he looks up at her to be sure she is not attacking him and he pushes away from her. Gavin, William, and Neil rush close and encircle her and Tony with a big untidy hug, little arms searching for a place to rest, lifting, alighting, and settling on part of a back or shoulder before the whole bundle rocks back and forth, all of them crying aloud.

At last their mother breaks the spell. All right, that's enough. He doesn't deserve our tears. You want to sleep or shall we go for an ice cream? The mention of ice cream flicks a switch in the room, casting away the gloom and stillness. The children break from their embrace and spin on their heels and run for their coats and return in no time to face her. She tries to move fast to match them. She grabs her coat, her purse, and her keys and they leave the front room and step out into the March air. You must walk in pairs and hold hands and no running on the pavement and never cross the road without first stopping and looking and make sure you stick together. They nod and walk along with William and Tony holding her hands and Gavin and Neil in front, side by side but not touching. The two in front glance back at her. They forget how tired they are and breathe out hard, or *smoke*, as they call exhaling in the cold. At the small café they file into a corner booth. Their mother explains the menu and the waitress takes the orders for four ice creams and one tea. The boys gobble and lick their spoons.

Eat slowly, boys. It's not going to run away.

Their mother laughs and sips her sugared tea. Neil says, Uncle Iqbal seems nice. She says, Yes, he is a kind man. He likes children. They switch to talk about how the ice cream needs to be warm like the orange juice and that would crown the occasion. Neil thinks warm ice cream could make someone a lot of money but William wants to know how the ice cream would work in scoops if it were warm. It wouldn't be ice cream if you couldn't scoop it, he says. They shiver and smile and scoot closer together. Gavin tries to convert the cost of the cones into cents and the others marvel at the expense of the treat. Their mother says things are expensive and she has to be careful since money is scarce but England is a good place for education and opportunity. They nod. Tony says, Opportunity, as if the word means another flavor of ice cream. He falls asleep before he finishes his ice cream and his three brothers dip their spoons in his cup and clean it out. Their mother carries him. The others race back to the house not by running but with rapid, small steps, toe to heel, stopping at the curbside for their mother to catch up and cross the road with them. That night they sleep like logs and well into the next day. She rises early and spends the morning listening to her children snore. She hums a Bible tune and unpicks the stitching of clothes sewn the wrong way. She leaves them to go shopping for groceries and the boys get into a big pillow fight of all three younger brothers against the eldest. They are so noisy that the corduroy couple from upstairs and their daughter descend the stairs and knock on the door. The woman and the man offer broad smiles and speak together as though they had rehearsed. Boys, could you please be quieter? Please? Gavin apologizes on behalf of his brothers, who hide behind the sofa.

Sorry, Mr. and Mrs. Dunstan.

He smiles at Jennifer, who looks at her stern parents and decides it is best not to smile back. Their mother returns, hears from the couple upstairs, and reprimands her four boys. She singles out Gavin, gazing at him through narrow eyes. He straightens as if called to attention. She says that she expects better from a thirteen-year-old and the eldest at that.

This is how their mother sees things as the weeks unfold: hard days ahead, her unfaithful husband who abandons her and the children ends up losing the most by missing out on moments exactly like this one, life lived at close quarters in these two rooms crowded with her and her progeny. She would not change a thing. Her children rise and shine for her. And for her they pitch in with the unpicking of clothes sewn the wrong way, which she resews, this time the right way. Uncle Iqbal comes with more pieces of garments and leaves with finished dresses and jeans and jackets. He takes them to the zoo, for more ice cream, to Trafalgar Square and Piccadilly Circus for little tin trinkets of Big Ben and Buckingham Palace. One bright Saturday he buys each a shining bicycle, one without gears for Tony, one with three gears for William, one with five for Neil, and one with ten for Gavin.

The boys' mother asks, What do you say, children? They say, Thank you, in unison. And before she can ask, Thank you, who? they add, Thank you, Uncle Iqbal.

The two adults argue late at night in hushed tones on the pullout sofa bed.

Mavis, your boys need a father figure.

They can make do with me. I'm their mother.

Aren't I allowed to have an opinion?

Yes, but not so quick with the father stuff. They're not bad children. You talk as if they're delinquents or something.

I think they need a clear path and a firm hand in this lax country.

She fumes. He tries his magic touch and Urdu poetry delivered in whispers and saves the evening. Another time the same subject of her rowdy children arises and this time she does not shut him down. His inquiring tone matches the one used for his poetry delivery. She wants to hear more from him.

Boys need a firm hand.

What more should I do? I am alone.

You have me. We should be together in this. I think Islam can provide them with strong guidance and make them successful in this difficult country.

But I want them to be happy.

Islam fulfills the spirit and leads to great happiness.

She sees that the man cares and decides to give his system a try.

On another Saturday he asks the four boys if they know what a Muslim is and if they might like to see what Muslim children do with their Saturdays. They nod and he drives them to a house full of children sitting in rows chanting the Arabic alphabet and lines from the Quran. The eldest smiles at the chorus of unknown words and imagines a flock of geese lifting off the wrinkled face of a lake. They eat with the children, boys divided from girls, and enjoy the day so much that they come back for a month of Saturdays.

The day arrives when Uncle Iqbal discusses the need for a small medical procedure to be done to them to complete their embrace of Islam. Their mother nods and repeats the word for Tony, who cannot get past two syllables, *Cir-cum*. She says it slowly and a little too loud, *Cir-cum-cis-ion*. The three boys look alarmed, and Tony, seeing the look on their faces, drops his smile and adopts a frown. Gavin asks, Is there no other way? Iqbal says, It will be painless and over in a jiffy. Their mother repeats, Yes, over in a jiffy. The boys resign themselves to the idea of losing a small portion of their bodies for a huge helping of spiritual well-being.

Uncle Iqbal chauffeurs the four brothers in his Ford van to the brick house with a menorah in the front window. Be brave for Mummy. They nod. They cannot speak through teeth clenched. London frost forces them to rub elbows when all they want is breathing space once outside their rented rooms. Their breaths boil and dissolve in brittle air. Ice repairs the cracks in the pavement. How can sun ever come back here? They take turns peeing in a wallpapered cubicle in a back room. Each of them stands there for a while and stares down at himself, trying to imagine how he will look after the operation and seeing for the last time a configuration he must bid goodbye. Each one presses two fingers to his lips and touches the end of his penis but thinks better of saying anything.

Up until now, Saturday mornings meant they were in someone's front room learning the Quran and Arabic, and Saturday evenings were spent in bed listening for Uncle Iqbal's late-night visits with their mother. Clothing in piles of separate pieces that she sewed together for him for a price led to this. They find prayers bewildering: their plosives ricochet in their heads and settle like marbles rolled into the sockets of their eyes. They genuflect countless times in a corner of the living room that doubles as their mother's bedroom and sewing room, guided by a little compass that tells them where to face. They plant feet on a mat woven with the Kaaba in ruby and cobalt and cushiony on their foreheads. Moisture from their ablutions keeps the air cool behind their ears. After prayer, the outside seems washed too—all the roofs and all the trees and a buffing of the light.

They take turns lying on the improvised operating table, converted from a dining-room table with a plain white tablecloth thrown over it. Gavin goes first. He raises a smile from the rabbi when he asks him not to take away too much since he wants something significant to please the girls. His bravery evaporates and he gasps when he sees the rabbi hold up a long needle and flick the tube full of the local anesthetic. The whole operation pivots on one swipe of the rabbi's pristine scalpel. In the middle of hearing the call to prayer, of seeing crowds at Mecca circling the black stone, of conjuring the feel of the prayer mat on their foreheads and the smell of a front room of children reciting the Arabic alphabet, each feels a tug and a burn that radiates and grows in intensity.

Uncle Iqbal seems to hit every bump in the road on the drive home, although other drivers honk at him for taking his sweet time. The children are, after all, precious cargo. Their mother says over and over how proud she feels, and how brave they are, until Gavin asks her through gritted teeth to please shut up. The rest of the drive they listen to traffic and each other's groans. They walk to the house and their bunks with feet wide apart, on tiptoe, with a rock and roll from side to side, as if the rabbi added to their girth rather than subtracted from it.

Who will be the first to try and pee? Each holds out by avoiding fluids. Tony relents first. As he pees he screams so loud the others think he might burst a blood vessel in his temple and open his wound afresh.

The challenge for the rest of the boys turns out to be how to keep from screaming. Neil stuffs a sock in his mouth. But when he emerges from the loo his eyes show so much white the others worry that his eyes will pop from his head. William sucks in air fast and fills his chest to bursting as he pees a scalding rope of straw. Gavin sees himself as if he has burst into flames and the fire brigade's engine number one hose happens to be operated by him as well. All he has to do is turn it on himself.

Their mother feeds them whatever they ask for and she grants permission for them to stay up late and watch TV. From now on they cannot socialize with girls. And to Gavin, she says, Especially Jennifer from upstairs. The boys lie in bed, unable to sleep. They hear their mother and Uncle Iqbal crooning in the next room. The two giggle from time to time. Gavin thinks about Jennifer and how he might fraternize with her, as his mum puts it, without contaminating his pure mind and body. It will mean talking to her but facing the opposite direction, looking at her in his mind's eye and making shapes with his hands in the air as if the air took her shape, and that way there would be no contamination of sight and touch. When the two adults fall quiet the children listen harder, but all they hear is their blood tuned to the pain between their legs.

The children force themselves to lie awake until overcome by an imperceptible slip and slide from their aching bodies, first the youngest, Tony, and next, William and Neil, and last to hold out because the eldest must always be first or last in everything, Gavin. He whispers each of his brother's names and no one answers. From their slow and even breathing he guesses they must be asleep. He releases a little boat on a lake with Jennifer seated in it and waves at her as the boat drifts from him. He performs this goodbye task by looking askance at Jennifer, at the lake's reflection of the boat with her in it, and so no pollution of himself. He sees himself seated before a sewing machine and applies butterfly touches to the pedal with his foreskin under the needle as he labors to reattach himself to himself. He floats off, no boat nor water, just his body lowered into a dark that shuts down his conscious thoughts, replacing them with more rhapsodic alternatives.

Uncle Iqbal, how come a rabbi circumcises Muslims?

We are all cut from the same cloth, son. He and I are in the same clothing business, I trust him completely. And there's less of a drive. The imam lives all the way across town.

What did the rabbi do with our foreskins?

Buried them in his back garden before sunset.

Upon hearing Uncle Iqbal, the boys become pure muscle and weightless. They curve around the city on bicycles at the ten speeds of light. They pray so hard they make their foreheads darken with a spiritual bruise. They discuss Muslim names and try to come up with ones that sound close to their Christian names. Soon they stray toward the most famous name, Mohammed. They all want it. Their mother tells them, You can't all be Mohammed. Imagine if I'd named you all Tony, or Gavin, then what? It would have to be followed by a number, Neil offers. But their mother is firm. How about Shaheen? Too girly. Uncle Iqbal interrupts with a suggestion that the name might be best if it came from the imam, someone with the authority to confer a name for all time.

It does not matter that their mother breaks up with Uncle Iqbal six months later because he proposes to her that she become wife number two. What a cheek, she tells her confidant, Gavin. She lines up the boys and they shake hands with Iqbal, and together they thank him for everything, barely able to say the Uncle part that's synonymous with his name. She throws a sheet over the sewing machine and uses it as shelf space, its ornate metallurgy mothballed for a season of futures. They never see Uncle Iqbal again and never mention his name. Maybe one of them remembers the tune of the song he liked to hum in the van. If so, no one mentions it. But their mother remembers. Her memories made up of him touching her in the dark front room, breathing in deep to stop herself from making any sound that might wake her kids in the other half of the room, and his poems in Urdu, whispered in her ears and sometimes fragments of it translated.

On Saturday mornings the children switch from Quran class to watching *Looney Tunes*. Bowls of cereal, drowned in boiled milk, and hot orange juice, swell their bellies. Marmalade sandwiches for lunch and sometimes supper too. They sing in helium voices, resurrected as Hanna-Barbera animals, armed with boom, bam, and ka-pow, Acme bags full of tricks. No more left hand for toilet, right hand for eating. No more always lead with the right and let the devil take your left hand. Truth turns ambidextrous for the boys, and for Gavin it takes the form of Jennifer, in her yellow cotton print dress and brunette bangs. Her parents leave the house and she invites him up to a bedroom that she has all to herself.

Show me yours and I'll show you mine.

You go first.

No, after you.

Promise to show me yours if I show you mine first.

I promise.

Gavin's impatient to take his turn as Doctor. Jennifer gently touches Gavin with her index finger and asks him how he got his scar, and if it still hurts. No, he says. But too quickly. So he adds, Maybe. He yearns for her touch once more. She traces the scar with her middle and index fingers. His head falls back and he pulls in his stomach involuntarily. Not a needle's deep puncture, nor a scalpel parting skin, but the flock that rises from the Quran as its throat opens and the menorah's many-limbed flames, and his mother in the arms of her first lover, and only love, his father, with Iqbal's song on his lips, father, who wants nothing more from her than the four children she has given him: *Alif, baa, taa, tha.*

Nominated by Conjunctions

TOWARD A UNIFIED THEORY

by WAYNE MILLER

from AMERICAN POETRY REVIEW

THE CHILDREN
Condemned to live

inside the weather
of our moods

JOY
What are you doing?

Filling this bucket with water
and dumping it into the water

HISTORY
They can't excavate the amphitheater further

because it extends back
beneath the houses

DEATH
We close their eyes

not for them
but for us

POETRY
One mouth moving
another

ZOO
The plexiglass
separating us from the animals

brings them closer

FRIENDSHIP
In the instant we both blink
we're blind to each other

it doesn't matter

HISTORY
The man in the grocery store
wearing an ankle monitor—

tube sock pulled up over it

MYTH
Cyclops—
who must wander the earth

with an I in his head

MEMORY
His suffering inside that house

became
the house

PANDEMIC
My son's recurring dream:

sailing a balloon
over an endless ocean

MYTH
Whose?

THE FUTURE
Our dead are approaching—
how should we

prepare for their arrival?

POLITICS
When the plane is going down
all you can do

is hold on
to the thing that's falling

SPOLIA
Gravestones became the walls
of the city, then

the walls
of the houses

DEATH
As the pepper grows
so does the air inside it

ANATOMY LAB
It wasn't that she saw herself
in that grayed entanglement—

She saw no one

POETRY
What are you doing?

*Filling this bucket with water
and dumping it into the water*

JOY
All these marks in the grass
left by the carnival—

the weight of which
we never considered

not once

MEMORY
Whose?

CATARACT
Between the mind and the page—
the body

THE CHILDREN
For whom each *species* is a character

FAITH
After his daughter died

he came at last
to believe in God

so he had something permanent

against which
to direct his rage

LOVE
When I was four time zones away from you

I never reset my watch

REVOLUTION
And yet?

Stet.

CATARACT
The eye is still my eye

with a little corporate lens
gripped inside it

ROMANTICISM
O luna moth—
born without a mouth!

ELEGY
On her last visit to the mountains
her window
opened onto a stream—

so comforting, she said, to sleep

beside that forever
sound of leaving

EXILE
They built their houses
from the timbers of their ships

DOOR
Means a wall can be broken

and can heal

FIRE DIVER
It's not passing through the fire
you worry about

it's resurfacing

MORTALITY
In your Zoom window
the daylight was rapidly diminishing

Here it was noon

GHOSTS
Whose?

AUDIENCE
Your death became a kind
of microphone

HOPE
In the middle of the drought
the white noise machine

filled our room
with rain

MARRIAGE
And yet?

Stet.

POLITICS
It's good to say:
if the plane goes down

the pilots do too

LANGUAGE
In which death can be
possessed

HISTORY
Condemned to live
inside the weather

of our moods

LITERATURE
Below the flat surface
of the flood:

the city

HISTORY
What are you doing?

*Filling this bucket with water
and dumping it into the water*

Nominated by American Poetry Review, Kevin Prufer

BUTTERFLY

by PETER KESSLER

from CHICAGO QUARTERLY REVIEW

My father's boyfriend, at least for a time, was a short, muscular man with warmly vacant brown eyes and a thick Argentinean accent. His name was Carlos. His eyelashes stretched like awnings over his face, and when a coquettish mood took him, which was often, he would bat them at me with all the promise of a storefront opening for business. He was standing now on the stoop of my father's house in a wifebeater and boxers, grinning into the sun of a June morning, and I was loading the trunk of my father's coupe.

"I'll put your stuff in the car," I said to him, and I edged past him, brushing against his studied reverie, picking up a small mustard-colored satchel in the entryway, backing out again.

Sun-bathed and beautiful, he conferred on me a bounteous smile, his teeth little gleaming dominoes. Carlos was stronger than me, but the lifting, carrying, and stowing of things was not his custom. He smelled strongly of cinnamon-ginger cologne. "Yes, you are always so very kind to me," he said.

"My pleasure," I said.

"You must find your pleasures somewhere," he said dreamily.

Just then, my dad returned from his early morning jog. His legs were streaked with sweat, and a heavy deodorant rolled off his body. The jogging was part of his daily fitness regimen, which in different seasons also involved bicycling, swimming, and hundreds of pushups. In those years he did everything he could to remain fit. He ran vigorously to the car, and he took Carlos's satchel from my hands and began to calculate how best to position it. I mounted the steps again and grabbed Carlos's little suitcase from inside the foyer.

"My valise!" Carlos hissed. "Please kindly care for this luggage as you care for all my packages."

"I'll handle it," my father said, running up the steps and taking the suitcase from me, running down the steps, negotiating it into the trunk.

"Oh, stop with your insinuations!" said Carlos.

"I will not stop," my father said. "I will not!"

"Then you will ruin me forever."

"I will ruin you, all right," said my father.

"You have already ruined me for anythings," said Carlos.

He shivered as if stricken by a breeze.

My father was beside him now, the sweat shining in his grey sideburns. It was the 1990s, and my father was at last fully out of the closet. He compensated for the years of concealment with a deliberate exaggeration, a bravado that I had not seen in him throughout my boyhood. He put his arm around Carlos and squeezed, his face warm with a luxurious and childish joy, and he kissed Carlos on the ear.

"There is plenty more spoiling to come," my father said.

❖   ❖   ❖

I was home from my junior year of college, and it was early in the summer, and I was young enough to think nothing of a vacation with my father and his lover. My father and I were still at a stage where we were doing everything together. I was not quite a boy and not quite a man but was nevertheless tethered to him for allotted times, and during such times, I lived as best I could the life of a student, while my father openly and belatedly lived as best he could the life of a romantic.

My father drove the three of us out of Boston. Shortly after lunch we found ourselves on Cape Cod, where my father at great expense had rented two little shacks side by side overlooking the beach at Provincetown. Not far from the shacks was a festive bar with a faux thatch roof, and not far from the bar, facing the ocean, was a row of sun umbrellas.

We arrived at the beach as the sun passed its peak, and we planted ourselves in front of the umbrellas, strategically outside of their shade, my father and Carlos draped like drying laundry across a pair of wooden chaise lounges, sipping mai tais and wearing Speedos. I wore a clunky pair of swim trunks.

Carlos was tan, compact, glistening. He applied cocoa butter to his chest upon arriving at the beach, and he glittered like a totem.

"But what about your back?" my father said to him, holding up the bottle of tanning lotion.

"You can have my back," Carlos said, flipping over.

Again my father was invigorated. He stood above Carlos, squirting suntan lotion across his shoulders and down his spine, my father's arms jiggling while he rubbed the lotion in. My father faced me with his immense happiness, partly as a father to his son, but also partly as something less rigid—and I found myself slipping into a role that was foreign to me, for all that I was only twenty-one, rising up to the moment, stirring, until from within emerged the strength to wink a conspiratorial approval at my father.

When my father was done, I turned to Carlos, and in my most cordially accented Spanish declared: "Ahora podrías freír un huevo en tu piel." Now you could fry an egg on your skin!

Carlos faced me in his dewy way, swatted at me with an exaggerated reproach. "You are silly!" he said. "You are like your father. Both sillies."

"And you, my dear?" asked my father, hunching down beside him.

"As if you have to ask, silly!" said Carlos, now swatting my father.

My father collapsed into his seat, lightly winded, the salt breeze dragging furrows through his hair.

*　*　*

The beach was jammed with people that afternoon, a mixture of the young, the hip, and the gay, and while I was at least young, I nevertheless felt that my presence on the beach was more that of an ambassador than a citizen. I did not like this feeling and knew that this sense of remove was peculiar at my age. Yet my life was peculiar, and there wasn't an easy exit. I was only now getting to know my father as an adult with romantic aspirations, even as he himself was only now beginning a more explicit, more public journey of allowing others to know him, too. My main task, it sometimes seemed, was to be a spectator to his Dionysian adventure without having to dampen his enthusiasm by too strenuously declining to be a participant. I drank a single beer. The beer, combined with the sun, sank me deeper into the folds of the beach.

We all were quiet for a time. Then a young Latina in a yellow bikini passed by our chairs, bronzed and grinning in all directions, her bleached blond hair falling like corn silk about her shoulders.

"Look at that woman," said Carlos to me. "A hot mami."

She was pretty, I conceded—but I added she was not my type. I really doubted that we would have anything to say to each other. "I suppose," I said.

"But that woman will keep you awake all night," said Carlos. "And then it will not matter what you say."

"I suppose," I repeated faintly. She really was lovely, in the way that anyone young and happy is lovely—but I was seeking a peer, a spitfire, a fellow chess player, both a spider and a waif. I could not say if the woman in the yellow bikini was any of those, but I doubted the odds and expected that she was at once too little and too much. I scraped the sand off the bottom of my feet.

"Trust the boy to know his own tastes," my father said, sipping at his mai tai on the other side of Carlos.

"Tastes?" said Carlos. "You speak to me of taste? But who does not like filet mignon?" And then to me: "You are too shy. Life will pass you by while you just sit waiting, denying this strength that lies inside of you."

He always spoke in this odd way, and the oddness drew Spanishisms from me in return. "Just where," I asked, "is the strength in introducing a dog to a cat and asking them to become lovers?"

Carlos giggled and swatted me. "Sillies. You are not looking now. The outside is soft, but the inside, she is strong, like your father."

Of course that right there was the tip-off that Carlos did not know my father. It had developed that my father was drawn to younger men, and they to him, he acting as some type of surrogate father, and they acting in the manner of passive young sons. It was my father's posture to be mature and level—a posture that he struggled to maintain for the duration—but he lacked the cool reserve of someone who was in fact truly settled. He suffered in his core the same weaknesses and caprices as the men who turned to him, and when all the young men discovered my father's fragility, they were repulsed, and his affairs ended with a speedy leave-taking. It was ever the same.

The blond Latina in the yellow bikini wandered past again, carrying in her arms several drinks from the bar. "You go, mami," Carlos shouted to her. "You know you've got style!"

"Thank you, papi."

"Come sit with me and my boyfriends," shouted Carlos. My father, nursing his mai tai, shrank into the chaise lounge.

"You're too much, papi," she said, ambling on her way.

✳   ✳   ✳

377

That night we retired to our two bungalows not far from the beach, free-standing but separated by only ten feet of sand. They were rickety structures painted in light shades of blue, orange, and pink, with mosquito netting across the windows. Portions of the walls had been made of particleboard, and the floor was cold underfoot. We turned in early after drinking a few beers. I lay in bed reading War and Peace by a dim lamplight, gripping the book against my chest and straining my eyes while next door my father and his lover amused themselves. At first I could hear them talking and laughing, various noises through cracks in the ceiling. Later, they were quiet, though it was a deliberate sort of quiet, different from my father's snoring. I supposed that I should be happy for them, and happy for myself, reading as I was, and yet I missed my father, and when at last I folded the book onto the side table and turned out the light, it was with a heaviness that was hard to comprehend.

✻　✻　✻

At breakfast the next morning, my father looked delighted, though he had dark circles under his eyes and held his coffee close to his body, sipping it constantly and with eager need. "I like a lotta caffe latte!" he exclaimed brightly. "Lotta latte! Get it?"

"For me it is orange juice," said Carlos, evenly. There was nothing bad-humored about him, but he lacked my father's ebullience.

"I'll squeeze your juice!" my father said.

None of us even smiled, and thereafter we ate our breakfast mostly in silence, pushing eggs around a slurry of strained tomatoes.

The beach that morning was warmer than the day before, but I was in an impatient mood. It was in part because we would be driving home in the afternoon and in part because after only a few hours the novelty of the beach had worn off. In fact, I have never really been much for beaches. I was already tired of looking at grains of sand and the small, broken bleached-white shell two feet from my nose and the scrap of blackened seaweed crumpled like wires beside it. Things were more businesslike all around, and my father and Carlos talked about a man they both knew named Ricky and a relationship Ricky was having with a fellow named Bud, who had only just recently left his wife, his house, and his two kids in Wellesley to pursue a new life as a high-spirited bon vivant in a walk-up in Jamaica Plain. From the way my father and Carlos talked, it was clear that they, too, were passing the time, and that their interest in Ricky, Bud, and Bud's erstwhile family was recreational at best. Hearing about Bud, I considered my own mother, but then I began to feel bad and decided that it would be better to have a drink.

I announced that I was getting a beer. My father and Carlos asked for mai tais. I stood up and stumbled over a sharp-edged shell. I ordered at the bar, and then waited, rubbing my feet against the barstool to remove the sand.

A woman with bleached blond hair appeared beside me in a yellow bikini, her skin smelling heavily of boysenberry suntan lotion. At first I did not recognize her, but then I realized that it was the same woman in the yellow bikini from the day before. Her skin had grown darker in the last twenty-four hours, except for small rings around her arms where she'd worn bangles. She was prettier up close, though she was also older than I had thought—probably in her early thirties, a good decade my senior.

"So what's the deal with you, bebé?" she asked. "Are you having a good time?"

"That's my dad and his boyfriend," I said. "We're here for the weekend."

"You've got quite a family, bebé," she said.

"I do."

She smiled, a luxuriant flash of satin. "It's nice to be on vacation with your sugar daddy. You like girls?"

"I do."

"Really?" She crossed her arms under her breasts. The effect was to puff them up bigger. "It's okay, don't lie to me."

Something about her response offended me. It made her at once more attractive but also immediately repugnant, and I felt that I could no longer speak to her except with an air of cynicism. "Actually, I didn't before . . . but there's something special about you that changes my mind."

"You're funny," she said, uncrossing her arms. Her breasts shrank down again. "Okay, that's nice. So what are you ordering?"

"A beer and two mai tais?"

"I love mai tais," she said. "You know what's even better? A mango smasher."

The bartender put down my drinks. I paid for them and gathered them up.

"You sure you're not a chip off the old block?" she asked.

"I'll prove it to you," I said, though even as I said it, the words, the tone, were utterly wrong. *I'll prove it to you.* How many ships had been burnt, how many towers stormed, how many sieges laid and fields left burning? How many women left weeping, hearths dashed against the rocks over that paltry, boyish exigency?

"Ew," she said. "Look," she said. "I thought you were nice and all. But you're really not that nice and I'm not interested in your projects."

"Nice to meet you," I said, turning on my heel.

"You have a good day with your boyfriends now, okay?"

I didn't respond, though when I arrived back where my father lay, I discovered that I was shuddering.

I handed down the drinks.

"Thank you for the mai tai," my father said.

"Thank youuuuu!" sang out Carlos.

My back was turned to the beach, and I could feel the footsteps passing close behind me, see the bronzed form reflected in Carlos's sunglasses, smell the wave of boysenberry suntan lotion. Carlos was watching her, and in his sunglasses I noted a quick flicker of yellow, and he registered a mild surprise. The footsteps receded.

"Pup looks sad," said Carlos softly.

My father inspected me carefully. He almost spoke, but then hesitated, holding his mai tai against his belly.

"Pup should go swimming," said Carlos, jabbing his toe at my foot.

My father considered a bit longer, then blinked. "Another hour and we'll hit the road," he said.

"There is no need for the Mr. Big Grumpy," said Carlos to my dad. "There is always the sun, the sea, and the sand."

"Just the same," my father said, staring at the sand.

"Boo!" said Carlos. "Boooooo!"

* * *

It was a week later, perhaps a bit ahead of schedule, when Carlos left my dad. He did not announce it ahead of time. Instead, he told my father that he was going to meet a few friends to go shopping for blue jeans, and hours later my father realized that all of Carlos's clothing had disappeared. And then, of course, my father deduced that Carlos had disappeared, too.

My father took it like he'd taken the others. He spent the next several days wandering about the house in his underwear, the shades drawn, talking to himself and sighing. At night he slept fitfully, and in the morning he woke hollow eyed and dry in the mouth. Now and then he would wince as if at a blow. I made him dinners—always ribbon pasta with garlic and tomato sauce, and every few days a slab of steak from

380

the grill. He ate the food wolfishly, which underscored that he was forgetting to eat otherwise and that he did not comprehend the depths of his own hunger. Every supper, I put a tall glass of milk before him, and he drank that greedily, too.

"You didn't really know him well," I reminded him at one of these pasta dinners. "And you didn't have so much in common."

"Maybe that was what I liked about him," he said sullenly.

"Still, it couldn't have lasted."

He pursed his lips in bitterness. "I wish I could have been the one to conclude that first."

I would watch him chewing, his jaw slack and his eyes glassy, and feel as though I were witness to a protracted accident. The carnage happened so slowly, pimpled my father day upon day so minutely, that it seemed less a crack-up than the downward arc of a life. I resented him terribly for this behavior, and yet this very resentment induced in me a pervasive guilt. I was forever judging him, even as I hated that I was judging him. And then we would go jogging together into the clutter of Dorchester, past the bay where the men windsurfed in the early summer morning, and I would push myself to surpass him, and then push myself to keep up with him, marveling at his resilience, and when I broke and had to stop jogging, my lungs ragged and aflame, I would be grateful to find him stopping beside me, walking with me the mile it took to get back home, sometimes walking in silence and sometimes talking about the world, and I would repent of all my judgments.

And then I would reflect that there was a time it might have been different for him—that in my earlier years he might have broken entirely with me, and with his past, and moved to a place that better catered to his being. He might have moved to San Francisco and lived in a third-floor walk-up in the Castro, or moved to New York and lived in Chelsea, passing his late nights frequenting the leather bars, and there in his relative youth he might have acquired the discipline and savvy necessary to now, in his later years, with confidence lead younger men around on a leash. He might have done this. Many men do.

"Have I been all right for you?" he murmured to me some days later, over the course of another of those ersatz pasta dinners, as he began to pull himself back up. His eyes were blanched from a flare-up of his allergies, his nose runny, and he was wearing a Red Sox T-shirt and boxer shorts.

Is this ever a proper question? They give you shelter, and then you grow and give them shelter in turn, and who among us can step outside of that arrangement to deliver a proper accounting? "You're a wonderful father," I offered.

"What if that's not my question?" he asked.

I searched within myself and hit upon a vacancy. I shoved a meatball into a slurry of sauce, placed my fork upon my plate. I had to add something. "I just want you to be happy," I said.

His shoulders fell down about him. And then I regretted that I had named it, that I had placed upon him the weight of my own expectations, that I had betrayed a metric of my judgment. I was so very young, and it seemed so very important then—*happiness*—and it also seemed so attainable, and so much a matter of personal choice.

"I'm really trying," he said.

*   *   *

Two weeks later, the day that I was scheduled to depart on a long, solo cross-country drive, Carlos reappeared on my father's doorstep. I was in the other room gathering my last items when my father opened the door. By the time I came to investigate the silence, Carlos was already leaning into my father, his slight weight collapsing into my father's solidity. Carlos mewed over my father's shoulders, and my father hugged him close.

"I don't know what came over me," said Carlos.

"It's all right," my father whispered. "We do silly things."

"Yes, I am a sillies," Carlos said, his eyes shut tight.

My father smoothed his hair, the wispy fur of a colicky baby. Carlos was missing part of his front tooth. His clothes were a shambles, and he had lost whatever luggage he had taken with him. I already knew he was penniless.

Carlos broke from my father's shoulder and took himself upstairs. And then my father walked past me, gaze averted, avoiding comment. From upstairs, we heard the kick of the shower.

"I'll be heading out soon," I said.

"I know," my father said. He went to the hutch, brought down his case, and arranged his music upon the stand. After days of silence, he took out his violin.

I should note that even as a boy, my father was reportedly entranced by the violin. Whenever he received his allowance, he visited the record store to shop for recordings by any and all of the old masters, chief among them Jascha Heifetz. Years later, classical music remained his great passion. As it had been when he was a boy, he played his instrument most every day, and when he played, his nostrils flared bull-like from the labor of breathing, and his expression grew soulful, and when the music quickened, so too the blood rose to his face. When he played, he seemed more truly centered in himself than at any other time.

It was a curious feature, too, of his playing that he liked to stare at the listener full on. He was able to do this, I think, because his eyes were only half alighting on what they saw, and his gaze arose from a place of purity. I think he stared, too, because it was an opportunity to perform. So it was that while Carlos was rummaging through my father's closet upstairs for a suitable change of clothes, I sat on the sofa and watched my father attack Tchaikovsky, moving at a respectable clip through the first movement of his violin concerto, staring at me soulfully.

My father was still playing when Carlos came downstairs in an orange bathrobe, his hair kinky with moisture, his feet in puffy rabbit-fur house slippers.

"I had thought you would already be driving the wide yonder," Carlos whispered to me mirthfully.

"I'll be leaving in an hour," I said.

"That's a good trip," said Carlos, nodding. "Breaking away."

He ruffled his hair with a hand towel, and the bathrobe slipped away from his legs, exposing the soft interior. Carlos sat beside me on the sofa and began rubbing my father's slippers into the carpet.

"I'm glad you'll be gone," he added. "I mean, for you. To be away, it will be good for you."

I smiled at my father and nodded to the prodigal beside me. I wanted to tell my father that he should look to his lover, but my father looked to me instead, his eyes brown and full, the lashes lengthy like my own. His bow skittered across the strings.

"You and your pretty little music box," said Carlos to my father, staring up at the ceiling in a pantomime of dream. "He is so strong when he plays," Carlos said to me, adjusting himself on the sofa cushion. "Though he could be a little less rude."

"It's lovely, Dad," I added, and my father breathed in deeply, growing larger before my eyes, a whirling firecracker of horsehair, rosin, and sound—and then he exhaled and again shrank back into someone normal, or oddly small.

❀   ❀   ❀

I have now passed the age my father was then. In most respects, I am my father's son. For all my world-weariness, I am prone to bouts of emo-

383

tive fancy, just as my father was before me, and if I were not so firmly tethered to a family and a home, it would be a monumental struggle to keep from being blown utterly apart.

Carlos was a little leaf drifting atop the ocean. My father was the ancient rocky crag upon which Carlos had once again alighted, only to feel himself, within minutes of his arrival, coming dislodged again, tugged back toward the broad, dark, wind-crazed world. Carlos had no part of the adamantine pull between father and son, and he was dishonest in so many of the ways that mattered, yet unlike some of those who followed, Carlos had the grace, when at last a short time later he left for good, to take only what he had brought with him. In that regard, I see even more clearly now that the love affair between Carlos and my father, however short-lived, had been predicated on a feeling that was real. For this I offer Carlos my retrospective gratitude. Sometimes only after twenty years are gone do you realize that you were fairly dealt with.

Chanteuse of late summer, bringer of my father's joy!—you, too, must be in your fifties now. On whom did you permanently alight?

Nominated by Chicago Quarterly Review

DEAR DAMAGE

by ASHLEY MARIE FARMER

from DEAR DAMAGE, (Sarabande Books)

On January 19, 2014, my grandfather Bill walked into my grandmother Frances's hospital room with a loaded gun he'd purchased that morning. He set their Neptune Society cards side by side on a nearby table and kissed his sleeping wife of sixty-three years. Then he shot her once in the chest. He tried to shoot himself, too, but a spring popped from the pawn shop gun and the weapon broke apart in his hands. Correctional officers who were at the Carson City, Nevada, hospital that day arrested him. According to subsequent news stories, he wept as he was apprehended. "I failed in my mission," he said.

Sun dotted my Long Beach, California, apartment as my sister relayed this news over the phone. I'd been grading student essays on a weirdly warm winter morning, and now my brain flickered, and it felt like a hand had my throat. I interrupted her to tell my husband, Ryan, what happened—"My grandpa shot my grandma and now he's in jail and she might die"—and then shock propelled us: we slipped on our shoes and walked quick miles down Ocean Boulevard with the sea shimmering below us. I thought of the people in the hospital who heard the gunshot, how horrified and panicked they must've felt, and then the word *ruined* echoed in my brain, a powerful certainty that everything good about our close-knit family was finished. My grandmother shot, my grandfather in jail: these two people I love so much and know so well now shattering— and my mom, who lived with them both, left to pick up the pieces.

Ryan and I shared an American Spirit on a park bench—I wasn't even a smoker—and I took my shoes off and stood on the shore where the tide washed over my toes. The sand looked tiger-striped and glittered with flecks of mica, and I thought about how many times Frances, who was born and raised in Los Angeles, swam in this same ocean or, years later, depicted it in dramatic oil seascapes I've memorized. I figured I should be exactly there, feet freezing in the water, when someone inevitably delivered the news that she'd passed. But amid the flurry of phone calls from my siblings and mom who now drove to the hospital, news of Frances's death didn't arrive: doctors declared that she wouldn't survive her injury, but it could be hours before she left us, days.

When we returned from the beach, my students' essays on the American Dream sat where I'd left them, a collection of sunny, abstract relics from just a few hours ago, the era of before, not after. I couldn't focus enough to make sense of their words, and maybe words would never make sense again. *Gun?* I thought. *Shot?* I thought. *Ruined.* Surely this cataclysm must be a mistake and this nausea gripping me must belong to someone else.

I Googled *Carson City shooting*: news crews already filmed in front of the hospital crime scene tape—a violent tableau that somehow belonged to us. At a different link: footage of my siblings' backs as they rushed toward the entrance. Other news outlets reported from the jail where they now had my grandfather on suicide watch. In yet another piece I'd view hours later, a woman held a microphone outside my grandparents' home, the home that belongs to all of us, the site of Christmas dinners and sagebrush Easter egg hunts, the house my grandpa built by hand, the one we picked out moss-covered rocks for from the old mine. The house where you'll find us grandkids' names scratched into concrete beside our small handprints. Where my grandparents' initials are ringed with a heart in Frances's perfect script—an image the cameraman came close enough to film.

* * *

This isn't a story I often share. I've feared others' judgements, and I become flooded with the temptation to explain—we're not gun people and my grandparents are more than just grandparents and, and, and. . . . Plus, despite the public nature of this event and the fact that strangers have dissected it in their own articles and posts, I've wondered which parts are mine to tell. There's also this: the few times I've shared it— with a coworker, a stranger, an old friend over a beer at a writing conference—I've watched their faces tense, grimace, wince. Even if I offer a warning or soften it, a story like this can, for the briefest moment, drop an anvil on a listener. And I've decided in these past few years that if there's one thing I don't want to do, it's contribute more pain to the world.

Instead, I've made a quiet study of pain, the blinding, bewildering strain you don't see coming, the pain of reality biting the dust, of looking toward the horizon to see pain extending forever into the future, an unforgiving desert. Or maybe pain has made a study of me, taking up residence in my body, thrumming in my chest, skyrocketing my blood pressure to ER levels and throttling me from sleep at two a.m. until night eases and the sun slides up. Because there's grief, yes, but it's complicated, too: What do you do with pain caused by someone you love, for actions you don't agree with but, on some level, understand? For a gunshot—a gunshot in public, no less—in a time of mass shootings? For my suffering grandmother? For my weeping grandfather who tried, but failed, to leave us and was now condemned to live?

This disorienting grief proved to be a baptism of sorts: even though I've barely been to church, I found myself in the months afterward praying in LA freeway traffic on my way to teach, tossing up pleas of *no more tragedy* to clouds or smog as I sailed between adjunct gigs. And if begging couldn't change the circumstances, I figured I could at least find the sterling takeaway, a thesis statement with supporting evidence leading up to a tidy "In conclusion . . ." like I'd find in a student's semester-end reflection essay. I wanted to make sense of not only my grandfather's actions and the ramifications, but also of pain itself because pain, after all, was not only the result but also the cause.

See, two weeks before my grandfather bought the gun, my grandmother tripped as she walked across their living room. It was a swift accident on an ordinary day when she'd just shared a late lunch at Katie's Country Kitchen in Minden, Nevada, with my grandfather and my mother and stepfather, Cindy and Earnhardt. It's the kind of thing that could happen to any of us moving quickly across a room on a winter afternoon except, in Frances's case, her body crashed in the most devastating way possible: her chin hit the floor and her neck essentially broke. A freak thing, as they say.

"I'm paralyzed, aren't I?" she asked my mom after paramedics wheeled her down an ER hallway where they'd wait for hours, other emergencies whizzing past them.

"I hope not," my mom said. Then she leaned over her mother's chest and sobbed.

Doctors later compared the damage in my grandmother's neck to that of a victim of a motorcycle wreck. In the weeks that followed, her

387

condition didn't improve. She had, in fact, been especially unlucky: not only was she now quadriplegic—a life-altering condition that occurred in an instant—but she experienced a type of neuropathy that causes an unrelenting pain that the strongest drugs don't touch. Doctors weighed options. While they did, my mom tended to Frances by rubbing lavender lotion into her feet, by applying Frances's makeup the way she wore it, by dripping drops of Starbucks onto her tongue since Frances could no longer eat or drink. The family rallied, hovered. Frances slurred to me over the phone the lie that she was "getting better every day, in every way."

Finally, doctors convened to deliver the grimmest prognosis: there would be no surgery, no healing, no returning to her living room to pick up where the strange day of the accident left off. This would be her new life instead. But in a nursing home. In perpetuity.

"I want to die," Frances pleaded more than once. To my mother, with whom she shares a birthday, the two of them stitched together, best friends. To my grandfather, always her anchor. "I want to turn the corner," she pleaded.

And for those reasons, Bill, my quiet, Navy veteran grandpa who'd whistle as he made coffee before anyone else was awake each morning—the most practical, rational guy I've known—said a word to no one about his plan, ate a sit-down breakfast that Earnhardt had prepared, and left to purchase a gun. Then he drove to the hospital with the weapon while families hiked near Lake Tahoe, brunched at noisy casino buffets, prayed at church. A "mercy killing" the reports months later declared.

❖   ❖   ❖

What can I do with this narrative of suffering? It's less than straightforward, a kaleidoscope of surreal moments from a movie I don't recognize. It involves us viewing my grandfather's televised arraignment, him reading a novel under the jail psychiatrist's cautious eyes before being released on bail late one night. It involves me hugging him in the kitchen the morning after, then sitting in the porch sun together before he gifts me Frances's wedding ring, him remarking that my gray-and-black striped dress matches his mug shot attire. It involves my mom declining to speak with politicians and network news shows that call the landline in the wake of high-profile assisted suicide cases. It involves me writing a note in support of my grandfather to the public defender and being surprised to see my words later quoted in newspaper articles, discussed in opposing ways by people who either support or condemn my grandfather's actions.

Beyond the personal? I've had five years to consider that morning within a broader context: right-to-die laws, violence and privilege, the US healthcare system, the US gun system, the way we collectively view aging, the way we grapple with suffering, the way people engage in comment sections without knowing the nuances of a story or realizing that families might read every remark.

But my hands are empty: five years later, no sparkling realization, no rock-solid thesis. My grandparents are both gone now, and I'm not the person in that Long Beach living room anymore: the shock has long lifted and California is a speck behind me. Yet part of me still stands at the edge of the Pacific with my feet in the surf—still pauses on that tiger-striped beach knowing that, like the tide, more pain will eventually come. It's human and inevitable.

Knowing that simple truth has reshaped my DNA. At a moment when the facts of our world compel us to sharpen ourselves each morning, I'm simultaneously more aware of the softness of others, their sore spots and shadows, the stories they don't spill when we share an airplane row or elevator. I've paradoxically become less afraid of tragedy by knowing that there's nothing you can do to stop it from demolishing a January morning. And, as anyone who's been changed by grief can attest, clichés take on surprising truth: for me, it's that one about every person fighting a private battle. It's the kind of line I'd have spotted in a former student's essay, a sentence I'd have circled in green pen. "Cliché?" I might have scribbled, a question mark to temper the judgment. But here I am, writing it. Both easing up on others and loosening my grip.

In conclusion, I have no conclusion, except this: while I'm skeptical about mining beauty from pain (Frances certainly didn't find her pain beautiful) or landing on a diamond takeaway or even claiming good can come from it, I've learned that time-freezing anguish makes for micromoments of unexpected reverence. Even when grief scrambles the big picture and clarity remains decades—or maybe forever—out of reach, the particulars come into focus. Like my sister's voice that first day, her voice identical to mine, and the care in it as she relayed terrible news. My mother dripping coffee onto her own mother's tongue. How, in those first days when our family paced my grandparents' house, sick and sleepless and shocked to our marrow, strangers left meals wrapped in cellophane on that same front stoop next to my grandparents' initials. One time, a card and carnations. One time, a bottle of wine like a sacrament. Holy, these details, even to me, a heathen fumbling prayers on the 405.

The tide comes for each of us, the phone call we can't predict, the suffering that refuses comprehension, the moment we're waiting for without knowing it. But there's still sand beneath our feet. And those tiny, glimmering flecks, as unexpected as gold.

Nominated by Sarabande Books

THE REAL INDIA

fiction by A.J. BERMUDEZ

from VIRGINIA QUARTERLY REVIEW

The centerpiece of Lark's studio is the *Cunt Bodhisattva*, an eight-foot architectural marvel of sedimentary vermiculite clay, sustainably retrieved from someplace in South Africa, molded in the shape of a woman bent backward in an Ūrdhvadhanurāsana pose, feet planted, legs spread, and vagina on display, stomach arching toward buoyantly upside-down tits and a neutral, choiceless face, palms firm on the ground astride a thicket of load-bearing hair.

"What do you think?" Lark asks.

"I think it's a striking confluence of the obverse elements of female fetishization and empowerment."

"I want her to feel playful. Does she feel playful?"

"She does."

"Really?"

"Extremely playful."

"Mark hates it."

"Of course Mark hates it," I say. "Mark's the embodiment of the white-male heteronormative art complex." Lark nods. These are words she knows. "He lives in fear that the Paleolithic Venus sculptures he curates will come to life in the night and strike a pose like this one."

"She doesn't look frightening?"

"Frightening how?"

"Like is her pussy the right shape?"

I look, really look, at the docile squiggles of the labia, the pinch of the clitoral hood, and the pearl of clay beneath, the elegant, apologetic dot of the urethra, all probably carved by her assistant Andrew, who's here on a fragile O-1B visa, and say, "There is no right shape." Lark nods, pleased but not sold. "But yes, it's a beautiful pussy."

She smiles. "I think so too."

When she begins to understand something like this, something she's made, you can't help but believe that it's your doing. You've taught her the words for this, penned index cards thick with the micro-vocabularies of feminism and post-feminism and post-post-feminism. You've gently guided the pronunciation of *eurocentrism, hegemony, intersectional transmedia narrative.* You've tenderly explained why *transgender* is apropos and *tranny* is verboten; explained why *hermaphrodite* is fine for bivalve mollusks but not for humans who contemporarily identify as intersex.

"Why?" she's said. "Why though really?"

"Because a community decides what they want to be called."

She accepts this and will regurgitate it back to a curator sometime. You've prepped her for this, marked the signposts of Native to Indigenous to First Peoples, POC to BIPOC to People of the Global Majority. You've explained what each letter of LGBTQIA+ and QUILTBAG signifies. She's exhausted by the quantity but eager to learn, consults the cheat sheet you've made for her. You've walked around the studio, sidestepping the massive swaths of canvas drying on the floor, admiring whatever's been pinned to the wall as a kind of low-key test, and discussed her work in terms she'll adopt and re-present: the homages to Nan Goldin and Laura Mulvey, the dovetailings with Nam June Paik and Mika Rottenberg. The sentences, read and reread, have been meticulously memorized until someone else's words sound like they've lived in her mouth for years, soundbites that will make it seem like she's read the whole thing.

It occurs to me, often, that I'm a traitor to the authors of books she hasn't read, the artists who couldn't afford the buy-in, the other artists whose work has nothing to do with her work but whose catalogs are referenced in her list of influences; to women, to PhD candidates, to people whose last names end in *−ez*, like mine.

Nonetheless, I cash the checks, and this is the thing that Lark has always understood. To be paid for something is to consent to it. To endorse it, as it were.

One day, between the vat of drying resin and the overexposed photographs, Lark says: "Let's go to India."

On its surface, this exclamation has the pastiche of a whim, but if you listen closely, you can hear the machinations. The impulse is spontaneous in the way that midcentury housewives would sometimes, suddenly, fully out of the blue, swallow dishwashing liquid instead of rosé.

"I have the miles," she says. "Enough for two seats in first."

Already I can imagine the thrill and stress of it. Unfettered access to the finer things, with Lark watching every selection like she's keeping score. How chic you are, how worldly you are, how alcoholic you are. How many times you've done this before (if none, a rube; if several, then why are you working for her?). She enjoys introducing people to things, like how the vegan meal is unfailingly better than the chicken or steak option, even if you eat meat, because it's rarer and more intentionally prepared. But sometimes she grows weary of her calling as a missionary of prestige and simply gifts you a copy of the *Tiffany's Table Manners for Teenagers*, because, as we all know, you'll never be taken seriously if you hold your fork wrong.

She likes you to wear good clothes, but she likes to pick them. She brings you the latest issue of *Vogue*, asks you to circle what you're attracted to. You select safely. You are good at tests, but there's no timer set, no rubric. No rules. When she finally returns, she looks at your selections. After each, she nods or tilts her head. "No," she says, more jaded than critical, "not for your shape."

She listens raptly to your stories of travel, stories she's asked to hear, threshing them for points of interest, exotic kernels of potential that prove how interesting you are. Occasionally she lights up and ends stories for you with a single, often incorrect sentence like, "So you hopped the next flight and came home immediately," or, "But that's the brother you lost your virginity to."

She takes you to a cake restaurant, exactly what it sounds like, right after she's hired you, and buys you a slice of cake. Ten feet from your table, a baby shower is in the throes of learning how to make custom cakes from a comically good-looking instructor, all elbow-deep in nonpareils and piping paraphernalia and strips of festively tinted fondant. Lark, who's been laughing and waving her thin arms around and talking about the importance of eating cake, how you only live once, sets down her fork and takes your chin in her hand. "Oh," she says. You've also stopped eating cake, since your chin is no longer your own. "You know, you can get almost anything done in L.A.," she says. "Anything. Places are so good here. It's amazing." Then, because you might not have understood: "Laser hair removal treatment," she says.

You don't brief her on your awareness of the field, your extensive history of borderline-unaffordable Groupons or the realities of genetics extending through your maternal and grand-maternal lineage presumably back to the Iron Age, when this flaw must have indicated some now-defunct evolutionary advantage. You don't tell her you're doing your best, and you don't cry in the cake restaurant. "Thank you," you say.

Every time you're dressed wrong, for years, you blame the East Coast. "It's a different aesthetic," you say, as though you're still getting the hang of things here in cryptic L.A. As though you could afford the low-rung sample-sale shift dresses and harem pants, all size zero or zero-adjacent, one-size-fits-all, "all" being a subgroup to which you apparently don't belong.

She tells you, on one occasion, about her abortion, and all you can think is, *That's probably for the best.*

Lark is insistent on the real India, not the postcard India or the *Darjeeling Limited* India, the tourist India or Hilton India. She's been before, multiple times, years ago. She says her soul is there. She hopes to be buried there.

You know that you will never go to India without Lark. So you say yes.

The night before our departure, I stay up till sunrise, an attempt to acclimate myself to the new time zone—the exact opposite of Los Angeles—and to sleep through the flight. When I wake up in first class, Lark's fallen asleep beside me, and I take the opportunity to order a scotch. "Poison," she'd say, were she awake, although the first thing she'll do when we land is find and buy heroin. By the time she wakes up, I've had two glasses of scotch and swapped the glass out for a cup of tea. She immediately, briskly summons a flight attendant, as though she's been waiting all this time, and orders two flutes of champagne. "Live a little," she says, handing my mug of tea to the attendant with the lithe, performative grace of a fairy godmother.

When the champagne arrives, Lark studies it and then smirks, like she'll allow it. "Not real," she says. "What's that word?"

"Ersatz," I say.

"That's right. Ersatz champagne." It's clear now, with twelve collective ounces of brut or blanc de blancs or whatever is bubbling before us that Lark has set me up. That whatever she says next will have the de facto portent of a toast. "I've been thinking," she says, "about the real reason for India." She leans in, conspiratorially. "It's the *Cunt Bodhisattva.* Imagine her sixty feet tall, arched over the border between Jammu and Kashmir, half her body in one state and half in the other,

her belly button skyward right at the border. Body the same color as the sand."

I nod and, because I'm exhausted and secretly drunk and trapped on this airplane, I say, "Yes. Of course yes. You're a genius."

"You get it though, right?"

"Of course. It's the interstice of postcolonial conflict literally embodied by the intrinsically female dichotomy of religious idolatry: the contraposed irony of deification and objectification."

Lark smiles, lifts her glass. "Exactly."

Of course it's work. It was always going to be work.

Lark's hired a driver, and the moment we get in the car you can tell it's only a matter of time before she fucks this guy. He introduces himself as Sai, a name she leans forward and asks him to sound out twice, despite its being only one syllable. Sai gratifies her request, foreplay-slow, then smiles like the bushes are full of paparazzi. The way he smiles, the snug fit of his Henley, you can tell Sai understands how money works.

Lark settles into the seat beside me and says, "Remember what I said back in L.A.?"

I do. I remember everything, although I'm not sure to what she's referring.

"White linen," she says, and when she looks at you she closes her eyes, maybe imagining something else. Some other you. "You have white linen, right?"

"I do."

Lark leans back, briefly closing her eyes again, maybe this time in a small expression of gratitude to the universe, and says, "This is going to be an electric trip."

Her hand is still on my knee, nails polished with a color that is the exact same shade as her actual nails, and she's right, I guess, I am wearing black, all black, which is not what we've discussed, and although laboriously selected for chicness and comfort and some je ne sais quoi factor that's really just a guess, at best it is 100 percent the opposite of what we'd talked about, and in a way, she's extra right because I'm noticing it for the first time now too.

On the half-hour drive from the airport to Haveli Dharampura, Lark leans against the window, enraptured by some frequency I can't hear. In the tighter side streets—shortcuts, Sai avers with a wink—people turn and look through the untinted back windows of the car. Lark is making eye contact with as many people as she can. Her soul is here, so I guess she knows what she's doing. I feel a pang of the same schaden-freude I get sometimes in Venice, seeing the tourists lifting cameras on straps around their necks, dodging skateboards, huddling together over an iPhone to compare restaurant reviews, although now I'm the tourist and there's no joy, so it's really just schaden sans freude.

"What do you think?" says Lark. Her eyes are shining, and in this moment I wonder if I've just missed her all this time. If perhaps she was right all along, a savant for the things that are ugly and aren't, cor-rect and incorrect, repugnant and resplendent. Maybe I read too much. Maybe I don't read the right things. Maybe, in this place, in the unpre-dictably scrawled circle of her magic, I can contort and flourish into some other thing.

"I'm so happy I'm here," I say. And I am. "Thank you."

I squeeze her hand and she squeezes back. She smiles, and I feel my-self breathe into a part of my chest I haven't felt in weeks. I'm ex-hausted, dehydrated, and nauseous from the ride, but she—this—is how the sun is. When it shines, it shines hot.

Through the meticulously clean glass of the backseat windows, I try to see the world as Lark does. Low-slung blocks of concrete scroll past, ribboned with color and signage, carts and bikes, smoke and sound, and I wonder if these are, to her, the real India. The window is cold against my forehead, and my eyes keep slipping closed. Despite what looks like a melee of sensory detail, all I can smell is the pine of the air freshener, fake as grape candy, and the delicate bite of Sai's aftershave.

We're six minutes into the ride when Lark leans forward, touches Sai where his deltoid meets his biceps, and asks, in a way I recognize from the DeVotchKa concert in Las Vegas, the balcony of The Box in New York, the parking lot outside the Nordic pavilion at the Berlin Biennale, in a manner at once sexy and inarticulate, where she can score some black tar heroin.

The hotel is a masterpiece, blessed by UNESCO, and though it's been around for two centuries, Lark still looks over her shoulder as we as-cend the steps, immensely self-satisfied, as though she discovered it. "See?" she says. I nod, doing my best to look enchanted.

Behind us, illegally parked along the too-narrow street nearest the entrance, Sai unloads our luggage. As I turn he winks, and it's unclear whether this gesture represents a stray bit of buckshot from his tactical flirtation or a private, conspiratorial acknowledgment of our member-ship in the same servant class.

A concierge and team of receptionists, all clad in white linen with brightly colored nylon vests, are poised to greet us in the lobby. I wonder if the different vest colors denote different teams or roles, like in kickball or an Atwood novel. Lark places her palms together and lightly bows to everyone at once. I abstain, feeling in this gesture the same discomfort I've felt at the end of yoga classes in West Hollywood amid an ocean of balayage, all blond and blond-adjacent, pre- and post-blond, women netting six figures per annum from their first divorces and more recent real estate licensures, reverently whispering *namaste* to one another. This, I'm quite certain, is not the real India. In any case, we've arrived. As we receive our keys, Sai confers with a bellhop, ensuring that our luggage will arrive at the rooms before we do. Lark has been rattling off the names of local specialties, none of which I'll remember. "Let's have dinner on the roof," she's saying. "Seven or eight. Eight is better." I nod, with the tacit understanding that I'll hang back and make the reservation. "Don't sleep," she advises. "You'll want to." I nod at this too—she's not wrong, this is the core principle of outwitting jet lag—although the only thing I've been able to think of since the flight is a nap.

After making arrangements for dinner with the concierge, I head up to my room and lie down. The bed is a mint-green queen, nested beneath a scalloped interior archway, one among a sprawling conundrum of scalloped interior archways, facing a simple flatscreen TV. On the balcony, two small rattan chairs overlook a spacious multistory courtyard—the jewel of the hotel's internet presence—and flank a small outdoor table, exactly the right size for a pot of tea with two cups and saucers. The bathroom, which I've only visited to splash cold water on my face, is white faux marble with touches of brass, complimentary toiletries, and washcloths all the same shade of faded persimmon.

I lie on top of the duvet to avoid any imprints on my skin from the seams of the sheets, pull my hair upward from the nape of the neck to ward off the telltale flatness of the hair, indisputable evidence of napping. I close my eyes, but have set a timer for fifteen minutes. Lark used to model, ages ago, to what degree I'm unsure (there's been mention of a Pepsi ad), but to a sufficient extent that she knows, as surely as an MD with a stethoscope clocking a heartbeat, when anyone has taken a nap. "It's in the eyes," I've heard her say, "you can tell," although I myself cannot. I don't know if it's a puffiness akin to the aftereffects of drinking or a hot shower, if either of these would enhance or negate the appearance of a nap, so I do nothing. My top priority is to stay awake, against all odds, so that I can appear to be awake.

When the alarm goes off, I pull a set of white linen clothing—drawstring pants and a tunic top—from my suitcase, hang the ensemble on the rod of the shower, and turn on the water as hot as it will go to steam out the creases. This is among the few pieces of sartorial intelligence I've arrived at on my own, uninherited from Lark.

Hers is the room next to mine, and when there's a knock on her door I jolt. I relax upon hearing the door open, then the sound of chatter, Lark's laugh. In nondescript language sounds: an invitation. In nondescript language sounds: a polite decline. The door, again.

Dinnertime is the equivalent of dawn in Los Angeles. Lark arrives fifteen minutes past eight o'clock, relaxed and wise in a way that suggests she's smoked a half gram of heroin. Everywhere there are tiny scallops in the walls, each set with a tea light. Each glints off her eyes the way that fire licks and then swells against the window of a burning building.

"You were gone a long time," she says.

I've only been in my room, timing everything out, but "Yes," I say, "it's been a long time."

I order the things from the menu that I think I remember her saying, but nothing is right. She presses the plump exterior of every object that arrives, pale beige nail against pale beige skin against pale beige dough, with the pad of her index finger, testing each piece, then ripping a section of food from its body and setting it aside, like she's done it a favor. "You don't seem happy," she says. But I am happy. I'm plenty happy—not heroin happy, of course, but happy. "I'm just quiet," I say. "Happy quiet."

Lark nods, dissecting another roll with her fingers. "Tomorrow we'll find a musician," she says. "We should have done it already."

This impulse, something she apparently picked up on a previous excursion, is one I've been dreading. In the days leading up to the trip, she's often hailed the importance of hiring a driver, then a musician, as the only real way to travel through India. "Should we ask Sai if he knows someone?" I say.

Lark looks at me like I'm insane. "No," she says, "it's essential to get a vibe."

The sun has only just set, but the sky to the west has turned a violent orange, leaking upward toward a murky swath of Liatris blue, looking less like an actual sunset and more like a cocktail named after one. "I photographed the light here once," she says. "Before your time. Leica, obviously. I blew the image up to four thousand percent. Four thousand.

Huge." She bobs a dead bag of English breakfast tea in the silty, tepid water of her china cup. "Artists do that now—you saw that fucking shit at Barry-Platte last fall? I came up with that."

"I've seen the photographs. They're beautiful."

Lark's expression stiffens, like I'm not getting it. Like no one is. She suddenly looks extraordinarily tired, a bit confused, like a baby that's about to cry. "Nature belongs to all of us," she says, eyes glassily fixed on a sherbet-hued minaret. "People think nature belongs to no one, but that's not true. It belongs to all of us."

She sits back from the table. On her plate, the mauled corpse of a dosa, translucent and jettisoned like the skin of a snake, sits hollowly amid a bay of decorative cilantro.

"In the morning," she says, apropos of nothing, part promise, part threat.

She tosses her cloth napkin onto the plate and three servers appear as if by magic, clearing the table with the alacrity of mafia novitiates purging a crime scene.

In the morning, the sky has turned from bruise-black purple to a scabbed-over white-gray. Lark has a headache, so we meet on her balcony for breakfast, avoiding the clattering dishes and silverware of the restaurant. "So," she says, "what are we going to do about this statue?"

"Well, first thing is to find a fabricator."

Lark nods. She pensively rips apart a ball of idli, sets the pieces back down on her plate. "And we'll need a clay guy."

"Do you know anyone? Here?"

Lark smushes a wad of idli between her fingers, then brightens with what must be a wonderful idea. "Let's ask Sai!" she says. "I'll bet Sai knows someone."

"Okay," I say.

Sai, to my chagrin, does know someone. His "clay guy," one of many stars in the constellation of Sai's rolodex, will laugh, bewildered and overjoyed by the project—he, too, "would enjoy seeing a pussy of this magnitude"—before recommending that the body of the *Cunt Bodhi-sattva* be constructed in eight parts: two arms, two legs, the upper torso, the middle torso, the lower torso/nethers, and the head. He will painstakingly coat the conglomerations of metal and wire crafted by the fabricator, an underpaid sophomore at the Delhi School of Art, before loading and transporting all eight sections of the eponymous bodhisat-tva via convoy through the tortuous curves of Himachal Pradesh to the border of Kashmir and Jammu, some middle-of-nowhere set of coordinates I've been tasked with identifying through a combination of Google Maps searches and hearsay, where we are unlikely to be disturbed by armed guards (fingers crossed), before assembling, photographing, and generally reveling in the majesty of the statue and all it exemplifies before returning to our boutique hotel in Udhampur.

But first, before any of this, we must find a musician.

As we near Connaught Place, Lark lowers the backseat window of the car and props her elbows on the door. She leans out, eyes closed, and inhales deeply. Amid the cacophonies of the milieu—bicycles, carts, vendors, children—she perks up at some sound: an egregiously out-of-tune sitar, stabbing at a melody that sounds a bit like "Over the Rainbow."

She asks Sai to pull over and, sussing out the source of the music, approaches an older gentleman who has what she'll describe as a "kind face." From the car, I watch with Sai as Lark speaks to the man slowly and clearly, bent at the waist in the posture of a black-and-white film heroine, couture-clad on a visit to the orphanage, dripping with beatific elegance and the salvific promise of white picket fences, hydrangeas, suburban reincarnation. The man is dressed in white linen and loose sandals, a weathered sitar nested in his lap. He nods as Lark draws a map in the air with the full length of her arms, then smiles, creases bundling along his eyes and mouth. He does, indeed, have a kind face. At last, the man gets to his feet and follows Lark to the car.

As we pull onto Ghanta Ghar Road heading east, Lark turns backward in her seat and places a hand on the musician's knee. "Play something, Rishi," she says.

Rishi dutifully plays a warbling riff, the neck of the sitar bobbing toward the roof of the car. Lark seems rapturously oblivious to the sourness of the instrument's tuning. Or perhaps this is why she chose him. Perhaps this is the real India.

Sai and Lark are in their own world up front, the principal cast of a madcap road trip. Lark leans against the glass with her chin tilted at an attractive angle, a pose of extremis, lips ever-so-slightly parted. You can almost imagine the Pepsi dripping directly into her mouth. Sai glances in her direction from time to time, aware of the bait, taking the bait.

Lark and I went sailing once, with her then-husband and my then-girlfriend, and this is the face I remember, tilted expectantly toward the sun, Ferruzzi's *Madonnina* by way of gang-bang denouement, before she leaned over the helm to slap the side of the boat, a trick to at-

400

tract dolphins. I was beguiled, shocked when it worked. This is how I picture her at times, flanked by dolphins, white linen on white deck, cosmically at ease with her own fortune.

The "clay guy," whose name is Varesh but to whom Lark will continue to refer as the "clay guy," passes the test, predominantly by being nearly as charming as Sai. There is a great deal of forearm touching and laughter as they review various samples of clay. Lark believes herself to be an impeccable judge of character, and of clay. She has been ripped off numerous times.

They settle on a natural gray-gold variant, a terra-cotta hybrid, and the way the clay guy keeps referencing the spectacular beauty of the dunes of the Thar Desert, just west of majestic Rajasthan, without explicitly saying that this is where the clay has been sourced, you can tell he bought it online. Lark delicately trails her fingertips over the sample, testing the texture and color against the sun jutting through a slatted skylight. "It's perfect," she says.

On the drive back toward Haveli Dharampura, Sai takes a shortcut through a settlement comprised of scattered brick and concrete structures, splashes of paint on the walls and laundry strung above the road. He works the horn with staccato precision, jarring cyclists and pedestrians to one side of the road or the other, while Rishi obediently continues to play.

A handful of women look up from their work. Hauling, washing, selling, building, cooking, hustling. One has to imagine what one of these women would do had she been born into wealth. If someone had just handed her money. It isn't until Lark turns back to look at me that I realize I've said this aloud.

"Do it," Lark says, perfectly calm, her expression a dare. "Just hand her money."

I look out the window, and there are a lot of hers. "Who?"

"Does it matter?"

I understand that Lark's trying to make a point, but then, abruptly, there's a one-hundred-dollar bill in her hand, fished from the caviar-leather Chanel coin purse she uses when she wants to appear grounded.

"Go ahead," she says. "Pick someone."

I don't touch the bill. I smile, instead, like she's made a cunning joke. "The distribution of wealth is already a little too stochastic for my taste."

She slides the bill between my fingers. "Isn't it better for someone to have it? It'll mean more to her than to us."

Lark asks Sai to pull over the car. Outside the window, several people have stopped to look. Rishi continues to play, his sitar scaling an atonal crest and descending, oblivious. "I'd really rather not."

"Okay, we'll go back to the hotel. Everyone stays poor today."

"Wait."

I look out the window and try to choose someone. There's no telling who's better or worse off, who's the most virtuous, most generous, who has the most children, the best idea for a startup, the smallest living quarters, or most sinister disease. Who's having the worst day. Whose kid could write her own ticket if only the college application fees could be secured.

Before clutching and pressing the door handle, I try to do the thing Lark claims to do, getting a "sense for someone," scouring the features for lines that might mean benevolence or malice. I get out of the car and quietly move toward a woman in a blue sari, a skittish child curled against the slippery fabric at her thigh, and hand her the bill. I try to be subtle but am too obvious. There's no way not to be. The entire street has turned to watch. Everyone has seen.

It's clear now that I've coronated a target, if not of theft then of envy. The woman's face is only partly visible, but her eyes flicker with thrill and panic, a look not unlike game being hunted.

I get back in the car, where Rishi's sitar has picked up pace. "See?" says Lark. Outside the window, other women stare soberly, unchosen. I haven't just given a person one hundred dollars. I've given hundreds of people nothing.

Over the course of my tenure with Lark, I've often pretended to be her. Sometimes it's an art-world Cyrano de Bergerac stunt, a phone interview or email to a dealer, a rescue attempt from her signature vacillation between flirting and bullying. Other times it's to book tickets or lodge a complaint, to protect her from the anxiety of being on hold, of talking to people she can't see, or because I have all the numbers memorized and she doesn't.

That night, over Sazeracs in the hotel lounge, Lark announces a new interview. I wonder whether I've invited this, her tendency to ask me something after a drink, or if it's a maneuver that predates me. "It's a newish art magazine, London-based, super-chic aesthetics," she says.

"Alright," I say.

The interviewer (Ben) is young, self-possessed but with a tight, nervous laugh. You can hear him shuffling hardcopy notes over the speakerphone.

As Lark, the directives are to be breezy, cool, smart but not too academic. Witty but not corny. If you don't like a question, just say something else. You're an artist, after all.

The last time you did a phone interview on her behalf, she sat across the drafting desk and mouthed things, her lips wide with exaggerated shapes you couldn't possibly hope to interpret as words, let alone articulable suggestions, and when you hung up she yelled, "Why didn't you mention the post-Anthropocene!?" which seems to have been the one expression from that Donna Haraway article that stuck, and you said it was because it didn't pertain to the work at hand, and just when it seemed like she was about to flip the table with eight different cyan oil paints or fire you or pay someone to break your kneecaps in the night, the magazine wound up gravitating toward the wrong quotes after all, printed the wrong things anyway, and basically just supremely failed to understand her work in all its complexity and contemporary relevance, and this, at least, was not your fault.

This time, the questions are all softballs. "I saw something on your Instagram about a secret project in Jammu and Kashmir. Can you say anything about that?"

"I'll just say this"—Lark loves it when you say "I'll just say this"—"There's no way to create art that's situated in both nature and civilization without aggressively inviting the post-Anthropocene."

Three questions later, when Ben expresses his gratitude and clicks off, Lark is already handing you a glass of champagne. She gives you a theatrical kiss on the forehead, leaving an imprint you'll see later like a ghost in the mirror, a lanceolate of lipstick the exact same color as her natural lips. "Fuck Europe," she says. "Those fuckers'll love this."

After champagne, a miniature compact appears—vintage, Chinese cloisonné—with a wad of what looks like ossified gum inside. "Live a little," she says.

You will never try heroin outside of Lark. So you say yes.

The minute it hits your lungs, you get it. You're a fan. You understand perfectly why people do heroin. The world is fists unfurled, languid with welcome.

Lark is jaded, more experienced, lazy with bliss. "Do you remember that night at Basel, when we did molly?"

"After Versace."

"Yes! You remember."

"I remember, but I didn't do molly."

"Yes you did. We both did."

"I didn't. I drank the Blue Lagoon you ordered, because you don't believe in drinking blue, which I fully respect, and then we got to the airport right before our flight."

"But you did molly."

"No."

Lark smiles a vicious smile, looks at you like you're lying, like you're a prude, despite the fact that you've just smoked heroin in front of her. "Okay."

"I didn't."

"Okay."

Lark smokes again. You take the pipe and pretend, already lush with regret.

"We did good tonight," she says.

"Yes. Yes we did."

In the morning, sunlight lacquers the courtyard in a slick, soberly green-white sheen. Lark is already gone, presumably off haranguing the clay guy about the shape of the clitoris. I drag myself to the balcony, wishing for death. My hair smells like black tea and vinegar and, with a crest of nausea, I am decisively disenchanted with heroin.

Beyond the rollickingly hazy night of half sleep, dreams of granular gray-gold sand in my teeth and eyelids, the feeling of apathy but certainty that I've left the garage door open back home despite the fact that I don't have a garage, something else has gnawed me awake, something worse, something Ben said during the interview: "The border of Jammu and Kashmir and what?"

"And it's a surprise," I said, not understanding the question, spurred by Lark's guidance to create mystery when one is confused.

Now, down a rabbit hole of guessingly misspelled Google searches, I discover that I have a much, much bigger problem.

Jammu and Kashmir are not two places, as Lark believes, but one place. Worse, she believes these two separate places to be at war with one another. And worst of all, she thinks these two distinct, war-torn civilizations are in the middle of the desert, a desert intended to be a perfect visual match for the clay she's selected for the apotheotic, sixty-foot arc of the *Cunt Bodhisattva*.

All of this is my fault. I've been nodding so automatically, from the advent of Lark's vision to the momentum of its evolution, that I have accidentally nodded at sand, at wilderness, at scribbles on maps less cartographically sound than the New World as a volcanic swampland riddled with dragons. I've nodded us into a shared fiction, a nonexistent border in a nonexistent landscape, patrolled by nonexistent armed guards, lush with the mirage of artistic triumph. This nod, I realize now, is something I've picked up from Lark: the nod of attentive, partial understanding, of trust in one's own confidence above all, of willing one's own rightness into existence, of sorting it out later.

Historically, Lark has gone through assistants at a pace rivaling the wives of Chinggis Khan. I've lasted the longest. This is evidence of strength, I've always thought, although plastic outlives oak. Fake things always last the longest.

I'll be fired. Sued, maybe. She's done it before. I'll be ousted from the industry in L.A., a cautionary tale about giving your assistant every advantage, flying her to India even, only to be so cruelly and incompetently betrayed.

As I squelch back my gag reflex and study the map for any hope of a tenable lie, a figure appears on the adjacent balcony, outside Lark's suite. It's Sai, wearing only a towel and a watch. He smiles, surprised but unashamed. "Good morning."

"Morning."

Sai has brought a small tin with him onto the balcony. He cracks it open, retrieves a thin sheaf of rolling papers and a wad of tobacco. As he prepares to roll a cigarette, he appraises me with genuine sympathy.

"Heroin?"

"Yeah. Heroin."

Sai sprinkles a bit of tobacco and weed into the sharp crease of a rolling paper. He licks and presses it into a cylinder, then offers it to me, leaning over the cusp of the balcony. "It'll help with the hangover."

"Is that true?"

Sai shrugs. I lean out over the gap between the balconies, meeting him halfway, so he can light the cigarette.

"Something else, yeah? Worse than heroin?"

I have no reason to trust Sai. He is a half-stranger in a persimmon-colored towel on my employer's balcony. Nonetheless:

"I've made a massive mistake, Sai."

I tell Sai everything. He nods with the quiet, seasoned calm of a detective who's just learned the truth, neither predicted nor farfetched.

He lights a cigarette for himself, and when his phone rings, he answers it with one hand, smoking with the other. The conversation, in crisp Hindi, is liltingly familiar, curt.

"More H?" I ask when he hangs up.

He sets the phone on the small table beside his cigarette kit. "Don't call it 'H.' Makes you sound like a tourist."

"Lark calls it 'H.'"

Sai waves his cigarette in a gesture that says, well there you have it. "And no. That was my boyfriend."

"Oh." There's no graceful way to convey my curiosity or delight, or there is and I'm too hungover to achieve it, so I say, "I didn't know you were bi. Or pan or—whatever; I didn't know you had a boyfriend." It's the overloud tone of perplexed support I remember from my own youth, from parishioners who thought themselves hip, and I wince.

"I'm gay." Sai grins and smokes, pumping the cigarette between his lips as though he's fellating it, and also so that I can see the face of his new watch: a Chanel J12 with a quilted blue band.

"So Lark . . . ?"

Sai shrugs. "Which part of you is sacred?"

We smoke in silence, watching as shadows move through doorways across the courtyard. I feel a surge of envy at Sai's ease. "Still. Don't get too excited."

"About what?"

"About that watch. Her Chanel gifts are never real."

Sai rolls another pair of cigarettes, then tucks them both between his lips and lights them at once. He hands one across the rift between the balconies.

"I'll help you," he says. "We can drive out to Hikkim, through the Spiti Valley. There's a route where the signs are all in Devanagari. She won't know the difference."

I nearly ask him why he's helping, but he seems to sense this already. "People like you and me," he says, "we have to stick together. For as long as it takes."

"How long is that?"

Sai thumbs the ridges of the watch band. "Until we're them."

The following days are a slur of color and sound: the gumdrop-stained glass of Alsisar Mahal, the sunken gray riverbanks of the Yamuna River, swollen with hyacinth. Beneath everything, the tremulous lilt of Rishi's sitar.

It's difficult, in these days, to say what is and is not the real India. The raucous commerce of the Mochpura Bazar is the real India. The post-colonial wainscoting of the Surajgarh Fort is not the real India. Camels are the real India. Camel jerky sold at the entrance of the Mochpura Bazar is not the real India.

At nights, Sai and I drink ourselves into a state of ego, guessing (always underguessing) how often the bartender (who looks nothing like Dev Patel) will be likened to Dev Patel by a revolving contingent of white female tourists.

As the connective tissue of the operation, Sai has arranged with Varesh to transport the statue to the coordinates we've selected near Hikkim. Varesh, who's grown weary of Lark's impatient, overenunciated demand for the shape of the knees to "create more feeling," is more than on board. None of the eight drivers care, and all are loyal to Varesh.

We, meanwhile, are wending our way along a slightly more tortuous route to the west, a careful itinerary with the semblance of spontaneity—ancient temples and markets, pit stops for chai—half-built from Lark's memories, honed by Yelp reviews. The route is partly intended to disorient Lark, but Sai is right: between the sex and inscrutable signage, Lark has no idea where we are. By the time we arrive at what she believes to be the border between Jammu and Kashmir, the hired crew will have already unloaded the interlocking parts of the *Cunt Bodhisattva* and pieced them together in the spectacular sixty-foot arch she envisioned. Photos will be snapped, a short video will be made, and Lark, clad in the white mousseline linen Fendi dress she's brought specifically for the occasion, will bow in the sand and worship the idol of her own creation.

This, of course, is not exactly how it goes.

North of Kaza, in the skittish, half-quiet hours before sunrise, we barrel west along the jagged lightning bolt of an unnamed road. Even predawn, the air simmers with the threat of what will be an abnormally hot day. Sai drives with both hands on the wheel, more focused than I've ever seen him. Lark bounces in the passenger seat, a vintage Leica slung around her neck, raring to capitalize on the magic hour. Rishi, who has tried to make conversation once or twice over the past week, has apparently accepted that this is not the role in which Lark has cast him, and now plays a persistent, hypnotic melody that quavers grimly each time we hit a dip in the road. I sit beside him in the back, dodging the neck of the sitar, watching each crest and hairpin turn the way one might wait for a tornado to finally touch ground. My only job on this leg of the journey is to distract Lark with conversation as we near the Dhar Lung Wooh Statue Point, the one landmark she might try to Google when this is all over.

At last, the ruddy slopes on either side of the road give way to an expanse of desert, freckled with grass, gapingly empty beneath the sky. Threads of pink have just begun to claw up from the horizon like blood in a pool, casting a reddish glow against a massive, sinewy form towering six stories high: the *Cunt Bodhisattva* in all her glory.

Lark leaps from the car, giddy with her own magnificence. She runs toward the statue, beckoning me to record her running toward the statue.

Through the lens of the small camera we've brought, she looks like a ghost, her dress and skin both nearly translucent. She races beneath the arched back of the statue, then mimics its pose like a tourist.

Sai gets out of the car and stretches, flashing a thumbs-up toward Lark. He checks the face of his knockoff Chanel watch, then angles it in my direction: 5:18.

He winks. We've done it.

Rishi hangs back, plucks a few final notes, then stops. The valley is silent.

"Where are the guards?" Lark calls.

"Further east!" I shout back. "This section of the border is clear."

Lark nods. She looks around like someone who has loudly declared for months that she doesn't want a surprise party, who is now disappointed that there isn't one.

When she jogs back toward the car, I realize for the first time that she's barefoot. There's a pair of sandals in the go kit, but she refuses. They won't look right in the photos. In ten minutes, her feet will be bleeding all over the place, but that's fine. It'll become part of the art, somehow.

As the sun rises, each detail of the statue emerges with the drama of a freshly discovered ruin. The crew Lark hired finished their work during the night, just a few hours ago, but it looks as though it's been here for eons. The nth wonder of the world.

Sai pops the trunk and extracts four flutes and a bottle of '02 Pérignon. I once made the error of not properly observing some guerrilla exhibit—a wheatpasting fiasco in Portland—and have always budgeted for this moment since. The cork is popped. The glasses are poured. Lark untangles the strap of the Leica from her hair and snaps photos from every angle: the perfect curvature of the bodhisattva's toes, the soft gaze of her barely open eyes. The meticulous rift of the ass and the v-like crease of the thighs like a strap on either side. The subtly sculpted rings of the throat.

Lark stares down the neck of the viewfinder, then smiles. She makes her way back to the car, where she leads us all—even Rishi—in a sloppily joyful, sleep-deprived toast.

As the sun continues to rise, tipping now from the magic hour to something less magical, a new revelation unfolds:

The enigmatically sourced clay, which in this light has the look of gold covered in dust, has begun to crack. Varesh has coated it in a "cured artisanal epoxy" of some kind, and when the sun hits it, the sheen of plasticky gloss begins to melt, slurring over the details of the statue. The cuticles of the toes dissolve, flattening the bodhisattva's feet into what look like beveled fins. The same phenomenon takes her fingers, above which the beaded rings of carved jewelry have begun to drip down the vertical spires of her wrists and forearms. It's impossible to see from this angle, but I imagine the fragile comma of her belly button caving in a widening, hollowing swell, like a meteor impact in slow motion. The curve of her upper lip (closer to the earth, on account of her backward bend), painstakingly etched by some anonymous art student to convey a Mona Lisa smirk by way of Ishtar, dips and leaks toward the nostrils of her aquiline nose, which itself has drawn a seam between the molten divots of her eyes. Her tits by now are nebulous slumps, shifting the way patches of lava might, though not at the same rate, the perk of one nipple treading water while the other vanishes toward a dislocated clavicle. At the same latitude but the opposite side of the statue, the clitoris—lest we forget, the size of a basketball—has slipped from beneath its protective hood toward the underwhelming dip of the anus. Each labium has merged with the other labia; the majora/minora hierarchy has been fully dissolved. The focal cunt, of eponymic primacy, has slid into a glut of malformed clay and grainy silicon.

Lark's gaze, white-hot with adrenaline, already pulses with what will be a spectacular lawsuit, despite the fact that, as far as she knows, we're committing an act of vandalism on contested land. "It's the wrong clay," she says simply, each syllable a bullet of self-righteousness.

"It's the clay you chose," I say, and the minute it's out of my mouth, I know I'll be fired. Worse than fired, I'll fall within the concentric cancer of whatever legal action she devises. I'll be one of those trees that rips at the root before the local news has even announced a storm warning. When the first of the legs snaps, the other pieces crumple in surprising sequence, half cracked, half resilient, tethered together with the inelegance of yolky meringue. Here and there the epoxy clings to a tendril of wire, like a sack of skin in which all the bones have been broken. Someone, somewhere along the way, fucked up, and this error became the foundation for another error, then another and another.

In the end, there will be only the wires: stalwart and mortified as the masonry left after a nuclear test. A suggestion of something else: a city built for the purpose of being destroyed. Lark won't have to fire you; you'll agree on it together. You'll call the airline, one last time before she changes the numbers, to move up your flight.

You'll meet other Larks. There will be Sylvie, then Ava J, then Branwen. Each will take something from you and leave something else in its place. With each apple will come a bit more knowledge of your nakedness, a bit more comfort with leaving the garden. You'll start to meet her everywhere, but mostly she'll live in the voice you hear come out of your mouth sometimes, when you're tired and a server leaves your water glass empty, or when a valet doesn't reset your seats to their original position. You'll be free, but there will always be a shred of you in the timbre of tight skin and good cars, the tone of voice that sounds like money. You'll be alright, better than alright. But it'll be like a virus, treated but not gone. When Sai's car is stopped at a checkpoint—Lark's not a monster; he's driving you all back to Delhi, underscored by Rishi's increasingly reluctant score—a guard asks your purpose for visiting India.

"Just to see it," I say.

The guard sweeps both arms outward, boredly grandiose, as if to say: Here it is.

It's only land, as it's always been. Ambivalent dirt, rocks that have no idea where they are. Lark is exhausted by the checkpoint but pleased by the advent of Wi-Fi, scouring apps, scouting the next big thing. Because I'm free and sad and unmoored and have always wondered and the stakes are low, I ask, "Is this the real India?"

From the front seat, although it will certainly cost him dearly, Sai laughs, then the guard laughs, and although Rishi doesn't laugh, he stops playing, and together they cannot stop laughing.

Nominated by Virginia Quarterly Review, Jayne Anne Phillips

TARRY

by G.C. WALDREP

from PLOUGHSHARES

Big Spring, Arrow Rock, Mo.

The body records its absences. Water, you take water
into it—as presence, as absence, deep into the archive
of water you throw your mask. Also, your other mask.
We, being matter, are negotiated. I had not thought
to be angry, as such. But rage flexes its majestic undoing,
its sustaining negation. The reparations the body seeks
rest in time. Perhaps they *are* time. I am not insensible
to the sounds water makes flowing. Or not flowing.
Tune thy instrument, o Captor. This is the present.
I decline in it like a verb from some unknown tongue.
I knelt at the octagonal well-cap—no. Nothing
like that, not here. In this place of coming & becoming.
What did the life say to the light, runs a joke.
My blood, also running, as if in jest. I admired it
at the blurred edges. I am not unhappy, or not rigorously
so. I retain my privacies. The trees here, strange to me,
extruded. A man measures himself against such divers
entities. It is early (for me). Low musky trill of some
fledged form. As if ancient, as if an intelligence placed
its thumb just there, in morning mist. I, too, am broken
into majesties: rage; blood; lead. Cold-flow
of the soundscape around me, what chain have I forged,
this terrible vagrancy. I score it for judgment,

among the arteries my mouth has known. A new breeze
dries the sweat against my cheek, I lift my hand to it
(breeze; sweat; cheek) as if casting myself in some play.
I swing back the great bronze gate. *Tarry*, what is it,
what can it be *made* of. For surely it is constructed,
like a house, amidst this oxygen. We can step
inside & out again, tourists. Or, we can dwell. That verb,
to dwell—it hangs from the line, it flaps in the breeze,
it is not a cage because look, the cage is right here.
You may view it through polarized glass. You
may touch it (if you believe in the grammar of matter).
Make the scar tremble, yes, that's it. A small seed blows
or falls into the crook of the book, armored. Some feasts
are very small, we walk right past them, as if the moon
weren't real in daytime. It is real. In the day.
There, behind where the cage last stood, & rising.
Waters respond to it, we know this. I have been deceived
but not by matter, never. Not by the hands of princesses
or kings. I washed myself & laced myself into
a thought, a stance. Betook myself to an ancient place.
Refused memory, aside from language (itself a trace).
And now the miniature appeals, each from its petitioner.
It is too early for wonder but not too early for prayer.
—There. As cage this prayer. Touch it or else don't,
the day says, avid & prinked. There's no new distance
here. I rub my thought against it, as against the cries
from the forest which is, I am told, new in the scheme
of all things, that is, of men. A locust leaf lodges
in my beard. I was much smaller than this, I suspect,
when I had cancer, when I gnawed the red latch.
White white white of the non-sky with a moon
superimposed. These waters, unlocking for it. Both
those in my body & those at my side, those that still
bear within them the hair & spoor of the strangers' dogs,
splashing freely in the moment just before my arrival.

Nominated by Ploughshares, Bruce Beasley

412

READING CELAN IN DEARBORN MICHIGAN

by HAJJAR BABAN

from PARENTHESES JOURNAL

I had no one to choose and lived within the rocks.

My mother called herself an orphan after
her father had no longer, in their home, appeared. Though literally
   through war,
the same story seems to fill in me. The language I didn't learn
because of what my father's father made, caused disappearance,
because there's a clock that for us no one wants
to move. That for us, created
the word *sparse*

Nominated by Parenthesis Journal

WHERE I AM WHITE

by ANDY CHEN

from PLOUGHSHARES

in that realm, a man of straw
can pass for a man, sleep him
in the woods on a horse's skull—skull
so he dreams of echoes, horse so his heart
learns to gallop. unlearn him the language
of his starving mother, pull his shoulders back.
and he'll swagger, he'll see a blooming meadow and think,
build. he'll put scythe to stalk. touch him. marry him. happily
ever after him—and now the story begins
unraveling. wasn't the logic bound to fail
somewhere? and wasn't it always going
to be here? leave him in a field
to protect what grows. shift him nightly
so the starlings believe. don't pity
what's only straw.

Nominated by Ploughshares

FOUR MORE STORIES

fiction by PETER ORNER

from CONJUNCTIONS

Years later they met on the threshold of a motel room door. He'd driven through the night and still arrived too late. Henry died while he was still in Ohio on the interstate. He'd just passed the pocked lights of the derelict oil refineries of Sandusky when Claudia texted. He kept driving because what choice did he have? He couldn't just turn around now that his momentum was carrying him forward not just to Henry but to Claudia, and when he arrived, after four in the morning, at the motel across the road from the VA, he let her know his room number. At nine thirty she knocked and he, having not slept, not that he remembered anyway, leaped up but when his hand was on the knob he hesitated to turn it and open the door because of how he'd look to her—not just the two-day drive and his dishevelment but the years, how they'd piled up in his face like layers of permanent grime but what choice here too, just as he'd kept driving he opened the motel room door out of pure inertia. All he had left. Henry passed, she'd texted. He'd pulled over in the breakdown lane and tried to weep. Henry passed. Henry is past. Now, he opened the door and they looked at each other. She'd dyed her hair red. Before, it had been red but not this red. She was the same and not the same. But it wasn't her hair, it was her eyes, as always, eyes he'd never stopped seeing and here they were, all the visions merging with her actual breathing presence. Claudia stood there, the light behind her, the white-gray light. It was early November. Even back then they'd never had much to say to each other. What they wanted of each other was always lodged in their eyes. Words useless. Why say them at all? They both loved Henry. They loved each other. That was the way it was, the way it stayed. He'd arranged a transfer and left town because it was the only way to live without her and that was twenty-two years ago and he'd married, divorced, remarried, and still, look at her, standing in the morning doorway, the light behind her.

You made it.

Not quite.

I told him you were coming. He smiled. He did. He thought of you and he smiled.

They crumple into each other. If someone passing by on the two-lane between the motel and the VA happened to glance their way it might have looked like a woman fainted into some old man's arms. But really it's his knees that just buckled.

WEST LAFAYETTE

They'd lost a child. He fell out a third-story window. The screen gave way. I never got the full story. But I thought I could see the moment on their faces. A little more than arm's length will always be too far. By the time I met them they'd had a second child, a daughter. I wondered if it made any difference. If caring for the new baby lessened the visions. When the second kid was about ten months old they split up. This was in West Lafayette in the early 2000s. He was a writer, and she, if I remember, was finishing a master's in public health. This happened. I've become less and less interested in invention. Don't we have enough sorrow already? Why concoct more? But facts don't make any of this the truth. What did I know about them? Two people I was acquainted with for a couple of years? We were part of the same group of friends, mostly grad students and adjuncts at Purdue. All of us passing through West Lafayette on our way somewhere we were all convinced would be better, a lot better. Anybody could see that they loved that second child more than life itself. I wonder if this is what drove them apart. Because they also loved their first child, in death, with what I imagined was a kind of static love, crushing, motionless love. Imagine the pressure not to remember. After they split up both began to see other people within a couple of months. Of course, we talked about them. (Was there envy in our talk? Yes. They were the center of so much attention, those two. Tragedy had made them celebrities.) She was pretty and vivacious, short hair, big glasses that magnified her light gray eyes, eyes that were always coated with what I perceived to be a film of tears. She laughed a lot, sudden outbursts of goofy, barky laughter. Then, just as abruptly, she'd stop. In that pause of silence, somebody would change the subject, whatever it had been. Strange, as much as I still see her, it's him I think about now. I have no memory of his face. It must have been an unremarkable, unmemorable face. He was taciturn. An old-timey word, but that's what he was. He'd stare at you with his mouth closed. Those few words he did say seemed measured out in tablespoons. He was unpublished. He'd been working on a novel for years. The talk in our circle was that he was genius, biding his time before the world would know he existed. I don't think any of us ever read a word he wrote. This didn't make him any less threatening. He once loaned me a book. I'd said something about memory, some throwaway, a line about the past being more intense than what was in front of me. He said that reminds me of something. He went upstairs to his office in a closet and brought down the book. I still have it. I never finished it. A brief novel by Claude Simon called *The Trolley*. Every time I notice it on the shelf, I think of the couple in West Lafayette. Eventually, we did scatter. Our programs ended, our contracts expired. I'm holding it right now. *The Trolley* is a thin blue paperback, 107 pages. Now I remember. There's something off about this little book that has nothing to do with the story. A printing error caused the text to bleed all the way to the edges of every page leaving no margins at all. The small pages are too crowded with words. Once, before they broke up, the group of us met to hang out on a patch of grass down by the Wabash River. The rains had turned everything so green. The baby was crawling around and everybody was cooing over her. We were sitting on the grass watching the muddy river flow by. I watched their faces for signs of doom. She was laughing about something in her barky way and he too was laughing with his mouth closed. What made us all so sure we'd find a place better than this?

HER BROTHER

She'd show me pictures of him as a kid, how beautiful he was, how smart, how funny. She'd talk about how she was the first to notice, years before anybody else in the family, so that when he started crashing cars and having to be restrained by cops from beating up their father, she wasn't as shocked as everybody else, not that she'd known what it would come to, only that it would come to something. When I asked how she'd known she said she couldn't say exactly, just that it was something she'd seen in his eyes, how he'd be saying something, something totally normal but at the same time, with his eyes, he'd be pleading with her. Pleading what? That's the thing, she said, I don't think he knew exactly. Only that something was pulling him away. Something he sensed before he even started to change.

When he was doing all right he lived in a group home in Ames. He could hold down jobs, usually as a clerk. Once, for six months, he worked for a construction company. He'd always been strong and good with his hands. When the meds were the wrong combination or he stopped taking them altogether he'd either be silent or he'd go into rages and they'd have to get another court order to place him on a hold in the locked wing of the university hospital. After sixty or ninety days, they'd release him and he'd sleep in his old bed at home. Or sometimes at a friend's house. He always had two or three friends who'd take him in for a few days. Other times who knew where he went.

Mostly I remember him as gentle, with a hangdog but still handsome face, and there were always flashes of what she called his old wit, his old flair. Like he was some retired entertainer. As a kid she said he never stopped joking, never stopped moving, and when he walked he often danced. I'd see it too in his eyes, when he seemed to suddenly think of something clever to say. They'd open wider, not without a struggle, as if fighting against the droop. Sometimes he'd manage to get it out, to say whatever he thought of to say. Other times he couldn't and his eyes would cave in again.

CAROLINE

The son called the department and asked that somebody check on her. He might have driven the two and a half hours or so up from Connecticut and checked himself since he must have known what they'd find. But why expend yourself when all you have to do is pick up the phone? I happened to be driving by when I saw Simon outside the house looking up at the second-floor windows. There was nothing to see. Something about the way Simon was standing made me think he'd been out there a while. I threw the truck into reverse and pulled in behind Simon's car. Not a car; all the cops now drive SUVs. I joined him outside the door.

"You're not in uniform."

"Dispatch called me at home. Figured I'd come myself."

"How long you been out here?"

"Fifteen minutes."

"Locked?"

He looked at me. He didn't shrug but that's what his eyes did. Locked or unlocked, it didn't matter. I tried the door. Locked.

"Well?" he said.

"Well, what?" I said.

"Are you going to help me jimmy the door?"

I went back to my truck and brought back an ax.

"When was the last time you spoke to her?" Simon asked.

"Seventeen years ago."

"I believe it."

And it's true. In a small town it's easy to stop speaking to someone you see every day. You get out of the habit and it's easier to keep not talking than it is to begin again. Simon took the ax and wedged it in the crack in the door. A couple of tugs and the cheap lock gave way. Sounded like a tooth being extracted. I won't describe what we found. The smell alone. Simon called the coroner's office and we waited in the driveway. Years ago, we'd had something. It wasn't a secret. Word got around. We broke it off. Both of us married. We had some afternoons, not many, but enough to make me think, even now, of her each and every time I drive by her place to and from work. When Jimmy passed I went to the service and stood in the back, but I didn't offer any condolence. Now I wish I had. If only to touch her again. For years, she was town clerk. After she retired she volunteered part-time at the library. I stopped going to the library, at least on days I knew she'd be there. Caroline. She was funny. I remember once she said, So this is an assignation. A what? I said. An illicit love meeting. The thing with an assignation is that it needs to have a date and time. If it's spontaneous, it's not an assignation. And so we had our assignations. Dates and times. I remember she'd make me laugh and then put her hand over my mouth, I laugh loud, though there was never anybody who could possibly hear us. Short afternoons. Before we both had to get back to work. Extended lunch hours. We never ate. Caroline on a sunny afternoon, the shades up, squinting as she stretched out on the couch. She said she didn't want to sully her and Jimmy's bed. Also, she didn't want to have to remake it. I said, Do you think I give a damn where? Our silence, all that accumulated silence, there wasn't hostility in it. We got used to it, passing each other at Donahue's market without a word, just the weight of what we might have said. Maybe we both thought, even after years, that it was just a pause. That at some point we'd—Because we were stupid. Everybody's stupid. I stood there in the driveway with Simon waiting on the coroner. Simon said that I was going to have to sign a form now that I was a witness. We pushed the gravel around with our feet.

Nominated by Conjunctions

A PLACE I DIDN'T TRY TO DIE IN LOS ANGELES

by JENNY CATLIN

from THE GETTYSBURG REVIEW

The motel is permanently closed now. When I type "Nutel motel Los Angeles" into my laptop's keyboard, Google feeds me newspaper clippings and one-star Yelp reviews, along with a few photos of the sign, large and red and of another era, "iconic," according to the captions. A page deep into Google Images, I find a missing-person flyer with a grainy image of a shitty butterfly tattoo on pale skin. The picture of the shitty butterfly tattoo is also a picture of the thigh of a woman found rotting between mattresses in the motel thirty-three years ago. I say "rotting," but I guess that's an assumption. Above the picture of the shitty tattoo is a computer-generated image of the woman, of what she might have looked like: short hair, badly drawn-on eyebrows, crooked lips. There is no grainy picture of Jane Doe's face to match the tattoo, only this crooked-lipped rendering, and so I suspect she was either beaten beyond recognition or pretty decayed by the time she was found—that she was rotten or had rotten things done to her.

The motel had a string of names over the years, but while I was there, it was the Nutel. I still don't know the proper pronunciation, whether it was NEW-tell or NUT-tell. I just called it the Nut. The Nut was a squat, L-shaped building near the intersection of Third Avenue and Alvarado Street in Los Angeles, catty-corner from MacArthur Park. Although the motel was flanked on either side by lavanderias, my room never smelled like a home on a Sunday, never like detergent or oily sheets of fabric softener. Instead, the halls were saturated in the heavy stench of piss and Top Ramen. Rooms rented by the hour, night, week, or month.

In 2010, $695 would buy you a room for a month. I don't know how much it cost for the week, night, or hour.

Jane Doe's missing-person flyer says she was maybe white, maybe Hispanic, maybe fifteen, maybe twenty-three. It says her corpse wore a blue-and-white necklace, that a pair of earrings were found near her body. I wonder if she took the earrings off herself. If they were important to her. If she laid them carefully on the chipped brown nightstand with the wobbly leg and made sure they didn't fall.

✳   ✳   ✳

Somewhere there is a photo of me that was taken at the Nut by a friend of a friend of a friend from Denver, who was swinging through LA to buy a stolen identity. I'm sitting cross-legged on a sateen mauve bedspread that would have looked puke-ish even in the '90s. In the picture, I'm wearing a gray dress with a scoop neck. My tits look great—young and round. I'm thin. My Dollar Tree red lips are wrapped around the black barrel of his Glock 19 9mm. Though we were just drunk and fucking around, I liked the feel of that gun in my hand, cold and heavy. I liked the taste of it between my teeth, so much like the copper pennies I used to suck on as a kid.

I wasn't planning to die in that moment, that gun in my mouth, but I wasn't actively trying not to die either. The distinction is narrow, but for a person like me, it's a good idea to have an active plan not to die. It doesn't always come naturally.

In my head, I named the Nut's manager Not Carol because she reminded me of a woman back home who had cared for me in my twenties, a former bar boss with bottle-red hair and more patience for me than I ever earned. Not Carol and Carol probably didn't have much in common, except the long, skinny cigarettes that dangled perennially from both of their age-spotted hands. Maybe they also shared the same kind of hard lives that led to managing cheap motels and dive bars well into their sixties, so I morphed the Nut's manager, who had chrome hair, into a recognizable ally for no other reason than to build shelter in that wilderness. Back then, I spent a lot of time alone in the wild, looking for lodging.

It wasn't the streets themselves I felt lost in. Rough neighborhoods and anonymous places had always been my home. By the time I decided to move to LA, I felt like I had a corporeal relationship with every sidewalk crack and alley in Denver. I had worked in dive bars and low-end strip clubs all over the city. Like the place lazily named My Bar, far east on Colfax, where we fried our one menu item, french fries, in a vat of filthy oil behind the graffiti-covered bar. Or the Paper Tiger, with her crudely painted sign advertising Steak Specials, where the dancers changed cocaine-covered singles for quarters to slip into the jukebox at the start of their sets. I was on a first name basis with pimps, sex workers with heartbreaking back stories, people with a past, and those without one. Even Denver's roughest blocks felt, if not homey, at least familiar. Los Angeles didn't seem to work in blocks at all—it felt impossibly large and flat, like a place where I could live forever and never recognize a single face, never even make eye contact.

* * *

There were places I tried to die in Los Angeles: the Santa Monica Pier, drunk before dawn; the metro platform at Universal City Station; a studio apartment off Wilshire Boulevard, where in the evenings sweet, mournful cello music wafted through the open windows. But I didn't try to die at the Nut, not on purpose.

I spent most of the four weeks I lived in that motel room just hoping for the hours to pass, waiting for an unnamable something. I'd hum old LA punk songs, the Germs and Circle Jerks a bridge between me and the alien landscape of the city. I had a book of large-print crossword puzzles. When I finished the last puzzle of the book, I erased my answers and started over again.

The long, rectangular window of my room at the Nut overlooked the roof of the motel's garage. Razor wire circled the roof, but the wire had been clipped in spots, and motel guests could get up on the roof from the outside stairs. Hidden in my room from the goldenrod sun of the Los Angeles evening, I'd stare through the grimy window, which opened just a sliver, a thin line of rusted screen. Besides the roof, I could see a bit of the tienda where I bought tall boys and an obstructed square of shuffling shadow in the alley between those two buildings.

On Saturday mornings when the Alvarado Street Market was in full swing, when the steep sidewalks spilled bodies onto the blocked-off street and the brassy, accordion-rich polka of the mariachi danced the zapateado over the neighborhood, the thin rectangle of my window would rattle in its aluminum frame. Those sweaty Saturdays, the sweet corn smell of a hundred abuelas' tamales mingled with knock-off perfume and saturated the whole neighborhood. It smelled like a home I hadn't been invited to.

Sometimes a few people would gather on the Nut's garage rooftop, and I'd press my face against the strip of screen, trying to absorb the intoxicating singsong of laughter, the sickly sweet stench of blueberry blunt wraps.

One perfect pink dusk, a man punched a woman so hard blood erupted from her face like a geyser. I'd seen fights, of course, brutal and life-ruining ones even, but this was cinematic in its gore. I'd never seen blood act like that.

I didn't think there was much to be done. I'm not prone to calling the police, and even if I were, the Nut wasn't the kind of place I'd call them from. Instead, I just averted my eyes and noted how glad I was not to be that woman. I noted, too, that I didn't want to die there, in that room or inside that razor wire halo.

* * *

Every year, the Los Angeles County coroner's office pours the bony cremains of around fifteen hundred unclaimed bodies into mass graves in the LA and Boyle Heights cemeteries. At first, that number seems vast and distant. But if I had died at the Nut, I know no one would have looked for me at the morgue, and so that number begins to sound small. I knew then I had a body that someone might've stuffed between mattresses in a shitty motel, a body that when found would've maybe been photographed for a photocopied flyer and forgotten. So to me, fifteen hundred bodies sounds just like my body, like a custom-tailored black zippered bag.

Some hot November afternoon, I had to inch my way past two EMTs having an animated argument about the Laker's defensive game in the second-floor hallway. I stood in front of the door to my room, room 285, and watched them, young and vibrantly alive, gesturing over the corpse of some poor dead fuck laid out on a gurney between them.

I wished that I could reach between the bickering EMTs in their starchy blue uniforms, wished I could unzip the cheap black plastic and slip my hand inside, rest it on the swell of belly that used to be living flesh. I wished that I could lean down to those unhearing ears and whisper, "Good-bye and good luck, neighbor. Maybe the next trails will be happier ones."

What I'd left in Denver, in part, was a man with an infectious laugh, a dog with ears so large they dragged on the ground, and an apartment with a soft bed and clean sheets. I'd left a job with tips that paid my bills and a collection of people I ate big bowls of pho with on Wednesday mornings.

I'd wanted to marry the man with the infectious laugh, had hatched a plan with him, drunk at some off-the-strip Vegas bar. He was a person who made sure I got home safely.

My life in Denver had made me mostly happy, and that man had too, but I'd hidden monsters under that soft bed with clean sheets. Monsters that snatched at my wrists and ankles during dark and lonely 4:00 a.m.s. At the time, I think I thought I could outrun them. So they were also part of what I thought I'd left in Denver, those spindly fingered things.

In LA, my thoughts were loud, ugly creatures. When the Nut's "Color TV!" claim turned out to be false, I wondered about the cost of a little satellite dish every time I saw one poking out of the building's adobe facade. I thought that TV could be a companion or at the very least drown out my thoughts. I was hungry for distraction; I was hungry in general. But I was broke. I spent five dollars at the Jon's across the street from the Nut on two loaves of gummy, expired white bread, a bottle of store-brand yellow mustard, and a large pack of American cheese slices. Hoping that I was living a sad, drunk girl's version of the Hanukkah story, I convinced myself that these supplies would stretch past their possibilities. With fifteen slices per loaf, thirty slices in all, I allotted myself a single slice of bread with a slice of cheese and a little stripe of mustard every day. In the morning, as I peeled the cellophane wrapper from the neon orange cheese, my hands would shake in expectation. In addition to piss and Top Ramen and, on Saturdays, tamales and cheap perfume, my room reeked of cheap yellow mustard. But I was eating, trying not to starve to death.

Like Jane Doe with her shitty butterfly, if I died in that baby-shit brown room, during that hot November—five foot two, 145 pounds, almost surely white, almost surely not Hispanic, long past fifteen, past twenty-three—there wouldn't have been anyone to identify my body. Alive, my phone never rang. I'd already worn through the kindness and concern of everyone I had once known. People didn't look for me; no one would have even known I was missing. I'd wanted to get off the radar, and I'd gotten my wish.

If I had drunk myself into a slow slide—first unconsciousness, then coma and death—I wonder how decomposed I would have been before someone found me. I wonder which stages of death my poor unwanted corpse would have already passed through. Eventually, someone would have come banging on the door to room 285, looking for rent money. Someone would have noticed the smell.

I imagined yielding to death like that back then, slipping into the warm arms of booze, letting it hold me. But I didn't actually try to surrender. Not then, not at that time. Back then I was still fighting. Nevertheless, I wonder if there would have been a flyer, like Jane Doe's. One that said I wore a necklace engraved with the words "I don't exist when you don't see me."

Room 285 was on the west end of the second floor, and leaving the motel was a challenge no matter which of the three exits I chose. I didn't have much to do, was accountable to no one, responsible for nothing. It was easy to group my meager tasks together, leaving and retuning no more than once a day, but every time I opened my door to the dank hallway, my palms would sweat. I'd grind my teeth. I'd cross my arms tight across my chest, hoping to protect myself from the entire, terrifying outside world with its horns and sirens and loud arguments, and before I faced that world, I had to get out of the building.

There were internal and external sets of stairs and an old cargo elevator. All three exited onto the busy, busted sidewalks of Third Avenue, and all three scared me. The outside stairwell was at the opposite end of the hallway from my room, beyond a heavy steel door with a long defunct exit sign dangling from its own electronic intestines. On the small landing outside, I could climb through a cut in the razor wire to the parking garage's roof or take a short flight of concrete stairs to the street below.

A small alcove to the side of the landing was home to a woman named Star who mumbled ceaselessly into a bundle of blankets she cradled like a newborn. The first time I saw her, I thought it might be one. I don't know how I learned her name. Most likely, I was drunk and social on some brave daytime outing and asked. Maybe it was uttered in the halls by strangers. Star was a large woman. She seemed immovable, always draped in heavy layers of fabric. When I would start down the stairs, their edges lined with rusting metal, she'd block them with that large body of hers and jab her meaty palm toward me, opening and closing it in a pantomime of "gimmie." She wanted what the Stars of the world always seem to want: money, booze, a cigarette. Once, I handed her a half slice of my chewy, expired white bread, and she flipped her palm, dumping my offering on the concrete. She kept her big body blocking the exit and her chubby hand working until I fished a Bronco 100 out of my bag.

I wanted the same things the Stars of the world did, and I counted the hours between carefully rationed cigarettes and sips from the plastic pints of Popov vodka I kept in my purse. I didn't have much to share; cigarettes and booze were my most valuable possessions. Star was harmless, I suspect. Most of the residents and guests probably ignored her, but I was an easy mark. Anytime I saw that meaty palm, I relented a small something.

I'd flirted with homelessness throughout my teens and twenties. In Denver, I'd slept in a late-model Honda parked on side streets and in poorly lit parking lots. I'd learned to be crafty about meals, gathering day-old pastries from coffee shops and waiting until organic grocers threw out boxes of produce too ugly for the wealthy. I never went hungry, and I knew how to wash my hair and body in a rotating series of public restrooms without arousing suspicion from snooping clerks, knew which gas stations had the best smelling soap, the kind most like real shampoo. I knew that if I drove out past Tower Road, near the airport, I would find a 24-hour truck stop managed by a woman with a crimson bindi and bracelets that made music when she used the barcode scanner. Her showers were sparkling, and the long-haul truck drivers kept to their own stalls. In Denver, I'd known those things, so I never really felt lonely, and though I might have been without a house, I never felt without a home.

In LA, I was desperate to hold onto anything. When I needed to leave my room, I had to balance that desperation with my abject fear of the inside stairwell. It was usually vacant, but I had to hold my breath to screw up the courage to make the turn, mid second-floor hallway, into the echoey, enclosed, heavily tagged corridor. On my first day at the Nut, as I was bringing my things to my room (a single cast-iron pan and a few shiny black Hefty bags of clothes and books), I'd been cornered on the landing by a group of lanky men with faded deep-blue face tattoos. I was day-drunk and shaky on my feet in that strange, gleaming city. I would guess those men assumed a woman drunk and alone in the stairwell of the Nut motel, fists full of sagging Hefty bags, wasn't going to make trouble. If they'd been guessing that, they were right.

Those young men didn't physically hurt me, didn't do much of anything, really, except breathe heavy cognac and Swisher Sweets too close to my clamped-closed mouth. One guy cupped my chin in his long, thin fingers and brushed his chapped lips against my neck while the others made a show of pawing at my crotch and sticking their rough hands down the back of my jeans, moaning dramatically as they grabbed handfuls of my ass, fumbling and gesturing like schoolboys, which, in an alternative universe, they might well have been.

I stared at the tags on that concrete landing and kept my mouth shut, didn't move a muscle, didn't make a sound. I could see the ribbed-rubber handle of a 9mm pressing against a white T-shirt. I was afraid but unhurt. I suppose fear was probably the whole point.

For the rest of my time there, if I took the inside stairs, I scurried up and down them like a shifty packrat, clutching my bag to my chest, holding my breath. There was that old cargo elevator as well, its urine stench even stronger than the hallway's, but I had a pretty good idea of how long it would take to get help if I got trapped in there with another group of lanky guys who stashed handguns in their waistbands. I didn't know how long I could hold my breath, how long I could clench my jaw and stay silent. I never took that elevator. Not once.

There is a kind of alone that only exists in cities as large as Los Angeles. To be alone among four million people is staggering. That dumbfounding loneliness is at the center of all my memories of the Nut, and I was physically alone most of the time too. I went to the tienda alone for my tall boys of Bud Light; I was alone when I pulled the scratchy mauve bedspread over my head while someone with a booming voice pounded on my door demanding Julio. I remember washing my socks in the mildewed bathroom sink and hanging them over the shower rod to dry, alone; counting change for cheapo cigarettes, alone. Scouring want ads for any job that might have me, alone; making all those single-slice sandwiches, alone. It's true I was all alone during these tasks, but I had checked into the Nut with a boy named Cameron.

It's hard to remember what I thought at that time, what I hoped for or expected leaving Denver with Cameron. I was drinking hard and so sad. I think I thought I could drown all those hurts: memories of my face pressed into car upholstery while old men grunted behind me; memories of crawling through damp alleys close to home but too fucked up to get there; memories of all the broken bones and scabby knees and the trail of wreckage I always left in my wake. Maybe I thought I could bury shame with distance, thought that shoveling miles on top of my regrets would somehow absolve me.

Cameron was nearly ten years my junior and was being eaten alive by his own grief. He was leaving Denver to check into an exclusive rehab nestled in the Malibu hills. I tagged along, though I don't remember making plans to, don't even recall if he ever really invited me.

428

I was so provincial, when he'd first said "Malibu," I had confused it with Maui and thought we were going to Hawaii, not considering that Hawaii wasn't drivable. It must have looked like I left the man I'd once wanted to marry for Cameron, left the dog with the droopy ears and the friends I shared pho with on Wednesdays for just some guy. And maybe there was a bit of truth to that, but I think it was more about the leaving, period. That's how it seems now, anyway.

If someone asked me how it all happened, "I don't know" would be the only honest answer. I was in love and in Denver and then I wasn't.

Denver was the only place I had ever felt at home, and my exit was like an amputation—swift but brutal. I still feel the phantom pains of that home I don't live in, still feel the raw nerves of leaving. To me, though, rehab was the golden ticket, and Cameron had one. I'd been some shade of addicted since I was a child, cycling through drugs until I landed on and committed to drinking. I'd watched TV shows where people went to fancy rehabs and did yoga and got therapy and got sober, and I thought that's what I could do. I thought some formula could make me a person with a second chance, thought rehab could be some kind of answer, was sure that getting sober would solve everything.

But I wasn't going to rehab. I guess I didn't think much about not having my own golden ticket, didn't think about how I couldn't really cash in on his. I didn't know anyone in Los Angeles and had only the Deep Rock bottle full of quarters I'd taken from my Denver apartment to live on. I didn't even realize that I wasn't sure which freeway to take into Los Angeles until I was sitting in a different cheap motel room outside Barstow with a map splayed on the bed.

The day Cameron and I checked into the Nut, after hauling our meager belongings into the room, I told Cameron about the lanky boys in the stairwell, about their searching hands. He'd been watching a *Simpsons* DVD on the clunky laptop I had brought with me, which would end up tossed and broken in a drunken fight hours later.

I told him, and he said, "What the fuck do you want me to do?" And I said, "Nothing." I said, "I was just warning you that they had guns," which wasn't entirely true, that I was warning him. I don't know what the fuck I would have wanted him to do about it, but I wanted something, even if it was just sympathy. I shut the particleboard bathroom door and sobbed over the rust-stained sink, a halo of cigarette stains yellowing the rim. I thought about the 1,017 miles of bridges I'd burned, about how I'd left no way to get back to Denver, about how Cameron would leave for rehab in two days and I'd be alone in the Nut motel, nothing but lanky boys and searching hands and a change jar to my name. I thought about how I didn't want to die there, but I also thought about how I wasn't at all sure how not to.

As planned, two days later, on November 5, Cameron checked into rehab. It was my thirty-first birthday, and LA was warm and golden the way it can be in early November. I drove him to meet his mother, a woman who had likely never heard of me. She was kind, even though I must have seemed like one of Bukowski's women: shaking and sick, stinking of booze, looking all of my thirty-one years next to her son's twenty-four, all of my poverty next to their affluence. I'd tried to dress nicely, wearing that same gray dress, the only one I'd brought. I was trying to impress her, I guess, but in the glaring lights of the TGI Friday's where the three of us shared a banana split before heading over to the rehab center, it was clear my dress had a stain over the breast. It showed too much cleavage; the hem was unraveling, and I picked at the loosening thread all through Cameron's check-in.

The chasm between Cameron and me was vast that day and never closed. After a woman with enormous silicone breasts and a pink dress made of fabric that looked softer than anything I had ever touched lead him to his suite, explaining how to put in orders with the chef, what hours massages were available, I climbed into my twenty-year-old Toyota Corolla, the manual I bought after my Honda died, which I barely knew how to drive, and rode the clutch south on the 101 freeway in the hot traffic glare of a Los Angeles Friday afternoon.

The night of my thirty-first birthday, I drank beneath the Nut's rough bedsheets. I swallowed syrupy vodka from a jug Cameron left for me. "It's your birthday, and it's like my *rebirthday,*" he'd said, and I'd smiled and stutter-slurred, "Happy birthday to *us.*"

That night, I called the man I'd left in Denver. Hunting for what, I don't know. Sympathy? Companionship? Some kind of retardant to stop the fire that seemed to be consuming everything? The man said, "I can't talk to you. You can't call me for this." And, of course, he was right. I could have spent my birthday anywhere; I didn't have to be that kind of sad. I'd chosen to drink alone at the Nut in my baby-shit brown room.

Although I was in many ways at the mercy of my own madness back then, I had made choices. That night I curled into a ball and cried till dawn, then cried through the morning until I sobered up enough to decide again not to die there, even though dying seemed like the most natural choice. I gathered up the empty bottles and scurried down the inside stairwell to get rid of them. I went across the street to Jon's to buy lunch with quarters. I didn't cry again for years.

I lived in that alone space for a long time, probably still spend most of my nights there. I don't know that my lonely memories of the Nut would have been any less so had Cameron stayed. That solitary city was in my bones back then, and I don't think anyone else could have penetrated it.

So Cameron went to rehab and didn't get sober, and neither did I, at least not for a few more years. But I didn't die there in the Nut motel, didn't even try to.

There are only two stories for a woman like me in a place like the Nut. It's either a story of passing through, if you're as lucky as I was, or it's a place of staying forever, whether it's on the outside stairs, opening and closing a filthy, meaty palm, or between mattresses, earrings left on the nightstand. I wasn't the only woman to land in that baby-shit brown room. There are a thousand indistinguishable places and people like us scattered across the US. The Nut wasn't special, and neither was I.

Nominated by Gettysburg Review

THE OLD FAITH

by REV. ROB McCALL

from THE AWANADJO ALMANACK

First confession: I am not a Christian by any prevailing definition. Christians can say the Apostle's Creed without crossing their fingers. They believe in the second coming of Christ and the resurrection of the body. Christians are sure that accepting Jesus Christ as their personal Lord and Savior will gain them a place in heaven. Christians believe that God is three in one, Father, Son and Holy Ghost. Christians believe that Christ was born of a virgin, with no earthly father. Christians are confident that theirs is the only way, and do not hesitate to convert others by force or guile. Christians believe that humanity and the Earth are fallen and can only be redeemed by Christ. They believe that animals have no souls and that mankind is master of the Earth.

All my life I have read the same scriptures, prayed the same prayers and sung the same hymns as other Christians, but I have been led another way. I do not believe these things. Nor do I find much evidence that Jesus believed these things, either.

There is an Old Faith that survives out in the country, in small towns, tribal reserves, and the hearts of spiritual people all over the globe who want little to do with organized religion. It is the faith that was from the beginning. It is faith in the earth and the weather, the sun and moon, the land and the sea. It's anchored in the fertility of the earth and the changing of the seasons. It acknowledges the first Mother and first Father, male and female. It celebrates the healing power of the Creator spirit. It holds to the faith of the ancestors and works to pass that faith on to coming generations. It has two natural laws: "You reap what you sow," and "Do to others as you would have others do to you." It has

432

many teachers. It is the original faith of humankind and will never be extinguished.

Organized religions, born in the cities, have stolen from the Old Faith and then tried to stamp it out. But the Old Faith lives on, quietly and joyfully, in the country. That is why it is called 'pagan' and 'heathen.' Pagan comes from the Latin word for country; heathen means from the wilderness.

The Old Faith has no need for bishops or popes, celibates, catechisms, dogma, or inquisitions. Its cathedrals are the mountains and the shores. Its temple is roofed by clouds and illuminated by the lights in the sky. Everyone is a priest.

When I was younger I felt sorry for Native Americans whose old faith was over-ruled and dominated by organized religion four or five hundred years ago. I still do. But, after many years, the realization came that my people's old faith was over-ruled in the British Isles fifteen hundred years ago or more. White people have been separated from their old faith much longer, and have almost given in; but not completely.

If, when you hear Native American or Celtic or African or other tribal music, you get excited, it is because of the Old Faith still alive in you, the original soul and spirit, which will never die, and will always come to life again as sure as spring follows winter. We hear it in the fiddles and pipes, and the rattles and the drums. This is the Old Faith that always springs forth hopeful.

The Old Faith does not give men dominion over women. Women are not limited to being either virgins or witches. Women are the source of new life and the teachers of the young. Women are equal to men in the Old Faith, which honors both the circle and the cross, the earth and the four directions. It does not sacrifice children or animals to an angry deity. Its fundamental creed is life, not death. Its doctrine is love, not fear. It is satisfied with making the earth better for present and coming generations, not obsessed with what happens after we die, since we cannot know this. It wants a better present for all creatures, not just a better future in heaven for a select few who know the magic words and the secret rituals.

The Old Faith is quietly but vigorously alive in the country, small towns, tribal villages, and reservations all over the world. You can see its seasonal symbols everywhere if you have the eyes for it. See the orange and black of the harvest. See the green and red wreathes and evergreen trees at the beginning of winter. See the handmade baskets and herbal remedies. See the flowers of spring, the lilies and daffodils. See the gardens and orchards and wildflowers in bloom.

The Old Faith is not written only in books to be read by the elect and elite. It is declared far and wide to every creature in the Creation we behold. See the sun through the year as it goes higher in the sky, then lower, until it rises again. Hear the birds sing to the dawn. Theirs is the same old faith as ours. Watch the flowers turn their faces to the sun as it moves across the sky. Theirs too is the Old Faith. See the moon through its monthly changes and watch the tides rising and falling with it. This is the one original ancient faith, eons older than what Christians call the "old-time religion."

The organized religions of books, cities, and churches are breaking down all around. They are utterly bankrupt. Look at the disintegration of the "Catholic" church with its accumulated wealth and perversion, impoverishing and debasing the faithful while enriching and indulging the hierarchy. Look at the mainline Protestant churches with their fleeing multitudes and lukewarm faith. Look at the fundamentalists of all religions obsessed with fear and violence, desperately seeking the suicidal end of this world they so bitterly hate. All these organized religions are coming to an end.

Yet, we in whom the Old Faith still lives are afraid of practicing it, though plants and other animals practice it fearlessly day and night, summer and winter. Why are we afraid? The Old Faith has been brutally suppressed for thousands of years. Crusades, conquistadors, religious wars, inquisitions and burning at the stake, angry men with their punishing colonization of the earth and the human spirit have done everything they could to suppress the Ancient Faith. We have an ancestral fear of practicing it in the open, so we practice covertly behind closed doors or far out in the country where it still rules.

Today, the earth is being ravaged, the oceans are dying, the ice-caps are melting, whole species are becoming extinct, diseases like HIV/AIDS and malaria are visiting destruction among humans greater than anything since the Black Death, from the selfish pride of un-natural, urban, hierarchical religions erasing the ancient wisdom of the Creator and the Old Faith, and imposing rigors of the book to enrich and empower the few at the expense of the many. This is the work of demonic powers and principalities, kingdoms of this world trying to seize the power of the Creator for their own purposes.

It is time for the Old Faith to come out in the open and return to the prophets who preached about the vineyard taken away from those who would enrich themselves and given to those who would use it to enrich others. Jesus never meant to start a new religion of gilded cathedrals,

popes and bishops. He called down the laws and creeds of temple reli-
gion to return to the Old Faith. "Love God with all your heart, soul,
mind and strength," he said, "and love your neighbor as yourself." He
called down the Roman Empire for its slavery and exploitation, and was
tortured to death by it in the most hideous way. But, like the Old Faith,
he did not die.

To you whose religion is fishing or farming or gardening or handi-
craft or hiking or fiddling or drumming; to you whose saints are your
neighbors and children, to you whose temple is the earth and whose
creed is the turning of the seasons; to you whose matins are sung by
the birds and whose evensong is the rising moon and the setting sun; to
you who remember and remain fearless and joyful in the Old Faith:
Have courage. Your hour approaches. You are to be the redemption of
the world.

Nominated by Genie Chipps

DREAMING OF WATER WITH TIGER SALAMANDERS

by SAM KECK SCOTT

from LONGREADS

The big yellow machine casts up a brown blizzard of dust, adding to the trouble of seeing any small bodies attempting to run or slither for their lives. I chase the fleeing field mice and pocket gophers, pinching them at the backs of their necks, and stuff them into the pocket of my orange safety vest, already bulging with the wriggling bodies of alligator lizards and western skinks.

Better that pocket than the other, where a two-foot gopher snake is coiled up, its head poking out from this alien world of fluorescent orange, where it slowly unspools its slender body, the color of wet hay, up my torso. Again and again, I coax it back in using the heel of my palm, waiting for the mayhem to cease long enough to walk across the busy road to the edge of a dry creek bed, where I unceremoniously dump them all in a squirming pile below a blackberry thicket. Homeless, but alive.

To the rest of the construction crew, I must look ridiculous—stooped over, racing this way and that through a cloud of dust, filling my pockets with small creatures as the rotary mixer nips at my heels. But I've learned not to care. No matter how I appear, the biologist will always be the outcast on these projects.

When I walk away from the machine, I can't tell where the dust ends and the smoke begins. Once again, the air in California is lethal to breathe, bruised gray and purple, burning my eyes and throat as I stand in it day after day. But this year is different—this year I need two separate masks to juggle two separate calamities. When alone, the N95 with a one-way valve is superior for filtering smoke, but when close to others I quickly switch to my cloth mask for the virus, knowing the valve won't protect them from my potentially deadly exhalations. It's late summer, 2020, and we're all still beginners at learning to live with an invisible killer.

Some animals don't flee when the mixer comes. They hold their ground. Wait for the trouble to pass. But nothing in their evolution has prepared them for an eight-foot-wide drum covered in corkscrewing blades coming straight towards their soft bodies where they hunker in their meadow homes. The rotary mixer penetrates the ground 20 inches deep, turning the hard-packed earth into fluffy, aerated, hydrated soil in tidy rows. It's a dream machine if you need to turn a lumpy field into the future site of a housing development, but it's a science-fiction nightmare if you're a vole or a praying mantis or a king snake; a slender salamander, an earthworm, a deer mouse, or a Jerusalem cricket. The ones who don't flee will be ground into sausage and mixed evenly into the soil, and sometimes are so pulverized they become more mist than matter. Within an hour of the first pass of the mixer, crows appear by the dozens to peck at the peppered bits of the animals I failed to save.

My job is not to save any of these animals. But since I'm here, I try. The only reason the development company was forced to hire a biologist, as they are on every housing development being built on the Santa Rosa Plain, is for a small population of a single species of salamander—the federally endangered Sonoma County population of the California tiger salamander—an animal once prolific in this part of Northern California, now almost entirely wiped out.

Before European settlers colonized this area, one could scarcely come up with a place more perfectly suited to the unique needs of tiger salamanders than the Santa Rosa Plain—a lush mosaic of lakes, creeks, wetlands, vernal pools, riparian forests, grasslands, and oak savannah. A hummocky world of wet depressions and dry rises—as if the land itself was as amphibious as the salamanders who thrived there.

Tiger salamanders live a double life—they need both wet and dry places in close proximity. For most of the year, they stay underground in the burrows of other animals, or in large cracks in the adobe soil. But when the rains come, they emerge from their subterranean lairs to migrate in their slow, salamandery way: padding out across the land to a nearby breeding pond, which must be ephemeral to ensure no predatory fish can take up residence in them. After breeding, the adults move upland again, leaving their eggs to hatch into larvae, who metamorphose either quickly or slowly depending on the speed at which their pool is drying up. Once the larvae grow legs, maturing into juveniles who breathe air through lungs instead of gills, they too migrate upland to find an underground home, where they remain for the two to five years it will take them to reach breeding age.

I thought a lot about tiger salamanders during the early weeks of the pandemic, drawing inspiration from these masters of sheltering-in-place. I live in a trailer, which normally suits me just fine—I find small spaces comforting, and too many possessions stressful, so the trailer offers the perfect constraint. But when shelter-in-place began in March, my trailer quickly shrank around me. I morphed into a subterranean animal living in a narrow, aluminum burrow, aestivating during the dry months, waiting for rain. Waiting for a vaccine. Waiting for anyone to tell me anything that felt true or useful.

Time thickened, then congealed. I hunched over, shuffling around in my sweatpants. One step to the fridge, two to the bathroom, one to the bed, three to the door. This trailer was only meant to be a home base for my life on the move as a field biologist. A way to hack the Bay Area's obscene rental market—one of the highest in the nation. Not a place to weather a global pandemic. Alone.

After months of being stuck inside, treating my groceries like hazardous waste until I'd washed them with soap, and growing tired of my own cooking, it was tiger salamanders who finally coaxed me out of my burrow—or at least the possibility of them. A few months into the pandemic, developers had found their way onto the essential worker's list, and I got the call about 42 new townhouses being built in a vacant lot in Santa Rosa.

"Vacant" being a relative term. Without needing to see it, I knew the site would be home to many living things. And it was. The first day on the job, I saw fence and alligator lizards, a garter snake, western skink, piles of fox shit, many birds. I also found the recent remains of a human encampment, as I always do at the beginning of these projects. Vacant, according to the company preparing to develop the land, meant the lot was empty of any living thing willing to pay money to be there.

What I didn't find in that lot were any tiger salamanders. And I knew I wouldn't. They're endangered for a reason. The needs of tiger salamanders are far too specific for them to be living in a bone-dry, weedy lot like this, penned in by urban sprawl, and nowhere near a breeding pool—long ago amputated from the last life-supporting places of tiger salamanders in Sonoma County. But as the yellow machines stripped the land bare like a swarm of gargantuan locusts, I spent day after day looking for them anyway, filling the pockets of my safety vest with the struggling bodies of all those we aren't mandated to care about.

"You've been out here every day for two weeks and still haven't found one of them salamanders?" the foreman said to me one morning, appearing beside me and slapping me on the back while I watched an excavator dig up a waterline.

"Not yet," I replied, stepping away, his handprint glowing on my shoulder blade like a coronavirus starburst.

"Then what's the point of having you out here if there aren't any?" he asked me, maskless.

"Well, there's always a chance there are," I told him, despite knowing there almost certainly wasn't. "They used to be all over before we dried up the Laguna," I added.

He looked around at this dusty, flat, unremarkable place, surrounded by houses, a nearby high school, storefronts with blinking neon signs, busy roads. I'm guessing that's all he saw. I'm guessing he wasn't imagining what this place used to look like, only a few generations ago, like I was.

He stepped forward, peering into the eight-foot trench.

"There's too much fucking clay in this soil!" he barked, saying it to no one in particular, before walking away.

I wanted to yell at him that there's too much fucking clay in this soil because it used to be a wetland. There's too much fucking clay in this soil because this place once teemed with profusions of wet, aquatic life. But I kept quiet, staying in my narrow lane—only here for the nonexistent salamanders.

Before Europeans settled the Santa Rosa Plain and turned it into cow pasture and high-intensity agricultural land—smearing it with chemicals and shopping centers; bifurcating it with roadways and irrigation canals; before they dried it up, domesticated it, and sucked the green lush life from its spongy soil, turning the land and its grasses the dead-gray of roadside cardboard—the Santa Rosa Plain was dripping and oozing with life, sprinting, squirming, squiggling, crawling, flapping, splashing and growling across its skies and lands and waters.

Grizzly bears were here, wading up to their haunches in cool, clear water never touched by agrochemicals, hormones, antibiotics, or gasoline. Salmon pushed up rushing creeks and rivers, skipping over each other's backs, beating past the swiping claws of the bears, big as catcher's mitts. Waterfowl blackened the sky like living, billowing curtains, honking and calling, shitting an even coat of nutrient-rich fertilizer across every inch of the land, sending a chaos of plant life bursting skywards. Pronghorn grazed at the wetland's edges, stalked by cougar slinking down through the purple manzanita of the foothills, while condors with nine-foot wingspans cast sharp, slicing shadows over the land, searching for bloat, for stink, for blood—of which there was plenty. At night, bats swooped and hunted through a thick, sonic stew of frog chorus, and coyotes curdled the air with their manic songs whenever the silver moon rose in the east. And of course, there were people here then too. The Southern Pomo built tule balsa rafts and lived in tule huts all over the Santa Rosa Plain, fishing for salmon with hooks chipped from chert. Hunting black-tailed deer and pronghorn. Gathering fat acorns in baskets woven from willow branches. Coexisting with all this life.

And amidst the flurry, the tiger salamanders—their dark, stalky bodies splotched in archipelagos of sunlit buttercup as they ambushed spiders in the darkness of gopher burrows. Tiger salamanders, their yellow lips giving them the appearance of a dopey grin, twisting their wet, rubbery bodies around each other in breeding ponds. Tiger salamander larvae boiling in every vernal pool dotting the plain, the external lungs behind their heads swaying like aquatic lion's manes. Tiger salamanders dragging their heavy tails as they migrate by the thousands on the first big rain of the year: a clumsy procession of yellow speckles moving in slow motion over hills; through tall, swaying grasses; past the brown, humped mountains of sleeping grizzlies. A few getting speared and eaten by herons and egrets along the way, or batted in the air by bobcats, ground up by rapacious badgers, or swallowed whole by snakes. But they kept going, determined to get to their breeding ponds at any cost—determined to make more tiger salamanders. The only ones in the world who can.

This was not so long ago. This wasn't the Pleistocene or some other far-flung time in the past. This was less than 200 years ago. Individual koi fish have been known to live longer than that. Only 100 years ago the Santa Rosa Plain was closer to that throng of life than to what it is today—traffic, bad air, car dealerships glinting in the sunlight. Townhouses crammed between townhouses crammed between townhouses.

The reason tiger salamanders are no longer proliferating as they once did is not for lack of effort. Nowadays, on the first big rain of the year, they are run over by the dozens as they slowly cross busy roads separating their underground homes from breeding ponds, drawn by the strength of a giant magnet born of tens of thousands of years of instinct. Local biologists have learned where some of the busier crossings tend to be and will spend all night standing in the rain escorting salamanders safely from one side to the other, headlights whipping past them at 70 miles per hour. But these efforts are not enough to counteract what we've done to the land in Sonoma County.

In less than a geologic blink of an eye, 95% of the breeding habitat of the Sonoma County population of the California tiger salamander is now gone or under direct threat from development. And it isn't just the salamanders who are suffering. Some of the largest grizzly bears in the world used to live where I live—the last one shot by white settlers in California in 1922. Gray wolves were also trapped and shot into local extinction in California, though after 90 years of absence, a small pack has recently reentered the Golden State, mounting a quiet comeback—godspeed. Pronghorn, a short-necked relative of the giraffe, left the Santa Rosa Plain long ago, as did the California condor, after nearly going extinct due to lead poisoning from the bullets filling the bodies of the countless animals left to rot across the landscape.

According to the historical records of the Laguna Foundation in Santa Rosa, an individual hunter killed 6,200 ducks *by himself* in 1892 to supply markets in San Francisco. One morning I noticed seven Canada geese standing in the center of our project site. When the construction crew arrived, firing up the yellow machines, this anemic flock flew off to look for some other marginal place to scrape out an existence. As I watched them fly away, I didn't see seven geese in the sky above me—I saw the ghosts of the thousands of birds that were no longer there, replaced instead by a sky toxic with smoke.

None of this is normal, yet we treat it as if it is. And it isn't just Northern California that's changed—the entire planet has. All the way down to the fish in the sea.

As a species, we suffer from a sort of collective amnesia brought on by a phenomenon called "shifting baseline syndrome." Shifting baselines are what allow each new generation of people to be born into a world that appears "normal" to them, even as their grandparents loudly lament "the way things used to be." Those lamentations die with the older generation, and the new generation begins the process over, now bemoaning the changes they've witnessed in their short lifetimes, while their children and grandchildren are born into worlds that appear perfectly normal to them. And so on.

441

A classic example of shifting baseline syndrome was discovered by marine biologist Loren McClenachan when she found a series of historic photographs all taken in the same place on a wharf in Key West, Florida. The photos show people displaying their day's fishing catch in front of a hanging board throughout the decades, beginning in 1956 up until 2007. As the years slip past, the fish on display get smaller and smaller and smaller. At first, in the 1950s, they are mighty behemoths hanging from hooks, taller than the people who caught them, averaging 43.8 pounds. But by 2007, the average weight of the fish is only five pounds, held proudly in the hands of the anglers with no exertion whatsoever. Yet, what is most striking about these photographs isn't the shrinking fish, but rather the smiles on the faces of these pleased fisherpeople, which lose none of their brightness throughout the decades, even as their catches become preposterously diminished. *This* is shifting baseline syndrome. We keep smiling, ignorant to the fact that the natural world, which we rely on for survival, is disappearing beneath our feet, and in our very hands.

Recently, we've reached a point where the ecological changes are happening too fast and are too destructive for us to continue in this ignorance. Shifting baseline syndrome may have helped to bring the Big Bad Wolf to our door, but climate change, habitat loss, and pollution have blown the house down. Or in the case of my home state of California: burned the house down.

Growing up in Northern California, I never remember the sky filling with smoke. Not once. Wildfires, if I heard about them at all, were burning "over there" somewhere, out of sight, and nothing for me to fear. Not anymore. 2020 marked the fourth straight year Sonoma County was either on fire itself or smothered by the toxic smoke of other fires—or both—as it became the largest, most destructive fire season in California's history.

During a day off from looking for salamanders, I found myself stuck in my trailer again. The air quality outside—measured in PM2.5— was in the 370s. Anything above 300 is considered by the EPA to be hazardous to human health, and anything above 151 is categorized as unhealthy. The air temperature was 95°F. I had no choice but to keep every window and door sealed shut because of the smoke, but my trailer sits in direct sunlight, and the indoor temperature quickly outpaced the heat outside. Sweat poured down my body as if in a sauna at full furnace. My chest tightened. I felt squeezed by the hands of some invisible giant. I couldn't tell if it was claustrophobia or if I was actually running out of breathable air. I paced around my narrow home, leaving wet footprints across the wood floors—the air a hot, toxic porridge both inside and out. Panicked, I went to the window, looking out across the farm where my trailer is parked. Normally I see green hills and old red barns out that window, but on this day, I could barely see the outline of my truck, parked only 15' away—a vague shape in a brown-gray hellscape.

My chest squeezed tighter. I had to find some good air to breathe. I held the door handle, ready to burst out of this sweltering aluminum pillbox, but there was nowhere to go. I was trapped. If I opened the door, the air inside my trailer would only get worse. This wasn't simply the smoke of charred forests, but countless human structures as well, filled with paint, asbestos, burned-out cars, garages full of half-empty gas cans, lacquers, engine oil, cleaning supplies. I remembered two years earlier when the smoke from the fire that destroyed the entire town of Paradise settled over Sonoma County, and I'd wondered if I was breathing dead bodies. If the ash on my truck was someone's uncle, or mother.

Black bear, or rattlesnake.

I fell face-first onto my small couch, pressing my nose and mouth into a pillow, trying to calm down. I thought of the salamanders—how they breathe air through both their skin and lungs and how easily polluted their small, squishy bodies are. When the smoke rolls into their cramped burrows, what will this rancid air do to them? Will any tiger salamanders crawl out this winter when the rains finally come? *If* they come? Or will they all die in there? Smoked. Jerkied. Little golden-flecked mummies, hard as old bubblegum. Will anyone notice? Will tiger salamanders make the news if we kill off the last one? Will people finally realize how cute they were, and wonder why no one had told them earlier, before it was too late?

According to ancient belief, salamanders have nothing to fear from fire. The Talmud describes salamanders as being born of fire, and that anyone who covered themselves in the blood of salamanders would be immune to burning. In Greek, the name salamander means "fire lizard." Both Pliny the Elder and Aristotle claimed that salamanders could extinguish fires with their wet, icy skin. Leonardo da Vinci said that salamanders have "no digestive organs, and get no food but from the fire, in which it constantly renews its scaly skin." People also long believed that the fire-proof substance, asbestos, was made from the "fur" of salamanders. It's thought that these archaic misconceptions arose from

443

the fact that salamanders often burrow beneath, and sometimes inside of, rotting wood, and throughout history, as people placed these logs into their fires, salamanders would crawl out of the flames.

I found myself wishing the mythology of the fire lizards was true. As the August Complex Fire, California's first-ever "gigafire"—one that is larger than a million acres—burned to the north of me, and the nearby hillsides around Santa Rosa were an inferno to the east, and the Santa Cruz Mountains to my south were engulfed in flames until they ran straight into the sea, I wished that somehow, in the charred wake of all this destruction, millions of salamanders would materialize. Slow-motion phoenixes rising from the ashes with their long tails, fat legs, yellow spots, and a knowing look in their wet, protruding eyes that says: *We come from where you're headed, and you're not going to like it there.*

But of course, tiger salamanders, like most other lifeforms, will not emerge from these fires, but will instead be destroyed by them.

"Why should I care about some salamander anyway?"

It's a question I get from the construction crew on nearly every job site, and you can replace salamander with whatever species I might be there to protect: dusky-footed woodrats, Alameda whipsnakes, red-legged frogs, desert tortoise.

"We have houses to build for actual human beings; isn't that more important?"

Well, yes, sure. But also, no. We need tiger salamanders, and all other plants and animals, because what's killing them is also killing us. A California with a healthy tiger salamander population is a place where we're all healthier. Tiger salamanders need both undisturbed habitat and enough clean, unpolluted water to fill their breeding pools every year. They don't have it. It's the same reason you might not have enough water in your well. It's the same reason farmers can't keep their crops from drying out. It's the same reason cities are fighting over and diverting distant streams to keep the taps flowing. And it's the reason why California had its first gigafire last year, which will surely not be the last, just as the SARS-CoV-2 pandemic will not be the last virus to spill from the bloodstreams of animals into our own, with our endless, violent encroachment into wildlands.

My job is to protect the disappearing animal species of California. I think of these animals as ambassadors to the apocalypse. Tiger salamanders are trying to tell us something by their very disappearance—if the world isn't healthy enough for us, it isn't healthy enough for you either. We would be wise to heed the warnings of those species who are showing us where we're all headed, because there is no more urgent form of communication than going extinct.

*   *   *

I dream of water. Every day, as I wake to more smoke, more news of another fire ripping through nearby hills, I dream of heavy clouds galloping, gathering, rolling in from the sea—white-gray baskets sloshing with clean rainwater that burst open as they sweep across the West, drenching us, rinsing us, reminding us of what this world could, and should be. So much water that each dimple in the landscape fills up, turns green and writhes with life again. I dream of a world where people don't simply care about the many creatures we share this planet with, but celebrate them. A world where tiger salamanders migrate by the thousands on the first good rain of the year again—so many they walk over each other's backs—all of them wet and vigorous, breathing pure air through yellow-speckled skin, while the people come outside to line up and watch. Cheering them on.

Nominated by Longreads

BLUE

by ERIN WILSON

from BLUE (Circling Rivers)

There is a family story.

When my first husband and I were together,
we hiked a fairly arduous trail with the children,
young at the time.

At the top, our daughter,
believing she saw water in the distance,
ran toward the jutting precipice
and nearly jumped.

It was sky.

My ex caught her.

There is a second part to this family story. There was a second child
   running.

The father's arms were already full.

Nominated by Circling Rivers

THE ALMOST BRIDGE

by GEFFREY DAVIS

from SWAMP PINK

—*for D*

Weeks like this, the universe's dark shoulder
tapping seems determined. Over the phone

we swap our latest verses in that old
song of cosmic abandonment. I describe

three bad days on the river: the tender
girth of a drifter's pink dildo forsaken

beneath Tennessee's 400 bridge;
a wild rock dove drowning in the middle

of the muddied current; someone's body
outlawed for struggling to wash the living

from their clothing. Lucky for us, you—
and the bird that shat on your face years ago,

adding a coincidental laughter track
against today's temptation to prove the calculus

for sorrow's constant way with us. Although.
I do not mention my brother gambling

with more of my family's trust
in the haven of a father's hands. And I

have yet to tell you about the rat's nest
I upset earlier in the garden.

and dispatched the blind young in a t-shirt
knotted at its shabby neck, weepy

for another afternoon with loss
smeared across my own hands—: as I gathered

the deserted pups to smother in worn cotton
then a shallow bucket of water.

I recognized the hopeful edge of despair
sealed by their hard squeaks. And also the stunning

memory of a fox bounding onto the dark highway—
full-grace from the forest—

kept bucking my mind's efforts to build peace.
I didn't mean to end that fox

with my car. I didn't mean to stumble
again into the sorry church of shame.

heart vibrating with its new faith
in disasters . . . Before hanging up.

we reminisce about the landline's obsolete
dial-tone, how its eeriness could linger

with you after the warmth of a friend's voice
had been severed from any loneliness

at your ear. Just then the sky completes
its all-day promise and rain starts dotting

the street through sunshine. *I love you*, I say
aloud, and wait, once our call has ended.

Nominated by Danielle Cadena Deulen

TWO HALVES OF THE SKULL OF JOHN THE BAPTIST

by JEFFREY THOMSON

from MUSEUM OF OBJECTS BURNED BY THE SOULS IN PURGATORY (Alice James Books)

transparent crystal, sections of a human head, silver plate in the Amiens Cathedral, France, and the Basilica di San Silvestro in Capite, Rome

he was not the one

Salome wanted

he wore

his head

a goat's skin

she was the one

not the one

who cried

John

in her wilderness

he lived in

of palace

a wild desert

and moon

he was the coming of

there is always

the light

another

light shone

she was the one

450

in his face

       who took his head

he called the dove

       she looked

down

       upon his head

he was not the one

       shoulder bare

who walked

       bright

into a Jerusalem

       the silver platter

paved with palms

       spun with

there is always

       moonlight

another

Nominated by Alice James Books

BLACK LAND MATTERS: CLIMATE SOLUTIONS IN BLACK AGRARIANISM

by LEAH PENNIMAN

from TRANSITION MAGAZINE

In 2012, Hurricane Sandy, the largest Atlantic hurricane on record, swept across the Caribbean and the entire eastern seaboard of the United States. We were alerted to Sandy's arrival to Soul Fire Farm in the middle of the night, when we heard a deafening and perplexing roar from the forest. My spouse and I sat straight up in bed, looked at each other wordlessly, and headed outside. The powerful sound was coming from a newly formed "river" cascading from the forest and headed right toward our crop fields. It was dark, windy, and cold, yet we knew that if we did not act, we might lose our fall harvest. We woke up our young children, ages seven and nine, put shovels in their hands, and got to work digging a trench to divert the waters from the crops. After several muddy hours, we retired to our beds and hoped that our mounded soil would absorb the floodwaters. In the morning, news of devastation began trickling in. Both of the roads, Routes 2 and 22, which serve our town of Grafton were completely washed out, and residents were trapped. Neighboring farms had lost between fifty and one-hundred percent of their topsoil in the heavy rains. New York City was without electricity, with elders and people of color disproportionately adversely impacted. Our friends in Cuba, Haiti, Puerto Rico, and the Bahamas were facing homelessness and food shortages. Our youngest child wore a life jacket around the farm for days, terrified of being swept away by waters that were slow to recede.

The ice cores have spoken. As land and sea ice has accumulated over hundreds of thousands of years, it has trapped atmospheric gasses in varying concentrations across time. For millennia, the concentration of carbon dioxide (CO_2) in the atmosphere fluctuated, but it never exceeded 300 parts per million (ppm). Starting around the industrial revolution, the burning of fossil fuels, rampant deforestation, and soil tillage have driven atmospheric CO_2 exponentially up to its current level of 419 ppm. According to NOAA records, the blanket of heat-trapping CO_2 and other greenhouse gasses has driven a mean global surface temperature rise of one degree Celsius (2.12 degrees Fahrenheit) since the late nineteenth century. The glaciers are retreating, and the permafrost is melting. The rates of sea level rise are accelerating, and the ocean is acidifying. Extreme weather events like heat waves, floods, droughts, hurricanes, and tornadoes are increasing in intensity and frequency.

Within the US, the most severe adverse climate impacts, including flooding, heat waves, poor air quality, and workers' exposure to intense weather, disproportionately fall on racialized and poor communities. A comprehensive peer-reviewed investigation by the Environmental Protection Agency (EPA) released in 2021 found that Black American individuals are projected to face higher repercussions of climate change by every measurable index, as compared to all other demographic groups. From asthma rates to temperature-related death to flooding threats to damaged property and lost lives, black communities are on the frontlines.

These disparate and inequitable climate impacts are felt at a global scale. As explained in the *New York Times,* the rich and developed countries comprising twelve percent of the global population, including the United States, Canada, and much of Western Europe, are responsible for half of greenhouse gas emissions over the past 170 years. By contrast, the countries least responsible for greenhouse gas emissions are hardest hit by climate impacts such as sea level rise, tsunamis, drought, and irregular weather patterns. "If you're not affected by climate change *today*, that itself is a privilege," said climate activist Andrea Manning.

* * *

White supremacy is a major catalyst for the destruction of earth's life support systems. Embedded in the theory of the supremacy of white people over other races is the theory of human supremacy over nature. This is exemplified in the white supremacist philosophies of the

Doctrine of Discovery, private property, and Manifest Destiny, which led directly to the exploitation of land and natural resources, and the displacement of indigenous people globally. In 1846, Senator Thomas Hart Benton asserted, "It would seem that the White race alone received the divine command, to subdue and replenish the earth: for it is the only race that has obeyed it—the only race that hunts out new and distant lands, and even a New World, to subdue and replenish . . ."

The philosophies and practices of colonial conquest, subjugation, extraction, and commodification mutually reinforce each other, and simultaneously exploit racialized people and the earth. As European settlers displaced indigenous peoples across North America in the 1800s, they exposed vast expanses of land to the plow for the first time. According to K.W. Flach et al. (1997), it took only a few decades of intense tillage to drive over fifty percent of the original organic matter from the rich prairie loam soils. The productivity of the US Great Plains decreased by seventy-one percent during the twenty-eight years following that first European tillage. The initial anthropogenic rise in atmospheric carbon dioxide levels was due to that breakdown of soil organic matter. Land clearing and cultivation emitted more greenhouse gasses than the burning of fossil fuels until the late 1950s. As expressed by Mary Annaïse Heglar, "The fossil fuel industry was born of the industrial revolution, which was born of slavery, which was born of colonialism." In his chilling and unapologetic indictment, Wendell Berry stated:

It stands to reason that any hope of solving the environmental crisis will require an examination and uprooting of the white supremacist ideologies that underpin the crisis. The voices and expertise of black, brown, and indigenous environmentalists, amplified by all those who have eschewed white supremacy, must be heeded if we are to halt and reverse planetary calamity. Ecological humility is part of the cultural heritage of black people. While our 400+ years immersion in racial capitalism has attempted to diminish that connection to the sacred earth, there are those who persist in believing that the land and waters are family members, those who understand the intrinsic value of nature. The same communities that are on the frontlines of climate impact, are also on the frontlines of climate solutions. A new generation of black farmers are leading the way as climate stewards by putting carbon back in the soil where it belongs.

The truth of the matter is that black people have a 12,000-year history of noble, sacred, and dignified relationship to soil that far surpasses our 246 years of enslavement and seventy-five years of sharecropping

454

in the United States. For many, this period of land-based terror has devastated our sacred connection to soil. We have confused the subjugation our ancestors experienced on land with the land herself, naming her the oppressor and running toward paved streets without looking back. We do not stoop, sweat, harvest, or even get dirty, because we imagine that would revert us to bondage. Part of the work of healing our relationship with soil is the unearthing and relearning the lessons of soil reverence from years past.

* * *

We can trace black people's sacred relationship with soil at least back to the reign of Cleopatra in Egypt (69–30 BCE). According to Jerry Minich (1977), Cleopatra recognized the earthworm's contributions to the fertility of Egyptian soil and declared the animal sacred and decreed that no one, not even farmers, were allowed to harm or remove an earthworm for fear of offending the deity of fertility. According to a study by the USDA in 1949, the great fertility of the Nile River Valley was the result of the activity of earthworms. The researchers found the worm castings from a six-month period to weigh almost 120 tons per acre, approximately ten times the amount of castings on soils in Europe and the US.

In West Africa as well, the depth of highly fertile anthropogenic soils serves as a "meter stick" for the age of communities. According to James Fairhead et al (2016), over the past 700+ years, women in Ghana and Liberia have combined several types of waste—ash and char residues from cooking, bones from food preparation, by-products from processing palm oil and handmade soap, harvest residues, and organic domestic refuse—to create African dark earth, a veritable black gold. African dark earth has a high concentration of available calcium and phosphorus, likely due to the addition of animal bones. The bones in combination with the char also make the soil more alkaline, so it has a liming effect on soil chemistry. African dark earths store between 200 and 300 percent more organic carbon than typical soils in the region, reducing atmospheric greenhouse gasses, as well as 2 to 26 times the amount of pyrogenic carbon than regular soil, a carbon compound that persists longer in the soil and contributes to fertility and climate mitigation. West African farmers continue to produce and use dark earth today. The elders in the community measure the age of their town by the depth of the black soil, since every farmer in every generation participated in its creation.

In Northern Namibia and Southern Angola, farmers refused to be displaced from the soils they had built over generations. According to Julianna White (2016), the Ovambo people were clear that soil fertility was not an inherent quality, but rather something that is nurtured over generations through mounding, ridging, and the application of ample manure, ashes, termite earth, cattle urine, muck from wetlands, and other organic matter to increase its fecundity. When the colonial government attempted to force the Ovambo farmers off their land, offering them equivalent plots with "better quality" soil, the farmers countered that they had invested substantially into building their soils and doubted that the new areas would ever equal their existing farms in fertility.

Centuries later, this sacred and reverent connection between black people and soil was also commemorated by black land stewards in the United States. George Washington Carver was a pioneer in regenerative farming, one of the first agricultural scientists in the United States to advocate for the use of leguminous cover crops, nutrient-rich mulching, and diversified horticulture. According to Mark D. Hershey (2011), Carver was dedicated to the regeneration of depleted southern soils and turned to legumes, such as cowpeas and peanuts, as a means to fix nitrogen and replenish the soil. He believed that the cowpea, a crop indigenous to Africa, was indispensable in a crop rotation, noting that a soil's "deficiency in nitrogen can be made up almost wholly by keeping the legumes, or pod-bearing plants, growing on the soil as much as possible." In addition to promoting cover cropping, Carver experimented with and advocated for compost manuring to address the deficiencies of the Cotton Belt soils. In 1902, he spoke at the annual convention of the Association of American Agricultural Colleges and Experiment Stations about his use of swamp muck, forest leaves, and pine straw to fortify soils. He believed that the forest was a "natural fertilizer factory" containing trees, grasses, and debris that produced "countless tons of the finest kind of manure, rich in potash, phosphates, nitrogen, and humus." Carver sought to persuade farmers to dedicate their autumn and winter to the collection of organic matter. He advised farmers to dedicate every spare moment to raking leaves, gathering rich earth from the woods, piling up muck from swamps, and hauling it to the land to be plowed under. Carver believed that "unkindness to anything means an injustice done to that thing," a conviction that extended to both people and soil. A farmer whose soil produced less every year was neglecting proper care, and so proof that he was being unkind to it in some way.

His faith in the moral imperative to care for soil was expressed in the Bible verses he invoked while teaching farmers, such as Proverbs 13:23: "Much food is in the tillage [fallow ground] of the poor; but there is that is destroyed for want of judgment."

* * *

Black farmers in the United States have yearned to secure land tenure and the ability to implement their heritage farming practices that sequester carbon and honor the soil. This essay will now explore the historical journey of African Americans in that struggle for land. Chattel slavery, sharecropping, governmental discrimination, and land grabs served as institutional obstacles to land ownership. Lack of secure land tenure was a major threat to the continuing legacy of Black land stewardship practices.

After 246 years of toiling on the land of enslavers under threat of the lash, recently emancipated African Americans were eager for land ownership. The black community of Falls Church, Virginia wrote to the Freedman's Bureau in 1865, "We feel it very important that we obtain HOMES, owning our own shelters, and the ground, that we may raise fruit trees, concerning which our children can say—these are ours." At the suggestion of Rev. Garrison Frazier and a coalition of Georgia black ministers, General William T. Sherman confiscated 400,000 acres of land from Confederate landlords and allocated 40-acre plots to black families. Just a few months after 40,000 black freedmen were settled, Andrew Johnson overturned the order, evicted the black families, and returned the land to the very people who had declared war on the United States. The broken promise of "40 acres and a mule" was one insult in an egregious litany of black folks being dispossessed of land in the US.

Though forced into the debt peonage poverty-trap of sharecropping, black farmers held onto hope of one day owning their own land. In 1862, the Homestead Act provided federal land grants to Western settlers as a mechanism for transferring 270 million acres of stolen Native American land to white people. De facto discrimination generally prevented black people from participating. Instead, black families saved up money and purchased nearly sixteen million acres by 1910, representing fourteen percent of the nation's farms. The white supremacist backlash against expanding black land ownership was swift and severe. According to the Equal Justice Initiative, more than 4,000 African Americans were lynched between 1877 and 1950. Black landowners were specifically targeted for not "staying in their place," that is, not settling for life as sharecroppers. According to one investigation by the Associated Press, white people violently stole at least 24,000 acres of land from 406 black people, depriving the black farmers of tens of millions of dollars and often, their lives. For example, Kentucky farmer David Walker and his family of seven were attacked by the Ku Klux Klan on October 4, 1908. According to Cecily Andrews (2017), KKK members burned their house to the ground with one child trapped inside, shot and killed his wife and baby, and wounded the other children. The survivors were run out of town and the 2.5-acre farm was folded into the property of their white neighbor, whose family retains title to the present day.

The United States Department of Agriculture was also complicit in black land loss. Throughout the South, USDA agents withheld crucial loans, crop allotments, and technical support services from black farmers and excluded them from USDA county committees. For example, according to Carol Estes (2001), Mississippi farmer Lloyd Shaffer went to the USDA office to apply for the programs to which he was entitled. "On three separate occasions, the white FHA loan officer took Lloyd Shaffer's loan application out of his hand and threw it directly into the wastebasket. Once Lloyd was kept waiting eight hours, from the time the office opened until after it closed at night, while white farmers came and went all day long, conducting business." By the 1950s, USDA programs had been "sharpened into weapons to punish civil rights activity." The founders, according to Rosenberg and Stucki (2017), of the White Citizens' Council, an association of white supremacist organizations, drew up a plan to remove 200,000 African Americans from Mississippi by 1966 through "the tractor, the mechanical cotton picker . . . and the decline of the small independent farmers." Black farmers who held onto their land used their independence to support civil rights workers which often made them targets for lynch mobs and local elites. In 1965, The US Commission on Civil Rights, an independent agency created by the Civil Rights Act of 1957 to investigate and report on a broad spectrum of discriminatory practices, released a highly critical study revealing how the Agriculture Stabilization and Conservation Service, the Federal Housing Association, and the Federal Extension Service bitterly resisted demands to share power and resources with African American farmers, leading to a precipitous decline in black land ownership. In 1983, President Reagan pushed through budget cuts that eliminated the USDA Office of Civil Rights; officials admitted they "simply threw discrimination complaints in the trash without ever responding to or investigating them" until 1996, when the office re-opened. In 1920, 925,000 black farmers owned sixteen million acres of land, fourteen percent of the US farms. By 1970, the black community had lost ninety percent of its farmers and its farmland. "It was almost as if the earth was opening up and swallowing Black farmers," wrote scholar Pete Daniel.

Present-day black landowners often do not have access to legal services in order to create wills, so their property is inherited in common by their descendants, who become legal co-owners. According to Thomas Mitchell and Leah Douglas, an heir's property is usually not eligible for mortgages, home equity loans, USDA programs, or government housing aid, tying the hands of property owners who want to invest in their land. Heirs' property is also vulnerable to corrupt lawyers and predatory developers because they only need to convince one heir to sell in order to force sale of the entire property; this is known as a partition sale. Developers hunt down distant relatives, often in other states, and offer them cash for their share of the land, then force sale of the entire property at auction. It is estimated that over fifty percent of black land loss since 1969 was due to partition sales. According to the USDA census, today, white people own 94.4 percent of the agricultural acreage in the United States. "If we don't have our land, we don't have our family," says Queen Quet, chieftess of the Gullah/Geechee Nation. "This is the battle we're in now."

*　*　*

Despite immense challenges to land access, black farmers today persist in using heritage agrarian practices to capture carbon from the air and trap it in the soil. Their primary strategies are silvopasture and regenerative agriculture, solutions ranked #9 and #11 respectively in Paul Hawken's *Drawdown*. Silvopasture is an indigenous system that integrates nut and fruit trees, forage, and grasses to feed grazing livestock. Regenerative agriculture, a methodology first described by Dr. George Washington Carver, involves minimal soil disturbance, the use of cover crops, and crop rotation. Both systems harness plants to capture greenhouse gasses. "No other mechanism known to humankind is as effective in addressing global warming as the capturing of carbon dioxide from the air through photosynthesis," said Hawken.

USDA census data has consistently shown that the majority of black farmers nationwide are small and diversified—the majority operating on less than 180 acres, raising specialty crops like herbs and vegetables, growing vegetables and melons, or running a combined livestock and crop operation. This correlation between farm stewardship by black producers and the use of sustainable agricultural practices is notable. To humanize the data, this article highlights three black modern-day black farmers who are leading the way in climate healing agriculture, Leonard Diggs, Germaine Jenkins, and Keisha Cameron.

After working in an auto parts store during high school, Leonard Diggs swore that he would never have another job working indoors. True to his word, Diggs went on to manage sustainable farms in northern California for over thirty years. Currently, Diggs is developing a 418-acre incubator farm at Pie Ranch, where beginning farmers will establish their own carbon-neutral businesses. In collaboration with the Amah Mutsun tribal band and nearby farmers, Diggs is creating a landscape-level ecosystem plan that integrates forest, riparian corridor, native grasslands, perennial and annual crops. Unlike many incubator farms that emphasize annual crops and allow farmers to stay for just a few years, Diggs is working with a longer horizon. He plans to plant orchards and perennials, getting them established over ten years, and handing new farmers a working landscape. Instead of making them leave as soon as their businesses get established, he will move the incubator to a new area and the farmers can stay.

Diggs argues that we need to realize that working landscapes provide not just products but also ecosystem services like carbon sinks, water recharge, and evolutionary potential. He envisions a food system where farmers derive thirty to forty percent of their income from the value of ecosystem services and do not have to "mine" the soil to make a living. He is working with researchers to establish baseline data for the amount of carbon in the soil, and the composition of bacterial and fungal communities. The goal is for the farm to capture more carbon than it releases over time. He is working toward an agriculture that does not lose our carbon and does not deplete our people.

Not everyone in the black farming community is as excited about fiber as Keisha Cameron. Given the prominent role of the cotton industry in the enslavement of African Americans, many farmers eschew cultivation of textiles. She points out that black people are largely absent from the industry on almost every scale. Yet, these agrarian art ways are part of black heritage.

At High Hog Farm, Cameron and her family produce wool, meat, eggs, and milk from heritage breeds of sheep, rabbits, chickens, and goats, each integrated into a silvopasture system. Cameron introduced American Chinchilla rabbits into the farm's ecosystem this year, since

460

rabbits consume a wider diversity of forage than goats and their manure is highest in nitrogen. The family is working to establish tree guilds, a system where fruit trees are surrounded by a variety of fiber crops like indigo, cotton, and nettles. Their goal is a "closed loop" where all the farm's fertility needs are created in place. Each aspect of the farm supports another.

Though her family only farms five acres, she feels that is enough to make an impact. According to Eric Toensmeier, silvopasture traps forty-two tons of carbon per acre every year. This is because pasture stores carbon in above- and below-ground biomass of grasses, shrubs, and trees. Also, animals that are raised on pasture have healthier digestive systems than those raised in confinement and emit lower amounts of methane. That means that Cameron may be sequestering up to 210 tons of carbon annually.

When Germaine Jenkins first moved to Charleston, she relied on SNAP and food pantries to feed her children. She did not like that her family couldn't choose what they wanted to eat, and there were few healthy options. She was sick of standing in line and so decided to grow her own food.

Jenkins learned how to cultivate her own food through a Master Gardening course, a certificate program at Growing Power, and online videos. She promptly started growing food in her yard and teaching her food-insecure clients to do the same through her work at the Lowcountry Food Bank. In 2014, Jenkins won an innovation competition and earned seed money to create a community farm.

Today, Fresh Future Farm grows on 0.8 acres in the Chicora neighborhood and runs a full-service grocery store right on site. The neighbors are living under food apartheid, so all of the food is distributed using a sliding scale pay system.

Jenkins relies on what she calls "ancestral muscle memory" to guide her farming practices. Fresh Future Farm integrates perennial crops like banana, oregano, satsuma, and loquat together with annuals like collards and peanuts. They produce copious amounts of compost on site using waste products like crab shells, and they apply cardboard and wood chips in a thick layer of mulch. She repurposes everything—old Christmas trees as trellises and branches as breathable cloche for frost-sensitive crops. They even have grapes growing up the fence of the chicken yard so that the chickens fertilize their own shade.

Jenkins's regenerative farming methods have been so successful at increasing the organic matter in the soil, that they no longer need irrigation. They are also less vulnerable to flooding. One winter they had four feet of snow, and the soil absorbed all of it.

These individual farmers are not alone. Black land stewards, both legacy and returning generations, are working to build organization and networks of mutual support. Organizations like the National Black Food and Justice Alliance, the Federation of Southern Cooperatives, and Land Loss Prevention Project are working in coalition to save the remaining black farmland and to establish a Black "commons" of permanently protected agricultural land. The coalition worked on the Justice For Black Farmers Act which would, among many provisions, provide funding for the return of up to sixteen million acres of land to black farmers. Permanent, secure land tenure is essential to the capacity of black farmers to implement heritage regenerative practices that could heal the climate. According to Eric Toensmeier, for every one percent increase in soil organic matter, we sequester 8.5 tons per acre of atmospheric carbon. If all of us were to farm like Jenkins, Diggs, and Cameron, we could put 322 billion tons of carbon back in the soil where it belongs. That's half of the carbon we need to capture to stabilize the climate. Black land tenure is an essential part of the climate solutions matrix.

❋   ❋   ❋

When the waters of Hurricane Sandy receded, we found our farm relatively unharmed. The Ovambo-style raised beds, Dr. Carver-inspired cover cropping, and African Dark Earth compost made our once fragile soils resilient in the face of flooding. The excess water slowly seeped into the ground, supported by the high organic matter that had been restored to pre-colonial levels through Afro-indigenous farming methods. Our soil was not only capturing atmospheric carbon, but it was mitigating climate impacts. Our son could safely take off his life jacket and trust that food would abound.

As Larisa Jacobson, Soul Fire Farm's Co-Director Emeritus explained, "Our duty as earthkeepers is to call the exiled carbon back into the land and to bring the soil life home."

Nominated by Transition Magazine

SPECIAL MENTION

(The editors also wish to mention the following important works published by small presses last year. Listings are in no particular order.)

FICTION

Max Bell—Doppel (New Ohio Review)
Roy Parvin—A Name For Everything (Hudson Review)
Nicole Cullen—Trespasses (Idaho Review)
Tehila Lieberman—The Firmament And The Night Doll (Jewish Fiction)
Iheoma Nwachukwu—Spain's Last Colonial Outpost (Ploughshares)
Alice Hoffman—The Dark Lady (Five Points)
Charles Watts—Harbinger (Chicago Quarterly Review)
Jackson Saul—Only Be Good Things (Gettysburg Review)
S.L. Wisenberg—Bad Girl In Berlin (Narrative)
Kiik Araki-Kawaguchi—Columbo And The Sugar War (A Public Space)
Dolan Morgan—Launder (Another Chicago Magazine)
Becky Hagenston—La Mesa (Arts And Letters)
Kolena Jones Kayembe—Girls (Oxford Magazine)
Serkan Görkemli—Runway (Iowa Review)
J. Robert Lennon—Pingüino (American Short Fiction)
E.K. Ota—The Paper Artist (Ploughshares)
Cord Jefferson—The Front House (Yale Review)
Drew Calvert—Social Learning (Kenyon Review)
Mi Jin Kim—Pocket Money (A Public Space)
Jennifer Cook—Anaheim (Kenyon Review)
Marian Crotty—What Kind of Person (Iowa Review)

Meredith Talusan—Crosscurrents (Bellevue Literary Review)

Benjamin Inks—Love In The Time of Combat Injuries (As You Were)

Gothataone Moeng—Homing (Virginia Quarterly Review)

Emily Coletta—As Someone Who Knows Phillip Quite Well
(Catamaran)

Laura Venita Green—Stuck (Story)

Sena Moon—Porn Star (Kenyon Review)

Alec Niedenthal—The Patriotic Hat (The Drift)

Emily Mitchell—The Church Of Divine Electricity (Southern
Review)

William Pei Shih—Necessary Evils (Southern Review)

Valerie Sayers—A Good Looking Guy (Missouri Review)

Vida James—You Belong In Gray (Story)

C. Felix Amerasinghe—The Road To Revolution (Raritan)

Pritha Bhattacharyya—Surrogates (Southerm Review)

Kristina Gorcheva-Newberry—The Kyiv Symphony (Zyzzyva)

Robert Anthony Siegel—The Silver Door (Harvard Review)

Diane Williams—Each Person To Her Paradise (n + 1)

Cal Shook—Exotic Pets (The Common)

Jeremy Griffin—Raise Your Fists (Hopkins Review)

Wendell Berry—A Rainbow (1945–1975–2021) (Threepenny Review)

Alyson Mosquera Dutemple—Marvelous Freaks of Nature (Colorado
Review)

Josephine Rowe—Little World (Zoetrope)

Emma Cline—The Erl-King (Granta)

JP Gritton—Cowboys (Ploughshares)

Lidia Yuknavitch—Olga (Bomb)

Jamil Jan Kochai—The Tale of Dully's Reversion (Zoetrope)

Thomas Bolt—Area of Isolation (n + 1)

Russell Banks—Kidnapped (Conjunctions)

Richard Wirick—Flashbox (Santa Monica Review)

Nikki Ervice—Rabbit (Iowa Review)

Meghan Reed—Where The Animals Sleep At Night (Oxford
American)

Lindsey Drager—In Defense of Optimism (Iron Horse)

Jennafer D'Alvia—Staircase (Chautauqua)

David E. Lee—Heaven For Your Full Lungs (Black Lawrence)

Nur Turkmani—In The Line (Oyster River Pages)

Simon Han—The Trick (Virginia Quarterly Review)

Leslie Kirk Campbell—The Man With Eight Pairs of Legs (Sarabande)

Sarah Balakrishnan—Rouses Point (Narrative)

Vi Khi Nao—Ekalaka (Noon)

Deesha Philyaw—Mayretta Kelly Brunson Williams Bryant Jones (1932–2012) (Smokelong Quarterly)

NONFICTION

John Thomason—Have You Forgotten Him? (The Baffler)

David Stromberg—The Eternal Hope of The Wandering Jew (Hedgehog)

Rue Matthiessen—LSD and Zen (Free State Review)

Christina Rivera Cogswell—The 17th Day (Terrain)

Suzanne Scanlon—The Moving Target of Being (Granta)

Ucheoma Onwutuebe—A Nigerian Attempts Therapy (Bellevue Literary Revue)

Danielle Shorr—Grief Teacher (New Orleans Review)

Lauren Fedorko—Roe vs Wade (Kelsey Review)

Emily Pittinos—Ashes (Mississippi Review)

Jodie Noel Vinson—Self Portrait After Covid 19 (Ninth Letter)

Tan Tuck Ming—Departures (Kenyon Review)

Mary Milstead—Tenderness (River Teeth)

K Chiucarello—Water Works (Shenandoah)

Rosanna Warren—Foreign Affairs (American Scholar)

Pamela Macfie—Unlettered (Sewanee Review)

Toni Martin—My Father's Voice (Threepenny Review)

May-lee-Chai—Hungry Ghost (Alaska Quarterly)

Daniel O'Neill—Averted Vision (American Scholar)

Robert Pinsky—Magic Mountain (Salmagundi)

Kiyoko Reidy—A More Complete Truth (Crazyhorse)

Zoe Valery—The Ghost (New England Review)

Zoë Bossiere—The Beetle King (The Sun)

Nicholas Dighera—The Tree (River Teeth)

Bennett Sims—Portonaccio Sarcophagus (Georgia Review)

Dorthe Nors—Wandering Houses (World Literature Today)

Amelia Mairead McNally—On Throwing Things Away (New Ohio)

Gina Apostol—May Your Muse Still Be Singing (Hopkins Review)

Alexis Richland—My Body, My Theology (Gettysburg Review)

Elias Rodriques, Clinton Williamson—Sweet Little Lies (Baffler)
Christian Kracht—The Gold Coast (Paris Review)
Peter Wayne Moe—Bones, Bones: How To Articulate A Whale (Longreads)
Nickole Brown—On Memory And Survival (Orion)
Jeannette Cooperman—Thoughts On The End . . . (Common Reader)
Carolyn Forché—The Rest Of The Story (Yale Review)
Cristina Eisenberg—Lessons From The Mother Bear (About Place)
John Balaban—The Writing Life (Massachusetts Review)
Stephanie Anderson—Disturbance (Ninth Letter)
Andre Dubus II—Pappy (River Teeth)
Tamara Dean—Safer Than Childbirth (American Scholar)
Tom Quach—Goodbye, Little Saigon (Bennington Review)
Paul Susi—Here Lies (Oregon Humanities)
Mike Broida—Great Fortune (Colorado Review)

POETRY

Rosalie Moffett—Time And Place (West Branch)
Cathy Linh Che—Bomb That Tree Back . . . (Guernica)
Blas Falconer—Que Significa (Southern Post Colonial)
Terrance Hayes—The Kafka Virus Vs(Thursday) (Iowa Review)
Diane Seuss—Love Letter (River Mouth Review)
Jenny George—Quantum (Kenyon Review)
Bob Hicok—Butterscotch (Conduit)
Katie Ford—from "Estrangement" (American Poetry Review)
Rick Barot—Goodwill (Adroit Journal)
Derrick Austin—Jesus Year (Honey Literary)
Tyree Daye—Angels Come Down From Heaven (America Poetry Review)
Janiru Liyanage—Ars Poetica (Agni)
Marianne Boruch—Shards (New England Review)
Jennifer Franklin – Antigone's Decision (Bennington Review)
Robert Cording—Looking Around (Agni)
Brenda Hillman—The Mostly Everything That Everything Is (Tree Lines, Grayson Books)
Torrin A. Greathouse—Etymythology (Southern Review)
Jenny Browne—from "I Am Trying To Love The Whole World" (Ilanot Review)
Lee Ann Roripaugh—To My Cancer . . . (Florida Review)

Karen Paul Holmes—Send It, Send It (Lascaux Review)

Faylita Hicks—The Skybridge In This Divorce (America Poetry Review)

Dale Kushner—What Could't Be Said (3: A Taos Press)

James Davis May—Depression In Saint-Meloir Des Ondes (Sugar House)

William Keckler—Auschwitz Tourists (Modern Haiku)

Yuko Taniguchi—Two Views(After Tsunami) (Ecotone)

Marianne Boruch—Of Course Pliny Got Here First (Narrative)

David Kirby—The Fates (Rattle)

Rebecca Hazelton—More Husbands (Southern Indiana Review)

Elisavet Makridis—Endangered Dialect Lesson: Five Revisions (Inverted Syntax)

Maria Zoccola—Saint Somebody's (Orange Blossom)

Hannah Lee Jones—Longing Town (June Road Press)

PRESSES FEATURED IN THE PUSHCART PRIZE EDITIONS SINCE 1976

A-Minor
About Place Journal
Abstract Magazine TV
The Account
Adroit Journal
Agni
Ahsahta Press
Ailanthus Press
Alaska Quarterly Review
Alcheringa/Ethnopoetics
Alice James Books
Ambergris
Amelia
American Circus
American Journal of Poetry
American Letters and Commentary
American Literature
American PEN
American Poetry Review
American Scholar
American Short Fiction
The American Voice
Amicus Journal
Amnesty International
Anaesthesia Review
Anhinga Press
Another Chicago Magazine

Antaeus
Antietam Review
Antioch Review
Apalachee Quarterly
Aphra
Aralia Press
The Ark
Arkansas Review
Arroyo
Art angel
Art and Understanding
Arts and Letters
Artword Quarterly
Ascensius Press
Ascent
Ashland Poetry Press
Aspen Leaves
Aspen Poetry Anthology
Assaracus
Assembling
Atlanta Review
Autonomedia
Avocet Press
The Awl
The Baffler
Bakunin
Bare Life

Bat City Review
Bamboo Ridge
Barlenmir House
Barnwood Press
Barrow Street
Bellevue Literary Review
The Bellingham Review
Bellowing Ark
Beloit Poetry Journal
Bennington Review
Bettering America Poetry
Bilingual Review
Birmingham Poetry Review
Black American Literature Forum
Blackbird
Black Renaissance Noire
Black Rooster
Black Scholar
Black Sparrow
Black Warrior Review
Blackwells Press
The Believer
Bloom
Bloomsbury Review
Bloomsday Lit
Blue Cloud Quarterly
Blueline
Blue Unicorn
Blue Wind Press
Bluefish
BOA Editions
Bomb
Bookslinger Editions
Boomer Litmag
Boston Review
Boulevard
Boxspring
Brevity
Briar Cliff Review
Brick
Bridge
Bridges
Brown Journal of Arts
Burning Deck Press

Butcher's Dog
Cafe Review
Caliban
California Quarterly
Callaloo
Calliope
Calliopea Press
Calyx
The Canary
Canto
Capra Press
Carcanet Editions
Caribbean Writer
Carolina Quarterly
Catapult
Caught by The River
Cave Wall
Cedar Rock
Center
Chariton Review
Charnel House
Chattahoochee Review
Chautauqua Literary Journal
Chelsea
Chicago Quarterly Review
Chouteau Review
Chowder Review
Cimarron Review
Cincinnati Review
Cincinnati Poetry Review
Circling Rivers
City Lights Books
Clarion
Cleveland State Univ. Poetry Ctr.
Clover
Clown War
Codex Journal
CoEvolution Quarterly
Cold Mountain Press
The Collagist
Colorado Review
Columbia: A Magazine of Poetry and Prose
Columbia Poetry Review
The Common

Conduit
Confluence Press
Confrontation
Conjunctions
Connecticut Review
Consequence
Constellations
Copper Canyon Press
Copper Nickel
Cosmic Information Agency
Countermeasures
Counterpoint
Court Green
Crab Orchard Review
Crawl Out Your Window
Crazyhorse
Creative Nonfiction
Crescent Review
Cross Cultural Communications
Cross Currents
Crosstown Books
Crowd
Cue
Cumberland Poetry Review
Curbstone Press
Cutbank
Cypher Books
Dacotah Territory
Daedalus
Dalkey Archive Press
James Dickey Review
Decatur House
December
Denver Quarterly
Desperation Press
Diálogos Books
Dogwood
Domestic Crude
Doubletake
Dragon Gate Inc.
Dreamworks
Dryad Press
Duck Down Press
Dunes Review

Durak
East River Anthology
Eastern Washington University Press
Ecotone
Egress
El Malpensante
Electric Literature
Eleven Eleven
Ellis Press
Emergence
Empty Bowl
Ep;phany
Epoch
Ergol
Evansville Review
Exquisite Corpse
Faultline
Fence
Fiction
Fiction Collective
Fiction International
Field
Fifth Wednesday Journal
Fine Madness
Firebrand Books
Firelands Art Review
First Intensity
5 A.M.
Five Fingers Review
Five Points Press
Fjords Review
Florida Review
Foglifter
Forklift
The Formalist
Foundry
Four Way Books
Fourth Genre
Fourth River
Fractured Lit
Frontiers: A Journal of Women Studies
Fugue
Gallimaufry
Genre

The Georgia Review
Gettysburg Review
Ghost Dance
Glacier Journal
Glassworks
Gibbs-Smith
Glimmer Train
Goddard Journal
David Godine, Publisher
Gordon Square
Graham House Press
Grain
Grand Street
Granta
Graywolf Press
Great River Review
Green Mountains Review
Greenfield Review
Greensboro Review
Guardian Press
Gulf Coast
Hanging Loose
Harbour Publishing
Hard Pressed
Harvard Advocate
Harvard Review
Hawaii Pacific Review
Hayden's Ferry Review
Here
Hermitage Press
Heyday
Hills
Hobart
Hole in the Head
Hollyridge Press
Holmgangers Press
Holy Cow!
Home Planet News
Hopkins Review
Hudson Review
Hunger Mountain
Hungry Mind Review
Hysterical Rag
Iamb

Ibbetson Street Press
Icarus
Icon
Idaho Review
Iguana Press
Image
In Character
Indiana Review
Indiana Writes
Indianapolis Review
Intermedia
Intro
Invisible City
Inwood Press
Iowa Review
Ironwood
I-70 Review
Jam To-day
Jewish Fiction
J Journal
The Journal
Jubilat
The Kanchenjunga Press
Kansas Quarterly
Kayak
Kelsey Street Press
Kenyon Review
Kestrel
Kweli Journal
Lake Effect
Lana Turner
Latitudes Press
Laughing Waters Press
Laurel Poetry Collective
Laurel Review
Leap Frog
L'Epervier Press
Liberation
Ligeia
Light
Linquis
Literal Latté
Literary Imagination
The Literary Review

O. Blk
Obsidian
Obsidian II
Ocho
Oconee Review
October
Ohio Review
Old Crow Review
Ontario Review
Open City
Open Places
Orca Press
Orchises Press
Oregon Humanities
Orion
Other Voices
Oxford American
Oxford Press
Oyez Press
Oyster Boy Review
Painted Bride Quarterly
Painted Hills Review
Palette
Palo Alto Review
Paper Darts
Parentheses Journal
Paris Press
Paris Review
Parkett
Parnassus: Poetry in Review
Partisan Review
Passages North
Paterson Literary Review
Pebble Lake Review
Penca Books
Pentagram
Penumbra Press
Pequod
Persea: An International Review
Perugia Press
Per Contra
Pilot Light
The Pinch
Pipedream Press

Pirene's Fountain
Pitcairn Press
Pitt Magazine
Pleasure Boat Studio
Pleiades
Ploughshares
Plume
Poem-A-Day
Poems & Plays
Poet and Critic
Poet Lore
Poetry
Poetry Atlanta Press
Poetry East
Poetry International
Poetry Ireland Review
Poetry Northwest
Poetry Now
The Point
Post Road
Prairie Schooner
Prelude
Prescott Street Press
Press
Prime Number
Prism
Promise of Learnings
Provincetown Arts
A Public Space
Puerto Del Sol
Purple Passion Press
Quademi Di Yip
Quarry West
The Quarterly
Quarterly West
Quiddity
Radio Silence
Rainbow Press
Raritan: A Quarterly Review
Rattle
Red Cedar Review
Red Clay Books
Red Dust Press
Red Earth Press

474

Red Hen Press

Reed

Release Press

Republic of Letters

Review of Contemporary Fiction

Revista Chicano-Riqueña

Rhetoric Review

Rhino

Rivendell

River Heron

River Styx

River Teeth

Rowan Tree Press

Ruminate

Runes

Russian *Samizdat*

Saginaw

Salamander

Salmagundi

Salt Hill Journal

San Marcos Press

Santa Monica Review

Sarabande Books

Saturnalia

Sea Pen Press and Paper Mill

Seal Press

Seamark Press

Seattle Review

Second Coming Press

Semiotext(e)

Seneca Review

Seven Days

The Seventies Press

Sewanee Review

The Shade Journal

Shankpainter

Shantih

Shearsman

Sheep Meadow Press

Shenandoah

A Shout In the Street

Sibyl-Child Press

Side Show

Sidereal

Sixth Finch

Slipstream

Small Moon

Smartish Pace

The Smith

Snake Nation Review

Solo

Solo 2

Some

The Sonora Review

Southeast Review

Southern Indiana Review

Southern Poetry Review

Southern Review

Southampton Review

Southwest Review

Speakeasy

Spectrum

Spillway

Spork

The Spirit That Moves Us

St. Andrews Press

St. Brigid Press

Stillhouse Press

Stonecoast

Storm Cellar

Story

Story Quarterly

Streetfare Journal

Stuart Wright, Publisher

Subtropics

Sugar House Review

Sulfur

Summerset Review

The Sun

Sun & Moon Press

Sun Press

Sundog Lit.

Sunstone

Swamp Pink

Sweet

Sycamore Review

Tab

Tamagawa

Tar River Poetry
Teal Press
Telephone Books
Telescope
Temblor
The Temple
Tendril
Terrain
Terminus
Terrapin Books
Texas Slough
Think
Third Coast
13th Moon
THIS
This Broken Shore
Thorp Springs Press
Three Rivers Press
Threepenny Review
Thrush
Thunder City Press
Thunder's Mouth Press
Tia Chucha Press
Tiger Bark Press
Tikkun
Tin House
Tipton Review
Tombouctou Books
Toothpaste Press
Torch
Transatlantic Review
Treelight
Triplopia
TriQuarterly
Truck Press
True Story
Tule Review
Tupelo Review
Turnrow
Tusculum Review
Two Sylvias
Twyckenham Notes
Undine
Unicorn Press

University of Chicago Press
University of Georgia Press
University of Illinois Press
University of Iowa Press
University of Massachusetts Press
University of North Texas Press
University of Pittsburgh Press
University of Wisconsin Press
University Press of New England
Unmuzzled Ox
Unspeakable Visions of the Individual
Vagabond
Vallum
Verse
Verse Wisconsin
Vignette
Virginia Quarterly Review
Volt
The Volta
Wampeter Press
War, Literature & The Arts
Washington Square Review
Washington Writer's Workshop
Water-Stone
Water Table
Wave Books
Waxwing
West Branch
Western Humanities Review
Westigan Review
White Pine Press
Wickwire Press
Wigleaf
Willow Springs
Wilmore City
Witness
Word Beat Press
Word Press
Wordsmith
World Literature Today
WordTemple Press
Wormwood Review
Writers' Forum
Xanadu

Yale Review
Yardbird Reader
Yarrow
Y-Bird
Yes Yes Books

Zeitgeist Press
Zephyr
Zoetrope: All-Story
Zone 3
ZYZZYVA

THE PUSHCART PRIZE FELLOWSHIPS

The Pushcart Prize Fellowships Inc., a 501 (c) (3) nonprofit corporation, is the endowment for The Pushcart Prize. "Members" donated up to $249 each. "Sponsors" gave between $250 and $999. "Benefactors" donated from $1000 to $4,999. "Patrons" donated $5,000 and more. We are very grateful for these donations. Gifts of any amount are welcome. For information write to the Fellowships at PO Box 380, Wainscott, NY 11975.

Founding Patrons

Michael and Elizabeth R. Rea
The Katherine Anne Porter Literary Trust

Patrons

Anonymous
Margaret Ajemian Ahnert
Daniel L. Dolgin & Loraine F. Gardner
James Patterson Foundation
Neltje
John Sargent
Charline Spektor
Ellen M. Violett

BENEFACTORS

Anonymous
Russell Allen
Barbara Ascher & Strobe Talbott
Hilaria & Alec Baldwin
David Caldwell
Ted Conklin
Bernard F. Conners
Richie Crown
Cartherine and C. Bryan Daniels
Maureen Mahon Egen

Dallas Ernst
Cedering Fox
H.E. Francis
Diane Glynn
Mary Ann Goodman & Bruno Quinson Foundation
Bill & Genie Henderson
Bob Henderson
Marina & Stephen E. Kaufman
Wally & Christine Lamb
Dorothy Lichtenstein

480

Nelson DeMille
E. L. Doctorow
Penny Dunning
Karl Elder
Donald Finkel
Ben and Sharon Fountain
Alan and Karen Furst
John Gill
Robert Giron
Beth Gutcheon
Doris Grumbach & Sybil Pike
Gwen Head
The Healing Muse
Robin Hemley
Bob Hicok
Hippocampus
Jane Hirshfield
Helen & Frank Houghton
Joseph Hurka
Christian Jara
Diane Johnson
Janklow & Nesbit Asso.
Edmund Keeley
Thomas E. Kennedy
Sydney Lea
Stephen Lesser
Gerald Locklin

Thomas Lux
Markowitz, Fenelon and Bank
Elizabeth McKenzie
McSweeney's
Rick Moody
John Mullen
Joan Murray
Thomas Paine
Barbara and Warren Phillips
Hilda Raz
Stacey Richter
Diane Rudner
Schaffner Family Foundation
Sharasheff—Johnson Fund
Cindy Sherman
Joyce Carol Smith
May Carlton Swope
Andrew Tonkovich
Glyn Vincent
Julia Wendell
Philip White
Diane Williams
Kirby E. Williams
Eleanor Wilner
David Wittman
Richard Wyatt & Irene Eilers

Members

Anonymous (3)
Stephen Adams
Betty Adcock
Agni
Carolyn Alessio
Dick Allen
Henry H. Allen
John Allman
Lisa Alvarez
Jan Lee Ande
Dr. Russell Anderson
Ralph Angel
Antietam Review
Susan Antolin
Ruth Appelhof
Philip and Marjorie Appleman
Linda Aschbrenner
Renee Ashley
Ausable Press
David Baker
Catherine Barnett
Dorothy Barresi
Barlow Street Press
Jill Bart
Ellen Bass
Judith Baumel

Ann Beattie
Madison Smartt Bell
Beloit Poetry Journal
Pinckney Benedict
Karen Bender
Andre Bernard
Christopher Bernard
Wendell Berry
Linda Bierds
Stacy Bierlein
Big Fiction
Bitter Oleander Press
Mark Blaeuer
John Blondel
Blue Light Press
Carol Bly
BOA Editions
Deborah Bogen
Bomb
Susan Bono
Brain Child
Anthony Brandt
James Breeden
Rosellen Brown
Jane Brox
Andrea Hollander Budy

E. S. Bumas
Richard Burgin
Skylar H. Burris
David Caligiuri
Kathy Callaway
Bonnie Jo Campbell
Janine Canan
Henry Carlile
Carrick Publishing
Fran Castan
Mary Casey
Chelsea Associates
Marianne Cherry
Phillis M. Choyke
Lucinda Clark
Suzanne Cleary
Linda Coleman
Martha Collins
Ted Conklin
Joan Connor
J. Cooper
John Copenhaver
Dan Corrie
Pam Cothey
Lisa Couturier
Tricia Currans-Sheehan
Jim Daniels
Daniel & Daniel
Jerry Danielson
Ed David
Josephine David
Thadious Davis
Michael Denison
Maija Devine
Sharon Dilworth
Edward DiMaio
Kent Dixon
A.C. Dorset
Jack Driscoll
Wendy Druce
Penny Dunning
John Duncklee
Nancy Ebert
Elaine Edelman
Renee Edison & Don Kaplan
Nancy Edwards
Ekphrasis Press
M.D. Elevitch
Elizabeth Ellen
Entrekin Foundation
Failbetter.com
Irvin Faust
Elliot Figman
Tom Filer
Carol and Laueme Firth
Finishing Line Press

Susan Firer
Nick Flynn
Starkey Flythe Jr.
Peter Fogo
Linda Foster
Fourth Genre
Alice Friman
John Fulton
Fugue
Alice Fulton
Alan Furst
Eugene Garber
Frank X. Gaspar
A Gathering of the Tribes
Reginald Gibbons
Emily Fox Gordon
Philip Graham
Eamon Grennan
Myrna Goodman
Ginko Tree Press
Jessica Graustain
Lee Meitzen Grue
Habit of Rainy Nights
Rachel Hadas
Susan Hahn
Meredith Hall
Harp Strings
Jeffrey Harrison
Clarinda Harriss
Lois Marie Harrod
Healing Muse
Tim Hedges
Michele Helm
Alex Henderson
Lily Henderson
Daniel Henry
Neva Herington
Lou Hertz
Stephen Herz
William Heyen
Bob Hicok
R. C. Hildebrandt
Kathleen Hill
Lee Hinton
Jane Hirshfield
Hippocampus Magazin
Edward Hoagland
Daniel Hoffman
Doug Holder
Richard Holinger
Rochelle L. Holt
Richard M. Huber
Brigid Hughes
Lynne Hugo
Karla Huston
1–70 Review

Iliya's Honey
Susan Indigo
Mark Irwin
Beverly A. Jackson
Richard Jackson
Christian Jara
David Jauss
Marilyn Johnston
Alice Jones
Journal of New Jersey Poets
Robert Kalich
Sophia Kartsonis
Julia Kasdorf
Miriam Polli Katsikis
Meg Kearney
Celine Keating
Brigit Kelly
John Kistner
Judith Kitchen
Ron Koertge
Stephen Kopel
Peter Krass
David Kresh
Maxine Kumin
Valerie Laken
Babs Lakey
Linda Lancione
Maxine Landis
Lane Larson
Dorianne Laux & Joseph Millar
Sydney Lea
Stephen Lesser
Donald Lev
Dana Levin
Live Mag!
Gerald Locklin
Rachel Loden
Radomir Luza, Jr.
William Lychack
Annette Lynch
Elzabeth MacKieman
Elizabeth Macklin
Leah Maines
Mark Manalang
Norma Marder
Jack Marshall
Michael Martone
Tara L. Masih
Dan Masterson
Peter Matthiessen
Maria Matthiessen
Alice Mattison
Tracy Mayor
Robert McBrearty
Jane McCafferty
Rebecca McClanahan

Bob McCrane
Jo McDougall
Sandy McIntosh
James McKean
Roberta Mendel
Didi Menendez
Barbara Milton
Alexander Mindt
Mississippi Review
Nancy Mitchell
Martin Mitchell
Roger Mitchell
Jewell Mogan
Patricia Monaghan
Jim Moore
James Morse
William Mulvihill
Nami Mun
Joan Murray
Carol Muske-Dukes
Edward Mycue
Deirdre Neilen
W. Dale Nelson
New Michigan Press
Jean Nordhaus
Celeste Ng
Christiana Norcross
Ontario Review Foundation
Daniel Orozco
Other Voices
Paris Review
Alan Michael Parker
Ellen Parker
Veronica Patterson
David Pearce, M.D.
Robert Phillips
Donald Platt
Plain View Press
Valerie Polichar
Pool
Horatio Potter
Jeffrey & Priscilla Potter
C.E. Poverman
Marcia Preston
Eric Puchner
Osiris
Tony Quagliano
Quill & Parchment
Barbara Quinn
Randy Rader
Juliana Rew
Belle Randall
Martha Rhodes
Nancy Richard
Stacey Richter
James Reiss

Katrina Roberts
Judith R. Robinson
Jessica Roeder
Martin Rosner
Kay Ryan
Sy Safransky
Brian Salchert
James Salter
Sherod Santos
Ellen Sargent
R.A. Sasaki
Valerie Sayers
Maxine Scates
Alice Schell
Dennis & Loretta Schmitz
Grace Schulman
Helen Schulman
Philip Schultz
Shenandoah
Peggy Shinner
Lydia Ship
Vivian Shipley
Joan Silver
Skyline
John E. Smeleer
Raymond J. Smith
Joyce Carol Smith
Philip St. Clair
Lorraine Standish
Maureen Stanton
Michael Steinberg
Sybil Steinberg
Jody Stewart
Barbara Stone
Storyteller Magazine
Bill & Pat Strachan
Raymond Strom
Julie Suk
Summerset Review
Sun Publishing
Sweet Annie Press
Katherine Taylor
Pamela Taylor
Elaine Terranova
Susan Terris
Marcelle Thiebaux
Robert Thomas
Donna Talarico

Andrew Tonkovich
Pauls Toutonghi
Juanita Torrence-Thompson
William Trowbridge
Martin Tucker
Umbrella Factory Press
Under The Sun
Universal Table
Upstreet
Jeannette Valentine
Victoria Valentine
Christine Van Winkle
Hans Vandebovenkamp
Elizabeth Veach
Tino Villanueva
Maryfrances Wagner
William & Jeanne Wagner
BJ Ward
Susan O. Warner
Rosanna Warren
Margareta Waterman
Michael Waters
Stuart Watson
Sandi Weinberg
Andrew Wainstein
Dr. Henny Wenkart
Jason Wesco
West Meadow Press
Susan Wheeler
Mary Frances Wagner
When Women Waken
Dara Wier
Ellen Wilbur
Galen Williams
Diane Williams
Marie Sheppard Williams
Eleanor Wilner
Irene Wilson
Steven Wingate
Sandra Wisenberg
Wings Press
Robert Witt
David Wittman
Margot Wizansky
Matt Yurdana
Christina Zawadiwsky
Sander Zulauf
ZYZZYVA

CONTRIBUTING SMALL PRESSES FOR PUSHCART PRIZE XLVIII

(These presses made nominations for this edition.)

Abalone Mountain Press, 906 W. Roosevelt St., #3, Phoenix, AZ 85007

Abandon Journal, 8911 N. Capital of Texas Hwy, #4200-067, Austin, TX 78759

Abandoned Mine, PO Box 3782, Albuquerque, NM 87190

About Place Journal, 4520 Blue Mounds Trl, Black Earth, WI 53515-0424

Abstract Magazine TV, 124 E. Johnson St., Norman, OK 73069

Abyss & Apex, 116 Tennyson Dr., Lexington, SC 29073

Academic Studies Press, 1577 Beacon St., Brookline, MA 02446-4602

Acorn, 115 Connifer Ln, Walnut Creek, CA 94598

Acumen Literary Journal, 4 Thornhill Bridge Wharf, London N1 0RU, UK

ADI Magazine, 101 Martini Dr., Richmond Hill, ON L4S, 2S5, Canada

Admission Press, 12600 West Glen Court, Choctaw. OK 73020

The Adroit Journal, 1223 Westover Rd., Stamford, CT 06902

Aeon, C.A. McKean, Level 5, 100 Flinders St., Melbourne VIC 3000, Australia

After . . ., M. Owen, 57 Thorpe Gardens, Alton, Hampshire GU34 2BQ, UK

After Dinner Conversations, K. Granville, 2516 S. Jentilly Ln, Tempe, AZ 85282

After Happy Hour Review, 599 Blessing St, Pittsburgh, PA 15213

After the Art, RB Noble, 3000 Connecticut Ave. NW, #233, Washington, DC 20008

Agni Magazine, Boston Univ., 236 Bay State Rd., Boston, MA 02215

Airlie Press, PO Box 13325, Portland, OR 97213

Air/Light, English Dept., USC-Dornsife, 3501 Trousdale Pkwy, Los Angeles, CA 90089-0354

Aji Magazine, 414 N. Mesa Dr., Carlsbad, NM 88220

Alaska Quarterly, ESH 208, 3211 Providence Dr., Anchorage, AK 99508

Alaska Women Speak, PO Box 90475, Anchorage, AK 99509

Alice Greene & Co, PO Box 7406, Ann Arbor, MI 48107-7406

Alice James, Auburn Hall, 60 Pineland Dr., Ste 206, New Gloucester, ME 04260

Alien Buddha Press, 330 Mitchell St., Spartanburg, SC 29307

All You Need Productions, 1189 Laurel Ave., St. Paul, MN 55104

All-Story/Zoetrope, 916 Kearny St., San Francisco, CA 94133

Allbooks, PO Box 562, Selden NY 11784

Allium Journal, Columbia College, 600 So. Michigan Ave., Chicago, IL 60605

Alocasia, 218 N. 10ᵗʰ St., #3R, Philadelphia, PA 19107

Alta Journal, PO Box 14666, San Francisco, CA 94114-0666

Alternating Current, PO Box 270921, Louisville, CO 80027

American Diversity Press, 3624 Cline Rd., Chattanooga, TN 37412

American Literary Review, English, University of North Texas, 1401 W. Hickory St., Denton, TX 76201

American Poetry Review, 1906 Rittenhouse Sq., 3ʳᵈ FL, Philadelphia, PA 19103-5735

American Scholar, 1606 New Hampshire Ave. NW, Washington, DC 20009

American Short Fiction, PO Box 4152, Austin, TX 78765

Anhinga Press, PO Box 3665, Tallahassee, FL 32315

Animal Heart Press, Gordon, 300 Long Shoals Rd., #17-O, Arden, NC 28704-7764

Another Chicago Magazine, 1301 W. Byron St., Chicago, IL 60613

Apex Magazine, 318 Shore Club Dr., St. Clair Shores, MI 48080

Appalachia Journal, Woodside, 41 Bridge St., Deep River, CT 06417

Appalachian Heritage, Shepherd Univ., PO Box 5000, Shepherdstown, WV 25443

Appalachian Review, Berea College, CPO 2166, Berea, KY 40404

Apparition Literary, Robinson, 1220 Johnson Dr., #81, Ventura, CA 93003

Apple Valley Review, 88 South 3ʳᵈ St., #336, San José, CA 95113

Apricity Press, Mason-Reader, 3279 Coraly Ave., Eugene, OR 97402

April Gloaming, 4969 Algonquin Trail, Nashville, TN 37013

Arachne Press, 100 Grierson Rd., London SE23 1NX, UK

Archetype, 106 Earl Place, Toronto, ON M4Y 3B9, Canada

Ariel Chart Int'l Journal, 227 Laurel Landing Blvd., Kingsland, GA 31548-6185

Arizona Authors, 1119 E. LeMarche Ave., Phoenix, AZ 85022-3136

Arkana, UCA, Thompson Hall 324, 201 Donaghey Ave., Conway, AR 72035

Arrowsmith Press, 11 Chestnut St., Medford, MA 02155

Arteidolia Press, 1870 Cornelia St., Ridgeway, NY 11385

Arts & Letters, CBX 89, Georgia College, Milledgeville, GA 31061-0490

Ashland Creek Press, 2305 Ashland St., Ste. C417, Ashland, OR 97520

ASP, H. Grieco, 3009 N. Edison St., Arlington, VA 22207-1806

Aster(ix), Cruz, English, Univ. Pittsburgh, 4200 Fifth Ave., Pittsburgh, PA 15260

Atmosphere Press, 7107 Foxtree Cove, Austin, TX 78750

Atticus Review, K. Short, 973 E. 8ᵗʰ Ave., #2, Spokane, WA 99209

AutoEthnographer, 2200 NE 16ᵗʰ Ct. Fort Lauderdale, FL 33305

Autumn House Press, 5530 Penn Ave., Pittsburgh, PA 15206

Autumn Sky Poetry Daily, 5263 Arctic Circle, Emmaus, PA 18049

Awakenings, 4001 N. Ravenswood Ave., #204-C, Chicago, IL 60613-2434

Awst Press, PO Box 49163, Austin, TX 78765

Axon, Atherton, 601/341 Ascot Vale Rd., Moonee Ponds, VIC, Australia

Balance of Seven, 917 Stone Trail Dr., Plano, TX 75023-7109

Banyan Review, 1832 Brantley St., Winston-Salem, NC 27103

Barzakh, C. Syrewicz, English-HU 374, SUNY, 1400 Washington Ave., Albany, NY 12222

Bat City Review, English-UT, 204 W. 21st St., B5000, Austin, TX 78712-1164

Bay to Ocean Journal, PO Box 1773, Easton, MD 21601

Bayou Magazine, UNO-English, 2000 Lake Shore Dr., New Orleans, LA 70148

BC3, 250 Executive Drive, Cranberry Township, PA 16066

Bear Review, 4211 Holmes St., Kansas City, MO 64110

Bee Infinite Publishing, 2045 S. Oxford Ave., Los Angeles, CA 90018-1530

beestung, 218 N. 10th St., #3R, Philadelphia, PA 19107

Beir Bua Press, Co. Tipperary, Ireland (www.beirbuapress.com)

Bell Press, 202-1622 Frances St., Vancouver, BC V5L 1Z4, Canada

Belle Point Press, Dodd, 1121 North 56th Terrace, Fort Smith, AR 72904

Bellevue Literary Review, 149 East 23rd St., #1516, New York, NY 10010

Belmont Story Review, 1900 Belmont Blvd., Nashville, IN 37212-3757

Beloit Poetry Journal, PO Box 1450, Windham, ME 04062

Beltway Poetry Quarterly, PO Box 605, Washington Grove, MD 20880

Bennington Review, 1 College Dr., Bennington, VT 05201

Bent Key, 36 Owley Wood Rd., Cheshire CW8 3LF UK

Better Than Starbucks, O Park St, PO Box 673, Mayo, FL 32066

Beyond Words, (Inh. Gal Slonim) Hermannstr. 230, 12049 Berlin, Germany

BHC Press, 885 Penniman #5505, Plymouth, MI 48170

Big City LIt,, Cappelluti, 85 Creek Rd., Middlebury, VT 05753

Big Other, 1840 W. 3rd St., Brooklyn, NY 11223

Big Table, 632 Santana Rd., Novato, CA 94945

Big Windows, English-LA355, Washtenaw Community College, 4800 East Huron River Drive, Ann Arbor, MI 48105-4800

bioStories, 225 Log Yard Ct, Bigfork, MT 59911

Birmingham Poetry Review, English, UAB, 1720 2nd Ave. S., Birmingham, AL 35294-0110

BkMk Press, 5 W 3rd St., Parkville, MO 64152-3707

Black Lawrence Press, Goettel, 279 Claremont Ave., Mt. Vernon, NY 10552-3305

BlacKat Publishing, 18835 Curtis, Detroit, MI 48219

Blackbird, VCU, English, PO Box 843082, Richmond, VA 23284-3082

Blackwater Press, 120 Capitol St., Charleston, WV 25301-2610

BlazeVOX, 131 Euclid Ave., Kenmore, NY 14217

Blink-Ink, P.O. Box 5, North Branford, CT 06471

Blood Orange Review, WSU, English, Box 645020, Pullman, WA 99164-5020

Blue Bone Books, PO Box 2250, Santa Cruz, CA 95063-2250

Blue Cactus, 3910 N. 28th St., #512, Tacoma, WA 98407

Blue Heron Review, N66W38350 Deer Creek Ct., Oconomowoc, WI 53066

Blue Light Press, PO Box 150300, San Rafael, CA 94915

Blue Unicorn, 13 Jefferson Ave., San Rafael, CA 94903

Bluestem, EIU, 600 Lincoln Ave., Charleston, IL 61920

Bodega Magazine, 451 Court St., #3R, Brooklyn, NY 11231

Boiler Journal, 7547 Quiet Pond Place, Colorado Springs, CO, 80923

Bomb, 80 Hanson Pl, Brooklyn, NY 11217-1506

Book Post, 291 14th St, Brooklyn, NY 11215

Boomer Lit, 4509 Beard Ave So., Minneapolis, MN 55410

Booth, 4600 Sunset Ave., Indianapolis, IN 46208

Borda Books, 264 Santa Monica Way, Santa Barbara, CA 93109

Border Crossing, Creative Writing, 650 W. Easterday Ave., Sault Ste. Marie, MI 49783

Bottom Dog Press/Bird Dog Publishing, PO Box 425, Huron, OH 44839

Boulevard, 3829 Hartford St., St. Louis, MO 63116

Bourgeon Press, 1200 S. Courthouse Rd., #607, Arlington, VA 22204

Braided Way, 8916 Shank Rd., Litchfield, OH 44253

Breakwater Books, 1 Stamps Lane, St. John's NL, A1E 3C9, Canada

Breath and Shadow, Kuell, 12 Pleasant St., Danbury, CT 06810

Briar Cliff Review, 3303 Rebecca St., Sioux City, IA 51104-2100

Brick, A. LaSorda, 784 College St., Toronto, ON M6G 1C6

Brick Road Poetry Press, 341 Lee Rd. 553, Phenix City, AL 36867

Bright Flash Literary Review, 12520 Caswell Ave., Los Angeles, CA 90066

Brilliant Flash Fiction, 142 Capetown Court, #106, Weaverville, NC 28787

Brink Literary Journal, 450 Hwy 1W, #126, Iowa City, IA 52246

Broadkill Review, 25624 E. Main, Onley, VA 23418

Broadsided Press, PO Box 24, Provincetown, MA 02657

Broadstone Books, 418 Ann St., Frankfort, KY 40601-1929

Broken Spine, 32 St. Thomas More Drive, Southport, Merseyside, PR8 3FG, UK

Brooklyn Poets, 144 Montague St., 2nd Fl, Brooklyn, NY 11201

Brownstone Poets, Carragon, 8785 Bay 16th St/. #B-8, Brooklyn, NY 11214

Cable Creek Publishing, 12666 German Church St. N.E., Alliance, OH 44601-9505

Café Irreal, PO Box 87031, Tucson, AZ 85754

California Quarterly, CA State Poetry Society, PO Box 4288, Sunland, CA 91041

Capsule Stories, PO Box 11762, Clayton, MO 63105-0562

Carmel Creative Writers, R. Freedman, 15285 Cherry Tree Rd., Noblesville, IN 46062

Carousel, Laliberte, 1851 Oneida Court, Windsor, ON N8Y 1S9, Canada

Catamaran, 1050 River St., #118, Santa Cruz, CA 95060

CatsCast, 521 River Ave., Providence, RI 02908

Cave Wall Press, PO Box 29546, Greensboro 27429-9546

Central Conference of American Rabbis, 355 Lexington Ave., 8th FL, New York, NY 10017-6603

Červená Barva Press, PO Box 440357, W. Somerville, MA 02144-3222

Chamber Magazine, 1623 Old Post Rd, Gillett. AR 72055

Chaotic Merge Magazine, 1793 Amsterdam Ave., #12, New York, NY 10031

Chatwin Books, 735 S 4th St. W, Missoula, MT 59801

Chautauqua, UNC-W, Creative Writing, 601 S. College Rd., Wilmington, NC 28403

Cheap Pop, Russell, 801 O St., #260, Lincoln, NE 68508

Chestnut Review, 213 N. Tioga St., #6751, Ithaca, NY 14850

Chicago Quarterly Review, Haider, 517 Sherman Ave., Evanston, IL 60202

Chiron Review, 522 E. South Ave., St. John, KS 67576-2212

Choeofpleirn Press, 1424 Franklin St., Leavenworth, KS 66048

Cholla Needles, 6732 Conejo Ave., Joshua Tree, CA 92252

Cincinnati Review, English, PO Box 210069, Cincinnati, OH 45221-0069

Circling Rivers, PO Box 8291, Richmond, VA 23226-0291

Cirque Press, 3157 Bettles Bay Loop, Anchorage, AK 99515

Cloaca Mag, 13902 Bermuda Beach Dr., Galveston, TX 77554

Close to the Edge Books, Archbrook, Teignharvey, Devon, TQ12 4RS, UK

Cloudbank Books, PO Box 610, Corvallis, OR 97339-0610

Cloves, A. Barrios, 49 Winchester St., #1, Brookline, MA 02446

Coachella Review, UCR Palm Desert, 75080 Frank Sinatra Dr., Palm Desert, CA 92211

Coal City Review, English Dept., University of Kansas, Lawrence, KS 66045

Coastal Shelf, 3306 Country Club Dr, Grand Prairie, TX 75052

Codhill Press, 420 East 23rd St., #3H, New York, NY 10010

Coffin Bell Journal, 11950 Clifton Rd., Savannah, TN 38372

Cold Moon, Jacobson, 405 S. Jefferson Way, Indianola, IA 50125

Cold Mountain Review, Appalachian State-English, 225 Locust St., Boone, NC 28608

Cold Signal Magazine, 110 N. Arthur Ashe Blvd, Richmond, VA 23220

Collapse Press, 324 Kitty Hawk Rd., #101, Alameda, CA 94501

Collateral Journal, 7710 Newcastle Dr., Annandale, VA 22003

Colorado Review, CSU, English, Fort Collins, CO 80523-9105

The Common, Frost Library, Amherst College, Amherst, MA 01002-5000

COMP, Creative Writing, Piedmont Univ., 170 Ridgewood Way, Athens, GA 30605

Complete Sentence, J. Thayer, PO Box 92, Tolovana Park, OR 97110

Comstock Review, English, Univ. of Wisconsin, 800 Algoma Blvd., Oshkosh, WI 54901

Concho River Review, ASU Station #10894, San Angelo TX 76909-0894

Concrete Desert Review, CSUSB-PDC, 37-500 Cook St., Palm Desert, CA 92211

Conduit Books & Ephemera, 788 Osceola Ave., St. Paul, MN 55105

Conjunctions, Bard College, Annandale, NY 12504-5000

Connecticut River Review, 9 Edmund Pl, West Hartford, CT 06119

Consequence Forum, PO Box 371820, Las Vegas, NV 89137

Constellations, 127 Lake View Ave., Cambridge, MA 02138-3366

Contrary Journal, S. Beers, 615 NW 6th St., Pendleton, OR 97801-1317

Copper Nickel, UC-D, English - CB 175, PO Box 173364, Denver, CO 80217-3364

Crab Creek Review, 2027 NW 60th St., Seattle, WA 98107

Crazyhorse, College of Charleston, 66 George St., Charleston, SC 29424

Creative Nonfiction, 5877 Commerce St., Pittsburgh, PA 15206-3835

Cultural Daily, 3330 S. Peck Ave., #14, San Pedro, CA 90731

Current, English, Covenant College, 14049 Scenic Hwy, Lookout Mountain, GA 30750

Cutbank, Univ. of Montana, English, LA 133, MST410, Missoula, MT 59812

Cutleaf Journal, Lesmeister, 922 Pleasant Ave., Decorah, IA 52101

Cutthroat, 5401 N. Cresta Loma Dr., Tucson, AZ 85704

Dashboard Horus, M. Lecrivain, 6028 Comey Ave., Los Angeles, CA 90034

Deadlands, Markey, 2108 Foster Hill Rd, #1, East Calais, VT 05650

december, P.O. Box 16130, St. Louis, MO 63105-0830

Decolonial Passage, PO Box 35238, Los Angeles, CA 90035

Deep Wild Journal, 2309 Broadway, Grand Junction, CO 81507

Delmarva Review, PO Box 544, St. Michaels, MD 21663

Denver Quarterly, English, Univ. of Denver, 495 Sturm Hall, Denver, CO 80208

descant, Texas Christina University, bTCU Box 297270, Fort Worth, TX 76129

Diálogos Books, 3216 Saint Philip St., New Orleans, LA 70119

Diet Milk Magazine, 304 Druid St., High Point, NC 27265

Dipity Literary Magazine, 403 Pyramid St., Henderson, NV 89014

Disappointed Housewife, 2819 Cauchoo Ct., Cool, CA 95614

Divot Lit, 950 Seminole Woods Blvd., Geneva, FL 32732-9316

DMQ Review, 16393 Bonnie Lane, Los Gatos, CA 95032

The Dodge, College of Wooster, 1189 Beall Ave., Wooster, OH 44691

Double Dagger Books, 61 Waverly Rd., Toronto, ON M4L 3T2, Canada

Double Yolk, 3439 Hudson Hills Lane, Mason, OH 45040

Doubly Mad, Other Side, 2011 Genesee St., Utica, NY 13501

Down and Out Books, 1139 E. Ocean Blvd., #105, Long Beach, CA 90802

Dread Machine, 43 Lexington Rd., Avon, CT 06001-2958

Dream Boy Book Club., 402 E. Chestnut St., #2W, Bloomington, IL 61701-3160

Dreich, 45 Whitelaw Rd., Dunfermline, Fife, Scotland KY11 4BN, UK

Dribble Drabble Review, 43 Twelve Oaks Dr., Murphysboro, IL 62966

Driftwood Press, 14737 Montoro Dr., Austin, TX 78728

Drunk Monkeys, 252 N Cordova St., Burbank, CA 91505

Dunes Review, T. Scollon, 437 Hamilton St., Traverse City, MI 49686

earth love press, 58 Colinslee Dr., Paisley, Renfrewshire, PA2 6QS, UK

EastOver Press, Lesmeister, 922 Pleasant Ave., Decorah, IA 52101

EastWest Literary Forum, 19-22 22 Rd., Long Island City, NY 11105

Eccentric Orbits, 1882 N. Garland Lane, Anaheim, CA 92807

ecotone, UNC Wilmington, 601 S. College Rd., Wilmington, NC 28403

ECW Press, 665 Gerrard St. East, Toronto, ON M4M 1Y2, Canada

Eggplant Emoji, J. Martin, 1753 Old York Rd., Warminster, PA 18974

EGW Publishing, 3308 Selby Lane, Modesto, CA 95355

805 Lit & Art, S. Katz, 507 Bayview Dr., Holmes Beach, FL 34217

8th and Atlas Publishing, M. deParis, 911 Walnut St., Winston-Salem, NC 27101

86 Logic, 3621 30th St., #3, Astoria, New York, NY 11106

Ekphrastic Review, 1085 Steeles Ave. W., Ste. 1505, Toronto, ON M2R 2T1, Canada

Electric Literature, PO Box 1211, Kingston, NY 12402

Elegant Literature, Martens, 10410 Gary Rd, Rockville, MD 20854

ELJ Editions, PO Box 815, Washingtonville, NY 10992

Elyssar Press, Redlands, CA 92373

Emergence, S. Quinn, PO Box 1164, Inverness, CA 94937

Emerson Review, Emerson College, 120 Boylston St., Boston, MA 02116

Epiphany, 71 Bedford St., New York, NY 10014

Epoch, 251 Goldwin Smith Hall, Cornell University, Ithaca NY 14853

Escape Into Life, K. Kirk, 108 Gladys Dr., Normal, IL 61761

Essay Press, 1106 Bay Ridge Ave., Annapolis, MD 21403-2902

Essential Dreams Press, 33 Autumn Drive, Northampton, MA 01062

Etcetera Poetry, Naughton, 1817 Parker St, Vancouver BC V5L 2L1, Canada

Evergreen Review, 130 W. 24th St., #5A, New York, NY 10011

Evocations Review, PO Box 293, Tiverton, RI 02878

Exit 7, B. Shurley, 4810 Alben Barkley Dr., Paducah, KY 42001

Exit Studio, 1466 N. Quinn St., Arlington, VA 22209

Exit 13, 22 Oakwood Ct., Fanwood, NJ 07023-1162

Experiments in Fiction, 9 Waterside House, Carlisle CA2 5HF, UK

Exposition Review, PO Box 48542 Los Angeles, CA 90048

Eye to the Telescope, PO Box 6688, Portland, OR 97228

The Fabulist Magazine, 1377 5th Ave., San Francisco, CA 94122

failbetter, 2022 Grove Ave., Richmond, VA 23220

Fairy Tale Review, English Dept., Univ. of Arizona, Tucson, AZ 85721

Faith Journey, 3112 Arrowwood Dr., Raleigh, NC 27604

Fantasy Magazine, Sorg c/o Locus, 655 13th St., #100, Oakland, CA 94612

Farmer-ish, 302 Davis Rd., Eddington, ME 04428

Fatal Flaw, 122 E. 17th St., #3F, New York, NY 10003

Faultline, UCI-English, 435 Humanities Bldg., Irvine, CA 92697

Fauxmoir Lit Mag, 810 W. Clinch Ave., 5th Fl, #4, Knoxville, TN 37902

Feels Blind Literary, 603 S. Paca St., Baltimore, MD 21230

Fernwood Press, PO Box 751, Newberg, OR 97132-0751

Fiction International, SDSU, English, 5500 Campanile Dr. San Diego, CA 92182-6020

Fiction on the Web, C. Fish, 121 Leigham Vale, London SW2 3JH, UK

Fiction Week Literary Review, 887 South Rice Rd., Ojai, Ca 93023

Fictional Café, 5 Hollow Lane, Lexington, MA 02420

Fieldguide Poetry Magazine, 60 Avalon Circle, Smithtown, NY 11787

Fifth Wheel, 2905 N. Charles St., #213, Baltimore, MD 21218

The Figure 1, 2270 S. University Blvd, #328, Denver, CO 80210

Final Thursday, 815 State St., Cedar Falls, IA 50613

Fine Print Press, PO Box 64711, Baton Rouge, LA 70896

Finishing Line Press, POB 1626, Georgetown, KY 40324

First East, PO Box 486, East Aurora, NY 14052

First Matter Press, 221 SE 15th Ave., #A, Portland, OR 97214

Five Fleas, Itchy Poetry, 405 S. Jefferson Way, Indianola, IA 50125

518 Publishing. 1647 Spring Ave E., Wynantskill, NY 12198

Five Points, Georgia State Univ, Box 3999, Atlanta, GA 30302-3999

Flapper Press, 4400 West Riverside Dr., Ste. #110, #115, Burbank, CA 91505

Flash Back Fiction, Jendrzejewski, 2 Pearce Close, Cambridge, CB3 9LY, UK

Flash Flood, Jendrzejewski, 2 Pearce Close, Cambridge CB3 9LY UK

Flash Frog, 1010 16th St., #311, San Francisco, CA 94107

Flat Ink, Dilara Sümbül, 1/702 Fairview St., Berkeley, CA 94703

Flights, Flight of the Dragonfly Press, 21 Worthing Rd., East Preston, West Sussex, BN16 1AT, UK

Florida Review, English Dept., PO Box 161346, Orlando, FL 32816-1346

Flying Ketchup Press, 11608 N. Charlotte St., Kansas City, MO 64155

Flying South, 546 Old Birch Creek Rd., McLeansville, NC 27301

Flyway, English Dept., Iowa State Univ., 203 Ross Hall, Ames, IA 50011-1201

Foglifter, Flynn-Goodlett, 633 33rd St., Richmond, CA 94804

Folly X. O., 2615 Harris Ave., Silver Spring, MD 20902

Foothill Poetry Journal, 160 E. 10th St., B2/B3, Claremont, CA 91711-5909

Forge, 4018 Bayview Ave., San Mateo, CA 94403-4310

42 Miles Press, Indiana University South Bend, 1700 Mishawaka Ave., PO Box 7111, South Bend, IN 46634-7111

Four Way Books, 11 Jay St., #4, New York, NY 10013-2847

Fourteen Hills, SFSU-Creative Writing, 1600 Holloway Ave., San Francisco, CA 94132

Fourth Genre, 4198 JFSB, Brigham Young University, Provo, UT 84602

Free Fall, 250 Maunsell Close NE, Calgary, AB T2E 7C2

Free State Review, 3222 Rocking Horse Lane, Aiken, SC 29801

Free Verse Revolution, K. Reed, 1 Broome Grove, Wivenhoe, Colchester, Essex, CO7 9QB, UK

Freshwater Literary Journal, Asnuntuck Community College, 170 Elm St., Enfield, CT 06082

Frogmore Press, 21 Mildmay Rd., Lewes BN7 1PJ, UK

Fugue Journal, Univ. Idaho, 875 Perimeter Dr., MS 1102, Moscow, ID 83844

Full Grown People, 106 Tripper Ct., Charlottesville, VA 22903

Galileo Press, 3222 Rocking Horse Lane, Aiken, SC 29801

Gallaudet University Press, 800 Florida Ave. NE, Washington, DC 20002-3695

Gargoyle, Paycock Press, 3819 13th St. N., Arlington, VA 22201

Gateway City Press, 1163 Spencer, St. Peters, MO 63376

Geest-Verlag GmbH & Co. KG, Marienburger Strasse 10, 49429, Visbek, Germany

Gemini Magazine, PO Box 1485, Onset, MA 02558

Georgia Review, 706A Main Library, Univ. of Georgia, Athens, GA 30602-9009

Gettysburg Review, Gettysburg College, 300 N. Washington St., Gettysburg, PA 17325

Ghost Parachute, 617 N. Hyer Ave., #4, Orlando, FL 32803

Gibson House Press, 531 Stover St., Fort Collins, CO 80524

Gigantic Sequins, Southwick-Thompson, Jacksonville State Univ., 700 Pelham Rd. No., Jacksonville, AL 36265-1602

Gival Press, PO Box 3812, Arlington, VA 22203

Glacier Journal, English Dept., Indiana University South Bend, 1700 E. Mishawaka Ave., South Bend, IN 46615

Glass Lyre Press, PO Box 2693, Glenview, IL 60025

Glassworks, 260 Victoria St., Glassboro, NJ 08028

Gnashing Teeth, 242 E. Main St., Norman, AR 71960-8743

Golden Antelope, 715 E. McPherson St., Kirksville, MO 63501

Golden Dragonfly Press, 87 Colonial Village, Amherst, MA 01002

Golden Foothills Press, 1438 Atchison St., Pasadena, CA 91104

Gone Lawn, 2207 Anthem Ct., Brentwood, TN 37027

Good Life Review, S. Shehan, 13644 Seward Circle, Omaha, NE 68154

Good River Review, Spalding Univ., 851 S. Fourth St., Louisville, KY 40203

Granfalloon, Planetesimal Press, 157 Adelaide St., W., #175, Toronto, ON M5H 4E7 Canada

Granta, 12 Addison Ave., Holland Park, London W11 4QR, UK

The Gravity of the Thing, 17028 SE Rhone St., Portland, OR 97236

Grayson Books, PO Box 270549, West Hartford, CT 06127

great weather for MEDIA, 515 Broadway, #2B, New York, NY 10012

Green Linden Press, 208 Broad St South, Grinnell, IA 50112

Green Silk Journal, 228 N. Main St, Woodstock, VA 22664

Green Writers Press, 34 Miller Rd., W. Brattleboro, VT 05301

Greenbelt News Review, 15 Crescent Rd., Greenbelt, MO 20770-1887

Grimscribe Press, 1238 Fern St., New Orleans, LA 70118-3969

Ground Up, PO Box 8113, 421 8th Ave., New York, NY 10001

GS Press, Sanghri & Hogan, 3131 Landore Dr, Naperville, IL 60564

Guernica, Moore, 1368 W. Bertona St., Seattle, WA 98119

Gyroscope Review, PO Box 1989, Gillette, WY 82717-1989

H-Pem, Armenian Culture Platform, 12 S. First St., New Hyde Park, NY 11040

HaikuKATHA, Raychowdhury, 79 Laconia St., Lexington, MA 02420-2229

Hamilton Stone Review, PO Box 457, Jay, NY 12941

Hand to Hand Press, Jayne, 824 SE 30th Ave, #8, Portland, OR 97214-4077

Handtype, PO Boc 3941, Minneapolis, MN 55402-0941

The Harvard Advocate, 21 South St., Cambridge, MA 02138

Harvard Review, Lamont Library, Harvard Univ., Cambridge, MA 02138

Hayden's Ferry Review, ASU, P.O. Box 871401, Tempe, AZ 85287-1401

Headmistress Press, 60 Shipview Ln, Seq uim, WA 98382

Heavy Traffic, 416 Adelphi St., Brooklyn, NY 11238

Hedge Apple, Hagerstown Community College, 11400 Robinwood Dr., Hagerstown, MD 21742-6514

Hedgehog Review, Univ. of Virginia, PO Box 400816, Charlottesville, VA 22904

Helix Literary Magazine, English, CCSU, 1615 Stanley St., New Britain, CT 06050

Here, ECSU, English, Webb Hall 225, Windham St., Willimantic, CT 06226

Hermine, PO Box 70505, 2938 Dundas St., West, Toronto, ON M6P 4E7 Canada

HerStry, 2120 N 54th St., Milwaukee, WI 53208

Hex Literary Magazine, 28 Rich St., Worcester, MA 01602

Hex Publishers, PO Box 298, Erie, CO 80516

Heyday, PO Box 9145, Berkeley, CA 94709

Hidden Peak Press, 6875 N, Trailway Cir., Parker, CO 80134

Highland Park Poetry, 1690 Midland Ave., Highland Park, IL 60035

Hillfire Press, 2085 Dahlia St., Denver, CO 20807

Hinterland, Enterprise Centre, Univ. East Anglia, Norwich NR4 7TJ, UK

Hippocampus, 210 W. Grant St., #104, Lancaster, PA 17603

History Through Fiction, 3050 Old Hwy 8, #328, Roseville, MN 55113

Hole in the Head Review, 85 Forbes Ln, Windham, ME 04062

The Hollins Critic, Hollins University, Box 9538, Roanoke, VA 24020

Honey Literary, 908 S. Barstow St., #2, Eau Claire, WI 54701

Honeyguide, 60 Avalon Cr., Smithtown, NY 11787

Hopkins Review, 3400 N. Charles St., 81 Gilman Hall, Baltimore, MD 21218

The Hopper, 4935 Twin Lakes Rd., #36, Boulder, CO 80301

Horseback Press, 240 Guigues Ave., Ottawa, ON K1N 5J2, Canada

Howl, 17 Waterpark Green, Carrigaline, Cork, P43 DC85, Ireland

Hub City Press, 186 West Main St., Spartanburg, SC 29306

The Hudson Review, 33 West 67th St., New York, NY 10023

Humanitas, MUSC, 171 Ashley Ave., Ste 201, MSC 172, Charleston, SC 29425

Hunger Mountain, 3711 Glendon Ave, #305, Los Angeles, CA 90034

Hypertext, c/o Rice, 1821 W. Melrose St., Chicago, IL 60657

I-70 Review, 5021 S. Tierney Dr., Independence, MO 64056-6930

iamb, 57 Thorpe Gardens, Alton, Hampshire GU34 2BQ, UK

Ibbetson Street Press, 25 School Street, Somerville, MA 02143

Idaho Review, BSU-Creative Writing, 1910 University Dr., Boise, ID 83725-1545

Identity Theory, 107 Skytop Dr., Henderson, NV 89015

IHRAF Publishes Literary Journal, 4142 73rd St., #5M, Woodside, NY 11377

Ilanot Review, K. Marron, 75-54 113th St., Forest Hills, NY 11375

Illuminations, CC-English, 66 George St., Charleston, SC 29424

Image, 3307 Third Avenue West, Seattle, WA 98119

Improbable Press, 3460 Danna Crt., Eugene, OR 97405

Indiana Review, English, Ballantine Hall 554, 1020 Kirkwood Ave., Bloomington, IN 47405

Indiana Writers Center, 1125 E. Brookside Ave., #B25, Indianapolis, IN 46202

Indie Blu(e), 1714 Woodmere Way, Havertown, PA 19083

Indie It Press, 230 S. Catlin St., #102, Missoula, MT 59801

Inky Dink Press, 5552 N. 156th Lane, Surprise, AZ 85374

Intima Journal, 36 N. Moore St., #4W, New York, NY 10013

Intrepidus Ink, 1374 S Mission Rd., #521, Fallbrook, CA 92028

Inverted Syntax, PO Box 2044, Longmont CO 80502

Invisible City, USF, Ben Briggs, Kalmanovitz Hall, Rm 302, 2130 Fulton St., San Francisco, CA 94117

The Iowa Review, University of Iowa, 308 EPB., Iowa City, IA 52242

Iron Horse, Patterson, TTU-English, MS 43091, Lubbock, TX 79409

Irreantum, Jepson, 115 Ramona Ave., El Cerrito, CA 94530

Italian Americana, c/o Terrone, 35-56 77th St., #31, Jackson Hts, NY 11372

J Journal, English, 619 West 54th St., 7th Fl, New York, NY 10019

Jabberwock Review, MSU, Drawer E, Mississippi State, MS 39762

Jacar Press, 6617 Deerview Trail, Durham, NC 27712

Janus Literary, Leagra, PO Box 881, Garner, NC 27529

Jelly Bucket, Eastern Kentucky Univ., English/Theater, Mattox 101, 521 Lancaster Ave., Richmond, KY 40475

Jerry Jazz Musician, 2538 NE 32nd Ave., Portland, OR 97212

Jersey Devil Press, 1826 Avon Rd. SW, Roanoke, VA 24015

Jet Fuel, Muench, 1508 W. Erie St., #3, Chicago, IL 60642-6365

Jewish Fiction, N. Gold, 3778 Walmer Rd., Toronto, ON M5R 2Y4, Canada

JMFdeA Press, PO Box 235737, Honolulu, HI 96823

jmww, 2306 Altisma Way, #214, Carlsbad, CA 92009

The Journal, OSU - English, 164 Annie & John Glenn Ave., Columbus, OH 43210

June Road Press, PO Box 260, Berwyn, PA 19312

Kallisto Gaia Press, 1801 E 51st St., #365-246, Austin, TX 78723

Kelp Journal & Books, 1491 Cypress Dr., 475, Pebble Beach, CA 93953

Kelsay Books, 502 S. 1040 E, #A119, American Fork, UT 84003

Kelsey Review, MCCC, 1200 Old Trenton Rd., West Windsor, NJ 08550

Kenyon Review, Finn House, 102 W. Wiggin St., Gambier, OH 43022-9623

Kernel Magazine, 1636 Grant St., #B, Berkeley, CA 94703

Kestrel, 264000, FSU, 1201 Locust Ave., Fairmont, WV

kin press, J. Mlozanowski, 209 Killingworth Rd., Higganum, CT 06441

Kissing Dynamite, C. Taylor, POB 662, Scotch Plains, NJ 07076

Kitchen Table Quarterly, 4622 Prospect Ave., Los Angeles, CA 90027

Kitty Wang's Mambo Academy, PO Box 5, North Branford, CT 06471

Knot Magazine, 721 East 8th Ave., Springfield, CO 81073

Kore Press Institute, 325 W 2nd St., #201, Tucson, AZ 85705

Kweli Journal, POB 693, New York, NY 10021

Lake Effect, Humanities, 4951 College Drive, Erie, PA 16563-1501

Lakeshore Literary, 1590 44th St. SW, Wyoming, MI 49509

Lascaux Review, 3155 Pebble Beach Dr., #10, Conway, AR 72034

Last Leaves Magazine, 507 Airey Ave., Endicott, NY 13760

The Last Press, 23798 Whitman Deering Dr., Minnesota City, MN 55987

Latin American Writers Institute, Hostos CC, CUNY, 500 Grand Concourse, Bronx, NY 10451

Laurel Review, NWMSU, 800 University Dr., Maryville, MO 64468

Lavender Review, 4 Corley Loop, Eureka Springs, AR 72632

Left Books Ltd, 34 Johnston Place, Oldbrook, Milton Keynes, MK6 2JS, UK

Leon Literary Review, 2 Saint Paul St., #404, Brookline, MA 02446

L'Esprit Literary Review, 624 W. 5th St., #10, Long Beach, CA 90802

Light, Balmain, 1515 Highland Ave., Rochester, NY 14618

°Limp Wrist, 520 NE 20th St., #708, Wilton Manors, FL 33305

The Lincoln Review, English, University of Lincoln, Brayford Pool, Lincoln LN6 7TS, UK

Line of Advance, 2126 W. Armitage, #3, Chicago, IL 60647

Lips, Box 1498, Clifton, NJ 07015

Liquid Imagination, 7800 Loma Del Norte Rd. NE, Albuquerque, NM 87109

The Literary Hatchet, 345 Charlotte White Rd., Westport, MA 02790

Literary House Press, Washington College, 300 Washington Ave., Chestertown, MD 21620

Literary Mama, C. Ditiberio, 699 Oregon Ave., Palo Alto, CA 94301

Literate, W. Meiners, 1422 Meadow St., Mount Pleasant, MI 48858

Lithic Press, 138 S. Park Sq., #202, Fruita, CO 81521-2544

LitMag, c/o Berley, 23 Ferris Lane, Bedford, NY 10506

Litro Media, 33 Irving Pl., New York, NY 10003

Littoral Books, PO Box 4533, Portland, ME 04112-4533

Littoral Press, 622 26th St., Richmond, CA 94804

Livingston Press, Stn 22, Univ. West Alabama, Livingston, AL 35470

Loch Raven Review, 1306 Providence Rd., Towson, MD 21286

Lolwe Magazine, 11 Netheravon Rd.., W7 1DN, London, UK

long con magazine, 6380 Chebucto Rd., Halifax, NS B3L 1L1, Canada

Long Day Press, 2016 N. Kedzie Ave., Chicago, IL 60647-3704

Longleaf Review, 1275 Monterey St., Jacksonville, FL 32207

Longreads, C. Rowlands, 1228 Evelyn Ave., Berkeley, CA 94706

Longridge Review, 325 W. Colonial Hwy, Hamilton, VA 20158

Longship Press, 1122 4th St., San Rafael, CA 94901

Lookout Books, Creative Writing, 601 South College Rd., Wilmington, NC 28403

Los Angeles Review of Books, 6671 Sunset Blvd., #1521, Los Angeles, CA 90028

Lost Balloon, 1402 Highland Ave., Berwyn, IL 60402

Lost Horse Press, 1025 So. Garry Rd., Liberty Lake, WA 99019

Lothlorien Poetry Journal, S. M. Jones, 7 Baptist Walk, Hinckley Leics LE10, IPR, UK

Loving Healing Press, 5145 Pontiac Trail, Ann Arbor, MI 48105-9238

Lowestoft Chronicle, 1925 Massachusetts Ave, #8, Cambridge, MA 02140

LSU Press, 328 Johnston Hall, Baton Rouge, LA 70803

Lumpen Pockets, A. Kini, 60-12 69th Ave., #3, Ridgewood, NY 11385

The Lunar Journal, Grace Zhang, lunarlitjournal(at)gmail.com

Lyrical Iowa, M. Baszczynski, 16096 320h Way, Earlham, IA 50072

The MacGuffin, 18600 Haggerty Rd., Livonia, MI 48152-2696

MacQueen's Quinterly, PO Box 2322, Kernersville, NC 27285

Mad Swirl, M. Clay, 4139 Travis St., Dallas, TX 75204

Madville Publishing, PO Box 358, Lake Dallas, TX 75065

Main Street Rag Publishing, Douglass, 4416 Shea Lane, Mint Hill, NC 28227

Malarkey Books, 2401 E. 32nd St., #10-232, Joplin, MO 64804-3177

Manhattan Review, 440 Riverside Dr., #38, New York, NY 10027

Mantle Poetry, c/o Jackson, 4610 Carroll St., Pittsburgh, PA 15224

Many Worlds, 1814 Morehead Hill Ct., Durham, NC 27703

The Margins, Asian American Writers, 112 W. 27th St., #600, New York, NY 10001

Marrow Magazine, 1517 Proctor St., Tallahassee, FL 32303

Marsh Hawk Press, PO Box 206, East Rockaway, NY 11518-0206

Mayday, PO Box 1094, Grafton, WI 53024

McNeese Review, MS- English, Box 92655, Lake Charles, LA 70609

McPherson & Co. Publishing, PO Box 1126, Kingston, NY 12402

McSweeney's Quarterly, J. Yeh, 496 Broadway, 3rd FL, Brooklyn, NY 11211

The Meadow, English Dept., Vista B300, 7000 Dandini Blvd., Reno, NV 89512

Meat for Tea, Valley Review, 282 W. Franklin St., Holyoke, MA 01040

Mercer University Press, 1501 Mercer University Dr., Macon, GA 31207-1515

Michigan Quarterly Review, 3277 Angell Hall, 435 S. State St., Ann Arbor, MI 48109-1003

MicroLit Almanac, Parnell, 1189 Great Plain Ave., Needham, MA 02492

Mid-American Review, Bowling Green State Univ., Bowling Green, OH 43403

Midway Journal, Pennel, 2603 Ashton Crt., Endicott, NY 13760

Midwest Quarterly, PSU, 44 Grubbs, 1701 South Broadway, Pittsburg, KS 66762

The Militant Grammarian, 20 Chapel St., #C706, Brookline, MA 02446

Military Experience & the Arts, PO Box 821, Morgantown, WV 26508

Milk Candy Review, 3145 Grelck Lane, Billings, MT 59105

Milk House, Ryan Dennis, 9444 North Hill Rd., Arkport, NY 14807

Minerva Rising Press, 17717 Circle Pond Court, Boca Raton, FL 33496

Minison Project, M. A. Hernandez, 1 Embassy Dr., Cherry Hill, NJ 08002

The Minnesota Review, 331 Major Williams Hall (0192), Blacksburg, VA 24061

Minola Review, 669-A Crawford St., Toronto, ON M6G 3K1, Canada

Minyan Magazine, Marlow, 7683 Cross Village Dr., Germantown, TN 38138

Mississippi Review, USM, 118 College Dr., #5144, Hattiesburg, MS 39406-0001

Missouri Review, 453 McReynolds Hall, UMO, Columbia MO 65211

Mizna, 2446 University Ave. W., #115, Saint Paul, MN 55114

Mobius, Journal of Social Change, 149 Talmadge, Madison, WI 53704

Mocking Heart Review, 2783 Iowa St., #2, Baton Rouge, LA 70802

Modern Haiku, PO Box 1570, Santa Rosa Beach, FL 32459

Modern Language Studies, Susquehanna Univ., English, 514 University Ave., Selinsgrove, PA 17870-1164

Moist, H. VanderHart, 10 Linganore Pl., Durham, NC 27707

Molecule, Carey, 80 School St., Manchester, MA 01944

Mom Egg Review, POB 9037, Bardonia, NY 10954

Moon Park Review, PO Box 87, Dundee, NY 14837

Moon Pie Press, 16 Walton St., Westbrook, ME 04092

Moon Tide Press, 6709 Washington Ave., #9297, Whittier, CA 90608

MOONLOVE Press, 266 Clark Blvd., Massapequa Park, NY 11762

MoonPath Press, PO Box 445, Tillamook, OR 97141-0445

Moonrise Press, PO Box 4288, Sunland, CA 91041-4288

Moot Point Magazine, 1552 Brunswig Lane, Emeryville, CA 94608

Mouthfeel Press, 2967 Mockingbird Lane, Huntsville, TX 77320

Muddy River Poetry Review, 15 Eliot St., Chestnut Hill, MA 02467

Mudfish, Box Turtle Press, 184 Franklin St., New York, NY 10013

Mukana Press, Box 459, 1200 Franklin Mall, Santa Clara, CA 95052-6099

Muse-Pie Press, 73 Pennington Ave., Passaic, NJ 07055

MUTHA Magazine, 304 18th St, Brooklyn, NY 11215

Muumuu House, 16-566 Keaau Pahoa Rd. 188-168, Keaau, HI 96749

Muzzle Magazine, Rogers, 10496 W. Outer Drive, Detroit, MI 48223

n + 1, 37 Greenpoint Ave., # 316, Mailbox 18, Brooklyn NY 11222

Narrative, 2443 Fillmore St., #214, San Francisco, CA 94115

Nat 1, 89 Union St., #1021, Auburn, ME 04210

National Flash Fiction Day, Jendrzejewski, 2 Pearce Close, Cambridge, CB3 9LY, UK

Native Skin Lit Mag, 366 Fm 1488 Rd., #358, Conroe, TX 77384-4288

Naugatuck River Review, PO Box 368, Westfield, MA 01086

Neologism Poetry Journal, 365 South Mountain Rd., Northfield, MA 01360

New American Press, PO Box 1094, Grafton, WI 53024

New England Review, Middlebury College, Middlebury, VT 05753

New Flash Fiction Review, 2440 Princeton Pike, Lawrenceville, NJ 08648

New Letters, 5101 Rockhill Rd., Kansas City, MO 64110-2499

New Ohio Review, Ohio University, 201 Ellis Hall, Athens, OH 45701

New Orleans Review, Campus Box 195, Loyola Univ., New Orleans, LA 70118

New Territory Magazine, K. Foster, 304 N. 8th St., Oskaloosa, IA 52577

New Verse News, Greenlot Sambandha M-32, Kec. Mengwi, Kab. Badung, Munggu, Bali 80351, Indonesia

Next Page Press, 118 Inslee, San Antonio, TX 78209

Nifty Lit, PO Box 1205, Alamo, CA 94507

Night Picnic Press, PO Box 3819, New York, NY 10163-3819

Nightboat Books, 310 Nassau Ave., #205, Brooklyn, NY 11222-3813

Ninth Letter, English, 608 S. Wright St., Urbana, IL 61801

Nite Baby Nite, 1 West 126th St., Ste 5D, New York, NY 10027

Nocturne Magazine, 305 Frank St., #B, Edgerton, MO 64444

Noon, 1392 Madison Ave., PMB 298, New York, NY 10029

North American Review, Univ. Northern Iowa, Cedar Falls, IA 50614-0516

North Carolina Literary Review, ECU Mailstop 555 English, Greenville, NC 27858-4353

Novel Slices, 136 Muriel St., Ithaca, NY 14850

null pointer press, 86 Silver Sage Cres., Winnipeg MB R3X 0K2, Canada

Nunum, G. Miller, 23 Kipling Ct., Moncton, NB, E1E 4J7 Canada

Obsidian, Illinois State Univ., Box 4241, Normal, IL 61790-4241

Ocean State Review, C. Kell, 940 Quaker Lane, East Greenwich, RI 02818

Off Assignment, 1802 Massachusetts Ave., #32, Cambridge, MA 02140

128 Lit, 558 W. 162nd St., #1, New York, NY 10032-6001

One Story, 232 3rd St., #A108, Brooklyn, NY 11215-2708

Orange Blossom Review, 13228 Moran Dr., Tampa, FL 33618

orangepeel, 2144 Ravenglass Place, Apt. F, Raleigh, NC 27612

Oranges Journal, 43 Butlers Close, Bristol, BS5 8AW, UK

Orbis Quarterly, 17 Greenhow Ave., West Kirby, Wirral, CH48 5EL, UK

Oregon Humanities, 610 SW Alder St., #1111, Portland, OR 97205

Origami Poems Project, 1948 Shore View Dr., Indialantic, FL 32903

Orion's Belt Magazine, 157 W. 105th St., #4ER, New York, NY 10025

Ornithopter Press, 37 E. Merwick Ct, Princeton, NJ 08540

Osiris, 106 Meadow Lane, Greenfield, MA 01301

the other side of hope, Plasatis, 199 London Rd., Leicester, LE2 1ZE UK

Outlook Springs, 193 Leighton St., Bangor, ME 04401

Outpost 19 Books, 303 Coleridge St., San Francisco, CA 94110-5463

Oxford Magazine, MU- English, 306 Bachelor Hall, Oxford, OH 45056

OyeDrum, 1725 Toomey Rd. #200, Austin, TX 78704

Oyster River Pages, 26060 Wellspring Ave., Lewes, DE 19958

Paddler Press, 124 Parcells Crescent, Peterborough, ON K9K 2R2, Canada

Pages Literary Journal, A. Cates, 645 Cross Creek Dr., Wilmington, OH 45177

Paloma Press, 110 28th Ave., San Mateo, CA 94403

Pangyrus Lit Mag, 2592 Massachusetts Ave, Cambridge MA 02140

Panorama Journal, 87 Glisson Rd., Cambridge, CB1 2HG, UK

Papeachu Press, 6511 26th Ave. NW, Seattle, WA 98117

Paperbark, U Mass, South College W342. 150 Hicks Way, Amherst, MA 01003

Paranoid Tree Press, 3317 Pillsbury Ave S. Minneapolis, MN 55408

Parentheses Journal, 4065 Confederation Pkwy, #1309, Mississauga, ON L5B 0L4, Canada

Parliament Literary Journal, 1111 Central Ave, Highland Park, NJ 08904

Pasque Petals, PO Box 294, Kyle, SD 57752

Passages North, English, NMU, 1401 Presque Isle Ave., Marquette, MI 49855-5363

Passengers Journal, A. Winham, 180 Sterling Place, #11, Brooklyn, NY 11217

Paterson Literary Review, Passaic County Community College, 1 College Blvd., Paterson, NJ 07505—1179

Paul Stream Press, 49 Smoke St., Nottingham, NH 03290

Peach Magazine, 14 Fairfield Ave., Buffalo, NY 14214

Peatsmoke Journal, Wallace, 114 Cedarhurst Lane, Milford, CT 06461

Peauxdunque Review, 4609 Page Dr., Metairie, LA 70003

Pelekinesis, Givens, 112 Harvard Ave., #65, Claremont, CA 91711-4716

Pembroke Magazine, P.O. Box 1510, Pembroke, NC 28372-1510

Penmen Review, SNHU, 55 So. Commercial St., Manchester, NH 03101

perhappened mag, 2205 Wilkinson Ave., #2, Marquette, MI 49855

Perugia Press, PO Box 60364, Florence, MA 01062

Petigru Review, M.Picone, 3850 Maypop Cir. #107, Myrtle Beach, SC 29586-1381

Philadelphia Stories, 93 Old York Rd, Ste l/#l-753, Jenkintown, PA 19046

Phoebe, GMU, M10884, The Hub 1201, 4400 University Place, Fairfax, VA 22030

The Pinch, UM-English, 435 Patterson Hall, Memphis, TN 38111

Pinesong, NC Poetry Society, 131 Bon Aire Rd., Elkin, NC 28621

Pink Trees Press, 8237 61st Rd., Middle Village, NY 11379

Pithead Chapel, B. Terwilliger, 6865 Kirkville Rd., East Syracuse, NY 13057

Plain View Press, 1101 W. 34th St, #404, Austin, TX 78705

Planet Scumm, S. Clancy, 15 Mt. St. Mary's Way, #001, Hooksett, NH 03106

Plough, 151 Bowne Dr., PO Box 398, Walden, NY 12586

Ploughshares, Emerson College, 120 Boylston St., Boston, MA 02116-4624

Plume, D. Lawless, 740 17th Avenue N, Saint Petersburg, FL 33704

Poetry Box, 3300 NW 185th Ave., #382, Portland, OR 97229

Poetry Center, CSU, 2121 Euclid Ave., Cleveland, OH 44115-2214

Poetry International, English, SDSU, 5500 Campanile Dr., San Diego, CA 92182

Poetry Northwest, K. Kuipers, 4770 Duncan Dr., Missoula, MT 59802

Poetry Project, 131 East 10th St, New York, NY10003

Poetry South, 1100 College St., MUW-1634, Columbus, MS 39701

Poetryology, Abu Dhabi, Al Sila, PO Box 76753, Uchechukwu Agodom, United Arab Emirates

Poets Wear Prada, Hoffman, 533 Bloomfield St., 2nd Fl, Hoboken, NJ 07030

Ponder Review, 1100 College St., MUW-1634, Columbus, MS 39701

Porkbelly Press, 5046 Relleum Ave, Cincinnati, OH 45238

Porter House Review, English, TSU, 601 University Dr., San Marcos, TX 78666

Posit, Lewis, 237 Thompson St., #8A,, New York, NY 10012

Post Road, Boston College, English, 140 Commonwealth Ave., Chestnut Hill, MA 02467

Potomac Review, Paul Peck Humanities., MT/212, Rockville, MD 20850

Prairie Journal Trust, 28 Crowfoot Terr. NW, PO Box 68073, Calgary, AB, T3G 3N8, Canada

Prairie State Press, 1808 Cobble Creek Dr., Mahomet, IL 61853

Pratt Writing Program, 200 Willoughby Ave., Carroneer Ct., 1st Fl, Brooklyn, NY 11205

Presence Journal, 65 Clark Ave., Bloomfield, NJ 07003

Press 53, 560 N. Trade St., #103, Winston-Salem, NC 27101-2937

Prime Number Magazine, 560 No. Trade St., #103, Winston-Salem, NC 27101

Prism Review, 1950 Third St., La Verne, CA 91750

Profiles, Mayfield, 77 Lucan Rd., Chapelizod, Dublin 20, Ireland

Progenitor Art & Literary, Arapahoe Community College, Littleton, CO 80160

Prolific Pulse Press, 5921 Waterford Bluff Ln, #1418, Raleigh, NC 27612

Psaltery & Lyre, M. Tullis, 465 W. 200 S., Basement, Smithfield, UT 84335

PseudoPod, T. Bailey, 521 River Ave., Providence, RI 02908

A Public Space, PO Box B, New York, NY 10159-1047

Puerto Del Sol, NMSU, PO Box 30001, MSC 3E, Las Cruces, NM 88003-8001

Pulse & Echo, c/o Danville Public Library, 319 Vermilion St, Danville, IL 61832

Quarter After Eight, Walsh, 359 Ellis Hall, Ohio University, Athens, OH 45701

Quarter Press, Smith, 305 N. Masonic St., Millen, GA 30442

Quarterly West, Univ. of Utah, English/LNCO 3500, 255 S. Central Campus Dr., Salt Lake City, UT 84112-9109

Quartet, Blaskey, 10613 N. Union Church Rd., Lincoln, DE 19960

Querencia Press, PO Box 3229, Munster, IN 46321

Quiet Lightning, 256 40th Street Way, Oakland, CA 94611

Quill and Parchment, 2267 Lambert Dr., Pasadena, CA 91107

Quillkeepers Press, PO Box 10236, Casa Grande, AZ 85130

R. Graham Publishing, 10201 Flatlands Ave., #360111, Brooklyn, NY 11236

Rabid Oak, 8916 Duncanson Dr., Bakersfield, CA 93311

The Racket, Sanders, 2045 Grahn Dr., Santa Rosa, CA 95404

Radar Poetry, 19 Coniston Ct., Princeton, NJ 08540

Ram Eye Press, A. Bestwick, Blea Moor, Upper Hartshay, Derbyshire, DE56 2HW UK

Rat's Ass Review, 309 Chimney Ridge Rd., Perkinsville, VT 05151

Rattle, 12411 Ventura Blvd., Studio City, CA 91604

Ravenna Press, PO Box 1166, Edmonds, WAS 98020

Raw Earth Ink, PO Box 39332, Ninilchik, AK 99639

Razor Magazine, J. Sippie, 101 West End Ave., New York, NY 10023

Read Furiously, 555 Grand Ave., #77078, Ewing, NJ 08628-8043

Read or Green Books, 261 Burma Dr. NE, Albuquerque, NM 87123

Reckon Review, PO Box 1280, Flat Rock, NC 28731

Reckoning Press, 206 East Flint St., Lake Orion, MI 48362

red lights, 2740 Andrea Drive, Allentown, PA 18103

Red Ogre Review, 1254 S. Saltair Ave., #102, Los Angeles, CA 90025

Red River, Smti. Moramee Das, c/o Sri Ramen Das, P.O. Silpukhuri, Hsno 22, Happyvilla, Barwari, Uzanbazar P.S. Latasil, Guwahati, Dist-Kamrup (M), pincode 781003, Assam, India

Red Rock Review, 6375 W. Charleston Blvd., Las Vegas, NV 89146

Red Wheelbarrow, DeAnza College-English, 21250 Stevens Creek Blvd, Cupertino, CA 95014

Redactions, 182 Nantucket Dr., Apt. U, Clarksville, TN 37040

Redhawk Publications, 2550 US Hwy 70 SE, Hickory, NC 28602

Redivider, Emerson College, Ansin 1015B, 120 Boylston St., Boston, MA 02116

Reed Magazine, English Dept., San José State Univ., 1 Washington Sq., San José, CA 95192-0090

Rejected Lit, 103 N. Western Dr., Bozeman, MT 59718

Relief Journal, Taylor Univ-English 236 W. Reade Ave, Upland, IN 46989

Renaissance, English, Wayne Community College, 3000 Wayne Memorial Dr., Goldsboro, NC 27534

Reservoir Road, 49 Winchester St., #1, Brookline, MA 02446-2894

Revolute Literary, Randolph College, 2500 Rivermont Ave., Lynchburg, VA 24503

Rhino, PO Box 591, Evanston, IL 60204

Ribbons, S. Weaver, 127 N.10th St., Allentown, PA 18102

riddlebird, 1211 Gerry St., Woodstock, IL 60098

Ringing Rover, Belmont, Edale, Hope Valley, S33 7ZA, UK

Ripe Fiction, 1001 O St., #701, Lincoln, NE 68508

Rivanna Review, 807 Montrose Ave., Charlottesville, VA 22902

River Heron Review, PO Box 543, New Hope, PA 18938

River Mouth Review, 2023 E. Sims Way, #364, Port Townsend, WA 98368

River Paw Press, 706 Hayes, Irvine, CA 92620

River Teeth, English, BSU, 2000 W. University Ave., Muncie, IN 47306

Roanoke Review, Miller Hall, 221 College Lane, Salem, VA 24153

Rodney's Underground Press, Adelmann, Sternstrasse 14, D-44137 Dortmund, Germany

Rogue, J. Khoury, 5441 Covode Pl., Pittsburgh, PA 15217-1914

Roi Fainéant Press, 3247 Evergreen Hills Dr., #1, Macedon, NY 14502

Room, PO Box 46160, Stn. D, Vancouver, BC V6J 5G5, Canada

Rose Garden Press, Mam Tor House, Edale, Hope Valley, S33 7ZA, UK

Ruby Literary Press, 722 Duluth St., Durham, NC 27705

Run Amok Books, V. Smith, 2043 Hagen Ln, Flossmoor, IL 60422

Running Wild, 2101 Oak St., Los Angeles, CA 90007

Rust + Moth, 4470 S. Lemay Ave., #1108, Fort Collins, CO 80525

The Rutherford Red Wheelbarrow, Zirilli, 90 Kennedy Rd., Andover, NJ, 07821

Sable Books, 4403 Edgemore Rd., Greensboro, NC 27455

Sactown Magazine, 1017 L St., #671, Sacramento, CA 95814

Sagging Meniscus Press, 115 Claremont Ave., Montclair, NJ 07042

Sailors Review, VaChikepe And The 100 Sailors, 300 Swift Ave., Box 93813, Apt. 338, Durham, NC 27708

Salamander, Suffolk U., English, 8 Ashburton Pl., Boston, MA 02108

Salt Hill Journal, English, 401 Hall of Languages, 100 University Ave., Syracuse, NY 13244

San Diego Poetry Annual, M. Klam, 4712 Leathers St., San Diego, CA 92117

San Pedro River Review, Alfier, 5403 Sunnyview St., Torrance, CA 90505

Sancho Panza Literary, 16 Carleton Rd., West Hartford, CT 06107

Sand Journal, c/o Mason, Archibaldweg 28, 10317 Berlin, Germany

Sans.Press, 17 Rice's Corner, High Rd., Thomondgate, Limerick, Co. Limerick, V94 KT51, Ireland

Santa Clara Review, Santa Clara Univ., 500 El Camino Real, Santa Clara, CA 95053

Santa Fe Writers Project, c/o Gifford, 4916 Edgemoor Lane, Bethesda, MD 20814

Santa Monica Review, 1900 Pico Blvd., Santa Monica, CA 90405

SAPIENS, 655 Third Avenue, 23rd Floor, New York, NY 10017

Sarabande Books, 735 Lampton St., #201, Louisville, KY 11975-0380

Sard Adabi, F. Alharthi, 5663 Tecumseh Dr., Tallahassee, FL 32312

Saturnalia Books, 105 Woodside Rd., Ardmore, PA 19003

SBLAAM, Smoky Blue Literary and Arts Magazine, 36 Louisiana Ave, Asheville, NC 28806

Scoundrel Time, 6106 Harvard Ave., #396, Glen Echo, MD 20812

Scribes°MICRO°Fiction, PO Box 715, Kinderhook, NY 12106

Sea Crow Press, PO Box 966, Barnstable, MA 02630

Seaside Gothic, 6 Larch Close, Broadstairs, Kent, CT10 2LW, UK

Sequoyah Cherokee River Journal, 6143 River Hills Circle, Southside, AL 35907

Sewanee Review, 735 University Ave., Sewanee, TN 37383

Shark Reef, 66 Country Rd., Lopez Island, WA 98261

Sheila-Na-Gig, 203 Meadowlark Rd., Russell, KY 41169-1539

Shenandoah, English Dept., W&L Univ., Lexington, VA 24450-2116

Sheridan Press, 450 Fame Ave, Hanover, PA 17331

Shooter, White, 35 Langdon Rd, Cheltenham, 6L5 37N2, UK

The Shore Poetry, 843 Johnson Rd., Salisbury, MD 21804

Silverfish Review, PO Box 3541, Eugene, OR 97403

Sine Theta Magazine, Stella Li, 18 West Kincaid Dr., West Windsor, NJ 08550

Singapore Unbound, J. L. Koh, 3 West 122nd St., #5D, New York, NY 10027

Sixteen Rivers Press, PO Box 640663, San Francisco, CA 94164-0663

Sky & Telescope, Young, 1374 Massachusetts Ave., Cambridge, MA 02140

SLAB, English, Slippery Rock Univ., 1 Morrow Way, Slippery Rock, PA 16057-1326

Slag Glass City, English Dept., DePaul Univ., 2315 N. Kenmore Ave., Chicago, IL 60614-3261

Slapering Hol Press, 300 Riverside Dr., Sleepy Hollow, NY 10591

Sleet Magazine, 1846 Bohland Ave., St. Paul, MN 55116-1906

Slippery Elm, Univ. of Findlay, 1000 N. Main St., Box 1615, Findlay, OH 45840

Smartish Pace, 2221 Lake Ave., Baltimore, MD 21213

Smokelong Quarterly, Allen, 2127 Kidd Rd., Nolensville, TN 37135

Snarl, 512 Rockledge Road, #C4, Lawrence, KS 66049

So to Speak, MSN 2C5, The Hub Rm 120, 4400 University Dr., Fairfax, VA 22030

SoFloPoJo, O'Mara, 1014 Green Pine Blvd., #E-1, West Palm Beach, FL 33409-7005

Soft Star Magazine, Adkins, 1324 Downington Ave., Salt Lake City, UT 84105

Solstice Literary, L. Leonard, 10 Longfellow Rd., Arlington, MA 02476

Soundings East, English Dept., Salem State University, Salem. MA 01970

South Dakota Review, USD-English, 414 East Clark St., Vermillion, SD 57069

South 85 Journal, 923 King Richard Dr., Charleston, SC 29407

The Southampton Review, 239 Montauk Hwy., Southampton, NY 11968

Southeast Review, English, FSU, 405 Williams Bdg., Tallahassee, FL 32306

Southern Humanities Review, 9088 Haley Center, Auburn Univ., Auburn, AL 36849-5202

Southwest Review, PO Box 750374, Dallas, TX 75275-0374

Spare Parts Literary, Churchtown Farm, Lawhitton, Launceston, Cornwall, PL15 9NQ, UK

Speak Poetry, 110 28th Ave., San Mateo, CA 94403

Speculatively Queer, 7511 Greenwood Ave. N, #4108, Seattle, WA 98103

Spellbinder, A. Kennedy, 421 Thorney Leys, Witney, OX28 5NR, UK

Spiritus, M. Burrows, 8 Central St., Camden, ME 04843

Split Lip Magazine, 409 E. Cherry St., Walla Walla, WA 99362

Split Rock Review, 30330 Engoe Rd., Washburn, WI 54891

Split This Rock, 1301 Connecticut Ave. NW, #600, Washington, DC 20036

Splonk, 10 Mountpleasant Ave., Ballinasloe H53 R970, Co Galway, Ireland

Spoon River Poetry, ISU, Campus Box 4241, Normal, IL 61790

St. Rooster Books, Murr, 241 W. Walnut St., Oneida, NY 13421

Stackfreed Press, 634 North A St., Elwood, IN 46036

Stairwell Books, 161 Lowther St., York, YO31 7LZ, UK

Stanchion, 281 W. Lincoln Hwy., #402, Exton, PA 19341

Star 82 Review, PO Box 8106, Berkeley, CA 94707

Star*Line, 61871 29 Palms Hwy, Joshua Tree, CA 92252

Starship Sloane Publishing, 603 Splitrock St., Round Rock, TX 78681

Still: The Journal, 89 W. Chestnut St., Williamsburg, KY 40769

Stone Pacific Zine, Nasta, 2813 15th Ave. S., Seattle, WA 98144

Stoneboat Literary Journal, 407 Euclid Ave., Sheboygan, WI 53083

Stonehouse Publishing, PO Box 68092, Boonie Doon Shopping Centre, Edmonton, Alberta, T6C 4N6, Canada

The Storms, Effelstown Cottage, Station Rd., Lusk, Co Dublin, K45 HY84, Ireland

Story, 312 E. Kelso Rd., Columbus, OH 43202

Story Circle Network, PO Box 200, Idledale, CO 80453

Strange Horizons, 408 Highland Ave., Winchester, MA 01890

Stranger's Guide, PO BOX 15007, Austin, TX 78761

Streetlight Magazine, 56 Pine Hill Lane, Norwood, VA 24581

Subnivean, S. Frazier, 4748 Weller Hall Place, Clay, NY 13041

The Summerset Review, 25 Summerset Dr., Smithtown, NY 11787

The Sun, 107 North Roberson St., Chapel Hill, NC 27516

Sundial, Murphy, Lehigh University, 4 Farrington Sq., Bethlehem PA 18015-3033

Sundog Lit, 607 W. Edwards Ave., Houghton, MI 49931

Sunlight Press, 3924 E Quail Ave., Phoenix, AZ 85050

Surface Dweller Studios, L. Lavin, 509 N. 70th St., Seattle, WA 98103

Surging Tide Magazine, 123 Hearth Ct., Baltimore, MD 21212

Susurrus Magazine, 205 W. Montgomery Xrd, #608, Savannah, GA 31406

Swamp Pink, English Dept., College of Charleston, 5 College Way, Charleston SC

Sweet: A Literary Confection, 83 Carolyn Lane, Delaware, OH 43015

SWWIM Every Day, 301 NE 86th St., El Portal, FL 33138

Symposeum, A. Kominsky, 3701 Turtle Creek Blvd., Dallas TX 75219

Syncopation, N. Welsh, 4 Shady Glen Crescent, Bolton, ON L7E 2K4, Canada

Synkroniciti, 7603 Rock Falls Ct., Houston, TX 77095

TAB Journal, Chapman University, 1 University Dr., Orange, CA 92866

Talbot-Heindl Experience, 1250 S. Clermont St., #2-307, Denver, CO 80246

Tar River Poetry, ECU, MS 159, East 5th St., Greenville, NC 27858-4353

Taurean Horn Press, PO Box 526, Petaluma, CA 94953

TCU Press, TCU Box 298300, Fort Worth, TX 76129

Tell Your Story, C. Sowers, 5229 Brooks Bend, Greenwood, IN 46143

Terrapin Books, 4 Midvale Ave., West Caldwell, NJ 07006

Texas Review Press, SHSU, Box 2146, Huntsville, TX 77341-2146

Thimble, 47 Pleasantdale Rd., Rutland, MA 01543

32 Poems, Washington & Jefferson College, 60 S. Lincoln, Washington, PA 15301

Thirty West Publishing, J. Dale, 518 Wilder Sq., Plymouth Meeting, PA 19462

This Broken Shore, 15 Sandspring Dr., Eatontown, NJ 07724

This Works Press, 137 Linebrook Rd, Ipswich, MA 01938

Thornwillow Press, PO Box 982, Newburgh, NY 12551

Thorny Locust, S. Kofler, 700 W. 31st St., #308, Kansas City, MO 64108

3: A Taos Press, P.O. Box 370627, Denver, CO 80237

3 Elements Review, 198 Valley View Rd., Manchester, CT 06040

300 Days of Sun, H. Lang-Cassera, NSC, 1300 Nevada State Dr. DA126, Henderson, NV 89002

Three Mile Harbor Press, PO Box 1, Stuyvesant, NY 12173

Three Rooms Press, 243 Bleecker St., #3, New York, NY 10014

Threepenny Review, PO Box 9131, Berkeley, CA 94709

Thrush Poetry Journal, 889 Lower Mountain Dr., Effort, PA 18330

Timber Journal, U.C. Boulder, 226 UCB, Hellems 101, Boulder, CO 80309

Tikkun, Tiny Wren Lit, 99 Tabilore Loop, Delaware, OH 43015

Tipton Poetry Journal, 642 Jackson St., Brownsburg, IN 46112

Torch Literary Arts, 5540 N. Lamar Blvd, #39, Austin, TX 78751

trampset, 2519 36th Ave., Astoria, NY 11106

Transition, Hutchins Center, Harvard Univ., 104 Mount Auburn St., #3R, Cambridge, MA 02138

Trestle Creek Review, Lee-Kildow Hall 204, North Idaho College, 1000 W. Garden Ave., Coeur d'Alene, ID 83814

Troublemaker, D. Schweizer, 132 Polk St., Riverside, NJ 08075

TSR: The Southampton Review, 239 Montauk Highway, Southampton, NY 11968

TulipTree Review, PO Box 133, Seymour, MO 65746

Tupelo Press, PO Box 1767, North Adams, MA 01247

Twenty Bellows, J. Stuart, 3344 W. Walsh Pl., Denver, CO 80219-3313

Twenty First Century Renaissance, Glass House, Harbour Court, George's Place, Dun Laoghaire, Dublin, A96 P0A4, Ireland

The Twin Bill, 3778 Burkoff, Troy, MI 48084

Two Hawk Quarterly, 400 Corporate Pointe, Culver City, CA 90230

Two Mountain Press, 1901 Van Ness Ave., Reno, NV 89503

Two Shrews Press, 2550 Martha Ave., Green Bay, WI 54301

Two Sylvias Press, PO Box 1524, Kingston, WA 98346

Twyckenham Notes, 14223 Worthington Dr., Granger, IN 46530

Typehouse, V. Gryphin, PO Box 68721, Portland, OR 97268

Ubiquitous, Pratt Institute, 200 Willoughby Ave., Carroneer Ct., 1st Fl, Brooklyn, NY 11205

Ugly Duckling Presse, 232 3rd St., #E303, Brooklyn, NY 11215

Unbearables, Autonomedia Publishing, 30-73 47th St., #3F, Long Island City, NY 11103-1531

The Unconventional Courier, 1117 West 6th St., #39, Lewistown, PA 17044

Under Review, 1536 Hewitt Ave., MS-A1730, Saint Paul, MN 55104

Under the Sun, M. Highers, PO Box 332, Cookeville, TN 38503

Undertow Publications, PO Box 490, 9860 Niagara Falls Blvd., Niagara Falls, NY 14304

University of Arkansas Press, McIlroy House, 105 No. McIlroy Ave., Fayetteville, AR 72701

University of Iowa Press, 119 West Park Rd., 100 Kuhl House, Iowa City, IA 52242-1000

University of Nebraska Press, PO Box 880630, 1225 L St., #200, Lincoln, NE 68588

University of Utah Press, 295 South 1500 East, #5400, Salt Lake City, UT 84112-0860

Upstreet, M. Dorsel, 1420 Elmsford Lane, Matthews, NC 28105

Ursa Story Company, 4025 56th Ave. SW, Seattle, WA 98116

US 1 Worksheets, E. Carrington, 141 N 8th Ave., Highland Park, NJ 08904

Vagabond, 1507 Curtis St., Berkeley, CA 94702

Vagabond City Literary Journal, A. King, 2074 Sailmaker Dr., Lewisville, TX 75067

Vallum, 5038 Sherbrooke Ouest, PO Box 23077 CP Vendome, Montreal, QC H4A 1TO Canada

Vast Chasm Magazine, 6315 S. 176th St., Omaha, NE 68135

Véhicule Press, PO Box 42094, BP Roy, Montréal, Québec H2W 2T3 Canada

Veliz Books, 2550 Bonita, La Verne, CA 91750

Velvet Giant Journal, 951 Carroll St., #3A, Brooklyn, NY 11225-1924

Venetian Spider Press, 203 Amy Court, Sterling, VA 20164

Versification Zine, 2248 River Oaks Dr., West Columbia, TX 77486

Vestal Review, Galef, 65 Edgemont Rd., Montclair, NJ 07042-2304

Viewless Wings Press, 5424 Sunol Blvd., #10-557, Pleasanton, CA 94566

Viridian Door, Harper, 620 18th Ave E, #16, Seattle, WA 98112

Visual Art Source eNewsletter, 231 Cedar Heights Dr., Thousand Oaks, CA 91360

Vita Brevis Press, 4747 W. Waters Ave, #1613, Tampa, FL 33614-1436

Vita Poetica Journal, 2105 Linden Lane, Silver Spring, MD 20910

Voices de la Luna, 5150 Broadway St., #149, San Antonio, TX 78209

Volume Poetry, Gilmore, 55 Clifton Pl., #1, Brooklyn, NY 11238

Wandering Aengus, PO Box 334, Eastsound, WA 98245

Washington Square Review, Lucken, Lansing Community College, PO Box 40010, Lansing, MI 48901

Washington Writers' Publishing House, 2814 5th St. NE, Washington, DC 20017

Water~Stone Review, MS A1730, 1536 Hewitt Ave., St. Paul, MN 55104-1284

Water's Edge Press, 8241 W. Lapis Moon Ln., Tucson, AZ 85743-5246

Watershed Review, CSU, English, 400 West First St., Chico, CA 95929

Waterwheel Review, Smith, 52 Grey Rocks Rd., Wilton, CT 06897

Wax Paper, 856 N. Marshfield, #2F, Chicago, IL 60622

Waxwing Literary Journal, 1100 Camero Way, Fremont, CA 94539

The Way Back to Ourselves, K. Phinney, 4535 Cozzo Dr., Land O Lakes, FL 34639

Wayne State University Press, K. Giffin, 4809 Woodward Ave., Detroit, MI 48201

Wee Sparrow Poetry Press, Calle Pereira, 1, 2A, Cádiz 11009, Andalucia, Spain

Weird House Press, 8401 Old Stage Rd., #78, Central Point, OR 97502

West Branch, Bucknell Hall, Bucknell University, Lewisburg, PA 17837

The West Review, 994 Overlook Rd., Berkeley, CA 94708

West Trade Review, K. Harmon, 801 W. Trade St., Charlotte, NC 28202

West Trestle Review, P. Caspers, 220 Sierra Way, Auburn, CA 95603

West Warwick Public Library Press, 1043 Main St., West Warwick, RI 02893

Westchester Review, PO Box 246h, Scarsdale, NY 10583

Whale Road Review, 3900 Lomaland Dr., San Diego, CA 92106

Whiptail Journal, Lehmann, 134 White Birch Dr., Guilford, CT 06437

Whistling Shade, 1495 Midway Pkwy, St. Paul, MN 55108

Wigleaf, MU-English, 114 Tate Hall, Columbia, MO 65211

Wild Ink Publishing, 5 South Rupp Ave., Shiremanstown, PA 17011

The Wild Word Magazine, Zimmermannstrasse 6, 12163 Berlin, Germany

Willow Springs, 601 E. Riverside Ave, #442, Spokane, WA 99202

Willowdown Books, 52-5550 Admiral Way, Delta, BC V4K 0C4, Canada

Willows Wept Review, 17517 County Road 455, Montverde, FL 34756

Wolfpack Publishing, 9850 S. Maryland Pkwy, #A-5, 323, Las Vegas, NV 89183

Woodhall Press, PO Box 636, Fryeburg, ME 04037

Woodward Review, 454 Withington St., Ferndale, MI 48220

The Woolf, D. Miller, Postfach 409, 8803 Rüschlikon, Switzerland

Worcester Review, PO Box 804, Worcester, MA 01613

Word on the Street, S.B. Furst, 367 Windsor Dr., Fishersville, VA 22939

Wordrunner eChapbooks, 210 Douglas St., #311, Petaluma, CA 94952

Words Without Borders, Harris, 2809 W. Logan Blvd., Chicago, IL 60647

World Literature Today, 630 Parrington Oval, #110, Norman, OK 73019-4033

World Stage Press, Sims Library, 2702 W. Florence Ave., Los Angeles, CA 90043

World Weaver Press, PO Box 21924, Albuquerque, NM 87154-1924

Wrath-Bearing Tree, A. Williams, 8550 Cirrus Ct., Colorado Springs, CO 80920

Write Volumes, 728 Sheridan Rd., Chicago, IL 60613-3244

Writer's Atelier, 110 N. Orlando Ave., #12, Maitland, FL 32751-5533

Writing Disorder, PO Box 3067, Ventura, CA 93006

Wrongdoing, 718-650 Sheppard Ave E., North York, ON M2K 3E4, Canada

Yale Review, Yale University, PO Box 208243, New Haven, CT 06520-8243

Yellow Arrow Publishing, PO Box 102, Glen Arm, MD 21057

Yellow Medicine Review, SMSU, 1501 State St., Marshall, MN 56258

Your Impossible Voice, 4972 Farview Rd., Columbus, OH 43231

Zephyr Press, 400 Bason Dr., Las Cruces, NM 88005-3717

Zig Zag Lit Mag, 42 Munsill Ave., #E, Bristol, VT 05443

Zoetrope: All Story, 916 Kearny St., San Francisco, CA 94133

Zone 3, APSU, Box 4565. Clarksville, TN 37044

CONTRIBUTORS' NOTES

DOUG ANDERSON won the Kate Tufts Discovery Award.

RAE ARMANTROUT judges the Yale Younger Poets Award. She won a Pulitzer Prize and a National Book Critics Circle Award.

HAJJAR BABAN is a 2021 Soros Fellow and a recent MFA graduate from The University of Virginia.

LISA BELLAMY teaches at The Writers Studio and is the author of two poetry collections. Her "Wild Pansy" appeared in *Pushcart Prize XLIV*.

A. J. BERMUDEZ is editor of *The Maine Review*. Her first book is *Stories No One Hopes Are About Them* (2022).

MOLLY BRODAK published a memoir, a poetry collection and three chapbooks. *Cipher* won the 2019 *Pleiades* Prize. She died in 2020.

JENNY CATLIN holds an MFA from Eastern Washington University and a Masters in Ecopsychology from Naropa University.

KAI CARLSON-WEE is the author of *Rail* (BOA), and a former Stegner Fellow.

LAKIESHA CARR's debut novel, *An Autobiography of Skin*, is just published by Pantheon. She lives in Texas.

KAMERYN A. CARTER is founding Co-editor of *Emergent Literary*. Her poems have appeared in *Phoebe, Bat City Review* and *Best American Poetry 2023*.

ANDY CHEN's poems were published in *Ploughshares, New England Review* and *The Offing*. He lives in St. Louis

HEDGIE CHOI received her MFA in poetry from the Michener Center and an MFA in fiction from Johns Hopkins.

ALIX CHRISTIE's latest book is *The Shining Mountain* (University of New Mexico Press).

CHRISTINA RIVERA COGSWELL's "Two Breaths" is an excerpt from *My Oceans* (Curbstone Books). She won the John Burroughs Native Essay Award in 2023.

LYDIA CONKIN has been honored in several previous Pushcart editions and by a Stegner Fellowship and others. A story collection, *Rainbow Rainbow*, was published recently.

MICHAEL CZYZNIEJEWSKI has published story collections with Dzanc Books (2009) and Curbside (2012, 2015).

KRYSTYNA DABROWSKA lives in Warsaw, Poland. She is the author of five poetry books, translated into 20 languages.

DA-LIN was born in Taiwan. She won the PEN America Emerging Voices Fellowship and the James Kirkwood Literary Award.

GEFFREY DAVIS is poetry editor of *Iron Horse*. *One Wild Word Away* is due soon from BOA.

FRED D'AGUIAR's *Years of Plagues* is out from Harper and a poetry collection, *Letters To America*, is published by Carcanet.

EUGÉNIO DE ANDRADE (1923–2005) was Portugal's most honored poet. Alexis Levitin was asked to do this translation for the 2022 Festival of his work.

JACK DRISCOLL's story originally appeared in *Georgia Review* and was included in *Wanting Only To Be Heard* (University of Massachusetts Press).

SARA ELKAMEL is a prize winning journalist and translator. She lives in Cairo, Egypt and New York. Her chapbook is *Field of No Justice* (Akashic Books)

ASHLEY MARIE FARMER won the 2020 Rubery Award.

ZORINA EXIE FREY is an educator, writer and screenwriter. She holds an MA from Converse University.

MOLLY GALLENTINE last appeared in *Pushcart Prize XLIII*. She lives in Jersey City, New Jersey.

GLENN GITOMER is a lawyer in Philadelphia and a graduate of New York University's Tisch School.

JOY GUO is an attorney living in New York. Her work has appeared in *Chestnut Review*, *Smokelong* and *Passages North*.

JORIE GRAHAM teaches at Harvard. She is the author of fifteen poetry collections.

YONA HARVEY is the author of two poetry collections. She is the winner of the Believer Book Award and the Kate Tufts Discovery Award.

JULIE HECHT's "Taco Night" appeared in *Pushcart Prize XLIII*. She is the author of two story collections, a novel and a nonfiction work. Her next book is *Every Single Thing*.

ALLEGRA HYDE's debut novel *Eleutheria* was named a "Best Book of 2022" by *The New York Times*. She teaches at Oberlin College.

ONYEKACHI ILOH is a writer and visual artist from Nigeria.

LILY JARMAN-REISCH has published poems in *Mobius, One, Slant Poetry and Snap-dragon*. She lives in Baltimore.

KATERYNA KALYTKO lives in Ukraine and won the 2017 Joseph Conrad Prize.

PETER KESSLER lives in Philadelphia. His work has appeared in *Gulf Coast, Catamaran, GSU Review* and others.

SOPHIE KLAHR's books are published by Backwaters Press, Yes Yes Books and Fiction Collective. She lives in Los Angeles.

GREY WOLFE LAJOIE's debut collection *Little Ones* will be released in Fall, 2024.

JAMES LONGENBACH was the author of six poetry books and eight books of prose. *Earthing* was a finalist for The National Book Critics Award. He died recently.

REV. ROB MCCALL was paster at Blue Hill Maine Congregational Church until retiring in 2015. He was the author of three essay collections.

WAYNE MILLER edits *Copper Nickel*. His seventh poetry collection is Forthcoming in 2025.

MATTHEW NEILL NULL is author of the novel *Honey From The Lion* and the story collection *Allegheny Front*. He teaches at Susquehanna University.

PETER ORNER directs the writing program at Dartmouth College. His essays collection and other books are available from Catapult.

TRIIN PAJA lives in Estonia. Recent poems have appeared in *Black Warrior, Rattle, Thrush* and elsewhere.

LEAH PENNIMAN lives in Grafton, New York and is a farmer, educator and author.

MARY RUEFLE's latest book is *Dunce* (Wave Books). She lives in Vermont.

HAYDEN SAUNIER is the author of five poetry collections. She is the founder and director of No River Twice, a poetry performance group.

KATHRYN SCANLAN's latest work is *Kick The Latch* (New Directions). She lives in Los Angeles.

SAM KECK SCOTT is a writer and wild life biologist living in Northern California. His work has been featured in *Orion, Outside* and *The Atlantic*.

CLAUDIA SEREA is the author of seven poetry collections, most recently *In Those Years No one Slept* (Broadston Books, 2023)

DIANE SEUSS won the Pulitzer Prize for poetry. Her *Modern Poetry* is forthcoming from Graywolf.

JIM SHEPARD appeared in two previous Pushcart Prize editions. He teaches at Williams College.

TYLER SOMES live in Austin, Texas and is a lawyer.

SCOTT SPENCER is a playwright and has written 14 novels.

STEVE STERN's work has appeared in five previous *Pushcart Prize* editions. He lives in Ballston Spa, New York.

CLIFFORD THOMPSON teaches at Sarah Lawrence and Bennington colleges.

JEFFREY THOMSON teaches at the University of Maine, Farmington. He is a poet, memorist, translator and editor.

FREDERIC TUTEN is the author of five novels, two short story collections and the memoir *My Young Life*. His honors include a Guggenheim Fellowship and recognition from The American Academy of Arts and Letters.

LAURA VAN DEN BERG's next novel, *Florida Diary*, is forthcoming from FSG. She last was honored in *Pushcart Prize XXXIV*.

G.C. WALDREP's "The Opening Ritual" is out soon from Tupelo Press. He teaches at Bucknell University.

ERIN WILSON's work includes the chapbook *The Belly of The Pig* (Dancing Girls Press). She lives in a small Canadian town on Robinson-Huron territory.

TRYPHENA L. YEBOAH was born in Mampung, Ghana. Her chapbook, *A Mouthful of Home*, was published in 2020. She won the 2021 Narrative Prize.

INDEX

The following is a listing in alphabetical order by author's last name of works reprinted in the *Pushcart Prize* editions since 1976.

515

554